PRAISE FOR MARIAH

~The Wyndham Beach Series~

ALL THAT WE ARE

"Mariah Stewart writes beautiful books."

—*Bayside Book Reviews*

"A hopeful and emotional novel about twists of fate, enduring friendships, and life's never-ending surprises."

—@harlequinjunkie

"I have loved this entire series but this one is THE BEST ONE YET! I loved everything about this book—the characters, the story line, the pacing—all of it!"

—Owl Reviews on *Goodreads*

"The Wyndham Beach series is one of my favorite comfort reads . . . Everything that I love about this series is here in abundance—the gorgeous setting, the wonderful and now very familiar characters . . . the gorgeous female friendships, and a plot that is uplifting, comforting, and life-affirming."

—@Salboreads

"This is the final installment of the Wyndham Beach series and I am sad to see it end! I have loved this series because it isn't like your typical beach romantic story line . . . I appreciate that the series includes women not only in their 30s (the children) but the mothers play a prominent role. Stewart . . . looks at family dynamics in their entirety."

—@stumblingintobooks

"I love that this is a 'later in life' story and especially the warm, rich friendships."

—@brettlikesbooks

"Thank you for featuring real women with such positivity and zest for life. Well done to the author."

—Cozy Reader on *Goodreads*

"A new author for me and I loved this book! Beautifully written with real, complex character development, I felt like I'd known the main characters forever."

—Julia on *Goodreads*

"Longtime friends, family, and love weave a wonderful pattern in this novel . . . A thoroughly enjoyable and charming read."

—Paula on *Goodreads*

"From start to finish, I never put it down . . . Stewart's books are always chock-full of warm, vibrant characters who bring you into their lives."

—Gail on *Goodreads*

GOODBYE AGAIN

"Stewart returns to Wyndham Beach, Mass., for a lighthearted tale of love and reinvention refreshingly centered on an older heroine . . . The strength of the female friendships especially shines through, bolstering the love story. Readers will be eager for more."

—*Publishers Weekly*

"A wonderful story that will touch your heart. The book focuses on the friendship of three lifelong friends as they support each other through grief, new relationships, second chances, and hope."

—*Harlequin Junkie* (top pick, 5 stars)

"One of my comfort programs is *Virgin River*—it's a TV program I can unwind with. The Wyndham series by Mariah Stewart has become my bookish equivalent. I love that the ladies—Liddy, Maggie, and Emma—are in their fifties and navigating life and relationships as older women, as mothers, partners, and working women. This is a book filled with mostly nice people; with friendships, and family; with a glass of wine at sunset and a blooming, wonderful bookstore, and I really enjoyed my time at Wyndham Beach."

—@salboreads

"Mariah Stewart writes about women with real-world problems and does it well. A highly recommended series featuring mature heroines."

—*Bayside Book Reviews*

"An authentic portrayal of someone's messy life and there is a lot to relate to here. There's a couple of romances, lots of friendship, and some drama, too. Overall, a really enjoyable read, especially if you like character-driven stories in an idyllic setting."

—*Novelgossip*

"I love this series because it's a romance with generational characters. It is refreshing to read a romance that involves various ages and still covers real-life struggles and decisions, and is still topped with an HEA."

—@stumblingintobooks

"Mariah Stewart has been one of my favorite authors for such a long time. *Goodbye Again* has all the things I love so much. There are a lot of big themes in this book—there's substance along with the lighter love story. I love losing myself in the world Stewart builds, and if you haven't been there yet, I'd greatly recommend it."

—@shoshanahinla

AN INVINCIBLE SUMMER

"*Oh* my. This book was simply *gorgeous*! Each of the characters we're introduced to leaves a mark on your heart. The love that was both lost and found is enough to turn the biggest skeptic on to the idea of everything happening for a reason, and in its own time. All in all, it was a wonderful cast of characters with varied lives that are intriguing, heartbreaking, and uplifting in equal parts."

—*Satisfaction for Insatiable Readers*

"This is my first by this author, and it certainly won't be the last. Her writing is extremely engaging, and the author really brings to life the dynamics of longtime friendships and relationships and all the ups and downs that come with them. I couldn't help but fall in love with this book."

—*Where the Reader Grows*

"A multigenerational story line, an idyllic setting, and a new series from one of my tried-and-true authors? Yes, please! As much as I loved the setting and the premise of this one, the characterization is where it really shines. Maggie and her two lifelong friends were all such lovely, authentic women."

—*Novelgossip*

"This story hooked me from the beginning and kept me dangling all the way through: cheering, crying, and just absorbing the decisions as Maggie finds her path to true happiness. A wonderful story I just fell for!"

—*A Midlife Wife*

"What makes this book so readable are the relationships and how the past ties into the future. Isn't that the way it is for all of us? *An Invincible Summer* is a fast-paced, easy-to-read story delving into the relationships we have in life and how they both break and sustain us."

—*Books, Cooks, Looks*

"I really loved these characters and this story. The characters just felt real and flawed in the best of ways. I found myself caring about each of the characters, which has me really excited that this book is just the beginning to a series. I will definitely be continuing on, as I want to see what happens with some of these other characters. I just want more, if I'm being honest! Read this book if you are a fan of women's fiction, contemporary fiction, or are looking for a great summer read."

—*Booked on a Feeling*

"This book was raw and real. Stewart crafted beautifully imperfect characters that allow us to see ourselves in their struggles. I spent the majority of the novel on the edge of my chair, cheering for Maggie and her daughters. This book also gives off what I'd consider *Virgin River* vibes, so if you like that series, grab this one and give it a try."

—@stumblingintobooks

"What a down-to-earth, heart-filling, and sentimental read. Full of friendships, forgetting, and moving forward. The relationships and characters are realistic, charming, and the plot is a bit elusive to keep you on your toes. A very enjoyable read about love, loss, and second chances, and it is a page-turner."

—@momfluencer

"This novel by @mariah_stewart_books is what a women's fiction novel is all about. There's a bit of romance, friendship, and complicated relationships. I really enjoyed how this book highlighted the messiness that life can be, but [it was] done in a lighthearted way. And the overall theme of learning lessons from the past and the courage to move forward on to new phases of one's life was endearingly told."

—@tamsterdam_reads

"There is so much I loved about this read. The setting of Wyndham Beach is gorgeous. I could smell the sea air, feel the warmth of the sun as the women took their coffee and sat watching the horizon. I could feel Maggie's pull to return to her roots. I loved the female relationships in the book. Maggie is a strong but supportive mother who brings her children through crises but holds out for her own choices, and the independence of her own life. The gatherings with her friends are glorious—tattoos, rock concerts, and the warmth of conversations between women who really know and understand each other. This was such a celebration of life and especially of women of *all* ages."

—@salboreads

~The Hudson Sisters Series~

THE LAST CHANCE MATINEE

"Prepare to fall in love with this amazing, endearing family of women."
—Robyn Carr, *New York Times* bestselling author

"The combination of a quirky small-town setting, a family mystery, a gentle romance, and three estranged sisters is catnip for women's fiction fans."
—*Booklist*

"If you like the Lucky Harbor series by Jill Shalvis, you will enjoy this one. Stewart's writing reminds me of Susan Wiggs, Luanne Rice, Susan Mallery, and Robyn Carr."
—*My Novelesque Life*

THE SUGARHOUSE BLUES

"A solid writer with so much talent, Mariah Stewart crafts wonderful stories that take us away to small-town America and build strong families we wish we were a part of."
—*A Midlife Wife*

"Reading this book was like returning to a favorite small town and meeting up with friends you had been missing."
—*Pacific Northwest Bookworm*

"A heartwarming read full of surprising secrets, humor, and lessons about what it means to be a family."
—*That Book Lady Blog*

THE GOODBYE CAFÉ

"Stewart makes a charming return to tiny Hidden Falls, Pennsylvania, in this breezy contemporary, which is loaded with appealing down-home characters and tantalizing hints of mystery that will hook readers immediately. Stewart expertly combines the inevitable angst of a trio of sisters, a family secret, and a search for an heirloom necklace; it's an irresistible mix that will delight readers. Masterful characterizations and [a] well-timed plot are sure to pull in fans of romantic small-town stories."

—Publishers Weekly

"Stewart [has] the amazing ability to weave a women's fiction story loaded with heart, grit, and enough secrets [that] you highly anticipate the next book coming up. I have read several books from her different series, and every one of them has been a delightful, satisfying read. Beautiful and heartwarming."

—A Midlife Wife

"Highly recommend this series for WF fans and even romance fans. There's plenty of that sweet, small-town romance to make you swoon a little."

—Novelgossip

"These characters will charm your socks off! Thematic and highly entertaining."

—Booktalk with Eileen

~The Chesapeake Diaries Series~

THAT CHESAPEAKE SUMMER

"Deftly uses the tools of the genre to explore issues of identity, truth, and small-town kinship. Stewart offers a strong statement on the power of love and trust, a fitting theme for this bighearted small-town romance."

—Publishers Weekly

DUNE DRIVE

"Rich with local history, familiar characters (practical, fierce, and often clairvoyant centenarian Ruby is a standout), and the slow-paced, down-home flavor of the bay, Stewart's latest is certain to please fans and add new ones."

—Library Journal

ON SUNSET BEACH

"Mariah Stewart's rich characterization, charming setting, and a romance you'll never forget will have you packing your bags for St. Dennis."

—Robyn Carr, New York Times bestselling author

COMING HOME

"One of the best women's contemporary authors of our time, Mariah Stewart serves the reader a beautiful romance with a delicious side dish of the suspense that has made her so deservingly popular. *Coming Home* is beautifully crafted with interesting, intelligent characters and pitch-perfect pacing. Ms. Stewart is, as always, at the top of her game with this sensuous, exhilarating, page-turning tale."

—Betty Cox, *Reader to Reader Reviews*

AT THE RIVER'S EDGE

"Everything you love about small-town romance in one book . . . *At the River's Edge* is a beautiful, heartwarming story. Don't miss this one."

—Barbara Freethy

"If you love romance stories set in a small seaside village, much like Debbie Macomber's Cedar Creek series, you will definitely want to grab this book. I easily give this one a five out of five stars."

—*Reviews from the Heart*

The Head That Wears the Crown

The Mercy Street Series (Suspense)

Mercy Street
Cry Mercy
Acts of Mercy

The FBI Series (Romantic Suspense)

Brown-Eyed Girl
Voices Carry
Until Dark
Dead Wrong
Dead Certain
Dead Even
Dead End
Cold Truth
Hard Truth
Dark Truth
Final Truth
Last Look
Last Words
Last Breath
Forgotten

The Enright Series (Contemporary Romance)

Devlin's Light
Wonderful You
Moon Dance

Stand-Alone Titles (Women's Fiction / Contemporary Romance)

The President's Daughter
Priceless
Carolina Mist
A Different Light
Moments in Time

Novellas

"Finn's Legacy" (in *The Brandywine Brides*)
"If Only in My Dreams" (in *Upon a Midnight Clear*)
"Swept Away" (in *Under the Boardwalk*)
"'Til Death Do Us Part" (in *Wait Until Dark*)

Short Stories

"Justice Served" (in Thriller 2: Stories You Just Can't Put Down)
"Without Mercy" (in Thriller 3: Love Is Murder)

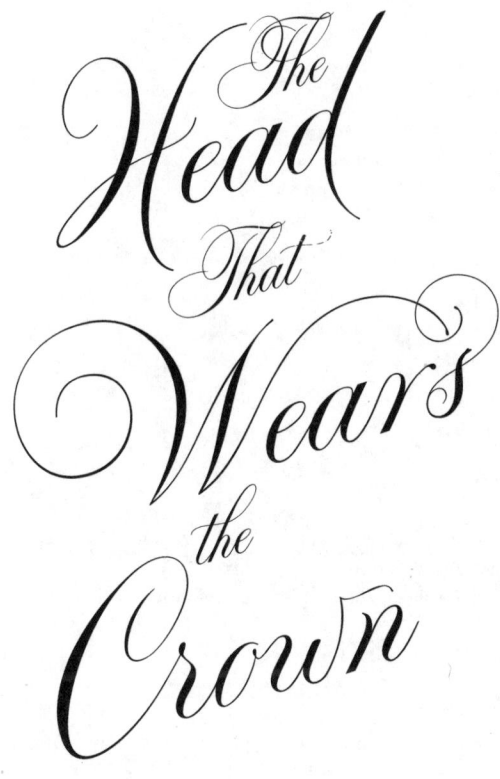

The Head That Wears the Crown

MARIAH STEWART

 Montlake

Published by Montlake, Seattle

www.apub.com

Amazon, the Amazon logo, and Montlake are trademarks of Amazon.com, Inc., or its affiliates.

ISBN-13: 9781662512728 (paperback)
ISBN-13: 9781662512711 (digital)

Cover design by Caroline Teagle Johnson
Cover image: © Zastavkin / Getty; © MirageC / Getty;
© Eugene Partyzan / Shutterstock; © Jade ThaiCatwalk / Shutterstock

Printed in the United States of America

For Robyn Carr

Chapter One

One thing I want to make clear: before this whole thing started, I was pretty much like anyone else. Maybe even pretty much like you. I worked five days every week, and took a one-week vacation every summer at the Jersey Shore with my ex-sister-in-law and our kids. I'm not going to tell you things didn't get . . . well, *tense* sometimes, but the house was free—thanks to the ex-sister-in-law, who owns it—and the kids got to spend the week with their cousins on their father's side, which is all my ex-sister-in-law cared about since the kids rarely saw each other and she was very fond of them (not so much fond of me).

Now that I think about it, they rarely see their father, either. He's more interested in his new wife and the new family—the one they started before he was my ex—which is perfectly fine with me, since he's not the man I thought he was when we got married. Of course, I was twenty-two at the time, but even so, I should have known better than to marry a man who didn't think Big 5 basketball was all that (it's a Philly thing).

Anyway, my seventeen-year-old son, Ralphie—why, why, why had I let his father talk me into naming that boy after him?—and my fourteen-year-old daughter, Juliette—who tells everyone her name is *Jules* because Juliette is *so* not cool—and I live a block off Porter Street in South Philadelphia in a row house that looks a lot like every other row house in the neighborhood. We have take-out pizza on Friday nights from Giorgio's and take-out Italian two nights a week. And by take-out Italian I mean I stop at my sister Roe's on my way home from work and pick up enough for the three of us of whatever she made that day.

Roe—short for Rosalie—is the youngest of us three girls. She can also be one of the most annoying people on the face of the earth (one-time runner-up for Miss Negativity USA), but we love her anyway. She's a fantastic cook—she cooks four weekdays at Robotti's Italian Garden—and feeds us on two of those days. Hard to bitch too much about someone who keeps you and your family well fed, but that's a totally separate issue from the fact that she's still a PITA a lot of the time. But, like I said, we love her anyway.

I was telling you how this whole crazy thing happened.

So I was at the Italian Market on Ninth Street on a Saturday morning in early April, lugging around the usual. Meat and cheese from Di Bruno's, pasta from Talluto's, thinking about stopping on my way home to pick up bread and cannolis from Isgro's, when I got the feeling I was being watched. You know that feeling, right, when those little hairs on the back of your neck start to tickle? I'd just remembered I'd said I'd pick up mussels for Roe when I noticed a dark-haired man staring at me while he was pretending not to. He was tall, dark, and, yes, handsome—the latter being a bit of an understatement.

Which begged the question: Why was he watching this fortysomething mom of teenagers, who was rocking the beginning of a few varicose veins and maybe a little arm flap? Not to mention the grays that my hairdresser expertly covered the first week of every month (the same hairdresser who'd been dropping some not-so-subtle hints that I might want to put a little Botox on my Christmas list this year). At first I thought I was imagining that it was me he was looking at—I mean, I need a little more maintenance these days, but don't get me wrong, I haven't exactly let myself go (I've been told I can pass for thirty-five in the right light—thirty if you're on your fifth beer and/or your third shot of Jack Daniel's). I will say with all modesty, all things considered, I still look pretty good in a pair of yoga pants.

So I moved on to the fish market. When I came out, I could swear I saw him again near the butcher shop, but Ninth Street was crowded, and when I looked back he was gone. By the time I'd gotten to my car, I'd forgotten all about Mr. Tall, Dark, and Handsome (as Sin).

On Sunday morning, I took the kids to Mass at Saint Monica's. Which was no easy feat, people, getting teenagers up early on a Sunday morning to go to church. But the last promise I made to my mother before she passed—God rest her soul—was that I'd keep the kids in the church. You make a promise to your dying mother, you keep it, right? I couldn't afford the tuition to Catholic school these past two years, but I could insist they go to church and to CCD (that would be Confraternity of Christian Doctrine, for those of you who never sat through Catholic education classes). When they balked, I reminded them they were doing it to honor their grandmother, who'd be turning in her grave if they didn't go. Since both my kids loved my mother, they went. Oh, sure, sometimes they grumbled, but they went.

So anyway, on Sunday, we were coming out after Mass ended, and I was standing on the steps talking to Mrs. Hill, who was an old friend of my mother's, when I looked out across the street, and there was the dark-haired guy from the market. Only this time he was with two other men. They were both shorter than him, one being somewhat squat and shaped like a fireplug and the other tall—though not as—and very, very thin. Like, cadaver thin, and he wore a bowler-style hat. The three of them were wearing black suits and white shirts and dark glasses. And they were all watching me.

My first thought—after thinking they were grossly overdressed for a warm day in April—was that they were human traffickers watching my daughter, who, while only fourteen, looks more like sixteen. She's petite, only five feet two—I'm only two inches taller—and she has long chestnut-brown hair and green eyes, both like mine, and she's perfectly proportioned, if you get what I mean. She's still growing into her looks, but already you can see she is going to be a stunner before she's of legal age. I looked around wildly for Juliette, who I found standing in the middle of a group of girls she's been friends with since kindergarten.

I excused myself to Mrs. Hill and tried to find my son in the crowd, but he was down on the sidewalk. At over six feet tall, he's not hard to pick out in a crowd. He has dark curly hair that he keeps just long enough to tumble over his forehead because some old girlfriend told him he looked adorable that way. His eyes are green like the rest of us, and he's built pretty well since he plays a lot of sports. I called his cell and told him to get his sister and take her home. Now. He started to argue—he was talking to some cute girl I vaguely recognized as an old classmate of his—but apparently something in the way I said "NOW!" convinced him to move. He grabbed his sister and hauled her off the steps and down the street. She was obviously annoyed at having her big brother interrupt her like that, so she was no happier than he was.

I watched the three men across the street, and, while I didn't want to prematurely overreact—there could be a perfectly logical explanation why they seemed to be everywhere I was—if they took so much as one step in the direction of my kids, I was hitting 911. But they hadn't moved and didn't seem to notice Juliette was gone. They were still watching me, which raised the question: Who traffics forty-four-year-old women?

I walked home with several friends who dropped off as we reached their streets, and I was watching over my shoulder every so often, but nobody was there. Soon it was just me on this sunny Sunday morning heading for home, alone. I convinced myself it was all in my imagination and laughed at myself for being so silly. Like a guy who looked like that would be looking for me, right?

I had a lot of explaining to do to my kids when I got home.

The next morning, I pulled into the parking lot at my office building in the far Philly suburbs where all phases of the business of insurance were conducted. It wasn't quite eight thirty in the morning, so I sat in the car for another few minutes listening to the local morning radio sports talk show on WIP. This morning they'd picked up on the ongoing argument from Friday's show: Which Philly team had the largest fan base, and was it deserved?

No-brainer. The Eagles. And yes. Yes, it was.

I listened to a few callers who tried to make a case for the Phillies or the Flyers, and a few 76ers fans called in before I turned off the car and opened the door, a cup of Wawa coffee in one hand and a tote bag in the other. I locked up and started through the parking lot.

I was one car row from the entrance when I saw them. All three of them, and I realized this was no coincidence.

My blood froze in my veins, and my legs turned to rubber. I dropped my coffee—and damn it, there was still half left—and ran for the door.

"What's your hurry, Annie?" Debbie Wilson, the receptionist for my department—that would be claims—had been halfway up the steps when she heard the splash.

I blew past her and rushed into the building, past the security guard, and hightailed it down the hall to my department as fast as my size seven-and-a-half ballet flats could take me. Once safely in my cubicle, I dropped my tote—pissed off more than I can tell you that I'd wasted a half cup of Wawa Colombian that had been fixed perfectly—and fell into my chair, gasping for breath.

I was so out of shape, and I regretted having dropped my gym membership back in the fall when I was going through a budget crisis. My heart was beating like crazy and my hands were shaking uncontrollably. I didn't know who those men were, but they were definitely following me.

Which made no sense at all. I mean, why?

I couldn't think of one good reason unless my ex's family put a hit out on me. Which wasn't inconceivable.

I sat for a moment to calm myself, trying to decide what to do. I walked back out to the lobby and stopped at the security guard's station, peering around the corner to make sure they hadn't followed me into the building, but the only people I saw were people who belonged. I tapped Glenn, the guard, on the shoulder.

"Glenn, there are three guys outside in the parking lot who don't work here."

Glenn shrugged, not bothering to raise his eyes from the newspaper spread out across his desk. "So maybe they're here for a meeting and they're early."

"I think they're following me."

He looked me over, head to toe, then back again. "Why would they be following you?"

"I have no idea, but maybe you could find out."

"Sorry. Can't leave my post."

So I went to the receptionist's desk, where Debbie was just getting set for the morning. Computer booted up, coffee on one side of the desk, and a cheese danish from the snack room on the other.

"Deb, did you see the—"

"Oh, hey. Too bad about your coffee. The stuff they're selling downstairs this morning sucks." She sat on her chair and swiveled around to look at me. "I think you got a splash there on your skirt."

I looked down. Yep, that was a splash of the coffee I should have been drinking. I grabbed a tissue from her desk and tried to blot away the evidence.

"Did you make it in time?" Debbie asked.

"In time for what?"

"The bathroom. Isn't that where you were rushing to?"

"Um, no. Listen, Deb—did you happen to notice three men in dark suits standing outside the building this morning?"

"Yeah, Rich, Lennie, and Joe. The undertakers. I mean, the under-writers." That Debbie. What a jokester.

"Not those three. Three different men. One really short guy, a medium-tall guy, and one really tall guy. The medium-tall guy looked like a cigar with a bowler, but the *tall* tall guy looked like your best fantasy." Surely Deb would have noticed him.

"Nope. Are you having a meeting this morning? Want to leave their names?" She opened the center drawer of her desk and took out a small notepad and a pen.

"I don't know their names. They were standing right out there next to the PARKING BY PERMIT ONLY sign." I tossed the damp tissue into the wastebasket next to her desk.

She shook her head. "There wasn't anyone there when I came in except Elena Crockett. She was having a problem parking that big new Benz of hers."

Elena was the president of Philadelphia Fire, Casualty, and Liability Insurance Company—PFCLIC—my employer.

I walked to the wall of glass that wraps around the reception area and looked out, but no one was there who shouldn't be.

I turned around, and Debbie was staring at me as if waiting for an explanation.

"These guys have been following me all weekend," I told her. "At least, I'm pretty sure they were."

At first she didn't say anything. Finally she said, "If you think you're being followed, you should call the police."

"You're right. Of course. Why didn't I think of that?" I nodded and went back to my cubicle, where I picked up the phone, then immediately hung up. Did I call the city police or the police out here in Chester County? Would that be the state police? Did the township we were in have their own police department?

I tried the state police. After reporting that I'd seen the same three men in the same places I'd been in over the past two days, I was asked a barrage of questions: Did I recognize any of them? Know their names? Did the men make contact with me? Did they approach me? Speak to me? Attempt to touch me? Threaten me in any way? Then the trooper on the other end of the line sighed and asked, "So what exactly did they *do* besides be in the same places you were in?" and I had to admit they'd done nothing *personal* to me but I felt they were following me.

"But you saw them in all public places, right? Not near your home or hanging out around your car?" he asked.

"No," I said quietly. Maybe I had overreacted.

"Okay, I have the report, but there's nothing I can do for you. You don't know their names and they haven't committed a crime. Let me know if they contact you. Or maybe try the Philly police since two of the incidents happened there." The trooper hung up before I even got out a thank-you.

While I looked up a number online for the Philadelphia police, the phone rang, and before I knew it, I was embroiled in hot negotiations with an attorney trying to push me into settling an accident case for which our insured had absolutely no liability since it was caused one hundred percent by his client. The man didn't know what he was in for. I was a crack negotiator.

Mondays were always tough, because we had people calling in to report accidents and we had our regular workload to deal with, so my phone rang nonstop. I'd skipped breakfast and was famished by one o'clock, which was my first chance to get up from my desk. I had about ten minutes to eat lunch and check in with my BFF, Marianne McDevitt, who worked in underwriting and was the person who put me on to the job I have now. Before I knew it, it was four thirty and time to leave. I managed to get out by five forty-five and still had to drive back to the city. Before I left the building, I stood inside the front door and scanned the parking lot, but I didn't see my three amigos. When I got to my car, I sent a text to both kids to see what was going on at home.

Homework, from Jules. **Nothing**, from Ralphie.

All the way home I thought about whether or not to call the police and what I'd say if I did. The state trooper had raised some good points. I decided to calmly examine the facts of the situation as I parked my car. Then I wondered what the facts really were.

Parallel parking on any street in South Philadelphia was always a challenge, so I focused on that. I grabbed my tote bag from the passenger seat, got out, and locked my car.

And walked smack into Mr. Tall, Dark, and . . .

"Who the hell are you, and why have you been following me?"

I tried to back away, but I was between him and my car. Tweedledum and Tweedledee were on the sidewalk on the opposite side of the street watching and standing in exactly the same position, their arms folded over their chest.

"You are Annaliese Gilberti Cancelmi." A statement, not a question.

I didn't bother to respond, since he already knew who I was.

"We've been looking forward to meeting you." I detected an accent in his soft voice. "You've no idea how much."

"So you could send me to Dubai in a shipping container?" What else could it be? I didn't owe the IRS.

"Why would we do that?" He appeared to genuinely ponder the question.

May I say, up close, he looked even better.

"Because that's what human traffickers do." I met his gaze head-on. I couldn't help but notice how chocolaty brown his eyes were. I momentarily wished I were thirty again, because he was clearly close to fifteen years younger than me.

He frowned. "Mrs. Cancelmi, is there someplace quiet where we can talk privately?" I was still trying to place his accent. Not quite French. Not quite Italian.

I'd heard it before—a long time ago.

"Who are you?" I asked again, this time in a somewhat more civilized tone. "Why have you been following me?"

"Please. We mean you no harm. On the contrary. Please. A few minutes of your time. Any place you choose. I swear on my life no harm will come to you."

That accent again. It floated through me like a distant echo.

I stared at him for a very long time. Finally, I said, "There's a coffee shop right down there at the corner. I'll meet you there in one hour."

"Thank you. Very much, we thank you." He looked relieved as he backed away and nodded.

"Watch the traffic." He was crossing the street backward, as if not wanting to turn his back on me. Rush hour around here, no one stops for anything or anyone. "And don't call me Mrs. Cancelmi."

I muttered under my breath, "I'm not Mrs. Cancelmi." My mom didn't change her name when she got married. Her family name was Gilberti, and she went by that, and we girls were given her last name at birth. If my father cared one way or the other, he never showed it. I didn't care either way, but when I got married, my mother asked me to respect her family name by keeping it, as she had, so I did, which was just one more reason my ex's family was happy to see me go. The kids of course carried their father's name. I tried hyphenating—you know, like the Brits do, so they'd be Gilberti-Cancelmi, but that didn't fly with Ralph Senior's family, either. Besides, can you see a six-year-old having to learn to print that in first grade? Yeah, me neither.

Anyway, I went into the house and closed the door behind me, wondering why I'd just agreed to meet with these guys, if I should just go ahead and call the police like I'd planned, or if I should hear him out.

In the end, it was the accent that pulled me in, that accent that conjured up memories of things I hadn't thought about in a long time.

Well, the accent and the fact that he was hotter than any guy I'd ever seen in the flesh. Besides, at that point, curiosity was killing me.

Chapter Two

It was Juliette's night to start dinner, so everything was ready when I went into the kitchen. I'd picked up a baked pasta dish from Roe the night before, so all it needed was thirty-five minutes in the oven. My daughter had made a salad and had the dining room table set. She'd picked a few tulips from my poor excuse for a backyard garden and placed them in a pretty vase that had belonged to my mother. I hadn't seen it in a long time so I wasn't sure where she found it, but I appreciated her effort to make the table look cheery.

"Smells good." I dropped my bag on the counter. "Looks like spring in the dining room, Jules. Nice."

Juliette rolled her eyes, but she wasn't fooling me. She was as pleased by the compliment as she was with how nice the table looked. She followed me into the dining room with a pitcher of water and began to fill the glasses.

"Call your brother and let's eat before it gets cold." I plated the pasta, and before I could pass the dishes around, the kids were seated at the table. Ralphie was always ready to eat, so getting him into the dining room was never a problem.

"So what's doing at school this week?" I asked, listening and eating, discussing the usual: sports, tests, the new kid who transferred from some school in Jersey and got suspended when drugs were found in his locker, the ongoing conversation about which colleges Ralphie wanted to visit in anticipation of sending out applications in the fall, and where he was most likely to get a scholarship, all the while keeping an eye on the clock. I didn't want to alarm the kids, so I didn't want to appear as if I was rushing through my meal. By the time we finished, over fifty minutes had passed.

"Ralph, it's your night to clear, rinse, and load the dishwasher." I stood as if I wasn't in a hurry, as if my heart wasn't racing wildly, and picked up my bag. "I'm going down to Barb's for coffee. I won't be long." I'd done this before on occasion, so there was no red flag.

"Could you bring us something for dessert?" This from Juliette.

"Sure. I'll see what she has tonight."

It took me two minutes to walk to the corner. When I arrived at Barb's, the three were seated at the only table occupied, the one closest to the back wall. They all looked up at the same time I walked in, but I didn't acknowledge them.

"What'll it be tonight, Annie?" Barb's daughter, Lynnie, was behind the counter.

"I'll have a large decaf," I told her as I eyed the pastry counter. "And put three cream puffs in a box for me, please."

I took the mug she passed over the counter and moved to the station to fix my coffee, willing my hands not to shake. I was trying to act normal. Dropping a container of half-and-half on the floor would blow it.

"Annie, your cream puffs," Lynnie called to me.

"I'll get them on the way out." My focus was on the table where the three men waited patiently for me.

When I got within five feet of the table, all three stood and the handsome one held my chair out for me. I felt Lynnie's eyes on me. I could almost see her jaw drop and hear the gossip chain revving up. I sat and put my coffee on the table and studied each of their faces in turn as they sat as well. Mentally I thought of them as the Fireplug, Dead Man Walking, and George. The first two were self-explanatory.

I thought of the good-looking one as George because he reminded me of a young George Clooney—in his *ER* days—only maybe even a little better looking and taller. He could also be more jacked than Clooney, but that was just a guess.

I realized they were studying me at the same time.

"Okay, what's this all about?" I asked as I took my phone from my bag and put it on the table next to my mug.

"We appreciate your meeting with us," George said softly. *That accent again . . .*

Fireplug and Dead Man Walking sat silently. Of course they knew exactly what was going on and were obviously content to let one man speak for them.

"What's your name? Where are you from? Why are you stalking me? What do you want?" I whispered as I glanced at my phone. I had 911 ready to go. All I had to do was hit the call button. "I'll give you five minutes."

The three exchanged a long look before George began to speak.

"My name is Maximilien Belleme. We"—he indicated his companions—"are from a small country in Europe. Saint Gilbert. I believe you've heard of it?"

He'd pronounced it *San Zjil-bear*, and that distant bell began to ring again, louder this time. *Saint Gilbert . . .*

"But I'm afraid our conversation is likely to take more than five minutes," he added almost apologetically.

"Saint Gilbert." I pronounced it as he had, and in that moment, I heard the soft voice of my grandmother. Grandmere, we called her when we were speaking to her. Otherwise, we usually referred to her as Gran.

"Grandmere." I didn't realize I'd said it aloud until George—er, Maximilien—said, "Ah, you remember her."

"Of course I remember her. She died when I was nine, but I remember . . ." I struggled to recall exactly what it was I did remember.

"Her voice. Her accent. Yours is the same. She smelled like violets. She spoke slowly and softly and very properly." I closed my eyes and she came into focus. "She always wore the same jewelry. Earrings that looked like golden roses. A ring that had a big red stone. She let me try it on once." I frowned as I opened my eyes. I hadn't thought about that in . . . God, I couldn't remember how many years it had been. And why was I babbling?

"Gran always seemed old, and she was sort of . . ." I searched for the right word to describe her as she was in my memory. "Otherworldly, maybe? She was tall and very beautiful, and her smile was always sort of sad, like she had a sad secret." I closed my eyes again, trying to picture her face, but the only face I saw was my mother's. I realized I was still babbling and snapped back to the present. "Why are we talking about her?"

"What do you know of her childhood?" he asked.

"Not much. But my mom said once that Gran had grown up in a house much larger than the row house we lived in. And one time when Juliette asked for a pony for Christmas, Mom made some comment about Gran having had a whole stable of ponies when she was little. Whenever one of us asked about her, Mom would say something like, 'It's complicated.'" I shrugged. We'd been pretty young when Gran died. "That's it. That's all I know."

"What do you know about her family?"

I tried to remember everything I'd heard over the years.

"Gran had sisters named Jacqueline and Amelia. Jacqueline died. Her mother's first name was Elizabet. My mom was named for her. Everyone would spell it with an *h* at the end to make it Eliza*beth*, and Mom would get annoyed and correct them. Eliza*bet*."

"What else?"

"Her parents died during the Second World War and so did her brother. He was older than she was. That might be when Jacqueline died, too, but I'm not sure about that. Gran had to leave her home because . . . I don't know why, I think it had something to do with the war. Someone helped her get to England—her and Amelia—and she met my grandfather there. After the war ended, she came here." I shook my head. "My mom never said much more than that. She said her mother didn't like to talk about the past. Mom's aunt Amelia visited one time. She lived in London, I remember that. Gran's house was big, and it was like a museum. There were so many fancy things there." Fancy things that had fascinated us as small children, things we were never permitted to touch.

Except sometimes when I got to visit with her all by myself. Memories flew past my inner eye with the speed of children running frenetically down a long, dark hallway.

"Is that all?"

I nodded. I wasn't sure where this strange conversation was going. "Why are we talking about all this, about *her*? Can we just get to the point?"

His eyes met mine as he leveled his gaze. A long moment passed before he spoke. For that moment, I forgot I was looking at a man I'd thought was going to pack me away and put me on a boat to Dubai.

Then he spoke, and the spell was broken.

"Your grandmother was Her Royal Highness, Grand Duchess Annaliese Emelie Sophia Elizabet of the Grand Duchy of Saint Gilbert."

"Huh?"

That's all that would come out of my mouth. I stared at him, then at the other two men, who were nodding silently.

Finally, I found my voice.

"Obviously you have her mixed up with someone else. My grandmother was a war refugee. She came to this country with nothing but her new husband."

"And the jewelry she managed to smuggle from Saint Gilbert in the hems of her clothing," he said softly. "And a small Bible with a white leather cover."

That got my attention. Actually, it sent a chill up my spine. My mother often read from it, but after she passed away, I'd mostly forgotten about it. Then three years ago I found it in a box of random things I'd cleared out from my mother's desk. Mom had been gone for almost eight years, but it had taken that long before I could face going through her personal space. The last time I saw that white Bible was a week ago on the top shelf of the small bookcase in my bedroom.

"How would you know what she took with her when she left her home?" *How could he possibly?*

"My grandfather was the man who helped her escape when the Germans invaded Saint Gilbert in 1941," Maximilien said with quiet pride. "He led her, her sister Amelia, and my grandmother through Switzerland into Italy and on to the coast of France, then to England. She met your grandfather there. He was an American war correspondent. They fell in love, married, and when the war ended and his work there was done, they came to America and settled near Philadelphia."

He seemed to be watching my face, so I tried really hard not to show any emotion whatsoever. I never knew my grandfather. He died when my mother was twenty, before I was born, but I did know he was a journalist and that he'd met my grandmother in England during the war.

"When your grandparents arrived in this country, they moved into a home outside the city. Your grandfather taught journalism at a college. You've seen the house, of course?" He paused. I nodded, and he continued. "Have you not wondered how a college professor in the late 1940s could have afforded such a home?"

I shook my head. I had no idea where this was going, but I remember that house. My mother grew up there, and both my grandparents died under that roof. It looked like a mini-castle surrounded by a black iron fence. It was furnished with antiques, some quite fancy. When we visited as a family we had to dress up and we had to wear gloves and we were told not to speak unless we were spoken to. Cecilia, who's two years younger than me; Rosalie, two years younger than Ceil; and I would sit quietly on a stiff dark-green velvet love seat with our hands folded in our laps, and we'd watch our grandmother chat softly with our mother on the other side of the large room while we squirmed uncomfortably on that horsehair-stuffed torture device. We were served tea in paper-thin china cups with gold roses painted on the inside, and we'd sit in the very formal dining room and eat delicious tea cakes that our grandmother had baked in her old-fashioned kitchen. Everything about that house was old fashioned, as was Grandmere. We never wondered why. We were kids, and that's who she was, and that was that.

After my grandmother died and the house and most of its contents were sold, a few furnishings were divided between my mother and her brother, and each of the grandchildren were given something from the house. I thought of the delicate set of china with its painted roses packed in boxes in my attic.

It occurred to me then that this man knew far more about my mother's family than I did, and I thought I had figured out why.

"I get it. You think I have the jewelry? That maybe my grandmother gave it to my mother and my mother gave it to me? Whatever my grandmother supposedly smuggled in her clothes? Well, you're too late. I have no idea where Gran's things went after she died. So if you've come to rob me . . . so sorry. You're wasting your time." I put my hands on the table, about to stand.

"We haven't come to rob you, Annaliese." Maximilien removed a leather pouch from the inside pocket of his jacket and placed it in the center of the table.

I stared at the pouch, then looked into his eyes. I saw nothing but sincerity there. Yes, I still wasn't sure I shouldn't call the cops, but there was something . . .

Anyway.

"Open it. Please." Dead Man Walking spoke for the first time. He, too, had that soft accent.

I reached for the pouch and slid it to my side of the table and opened it, my eyes still locked with Maximilien's. I could feel several objects inside, so I tilted it and lowered my gaze, watching, incredulous, as the contents tumbled out.

My grandmother's gold earrings. Her ring with the big red stone. A necklace I'd never seen before that looked like gold spun into gossamer threads where more red stones—some the size of my thumbnail—rested between the crossed filaments.

I know my jaw dropped. I picked up the ring and brought it closer, and knew it was the same one that had graced my grandmother's hand. In that moment, I could have sworn I smelled violets, and I had to fight back sudden tears.

Suddenly weary, I looked up and met Maximilien's eyes again.

"Will someone please tell me what this is all about?"

Chapter Three

I was still on the living room sofa staring blankly into space the next morning when I heard the kids moving around getting ready for school. It was too late to run upstairs and pretend everything was normal, so I curled up and pulled an afghan over me. I'd been up all night scouring the internet for anything related to Saint Gilbert and my brain was muddled, so I brushed over the fact that I'd slept downstairs in the same clothes I'd worn to work.

The kids bought my story that I hadn't been feeling well as they went past me into the kitchen. Some minutes later they came back through the living room, Juliette with a Pop-Tart in one hand and the other outstretched, palm up, for lunch money. I took care of her, then waited for my son to come along. He did, I handed over the cash, and off they went to catch up with their friends, arguing over the fact that Jules had taken the last Pop-Tart.

They closed the door behind them, and after waiting a few minutes to make sure they weren't coming back for a forgotten book or permission slip, I sat up, pushed off the afghan, and called my boss and claimed a migraine. Then I made coffee and called my sisters and told them to get over to my house immediately.

"I'm getting ready to go to work," Roe protested. "I can't drop everything on a whim."

"This is not a whim," I told her. "This is important. Life-changing, even."

"Oh my God, Annie! You have a life-threatening illness!"

"No, Roe, I'm not sick. I—"

"You met someone. I'm calling Ceil right now. We'll bring wine to celebrate."

"No new guy. Roe—"

"One of the kids got arrested. Oh God, was it drugs? You need bail money?"

"Dear God in heaven, Rosalie, just plead a migraine and get your ass over here."

I hung up before her imagination went totally off the rails, and I called Cecilia. No such craziness from her. Ceil was the practical one, the one with the most level head. I told her I needed to talk to her about something very important, and she just said, "On my way."

I could almost hear her shrug through the phone. It took a lot to rattle this woman, and since she had her own business as an interior designer, she could take time off when she wanted.

She was there before Roe, even though Ceil lived in Center City and Roe lived three blocks away. Ceil was the tallest of us and very slender. She had honey-blonde hair that was cut short and streaked with highlights, and she always looked very chic. Today she was dressed casually in black leggings and a taupe top over which she'd tossed a navy cardigan. She never forgot her earrings and always had some funky ring on one of her middle fingers and wore big, round tortoiseshell sunglasses that made her look like a VIP.

Roe, on the other hand, was somewhere in the middle, heightwise. Not as tall as Ceil, not as short as me. She had long, very dark curly hair that had a tendency to frizz in the humidity of Philly's summers and very long, dark curly eyelashes. She arrived wearing the white pants she always wore to the restaurant and a white tee. She carried about fifteen extra pounds because she was always tasting what she cooked and never had time to work out. I tried to get her to run with me in the early evening, but she was either still at work or too tired. She always looked—how to say this in a kind way—disheveled. Like she'd just rolled out of bed and hopped onto the subway.

I poured coffee for them and declined to answer any questions until the three of us were seated around my dining room table. Then I started off by asking them what they remembered about our grandmother.

"She was tall and beautiful, but she always dressed sort of strangely, like, not modern. And when we visited her, we had to sit on that old Victorian love seat with our backs ruler-straight and our legs crossed at the ankles." Roe wrinkled her nose. "We had to wear white gloves and use our best manners. I remember that was the last thing Mama always said before she rang the doorbell at Gran's house. 'Best behavior, girls.'"

"Gran was beautiful and very aristocratic. Elegant," Ceil recalled. "Just the way she held herself, and the way she spoke. I wanted to be just like her. She always liked you best."

"No, she loved all of us the same," I protested, though I knew Ceil was right.

For some reason, Gran warmed to me in a way that was different from the way she was with anyone else. The year I turned eight, things changed. At least one day every month, Mom would take me to Gran's and literally drop me off at the driveway. Gran would be waiting for me at the front door, and she'd hug me and close the door behind us as if shutting out the rest of the world. Those were very fun days for me. Gran and I would bake together, sometimes the little cakes she was so fond of, sometimes something else. On sunny days we'd go outside and explore the glory of her garden, where she'd planted so many beautiful flowers. She'd always let me pick a few to take home to Mom.

On those days, I saw a completely different Gran. She seemed happy to be with me and interested in every part of my life. Who my friends were, what I was learning in school. I'd always thought it was because I was her oldest grandchild, but I figured as my sisters grew older, they'd be invited to Gran's house for one-on-one time so they could get to know her better, too. Now I wasn't so sure that was her motive in wanting to spend time with me. I think it was more she wanted *me* to spend time with *her*, if you get the difference. Unfortunately, we never had time to explore whatever her real agenda might have been because of her unexpected death.

As if she could read my mind, Ceil said, "Annie, you were the only one she ever invited to spend time alone with her."

"Did you resent that?" I asked.

"Are you kidding? We weren't the ones who had to spend the afternoon sitting on those stiff chairs with the scratchy fabric poking through our clothes," Roe said.

That's not exactly what happened on my solo visits.

Ceil brought the focus back to where it belonged. "Gran always made me think of the old European royals you'd see in those 1930s movies Mom used to watch on TV."

I sighed and silently thanked Ceil for the segue. "Because that's what she was."

Roe tilted her head to one side as if she hadn't heard what I'd said. "She was what?"

"She was European royalty. Her Royal Highness, Grand Duchess Annaliese Emelie Sophia Elizabet of the Grand Duchy of Saint Gilbert."

My words hung over the table. It appeared my sisters were having the same problem processing it as I'd had. They turned to look at me at the exact moment wearing the exact expression, obviously waiting for me to say something that made sense, so I told them about the three men I'd met the night before and the story Maximilien—Max, by the end of the meeting—had told me.

I paused. "Actually, Max's grandfather was the man who helped Gran escape."

Roe looked up from her coffee and made another of her faces. This time it was her *WTF* face. "What kind of crazy shit is this?"

"I swear I'm not making this up."

"It sounds like a scam. They must want something." Roe frowned. "But what?"

"That was my first thought, too. But then they gave me this." I got up and got my bag and took the leather pouch out and spilled some of the contents across the table.

"What the hell?" Ceil picked up one of the earrings and turned it over in her hands. "I remember these. And this!" She reached for the ring, tears in her eyes. "Oh my God, I know this ring."

Roe took the earring from Ceil's hand, then shook the pouch and the other one fell out. She was speechless. Maybe for the first time in her life.

Then the two of them burst forth with a million questions at the same time.

"Stop. Please." I held my head. Now I really was on the verge of a migraine.

Ceil turned to me. "So they tracked you down to return the jewelry? How did they get their hands on it?"

"Max said that when Gran was sick and knew she didn't have much time, she returned it to friends in Saint Gilbert."

"There has to be an endgame." This from Roe.

"I'm getting to that. Here's the history in a nutshell. The Gilbertis ruled this little country for a very long time—like, hundreds and hundreds of years—and it is little, it's only about twelve hundred square miles according to the internet. Think Rhode Island. When the Nazis invaded the country, they killed Gran's parents and her brother and one of her sisters and some other assorted relatives, but Gran escaped, along with her sister Amelia, and made it to England, where they stayed until the war was over. Gran was only fifteen. She and her sister were the only members of the Gilberti family to survive."

"Oh my God, just like Anastasia," Roe gasped.

"Wow, she was just a little older than Juliette," Ceil said, ignoring Roe. "Can you imagine losing your entire family that way and being forced to flee your country? Poor Gran."

Roe and I both nodded. Poor Gran indeed. We'd never had a clue what she'd gone through.

"Anyway," I said after a moment's silence, "after the war, the Soviets 'liberated' the country from the Germans and made the country communist. When the Soviet Union was dissolved back in the 1990s, a lot of the small countries were gradually released and permitted to go back to self-rule."

"Saint Gilbert was one of them?" Ceil asked.

I nodded. "So over the past years, there was a lot of dissention and dialogue about what kind of government they should have. According to Max, they actually tried several—communism, socialism. Some wanted a democratic monarchy, like they have in the UK, some wanted a straight democracy. Some wanted a return to the monarchy because many of the citizens were old enough to remember that things were very good when the Gilbertis were in charge. Some even wanted to go back to being part of Russia. So earlier this year there was an election to settle things once and for all."

"And . . ." Roe gestured for me to hurry up.

"The people of Saint Gilbert voted to restore the monarchy."

"But there is no monarchy. Gran is dead, her siblings are dead . . ."

"So they looked for and found Gran's surviving family." Ceil always was quicker than Roe, bless her. "And with Mom and her brother gone, they found you. What do they want?"

"They want me to go back to Saint Gilbert with them and—well, reestablish the monarchy. And, ah . . . be the grand duchess."

In my mind's eye, I saw a sort of *poof* where this latest bombshell hit the table and exploded.

"Why you? Why not me? Or Ceil?" Roe asked bluntly.

"Because tradition called for the oldest daughter to inherit the throne. That would be me."

"What if there was no daughter?" Ceil asked.

"According to Max, that never happened. There was always at least one daughter per generation."

Another long silence.

"I call bullshit." Roe sneered. A real, honest to God sneer. You don't see many of those. "It's a scam."

"For what purpose? What could these people possibly want from me? I work my ass off to pay the mortgage on this little three-bedroom row house. I get child support but trust me, Ralphie eats through a month's worth in three days. What do I have that anyone could possibly want?"

I stared at Roe. Like I said, if anyone was going to be a pain in the ass, it would always be Roe. Only this time I didn't blame her. Not entirely, anyway.

Ceil reached across the table for the laptop and spun it around. I already had pulled up everything I could find related to Saint Gilbert, and she began to read through it.

"Saint Gilbert, the former Grand Duchy of Saint Gilbert, ruled for generations by the Gilberti family." Ceil looked up. "That's us, all right. Tucked into a corner between Italy, France, and Switzerland. Roughly the size of Rhode Island, like Annie said. Population about six hundred thousand." She read silently for another minute or two. "So far everything these guys told you about the history of the place checks out."

"Let me see that thing." Roe leaned over her and reached for it, and Ceil batted her hand away.

"Wait till I'm done."

"There isn't much here about the country's financial status," Ceil continued. "Doesn't seem like there's much going on there. No mention of manufacturing, nothing about agriculture, tourism, mining—nothing. Oh, wait, they do export wine and cheese—both cow and goat—mostly to neighboring countries." Ceil scanned the screen. "So how are the people supporting themselves? They can't all have cows, goats, and vineyards. Maybe the information wasn't available when this was written since the country was going through an upheaval of sorts." She looked at me over the laptop. "What are you going to do?"

"What am I going to do? You mean, what are *we* going to do? This is a family thing. It isn't just about me," I said.

"Annie, they didn't come here looking for Queen Cecilia. They sought you out to be their queen."

"Actually, there's no queen. It's grand duchess. That was the title Grandmere inherited. Max said her mother abdicated in her favor right before they sent Gran and her sister to flee the country." I was a little shaky on some of the details.

Silence again.

"Well, that explains a lot about her, doesn't it?" Ceil said. "Her bearing. Her elegance. Her . . . *presence*."

"Why aren't you jumping up and down and screaming?" Roe's eyes narrowed. "Why are you so calm?"

"I'm finding it hard to believe." I answered as honestly as I could. "How do you react to something like this? It's just too bizarre. Besides, this is serious stuff. This is life-changing. For real." I looked at Roe, who also wasn't jumping up and down screaming. In fact, none of us were. Which means we were all in shock and disbelieving, and/or we'd all watched *The Princess Diaries* three times the night before and had a call into the last video store in South Philly for a copy of *Roman Holiday*. Okay, that last part was probably just me. No one does *royal* like Audrey Hepburn. I figured I could learn a thing or two from her.

"Like I said. Crazy shit." Roe reached for the leather pouch and put the jewelry back in, pausing over the necklace. "I don't recognize this."

"I don't either." I looked at Ceil. "You?"

She shook her head.

"Well, it's too fancy for her to have worn on casual occasions, and we never saw her get dressed up. Those red stones are crazy big, though."

Roe held the necklace up to her throat. "Can you imagine if these stones were real? I bet they'd be worth a fortune."

"They're rubies, Roe, and they are real," Ceil told her.

"How do you know?" Roe held it up as if assessing its value.

"Remember after I graduated from Rosemont and I didn't know what I wanted to do? And Mom said the rule was you either went to work or—"

"Or you went to school. No exceptions." I repeated one of Mom's hard-and-fasts.

"Right. So she asked me what I was interested in, and I said jewelry, and she said to find out what I had to do to get a good job in that field. I talked to someone down on Jewelers' Row, and he said I needed to earn a certificate from the Gemological Institute of America. So I started taking the courses online. I only finished three of them." One by one, Ceil held up three fingers. "Diamonds. Colored stones. Gem identification. Trust me, little sister. Those are rubies, and they are flawless. And," she added, "they are undoubtedly worth a fortune."

"Wow." Roe's eyes widened. "We could sell them, and we could . . ."

"Over my dead body." I snatched the leather pouch from her. "They don't belong to us. They belong to the people."

"What people?" Roe made a face. "*Us* people. He gave them to you."

"They belong to the people of Saint Gilbert. And he didn't give them to me to personally own. He gave them to me to . . ." I hesitated while I thought it through. "To convince me to go there—to Saint Gilbert—and bring these with me."

Roe rolled her eyes.

Ceil ignored her. "Annie, did you tell the kids?"

"I wanted to talk to you first."

"Why?"

"Because it involves all of us. We're the granddaughters of the last grand duchess of the Grand Duchy of Saint Gilbert." My turn for a little eye rolling. "It even sounds goofy to say. It sounds so *Disney*, or like a Hallmark movie. But the point of this discussion is, what do I do now?"

"Did they invite all of us, or just you?" Ceil asked.

"Well, just me, I guess. It was more like, please come for a week or two or however long you want to stay and meet the people. See the country before you decide."

"Decide what?" Roe asked.

"Before she decides if she wants to be the grand duchess." Ceil, as always, went right to the heart of it. "And you're going, right?"

"Maybe. I don't know. I wanted to see what you guys think."

Roe grabbed the laptop, paused for a moment while she stared at the screen Ceil had been looking at, then turned it to face me. "This is a castle. A real castle. It's enormous. It has one hundred and ninety-seven rooms." She looked up. "That's even bigger than Caesars Hotel and Casino where I stayed in Atlantic City last year." She went back to the laptop. "It says this castle is where they lived. If nothing else, you should go for a vacation, check it out. Hey, maybe the stables where Gran kept her ponies are still there."

"I always thought that was something Mom made up. I never thought that was real." Ceil propped her elbow on the table, her chin resting in the palm of her hand. I felt her studying my face. "You're very solemn about this, Annie."

"It's solemn stuff. I almost feel as if I'm in shock."

"I could slap you a couple of times if you think it would help," Roe offered. I'm pretty sure she was kidding.

"Thanks, but another cup of coffee would be just as effective. Honestly, I don't know how I feel. This is about more than us. This is about six hundred thousand people who live in that country. So yeah, I'm waiting to have my 'yahoo' moment." Maybe because part of me still didn't believe any of it. Or maybe I'd hallucinated the whole thing. Except for Max, who I know is real.

Maybe I'd touched his arm a time or two last night, just to be sure.

"So what are you going to tell the kids?" Ceil asked.

"Just what I told you."

"How do you think they'll take it?" Roe scrolled through the pages she'd pulled up on the laptop. "Wow, there are some real high mountains there. And beautiful lakes. Oh, and here's another view of the castle. It looks like Cinderella's.

"'Built in 1740 of local white stone,'" Roe read aloud. "'The Gilberti family ruled Saint Gilbert from Castle Blanc, seen here in a recent photograph, until 1941, when the small duchy was overtaken,' yada yada. 'The last of the grand duchesses, Annaliese Emelie Sophia Elizabet'—that was Gran—'inherited the title upon the death of her mother,' blah blah. 'Immediately smuggled out of the country by a loyalist following the German invasion. Eventually she settled in the United States, where she lived quietly and raised a family, the details of which are not available.'" Roe looked up. "I wonder why she thought she had to keep it a secret."

"Maybe there are people in Saint Gilbert who didn't like the monarchy to begin with. Rebels, anarchists, socialists, whatever," Ceil said. "Maybe someone else who thought they should be on the throne. If there ever was to be a throne again."

"Then why didn't she change her name?" I wondered aloud. "She could have taken Grampa's name, but she didn't."

"Maybe because she was one of the last surviving members of the family, and she wanted to keep the name alive," Roe said. "Then again, I'll bet there are hundreds of people named Gilberti in this country. But why would anyone care? The country was in Russian hands for fifty years, or thereabouts, and she wasn't trying to make a comeback. Seems to me she was content to leave well enough alone." She tapped her fingers on the table. "It looks like this confirms everything they told you. Of course, they could have read the same Wikipedia page we did. Or written it."

"But what would their motive be?" Ceil bit the inside of her mouth, a habit she had when she was thinking what we used to tease were deep thoughts. "How can we find out what the political situation is there?"

"Google 'newspapers in Saint Gilbert,'" I suggested.

Ceil reclaimed the laptop and typed something.

"Doesn't look like much of a newspaper." She read for a few seconds. "But it does reference the January elections and the result. More than sixty-five percent of the voters want the monarchy brought back." She read for a few more seconds. "And it says a search is being conducted to locate living relatives of the last grand duchess." She looked up. "So there you go. Your three buddies were telling you the truth."

We sat in silence for a moment. Then Ceil said, "I think you should go and see for yourself. Check out the country, see what's what. They invited you and you should go. I would."

"It's hard to say no at this point. I mean, it could be real, and it could be a good thing." I wished I could be more decisive. Honestly, I'm usually not so wishy-washy, but this—this was different. It wasn't like choosing between basic black heels and slutty red ones.

"You could be walking into a trap," Roe warned.

"Right. A trap set by sex traffickers." I felt like Juliette, rolling my eyes as she does when she's invited to spend the night with a girlfriend and I call the girl's parents to make sure they're going to be home—even though sex traffickers had been my first thought, too. "Because there aren't enough middle-aged women in Europe to keep the traffickers happy."

"You need to go," Ceil announced. "Think of it as sort of a reconnaissance trip. You'll know if this is on the up-and-up. It could be very exciting and wonderful." She reached for my hand. "Whether it's worth uprooting your family, totally changing your life—all our lives, really—only you can decide. But I feel very strongly faced with the same decision, Mom would have gone."

She was right about that. Mom wouldn't have had to confer with anyone. She'd have had her bags packed and been out the door faster than you can say Annaliese Emelie Sophia Elizabet Gilberti.

"I think it's pretty clear Mom knew more about Gran's family than she let on," Ceil added.

I was thinking she was right about that, too. Why Mom chose not to share what she knew with us, I'll never know. But I do know she would have embraced this situation. I was starting to think I should, too. As Ceil said, it could be exciting and wonderful.

Or I could find myself in a large metal crate on my way to an auction somewhere to be sold to the highest bidder. If not sex slavers, maybe organ dealers.

"Ceil, is there any chance you could spend a week here, stay with the kids while I'm gone?"

"Sure. I can operate my business from here as well as I can from home. When do you want to leave?" she asked.

"I need to talk to the kids, and I'll need to talk to my boss. I have vacation time coming, so taking a week off isn't going to be a problem. I'll call the men I spoke with last night. Max gave me a card with his name on it." It was still in the pocket of my sweater.

"We need to go through your closet," Ceil said. "I bet you don't have a lot to wear in a castle."

"True. Mostly skirts, pants, a few dresses, and a couple of suits for big meetings or for those times when a judge orders me into court to make me face him during settlement negotiations." It was a tactic a few judges used to get the plaintiff money when the judge knew there was no coverage or no liability on our insured's part but they wanted to make sure everyone left their chambers happy. Well, everyone but the Philadelphia Fire, Casualty, and Liability Insurance Company. "I guess I could do some shopping."

Ceil nodded. "Saturday. I'll pick you up. We'll go to the King of Prussia Mall."

"Okay." I hoped Ralph Senior wasn't late with the child support payment this month.

"I think you should think it over a little more." This from Roe. Of course.

"I plan to. But I don't see any advantage in putting this off too long."

"I think you're crazy to go off alone with not one but three men you don't know. Why would you even consider that?" Roe asked. "You won't walk from here to that little neighborhood market by yourself at night."

"I want to see the country Grandmere came from. I want to see where she grew up." Even as I said it, I knew that deep inside, my decision had been made last night when I saw those rubies tumble from their pouch.

"It could be dangerous," Roe said.

"I'm pretty sure I'm willing to take that chance," I assured her in my calmest voice.

"I'd go with you if you didn't need me to stay with the kids," Ceil offered. "I think it sounds like an adventure."

"You can go." Roe turned to her. "I don't mind staying here."

I considered it for a moment before the thought of Roe spending a week in my house with my children, teaching them things I've tried hard to wean them from. Like whining. Like being afraid to try new things. Like not trusting your gut. Indoctrinating them with her religion—Negativity—and taking them to her chosen place of worship, the Temple of No.

I decided to go for mature and gracious and tried to sound sincere. "Thanks, Roe, I appreciate the offer, but Ceil can make her own hours, which you can't do."

"True." Roe reached for the laptop. "I want to take another look at that castle."

Ceil got up and headed for the stairs. "I want to see what's in your closet. Then we'll make a list of what we're going to buy."

"Easy does it, sissy. I'm not a duchess yet."

~

I told the kids when they got home from school in the afternoon. Neither believed me until I showed them the pages on my laptop and pointed out their great-grandmother's name right there on the screen.

Juliette sat up straight, her eyes shining. "Oh my God! Oh my God! We're royalty." She poked her brother. "You can call me Princess Juliette."

"Prince Ralphie." He stood and preened in the mirror over the sideboard. "Damn. That has a ring." He turned to face me. "Prince Ralph. I'll make the name cool again."

"As if it ever was," Jules muttered.

"I honestly don't know what your titles would be. Or if you even would have one." No point in feeding that fantasy just yet.

"This is the craziest shit I ever heard." Juliette dissolved into laughter that bordered on the hysterical.

"Language, please."

Ralphie demonstrated his best gangsta strut around the dining room. "We're going to *bring* it to that place," he told his sister.

I momentarily considered going to Saint Gilbert and staying there until they both graduated from college.

"Ralph, enough with that . . . whatever you call that . . ." I waved my hand in his direction.

Juliette got up and began to rush from the room, her phone in her hand, her thumbs moving wildly. "OMG, I can't wait to tell everyone! They're going to be so jealous! The look on snotty Tiffany Stout's face is going to be epic!"

I stood, both hands held up in front of me. "No! No! You will not tell anyone, do you hear me?"

My daughter stopped in her tracks.

"Huh? Why not? If it's true, then . . ."

"We need to confirm a few things. In the meantime, you are not to tell anyone—I mean *anyone*—about this. Do you understand?" I looked from one of my children to the other. They were both clearly still in fantasy land. "Promise me."

"I promise," Ralph muttered.

"Promise what?"

"I promise not to tell anyone."

"Juliette?"

My daughter bit the inside of her lip on the right side, and I could tell she was getting ready to plead her case.

"Can I just tell Marisa?" She folded her hands in supplication. "Please?"

"No. Marisa's mother has the biggest mouth in South Philly. Besides"—I knew this part would hit both my kids where they lived—"suppose there's been a mistake. Are you willing to look like the world's biggest loser in front of all your friends?"

They both turned white.

"So what are we going to do?" Juliette put the phone down.

"I am taking a week to go to Saint Gilbert and check things out. You are staying here with Aunt Ceil. If you want to talk to anyone about all this, feel free to discuss it with her or Aunt Roe. But no one else. Got it?"

My children nodded.

"Now go do your homework."

"Why can't we go with you?" Jules asked.

"Because I have no idea what I'm going to find when I get there."

Jules frowned, but nodded. She gathered her book bag and turned to leave the room. "Do you think there's a castle?"

"There is. There's a picture of it on the internet. Look up Castle Blanc, Saint Gilbert."

"Ohmygod." Jules looked about to hyperventilate as she and her brother headed for the stairs. "I'm going to be a princess! My family owns a castle! Top that, Tiffany Stout!"

I could hear them excitedly discussing the news as they climbed the steps. I waited until I heard their respective bedroom doors close, then I took the card from my pocket and dialed the number Max had given me the night before.

Chapter Four

"I still don't understand why I can't go with you." Juliette sat on the end of my unmade bed and pouted, ready to plead her case for about the fiftieth time.

"Because you have school, and last time I looked, you weren't doing so well in algebra." I stood in front of my (very small) closet and debated over whether I should take another pair of shoes. I'd already packed walking shoes—a.k.a. white tennis sneakers—my favorite ballet flats, a wear-with-just-about-anything pair of strappy heeled sandals, a fun pair of leopard-print flats, and of course, those fancy very high heels Ceil talked me into at Nordstrom. I'd also picked up a little black dress à la Audrey Hepburn (*Breakfast at Tiffany's*) and two sundresses since I read the summer temperatures in Saint Gilbert averaged in the eighties, and I'd hit up Chico's for some of their knit things that don't wrinkle even if you roll them up and stomp on them, so for the first time in my life, I wouldn't have to overpack. "And you have that big history test next week, am I correct?"

Juliette rolled her eyes.

"Jules? History test next week?" I closed the suitcase.

"Yes. Test next week. But if I'm going to be a princess—or whatever they call the daughter of the grand duchess over there—why would I need to know American history? I already know a lot. I know all about the Civil War and the Revolution."

"But right now you're studying the Second World War. Which, I might remind you, was when the Germans invaded Saint Gilbert and killed our ancestors and forced my grandmother to flee." I hoped by looping in some family history, she'd become a little more interested.

"Yeah, well, we won't be reading about that."

"History is history. And you know what they say. Those who fail to learn from history are doomed to repeat it."

"I want to see the castle." Jules was still pouting like a cranky three-year-old. At least Ralph had a baseball game after school—we'd said goodbye this morning—so I didn't have them both leaning on me. Ralphie does well in every sport, and even though my Wildcat heart would love nothing more than to eventually see him in Villanova blue and white on the basketball court, his heart is on the soccer field. He's really very good, if I may brag on him for a moment, but they don't play soccer in the spring here, and the boy needs to run off all that energy—and hormones—so baseball it is.

"I'll take pictures." I hoisted the suitcase off the bed and set it on the floor next to my carry-on bag, which held the necessities of life in case my suitcase went to Iceland as I was heading to Switzerland: toothbrush, toothpaste, underwear, the little black dress I'd bought on Saturday, two belts, two Chico's tops, their basic black sheath, and those strappy heeled sandals. If the worst happens, I won't have to be out and about for a couple of days in the outfit I'm wearing on the plane: a black pencil skirt, a long-sleeved rose silk shirt, a black tunic-length knitted cardigan, and the basic black heels I'd bought to replace the ones I'd been wearing to work every day for the past gazillion years. I carried the new black leather bag Ceil had bought me for the occasion. I'd wanted to wear pants, but Ceil reminded me I'd probably be arriving at the castle in whatever I wore on the plane, so I should go for the skirt.

Did I mention we were landing in Switzerland? Yes, Switzerland. Because Saint Gilbert doesn't have its own airport. What kind of country doesn't have an airport?

"Annie?" Ceil called from the bottom of the steps. "A car just pulled up out front."

"Okay, I'm coming," I called back. I ducked into the bathroom with the bag containing my makeup to touch up my face. I pulled out the face wash, my favorite moisturizer, and my all-in-one shampoo and conditioner and set them on the counter while I searched for my lipstick.

"And a man is walking up to the door . . . and, oh my . . ." Her voice trailed off.

Must be Max. I stuffed the lipstick back into the bag, tossed it into my carry-on, and grabbed my suitcase from my room.

I made it downstairs, dragging my suitcase—okay, Ceil's suitcase, since mine is a wreck having spent the last sixteen years schlepping kids' things back and forth to the Jersey Shore—and stopped next to the newel post to take a deep breath.

"You okay, Toots?" Ceil tore her gaze from the front window, through which Max could be seen approaching the front door.

"I'm good." I wasn't good. I was a nervous wreck. This was happening too quickly. I wasn't ready. I might never be ready. I'd been awake all night thinking about the potential consequences of this trip, and I was pretty sure I hadn't yet thought of everything that could go wrong.

Dear God, I was starting to sound like Roe.

The doorbell rang, and both Ceil and I lunged for it.

She got there first.

"Hi. I'm Ceil. Annie's sister. You must be . . ."

"Maximilien Belleme at your service, madam." He didn't exactly bow, but he did almost bend at the waist just a teeny bit when he dipped his head slightly.

Ceil sighed.

I'm pretty sure I know what kind of service my sister was imagining Max could perform for her.

"And I'm Juliette." Jules stepped forward, stars clearly dancing in her eyes. "Annaliese's daughter."

"Ah yes, Juliette, Her Highness's only daughter." Max, born to charm, took her hand and planted just the whisper of a kiss on her knuckles. Jules visibly swooned, and I admit I almost did as well. "And as such, second in line to the throne."

"What?" Juliette's eyes grew wide. "What?" She turned to me. "You never said . . ."

I shrugged. It had never occurred to me there'd be a second to the throne, since I wasn't sure I was going to be first.

Jules turned back to Max. "What will I be called when my mom is crowned—"

I cleared my throat.

"*If* my mom is crowned grand duchess?"

Max smiled. "You would be Her Royal Highness Princess Juliette Elizabet Terese."

"How do you know my middle name and my confirmation name?" Jules asked. Then the effect of what he'd said seemed to hit her all at once. "Wait—princess? Ohmygod, *princess*? I *knew* it! Princess Juliette. For real? Ohmygod . . ."

Max smiled again, then turned to me.

"Allow me to carry your things, Your Grace." I should point out here that he said those words without cracking a smile.

I'd asked him not to call me that—just Annie or Annaliese, but so far, it's been "Your Highness" or "Your Grace."

He gathered my bags and headed for the front door. He stopped halfway there and asked, "Shall we?"

"Wouldn't have to ask me twice." Ceil's eyes were fixed on Max, and they said it all.

That's right, my normally sensible, no-nonsense sister Cecilia was practically drooling over my new best friend, Max.

"Would you listen to yourself? He's at least ten years younger than you are," I whispered as I followed Max out the door.

"I can't help it. Besides, who cares how old he is? He looks like a young George Clooney. Only better."

"I know, right? Just like I told you," I said in total agreement, then I reminded myself this was a serious excursion I was embarking on. Depending on the outcome, this next week could change our lives forever. I needed to take it seriously, and I needed everyone else to take it seriously as well. I hugged my sister. "Thank you for staying with the kids. There's no one else I'd trust to stay with them."

"There's always Roe." Ceil hugged me back.

I smacked her lightly on the backside. "Not funny."

Max and the Fireplug were loading my bags into the trunk of the Lincoln Town Car. Dead Man Walking opened the rear passenger door and stood next to it as if he were standing at attention in front of Buckingham Palace.

"Mom, you have a *driver*." Juliette had followed me outside.

"I see that." The trunk lid slammed, and I turned to take my baby girl in my arms. "Be good for Aunt Ceil, hear?" She nodded. "I'll call or text every day. You'd better respond. Like, within five minutes unless you're in class."

"Why would you text me when I'm in class?" Jules hugged me tight.

"Because I'm not sure of the time difference over there. I'll figure it out and I'll try not to call when you're in school." I held on to her for as long as I could.

"And why do I even have to go to class since I'm going to be a princess?" she whined.

"Hey, you're not a princess yet. Don't count your tiaras before they're on your head."

"Mom?" she whispered in my ear.

"What, sweet pea?" God, I was going to miss this kid. And I was only going away for a week.

"Don't take this the wrong way, okay? I mean, I love you and I hope you live forever." She took a deep breath. "But when you die, will I really be the grand duchess?"

~

The plane took off on time, and by on time, I mean only forty minutes after its scheduled departure. I sat next to Max, and his compadres—who I now knew were John-Paul Laurent (Fireplug) and Marcel Barsotti (Dead Man Walking)—were directly behind us. I kept trying to think of something to say, but my mind was swirling. For one thing, I hate to fly, though I had to admit flying first class was way better than any other option. Except for maybe a private jet. That would be pretty great, too. For another, I still had to pinch myself to be sure this was all really happening. And then there was the matter of whether I'd lost my mind by agreeing to do this. I still wasn't sure. I kept telling myself it wasn't too late to change my mind—until it was because we were on the plane and it was headed down the runway.

I sat back and closed my eyes until we were in the air. Did I mention flying terrifies me?

"I'm so very glad you decided to return to Saint Gilbert, Your . . . ," Max began.

I jabbed him with my elbow.

"*Annaliese.* Your arrival is anxiously awaited at the castle."

"One, you can't return to a place you've never been. And two"—I sat up and opened my eyes, and whispered—"I thought we agreed there wasn't going to be any kind of announcement."

"There hasn't been. But arrangements had to be made for your stay, and certain protocols have to be in place."

"Why? Why can't you just put me up in a nice little B and B for the week and let me sightsee, if the purpose of this visit is for me to see the country?"

"I don't believe there are any bed-and-breakfasts in Saint Gilbert. There's very little need for them since tourism is nonexistent." He lowered his voice. "And there's the matter of your safety to be considered."

"What 'matter of my safety' are we talking about?" I turned to look him full in the face. Which under other circumstances I might have enjoyed. Did I mention how beautiful his eyes are, or that he has these long, dark lashes?

"There is a faction—a very small faction, I assure you—that opposes the return of the monarchy. We simply want to make certain you are . . . *well insulated* from them." He added hastily, "Few though they may be."

"I don't have a problem with a difference of opinion. Maybe they're right. Maybe the monarchy is yesterday's news. Maybe there's a better way for the country to be governed." I still couldn't believe anyone in their right mind would consider me suitable for governing an entire country. Have they met the man I'd married? That alone should speak to my decision-making abilities. "Maybe I should talk to them and find out what their objections are."

"That would be ill-advised, Your . . . Annaliese. Especially at this time."

"What do you mean, *at this time*?"

"Feelings are still running somewhat high so soon after the election."

"I thought you said the election was in January. It's the end of April. That's four months."

Max shrugged.

"Well, at some time, someone should have an open dialogue with these people. Me or whoever ends up, you know, taking charge." I could not bring myself to say the R word: *rule.*

"Perhaps in time," he conceded. "After things have settled down a bit and the country is on the right track."

"What track is it on now?"

"Things are a bit . . . muddled."

"Muddled," I repeat blankly.

"Politically."

"You said the country voted for the return of the monarchy." I thought for a moment. "But there must be some sort of governing body already in place. A council, or a parliament, or something."

"It's called the Duke's Council, yes."

"Even though there's no grand duke?"

"There was when it was first convened in 1682, and up until 1941. There are still some who inherited titles that ensure them a seat on the council."

"So what do they do? Make laws? Pass tariffs? Appoint judges? Aren't there diplomats who interact with other countries? Ambassadors? Are they in charge right now?" If I sounded exasperated, well, I was.

"Yes, the Duke's Council does those things and is in charge."

"So why don't they just stay in charge? Why do they need a grand duchess, whether it's me or someone else?"

"Because they cannot agree on anything." He sighed deeply, and it was apparent that this was of real concern to him. "Since 1993, the council has been comprised of hereditarily titled dukes. Some of those factions I mentioned have been at odds with each other before, during, and since the election. It is sad to say, but we are dealing with a tangle of egos. They will never agree on what's best for the people in our country because they're all concerned with their own interests."

Like so many in our Congress, I could have said, but did not. "So what makes you think I can talk them into agreement?"

"You don't have to. If there's a dispute, the monarch makes the final decision. In the absence of a monarch, majority rules."

"Which explains why certain factions might not be happy to see me arrive in Saint Gilbert." I couldn't believe I allowed myself to be put in this position, that I'd allowed myself to be talked into coming on this trip. "And wait . . . aren't dukes always men?"

Max nodded.

"So this council is comprised of all men? No women?"

He nodded again.

"Well, that's going to have to change," I muttered.

"That would be difficult to accomplish, madam. That would involve changing the Duke's Council to . . . something else. There would be resistance."

Of course there would be.

"What kind of resistance? Is anyone going to be, like, you know, *shooting* at me?"

"One would hope not, madam." Max's face was serious. "But you will always be well guarded. As royals should be. We are even now recruiting a new class of guards in anticipation of the restoration."

Right then and there, I decided I'd spend my week getting to know the land of my grandmother's birth before heading back to Philly after having given my final answer—thanks but no thanks—and waved buh-bye.

"You needn't be concerned about your safety. But you do need to know that the most important reason we need a grand duchess is that the majority of the country's assets are in a bank in Switzerland, not to be released until a rightful heir is coronated."

"So in other words, I—theoretically—hold the key to the vault?"

"In so many words, yes." Max sighed heavily. "Saint Gilbert needs help moving forward. It's not a rich country. We have few natural resources and, as I mentioned, no tourism to speak of."

"Why is that?" I wondered aloud. "Every European country has tourists."

"Where there are commercial attractions, yes." He tilted his head toward mine slightly. "Saint Gilbert has very little in the way of commercial attractions."

Swell. I'm being offered the chance to rule a country that has no prospects, a dueling council, and all its money stashed in a Swiss bank that only I—or someone like me—can access.

"You have a castle, right? Everyone wants to see a castle," I said.

"We have more than one, actually. However, some are not readily accessible, and others are in need of some . . . repair," he said cagily.

"But you have mountains, don't you? I mean, you're right there next to Switzerland. People go there to ski, right?"

He sort of half nodded his head.

"What, people don't ski in Saint Gilbert?"

"Yes," he said. "But mostly to get from one place to another in the winter."

"Meaning what, you don't have roads?"

"Some of the more remote areas . . . not exactly."

"Are you kidding me?" I shook my head in disbelief. "Gosh, this place sounds better and better all the time. Why aren't there roads?"

He hesitated for a moment. "There were roads once, roads that connected rural areas to the capital city, Beauchesne—that's where you'll be living—"

"Staying," I corrected him.

"Yes, yes, of course. Many of the roads to the rural villages were destroyed during the war, and after the invasion, while the Soviets promised to repair them, nothing was done to improve the infrastructure. They left the country with very little to work with, to put it mildly."

"What exactly do you expect of me?"

"The people of Saint Gilbert look to America as . . . how did your former president say it, 'the shining city on a hill'? When it was made known that the rightful heir to the throne was American, the idea to return the country to its monarchal state spread like wildfire. Everyone knows when the going gets tough, the Americans roll up their sleeves and get tougher. We all have heard of American ingenuity."

Dear God. He said it all with a straight face.

Then he added, almost apologetically, "I believe the people are looking to you to help them move forward into the twenty-first century."

My jaw dropped open as far as it would go, and it was all I could do not to laugh. Was he kidding?

"Look, I am not Joan of Arc or Mother Teresa or Indira Gandhi or . . . crap. I have no experience ruling anything. It sounds like you're all looking for someone to perform some sort of miracle. The only miracle I've ever performed was getting myself out of a bad marriage with my sanity. I'm a middle-aged single mother who's working her ass off to raise a couple of kids and keep them out of trouble and keep my head above water financially. I can balance my own budget, but barely. What makes you or anyone else think I can make a difference in Saint Gilbert?"

"Ah, but you know how to work hard. You're intelligent, as proven by your school transcripts. You graduated with honors from the esteemed Villanova University. We know of their excellent basketball."

I frowned. "How did you get my transcripts?"

Ignoring me, he continued. "Americans are known to be innovative problem solvers. Add the indisputable fact you are the heir to the throne, and there was no need for further discussion."

I started to protest, but he held up one hand.

"Don't overthink this. Please. Just visit our country. Stay in the city. Drive through the hills. Meet our people." He paused. "They're your people, too."

"Max . . ."

"Please. All I ask for now is you give yourself a chance to get to know us. Bring a fresh eye to the table, as you Americans like to say. See the country. Keep an open mind." He smiled. "And if nothing else, you're going to be spending a week in a European castle."

"There is that." I tried to force a smile, too, but I think the result may have been more like a grimace.

We sat quietly for a few long moments. Finally, I asked, "How are you involved in this?"

"I told you my grandfather was the man who brought your grandmother and great-aunt to safety after the Nazis came through Saint Gilbert."

"How did that happen?"

"They set out through Switzerland into Italy; however, I am not certain of the exact route they took."

"No, no. I meant, how did it happen that he was the one to help them?"

"He was the captain of the castle guard. It was his duty to protect the royal family."

"I see." After another moment passed, I asked, "And what is your duty, Max?"

"The same as his, madam," Max said. "The position is hereditary."

So the too-hot guy with the gorgeous eyes was my bodyguard. I could live with that for a week.

Chapter Five

We landed in Geneva, Switzerland, and oh, the view from the plane took my breath away. First of all, flying over the Alps is an experience this city girl could never have imagined. The mountain peaks actually went through the clouds in places! And Lake Geneva! It positively glittered in the morning sunlight. Looking out the window of the plane before we landed, I thought of the pictures of the castle in Saint Gilbert, which showed a lake.

I asked Max, "Does the lake in Saint Gilbert sparkle as much as Lake Geneva?"

"I would say more, but then you would think I was speaking from prejudice. So let me say only that soon you will be able to judge for yourself."

A car was there waiting for us. The four of us—Max, John-Paul, Marcel, and I—piled in. John-Paul took the wheel and Marcel rode shotgun, leaving Max to share the back seat with me. After several hours of driving, we stopped in a picturesque town for lunch, but I was so nervous I don't remember what I ate. Even though several weeks had passed between my first meeting with Max and company and getting off the plane in Geneva, it all seemed to rush toward me like an Amtrak commuter. I had a feeling in the pit of my stomach that grew more uncomfortable with every passing mile. Fight or flight was only valid if there was an option for one or the other. I had neither.

Okay, so maybe another little bit of confession is in order: I'm a little bit of a controlling person. I'm a Leo, so I don't feel I should be held responsible for it, but that's the truth. I try hard to keep it from getting out of hand, but sometimes my natural diva takes over, and then you just need to stand back and watch a master at work. Which is one of the reasons it's so hard for me to understand why I didn't take command of this situation from day one and be more decisive. Like Ceil had said, Mom would have been on the first plane out of Philly—and Mom was a Gemini. Maybe it was because my kids were still young, or maybe I was afraid it was all true, what Max had told me at that first meeting.

If it were true, I'd have to change my entire life. And imperfect as it was, I liked my life. Routine in some ways, sure, but they were routines because I'd chosen them. I had money problems at times, and my kids were far from perfect, and sometimes, yeah, I admit I missed the company of a great guy. I loved my friends—Marianne was like my sister from an Irish mother—and I liked my job. I'd been rolling along at my own sweet speed since I divorced Ralph Senior, and I was fine with the pace I set for myself. So all the hemming and hawing I'd been doing was so not like me.

Finding out there were some factions that might not be too happy to see me on Saint Gilbert soil added a whole new level to my anxiety.

Yes, I could have said no right from the beginning and let the boys go looking for someone else. Surely they could shake another branch of the Gilberti tree to find a suitable heir. My mom's late brother, my uncle Theo, had a daughter, Beth, who was three years younger than Roe. I haven't seen her in years, because Uncle Theo moved to Wyoming when he married his second wife. So I don't know what Beth's been doing since she was convicted of embezzlement—before he died two years ago, Uncle Theo said that whole thing had been a setup—but as far as I know she's still alive and out there, so if need be, there's a backup, right, once she's served her time?

And then there's always Ceil, I guess. I mean, if the oldest can't or won't accept the job, maybe it could fall to the next oldest, right? And there was that comment Max had made to Juliette about being "next in line." I obviously hadn't asked enough questions.

But here I was, in the back seat of a shiny black car that was speeding around corkscrew curves, John-Paul driving as if it were his last shot to qualify for a spot on the Formula 1 circuit.

The scenery, however, was to die for. Huge white snow-clad mountains slid down into deep green valleys, and when I say huge, I mean don't think the Poconos. These mountains totally dominated the landscape. The lakes reflected the highest peaks and the sky. And oh, the sky! It was bigger than I'd ever seen, even bigger than the sky hanging over the ocean in Margate, New Jersey, on a clear summer night. There were mountain passes that took my breath away—literally, since some of them were guarded from the steep slopes only by ropes tied onto posts. I hadn't been that scared since Ralphie shamed me into going with him on the roller coaster at Great Adventure (referred to as Six Flags by everyone except New Jerseyans and those in adjacent states).

We passed streams that ran alongside the road and meadows where cows the color of rich cream grazed. Now, I'm a city girl, and to me, cows are brown and white, maybe black and white. But I never saw white cows like these. I turned in my seat to look at them as we drove by, and Max must have noticed my curiosity.

"Charolais." He pointed to the white cows.

"Is that French? I don't speak French." Actually, I don't speak any language other than English. I've never even been outside the USA. "I don't know what Charolais means. Wait, do they only speak French in Saint Gilbert?"

"English is the official language," Max told me. Still looking out the window, he said, "Charolais is the breed of cow. Originally from Charolles, in Burgundy, in eastern France. Now they're bred in America and other countries as well," he explained. "There are several herds in

Saint Gilbert, but also there are other breeds as well. Montbéliarde, Abondance, Aubrac, Tarentaise, and of course, the Rouge, which are found only in Saint Gilbert."

"They're all kinds of cows?"

"Yes. Breeds."

"Right. Breeds of cows. You mentioned that cheese was an important export."

Max nodded. "There are certain cheeses made *only* in Saint Gilbert. You will, of course, be introduced to them."

"But they're sold in America, right?"

"We cannot sell our cheeses in America, madam. They're made from unpasteurized milk, the import of which your laws prohibit."

"Then why don't you pasteurize the milk if it would open a large market for the farmers?" I asked.

He looked at me as if I were speaking in tongues. His expression read *blasphemy*.

"It would alter the character of the cheese, Annaliese," he said kindly, as if speaking to a three-year-old. "Also, we could not produce enough to export to America. Our cheeses are made the exact way they were made generations ago. The cheese from each village has its own particular flavor. Heating the milk to pasteurize it would alter the flavor."

Chastised, I looked out the window and watched the mountains fly by.

We drove for almost two hours before John-Paul slowly pulled the car to the side of the road and turned off the ignition. Why stop now?

"Why are we stopping?" I asked.

John-Paul turned and looked at Max, who nodded, then opened the back door of the car, got out, and walked around the vehicle to open the door on my side. He leaned in slightly, his hand extended to me. It was clear he wanted me to get out.

"What?" I asked, confused.

"Please. Come." His hand hung in midair, and when I looked toward the front seat, both John-Paul and Marcel had turned to face the windshield.

It occurred to me then that I could have totally misread this situation from the start. For once in her negativity-filled life, could Roe have been right? My overactive imagination—fueled most likely by fatigue and nerves—caused my blood to freeze in my veins. I had visions of a painful departure from this world à la *Goodfellas*.

Had I been played big-time? Were the three of them members of the faction that had not wanted to restore the monarchy but to make certain it would never be restored? Starting with eliminating the next in line, which would be me.

I swallowed hard and took Max's hand and allowed him to lead me from the car. We walked a few steps into an open field studded with blue and yellow flowers. I squeezed my eyes closed tightly. When I'd thought about how I'd leave this earth, I never pictured myself standing in a field of wildflowers in Switzerland next to a gorgeous man who possibly was about to hasten my departure.

"Open your eyes, Annaliese," Max said. "I want you to see the exact spot where your grandmother left her homeland and entered Switzerland as she fled the German army."

My eyes flew open. "Huh?"

"This is the border between Saint Gilbert and Switzerland, the very place where the grand duchess and her sister made their way to freedom. From here they traveled to Italy, and from there, eventually, to England. But this is where their journey began."

I was so relieved I almost passed out. I was all but hyperventilating, and my knees barely held me upright.

"We thought perhaps you would like to make part of that journey in reverse," he continued, "by walking from Switzerland into Saint Gilbert."

"Oh. Of course. Yes." Hysterical laughter was barely under control at this point. "Yes. I'd love that. Thank you. So thoughtful."

He took my arm, and after several steps, he paused on the edge of a large, flat rock and gestured to the valley below us.

"Welcome to Saint Gilbert, Your Highness," he said softly.

Honestly, I don't know where it came from, but I had a lump in my throat almost as big as the boulder we stood on. I guess that was for Grandmere's sake, should she be watching. I had a powerful feeling she might be. She should have been able to come home, and while I'm pretty sure I'm no substitute for her, I resolve to do her proud with every step I take from here on out.

I looked down upon green hills and valleys where small stone farmhouses and barns stood along the roadside and tiny villages dotted the landscape. There were white cows like the ones we'd seen in Switzerland—the Charolais—and sheep and goats in nearby fields enclosed by ancient stone walls. The sky here was the clearest, brightest blue I'd ever seen, the mountains high and snow covered, and in the far distance, there was a lake of sparkly blue water kissed by sunlight, and ohmygod, as Jules would say, there was the castle, white and turreted and straight out of a fairy tale, next to the lake.

"It's . . ." I tried to find words, but I had none. I actually had to fight back tears.

"Indeed it is, madam." Max nodded as if he understood. "Shall we return to the car now?"

"Could we walk for a little? We've been sitting so long, first in the plane, then in the car, and the countryside here is breathtaking." Reasons enough to walk, I told myself, but deep inside, I knew what I was feeling went deeper than merely a need to stretch my legs. I still couldn't put my finger on it, but moments later, it came to me.

I felt my grandmother there with me then, as deeply as I'd ever felt the presence of anyone. Her light touch on the back of my head, once so familiar, and the scent of violets that always surrounded her were not products of my imagination. She was there. More than wanting to walk where she had walked, I wanted to walk her home.

And I did—well, part of the way. We started down the mountain road, and while I didn't know how far we walked, I held out as long as I could before I had to wave the white flag. I was exhausted, I'm not gonna lie. I was sweating and my feet were killing me since I'd talked myself into wearing the new plain black heels I'd picked up at Neiman Marcus when I made a super-quick dash at lunchtime on Thursday for a few last-minute things. I hated that I felt I had to dodge my best friend—Marianne and I always shopped together at lunchtime—but I just couldn't bring myself to talk about Gran and Saint Gilbert. I'll tell her when the time comes, and she'll understand. I hope.

Max and I barely spoke as we walked except when he would point out something he thought I might like to be aware of: the lonely ruins of a farm where the Nazis had torched the house and barn; a small village known for its particularly fine wine, the sunlit vineyards scrambling up the hillside; and the weathered remains of an old stone chateau where relatives of mine, long gone now, had once lived. They'd been routed by the Soviets, their vineyards destroyed. I wanted to ask Max if he knew what had happened to them, but the lump in my throat was too big for words to slide past. Gran must have known, though, because I felt a wave of sadness pass from her to me. Whatever had happened there hadn't been good.

When I finally had enough, I practically crawled onto the back seat. And just like that, I knew Gran was gone. I guess she just wanted to see my first reaction to her homeland, and she was satisfied.

Chapter Six

By the time we reached the outskirts of Beauchesne, I was having an out of body experience. I asked John-Paul to stop for a moment. We were on a hill outside the city, the castle and the lake below, and I rolled down the window for a better look. Ancient oak trees lined the road that led into the town square. From the square, the cobbled street led to the castle, which dazzled from any angle. Something fluttered inside me, like something coming to life.

"Beauchesne." Max nodded toward the city that lay before us. "It means 'beautiful oak.'"

Now I should put it right out there that I did, in fact, pretend to be a princess when I was little, like around four or five. (You too? I mean is there even a girl who never did? Never once?) I told everyone I lived in a castle that was surrounded by a dark forest of twisted thorn trees and a moat. I saw that scene in a book once, and obviously that picture made a lasting impression on my young mind. The castle I gazed upon was nothing like that. This castle was made of white stone, and it had real turrets that soared toward the sky and wings that led in different directions. There was no moat, but the beautiful crystal-clear lake met a stone wall behind the castle. From an arched opening in the wall, steps led down to the water. And yes, the lake *did* sparkle more brilliantly than Lake Geneva.

"What do you think?" Max asked as I stared wide-eyed.

"It's beautiful. I saw a picture online, but it was nothing like this. This is . . ." I threw up my hands. I couldn't even put it into words.

"Would you like to continue on to the castle now?"

I nodded and the car began to ease slowly down the hill and into the city, where the street narrowed. On either side were shops in a row of Tudor-style half-timber buildings. There was a bakery with piles of bread and displays of pastries and cakes in the window, a dressmaker, a bookshop, a restaurant, a chocolate shop, a pub, a hairdresser, and a café with small tables set outside on the cobbled sidewalk where a small group gathered and chatted in soft voices. If our passing was noticed, I saw no sign of it. A square complete with a fountain lay just ahead. There was a statue in its center but because of the trees, I couldn't really tell what it was. All I could see from the car was what looked like a huge fish tail.

Opposite one side of the square stood a large church made of the same white stone as the castle, its spires rising into the sky. Next to the church the road led to the white fantasy castle. John-Paul waved at a man in uniform who stood at one side of the tall stone pillars marking the entrance to the castle grounds, and my heart was pounding so hard I was afraid I'd pass out. We drove past the pillars and through a gate that opened for us, then along a winding road lined with neatly trimmed boxwood. I wondered if the view had changed much since my gran lived here, if this was the same as what she'd seen when she'd looked over her shoulder as she fled her home.

The castle was at the end of that road, and because of all the twists and turns, I'd been able to see it from different perspectives. It was so much bigger than I'd imagined, much more beautiful and imposing. I swear, I felt like I'd just stepped into the pages of a fairy tale. John-Paul stopped close to a square tower that jutted slightly from the front, in the middle of which was a very tall and wide arched wooden door. I was so turned around I wasn't even sure this was the front of the castle. Max held the car door for me, and when I got out and stared up at that magnificent structure, my breath caught in my throat as I tried to take it in.

This was no fairy tale. While the past few weeks had held the air of a daydream, the building in front of me was very, very real. Its size diminished me and for a moment, I was seven years old standing on the steps of the Philadelphia Museum of Art for the first time and feeling very small indeed.

When I tell you my knees shook and my hands began to sweat a little, you'll understand, right? It's not every day you get to stand before a castle from which your family once ruled an entire country. Even if that country was no bigger than Rhode Island, still, I was looking at hundreds of years of my family history. It was humbling, even a little intimidating. If not for the war, my mother would likely have grown up here, my sisters and I possibly as well.

I heard my mother whisper, *Annaliese, stand up straight. And don't forget your manners.*

And Gran: *Smile, child. Be gracious.*

I straightened my back, and together the four of us approached the enormous arched door, which swept open as we drew near. A call had obviously been made to alert whoever was inside that we were on our way, because the man who opened the door wore what looked like a military-style coat complete with all sorts of brass and ribbon badges and a red sash that went from his right shoulder to his left hip. Behind him stood a gathering of people who peered anxiously around him, apparently to get a good look at me.

"Your Highness." He bowed from the waist, his bald head nodding once. "We have waited for a very long time to welcome you."

I turned to Max and silently begged for help.

"Your Grace, permit me to introduce you to Vincens DellaVecchio, grand chancellor of Saint Gilbert and a ranking member of our council." Max touched my elbow. "Chancellor, it is my honor to present

Her Royal Highness, the Grand Duchess, Annaliese Jacqueline Terese Gilberti."

I wanted to remind him I was not the grand duchess yet and I didn't know if I ever would be, but I didn't want to embarrass Max—or incur the wrath of Mom—so I said, "How do you do." Something I never said—let's face it, where I come from a good *Yo* or *How you doin'* can mean pretty much the same thing—but it seemed right under the circumstances, considering the fact that I had no idea what a grand chancellor did, but he was obviously important enough that he wore a red sash and gold braid on his jacket, and he was the one who got to open the door.

"Your Highness, I cannot adequately express the joy your visit brings. You are the answer to our prayers." His voice was warm, smooth as silk, his words well chosen. He looked to be around midfifties and cut quite the fancy figure in his finery, I had to admit. I wondered how old that jacket was—did they even have an army here?—and how he'd managed to preserve the brass and the gold fringe.

I was about to set the record straight about my visit—I've never been the answer to anyone's prayers—when Max stepped forward.

"Her Highness has agreed to visit with us for a brief time," Max said, and there was something in the way he tilted his head and looked down into the face of Vincens the Grand that gave me the feeling he wasn't all that fond of the chancellor. My gut was telling me the chancellor returned the feeling.

Interesting. I tucked that away for another time.

"We are grateful for however long you will honor us with your presence." Again, a half bow from Vincens. "But I'm sure Your Grace is tired from her journey. Perhaps you'd like to freshen up, rest a bit, then join us later in the drawing room?"

"I would like that, yes, thank you. But my bags . . ."

"Are already on their way to your room," Max said, his tone more formal now that we were in the castle and surrounded by others. He turned to a woman who stood tall amid the crowd gathered in the wide entry. "Madam, if you'd be so kind as to show Her Highness to her quarters."

"Of course. If you would come with me, my lady." A beautiful woman with a gracious smile who looked to be around fifty stepped forward and bowed slightly from her waist, a sort of non-curtsy curtsy. She wore a shirtwaist dress the color of the spring grass we'd seen on the mountainside, and her white hair sat atop her head in a neat bun. She had the liveliest blue eyes and gorgeous skin, flawless and just the right amount of natural color to her cheeks.

Well, the curtsying—the curtsy is so yesterday—was going to have to stop. It made me uncomfortable, along with all the Your Highness-ing and Your Grace-ing. I needed to speak to Max about that. Again.

I glanced over my shoulder at Max, John-Paul, and Marcel, who stood watching me. Max nodded his head, and I turned to go with the woman to whom I'd been handed over.

Now that I'd made it past the gathering in the entry—smiling whenever someone's eyes met mine—I stopped to take in my surroundings. The large foyer—easily five times the size of the first floor of my row house—opened into a long, wide hallway that seemed to stretch forever. The floor was made of black and white squares—marble?—set in a checkerboard pattern, and the walls were the softest shade of almost but not quite yellow imaginable. There were tall arched windows that reached almost to the ceiling along the inside wall that looked out onto a huge courtyard, and in the spaces between the windows I noticed the telltale discoloration where paintings had once hung. I wondered what had happened to them.

"Madam." I stopped for a moment and addressed her as Max had.

"Claudette is my name," she said.

"Claudette, what do they call this . . ." I waved my hand around to indicate the hall.

"It's known as the gallery, my lady."

"Thank you." I resumed my steps, so she did as well.

We passed a series of closed rooms on the left. As if sensing my curiosity, my companion said, "Most of the rooms in the castle have been closed for many years. We've just begun to reopen them. We'd hoped to have them all refurbished before your arrival, but there wasn't quite enough time."

"Why were they closed?"

She paused in the center of the hall. "You know of course our history, how the German army came and took over the country."

"1941," I said. "The year my grandmother and her sister left Saint Gilbert after her family was killed."

Claudette nodded. "The Nazis had the reputation of confiscating anything of value. We didn't have time to hide everything, so some things that hadn't been hidden away were destroyed or stolen by the invaders. When the Russians arrived, they drove out the Germans, and the commander of the troops who came through Saint Gilbert liked the castle very much." She smiled wryly. "So much so that he made this his headquarters, which meant we had the enemy with us every day. The upside was that no further physical damage was done, but again, many of our treasures that hadn't been hidden away went with him when he left."

"Hidden away where?"

She smiled. "There are many secret places in a castle as old and as large as this one, places that came in quite handy during the war. I'll take you on a tour while you're here if you like." She resumed walking.

"What sort of things were hidden?"

"Those with the most value. Furniture that had been in the castle for generations. Some jewelry. The best silver and china services. Crystal. Artwork. Many portraits." She gestured to the empty walls. "Many very valuable paintings once hung on our walls. Of course, we knew we would lose part of our heritage to the invaders, but I will say we were successful in saving more than we lost—certainly the very best of our art and antiques—and that was and still is a consolation. When the Germans came and asked about the blank places on the walls, we told them we'd been hit by a rogue band of Russians. When the Russians came, we blamed the Germans."

We? Did she say *we?*

But that would imply Claudette had been alive back in the 1940s, and that was impossible. She couldn't have been more than midfifties at the very most, a contemporary of the chancellor, perhaps, though the years had certainly been kinder to her. But if she were in her fifties, that meant she wasn't born until the mid-1960s. She must have meant the collective *we.*

"Ah, here we are."

The hall flowed through a wide arched doorway into another hall that turned to the right and led to a stairwell that was straight out of a fairy-tale castle. Wide enough for six to eight people to descend side by side, it rose majestically to the second floor, framed by balusters, also of white stone, like the steps. My head was spinning like Regan's in *The Exorcist.* There was too much to see, too much to take note of, too many questions buzzing around in my head, but I had no idea where to begin. There were double doors to the left, and I supposed if you were coming down this set of stairs, you might be headed there.

"What's through those doors?" I asked.

"Oh, that would be the throne room." Claudette turned and took ten steps, pushed the doors open, then beckoned me to step inside. With one hand, she flipped some switches, and the dozen or so crystal chandeliers overhead and the sconces that lined the walls came to life. The effect was breathtaking.

The floor here was parqueted wood and stretched all the way to a dais at the opposite end of the long, wide room. There, two oversize chairs with high backs sat side by side, their seats and backs covered in deep-blue velvet.

"The thrones, my lady." She beckoned me to continue on to the end of the room. "They're quite interesting. The carvings are exquisite. Do look."

Have I mentioned how bizarre this all was?

"Ahhh, no, thanks. I think I'll save that for later. Right now, I'd like to freshen up." I was tired, and I felt as if I hadn't washed my hands or face since last week. I was so thirsty my tongue was starting to stick to the roof of my mouth, and to tell you the truth, I wasn't ready for the whole throne experience just yet.

"Of course." She closed the doors and proceeded to the stairwell.

"I read online there are almost two hundred rooms in this castle." We began to make the climb. I should note the ceilings in this place are about twenty feet high, which made for a long climb when you're tired.

"One hundred ninety-seven, counting all the different dining rooms and their anterooms, the drawing rooms, the many bedrooms, the—"

"Stop, please." I shook my head. "I grew up in a house that had seven rooms. I live now in a house that has six. The largest house I'd ever been in was my grandmother's. It had five bedrooms and a bunch of rooms downstairs, maybe six or seven, and I thought that house was enormous. This is overwhelming. I'll never learn where everything is in this place."

"Then you might be pleased to know you won't have to, at least not currently. Only this section and the east wing are accessible at this time. The entire west wing is closed, all floors. The roof has damage and it's leaked into the rooms on the third floor, and because the house was unoccupied for so many years after the Russians left, the damage went unnoticed for far too long. The floor is soft in some sections." She paused at the top of the steps. I was breathing hard from the climb, but my companion was cool as could be. "We'd hoped to have repaired it before someone from the royal family returned, but there weren't sufficient funds."

I nodded. Anything I said would have sounded weird. Even a simple "I'm sorry" could have been interpreted as, "I'm sorry your country is poor and I'm therefore sorry to have come here."

"This way, my lady." She paused and nodded in the direction of another long hallway.

"What's over there?" I'd stopped on the landing and pointed to the right.

"That would be the east wing. There are guest suites, a smaller library than the one on the first floor, a small kitchen, a billiards room, a small drawing room . . ."

"I got it. Much the same as downstairs only with bedrooms for visitors."

"More or less, yes."

"You said 'smaller library than the one on the first floor'? There are two libraries?"

Smiling, she nodded.

I might enjoy this visit more than I'd thought.

I followed Claudette along the hallway. There were more empty spaces on the wall similar to those in the gallery below, where something had hung long enough for the wallpaper around it to have faded.

"There were more paintings here," I heard myself say.

"We'd thought of hanging them, but I thought perhaps you should have the honor of selecting the works you most liked."

She paused outside double doors painted white with gold trim, her hands on the doorknobs. "This was the suite the last grand duchess occupied, your great-grandmother. We've restored it as best we could, but of course, should you decide to stay, you may change whatever you like."

She threw open the doors to the suite. I glanced inside at what I guessed would be a sitting room and stifled a gasp.

My first impression was that the room was all gold, but in actuality, the walls were a rich shade of cream made vibrant by the sunlight that burst through the casement windows and made everything in the room glow. A sofa upholstered in white-on-white damask faced a fireplace of more white stone and was flanked by armchairs also in white. Several more chairs stood near the fireplace, all in damask but gold rather than white, and there was an Oriental rug in shades of rose and pale blue on the floor. Tapestries hung from the ceiling to almost the floor and covered two walls, and there were several doors leading who knew where on both sides. An enormous vase of dark-pink roses stood on a side table.

"The bedchamber is through here, madam." Claudette opened a door on the left and stood to the side.

The bedroom was something else. It was enormous and high-ceilinged and luxurious in the way you'd see in *National Geographic* magazines featuring centuries-old European castles. There were gilded mirrors and a dressing table with a gold lamp that had a fringed silk shade. More vases holding colorful flowers were set here and there about the room. The bed was some sort of dark wood and had posters that had to have been seven or eight feet tall on the four corners. Atop the posters perched birds in various stages of flight.

"What are those birds?" I asked.

"Falcons, my lady. The Gilbertis were great falconers," she explained with a smile. "And please, I would be honored if you would call me Claudette."

"Only if you call me Annaliese." I returned the smile and waited for her response, which seemed to be a long time coming.

"I couldn't . . ."

"Of course you could."

"I wouldn't feel comfortable."

"What is your position here, may I ask?"

"I'll be your—what did my son call it?—your right hand. I'd been granted the privilege of overseeing the preparations for your arrival and your stay. My official title is senior lady-in-waiting, but think of me as your 'go-to' person."

"So you'll be the person I'll be spending the most time with. The person who'll answer my questions—that sort of thing?" Is that what a lady-in-waiting actually did?

"Yes. More or less."

"Then you absolutely need to call me Annaliese." I held up my hand when she began to protest again. "I am not comfortable being called 'Your Highness' or 'my lady' or any of those other titles. I don't know if I'm ever going to be those things. I'm here because I thought in all fairness I should come and see for myself where my grandmother was born and see where she lived and where her parents died. But I don't know that I'm going to be staying. I'm asking you to please call me Annaliese."

"Shall we compromise, then? 'Your Highness' when we are in company with others, 'Annaliese' at other times," she suggested.

"Deal. Thank you." It was progress. "Oh, and please—spread the word that I don't want to see anyone curtsying."

"Consider it done."

I walked around the room suppressing the urge to pinch myself. I just couldn't take it all in. I opened each of the closed doors and peered into the spaces beyond. Behind one was what I suspect had been a huge closet the size of a room. Behind another, a room with yet another fireplace that I assumed was a more private sitting room. The others . . . I have no idea.

What in the name of all that's holy was I doing here?

In times like this, when I felt unsure of myself, I found it eased my anxiety to get the person I was with to talk about themselves.

"You mentioned your son said you'd be my companion," I asked as I made my way around the room. "Have I met your son?" Hopefully not a member of one of the factions Max warned me about. The ones who *hopefully* wouldn't be shooting at me.

"Yes, my lady. Maximilien is my son." She smiled apologetically and tried again. "Annaliese."

"Maximilien who?" Had I met another Maximilien? There'd been so many people milling about downstairs, I wasn't sure.

"Maximilien Belleme." Claudette laughed. "Please don't tell me my son has left so little an impression on you that you have forgotten him already."

I'm guessing the *WTF* look on my face gave me away, because Claudette laughed good-naturedly. "I am his mother."

"What? How is that even possible? You're way too young to be his mother. Did you have him when you were about five?"

She laughed again. "Maximilien is my youngest. I was thirty-six years old when he was born."

"But he's in his, what, late twenties? Thirties at most?" I paused. Math had never been my strong suit, but that would make her in her sixties.

No freaking way.

"My son is forty-two, madam."

My head began to swim. "But that would make you . . ." The numbers didn't compute. And in what world did Max look to be in his forties? Not the world I've been living in.

"Seventy-eight on my next birthday, yes." She nodded and moved to open a door to the left of the bed.

When I finally shook off my disbelief, I followed her, still trying to figure out how a woman who was almost eighty could look—and move—like she was thirty years younger.

A special diet consisting of foraged greens from the forest floor? Long walks in the mountain air? Bathing in the milk of the Charolais? A strict diet of unpasteurized cheese and wine?

She opened the last of the doors. "Your bathroom, my . . . Annaliese."

I probably said something like *thank you*, but I can't be sure. I was stuck on the fact that she looked years—*decades*—younger than she claimed to be. There wasn't a wrinkle on her face, nor an age spot anywhere I could see. The skin on her hands was as luminous as the skin on her face.

Whatever else I might learn about the home of my ancestors over the week I'd be here, the secret of Madam Belleme's youthful beauty had just earned a spot high atop the list.

Chapter Seven

Minutes after she left my room, Claudette had tea sent. It was hot and arrived in a silver carafe and was accompanied by a delicate cup and saucer, a small china bowl of honey, several sugar cubes in a silver bowl, some small sandwiches, and a plate of the same little cakes my grandmother had baked with me so long ago. Looking at that plate took me back almost forty years, and unexpectedly, my eyes began to tear. Someone had once made these exact cakes for Gran here in this very castle, and she'd brought the recipe with her to America via what must have been, for a fifteen-year-old who'd lived a life of luxury, a tortuous and scary route through the rugged Swiss mountains.

Much as I tried, I could not wrap my head around the ordeal my family had endured. Thinking about her flight had me wondering about the assassinations of her parents, her brother, one of her sisters, and who knows who else. That line of thought made me wonder where the assassinations had taken place. In the castle? In the woods? Where were they buried, and by whom? Are their graves marked, or are they lost forever?

Macabre thoughts for sure, but that was my mood. This was all so new to me, and I had so much going through my head at the same time I thought it might explode.

I poured myself a cup of tea and sipped it as I walked around the bedroom, trying to convince myself this was no different from any room in any upscale hotel. I was doing okay with this line of thinking until

I sat on the stool in front of the dressing table and saw the hairbrush and hand mirror there. They were made of gold-colored metal, and for all I knew, it could have been real gold, considering where I was. On the back of both the brush and the mirror was a stylized *G* set with red stones. More rubies? Ceil would know. I wish I had her eye for gems.

I made the mistake of picking up the brush and turning it over. There amid the bristles several thin strands of hair were entwined. Few though they were, I could tell the hair was the same cinnamon brown as my own. Suddenly everything made me sad—the castle that was partially boarded up, the room, the hair in the brush, my murdered relatives, my exiled grandmother. Everything made me want to weep.

One thing I learned about myself when I was a kid was that when I wanted to cry, I should just let it rip. So I did. I sobbed. I wept buckets. I moved to the sofa and cried my eyes out. I stood at a window and looked out at the lake and the fields and the woods that stretched for as far as the eye could see, and the mountains, all things that hadn't been visible from the front of the castle. I went to the window on the other side of the room and took in the vast gardens that went on forever and the courtyard—I bet you could fit half of Lincoln Financial Field in there—and the outbuildings that I supposed were stables and who knew what else, and I cried until I stopped.

Then I took a deep breath, and I felt one hundred percent better. I was still sad for my ancestors who were murdered or exiled, but the pain wasn't as overwhelming as it had felt twenty minutes before. And now I had to remove the telltale signs of my sob-fest. Some cold water, some eye drops, some concealer, and I'd be good as new. I grabbed my carry-on and went into the bathroom to repair the damage.

The bathroom was charmingly old-fashioned, with a large tub set into the floor like a pool surrounded on two sides by walls tiled in blue and white and pastoral scenes that reminded me of some old porcelain vases my mother had. The tub was clearly large enough for more than one person, which made me wonder if the last duchess had entertained in her tubbie, and if so, who. Several large towels the color of just-fallen snow sat on the wide ledge around the tub alongside bowls of soap. The fixtures, by the way, were copper—so trendy these days, right?—and the sink was round, the pedestal on which it sat fancy, like a Greek column. The large oval bowl was a painted woodland scene depicting a variety of wildlife: rabbits, deer, fox, and birds. The birds all had rounded heads. Marked by yellow beaks that were short but curved, with yellow circles around the eyes, they all looked alike to me. The tops of their heads were reddish, their chests were white with dark spots, and the backs and wings were brown on some, more like gray on others. Falcons, Claudette had told me. I'd never seen one, though I'd read they were nesting on some window ledges in Center City, Philadelphia, where hopes were high they'd help control the pigeon population. If ever a bird looked as if it meant business, it was the falcon with its sharp eyes and talons.

Behind a half wall—also tiled in blue and white—I found the toilet. The area was set off to itself, and as toilets go, it was pretty fancy and much more contemporary than I'd expected. I pushed the handle to make sure it worked, and a rush of water flowed into the bowl, so no problem there.

The entire bathroom was way bigger than my bedroom back home, and it was so beautiful, with the colored tiles and the painted sink. But my favorite thing was the shower. It was set into a deep niche in the wall, like the one that held a life-size statue of the Virgin Mary I saw in a church I was in once at the Jersey Shore. The niche was so far into the wall, when I stepped inside my entire body was beneath the overhead shower. The whole thing was made of marble, and it was so cool I wondered why we didn't have these things back in the States, though maybe some people do. I couldn't wait to use it. I was tired and I felt travel weary. I'd been on a plane for hours, then in a car for several more, and I felt dusty and dingy from the walk I'd taken with Max. I didn't want to meet whoever was going to be downstairs later in the condition I was in. Actually, I didn't want to meet anyone downstairs, period, but that was apparently beside the point.

I went back into the bedroom and struggled to get the suitcase onto the bed. The thing weighed about sixty pounds. I opened it and took out my hair dryer and the adapter Ceil bought me to make sure I'd have power to use it. I tested it in an outlet and it seemed okay, so I could wash my hair without worrying that I'd look like a drowned rat for the rest of the day. I took a minute and laid out the dresses I'd brought with me on the bed. I'd hang them up later.

I was annoyed more than I can tell you that I couldn't find my face wash and shampoo. I couldn't believe I'd left all that plus my moisturizer at home, but I must have forgotten to tuck them back into my bag after I'd used them early that morning. I had seen soaps in the bathroom, and I supposed I could get by with those, but I'd miss my moisturizer. (What woman over the age of twenty-five leaves home without it?)

The shower was perfect in every way. The water temperature adjusted to my preference, and even the soap was lovely, creamy taupe in color with streaks of purple. It smelled beautiful, like violets after the rain, which of course made me think of Gran, which made me wonder if she'd stood in this same shower once upon a time. The soap lathered like a dream and was so rich I didn't even miss my shampoo and conditioner when I washed my hair. The fragrance surrounded me completely to the point I was almost drunk with the scent. When I finished and dried myself, I was so refreshed, I felt I was ready for anything.

First things first. I plugged in the hair dryer and proceeded to blow my hair out straight. The air in Saint Gilbert was dry, which meant there was no frizz, which was a big win for me. Next, makeup, which THANK GOD was in my bag. I'd blown a bundle at Sephora in the mall, and I'd be really pissed if every last piece hadn't made it to Saint Gilbert with me. But it was all there, right down to the cream eye shadow and the concealer. I stood in front of a full-length mirror in the bathroom while I put on what I hoped would pass as a happy face.

I hung clothes that needed hanging in the massive closet and tried to decide what to wear. My gut told me to go with black. I went back and forth between two black dresses—I'd brought several with me, but how to know which would be more appropriate for this afternoon's get-together? I held up first one, then the other before placing them side by side on the bed and asking myself, what would Audrey wear?

There was a knock at the door, and before I opened it, I put on the robe (pure silk, I was positive) that had been left in the bathroom.

"I thought perhaps you might need some assistance, Annaliese," Claudette said kindly.

She wore a beautiful dress with a round neck, long, sheer sleeves, and a chiffon skirt in shades of blue and green on white, and it flowed around her hips like a cloud. The stones in her ears were clear but sparkly as all get-out, and they matched the large round stone in the ring on her left ring finger. I hadn't been a GIA student like Ceil, but I'd have bet my next year's mortgage payments those suckers were diamonds, and I don't mean the fake stuff like they sell on TV. Her hair was white, but the kind of white that women want—if they *had* to go white, if you know what I mean. Her skin was luminous—there's no other word for it—and her smile radiant. I know I said it before, but I still couldn't get past the fact that she claimed to be seventy-eight years old. Honest to God, she looked like she was in her midfifties. *Barely* in her fifties.

How in the name of all that's holy could this woman be Max's mother?

"You look gorgeous," I told her, still marveling at that flawless face. "You look more like a duchess than I do."

She dismissed my comment with a wave of her hand, but I could tell she enjoyed the compliment all the same.

"I would love your assistance, Claudette. I can't decide what to wear. I don't know exactly what type of get-together this is supposed to be." I stepped back, and she went straight to the bed where I'd left the dresses.

"This will be very informal," she said. "I would have preferred putting off any such reception until tomorrow, but everyone was so excited about your arrival, it was decided it would be best to have a very small gathering with members of the Duke's Council as well as some old friends of the monarchy in attendance in a very relaxed setting." She turned back to the more immediate issue. "Either of these dresses would be perfectly appropriate."

I'd started to feel a little overwhelmed, and it must have shown on my face, because Claudette assured me, "My son and I will be there to introduce you to everyone, and I promise, the reception will not last more than ninety minutes at the very most. The people you will meet today are dedicated to the Gilberti family and are thrilled that you are here." Before I could protest, she added, "Whether or not you decide to stay, your great-grandparents were very popular, and your grandmother had many friends who are delighted at the opportunity to meet her granddaughter."

Right. But no pressure, Annie.

"So you think maybe this dress?" I held up the short-sleeved sheath with the scoop neck I'd bought on a whim at Chico's during my fly-by shopping at the mall last week.

"Absolutely, yes. We can dress it up with a bit of jewelry, and it will be perfect."

"I don't have any jewelry," I told her. "Maybe one of the scarves I brought might work." I searched in my suitcase for a scarf that looked summery in pinks and white and black and draped it around my neck.

"Perhaps," she said.

I could see she wasn't down with the scarf idea, but she picked up the dress we'd agreed on, and when I took off the robe she slid the dress over my head. Just that quickly Claudette reached for the robe and hung it on one of the padded hangers.

"Whose robe is that?" I asked.

"Yours, now, if you'd like. It was made for your great-grandmother, but we found it with your grandmother's things, so I suppose she'd borrowed it from time to time. But like so many of her lovely things, it was left behind the day she fled the country."

I slipped into my shoes—I'd been debating between the leopard-print flats, which were my favorites, and the smooth black leather heels I'd been wearing that day and decided the black ones would probably be best for this first outing. Everyone knows you only got one chance to make a first impression. My sisters had an argument once about who first said that. Roe said it was Will Rogers and Ceil said it was Oscar Wilde. We looked it up and found out neither had actually said it, but it had been used in an ad for men's suits back in the 1960s.

"Annaliese." I'd been almost to the door when Claudette stopped me. "You need jewelry."

I started to repeat what I'd said earlier—that I didn't have any—when I remembered the pieces that had been returned to me. I dug in my bag for the leather pouch.

"Max brought these to me when we met in Philadelphia," I said as I emptied the pouch onto the bed's white coverlet. "I remember my grandmother wearing these earrings."

"They're lovely. Rubies have always been a favorite of the royal family. But perhaps you'd like a choice now that you're here."

She picked up a long white box from the dressing table. I hadn't seen it before, so I suspect she'd placed it there when she came in and I simply hadn't noticed.

I stared at the box for a long time, almost afraid to open it, so Claudette did. She appeared nonchalant as she dipped into it.

"You should always wear earrings, especially when you wear your hair tucked behind your ears. It looks lovely pulled back." She handed me a pair of gold earrings similar to the ones my grandmother had always worn, but these were much larger, and the centers of the roses held oval-shaped rubies. My jaw dropped.

Oh, they'd make an impression all right.

"As I said, rubies have long been favorites of our royals. Your great-great-great grandfather brought many pieces with him as gifts for his bride when he came to Saint Gilbert from France to marry the grand duchess of the day." She stood back while I fastened them in my ears with shaking hands. The last time I bought a pair of earrings for myself, they were from Macy's. The year Ralphie was born, my ex bought me a pair of silver knots from Tiffany's in the mall for Christmas, but they disappeared when we divorced. I figured he took them with him when he left, and I suspected that wife number two was the new proud owner. Not that I cared.

"They are perfect on you. Now, for around your neck." She lifted a strand of pearls as big as pigeon eggs from the box. And yes, I have so seen pigeon eggs. My ex's fool brother used to raise them on the roof of his row house in South Philly before the neighbors complained.

Before I could say a word, she'd fastened the pearls around my neck.

"For your wrist . . . I think . . . yes, this is perfect." She held up a gold bracelet that reminded me of the necklace I'd left on the bed. The strands of gold wound around my left arm from my wrist to three or four inches above it, but unlike Gran's necklace, the bracelet had no stones.

"Last piece." She smiled and opened her right hand. On her palm sat several rings. "You choose."

I stood there staring for what seemed like forever. I think I may even have pinched myself. Like I said, I didn't own a lot of jewelry. Not that I didn't love it. I just hadn't been able to afford anything that even came close to what Claudette held in her hand. I didn't think I could even afford reproductions. That each piece was solid gold and the gemstones real was a given. There was an oval ruby solitaire that could put out someone's eye (the royal equivalent of brass knuckles?), a large pure-white pearl surrounded by rubies, a pearl surrounded by smaller pearls, and a hefty piece of gold that looked like twisted rope. I liked the rope, but it didn't seem to go with the other things I was wearing, so I chose the ruby solitaire and put it on my right-hand ring finger, but it was too big. I switched it on to the middle, and it was perfect.

"Excellent choice," Claudette assured me. "You look very much a Gilberti, Your Highness."

She steered me toward the floor-to-ceiling mirror on the wall opposite the windows and stood back to allow me to look at myself. I barely recognized my own reflection, mostly because I couldn't look away from those big honking rubies in my earlobes. Seriously, though—I had to admit I looked good. If not like royalty, at the very least an heiress. Or a debutante. Okay, maybe a former debutante.

"Oh my God" was the only thing I could think of to say as I touched the pearls that hung around my neck. "I thought you said this would be very informal. Where I come from, the only people who wear this much bling are Mummers, and only on New Year's Day."

Claudette smiled.

"Are you really sure I should wear all this?" I turned my head again to check out the earrings. "It's all so . . . fancy. So . . . so . . . regal."

"These are a very small part of the collection that makes up the crown jewels, the majority of which rest in a Swiss bank."

I stared at the pearls for a moment, then touched the huge earrings. "These are beyond gorgeous, Claudette, and I would love to wear them." I unhooked the pearls and handed them to her. "But another time. I think today I'd like to wear the pieces that I brought with me."

I took the earrings from my ears and placed them in the box she still held. I went to the bed and picked up the smaller pair and slipped them into my ears. I put on the necklace, and it fit perfectly within the scoop of my neckline.

"The bracelet is part of that set, Annaliese," Claudette told me. "You should wear it."

I smiled and returned to the mirror. I liked what I saw much better. The pieces Claudette had brought in for me were gorgeous. Seriously, a king's ransom in rubies and pearls. But I knew these earrings. I remember these gracing Gran's ears. I never saw her without them, and if I'd ever really thought about it, I might have guessed she'd been buried wearing them. Now, in her castle among her people, I wanted to wear them for her. I feel pretty sure that somewhere she is smiling and nodding in agreement.

I'll try not to embarrass you, Gran.

I left the ring with the big stone on my right hand and slipped Gran's ring onto my left. I know she would have approved.

"I know these pieces. They feel right to me."

"They belong to you, Annaliese."

I shook my head. "Only if I stay."

"Which we're all hoping you will decide to do."

"You don't know me. I could be a dud." I held up my hand to admire the ring and immediately regretted canceling the mani appointment Ceil had made for me.

She laughed. "I seriously doubt that. My son is an excellent judge of character. He is totally convinced that you are the right person to lead this country and—"

"Please," I interrupted her. I didn't want to hear it. "I appreciate Max's faith in me, but please let's wait to see how things go."

"As you wish, of course." She opened the door and held it for me.

"My grandmother wore these"—I touched the earrings and held up the finger where her ring sat, big and bold—"for as long as I can remember. So how did they end up with Max?"

"My father, and later my brother, Emile, had been in contact with your grandmother from the day she settled in Pennsylvania. When she knew her time was coming to an end, she asked that we take the jewels back here, to save them for the next duchess."

"Did she think that would be me?"

"I believe she hoped it would be your mother first, then you."

"I see." I felt a little let down that Gran's wish for Mom hadn't come true. "I don't think my grandmother had all those other jewels with her. So where have they been since 1941?" I asked as I walked toward the door.

"A story for another time. The guests have arrived, and they're gathering in the drawing room. Many have waited years for this day." She took my elbow and guided me in the direction of the stairwell. "Shall we?"

As we went through the hall on our way to the steps, I remembered I hadn't taken any photos to send back to the kids. Maybe Claudette could take a few for me on my phone. I know my sisters would die when they saw me wearing Gran's jewels, not to mention that ring with the gigundo stone. I almost did.

Chapter Eight

When we entered what Claudette referred to as the main drawing room, every conversation stopped and every eye in the room turned to look at me. I channeled my best Audrey Hepburn (and maybe a little of my homegirl, Grace Kelly) and told myself I had Gran's royal blood in my veins, and if for no other reason, I belonged here.

Stand up straight, Annaliese, I swear I heard my mother and grandmother whisper at the same time.

Do me proud, child, Gran added. I blinked back a tear and silently promised her I'd do my best.

There was a harpist playing in front of the enormous fireplace, a young woman in her twenties, I guessed. Her fingers never missed a string even when the entire room went silent.

Claudette nodded to Max, who stepped away from the group he'd been chatting with and came forward to take my hand. He bent at the waist and brushed his lips over my knuckles, and I admit I felt a tingle up my spine.

"Your Grace, if I may be so bold as to present you to your—"

I cleared my throat. If he said *subjects* or anything that even sounded like that, I was ready to bolt, royal jewels or not.

But he'd gotten the message.

"To friends of the crown who have been waiting to meet you."

I nodded because I didn't know what was appropriate to say, and I allowed him to lead me around the room.

We were in the castle's main drawing room, a long rectangle with windows from which I could see the lake. The walls were paneled floor to ceiling in a dark wood, and here and there a portrait hung. Relatives, no doubt. There were little private seating areas with lovely furniture that struck me as being sort of French in style and tables adorned with vases filled with peonies, which are my favorite flower. When I mentioned this to Claudette, she smiled. "A favorite of your great-grandmother's as well."

"Is she in any one of those?" I asked, nodding toward the portraits.

"No. But there are many portraits of her in the castle. I'll be happy to show you." She gestured to a server, who produced a tray holding several different wines.

"What is your preference?" Claudette asked.

"I don't know. I don't know the choices."

"What wine do you fancy when you are home?" she asked. "What do you buy when you buy wine for yourself?"

"Pinot grigio," I told her. No need to tell her the stuff I bought usually came in a box or that for me, a splurge was when I ordered from one of the TV shopping channels.

She looked over the tray before selecting a glass and handing it to me, saying, "I think you might enjoy this one."

I took a sip. The wine tasted pure and perfect, the flavor magical, and was unlike anything I'd ever tasted. I wished my bestie, Marianne, was here to share it with me. That girl did love a good glass of wine. I know back home she must be pissed at me, that I'd taken "vacation" without even telling her I was going. She would have wanted to come with me, regardless of where I was going. I didn't want to have to lie to her, and I didn't want to tell her the truth, so I figured I'd just have to deal with her hurt feelings when I got home. Once I knew what I was going to do, I'd tell her everything.

Overall, the reception was an experience I'll never forget. I wish I'd brought a little notebook to write things down, because I didn't trust myself to remember every detail and every face. It was the most memorable ninety minutes of my life. Unbelievably, I met people who actually knew my grandmother. I knew she was fifteen in 1941, which meant she was born in 1926. Which means she'd be ninety-seven years old if she were still alive, right? There were women who'd grown up with her, who got into mischief with her and played with her as a child. They shared stories of first crushes and first kisses. These were women who knew her strengths as well as her insecurities and her secrets.

And there were those who were with her when she found out her parents and her older brother and sister had been arrested, who understood if she didn't leave the country that day, that *hour*, she'd quickly be arrested as well. I swear I could feel her anguish and her fear at having to flee into the mountains, knowing her family would be dead before she reached the Swiss border.

Oh, Gran . . .

I promised myself before my visit here was over, I would speak with every one of those beautiful ladies. And beautiful they were, by the way. Barely a wrinkle on any of their faces, no sign of that nasty crepiness that comes with age, no little brown spots on their faces or their hands. Oh, sure, the oldest in the group—the ones who had been Gran's compatriots—had a touch of crow's-feet and just the slightest bit of laugh lines, but I'm telling you, most of these ladies had skin better than mine.

"Do you mind if I ask what you use on your face?" I asked Francine, whose last name I never did catch but she claimed to be in her mid-nineties. Looked maybe sixty, and by sixty, I mean good sixty. Like Jane Seymour sixty. Like Christie Brinkley sixty. Yeah. That good.

She stared at me before shrugging. "I don't understand. Use on my face?"

Maybe start with the basics, I thought. "What do you wash your face with?"

She frowned as if she thought the question was either rude or stupid so maybe she did mind, but I couldn't help myself. I had to know, and since the person asking her was either the next grand duchess or merely the granddaughter of the last one, she felt compelled to answer.

"Soap," she said as if there could be no other answer.

"Soap? That's all?" I was incredulous. "What kind of soap? Dove? Ivory? Aveeno? Something made in France?"

"Just . . . soap." Francine looked increasingly confused. "I don't know those other things you said."

"What kind of soap?"

"Just the soap we make here."

"You make your own soap?" I pondered this for a moment. "What do you put in it?"

"Just the usual. Goat milk and a few violet petals, as we've always done. Nothing special."

"So it's just soap and water?"

"Of course with water." At this point, I'm sure she thought I was not worthy to call myself a Gilberti.

"I'm sorry, I don't mean to be personal." Oh, but yes, I did! "It's just that your skin is absolutely beautiful." I glanced around the room. Actually, everyone there had really great skin. Even the men. Everyone simply glowed.

"Oh. Thank you. I apologize for hesitating, but the question caught me off guard. I never think about it, you see."

"You never think about how your skin looks?" She had to be kidding. If I had skin like that, I'd be looking at myself in the mirror twenty-four seven. I'd probably never stop looking at myself.

She shook her head. "It's just *skin*, my lady."

Right. And the *Mona Lisa* was just a painting.

I'm sure I made an odd impression—not to mention a lasting one—on each of the ladies I quizzed about their skin. To a woman, they all seemed to have the same attitude: "It's just skin." Skin that hasn't sagged, lined, wrinkled, or creped in seventy, eighty, ninety, close to one hundred years? How is that ever *just?* How is that even possible?

Of course I met everyone in the room—Claudette and Max saw to that. If one didn't have me by the arm, the other did. Vincens DellaVecchio was there with his son, Philippe, a balding middle-aged man a little on the paunchy side who seemed a bit too interested in the fact that I was wearing my great-grandmother's rubies. If he wasn't staring at my boobs, he was staring at my ears, my neck, or the middle fingers of both my hands. I made the mistake of asking him if his wife was in attendance. He smiled waaaaay too brightly when he told me she was deceased. As if I were interested in his status. Ugh.

Anyway, I met the other dukes who made up the Duke's Council and their wives and children. My head was starting to spin. I couldn't keep them all straight.

I did meet several charming people I wouldn't mind seeing again. A sweet man named Louis confided he'd been in love with Gran from the time they were five years old and had been heartbroken when he found out she was gone. He assured me he'd had a happy life with his wife, Antoinette (who I met later when I'd made the rounds of the room and who—surprise, surprise—had skin like a baby). They'd had five children together and lived at the far end of the city.

"You must come for tea," Antoinette said after we'd been introduced.

"I would be honored," I assured her. It sounded like the sort of thing a grand duchess would say, doesn't it? I was discovering there's a lot to be said about role-playing. I was beginning to like it.

I met a woman named Marguerite who claimed to have been a distant cousin of Gran's and a daughter of one of my great-grandmother's attendants. She professed to be in her nineties. I was hoping to spend some time with her since I knew absolutely nothing about Gran's mother, but I was whisked away to meet someone else on the council whose name I can't even recall at this point. There were so many people, so many names. I did find it interesting, though, that the older generations in Saint

Gilbert seemed to be a melting pot for most of Europe. This one was of Italian descent, that one of German, this one Belgian, that one French, another was Swiss. I was grateful the official language was English and taught in the schools.

I made my way around the room, sampling different varieties of local cheeses that I can say without prejudice were hands down beyond delicious. There was a soft ivory-colored cheese that looked like brie and was to die for, creamy and mild and topped with sour cherries. The South Philly in me wanted to snatch the entire tray and sneak off with it to the back porch, or as they say here in Saint Gilbert, the south veranda. Oh, and they served a cheese that was sort of like a baby Swiss that was luscious with the thinly sliced dark bread it topped. There were several others, all served on pretty silver trays passed by good-looking young men in white shirts open at the neck and plain black pants. I don't know who they were, but I guarantee Juliette would have been taking pictures with her phone and sending them back to her friends.

And okay, I admit I covertly took some pictures to send home when I got back to my room. Which I was hoping would be soon because I was dead on my feet.

By the way, each of the wines I sampled were as exceptional as the cheeses, and I could see where these two products could have carried the country through difficult times. They needed a wider distribution of both, though, and something more to bring them into this century. The castle wasn't going to get fixed and the roads weren't going to be repaired without another product, and whatever that was going to be, it would have to be available on an international level. I made a mental note to mention that to Max later. Whether or not I stayed, someone needed to take matters into their own hands and make something happen.

I wanted to remember everyone's name, but it wasn't going to be possible. As fascinating as the company was, I was fading fast. Thank God, Claudette appeared at my elbow at the exact moment I realized I'd had enough, and she escorted me from the room, leaving Max behind to close out the reception.

"You are exhausted," Claudette said as she saw me to my room. "I'd thought perhaps we'd have a private, quiet dinner with you this evening, but that's clearly out of the question. I'll have dinner brought to you whenever you like. All you have to do is open your door and tell Sebastian."

"Sebastian?" I asked as we rounded the corner in the hall.

"The guard outside your room. Whatever you need, whenever you need it, tell him or whichever guard is on duty, and it will be arranged."

"Do I really need a guard outside my room?" I whispered as we drew close to the man who stood like a sentry, straight and tall and staring directly ahead. He wore crisply pressed white pants and a navy jacket that looked like a military uniform, with some of that gold braid on the cuffs and shoulders and a large sword hanging from his waist.

"The guard is ceremonial, of course, but he's also your means of communicating with me or Max or whomever it is you need or want."

"Is that real?" Pointing to the sword, I addressed him directly when we arrived at the door to my room.

"Yes, Your Grace," Sebastian replied.

"And you know how to use it?"

"Yes, Your Grace." Sebastian was apparently a man of few words.

"Well, what would you do if someone came running up the hall brandishing a gun?" I said, thinking of the old *don't bring a sword to a gunfight* trope. "What good would a sword be?"

"None at all, Your Grace." To his credit, he remained stoically still. "In such case, I would shoot him." He patted his left side.

"Good answer." I opened the door and an amused Claudette followed me into my room.

"I'm a little confused about the communication chain around here," I said after the door closed behind us. "I have Max's cell number, but that's all."

"Sebastian and his morning replacement have access to everyone in the castle." She closed the heavy drapes to darken the room. "Is there something you need?"

"Not at the moment. I guess the only thing I need right now is a nap." She began to turn down the bed.

"Oh, I can do that," I began to protest, but she was done in a flash.

"Is there anything else I can do for you?" she asked as she smoothed the pillow cover.

"No, thank you." I watched her walk toward the door. "Oh, wait. There is one thing. If I could have a glass in case I need a drink of water . . ."

"I'll have it sent up immediately."

"Thank you." I walked back to the bed and touched the pillowcases. They were soft as silk and just as cool to the touch.

Claudette left the room before I remembered I was wearing all this jewelry, and I wondered if I should have given it to her for safekeeping. But apparently she trusted me and the armed guard at my door. I took it all off, piece by piece, studying each before returning it to the leather pouch. I took off my dress, and if I'd been home in my own house, I'd probably have dropped it where I stood and fallen face forward onto the bed, I was that tired. But being in the castle, I hung it in the closet on one of those silk-padded hangers someone had brought in just in case Gran was still watching.

I went into the bathroom and washed off my makeup. I was tired, but I wasn't about to smear my face all over those lovely pillowcases on the bed. I was still annoyed with myself for leaving my face wash and moisturizer in Philly, but I had to admit, the soap in the bathroom removed every trace—even the mascara—and my skin still didn't feel dried out. *Hmmm*, I thought. Twice today I'd washed my face with soap—something I hadn't done since I was about twelve and found the stuff Mom used—and I'd gone without any sort of face cream, and yet my skin felt as if I'd been to a spa, without a trace of that tight masklike pucker it would get when I washed it with even a mild cleanser. Curious.

When I came out of the bathroom, I found a carafe and a crystal glass on a pretty tray on the bedside table, though I hadn't heard anyone come or go. I slipped into the robe before opening the door. I peered out, but there was no one in the hall except Sebastian. I gave him a thumbs-up and went back into the room.

I draped the robe over a chair, then pulled a nightshirt over my head before I crawled under the sheet and sank into that soft mattress. I'm pretty sure I sighed with pleasure. I closed my eyes, and for a few moments I started to drift away. I smiled and waited to sail off into la-la land.

But no. The questions that had been building up since I walked into Castle Blanc started popping inside my brain like dried corn in a closed container over high heat and ran the gamut from how did all the furniture and fixtures inside the castle survive not one but two invasions to how is it that the crown jewels weren't stolen? How did they get into a vault in a Swiss bank? Max said something about the country's money being tied up in a Swiss bank, too. How did that happen? The castle seemed well staffed—but if no one has lived here in decades, who are all these people and where did they come from? Who is cooking and cleaning and baking and bringing me water? How is there a castle guard when there's been no one to guard for all these years? And now that I'm here, what exactly do these people expect me to do? How will I tell my friends from my foes? Max gave me the impression he was on it, but how do I know Max isn't going to turn out to be the bad guy after all? If he isn't at my elbow, his mother is. Are they really trying to assist me, or are they just trying to keep an eye on me and control who I come in contact with, who I speak with, where I go? Who should I trust?

Fatigue plus uncertainty equals confusion and paranoia.

It was pretty clear I wasn't falling asleep anytime soon, so I got up and looked for my phone. I took pictures around the suite—the bed, the fireplace, the bathroom, the sitting room with its fancy wood-carved fireplace surround. I was tempted to take pictures of the jewels but decided that could be asking for trouble. I was on a group text conversation with my kids and my sisters, so I sent the photos to everyone at the same time. My accommodations this week, I typed over the images from the bedroom. Just call me Your Highness, I jested when I sent the photos from the reception.

Moments later, I had a slew of return comments.

From Juliette: OMG, Mom! That party looks AWEsome! I wish I was there! What did you wear?

From Ralphie: Cool. Who's the cute chick in the blue dress?

From Ceil: Oh, man, that bed looks amazing! The bathroom looks fabulous! Are you having a good time? How's Max?

From Roe: I hope you don't have to make that bed and clean that bathroom before you leave. Or is there maid service? Don't leave your wallet laying around.

We all texted back and forth for about twenty minutes. It seemed my family had as many questions as I did. Finally, I signed off after promising to send photos of inside and outside the castle, the gardens (for Ceil), the city (for Juliette), and any cute girls Ralphie's age (for—duh—Ralphie).

I leaned on the window ledge and looked out across the lake and wondered if the last person who'd called this room hers—my great-grandmother—had looked out at this same view in those dark days when the country was being invaded. Had she known what was coming?

Thinking about it made me so sad. I tried to turn it off, but I couldn't. I felt surrounded by something I can't explain. I'm not gonna say *ghosts* because I don't believe in them, so let's just say some energy I wasn't familiar with and leave it at that. It was odd to be filled with so much sorrow for people you've never met, but I guess there's a connection there, one I'd never been aware of. If I do nothing else while I'm here, I'm going to find out what happened to them—my great-grand-mother, my great-grandfather, my great-uncle and aunt, and whoever else met their fate at the hands of the Nazis.

That was my last coherent thought. I went back to bed and closed my eyes, and bam! Gone till morning.

Chapter Nine

When I woke up my first morning in Saint Gilbert, I pinched myself about eighty times. Had I really spent the night in a castle? And not just any castle. This was Castle Blanc, in Beauchesne, the capital of Saint Gilbert. Home of my ancestors. The place where my grandmother was born. I'm pretty sure my expression was just like Roe's *WTF* face.

I got up and took care of business. I washed my face with the taupe-y soap again—still missing my face wash—and I was ready to take on the world. Except I was so hungry I could eat one of those beautiful white cows we saw on the drive in yesterday.

Was that really only yesterday? I'd completely lost track of time. So much had happened since I left my house and got into the Lincoln and headed for the airport.

I stood inside the closet debating what to wear. The sun was out, and if yesterday was any indication of what a sunny day felt like around here, it was going to be warm. Maybe not South-Philly-in-April warm, but warm enough. I decided on a blue cotton knit tank dress and a blue-and-white-striped linen shirt to wear over it. I could tie the shirt at my waist and roll up the sleeves. My only other decision was what to put on my feet. I stared at the shoes I'd brought with me until I realized I couldn't make a big decision like that without coffee. There was a reason coffee was known in our house as the elixir of awareness.

I opened the door to the hall, but instead of Sebastian, another tall man in a navy-blue-and-white uniform stood at attention outside the door.

"Good morning," I said as cheerfully as I was able.

He nodded. "Your Grace."

I needed coffee too badly to get into the whole *Call me Annaliese* thing, so I asked if he could arrange somehow for a tray to be brought up.

"Of course, Your Grace."

I thanked him and went back into my room and stared at my shoes trying to choose until there was a knock at the door.

"Please come in," I said.

A pretty young blonde woman wearing a white shirt and black pants came in carrying a tray.

"Where would you like this, my lady?" she asked.

I looked around, then pointed to the table in front of the sofa. "There would be fine, thank you . . ."

In my ear I heard my mother's voice: *How many times have I told you not to point?*

"Andrea," she replied with a shy smile.

"Thank you, Andrea."

"You're most welcome, my lady." She carried the tray to where I'd requested. "Would you like me to pour your coffee?"

Being a mom, I'm used to waiting on others but not the reverse. It makes me uncomfortable to feel as if people are fawning over me. So I simply tell her, "Oh, no thank you. I can do that."

"Will there be anything else?"

"No, thank you . . . oh. One thing. Do you know the name of the man outside the door?"

"It's Hans, my lady."

"Thank you. There won't be anything else."

She left quietly, and I sat down to pour myself a cup of coffee. There was cream in a small china pitcher and tiny dark cubes of sugar in a little matching bowl. Once I'd doctored my coffee to my satisfaction, I sat back, tasted, and sighed, content. Best coffee on the planet. After a few delicious reviving sips, I lifted the silver domes that covered the other items on the tray. I found a pretty pale-blue plate with tiny white flowers painted around the edge, in the middle of which a pat of butter shaped like a flower was nestled next to a croissant. There was also a small bowl of honey and another containing some of the same sour cherry compote that had been served with cheese at yesterday's meet and greet. Another dome hid a bowl of strawberries that were half the size of my fist. I am not exaggerating. I could have eaten my weight in them.

I drank my coffee and nibbled at the croissant—first plain, which was delish, but then I decided to go for broke and slathered on the butter and the cherries, and wow. I never tasted anything so amazing. Those cherries were from God, I swear. By the time I finished, there was nothing left, not a crumb. But in my defense, I hadn't eaten since snacking on bites of cheese late yesterday afternoon, so I wrote off any calories I might have ingested.

I have to admit there's a part of me that could easily get used to living like this. Just having someone else figure out meals on a daily basis was almost enough for me to pledge my allegiance to the flag of Saint Gilbert.

So there I was, well fed and happy and on my way to being suitably caffeinated, when there was another knock on the door. I opened it and Claudette stood in the hall.

"Did you enjoy your breakfast?" she asked pleasantly after I'd invited her in.

"Every bite. If you're responsible for what was on that tray, I can't thank you enough. The coffee was amazing, and the croissant was baked by angels and the fruit was delicious." I gestured for her to sit; then I realized she was waiting for me to sit first, so I did. "But I have to know: Where did you find the strawberries?"

"In the castle garden. I'm so glad you enjoyed them. Starting the garden was an act of optimism on our part that you would be joining us. The plants were originally in a garden at one of the farms outside the city," she explained, "but after the vote in January, when we realized we were going to need a source of fresh food at the castle, we decided to move some of the plants here once spring arrived."

"Who tends the garden?"

"There is a full-time gardener but also several volunteers, men and women who were more than willing to lend their time and their expertise to ensure that you and your family had the very best Saint Gilbert had to offer. If you look out the window you will see the garden inside the stone wall."

"I did see it, last night and again this morning. I hope I get to meet the gardeners while I'm here."

"They would be honored, I am sure."

I finished my coffee, all the things I wanted to ask and wanted to know swirling around inside me.

"You look troubled, Annaliese," Claudette said.

"It's frustrating to have so many questions, I don't even know where to begin."

"What's the very first thing that comes to mind right now?" she asked. "The most immediate question?"

"Who are all the people inside the castle and how did they get here and who trained them? Who got the farmers together, and how did they know someone—if not me then someone else—might be living here?"

"Ah, those are easy questions. Once the election was over, there were a number of meetings organized by the Duke's Council."

"Would you tell me again who is on the Duke's Council?" I know I met them all yesterday, but I could remember only one or two. Whether I stayed beyond this week or not, I should know who these people are.

"Of course. Currently, Vincens DellaVecchio, Dominic Altrusi, Pierre Belloque, my brother Emile Rossi, my son Maximilien, Andre

DiGiacoma, and Jacques Gilberti, a distant cousin of yours. Vito Benocci passed away earlier this year. His position has yet to be replaced."

"So your family has been in Saint Gilbert for a long time," I said. "Max said his grandfather had been with the castle guards before him."

"Captain of the guards, as was my brother in his youth, as is my son now," she said proudly. "My family has been closely aligned with the Gilbertis since the country was founded hundreds of years ago. We've always played a prominent role. My mother, as I may have mentioned, was the principal lady-in-waiting to your great-grandmother. Had things turned out differently, I would have done the same for your grandmother and possibly your mother as well. My mother had trained me for the position, but sadly, it was not to be."

"And now you're my—you're the principal lady."

"I am at your service. And if you fear that I am perhaps too old"— she smiled in a self-deprecating way—"my granddaughter Madeleine is being trained to take over the duties one day. She has been invaluable in getting the castle ready for your arrival. As I'm sure you understand, there were many roles to be filled."

"How did you manage to find people for the kitchen, to clean, to do laundry, to serve, to . . . to do all those things I've seen happening here? The guards at the door. The girl who brought me coffee this morning."

"Our challenge was to find the best people for the positions, regardless of their age or family connections. There was no shortage of applications once it was made known that we were actively seeking to bring you here. That many new jobs would be available. Many of our young people have left the country, and we were hoping to convince more of them to stay."

"Any particular reason they left?"

"University in other parts of Europe or in America, mostly. They go away to school, they make lives for themselves, they decide not to come home. There are admittedly more opportunities for them elsewhere, I cannot argue the reality. We would like to change that, but I'm not sure how that will happen. My oldest son Andre, my daughter Felice, and several of my grandchildren are gone and come back only for holidays." She shrugged. "So it will remain until we can offer them a reason to stay. I'm hoping we can find such reason over time."

"Where does the money come from to pay them?" I'd been wondering where the money came from to do *anything* around here—restoring the castle being the most significant, though they had a long way to go before that project was completed.

"The country still has some revenues." Claudette smiled. "But mostly from the Grand Duchess and Duke of Saint Gilbert."

I believe my expression went from merely curious to *say what* in less time than it takes for a heart to beat.

"When the certainty of German aggression was recognized, your great-grandparents transferred the country's wealth, along with the crown jewels, to a Swiss bank, where it remained safe through the years. While it is true that the bulk of the funds can only be released once the monarchy is fully restored, the bank officials recognized our plight. They advanced some in good faith after the January vote and with the assurance from the Duke's Council that every effort was being made to place the proper heir on the throne, which is what your great-grandparents not only envisioned but assumed, which is why the funds were held until such time as one of their descendants took the throne. I believe they thought in time your grandmother would return to rule the country, but of course, they had no way of seeing into the future, no way of knowing the Soviets would prove to be as great a threat as the Germans." She smiled sadly. "It is very difficult for a very small country such as ours to maintain our sovereignty."

"And if no proper heir agreed to sit on that throne, what would happen to those funds?"

"I imagine they would stay in the bank and continue to amass interest, as they have since 1941, until such time as an heir was crowned."

"That's a lot of interest."

"It is indeed, Annaliese."

"But there are other branches of the family who could be tapped to be grand duchess or duke, right?" Please. The last thing I needed was to carry the weight of guilt that I'd deprived future generations of Saint Gilbertians of their country's wealth if I decided not to stay, which was a distinct possibility.

"Not especially suitable, but I suppose if we had to make do, we could. For a time, anyway." I swear her nose partially lifted as if in disdain of any of those other Gilbertis. I wondered who they might be. Which left me to question if I were the pick of the litter, what must *they* be like?

"So who are these relatives, and will I meet them?"

"I believe you met your grandmother's cousin Marguerite yesterday. And then there's Vincens DellaVecchio."

"The grand chancellor is a relative?" Something about that possibility made me recoil in a sort of horror. Maybe it had something to do with the way his son tried to look down the top of my dress.

"No, but there is a small amount of shared blood. Vincens's grandfather and your great-grandfather were brothers." She averted her eyes and glanced out the nearest window.

"Claudette, is there something about the chancellor I should know?"

"I am hesitant to say something that might be construed as gossip or would appear to be mean-spirited or in any way give you reason to think there might be ulterior motives on my part."

"I'd like your opinion anyway." I really did. So far, she seemed like a straight shooter.

"It is my opinion and that of my brother and my son and some others that he is not to be completely trusted, Annaliese."

I remembered the mutual stink eye exchanged between Max and Vincens the day before. "Do I need to know why?"

"There are some who believe he would attempt to exert undue influence over you if given the chance. He is well aware that any road to the throne, to legitimacy of his family, goes through you." She took a deep breath. "It is thought he harbors certain . . . aspirations. His son, Philippe, is a widower and you are a divorcée. His younger son is also divorced."

"You mean he thinks I might be interested in . . . oh God no." I laughed at the very thought of touching Philippe beyond a simple—and quick—handshake. The other son, even sight unseen, was a definite no. "That will never happen."

"You have two sisters and a daughter. He has a grandson a few years older than your Juliette. Philippe's son is seventeen."

"And that *definitely* ain't happening." My daughter and the spawn of paunchy Philippe? The very thought brought out the South Philly mama in me.

And my sisters? Almost as funny. Ceil would eat him alive, and Roe would have him running from the castle screaming like an overtired two-year-old who lost his blankie. It's Roe's superpower. There's a reason she's still single.

"So he thinks there's a potential to marry up, so to speak, and that would get him closer to the throne?"

Again, she appeared to choose her words carefully. "It has been rumored he has such aspirations."

"Then the chancellor will find himself very disappointed."

I stood, dismissing the thought of anyone named DellaVecchio getting chummy with anyone named Gilberti, and Claudette stood as well. Apparently we were both of the same mind as far as *that* family was concerned.

"What would you like to do today?" she asked.

"I'd like to see the city. Maybe poke into a few shops and visit sights a tourist might see." If of course Saint Gilberti had tourists. "And I would like to see the church." I paused. "Were my great-grandparents found after . . . you know? Were they properly buried?"

Claudette nodded. "They are buried in the churchyard."

"They are?" I smiled. That they'd been respectfully treated in death made me happy.

"They are there along with the others."

"The others who died with them?" I asked.

"Your great-uncle, your great-aunt. Several members of the royal household."

"Do you know where it happened?"

"They were taken two by two to the opposite side of the lake and into the woods, where they were blindfolded and shot." Her face was rigid. The telling was obviously unpleasant. "But even aware their deaths were imminent, they took care to provide for their country. To preserve as best they could for generations to come, abdicating in favor of their daughter and planning her escape, in addition to protecting the country's assets, as we've discussed. That your grandmother survived was due solely to their foresight. They sent her away uncertain if she'd escape alive, but they knew she would surely die with them if she remained in Saint Gilbert, so they trusted her fate to God. She resisted and fought leaving them and her siblings, but in the end, she conceded to her parents' wishes and left before the sun came up. By noon on that same day, her entire family had been murdered."

"They must have been very brave and very wise."

"They are the heroes of our country, madam."

"As was your father."

She smiled and nodded. "Yes. He led them to safety. My mother accompanied them so they appeared as a family."

"Why weren't my grandmother's brother and her other sister—Jacqueline—sent away with her?"

"Her brother was eighteen and felt a duty to remain with his parents. Jacqueline was younger—eight or nine—and refused to leave her mother. Trying to convince her to go with her sisters only served to delay their departure, as the story was told by my father. In the end, the grand duchess was forced to permit her older two daughters to escape, knowing her youngest would be killed along with her."

We both reflected silently for a long moment. Then, because I sensed she was hoping we'd put that topic aside, I looked over the row of shoes I'd left in front of the armoire. "So I guess if I'm sightseeing today, tennis-type sneakers would be the best bet. I mean, given the selection."

"Undoubtedly they would." Her light mood returned as she watched me tie on my white Keds.

"Not very royal," I muttered.

I'd worn this same type of sneaker since I was three, and they were still my favorite. You can keep your walking and running shoes with those big ugly soles and the flashing lights and their promises to make you run faster and stronger, lose weight, and help you meet your daily minimum number of steps, thank you very much. I go old school, and I'm okay with that despite the fact that my children would mock me unmercifully if they saw me tying them on.

"Is Max around?" I asked casually.

"I'm not sure what his schedule is this morning, but if you'd like to speak with him, I'd be happy to call him."

"I thought maybe he'd be a good person to show me around Beauchesne."

"I'm sure he would be happy to, Annaliese. I'll have him come for you." She began to make her way to the door.

"Oh, I can meet him downstairs. I thought I'd check out the garden."

"As you wish." She opened the door and waited to see if I was ready to leave. I was, so I grabbed my bag and followed her out the door.

I still had the feeling of being in a very luxe hotel as I accompanied Claudette down the stairs.

We reached the bottom of the stairs, and I looked back over my shoulder. The steps rose behind us, and I felt like pinching myself again. I'd fallen into someone else's life, and I wasn't sure what was going to happen when that someone showed up and wanted it back.

Chapter Ten

Claudette left me alone in the drawing room while she contacted Max. I wandered around the room, studying the faces in the portraits. Some, I supposed, were my ancestors who'd ruled this country. I wondered what kind of ruler my gran would have been. In my heart, I knew she—or my mom if it had come to that—would have been great, that they both would have done good things. Which of course led me to wonder what I might be like if I had wealth and power, what kind of a ruler I'd be.

Then I reminded myself where I'd come from and what I'd left behind. Growing up, our house was governed by the Golden Rule: do unto others as you would have them do unto you. My mother believed that with her whole being. That was the most important moral lesson my sisters and I received from Mom, and she made it cover a lot of ground. There were few situations she couldn't apply it to. It was right up there with "stand up / sit up straight / stop slouching" and "mind your manners."

The double doors opened, and Max walked in, tall and handsome (I know I've said it a million times, but it bears repeating: the man was *fine*) and totally regal in his bearing. He was casually dressed in tailored slacks and a light-blue button-down shirt with the sleeves rolled to the elbow much like mine were. The difference between us was that he looked like he belonged in a castle drawing room. I looked down at my tank dress that I'd bought off the rack on sale at H&M and my white tennis shoes, and it was glaringly obvious where I belonged. It occurred to me then that I should've called on my patron saint of fashion, Saint Audrey, before I ventured out of my room. I momentarily tried to picture myself in the outfit she wore in *Roman Holiday* when she set off to explore the city—that white shirt with the little scarf tied around her neck, the belted cotton skirt—and I sighed. Not with these hips.

I guess it's true what they say: you can take the girl out of South Philly . . .

"You wished to see the city, Annaliese. It would be my pleasure to accompany you. Is there any place in particular you'd like to see?"

Just looking at him made me smile.

"I'd like to see the church, and a few of the shops. I should think about souvenirs for the kids and my sisters."

"It's an excellent day for an excursion." He walked to the door and held it open for me.

"Could we stop in the garden before we leave?" I asked as I went into the hall.

Max paused for a moment. "Might I suggest we save the garden for last?"

"Sure." I shrugged. It really didn't matter whether we started or ended there. I just wanted to see the flowers that grew here. Maybe even pick a few for my room. I thought of the garden I strolled through with Gran during my solo visits to her home, and I wanted to know if she'd planted certain flowers because they reminded her of the gardens here. I know all I had to do was ask, and someone would pick them for me. But I'm a city girl, so when I have the chance to pick flowers on a sunny day in a beautiful garden, that's what I want to do.

Max and I followed the hall into the gallery I'd come through the day before and out to the reception area. I glanced up at the fancy staircase.

"Why are there two fancy staircases?" I asked, thinking of the one Claudette and I had used earlier.

"The one you generally use leads to the back of the castle, where the private rooms are located. This one"—he nodded at the stairs in front of us—"leads to more public rooms. The ballroom, for example."

"There's a ballroom?"

"Of course." He smiled as he took my elbow. "Every castle has a ballroom."

"Have you ever been to a ball here?"

He shook his head. "There have been none since 1941."

I had this insane vision of me in a light-blue Cinderella ball gown being spun around the ballroom floor by Max in a military uniform dripping with gold braid and medals, sort of like the one Vincens wears. There's an orchestra playing and . . . okay, we all have our fantasies, right?

"Shall we go?" Max stood at the doorway.

Today there was no gathering of the castle staff, but when we stepped outside, there were guards at the exterior door. Two on each side of the entrance, all four wearing the blue-and-white uniforms I'd seen on Hans that morning. They all nodded formally as I passed by, and I wondered if they were supposed to keep silent, like the guards outside Buckingham Palace. Three cars were awaiting us in the drive directly in front of the castle, and Max accompanied me to the passenger side of the one in the middle.

"I took the liberty of assuming you'd not want an official royal escort this morning," he said as he opened the door for me. "But an unofficial one is in order."

I glanced at the car ahead of ours, then turned to look at the one at our rear.

"Why?"

"It is required anytime a royal leaves the castle, madam."

"I'm just like any other visitor to Saint Gilbert," I protested.

He laughed as he closed the door. "Any other visitor upon whose head we might place the crown."

The crown? I hadn't thought about a crown. I hadn't even thought about tiaras except to tease Juliette. I wondered what the crown looked like. Would it look like that fancy number Queen Elizabeth II wore, dripping with jewels and sporting fur? (Was it ermine?) I'd bet that sucker had been heavy, though. Maybe Saint Gilbert's crown was more like the fat-free yogurt of crowns, the same basic look but lighter.

I got into the car—a very cool dark-green Jaguar that would have brought out all the neighbors on my block back home to take a closer look—and fastened my seat belt.

"Is that really necessary?" I was turned in my seat looking over my shoulder. "The guards?"

"Necessary in the sense that you are under my protection, and I take that responsibility very seriously."

"Because you think one of those people who didn't want the monarchy to return is going to take shots at me?"

"I don't rule out anything when it comes to your safety, Your Grace. But don't worry. When we get into the city, you won't even know the guards are there." He put his arm out the window and signaled to the car ahead of us.

"But if I walk around with half a dozen guards, everyone will know I'm not just another tourist."

"No one will know they're there," he repeated. "Relax, Your—"

"Annaliese," I snapped. "Enough with that 'Your Grace' stuff."

Max settled behind the steering wheel while I tried to settle my nerves. I rolled down my window and looked straight up at the top of the castle wall, where flags swayed in the light breeze.

"Is one of those the flag of Saint Gilbert?" I asked.

Max leaned over me slightly. He smelled of the same soap I'd been using, and I wondered if there was some sort of law that prohibited use of any other. I'd caught the same scent from his mother and the young girl who'd brought my breakfast earlier that day.

"Our national flag is the one in the middle, the blue-and-white one. The others represent various houses that had married into our royal family over the centuries."

"Families have their own flags?" I wondered what ours would look like back home. Probably a large pizza—pepperoni and extra cheese—on a background that looked like our kitchen counters, which unfortunately are still the same faded red Formica that was there when I bought the house. Kitchen reno was on the list of things to do after paying off my college loans and getting my kids through school without taking out a second mortgage.

"Some families do. Or did."

"So the country's flag has . . . that looks like the castle's tower in the center." The breeze folded the flag in several places.

"It is the tower. It's the symbol of our nation. It stands for strength and the fact that we will defend our sovereignty."

"Is there an army, then?"

"Not at the present."

I nodded and thought it wise not to ask how a country without an army defended itself. Instead, I tilted my head to watch a bird that flew past the tower at a high rate of speed.

"Wow, did you see that?" I leaned out the window hoping to follow its flight, but it was gone already.

Max smiled. "Ah, that is a falcon. Our national bird."

"Your mother mentioned that the Gilbertis were falconers."

He nodded as he turned the key in the ignition. "Every generation since the country was established, so they say. My grandfather told me the last grand duchess took her falcon to hunt every morning and again later in the afternoon. She was most fond of that bird, he said."

"I wonder what happened to it."

"It's said that when the duchess realized her fate, she let her falcon fly free, but the bird circled the castle for days, calling for her, before it finally gave up and flew off into the forest." He put the car in gear and made a U-turn in the drive, then drove through the stone tunnel. "So that bird we just saw could be a descendant of the duchess's falcon."

I thought about that for a moment, wondering how it might feel to have a bird like that land on my arm. I thought I might like it. If I were to stay in Saint Gilbert, I'd definitely bring back the practice. Not that I was planning on staying, but if I did, I'd do the falcon thing.

At the end of the lane, Max waited while the gate opened for the first car in line. He nodded to the gatekeeper—that word always makes me think of *Ghostbusters*—and drove past the gates and onto the cobbled street. A short distance from the castle, he pulled to the curb and stopped the car. The other two cars stopped as well.

"The church is just around that bend in the road, but there's no place to park there. We should walk from here," he said.

"That's fine. I could use a good walk." Without waiting, I unhooked my seat belt, opened the door, and hopped out. When Max met me in front of the car, he looked amused.

"What?" I asked.

"I would have expected you to have waited for me to open the door for you."

"Where I come from, girls learn at an early age to open their own doors."

I meant that figuratively as well as literally. I always knew if I wanted something, I should figure it out for myself. Mom said we each needed to choose our own path, make a plan, then follow it through. I followed that advice all my life, and it never failed to get me where I wanted to go. Okay, there was that marriage to Ralph Senior, but everyone's entitled to stumble once in a while, right? And besides, I wouldn't have my children if I hadn't married him, so no harm, no foul.

I watched, but so far no one had exited the other two cars. Maybe they were just supposed to do surveillance from the front seats.

We walked along a cobbled sidewalk, and it seemed the farther we walked, the steeper the path. I was glad I'd worn my Keds, because those stones were round and uneven, and if I'd had anything else on my feet, I'd have taken a header and it wouldn't have been pretty.

We rounded a bend and the church came into view. It was shining clean and white, like the castle, and the stained-glass windows sparkled.

It was glorious, and I thought being buried in its shadow wouldn't be such a bad thing. I mean, if you had to be buried, and eventually we all would be. Unless we opted for cremation. As if dying wasn't a scary-enough thought.

A black iron fence enclosed the churchyard, and the closer we got, the faster my heart beat. There were only a dozen steps leading to the church's front doors, grand arched things of highly polished wood.

"Would you like to go inside?" Max asked, and I nodded.

"Yes, please."

I should explain here that I am a highly emotional person. I cry at weddings, funerals, christenings, Hallmark commercials, those Budweiser beer commercials with the Clydesdales, Ray Charles singing "America the Beautiful," Louis Armstrong's "What a Wonderful World," and every play or musical event either of my kids had ever been in. I have even been known to shed a tear at presidential inaugurations (depending on the president, of course). I had a lump in my throat while Max was telling me the story about my great-grandmother and her falcon. So it shouldn't surprise anyone that I walked up those steps with my eyes stinging and my bottom lip trembling (and I really do cry ugly). I can't even describe the feelings that swept through me when Max opened one of the doors and led me inside.

It took my eyes a moment to adjust to the lower light, but I could see the ends of the pews were beautifully carved, the seats themselves hewn of thick, dark wood. The altar was white marble, and the statues that stood on either side—the Virgin Mary with another woman on one side of the altar, Christ on the other—were life-size and lifelike. The stained-glass windows told the story of Jesus from birth to his death and were stunning in their design and color. I'd been in a lot of churches, but I'd never seen anything like this one. It was so beautiful and so serene and felt so holy, it would make a believer out of just about anyone. Okay, maybe not, say, Arlene Mulroney, the meanest of mean girls from my sorority, but probably everyone else.

"The saint with her arm around Mary . . . ?" I asked. I felt I should know, but I couldn't remember who she could be.

"Saint Ann. The patron saint of Saint Gilbert and the mother of the Virgin. Grandmother of Christ," Max whispered. Even though there was no service going on, it still felt right to whisper. "The first duchess was named Ann."

I should have realized it was Saint Ann. Who else could have been so familiar with the mother of the savior than the woman who'd given birth to her?

I walked all around the perimeter of the nave, studying the stained glass. I became increasingly aware of Gran's presence as a slight pressure on my right arm.

It's okay, Gran. Lean on me . . .

After I completed my round with Gran and cleared my throat of the emotions that had been building up, I asked Max, "How was this all preserved during the war?"

"The windows were removed and hidden in a number of secret places. Then the openings were covered over with wood."

"And the Germans never asked where the original windows were?"

"Of course. They were told the Russians took them."

"And they believed that?"

Max shrugged. "The Germans believed the Russian were barbarians and vice versa. When the Russians came, we told them the Germans destroyed them."

I could swear I felt the warmth of Gran's smiling approval.

"Where were the windows hidden?"

"I will show you sometime before you leave. I think it might amuse you." He glanced at his watch, and I wondered what other obligations he'd put off from the morning to usher me around the city. "Is there anything else you'd like to see here?"

"Your mother said my great-grandparents and some other relatives are buried in the churchyard. I'd like to see their graves."

"Of course." He took my elbow and led me through a side door near the altar that opened onto the peaceful fence-enclosed churchyard.

My great-grandparents rested beneath a huge black obelisk upon which stood an angel of snow-white marble. She looked down on the graves, wings fully unfurled. She was beautifully carved, her face both earthly and ethereal.

Their names—Grand Duchess Elizabet Maria Jacqueline, the Grand Duke Theodore Philippe Emile—were carved into humble flat white stones level with the ground. I walked around the obelisk and found the graves of their son, Prince Theodore William, and a daughter, Princess Jacqueline Cecilia, side by side. Gran's brother and sister. The moment was surreal. Just weeks ago their names were only echoes of something I'd heard as a child—and yet here I stood, feeling a connection so strong and so real.

The pressure on my arm increased, and I felt Gran's smile fade.

I couldn't explain why, but at that moment I wanted my sisters with me. I wished my kids were here. I felt a sadness I honestly hadn't expected, a bond I couldn't explain, as if strands of DNA were twining like vines from beyond the grave. I wondered what *they* thought of me, if they thought me worthy to bear their name, to follow in their footsteps.

I wondered if right then Gran was thinking about how she'd been sent away, spared by the love of her parents and the loyalty of their subjects from certain assassination. If she, like me, might be wondering how, had it not been for the insistence of the former and the diligence of the latter, I wouldn't be standing there, my children would never have been born. I hadn't expected the emotions—the gratitude and respect and the love—that washed through me for these people I'd never met and, up until a month or so ago, had never even heard of.

And because my grandmother had never gotten to do so, in her honor I knelt next to the graves of her parents and prayed for their brave and good souls. When I'd finished, and stood, I realized the pressure I'd felt on my arm was gone, and so was she.

Chapter Eleven

"Where would you like to go next?" Max held open the smaller of the two gates that fronted the graveyard.

"I think I'd like to check out the shops we passed yesterday when we drove into the city."

"We can cut through the square," Max said as we crossed the street. "There are several places that might be of interest to you."

It was cooler under the high canopy of the oaks for which Beauchesne was named. Two black squirrels ran across our path, and birds flew from one branch to another. Were they the same birds as back home? I didn't know, and was just about to ask, when I heard splashing water.

"The fountain?" I tilted my head to one side, listening, the birds forgotten.

Max nodded.

"All I could see from the car was the tail of a really large fish." I walked a little faster as we drew closer, then called back over my shoulder. "In Philly, there's a fountain on the Ben Franklin Parkway right in the middle of a traffic circle, Eakins Oval. It's named for Thomas Eakins, a famous painter. It's by the art museum. You know, where the *Rocky* statue is?"

Max smiled but didn't comment as he followed along, his hands in his pockets, dark glasses covering his eyes.

"There are actually three fountains," I went on as I drew closer to the sound of water. "The one in the middle is George Washington on his horse, and all around him are—"

The fountain came into sight and I stopped in my tracks. "Oh."

Max smiled. "As you can see, there's only half a fish. The other half is . . ."

"A mermaid." I walked closer, mesmerized.

She was lovely, even in stone, exquisitely carved, with hair that curled around her face and fell all the way to her waist, covering all but a glimpse of cleavage. Her face was so lifelike, I could almost believe a real mermaid had sat for the artist. Her arms were stretched upward gracefully, and water flowed from her fingertips like offerings.

"She's beautiful," I said, awestruck.

"Serafina," Max addressed the mermaid, "I am pleased to present Grand Duchess Annaliese Jacqueline Terese Gilberti."

"Not yet," I reminded him.

He folded his arms over his chest as he addressed the fountain in a mock whisper. "We're doing our best to convince her to stay."

I pretended not to hear.

"Tell me about Serafina."

"She's been a fixture in Saint Gilbert since the duchy was established. The legend is that a farmer and his wife came into the city to sell their cheese. The wife wandered away, got lost, and in the dark, she stumbled into the lake. From the courtyard, the duchess witnessed the fall and rushed as fast as she could to the water to save the farmer's wife, but she was too late. The woman had drowned. The duchess sat by the water and wept with guilt that she'd been unable to save her. But the spirits who lived in the lake heard the duchess weeping and took pity on her. They changed the drowned woman into a mermaid who would live in the lake for as long as there were Gilbertis living in the castle."

"So I guess Serafina's been gone for a long time."

"Close to eighty years." He glanced down at me, a hint of mischief in his eyes. "But maybe she'll be back now that you're here. Once word of her return spreads, the streets will be jammed with flocks of tourists hoping to see her. The restaurants will be filled, and the shops will—"

"Ha! Don't even try to put that kind of guilt on me; it won't work." I walked around the fountain, admiring Serafina from every angle. I didn't believe in mermaids, of course, and despite the attitude I was throwing at Max, I was touched by the story. "I'm a mother. I know guilt. I know how to inflict it and I know how to deflect it."

He stood on the opposite side of the fountain, looking up at the statue, his hands palms up. "I tried, Serafina. I tried."

"Very funny, you." I arrived back where I'd started. "Let's go see this city of yours."

"This city of *yours*, madam." He fell in step next to me, guiding me toward the path that led to the shops.

"You're really pushing this today, aren't you? I have no idea what I'm going to do, so could we please put all that aside?"

"As you wish."

I laughed. The line always made me think of *The Princess Bride*. It had been one of my favorite movies forever. I watched it at least once a year with my sisters and Juliette.

We emerged from the park onto a street so narrow, I wondered aloud how two cars could pass without sideswiping each other.

"This is the oldest section of the city," he explained. "When it was built, people traveled by horse, or by carriage."

"Late fifteen, early sixteen hundreds."

"Someone's done her homework." A smile tugged at the corners of Max's mouth.

"Don't read anything into it. I looked it up on Wikipedia." I glanced around as we headed up the street. "Where do people park their cars around here?"

"It's a problem," he acknowledged.

"One of the first things I'd do if I were in charge would be to build a parking lot somewhere."

He raised an eyebrow but didn't say anything.

"Don't read anything into that, either. I just mean, if you want tourist business, you need to be able to accommodate them."

He started to say something, but I cut him off. "Could we stop here?" I paused in front of a coffee shop. I couldn't stop thinking about the delicious brew I'd had that morning.

"Of course." Max opened the door of the shop and we both went inside.

The coffee shops back in Philly varied greatly from dingy neighborhood deli-type places with worn linoleum floors to modest like the one at the end of my street, with its polished hardwood floor and antique wooden counters, to upscale cafés. Of course we had Starbucks, and we had Wawa—whose coffee I preferred—and we had donut shops that serve coffee and any number of little places dotted throughout the city. But this coffee shop in Beauchesne had them all beat when it came to ambience—and to the coffee.

There was an ancient-looking glass case displaying several varieties of croissants and scones that looked like a spread in *Martha Stewart Living*, and little plates of tea cakes that had been iced in pastel colors, also very Martha, and therefore were almost too pretty to eat. Almost.

While Max placed our orders and chatted with the woman behind the counter, I looked around the room. Dark wood, a small fireplace with a white mantel, some tiny tables each with a vase holding one or two spring flowers, a well-worn wood floor. There were paintings on the wall, and while I did not recognize the name of the artist, I could tell they were originals. I could imagine sitting there near the fire on a chilly morning, sipping coffee and eating a scone or two.

Max introduced me as a friend to the woman who was preparing our coffee, Clothilde. After I'd admired the shop, I asked about the paintings.

"Ah, those." She waved a hand as if to dismiss their importance. "My son fancies himself an artist, so to humor him, my husband began to hang his work here in the shop. We should probably replace them now that he's moved to London."

"They're very lovely," I said. They were. Gentle landscapes and scenes from nature. I paused in front of a painting of a falcon in flight. It arced over the castle tower and flew toward the woods much like the real one we'd seen earlier. I thought perhaps at the end of my stay I might return and buy it if Clothilde was willing to sell it and I could afford it.

Max and I took our coffees, his croissant, and my scone, and we sat outside at a table shaded by a red-and-white awning. I tasted the coffee and grinned.

"I will say this. The coffee in Saint Gilbert just might be the best in the world. Not that I've had coffee from everywhere in the world, but I can't imagine any better."

"Ah, something in our favor. I'll take it."

Max took a bite of his croissant and I attacked my scone. You'd think that after the breakfast I'd eaten, I'd be good for most of the day, but nope. The scone was delicious, every bit as yummy as it had looked in the case, and I said so.

"Two things in our favor. Things are looking up," Max said. "I'd say our prospects are improving."

"And I'd say this is still only my second day, and there are so many unanswered questions."

"Ask, then."

"How is it that so much survived not one but two invasions? All the beautiful furniture in the castle, and the artwork, even the jewelry your mother showed me last night. Why isn't it all in Russia, or Germany?"

Max took a sip of coffee and nodded his head as if he'd been expecting those questions.

"We'd had word that the Germans were on the move and likely headed this way. We are a very small country, but we were not without our riches. Knowing what was likely to happen—not only to herself, but to her family, her country, her castle—your great-grandmother had the rooms stripped of as much as could be hidden. Furniture, tapestries, art—everything that could be moved quickly, in anticipation of the invasion, leaving just enough that the castle did not appear barren."

"I get that. But where could you hide so many things?" I knew I was making a face, but I couldn't help myself. "There's one hundred ninety-seven rooms in the castle. That's a whole heap of chairs and settees and fancy tables, my friend. Where did they go?"

"Have you seen the castle's dungeon, madam? It's most interesting, not just because of its size, but it's said there's a labyrinth of secret rooms." That little bit of mischief was back in his eyes again.

I found myself whispering, though I wasn't sure why. "They hid stuff in the dungeon?"

"There are sections that are quite dry and suitable for storage. There are also hidden rooms within the upper floors of the castle where artwork was stashed. Much of the china, silver, many of the accoutrements of castle life found a place behind this wall or that."

"Stuff was hidden in the dungeon. Huh." I thought about this for a moment. Pretty clever. Especially since it worked.

I remembered then that we'd been accompanied into the city by two cars. I looked around but didn't see any guys hanging around. "Where are your men? The ones that are supposedly guarding me?"

"Ahhh, Annaliese. You assume."

"Assume what?"

"Assume that all of my men," he said as he picked up our plates and cups to return them to the shop, "are men."

I looked up and down both sides of the street. Here and there were couples walking along or pausing in front of this shop or that. Across the street, a pair of women stood, their arms around each other, admiring something in a shop window. Next to where I stood was a butcher shop where a man and woman were discussing whether to have beef or lamb for dinner that night.

"Are they . . . ?" I whispered to Max when he returned.

"If I told you our secrets, they wouldn't be secrets anymore." He held his arm out to me. "Now, which shop would you like to go into?"

I looked up and down the street. "All of them."

The doors to all the places I'd noticed on our way into the city yesterday stood open. I couldn't wait to see inside each and every one.

And that's what we did. It was hard to take it all in, so I snapped a whole bunch of pictures on my phone. Everyone was so friendly and so proud of their shops and their wares. Having Max as my guide made the day seem even more special. I could almost imagine that we were . . . ah, never mind. It would never happen. For one thing, if I declined the opportunity to put *duchess* before my name, I'd never see him again. For another, he was so out of my league it wasn't even worth fantasizing. Even though I did.

I met a dressmaker whose displays made me wish I were twenty pounds thinner and five inches taller, because her work was truly showroom quality. I wasn't personally familiar with haute couture showrooms, but I'd watched enough award shows on TV to know perfection in design when I saw it. The woman, Gisele, was young—maybe midtwenties—and said she'd inherited the shop from her parents, her father who'd been an excellent tailor, her mother a clever designer. It was clear she'd inherited gifts in equal measure from both. She'd designed and made everything in her shop, and most items were one of a kind. There were sheaths made of wools so light and fine they almost felt like cashmere, and finely tailored suits. Dresses and blouses in silks that floated through your fingers like a soft breeze when you touched them.

Boy, this woman would clean up on Philly's Main Line, in Gladwyne or Bryn Mawr, or in one of those little boutiques on Chestnut Street in Center City. But here business was slow, she explained, since she'd just started out, but she was sure things would pick up after the American duchess came to Saint Gilbert.

I couldn't even look Max in the eye.

"Who told her there might be an American coming to Saint Gilbert, eh?" I asked Max after we'd left Gisele's shop.

"After the vote in January, it was well known that we were exploring that option," he said.

"Thank God she didn't know it was me," I said, then paused, wondering how many American women in the company of a member of the Duke's Council—the captain of the castle guard, no less—had dropped into her shop this week.

She might well have suspected. If she did, I'm pleased she didn't ask. If I ever do become the duchess, she was going to be my go-to for clothes.

We heard much the same optimism from other shopkeepers about business prospects looking up now that there'd be a Gilberti on the throne again: "After the American comes," or "After the monarchy has been restored," or "When our duchess has been crowned." I was seriously glad Max did most of the talking, lest my American accent be detected. Which it would have been since it was hard to disguise I was from South Philly.

Anyway, I had to admit I found the oldest section of Beauchesne truly charming. There was a cheese shop that sold only local cheeses and a wine shop across the street that sold local wines. I wish I could recall exactly which cheeses I'd eaten and which wines I'd drank the day before because I'd love to take home some of each. A market displayed the most beautiful produce next door to a bakery I recognized from our drive through the previous day. We also passed a stationery store that sold books and newspapers, and a candy shop whose owner claimed to be a sixth-generation Swiss chocolatier and where I picked up some goodies for the kids. There were several restaurants that didn't appear particularly busy at that hour, though an outside table or two had patrons. Each posted their menu in their front window, and while they each offered different items, I had to note there wasn't a Philly cheesesteak on any of them. If I were the duchess, that would change. Of course, the baker would have to duplicate the rolls so they're like the ones from Amoroso's or Liscio's, because everyone knows it isn't a Philly cheesesteak if the roll isn't right.

All things considered, the town had definite tourist appeal, and when I mentioned that to Max, he reminded me there were no places that offered accommodations that he knew of, and there were few attractions that would make people want to spend their money in Saint Gilbert as opposed to Italy or France or the UK.

"There has to be something," I murmured.

"We're hoping those fresh American eyes of yours will come up with it." Max was only half kidding. "Something that would make Saint Gilbert a destination. Something that sets us apart from those other places where people go to spend their vacation money."

"I'll let you know if anything occurs to me." The half of him that wasn't kidding was starting to get under my skin. I didn't appreciate having the onus put on me. It was a burden I didn't want and didn't feel I deserved. But since this could be my only visit to Saint Gilbert, I let Max dwell on his little fantasy of me flying in to save the day before he realized they'd have to move on to plan B. Assuming there was a plan B.

Then, because I didn't want to discuss it further, I took a quick right into a tiny gift shop, and after I picked up some beautifully wrapped soaps to take home for Ceil, Roe, and my bestie, Marianne, assuming she was still speaking to me, I was ready to go back to the castle.

We walked back to the car and because the street was too narrow to make a U-turn, Max drove straight up the hill past the church. This section of the city was residential, and while I didn't let on to Max, I fell in love with the rows of attached houses. Max called them town houses, but in Philly, we said row houses (tomato, tomahto). They were, like the shops, half-timbered and looked Tudorish, with casement windows and arched doors and little front gardens that were longer and wider the farther we drove up the hill. The front yards were all in bloom, and there were roses and other flowers I couldn't identify from a distance, and window boxes that overflowed with trails of color. All in all, Beauchesne looked exactly the way I pictured an old European town to look. The effect was totally enchanting, and in spite of myself, my mind immediately began to envision ways to market the city to attract visitors before I shut that exercise down. Totally unlikely, I reminded myself, and at best, premature.

Even so, God forbid Max knew what I was thinking.

Chapter Twelve

"Tomorrow the tour of the countryside, yes?" Max parked the car and left it in front of the castle door where we'd picked it up that morning.

"Yes, but right now, I want that garden tour."

"Of course."

Max laughed when he saw me get out of the car. We met up at the hood.

"You know, there may come a time when someone will always be there to open your door for you," he teased.

"Only if I let them."

We went into the castle, and I followed Max into the gallery and through French doors I'd originally thought were windows that opened onto the courtyard. Flowers grew in neat beds around the perimeter of the courtyard, so the area was awash in color—red, purple, cream, rose, yellow, pink, orange. The grass was carefully trimmed, and the cobblestone walkways were pristine.

"What is this area used for?" I asked.

"What would you like it used for, Your Grace?" Max asked with a straight face, but his smiling eyes gave him away.

"Flogging annoying members of the Duke's Council comes to mind."

"There are some on the council who might enjoy it."

I held up a hand. "Please. Don't tell me who."

"My lips are sealed, madam."

I laughed in spite of myself. "So what is this area used for?"

"At one time, outdoor entertaining. Garden parties and such. Perhaps one day . . ."

I could imagine beautiful women in light summer dresses from another era gracing the grounds. It would be lovely. "And where do we find the garden?"

"Around to the left, Your Grace."

"What happened to 'Annaliese'? I thought we had an agreement," I said.

"Apologies. Here at the castle I'm inclined toward formality. I'll try to be more mindful."

We walked around the side of the castle and found the garden I'd seen from my windows, which was even more spectacular when you were right there in it. The rose garden alone was breathtaking, and I said so.

Max smiled that half smile that I have to admit was growing on me. Maybe a little too much so.

I walked through the rows of blooms, stopping to—yes, smell the roses.

"Do you have a favorite?" Max walked behind me, slowing his pace to match mine.

"They're all beautiful, though this pale-pink one is lovely, and it's incredibly fragrant." I took another sniff, then stood back and gestured for Max to smell a particularly large bloom.

"Some of the bushes are original. I understand that some cuttings have been made over the years. The gardeners have been vigilant, as you can see, and have taken excellent care."

"Original? You mean from when the garden was first planted?"

"Yes. But don't ask me the year. I know it was long before my mother was born, because the rose garden was well established when she was a child."

"I had no idea rosebushes could live so long." I walked around the rest of the garden, admiring flowers I didn't even recognize.

I stood in the midst of all that color watching butterflies hover and flit, and I felt like I should be wearing a straw hat and pair of dusty overalls like Rebecca of Sunnybrook Farm. "Do you think I could cut some for my room?"

"Of course." Max held up a finger. "One moment, if you would . . ."

He disappeared behind the corner of the castle wall, and I wandered through the entire area a second time. I thought maybe once I got back to Philly, I'd check out some of the famous gardens in and around the city, like Bartram Gardens and Longwood Gardens, neither of which I'd ever been to.

Max appeared at the corner he'd rounded a few minutes earlier, a pair of clippers in one hand and a bucket in the other.

"Roberto said he'd be happy to cut a bouquet for you, but I told him I believe you wished this pleasure for yourself," he was saying as he came closer.

"You believe correctly."

I watched him stride on those long legs across the lawn and into the garden. The sun played off his dark hair and . . . damn.

Just . . . damn.

He was saying something else, but for a moment all my attention was elsewhere.

". . . and they'll stay fresh longer." He handed the clippers to me.

I should have asked him what he'd said, but then I'd have to own up to being one of those shallow women who get distracted by a really great-looking guy, so I just said okay. Most of the time I could control myself, but every once in a while, his handsomeness struck me all over again.

I'd been wondering about his relationship status, and while I hadn't wanted to appear, you know, predatory, I really wanted to know. It was inconceivable to me that a man as fine as Max would be unattached. So I took a deep breath and asked, "Are you married?"

"I was. My wife died six years ago."

I hadn't expected that.

"I'm so sorry." I was. Really. I don't wish death on anyone, even someone whose husband makes me sweat just looking at him. He looked mildly uncomfortable, so I didn't ask him the question on the tip of my tongue: How did she die?

"Do you have children?" I asked.

"A daughter. Remy." He added, "I believe she's Juliette's age."

I wondered if she was one of the young girls I'd seen around the castle. I wondered if she looked like him, then I wondered what his wife had looked like. Probably a supermodel.

I spent the next ten or fifteen minutes pondering the private life of Maximilien Belleme while cutting flowers and plunking them into the bucket. When I finished cutting, the bucket was jam-packed with flowers of every color, size, and shape.

"Do you think I overdid it?" I asked.

"Do they make you happy?"

"They do." I looked up at him and smiled. For a moment I almost forgot who I was: a forty-four-year-old divorcée living out my six-year-old self's princess fantasy, complete with a handsome—if not a prince—duke. Then I tapped myself on the shoulder to reel myself back in. Annie? Anyone home? Bueller?

"Permit me to carry those for you." Max held out both hands, and I passed over the bucket. "Would you like to see the kitchen garden while we're here?"

"Is that where the strawberries are grown?"

He nodded and gestured for me to follow him through a gate beyond which all I saw were trees. But once we stepped through it, there were rows and rows of green growing.

"My mind is spinning," I told him. "It's hard to take this all in."

"The orchard has been here for many years, but the garden is new. We tried to prepare for the event that you and your family would be living here," Max said. "And of course, it follows you'd be entertaining."

"So what happens to all this if there is no duchess, no royal family living in the castle?"

A cloud passed over his face. "I imagine we'd take it to the market while we explored other options," he said.

"So you do have a plan B."

Off to the left lay the lake, which I'd yet to see up close. I started off in that direction, and Max fell in step with me. We walked in silence until we reached the waist-high stone wall that separated the castle grounds from the water. I leaned on the wall and peered into the lake.

"Serafina's children?" I pointed at the water below, where a school of small fish swam in a sort of zigzag pattern.

"Perhaps." He placed the bucket on the ground.

I watched the fish for a few minutes. They looked like minnows to me, but then, where I come from, we call all tiny fish minnows.

"I can't rule a country I know nothing about," I said, finally understanding why I felt so much inner confusion and, yes, frustration. "Even the most basic things. I don't know your birds or animals or fish or flowers. Except for how it pertains to my family, I don't know your history. I don't know your heritage, your culture, your legends."

"We're happy to teach you."

"No, you don't get it. When you grow up in a country, you learn those things gradually, starting from the time you're little. Like, I don't know, Betsy Ross. George Washington and the cherry tree. Johnny Appleseed. Paul Bunyan. Pecos Bill. Bigfoot. The Jersey Devil." Which my cousin Frank swears he saw one night in the Jersey Pine Barrens, but I'm pretty sure he was drunk at the time. "Trying to learn someone else's legends seems like trying to learn the words to a song long after everyone else did, you know?"

"Does it matter who learned first, as long as you learn?"

"I don't know. It seems sort of . . . phony. Like trying to be a Saint Gilbertian when you're not really."

"With my most sincere apologies, I cannot agree. If someone comes into your country and is granted citizenship, is he any less American than you when he pledges his allegiance to your flag? Should he feel like a 'phony' because he wasn't born there? Should he be less proud, feel less devoted?"

I thought it over for a moment, acutely aware right then that I was the granddaughter of more than one immigrant. "No. He should feel proud of his citizenship."

"Well, then." He turned his back to the lake so he was facing the castle. "The things you mentioned are all easily learned. Our birds? Much like those in America. Golden orioles, cranes, ducks, geese. You already know we have falcons, but we have other raptors as well— hawks, owls, eagles. Here at the lake, we get ducks and geese, like any lake in America. We have the great blue heron, thrush, larks, pipits, sparrows. Nothing unusual there. Fish? The same as your freshwater lakes and ponds and streams. Pike, bass, trout, perch. Flowers? Again, the same. Roses, iris, peonies, daisies, lilies, as you have seen—and of course, violets."

I thought about this for a moment. I had to admit that even back in Philly, I doubted I'd be able to identify any of those fish if I saw them in a stream, though the birds I probably knew. The flowers, I knew the common ones. So maybe not so different. So I did feel a little less like a—ha!—fish out of water.

God, I sounded like my father, the great jokester of the family, a man who never met a pun he wouldn't repeat. He was such a happy soul, right up to the minute he had an out-of-the-blue, totally unexpected widow-maker of a heart attack and died on the spot. I wondered if he was aware of my mother's heritage, that his mother-in-law had been royalty. Until, that is, the world swept away her family and her country and her friends and everything else she knew and loved.

I hated thinking about that. Best to ignore the past and focus on the present, as my dad's Italian mother, my nonna Rose, used to say. She was one whose eyes were always clearly on the path ahead. I decided to channel Nonna Rose for a change and stay in the moment.

"What are those little fish swimming down there in the lake? Those tiny silvery ones," I asked.

"Sunbleaks." Max looked pleased that I'd asked. "We're keeping an eye on their population because somehow a fish that originated in Asia called the topmouth gudgeon was introduced into some streams in France. They eat the sunbleak's eggs, and they also pass on a parasite that renders sunbleaks unable to spawn."

"Who brought them here?" I asked, annoyed at the thought of interlopers interfering with the native fish. Cheeky buggers, those damned topmouth gudgeons! Like the pythons that some idiot let go in the Florida Everglades that ended up destroying the habitat by eating the native animals. Were people really that clueless, that thoughtless?

Never mind. We all know the answer.

"It's not known how they first moved into European waters," Max was saying, "and at this point it's almost immaterial. What matters is that we destroy the ones we find."

"Is anyone actually looking for them? I mean, does Saint Gilbert have a—I don't know what you'd call it—a fish and stream department?" I thought for a moment. "Fish and game? Wildlife conservation?"

"Nothing formal, but it's an excellent idea. When the Duke's Council meets next week, I'll propose that such a post be established."

"Is there a lot of sportfishing in Saint Gilbert?" I asked as we started back toward the castle, Max carrying the bucket of flowers.

"We have several picturesque lakes and streams, and fishing is popular here in the city," Max said thoughtfully. "The areas further from the city aren't as . . . accessible."

"Ah yes. The old the-Russians-were-supposed-to-fix-the-roads-but-didn't story." I recalled he'd mentioned that before. "Can't the Duke's Council vote on doing something about that?"

"There has been discussion but no consensus, but since the funds have been lacking, the arguments were moot. And there are other issues, madam."

"We must be close to the castle. I'm 'madam' again," I teased, but Max didn't smile. "So what other issues, besides the fact that your country only has two exports and you can't sell either in America."

"We could probably sell the wine, if we had a wine merchant who isn't married to the vineyards in France and Italy. Unfortunately, that is a hereditary post, and the man has singular vision. If he sold our wines on a broader international scale, he'd sell less from his family's vineyards."

"That's a clear conflict of interest. He should be removed." Something else to add to the list of things I'd change if in fact I were grand duchess. The thought had come quickly, and just as quickly, I swatted it away. "So what else? Infrastructure? Tourism? Other ways for people to make a living?"

He nodded slowly. "All those, yes."

"And by the way, you have a massive PR problem in that no one outside my family or who took a wrong turn at the Alps has ever heard of Saint Gilbert."

"That too." He nodded glumly.

"Maybe what you need isn't a duchess, Max. Maybe what you need is a good PR firm."

And quick access to those funds that have been collecting interest since 1941.

Chapter Thirteen

I had dinner that night with Max, Claudette, and several loyalists who'd been key supporters of the movement to return to the monarchy. We ate in a formal dining room—the smallest of several—and I had to admit, the food was every bit as good as the best I'd had back home. Actually, in some cases—as in the salmon and the vegetables—it was better. Dessert was better, too—some chocolaty thing that had layers of something that tasted like shortbread cookies covered with raspberries before the chocolate was artfully poured on.

If they kept feeding me like this, I'd be lucky if any of my clothes still fit by the end of the week. Then again, I might not care. Besides the fact that everything I'd tasted was delicious, there was something so decadently wonderful about having someone grow your food for you and someone else preparing fit-for-a-king meals. Or in my case, fit for a duchess. Part of me could totally get used to it.

The other part of me was still very conflicted.

I loved the good old US of A. If I moved to Saint Gilbert, I'd miss my friends and my life, my city, my job. Did I really want to leave everything behind to make a new life in a foreign country? Even if they do speak English here, and even if my family's roots are here, it's still foreign to me, right?

Of course, if this had happened right after my divorce, I might have jumped at it. Timing is everything.

Anyway, it was quite an experience, sitting at the head of the table in that beautiful room. The walls were papered with little gold crowns on a dark-blue background, and there was a rug on the floor that looked like it was older than God. The colors were faded, but even so, the blues and reds and creams were pretty. The table was covered in ivory damask and set with beautifully painted china—creamy white with a dark-blue border set with a gold crown. (BTW, the plates were set so the crown was at the top. Every time I looked down, I was staring at that crown. Subtle.) The flatware was ornate and heavy silver, each piece topped with, yep, that crown. A large round bowl in the center held a mass of peonies flanked by silver candelabras that looked like they could knock someone out, or at the very least raise a good-size goose egg. The overall effect was elegant, and I have to admit, it humbled me to think they'd gone through all that trouble for me. I'd never been treated like royalty before in my life. No one was royalty in South Philly, except maybe our sports heroes.

Like I said—conflicted.

The evening had been formal and a bit stilted, and I can't say I enjoyed the company since everyone was on their best behavior and the conversations were very dry and lacked animation. I understand it was a political necessity—these were descendants of the people who'd contributed to my grandmother's support and kept the fire of the monarchy burning all these years. Sort of like a White House dinner to thank the big donors who helped the president du jour get elected. But I still felt a little let down. At the end of the meal, we walked the guests to the reception area to see them off, but as soon as they'd departed, as if he'd read my mind, Max offered to show me the dungeon.

Now, back home, if a guy asked me if I wanted to see his dungeon, I'd run like hell. I heard there's a house somewhere on Catharine Street that had something kinky in the basement. It was supposedly owned by a guy who tended bar in Queen Village, but I personally had never met him. At least, I didn't think I had, so I cannot confirm the rumor.

Anyway, so there I was. It was dark outside, and the lighting in the castle wasn't all that great, and Max handed me a flashlight. He left the room and came back with a second light and said, "Just in case." Though he didn't say just in case what. I trusted him, so I followed him through the castle. We walked through an arch that led into the kitchen, where the basement stairs were located. Max turned on the overhead light, but he was wise to bring flashlights. We went down fairly wide stone steps that ended far below the first floor. The room at the bottom of the stairwell was wide and windowless and had—yes—chains bolted to the wall. I'm not making this up. I was thinking about how my kids would love to have a Halloween party down there.

All of a sudden, I started to giggle. Now, normally, I'm not a giggly woman, but can't you picture it? Me, following Max through some darkened rooms, flashlights in hand, down into the depths of the castle dungeon where chains are hanging from the walls?

"What?" Max asked.

"Sorry," I whispered, "but I feel like we're in an episode of *Scooby-Doo*."

"Who?" He stopped and turned around.

"*Scooby-Doo*. It's a cartoon dog, like a Great Dane? My kids used to love it." Max still looked blank, so I said, "Never mind." I gestured for him to keep going. How did you describe Scooby to someone who'd never had the experience?

"Was anyone ever . . ." I pointed to the chains dangling from the stone wall.

"Not in my lifetime, but I always thought they must have been put there for a reason, so who knows?"

I walked around the large room trying not to imagine some poor sucker suspended from those chains when I noticed there were several doorways leading off to the left and a dark hall to the right. "I guess those don't lead directly to the secret rooms."

"Correct, madam. Otherwise, they wouldn't be . . . ," Max teased.

"Secret. Right." I rolled my eyes à la Juliette. "So where are these hidden rooms that were large enough to store a castle full of furniture and other goodies?"

"Well, they didn't hide everything. That would have been too obvious. They had to leave some furnishings and some trappings of a royal home lest the Nazis become suspicious."

I followed Max down the dark hall into a rabbit's warren of tiny rooms.

"Cells?"

Max nodded, so I asked, "Were prisoners kept here? For real?"

"Some, but I doubt there was much real torture involved, if that's what you're wondering. I think at one time the castle dungeon was used more or less as the city jail. There would have been thieves, the random highwayman, probably the occasional murderer kept down here."

He opened the door to one of the cells and walked in and appeared to be scanning the stone walls. He stepped closer and ran his hand over a course of irregularly shaped stones, then said, "Ah, here we are."

With a push against the corner of one stone, a portion of the wall began to open inward.

"Oh my God. It's just like in the movies!" came out of my mouth before I had time to realize how goofy that must have sounded.

Max laughed and swept an arm forward. "After you, Your Grace."

I stepped inside and for a moment wondered if there was a safeguard in case there was a glitch and the wall closed by itself.

"Anyone ever get stuck in here?" I imagined some poor soul weeping inconsolably when they realized they were locked in.

"Once or twice, but their bodies were found before they decomposed so they could have decent burials."

At my look of horror, Max laughed again. "Just kidding, Annaliese. There is a way to both close and open from the inside."

He showed me the lever, and I was able to exhale.

I was seriously relieved. I doubted there was a cell phone in the world that got reception down here, so far underground and surrounded by thick walls of solid stone.

Of course, getting locked in with Max for a while could have its perks. Heh.

I chastised myself—but not too much—for letting my mind go there. I mean, it was inevitable. The guy was just about everything any woman would want. And he was within arm's reach every day. A girl could dream, right?

I brought myself back to reality. "So this is the secret place where the castle stuff was stashed." I walked around the room, which was large but maybe not large enough for an entire castle's worth.

"One of several." Max leaned against the wall, his hands in his pockets, one foot crossed over the other.

Damn. I really did like a casual guy.

"Would you like to see the others?"

"How many others? And are they all as empty as this one?"

"Several others. And yes. All empty now."

"Not much point in going from one empty room to another." I walked back out into the cell. "Didn't the Germans or the Russians wonder why there was so little space down here? I mean, it's a huge castle with an enormous footprint. Even I would expect the basement to be much bigger."

"There are many halls that lead to other halls, and altogether, they effectively create a sort of maze. Each hall has any number of cells, but to go from one hall to another can be confusing. The hall leading into the next hall can appear to go on forever to one who isn't familiar with the design. I doubt either of our invaders thought this was anything other than what it appeared. A prison with different . . . cellblocks, I believe you'd call them."

Max pushed the stone back in and the wall closed up. When the opening was completely closed, I couldn't tell where it had been. Whoever had designed and built it had been extremely clever.

We started to walk, and while I wasn't sure where we were in relation to where we began, we found our way back to the stairwell in no time. We went up the steps, guided by our flashlights.

At the top of the steps, Max asked, "Where to next?"

"I think I'd like to turn in. I am exhausted." Jet lag had finally gotten its teeth into me, and suddenly it was all I could do to keep my eyes open.

"Of course. I'll see you to your room."

"No, that's all right. I remember the way."

"I'm sure you do but still, you should not be unaccompanied."

I started to ask what he thought could possibly happen to me between the first and second floors, but I remembered there could be people around who might not be happy with my presence in the country, who *hopefully* wouldn't be shooting at me. So instead of taking off, I allowed him to walk me to my door.

"Thanks for everything today, Max. Taking me to the church, the tour of the town." I smiled. "For showing me the dungeon."

"You're most welcome, Your Grace," he said, adding that last part, no doubt, for the benefit of Sebastian, who'd taken up his post outside my door again. "It was my pleasure."

"Good night, then. And good night, Sebastian." The guard nodded his head in acknowledgment, and I went into my room and closed the door behind me.

I heard them talking while I toed off my heels and pulled my dress over my head, glad I'd had time for a shower before dinner so all I had to do now was wash my face and fall onto the pillow. And that's exactly what I did.

Chapter Fourteen

I called Ceil when I awoke the morning after my excursion to the dungeon. While we chatted, I sat on the little sofa in my sitting room, my bare feet resting on the table in front of me, the phone nestled on my shoulder. I rubbed my temples with the fingers of both hands, hoping to make the headache go away. It felt like a hangover headache, but I didn't think I'd had that much to drink the night before. Sure, wine with dinner and a nightcap of something—I don't remember what—but I felt fine until I got up this morning and I swear, there was a tiny elf sitting behind my eyes tapping teensy nails into the heels of little elf-shoes with his tiny hammer. It could have been the combination of everything: the flight and the subsequent jet lag, the wine, the overwhelming experiences of the past few days. All that.

"The cemetery is very quiet and dignified, and oh man, the emotions standing right there where our murdered great-grandparents and great-uncle and aunt are buried. I really wish you'd been with me, Ceil. It was such a *moment*."

"I can't even imagine. Maybe I can go back with you sometime and you can show me," Ceil said. "The town sounds wonderful, and all those little shops sound so charming. I'm really sorry I didn't go with you."

"Next time you will come with me, and we'll bring the kids. Roe, too, if she wants to come."

"Think there'll be a next time? Crap, I just spilled my coffee." I could hear Ceil's footsteps as she went from the dining room into the kitchen for paper towels.

I waited, giving her a minute while she cleaned up. I used almost all of that minute to wonder if there would be a next time.

"Annie? You there?" Ceil came back on the line. After I assured her I was still there, she said, "It all sounds so magical, like the real Magic Kingdom. We should all go, even if we're not going to be the royal family."

"We will. I really want you to see this place. You'll love it, I know you will."

"Sounds like you're warming to it."

"Oh, I'm warming. I really do like it here. Does that mean I'm staying?" I sighed. "I'm not there yet, Ceil. There's too much to sift through before I even start to think about what that even means."

"I get it. So how'd they let you out to roam around the country without security? Do they have a Secret Service there?"

"Well, I'm not a prisoner, ya know. And they have the castle guards. But yes, there's security, and I was never alone." I told her about the two cars that accompanied us yesterday. "There were a few times when out of the corner of my eye, I'd see Max looking off somewhere, almost as if he'd made eye contact with someone, but there didn't seem to be anyone there. Of course, if you're in a sort of Secret Service, you'd know how to remain secret. And there were other people in the city, looking at the shops or sitting outside one of the restaurants. But no one overt or all dressed in black."

"It sounds like a movie," Ceil said. "It all sounds so dreamy."

"I wish we'd known about all this when we were kids so we could have talked to Gran about, well, all of it." I didn't want to share the fact that I was pretty sure Gran was here with me. Probably Mom, too. I wasn't sure if the woo-woo factor would intrigue her or have her question my sanity.

"Maybe she wouldn't have wanted to. I bet it was all too painful for her. Mom didn't even talk about it, so the pain must have gone really deep."

"I'm sure it did. Ceil, have you ever driven past Gran's old house? The one we used to visit when we were kids?"

"A couple of times," she admitted. "That black iron fence that surrounded the property is gone, and it looks like the neighborhood has gone downhill. A couple of the houses on her street looked kind of shabby. Like they were in need of attention. It made me so sad. Did you ever go?"

"When the kids were little, yeah. One time, I parked in front—the fence was still there then—and just . . . remembered. I thought it would be nice to tell the kids about her, you know? Show them the house she lived in, the house Mom grew up in. Tell them a little about how we used to go visit."

"How'd that go?"

I snorted. "The two of them were beating the crap out of each other in the back seat and never heard a word I said." My nostalgic moment ruined, I'd driven away, wondering why I'd thought three- and six-year-olds would rather look at an old house through the car windows than beat up on each other.

I hung up after texting her the photos I'd taken the day before, thinking how everyone in the family would find something to love here. I thought briefly about using "the REAL Magic Kingdom" in a hypothetical marketing campaign intended to introduce Saint Gilbert to the rest of the world, but I think Disney had "the Magic Kingdom" in a lock. A country that couldn't afford to fix its roads couldn't afford to take on Disney.

I looked out the window that faced the lake and thought about Serafina. The water was perfectly calm and so blue, the scene so inviting, that I couldn't resist. If there really was a mermaid, I was pretty sure she'd show herself on a morning like this.

Not that I believed there really *was* one. Besides, she'd been gone since 1941. Not that I believed she'd ever been there for real, of course.

I opened the door and found Hans at his station.

"Any chance I could have my morning coffee down near the lake? Like around the arch?" I asked.

"Of course, madam." He maintained that stiff upper back thing, standing ramrod straight and staring directly ahead. "I shall arrange it immediately."

"Thank you." Believe me, no matter how this whole thing worked out, I would cherish those three little words—*of course* and *immediately*—till my last day.

I'd thought about my plans before I got dressed, so I was appropriately attired for seeking hidden rooms and exploring the countryside with Max. The breeze blowing into my room was a little cooler than yesterday, so I'd put on a long-sleeved shirt that was a sort of sea-glass green—one of my favorite colors—and a white pencil skirt. I had become conscious of how I looked when I was going to be with Max. He always looked so *GQ*, and I always felt so like the losing side of *Who Wore It Better?* when I was with him. So I brushed my hair out straight and tucked it behind my ears (Claudette said it looked best that way) and proceeded to walk that fine line when I put on my makeup. You know, the line between making yourself look naturally good and looking made up.

I noticed the lines around my eyes seemed to be softening a bit. My job must be more stressful than I realized if four days out of the office made the crow's-feet less noticeable. Then again, it was probably just the lighting.

Sadly, my shoe choices were the same as they'd been yesterday. I sighed, going once again with my Keds. If we were going to be out in the countryside, I might be called upon to walk around on uneven ground, and since I already knew what it felt like to walk those country roads in heels, this time I went for comfort.

By the time I got outside, a small table had been set up in precisely the spot I'd envisioned. There was a tray much like I'd had for breakfast my first morning, and a small vase filled with wildflowers. I sat in a comfy chair and poured myself a cup of coffee and just felt like, *Ahhhhh.* You know that feeling, right? When things are just the way you wanted them to be, and it makes you happy? Like kicking off tight shoes or taking off your underwire bra after a long day? That's how I felt. I sat in the morning sunshine and gazed out at the beautiful lake and nibbled my scone and ate more of those incredible berries and drank my coffee and just . . . *ahhhhh.*

For just those few moments, I felt like a duchess at home in her world, where all was well and good.

Then I saw Max walking toward me from the castle, and the morning got even better.

"Good morning," he called as he drew closer.

"Morning to you." I sat a little straighter as he approached, and I didn't even need Mom to remind me. I'd been slightly hunched in the chair before I saw him, and slouching wasn't a good look for anyone. "Want to join me?"

I looked at the tray and realized there was no extra coffee cup.

"Well, I'd invite you to share my coffee, but . . ." I pointed at the table. "Only one cup."

"Thank you, but I've had my morning limit." He stood with his hands on his hips looking down at me.

Be still, my flip-flopping heart.

"Almost ready for that drive about I promised you?" he asked.

"Sure. I just have to run back up to my room for a minute." What I wanted to do was check to make sure there were no little strawberry bits or seeds in my teeth.

"Of course. I'm not rushing you."

"I'm finished here." I touched the corners of my mouth with the napkin—surely the softest linen on the planet—and stood.

Walking back up to the castle, I had the opportunity to see that structure in all its magnificence.

"Whoever designed this place was a genius," I said.

Max nodded. "It is quite the castle."

"And you're quite the master of understatement. It's the most beautiful building I've ever seen."

Max smiled, no doubt hoping I was about to say I'd like to live here for the rest of my days, but I was nowhere near making that sort of decision.

I finished upstairs—teeth, makeup, hair—and was back downstairs with the escort who'd been waiting outside the door to my suite. I guess they were taking this guard-the-potential-duchess thing more seriously than I was.

But once again, outside there were three cars waiting. And once again, Max took my arm and led me to the middle of the three.

"Security detail in place?" I teased after he'd opened the passenger door for me and I slid across that cushy leather seat.

He wasn't amused.

Max got in behind the wheel and started the car. "Security is not a joke, Annaliese. It's a responsibility I take very seriously."

Chastised, I said, "I'm sorry. I'm just not used to having anyone worry about me."

"You'll get used to it."

"Only if I come back."

He ignored my remark and instead said, "I thought today we'd do a tour of the southern part of the country. You saw much of what the north is like on our drive from the airport the other day."

"What will we see in the south?" I asked.

"Villages, farms, a few vineyards. Lots of mountains, especially as we get closer to Italy."

"You said my grandmother's escape route went into Italy." I recalled the story, every detail I'd been told. But I knew I hadn't heard it all.

"Unfortunately, I don't know exactly where they crossed from Switzerland into Italy. I doubt if anyone knows the exact place." So apparently Max hadn't heard it all, either.

We drove along winding roads, some more narrow than others, and I could see where a little roadwork would make the travel from one village to another much more pleasant. It was uncomfortably bumpy in many places.

"Whoa!" The car hit a rut, and I was jarred in spite of the seat belt. I recovered my composure enough to say, "Well, that was impressive."

"One of the many roads that need improvement." Max swerved to the right to avoid another deep rut.

"Why haven't they been fixed? Surely there's been plenty of time to repair the roads."

"Plenty of time, but insufficient funds. Remember, most of the country's wealth is sitting in a bank in Switzerland." He slowed a little and glanced over at me. "Just waiting for the duchess to unlock that vault."

"I hate feeling responsible for all of Saint Gilbert's problems." I know I was whining, but I couldn't help it. "Don't think I'm not aware of what I could do *if* . . ."

"You shouldn't feel it's all on you. Even once the funds are returned, the council will have to agree to the repairs."

"But I—theoretically—would have the final say, right?"

"I'm fairly certain, yes. But remember, we haven't had a duchess ruling our country since 1941. The Duke's Council has made all decisions unopposed since the 1990s when the Soviet Union broke up. I don't know what precedents applied before that."

"So they—this group of all men—have never been challenged."

Max's smile was barely detectable, but I didn't miss it. "You'd be the first. Theoretically."

"How do you even learn to rule a country? How do you know what to do when you're asked to make decisions that will affect the lives of several hundred thousand people?"

"I admit our situation would be a challenge since there's no one in place to show you everything you need to know. So in that respect, yes, I agree it would not be easy. But there are those with whom you can consult. There's the council, of course. Some members may be more helpful than others."

"The chancellor?"

Max shrugged. "His position is traditionally that of a principal advisor. There are some areas in which he could be invaluable. Diplomacy, for example. He's very good at that sort of thing. He's known to heads of state outside Saint Gilbert, and well liked, from all I've heard."

I made a mental note of that.

"But not in the everyday running of the country?"

"In those matters, I would rely on my instincts." He cleared his throat. "Your instincts are quite good, Annaliese. My best advice to you is that you trust yourself."

"What makes you think my instincts are worth trusting?"

"You followed them to Saint Gilbert, didn't you?"

I guess he had me there.

"What if I want to do something but the council doesn't agree?"

"You would have to find a way to convince them to want what you want." He smiled again. "I have no doubt you are well capable of getting your way once you set your mind to it."

Well, there is that . . .

"There's a very pretty village less than a mile from here," Max said without segue. I guess he felt he'd made his point. "We could stop and have lunch, if you like."

"I'd like," I told him, then looked out the window to the mountains up ahead. "Are those the Alps?"

"Yes. That's Italy in the distance. The Alps run through Italy, France, Switzerland, Liechtenstein, Austria, Germany, and Slovenia, as well as Saint Gilbert."

I nodded. I remembered those mountains. "So there should be ski lodges and slopes for tourists."

"I agree. I'm sure the next duchess will find a way to bring tourists to Saint Gilbert." He reduced the speed as we entered a small village.

I frowned. "Stop dumping everything on the duchess."

"I'm not dumping on her, as you say. I'm challenging her. My instincts tell me she's a woman who enjoys a challenge." He parked the car along a tree-lined street and unhooked his seat belt. "I doubt she's one to back down."

I refused to pick up that gauntlet, though I had to admit, apparently he, too, had damned good instincts.

We had a terrific lunch in a beautiful café, and afterward we popped into a few of the little shops. But we avoided any further discussion of why I'd come to Saint Gilbert and just enjoyed the rest of the day. On the way back to the city, we took a side road that led to a castle that had a moat without water, and since no one lived there we couldn't watch the drawbridge come down, but it would have been fun. The hillsides were dotted with chateaus, and we drove through a number of perfectly picturesque villages. We stopped at several farms where Max knew the farmers, and as a city girl, I have to say I was loving the countryside and all the people we met. But by the time we arrived home—that is, back at the castle—I was ready for a nap and an early evening. I was in my room for the night by nine, in bed by ten.

When I closed my eyes, I could still see the faces of the farmers we'd met. They'd offered me wine and cheeses, and one even gave me a basket of wool he'd shorn from his sheep.

It was really thick and, frankly, didn't smell all that great, but I was gracious and accepted the gift with a smile. After we left, Max told me the wool from the local sheep is highly prized, but when I asked if any of it was made into yarn and exported, he said, "Not to my knowledge." Another opportunity lost, like the wine and the cheeses, if you ask me. He said he doubted the sheep farmers have the start-up money for anything more than what they're doing, which is basically selling their wool to a woman in the city who makes it into yarn. He wasn't sure where it goes from there. I told him that knitting is huge in the States, and he just said, "Hmmmm."

I was starting to get frustrated with all the opportunities wasted here. I realized people didn't have a lot of disposable cash—neither did the government, apparently, since my great-grandparents spirited away most of it into a bank in another country for safekeeping. Which was a better idea than letting an invader or some unscrupulous Saint Gilbertian loot the coffers, but it wasn't doing anyone any good where it was. Yes, I was increasingly aware that I could solve that little problem for them, but at what cost to me? To my family? It was one of those things I didn't want to think about right now.

I turned over and went to sleep thinking about American tourists oohing and ahhing over skeins of brightly colored yarn displayed in the window of one of those cute shops in Beauchesne.

Chapter Fifteen

"You'd asked about the portraits of your family," Claudette said the next morning when she'd come to check in with me after breakfast. "Perhaps you'd like to take a walk with me?"

"I would." Especially after having eaten several of those yummy croissants. This morning's were filled with a soft cheese and strawberries. So delicious.

I followed Claudette around the hallway to the main stairwell. At the top of the steps was a huge open area that I assumed was some sort of reception hall.

"Indeed it is, Annaliese. Guests would wait here before being announced to enter the ballroom." Claudette kept walking, then flung open a set of huge—I mean *huge*—double doors.

The ballroom was immense, the biggest room I'd ever been in, bigger than a basketball court.

"They must have had really fancy balls here," I murmured.

"Oh, most certainly. Your great-grandmother loved nothing more than a grand party. There'd be a full orchestra and the room would be filled with flowers, and everyone would wear their most fabulous gowns and jewels. Not just the local lords and ladies, but others as well. From France and Italy and Germany and the British Isles. India, even. At one time, Saint Gilbert was known for its excellent hospitality." She sighed. "It must have been a sight to see."

I raised an eyebrow, and she laughed.

"My mother told me how the music would play and couples would dance. And how, as a child, she had a little secret place above the ballroom." She pointed upward to where there were what looked like those box seats you see at the opera were located. "She would hide and imagine the scenes her mother described to her."

I knew without asking that as a child, my grandmother also had hidden in that secret perch and listened to the music, watched her parents and their guests swirl around the ballroom floor. To a little girl, it all must have seemed like . . .

"Magic," I said aloud. I suspected Gran was there with us, a smile on her face.

"Oh yes, in my mother's day, everything seemed touched by magic. It must have been a wonderful time to live in Saint Gilbert." She turned to me, her eyes still shining from a memory of a long-ago night. "My mother always went to Paris for her gowns—Paris, of course, came to the duchess—and she'd wear her best jewels. My father would wear his uniform. As captain of the castle guard, he must have been quite a sight, all those medals and gold braid. They tell me it was a time like no other. A time of peace and prosperity."

"No wonder the vote came in on the side of the monarchy," I said, not for the first time my mind darting to the vision of Max in one of those fancy uniforms. Most definitely a sigh-worthy sight.

"No wonder at all." She took one last look around, then turned back to me. "But we're here to look at portraits. If you'll follow me . . ."

I reluctantly left Max in the ballroom wearing his gold braid as we walked out to the reception area and took a left. Three doors down, the hall overlooked the first floor on one side. Claudette unlocked a door, opened it, and stepped inside. She turned on the light and I followed her into the room. She pushed on the head of a falcon carved into the mantel, and the wall next to it silently slid open.

My jaw dropped. There were paintings *everywhere*. I mean, stacks leaning against every inch of wall, and lining the walls.

"Oh my God." I stood in the doorway trying to take it all in.

"I admit it's a bit much, but I thought you'd like to see them all while you're here."

"It's almost spooky that the builders of the castle had the prescience to include these secret rooms. It's almost as if they expected something dire to happen," I said.

"Actually, the story is that the secret rooms were built for the sons of the first duke and duchess. They had seven sons and one daughter, who were apparently a rowdy bunch. When the castle was built, the duchess requested a series of rooms such as this hoping her children would be kept occupied playing hiding and finding games," Claudette explained.

"We call that hide-and-seek back home, though we never had secret hidden rooms. Mostly we'd play outside and hide behind parked cars." I walked around the room for a moment, imagining my kids and their cousins playing such a game. "I wonder how many times one brother locked another inside."

"There's a safety latch in every room," she said, pointing out the lever on the wall. "You couldn't get stuck inside unless you chose to." She paused in front of a large painting, then stepped aside. "This is a portrait of your grandmother as an infant in the arms of her mother. I think it's particularly lovely."

"Oh. Oh . . ." I walked over to the painting for a better look. It was maybe four feet wide and more than twice as tall, and it took my breath away. Baby Gran was wrapped in a white blanket, her eyes closed, nestled in the arms of her mother, who smiled at her sleeping dark-haired daughter with undeniable love and pride. My great-grandmother wore what looked like a wrap or robe, crimson in color and trimmed in gray fur, and she wore gold earrings and a gold cuff studded with red stones. On her head sat the most gorgeous crown.

"I'm betting those are real diamonds in her crown," I said.

"Not a crown, Annaliese, but her favorite tiara. And yes, of course the diamonds are real."

"Wow, if that's her tiara, I can't even imagine what the crown must look like."

Claudette smiled as she went through a stack of several large paintings that stood against the wall. "Here you can see what the crown looked like as it sat on your great-grandmother's head."

I helped her extract the painting from the stack and took a few steps back to take it in.

"Jesus, Mary, and Edna," I said, my mother's late next-door neighbor's favorite expletive escaping from my mouth without me realizing it had.

The portrait was life-size, and the woman portrayed was stunning. She stood against a backdrop of perfect blue—not baby blue, not marine blue, but something in between. At her feet, a small brown-and-white dog sat at attention, and on her head sat the crown. It was gold, studded with rubies and diamonds, and looked like it weighed a ton. It was beyond what I could have imagined, and my great-gran wore it proudly. Her dark-brown hair was gathered from her face and held up at the back of her head, and she wore the most gorgeous white dress I'd ever seen. The neckline was a deep V and hung slightly off her shoulders. The sleeves were caught up on each side of the bodice by a gorgeous diamond, ruby, and pearl pin. The skirt that flowed from the sashed waist draped beautifully, perfectly, to the floor. She was exquisite, and I said so.

"Oh yes, she was quite beautiful. Even after her marriage to your great-grandfather, nobles from all over Europe tried to woo her." Claudette said this with a smile on her face.

"Do you suppose she ever succumbed to their, you know . . ."

"Not that I ever heard. She was totally devoted to her husband. They were very much in love, soulmates, it was said."

I stepped closer to the portrait. "She was so tall, and her eyes are so green."

"As were your grandmother's." She added, "As are yours. But she wasn't tall. I don't think she was more than two inches past five feet."

"Juliette's height." I stared at the image expertly done in oils. "Actually, Juliette looks a bit like her. The eyes and the mouth are very similar."

"So my son told me. He saw a resemblance immediately upon meeting your daughter. It is our hope she will see the portrait for herself one day, madam." She rested the painting back against the wall.

I recalled all the empty spaces on the walls where paintings had once hung. "It would be nice if the walls were filled again. But the one of Gran and her mother—could that be hung in the room where I'm staying? Just for now?"

The portrait was so intimate, such a beautiful moment between mother and child, I didn't feel it belonged on display for just anyone coming into the castle to see. Maybe I'd change my mind, or maybe whoever was going to be in charge under plan B would feel differently, but for now, I would love for Gran and her mama to stay with me.

"The dog in the painting," I asked. "What breed is that?"

"That's a Gilberti spaniel, Annaliese. Very rare. They were bred here, but the Russians took many with them when they left and interbred them with something else. For a while, it seemed the breed had died out. However, with the newly resurrected sense of nationalism, I've noticed a few around the city. Perhaps the breed was kept alive in the villages or the countryside. Whatever, the dogs, too, are enjoying a slight comeback." She gazed out the window and said with a hint of pride, "Just like our city. Our country."

I didn't want to dwell on the reason for the comeback.

"It's a very cute little dog." It reminded me of a cross between a Cavalier King Charles spaniel and an English spaniel.

"That was Josephine, Her Majesty's favorite. The duchess had her portrait painted with her several times. Would you like me to procure one for you? Perhaps a pup?"

I had a fleeting vision of myself seated in a fancy chair surrounded by any number of Gilberti spaniels, like the late Queen Elizabeth II with her corgis.

I have to stop thinking like that.

"Oh no. But thank you." I sort of hated to pass, but I'd never had a dog and I wouldn't know what to do with it. I worked during the day, and the kids would be at school. Still, it was damn cute, and the kids would love it.

For the next several hours we went through all the paintings, Claudette making notes in a black notebook as she recalled as much as she could about who was depicted and where each had originally been hung. When we'd finished, every piece of art had been cataloged, and she and I had discussed potential places where each might hang. It had been a fun exercise, and besides learning who was who in my family tree, helping her made me feel I'd accomplished something for the first time since I arrived.

My eyes kept going back to the white dress in the first painting I'd looked at. I couldn't even begin to imagine what such a thing might cost today, and I had to ask. "Was the dress stolen?"

"Oh no. Great pains were taken to preserve it and the many others."

"Where . . . ?"

"This way, madam." Claudette secured the secret chamber, then escorted me into the outer room, where she turned off the light and locked the door behind us.

Across the hall and almost to where it met another hallway was a room comfortably furnished with a small sofa, several chairs, a bookcase full of books.

"When the castle was endangered, many of your great-grandmother's gowns along with her mother's and her grandmother's were hidden away lest they be stolen or destroyed." She pulled a book from the shelf, and the wall spun around to reveal a room. "As you can see, much was saved."

Oh, how I loved all these hidden rooms! It was like living inside a treasure hunt!

"Holy crap," I muttered as I followed Claudette into the room, my head feeling as if it were spinning out of control. There were gowns everywhere I looked. One thing I could tell for certain: my great-grandmother—and apparently her mother, and *her* mother— loved having jewels sewed onto her clothes. There had to be a fortune just in the rubies alone, and I said so.

"Yes, the Gilberti women have always been fond of pretty stones." She adjusted what appeared to be a ball gown on its hanger. "Some of these gowns and day dresses go back more than a hundred years, Annaliese."

"They've obviously been well preserved. Why weren't these sold and the money used for the things the country needs?"

"Everything you see here was personal property. All will remain under lock and key until the rightful heir is crowned. She may do whatever she wishes with them."

"You mean me."

"Should you decide to be that person, yes."

And with that, my head finally exploded. I looked around the room at the racks of clothes, the glorious colors, and all the finery, and I just couldn't take it anymore. The responsibility was too great. Did it make me shallow that I didn't reach my tipping point until I was faced with a room full of jewel-encrusted gowns?

"I think I've had enough for one day," I told Claudette as I headed for the hallway. "I think I'd like to go to my room for a bit."

"Of course." Claudette locked the door behind us. "There is a dinner scheduled for tonight, but if you're too tired, we can simply cancel it."

I admit I did think about bailing, but in the end, I shook my head. "No, we'll do it. I know I said I'd meet with all of Gran's friends who wished to come."

I was really tired, but since I might not have this opportunity again, I couldn't bring myself to back out. I'd take a little nap and a shower, and I'd be good to go to meet Gran's friends. I was looking forward to it.

~

The dinner was lovely, though I only made it downstairs with seconds to spare. I dressed in black—because everything I'd brought with me was casual or black—and Claudette draped my neck with a mile-long string of pearls that, honest to God, I could have used as a jump rope. She wound it around my neck several times, then let it fall until the longest loop hit right around my waist. Pearls and diamonds in my ears, and then for a change, diamonds and emeralds on my fingers. I had to say, this much bling made my very simple black dress look glamorous. I took as many pictures as I could, because I will probably never look like this again.

And what's that, you ask? How did I look? I looked *royal*. Truly royal. I walked into that dining room feeling like a million bucks. Well, yeah, since I was probably wearing a million bucks worth of jewels.

Like I said before, I didn't own any real jewelry, and I wasn't the fancy type. But I don't care how plainly you think you like to dress—let someone wrap you in sparklies like the ones I had on, and trust me, you will like it. A lot.

This dinner was the polar opposite of the dinner with the donors, as I liked to think of that first formal event. Gran's friends—such delightful ladies!—had all dressed for the occasion, and I found it very touching that they'd taken such care with their appearance. I made an effort to speak with everyone and used my phone to have Claudette take my photo with each individually. I promised to send them a copy, but I'd really taken them for myself so I could show my sisters Gran's beautiful friends. The cocktail hour had been a bit subdued, but once we were seated in the dining room, the ladies began to reminisce, and I could feel Gran's bittersweet emotions.

"Oh, Princess Annaliese was such a devil when she was younger," a giggling Martine said. "She loved to move things around from room to room so as to confuse the adults. She would make us help her, then we'd get in trouble, but she always admitted that she was behind the mischief."

"Remember when she moved all the furniture around in the drawing room and Her Highness came into the room and wasn't watching where she was going and almost tripped over a footstool?" Alma tried to hide her own giggles behind her hands.

"And when she dyed one side of her sister Jacqueline's hair with beet juice? It was such a horrible shade of maroon." Marguerite laughed.

"Oh, she got into such trouble for that," Louisa said.

"Her hands were stained from the beets so she couldn't even deny it had been she who'd done the deed," Edwina said, her eyes dancing with the memory.

"Oh, and when she put salt in the sugar bowls and sugar in the salters," Alma reminded them.

"The kitchen was in a tizzy that time," someone added, and they all laughed heartily.

And so it went throughout the meal, the ladies sharing their fondest memories of life in the castle in those days. The laughter sounded as if it had been bottled up inside them for a very long time, and they were happy to let it out.

Until Louisa said, "And the way she used to fly across the fields on her big black mare. Like she was chasing the very wind." She paused as her eyes filled with tears.

"Katrinka," a subdued Elena said. "The horse's name was Katrinka. Her Highness used to admonish the princess that she rode too fast, that she was too reckless, but the princess never failed to give Katrinka her head and let her fly. She said it was good for the horse and good for her." She dabbed at her eyes with her napkin. "I often wondered what became of that horse."

"Taken by the Germans," tall, noble Patrice declared as if still angered by the memory. "My father told me they'd emptied the stables and took all the horses. The best went to the officers, so I imagine Katrinka was spoken for by someone who ranked high."

"Hopefully someone who appreciated her and took good care of her," Elena said softly.

For a moment, the dining room fell into silence as the ladies sat with their sad memories surrounding them.

Hoping to lighten their mood, I raised my wineglass. "I'd like to propose we drink to Katrinka and my grandmother. Perhaps they've been reunited in the hereafter and are, at this moment, racing across the fields."

"That's a lovely thought, Your Grace." Louisa raised her glass, and the others followed. "To our beautiful friend, long gone now, and the beautiful memories she left us."

"We were blessed to have lived in that time, and to have known her. She was a bright soul even then," Alma added. "I'm grateful to have shared a childhood with her." She turned to me and placed a hand on my arm. "As I'm grateful to be sharing this time with you. Seeing you has been a reminder of the good times we shared with her, before the bad times came and she was forced to leave us. Thank you for bringing us together again, here in this place where we spent so many happy days with the friend we loved so dearly and missed so much."

"Still miss," Marguerite said.

"Here, here," someone added.

The ladies all tilted their glasses in my direction, and I murmured a thank-you. It was all the lump in my throat would allow.

I closed my eyes and imagined I could see Gran on that beautiful black mare jumping over clouds and flying toward the horizon. I wondered if in fact she had been able to see her horse again since she'd left this life, but who the heck knows what happens after we pass. It was enough for me to know that Gran was finding some peace in the company of her beloved childhood friends and in their remembrances of her.

$$\sim$$

I slept late again the next morning, and I was pretty sure everyone in the castle must be gossiping about the lazy American who did nothing but eat, drink, ride around with Max, and sleep. When I left my room for breakfast—I thought I'd dine in the small morning room that overlooked the castle grounds for a change—I found my great-grandmother's picture hanging between the large arched windows. It was one of the portraits that had caught my eye the day before, one of the many where she'd been painted in a white dress, though not the same as *the* white dress. Judging from the number of paintings I'd seen the day before, white was a favorite of hers. In this one, she wore lots of emeralds. I mean, she dripped in big, fat green stones.

"Gifts," Claudette told me when she joined me, "from an Italian count who'd courted her when she was younger, before she met and fell in love with your great-grandfather."

"And I guess they're in the Swiss bank with the crown and the tiaras and the ropes of pearls."

She nodded. "The duchess wanted those most valuable and sentimental pieces secured for her daughter."

"Who never got to wear them."

She patted me on the arm. "But perhaps a great-granddaughter—perhaps someday even a great-great-granddaughter will wear them. I believe that would please her."

I sighed at the thought of having that emerald-and-diamond necklace around my neck and that emerald crown—excuse me, tiara—on my head, then pushed the thought away. I couldn't let my decision be influenced by the fortune in jewels awaiting me in Switzerland, as lovely a fantasy as that was shaping up to be.

Later that day, Max took me on a complete tour of Castle Blanc from the first floor to the third—except for the west wing—and I have to say, my ancestors had their priorities straight. I'd never even dreamed of a time where I might have two libraries. I'd peeked into the small one on the second floor one morning and found it charming and cozy. But the one on the first floor! Now that was a library! When I opened the door and found those sky-high shelves packed with books, I almost fainted. There was so much history contained in that one spacious room, and in so many languages: not just English but French, Italian, German, and several I didn't recognize. I wanted to see a fire blazing in its two—*two!*—fireplaces, one at each end of the room. I wanted deep, cushy chairs and good reading lamps and something to prop my feet on. Oh, and soft, warm throws, the plushy kind. I could have spent an entire day there exploring the shelves. If I decided to become the duchess, I would have a library hour every day. One hour, in here, discovering the books my gran and the other Gilbertis read.

The music room was at the end of the hall, and it, too, was spacious with a high ceiling. I could easily imagine little concerts here back in the day when there'd probably been a piano and maybe a harp and some other instruments. Now it was just a large empty space with a dusty floor. I wondered if I listened very carefully I'd hear echoes of music from long ago, but I couldn't stand still long enough to find out, and besides, that's a little too woo-woo for me.

I remembered my mother talking about how she'd taken piano lessons when she was young. She'd wanted us three girls to play as well, but none of us wanted to. Along with that memory came the image of Gran playing for me once when I'd spent the day with her. I'd watched the way her hands seemed to float over the keys, spinning music from her fingertips. I remember thinking I'd been a bit hasty in my refusal to learn. I wondered if it was too late now.

I fantasized for a moment, about being the duchess and taking lessons on that same piano my gran played, but I quickly brushed the thought away. Gran had had beautiful hands, with long, gracious fingers. I looked at my stubby fingers with gnawed nails that my ex used to call peasant hands, a stark reminder of who I was and who I was not.

Was it possible to step out of myself and become something more? I really didn't know.

There was only one way to find out, but in my heart, I was further from making that decision than I was when I got here. What had at first seemed *big* now was more than big, more than life-changing. It was *world* changing, for me and my family, and would alter the course of our lives—our collective history—forever. It was frightening to hold that kind of power. Was I worthy to make that decision for my children, my sisters, even for myself?

The truth was, I was afraid to take the chance to find out.

Chapter Sixteen

The night before I left for home there was yet another dinner, and many of the people I'd met during the week had been invited. It was held in the gallery, which had been lit with hundreds of white candles in silver candleholders. Paintings had been hung on the walls—Claudette's doing, for sure—and there were flowers everywhere. We drank local wines, and there were toasts and well-wishes from around the table. I knew that I'd look back on that night when I got home and wish I'd said more, but my heart was in my mouth when I'd been asked to speak.

"I'm trying to find the words to tell you what this week has meant to me. I can honestly say I've loved every minute I've spent in Saint Gilbert. The country is beautiful beyond what I could have imagined, and you are all so gracious and kind and welcoming. I've made memories that I know will last my lifetime. It's been wonderful to see where my grandmother was born and grew up, to meet her friends who knew and loved her and who kept her alive in their memories even after her time here was cut short. I'm grateful to you for teaching me about my family, my heritage, things I never would have known or even suspected before I came here, and I thank you from the bottom of my heart. I only wish my mother was alive to have come with me, but I can say without embarrassment that I have felt her here with me, just as I have felt my gran—your last duchess—around me every day. So for them, and for my family, I thank you for inviting me to come as your guest to this wonderful place. Thank you for opening your country to me."

I guess I could have said more—maybe there were those at the table who'd been waiting for me to make an announcement—but I was so close to tears I couldn't have said another word. After I'd finished, everyone present stood and applauded, and I had to bite my lip to keep from out-and-out bawling.

I'd been made to feel such a part of this place all week that it felt almost like leaving home. I don't know how else to explain it. When I went to bed that night, it was with a thousand voices, sights, and sounds in my head, and I was still awake in the morning.

So I got up with the sun and attended an early-morning service at Saint Ann's in the city, after which I stopped in the churchyard for one last visit with Gran's parents and siblings before I left. I wanted them to know that even if I never came back, I would never forget them. No way could I have left Saint Gilbert without saying goodbye. I could feel the presence of my mother and grandmother—both overwhelmingly sad—and hoped that there'd been a reunion of spirits, so to speak.

I'd invited Max and Claudette to have breakfast with me by the lake, and when I asked Max to tell the castle guards to see we were not disturbed, he smiled and said, "Tell them yourself, why don't you. You're still the heir to the throne for as long as you're here."

So I asked that our party remain private, and I had to say, I enjoyed my last chance to be waited on for probably the rest of my life.

It was another glorious morning. The lake was sparkly like it had been the day I arrived. We made small talk and I sipped my delicious coffee (I was *so* going to miss my coffee!), but I noticed Max glanced at his watch several times, so I knew it was time to leave. I secretly waved goodbye to Serafina, then we walked back to the castle without saying much. I went up to my room to make sure I hadn't left anything behind, and moments later Claudette knocked on the door.

"Is there anything else I can do for you?" she asked.

"No, but thank you. You've been so wonderful, Claudette. I'm so grateful to you for all you did for me this past week. I don't know how I would have survived without you. I'd have been lost every day." I swallowed the now-familiar lump in my throat.

"It was my pleasure to assist you, but more, it was the greatest honor to have met you. You are truly a daughter of Saint Gilbert, and everyone who's met you hopes—*prays*—for your return." She handed me a package wrapped in white tissue and tied with a simple yellow ribbon. "Soap to take with you. I heard you say last night that you'd bought some but had hoped to buy more before you left because you enjoyed it so much." She smiled. "The duchess should never have to buy soap in her own country."

"Thank you, Claudette." I think I surprised her by hugging her, I was so touched by her thoughtfulness. I couldn't imagine leaving here without a hug for the woman who'd been so kind—almost motherly—to me.

"You're most welcome." For just a second she dropped her guard and returned the hug. Then, "I believe your car and driver are ready, Your Grace."

On the way out of the room, I stopped to say goodbye to Hans, who acknowledged me with a little smile and nod of his head. Claudette and I walked the now portrait-lined hall to the landing, then down the steps and through the gallery. The tables and chairs and candelabra from the night before were gone, so our footsteps echoed as we walked through the long, empty space.

As on the day I arrived, the castle staff assembled in the grand entrance, and I took a few seconds to say goodbye and thank each of them for their part in welcoming me and taking care of me. Then I was in the car, with John-Paul and Marcel in the front seat and Max next to me, one black car in front and another behind us, and we were moving toward the drive. I turned back to the castle and watched the blue-and-white flag snap in the breeze at the top of the tower. Then I saw a dark flash across the sky from the woods to the castle.

"Max, I think I saw the falcon."

"Come to say goodbye, no doubt." He looked over his shoulder as the bird disappeared around the castle wall.

"Well, *I* doubt, but it's a nice sentiment." We paused as the gate was being opened, and the cars passed through before heading out of the city the same way we'd entered a week ago. When I looked back, I could see the tip of the spire on the Church of Saint Ann above the treetops in the park.

"Which reminds me." Max reached into the pocket of his suit coat—a luscious dark-blue jacket that was soft as silk—and brought out a small box. "Something to remember us by."

"Max, you didn't have to . . ."

"Open it." He leaned back as if watching for my reaction, so I knew whatever was in the box had meaning.

I pulled off the leather cord that wrapped around the box several times and raised the lid.

"Oh . . ." I lifted the silver falcon pin from the box and held it up. The workmanship was incredible. "It's gorgeous. Just . . . perfect." I leaned back looking for a place to pin it and decided on the collar of the white short-sleeved blouse I'd worn with the same black pencil skirt I'd worn on the trip over.

"Here, permit me." Max smiled and took the pin from my suddenly inept fingers and secured it to my collar. His fingers brushed soft as a whisper against the side of my neck, and I felt it in every part of my being. I mean, like, body and soul. If circumstances had been different I'd have kissed him, a for-real kiss that would never happen. I guess he was just part of the big fantasy. You know, single, middle-aged mom inherits a crown and moves to the castle where she meets a handsome . . . oh, you know the rest. It's a favorite trope. Except of course no one fantasizes about being middle-aged.

"I love it, Max." I touched the pin with the tip of my right index finger. "Thank you."

"You are most welcome. I hope you will think of us whenever you wear it."

As if I needed anything to remind me of Saint Gilbert—or Max.

Too choked up to respond, I merely nodded. The words that were on the tip of my tongue stayed stubbornly where they were.

I tried to settle into my seat as John-Paul drove on through the countryside, a silent Marcel in the passenger seat lost in his thoughts. We passed the old farms with their stone houses and barns, their fields full of goats or cows. The little villages Max and I had driven through a few days ago, and the kind and gracious people I'd met there, went by in a blur, along with the chateaus and castles perched on distant hilltops. I regretted not having visited them all and learning their stories. Before I knew it, we'd passed the boulder from which I'd taken my first step into Saint Gilbert, and from there, it seemed we flew into Switzerland.

Why is it that the ride *from* always seems shorter than the ride *to*?

Soon we were at the airport, and then blink! I was on the plane heading home, my entourage of three in attendance, seated as we'd been on the flight over the week before: Max at my side, John-Paul and Marcel in the seats in front of us. I closed my eyes during the takeoff and didn't open them again until Lake Geneva was growing smaller by the minute in the distance. I watched from my window seat as the lake, then the mountains faded into the distance.

I knew Max had questions, but I still had no answers. He'd brought me to Saint Gilbert for one purpose, and I sensed that my leaving without having committed to the country must be making him feel as if he'd failed. I wanted to assure him it wasn't him, it was me, but that was what you said when you broke off a relationship with someone you were never really into in the first place. I felt conflicted and emotional and just a little guilty that I hadn't been able to be what they all hoped. There was nothing I could say, so I pretended to sleep, and eventually,

I did. I woke up just as the movie he'd selected began, so for the rest of the flight, we had something neutral to talk about—*Aquaman*, and the visual splendor of Jason Momoa.

There was a three-hour delay due to some mechanical problem when we stopped at Heathrow and another delay landing in Philly, so with all that and changing planes and sitting around, it was midafternoon by the time I arrived at my house. Jean-Paul parked the long black rental car in the middle of the street because there was no other place to put it, and he and Marcel stood guard and waved cars around it while Max got my luggage out of the trunk. I stood on the sidewalk waiting for him and noticed Mrs. Santangelo two houses down trying not to look at us as she washed her front stoop. It was white marble, like so many of the others on our street, and like so many of the residents around here, washing the front steps was an obligation only a little less sacred than Mass on Sunday. I waved to her, but she pretended not to see me. Just like she pretended she didn't see Max gather up my luggage and follow me into my house.

"That you, Annie?" Ceil called from the dining room after I shut the front door behind us.

"It is." I turned to Max. "You can leave my bags here. Thank you for bringing them in for me."

"Well, it wouldn't do to have tossed them onto the sidewalk as we drove by, Your Grace."

"Stop with that. We're not in Saint Gilbert, and I'm not your grace." My words came out sounding more harshly than I'd intended. "I'm sorry. This whole thing, the past week, has been . . ." I didn't even have words.

"I understand, Annaliese." His voice was soft and, I don't know, so sincere that I felt tears forming in my eyes. "You know what I and so many others are hoping, but I will not press you. I know there are many factors to be considered, and I trust you to make your decision, whatever it may be, for the right reasons. Take what time you need. Let me just say that I hope you enjoyed your stay with us as much as we enjoyed having you. You know how to contact me once you know what you want to do. I would ask only that you give serious consideration to what we've offered you. And if your desire is to decline, you let us know in order we might begin our search for an alternative. But whatever you do, know you have earned our respect and our deepest regard, and that you were always our plan A."

I barely trusted my voice, but I was able to squeak out, "I'll do my best not to make you wait too long. I promise."

"That is all we ask." His eyes were locked on mine the entire conversation, and sensing there was little more to say, Max took my hand. He brushed his lips across my knuckles, lingering several beats longer than was most likely necessary. "Goodbye, Annaliese."

"Thank you for everything, Max. No matter what happens, I'll never forget my time in Saint Gilbert." I took a deep breath. "I'll never forget you."

"Nor I, you." He smiled—somewhat reluctantly, I thought, but maybe that was just me wanting him to feel the same things I was feeling. He bowed slightly from his waist, then turned and left. I watched him get into the car and raised my hand to wave goodbye to John-Paul and Marcel, who took one look back at me. We'd said our goodbyes in the car, but honestly, I was going to miss them, too. They always came off like a couple of big lugs, but they'd grown on me.

"Well, that was some sweet sorrow." Ceil joined me at the front door and waved at the car as it pulled away. The windows were tinted, so it was hard to tell if anyone saw her or waved back.

Long after there was nothing left to see, I closed the door and slumped against it.

Chapter Seventeen

"You look like crap," Ceil told me. "Come into the kitchen. I'll make coffee, and you can unload it all on me."

"It's too soon to unload," I said, my back still to the door. "And no offense, but the coffee in Saint Gilbert has ruined me for the bargain brand I buy."

"Too bad." She grabbed me by the arm, walked me into the dining room, and deposited me in a chair. "You're back to reality, duchess. But I brought my coffee with me, and it's a hell of a lot better than yours."

"Okay, then." My elbows were on the table, and without Mom there to chastise me, I didn't care. "Where are the kids?"

"I made them go to school today since we weren't sure what time you'd be back. They have exams next week, and I didn't want to give them an excuse if they don't do well." Ceil walked into the kitchen.

"Excellent move. Are you sure you never had kids?" I called after her.

"Positive, but I have a sister who has two firecrackers, and I learn fast." I could hear Ceil pouring water into the coffee maker.

"How were they? Did they give you a hard time?"

"Nah. They save that for you."

The water was dripping into the pot, and I could smell the coffee as it began to brew. If I'd had more energy, I'd have gotten up and dug through my suitcase to find the bags of coffee I'd brought home with me.

Minutes later, Ceil came into the dining room carrying a tray that held two mugs of coffee, two spoons, a container of half-and-half, and a couple of pink packs of sweetener.

"Now spill." She handed me a mug and a spoon. "Start wherever you want, but start."

I spilled as I sipped. I told her everything, showing her pictures on my phone to illustrate a point now and then. I talked and cried and laughed and remembered. Even knowing I was going to have to repeat it all to Roe and the kids, I spilled it all.

"There's something different about you." Ceil studied my face and poured a second round of coffee into our mugs. "Not sure what it is. But your face . . ."

"Fatigue? Stress? By the way, this coffee is better than mine, thank you. Still not Saint Gilbert phenomenal, but better. I did bring home some of the great stuff, but it's buried in the suitcase."

"I can't wait to try it, but don't change the subject. You were stressed before you left."

I shrugged. "Stress is stress. Oh, I have something for you."

I went into the living room and opened my carry-on bag and took out the soaps in the pretty wrappings I bought in the gift shop in Beauchesne.

"This is the coolest soap," I told her. "They make it in Saint Gilbert with goat milk. Like an idiot, I left my face wash and moisturizer at home, but after a day or so, I didn't miss them. This soap didn't dry my skin at all."

"It's pretty." She sniffed it. "And it has such a nice light fragrance. Sort of like . . ." I waited to see if she picked up the same scent I did. "Violets. Like Gran's violets."

"I thought so, too. See the little flecks of purple in the soap?"

"I do." She sniffed it again, and she smiled. "It smells like Gran. Funny, isn't it, how scents can stay with you so long and bring back so many memories?"

"It's been scientifically proven. The sense of smell is the strongest link to memory of all the senses. Memory and emotion. Both can give you that ping of recognition from smelling something. Like the way tuna sandwiches always take me back to the lunchroom in grade school. And the smell of lilies always take me back to Dad's viewing and the grief I felt standing next to his casket." I choked back tears.

Ceil nodded. "Me too. Same memory. Every time I smell lilies I have that same overwhelming urge to vomit I felt that night. Gross but true."

We each took a moment to remember our dad and to compose ourselves.

After a moment, Ceil cleared her throat. "Anyway, I find it hard to believe you haven't used anything on your face but this soap. Your skin looks really good. *Really* good. Way better than when you left." She leaned closer. "Your crow's-feet are almost gone."

"I know. I guess I smile more at the office than I knew."

Just then the front door blew open and the hurricanes that were my children blew in.

"Mom's home! Mom!"

"Mom! Where are you?"

"Dining room." I got up and braced myself for the onslaught of my children. Say what you will, there's no feeling like having your kids so happy to see you that they damn near drive you into a wall.

And nothing will make your head explode quite like having them throw questions at you like fast pitches. The noise level in the room rose about a thousand percent.

Finally, "Okay, guys, I missed you both, too. So much! But let's slow down. You're going to give me a heart attack. Plus I can't talk that fast."

They each pulled up a chair and sat, and their interrogation began.

"So what was it like? Is the castle really huge and fancy? Like Cinderella's?" This from Juliette.

"What's the city like? Are there a lot of hot girls? Is there a soccer team?" This from guess who. "All countries have soccer teams, right? Can I try out if I'm the prince?"

And so on until it was time for dinner, which Roe was bringing. Once she arrived, we started all over yet again. My jaws and mouth were tired from so much talking and laughing. After we ate, Ralphie took my phone upstairs to print out my photos while he studied for his math exam. Juliette was almost in tears when she was denied the pleasure of sending photos of the castle around to all her friends.

"I'll send it anonymously, I promise!" she insisted.

"Nope. Not till I know what we're going to do," I reminded her. I'd only told them eighty-five times over dinner that I didn't know what that was going to be.

"But . . ."

"Stop. Let it go for now."

"But, Mom, you have to say yes. We have to live in that castle." She draped her arms around my shoulders and whispered, "I really, really, really want to be a princess."

"I know, sweet pea. But there are other factors that have to go into my decision."

"Like what?" My son came back downstairs and raised an eyebrow, like there could be any decision other than *Yes! We're going to Saint Gilbert to live in a castle!*

"For one thing, you won't see your father except maybe for visits on holidays," I began.

My son blew that off with a snort. "Which is different from when we see him now how?"

The boy had me there. "Okay, but your friends . . ."

"Will all be going to different colleges in another year anyway." He smirked devilishly. "But none of them will be a prince."

"I'd have to give up my job, which is a position I've had to work long and hard for."

I had. That old saying, a woman has to work twice as hard to be thought half as good as a man? Yeah. Alive and well.

"Your job gives you migraines, Mom," Juliette added. "You always say if you won the lottery, you'd quit in a Broad Street minute."

"Do you mean Broadway minute?" Ceil asked.

"Philly style, Aunt Ceil." Juliette kissed me and both aunts and picked up her book bag, which she'd dropped on the floor. She started out of the room, then turned and asked, "Is there a high school in Saint Gilbert, or will we have a private tutor?"

"Go study for your exams." I pointed toward the steps, and the two of them headed upstairs, whispering to each other. I turned to my sisters and said, "They're plotting a full-out attack. They think they can wear me down."

"Will they?" Roe asked. "'Cause it sounds to me like you really liked the place."

"I did," I admitted. "Actually, I loved it. It's impossible not to. The country is beautiful, the people are charming and friendly and welcoming, and the accommodations were out of this world. I never expected to be treated the way they treated me there, not even in my wildest imagination. The food was fabulous and the wine delicious. Then there was the matter of our family. The history. Our great-grandparents' tragic story. How they knew they were going to be murdered and how they plotted to secure the throne for their family. They were so brave and so smart. Roe, you stand there on their graves and you feel so *connected*."

"You stood on their graves?" Roe wrinkled her nose. "That's kinda crass, don't you think? And I'm pretty sure it's bad luck."

Ceil and I both rolled our eyes at the same time.

"I guess you had to be there to appreciate it," I said, dismissing her comments.

"I'm sure they were happy that one of their descendants made a point to seek out their graves and acknowledge them. Annie"—Ceil turned to me—"did you pray for them?"

I nodded. "I did."

"On your knees?" Roe asked.

"Of course."

"There you go." Ceil threw up her hands. "I bet they were thrilled. Assuming they were someplace where they knew what was happening."

"True," Roe conceded. "I'll bet no one even thinks about them anymore."

"Au contraire. They are well remembered. Revered," I told her. "And I even met people who remembered Gran and shared their wonderful memories of her."

I repeated all the stories my jet-lagged brain could remember, and when Ralphie came downstairs with a stack of photos in hand, I took them on a photo tour of Saint Gilbert and the castle. I showed them the portraits, explaining who everyone was as best as I could recall. I admit after a while my brain and my mouth weren't synced as well as they could have been, but they got the idea. They pored over the photos, and seeing their reactions to the gowns and the jewels was epic. Like, jaws-dropped epic.

"Wow!" Roe's eyes were wide and round. "The crown jewels! Did you get to try them on?"

"No, those are still in a vault in Switzerland." I explained our great-grandparents' plan to keep the country's wealth from being plundered, which everyone agreed had been brilliantly clever. "I don't think they ever imagined it would be so many years before there'd be an heir." I tapped the photos. "They hid furniture and paintings and other valuables in secret rooms in the castle."

"Secret rooms? That's so cool! Mom, you have to say yes." Juliette, who'd followed her brother downstairs, pulled a photo from the pile. "I need to wear this tiara to my prom."

"Baby, there is no freshman prom," I reminded her.

"Oh. Right." Her expression darkened, then a moment later brightened again. "I could come back for junior prom with my class, right? I could wear it then. Or I could wear it for a prom there, in Saint Gilbert. There has to be a school there. They must have . . ."

My head began to split open, and what was left of my brain started to leak out onto the table. "Enough for tonight. Guys, I have to go to bed. I can't even think anymore." I kissed everyone good night, then went into the living room to head for the stairs. My suitcase still stood in the middle of the room, another reminder I'd been away and now was home. I called the kids and gave them the chocolates I'd brought back, and Ralphie carried my suitcase upstairs. Roe left, and Ceil decided she'd stay over and leave the next day. We argued over who got to sleep in my bed—where she'd been sleeping all week—and who would sleep on the sofa. She insisted the sofa was fine—it was a sleeper sofa, but we rarely opened it. I gave up and went upstairs, undressed, and went straight to bed.

I was so happy to be in my own bed again, I barely had time to appreciate the feeling before I fell into a deep sleep. I didn't bother to set an alarm. After all, I got up with the kids every morning like clockwork, right? Not this time. It was almost eleven when I woke the next day. Thank God Ceil was still there to get the kids off to school, though they probably would have been okay on their own. They might have balked at having to spend their own money for lunch, though. When I finally got my act together, I went downstairs and found Ceil working on one of her design projects at the dining room table.

"I made scones," she said without looking up. "They're on the pan on top of the stove."

"Thank you, God," I said. "Oh, yum! Cranberry-orange! My fave. Thank you, Ceil." I poured a cup of the coffee she'd made, placed two scones on a small plate, and stood in the doorway between the kitchen and dining room. "Let me know when you want to take a break."

"Two minutes. I just want to . . ." She was shaking her head, looking at the room she'd been designing. "Oh, yeah. The black-and-white check for the window treatments. Definitely."

A few minutes later she looked up. "I can break now for a few."

"Come in and talk to me." I sat at the kitchen table, and after she poured herself a fresh mug of coffee, she sat across from me. "I can never repay you for staying with the kids, Ceil. If I'd had to worry about them with everything else that was going on . . ."

"You've already thanked me. It was my pleasure. It really was. I'll stay with them anytime."

"So bring me back to reality. Tell me what's been going on around here while I was gone. What did I miss?" I hadn't heard any local gossip in a week, and I was pretty sure I was entering a state of withdrawal.

"There was one thing." Ceil's eyes had a wicked sparkle, a sure sign that something of note had happened. "The day after you left, Karen Bustamonte died."

"She *died*?" My chin all but hit the table.

"Yeah, not to be confused with *dyed*."

Ceil. The punster. A chip off the old block.

Karen Bustamonte owned a local hair salon, Do Me, Do My Roots, on Broad Street. I have it on good authority that she was doing Ralph Senior within six months after we'd said "I do," but I guess that was old news. Everyone in the neighborhood knew she'd been a . . . how to put this delicately? She'd been paid for her "companionship," which is how she earned the money for the down payment on her shop. She'd been married . . . I dunno, five times? I'd lost track.

"How did she die?"

"She was hit by a garbage truck that was backing up while she was crossing Broad Street at seven in the morning. Tied up traffic for hours while they picked all the trash off her."

After a long moment of silence during which time both of us, I'm sure, were mentally picturing the scene, I asked, "So did you go to the viewing?"

"I wasn't going to, but Ralphie said he went to grade school with Karen's son Joey, and how he felt bad about it, and how he was pretty sure Joey'd show up if that had happened to you, so yeah, I took Ralphie." She took a sip of coffee. "I thought it would be okay with you."

"Yeah, it's okay." It was nice of Ralphie, who always did have a soft spot for his old friends. "Thanks for taking him. I'm sure Joey appreciated it."

"Everyone asked where you were," she said. "I told them you were away for a week on business. Technically, not a lie. Family business is business."

I nodded and took a bite of a scone. "True enough. And this is delicious, by the way."

"Thanks. So what do you think you're going to do?"

"I don't know. I really liked it there."

"Duh. Castle life."

"That was part of it, I'm not gonna lie. But it was everything. The history, the church, the lake, the shops, the countryside. And oh, Ceil, there are castles just waiting to be renovated. Right up your alley. And the hillsides—a chateau here, a farm there. And the food! I drool every time I think about the food. The wine . . . dear Lord, the wine. And the people . . . so friendly, so open and kind. So . . . patiently waiting for the American to come and turn things around." This last was a downer for me. "I'm damned if I don't go, and I'll be damned if I do go and I can't make anything good happen."

I took a few more bites of the scone. "Except of course I'd bring back a lot of money that's been sitting in a Swiss bank since 1941."

"I know I said it last night when you talked about that, but that really was pretty clever. At least it couldn't be stolen."

"Yeah, but if I don't go back and get crowned, the money stays there until they can find someone else. Honestly, I'm between a rock and a hard place." The scone went down in one last bite. I eyed the second one hungrily.

"You don't have to make a decision right now. Take some time and think it over. What's going to make you happy? What's best for the kids? What's best for the people of Saint Gilbert?"

"Well, obviously, it's best for them if I go back and make sure all that money's returned. It would mean new roads, schools, a bigger hospital. Crap, maybe even an airport. And I'm still not convinced there isn't some way to market the country to bring in tourists. It's a beautiful place that no one's ever heard of. I think once people find out about it, they'll want to go."

"Where are the photos Ralphie printed out?" Ceil asked. "I want to look again."

I went upstairs and retrieved the stack of pictures and handed them to Ceil when I went back down. She went slowly through the pack, paying closest attention to the countryside scenes.

"I could see marketing destination weddings at those castles once they're renovated." Ceil got a faraway look in her eyes, and I could see the wheels start to turn. "Think of what *that* could bring into the country. We could do an entire campaign around weddings alone. What starry-eyed girl wouldn't want to get married in a castle? We also could market the castle as a B&B to groups—corporate retreats, girl getaways, family reunions—and offer wine and cheese tours as part of a package."

She sat quietly, tapping her finger on the side of her mug, and I knew what that meant: she had something she wanted to say, but she didn't really want to say it.

"Okay, enough of the tapping already. Spill."

"I know it's strictly your choice, and I will respect whatever you decide to do, I swear it. But . . ."

"But . . ." Honest to God, sometimes it was like pulling teeth.

"But I was just thinking. You have the chance to do something that will change people's lives probably for generations. How often does that happen? Even if the only thing you do there is fix the roads, that's still making the place better than you found it."

I broke the second scone in half and put both pieces on the plate before I looked up at my sister.

"If I give up my life here to go there, I'm damn well going to do more than build a couple of roads."

Chapter Eighteen

On Monday, it was back to the salt mine we call PFCLIC. Getting up and dressed for work, driving out of the city via the expressway and into the county, it felt as if my week in Saint Gilbert had never happened. Like the trip, the castle, the people. Max—like none of it had been real at all. Like I'd stepped out of my life for a little while, and now I was stepping back in.

I pulled into a parking place in front of the building and turned off the radio and that morning's discussion of the latest Eagles trade and last night's Phillies game. I grabbed my coffee and my bag, and got out of the car, as I'd done a thousand times before. Walked into the building, past the reception desk, grateful that Debbie wasn't in yet so I didn't have to stop and talk. I loved her, but I just wasn't ready for the whole "how was your vacation" chitchat.

On to my cubicle where I found stacks of files on my desk, some with notes, some with bills that needed my authorization to pay. I sat down and within minutes my phone rang, and it was the same old, same old, like I'd never left. Nothing had changed at all. I glanced at the pile of phone messages and pushed them to the side of my desk. There was no one I really wanted to talk to.

It really was depressing. I'd pinned the falcon Max had given me onto the collar of my blouse that morning, and every once in a while, my fingers found it.

Around ten thirty, Marianne came into my cube. While I finished up the call I was on, she moved the files from my visitor's chair, sat, and waited for me to hang up.

"So, what, you couldn't tell me you were taking vacation?" she asked the second the call disconnected.

"It was a spur of the moment thing. But you're right. I should have told you. I'm sorry I didn't." Actually, I was sorry I couldn't, but that wasn't the same thing.

"So how'd you spend your week? I tried calling you a few times, but for some reason the calls wouldn't go through. I thought you'd have called at least once while you were off." She pulled her chair closer to my desk. "Tell me you didn't have a secret rendezvous with some tall, dark, and handsome someone."

Close, but not exactly the type of rendezvous she had in mind.

I forced a laugh. "No, just some R and R. You know."

She narrowed her eyes and stared at my face. "R and R my ass. You went to a spa. Dammit, why didn't you tell me? I'd have gone with you."

"What? No! Like I could afford a week at a spa."

"Annie, the lines around your eyes are gone. So are the elevens between your eyes. So you had Botox. You can admit it. No judgment."

"Mare, I didn't have work done on my face." My fingers went to the space where my eleven-lines used to be. I say used to be because I couldn't feel them, which was odd because they'd been so deep, I'd started referring to them as the Mariana Trench. "And you know I'm such a wuss; the last thing I'd let someone do is stick needles in my face."

Marianne pulled a small mirror from her bag and handed it to me. I took a good, long look.

"I guess I should take more time off. Just one week away from all the stress around here . . ." From the cubicle next to mine, my fellow examiner was screaming at someone on the phone. I nodded in that direction. "Point proven. You're in underwriting, Mare. You don't deal with the assholes we have to deal with."

"You know, you've taken time off before, and you didn't come back looking this good. You look almost . . . radiant." She was staring again. "Actually, you look like you've been having really good sex. A *lot* of really good sex."

Nothing forced about my laugh after that.

"No. *Hell* no. No surgery. No Botox. No spa. And definitely no sex, good, bad, or otherwise."

"So where did you go? What were you doing that you couldn't get a phone call?"

I debated whether to tell her the truth—I was dying to tell her the truth—but the phone rang, and I was literally saved by the bell. "We'll catch up later," I told her. "Let me take this call . . ."

I managed to avoid her through lunch by not taking the allotted hour, for which I had a legit excuse (all those files and phone calls to catch up on), and I was on the phone when she stuck her head into my cubicle at five. She whispered, "Call me," and I nodded. I still hadn't figured out what I'd tell her, but I knew I had to tell her something.

Driving home, all I could think about was the decision I had to make. I'd talked to Ceil again that morning before I left the house, and it was clear what she thought I should do. Ceil is always thinking about the other guy, so of course the first thing she'd think of is how I had an opportunity to impact an entire country and do good things for the people living there.

It felt strange returning to the routine of work, eat, sleep, and repeat, but that's how the next couple of weeks felt, except I had to come up with a story to tell Marianne. So I told her I'd gone to see some family of my mom's in Nebraska I hadn't met before who I'd just learned about—sort of the truth—and she seemed okay with that. I hated lying, but when the time came I could tell her the truth, she'd be okay with it.

While I still loved everything about my life I'd loved before I went to Saint Gilbert, it was pretty hard not to see that my time was spent focused on myself and my kids and little else. What was I going to focus on a few years from now when the kids were off to college? It wouldn't be too long before my nest was empty.

And then there was the fact that I was missing Max more than I expected—a fact I didn't feel I could discuss with anyone, not even Ceil. I'd spent so much time with the man, we'd developed what I'd thought of as, at best, a special relationship, and at the least, a good rapport. I wondered if he thought of me, too. I'd never felt that deep a connection to any man, not even—here I am tempted to make a joke, but I'll let it go—the one I married.

"You know, you've been at work for two weeks, and the lines you used to have on your face—the ones you attributed to work stress—still haven't come back," Ceil observed on Friday night while we waited for Roe to arrive with dinner. Both kids were out—the all-grades dance at the high school. They'd left the house arguing over whether Juliette's friends were too young for Ralphie and if his friends were too old for Jules.

"It's just a matter of time before they do." I looked closer at her face. "But are you using something new on your skin?"

She shook her head. "Just the soap you brought me. Why?"

"You skin looks . . ." I thought back to what Marianne had said to me, then got up and looked in the mirror hanging over the sideboard. My eyes met Ceil's in the glass. "Radiant. Like you've been having a lot of great sex."

"Ah no. Regrettably, no. Just your soap." She got up and stood next to me in front of the mirror. "Although we do both look . . ."

"Pretty damned good."

"Younger."

The front door opened and closed with a slam. "I'm here and I brought dinner," Roe called from the front room. She came into the dining room with a large white bag. "Capellini with spring vegetables and ham. The sauce is to die for. And yes, I made it myself because Albert was . . ." She paused and glanced from Ceil to me and back again. "Why are you two standing in front of the mirror? That's so weird."

Ceil and I stared at Roe, then looked at each other.

"Roe, come here," Ceil beckoned her.

"I have to put this down in the kitchen, then I'll . . . ," Roe began, and Ceil cut her off.

"Put the bag on the table and come here," Ceil told her.

For once, Roe did as she was told. "What?" she asked when she joined us.

Ceil and I studied her face.

I took a step closer. "You've been using the soap I brought you."

"Well, yeah. Wasn't that the idea?" Roe backed away from our scrutiny.

"Have you taken a good look at your face recently?" I asked.

"Like I have time to stand around and stare at my face?" she scoffed. "Unlike some of us."

"Roe, take a good look at yourself." I pointed to the mirror.

Roe exhaled loudly and frowned, but she looked in the mirror anyway. She stared for a very long moment before touching her reflection. "Something's different."

"There's hardly a line on your face," Ceil pointed out.

Roe continued to stare. She looked at Ceil, then at me. "You two as well." She leaned almost into my face to get closer. "You had those lines like Mom had. Huh." She touched the space between my eyes. "But they're gone. And the lines at the corners of Ceil's mouth . . ."

"The soap," Ceil and I said at the same time.

"That has to be it," I said, "if none of us has had Botox or some other treatment."

They both shook their heads.

"There has to be something in it," Ceil said. "Maybe it's the violets."

"I don't know what they put in it, other than goat milk and violets," I admitted. "But I told you I didn't see one single person in Saint Gilbert who had so much as a frown line." I turned away from the mirror. "I mean, even old people. Like in their eighties and better. Everyone there has this gorgeous skin, men and women, and looked years—*decades*—younger than they were. And the funny thing was, everyone acted like it was no big deal. Like the women I talked to hadn't even noticed how fabulous their skin looked. When I asked them what they used on their faces, they said just soap."

"If that's it—if it's something in the soap you brought back . . ." Ceil's eyes went wide as she grabbed my arm. "They're sitting on a gold mine."

Ceil and Roe started talking excitedly at the same time, and I covered my ears. I hadn't seen much of any industry in Saint Gilbert, but this could be a turning point in the country's fortunes. If this soap could erase lines in my forty-four-year-old face in a week, imagine what it could do for women—and men—in their sixties, seventies, and beyond.

Wait. I'd already seen what it could do.

"Maybe we're jumping the gun. Maybe we're just imagining this," Ceil said.

"Yeah. Maybe this is sort of like mob hysteria." Roe.

"So maybe we need to test it out a little more." I sat at the table and thought how best to do that. "I still have the bars Claudette gave me. Maybe if we get a few other people to try it . . ."

My sisters nodded.

"I'll give a bar to Marianne. She commented on my skin the first day I was back." I bit the inside of my cheek while I thought this through. "She has those lines from her nose to the side of her mouth." I traced an invisible line to make my point. "If they go away, we'll have to agree, we could have something."

"If you have extra, I'll give a bar to my landlady. She's about ninety." Roe had a tendency to exaggerate. I'd met her landlady. She was twelve years older than me.

"I can give a bar to my assistant, if you have enough," Ceil offered. "She's your age, Annie, but she looks a lot older."

"I have enough to go around. I'd bought some and Claudette gave me some before I left. I think I'll call Marianne and see if she's planning on going to the market tomorrow and if we could meet up for lunch."

"Will you tell her where the soap came from?" Ceil asked.

"I think I'm going to have to. She's my best friend, and I've been holding out on her and it's killing me."

"So tell her. She'll be excited for you," Ceil said.

And dear God, was she ever!

I was so glad I was smart enough to not have that conversation in the office. She squealed so loudly the woman in the booth behind us dropped her fork on the floor.

"Shhh." I looked around to see who'd turned to look at us. Enough that I knew we had to lower our voices. "Mare, listen to me. I don't want anyone to know about this. At least until there's some decision made. It's a secret, okay? We can't talk about it at work. Which is why we're having this conversation now."

"Okay. Okay. I'm good. I'm calm. But honest to God, Annie . . ." She patted one hand over her heart. "This is the wildest thing I ever heard."

"Believe me, I know."

"Did you take pictures?"

"I did." I pulled out the few I'd stuck in my bag that morning and put them on the table. "See, this is—"

"Oh my God." The words came out in a whisper of reverence. "It's a castle. It's a real castle." She glanced from the photo to me. "This is the place where your grandmother was born? You stayed here?"

I nodded. We went through each of the photos, and when we finished, she wanted to see them again. Then she stacked them like you'd stack a pack of playing cards and said, "I don't understand why you're even hesitating."

"A number of reasons." I reached out for the photos, and she pulled them back.

"Is this where the spa was?" she asked.

I laughed and she handed over the pictures. "No spa." Not yet, anyway. "Which reminds me. I brought you a little present from Saint Gilbert." I found the bar of soap in my bag and handed it to her. "This is made there. This is all I had to use the entire time I was there because I'd left my face wash home."

"You used soap on your face? Every woman over the age of twenty knows that's a no-no."

I returned the photos to the zippered compartment in my bag. "Did I come back looking wrinkled and dried?"

"No," she admitted. "You looked pretty good." She narrowed her gaze. "Still do, actually."

"What you said was I looked like I'd had a lot of really good sex," I reminded her.

"And this was all you used? You swear it, Annie?"

I crossed my heart. "I swear."

"Huh." She sniffed the soap. "Smells pretty good."

"Just use it. Promise. Nothing else but this. No face wash, no creams, no serums." I reached across the table and tapped the soap. "Just this."

She studied my face for a minute before nodding. "Okay. Yeah, I promise. What the hell? At least I'll smell good."

～

Within five days there was a noticeable difference on Marianne's face, and trust me, I looked carefully every single day. By Thursday morning, it was pretty clear that the soap was doing its thing for Mare. That night, when Ceil and Roe both reported in that the women they'd given the soap to had the same results—nothing dramatic in that short amount of time, but diminished facial lines—we knew we were onto something. I wasn't sure what was in that soap, but it was powerful.

I thought of Claudette and her flawless face, and I immediately thought of a spa where all the products were made from . . . whatever it is the soap is made from. I imagined women—and men—from all over the world opting for a few weeks in Saint Gilbert instead of a surgeon's knife or an injection of something into their faces. Ceil was right: Saint Gilbert was sitting on gold. And I was pretty sure I knew how to mine it.

Which was the moment I decided to trade my South Philly row house for a castle in Saint Gilbert.

~

In fairness to my kids, I had to wait until the school year had ended to even tell them what I'd decided. I thought they should finish taking their exams and Ralphie should go to his prom. Who knew what would happen in the long run? If we ended up coming back to Philly for whatever reason, I wanted to make sure everything was smooth for them with school. But on the day after our soap revelation, I called Max on my cell from my car.

"I hope this call brings good news," he said after we'd finished our initial greetings.

I couldn't even put into words how good it was to hear his voice again.

"I hope so. I mean, I hope it works out well for everyone." I took a deep breath. "I'd like to come back if you still want me. I mean, if the council or the country or . . ."

He fell silent for a moment, and I wondered if they'd started a search for someone else and came up with a better candidate.

"Annaliese, are you sure?"

"As sure as I can be. I think."

I could feel his smile through the phone, and it made me want to weep. "You've no idea how happy you have made me." He added quickly, "And of course everyone who's been waiting to hear from you, Your Grace."

"Don't start with that already."

He laughed. "You'll get used to it, I promise. But only, as you wish, in public. I'll try to remember. So when can we come for you?"

I explained to him about the kids' school schedule and that I wasn't telling them until after school was out for the summer in a few weeks, but I thought we could probably wrap things up here by the end of May.

"Please, can we keep this between us? Just for a little while longer? I don't want it to become public and somehow get back to the kids until I tell them."

"I will need to tell the members of the Duke's Council," he said, "but I will ask them to consider your situation and to respect your wishes. I feel certain they'll be more than happy to comply. Our country's been without our royal family for so many years, another few weeks should not matter."

We talked about dates and logistics and I don't even remember what, because my heart was pounding so loudly in my ears, I missed half of what he was saying. After we'd hung up, all I knew was the date of our departure had been set and I'd promised Max I'd talk to my sisters about making the trip with me. I couldn't imagine either of them would decline the invitation.

Neither did.

Ceil had just enough time to finish up work she was doing for a client, and Roe had time to help her boss find a replacement for her.

I'd planned on keeping the whole thing under wraps so we could make our departure as quietly as possible. But as the saying goes, man plans, God laughs.

I planned to meet with my boss at the end of the week, at which time I'd hand him my resignation along with my two weeks' notice. I was still rehearsing what I was going to say when my cell rang.

"Oh my God! Mom!" Juliette was shrieking. "We were in English class and Mr. Porterfield read news from his phone, and it said that you're the duchess and that we're going to live there in the castle and . . ."

Off she went, breathless and babbling. I leaned against the wall, wondering what had happened. Who'd released the story to the press? I felt certain it wasn't Max, but apparently someone on the council couldn't keep his mouth shut. "And now everyone knows I'm a princess, and OMG you should have seen the look on Tiffany Stout's face. It was . . . it was . . . *awesome*. It was the best moment of my *life*."

A click on my phone indicated a call was waiting. Ralphie. I hung up with Jules and listened to more of the same from my son. No, I didn't know how the story got out. There was no way to deny it, so I told Ralphie we'd talk about it when he got home but, in the meantime, for him to downplay it as much as possible. As if.

I walked into Lenny Scott's office and sat on one of the two chairs that had been placed directly in front of his desk in such a way that you had to look him straight in the eye. Yuck. Anyway, the news had preceded me, even here.

He held up his phone and said, "This really you?"

I didn't need to see what was on the screen to know what he was referring to. Reluctantly, I nodded.

"Really? Wow. Is that crazy or what? How long have you known?" And off he went on a stream of questions, none of which I got to answer because he was talking so fast. Easily as fast as Ralphie, though Juliette still had them both beat when it came to speed-speech.

"So I guess you'll be leaving us. Damn. Who'd ever have guessed you were a *royal duchess?*"

After he came back to earth, we agreed on a last day for me— that would be that very day, since we both knew the interest generated locally if not nationally soon would prohibit any work from being done in any department, so I might as well leave right then before the television crews started showing up.

A glance out the window behind him proved we were already late on that score.

I went back to my cube to gather my things, still feeling jumbled. I packed my personal belongings—the pictures of my kids, my philodendron and Boston fern, both of which were doing supremely well, an old pair of running shoes from when Marianne and I were walking the parking lot at morning and afternoon break times to try to drop a few winter pounds—then I picked up the phone and called Marianne to tell her I'd been publicly outed on social media.

But too late. She'd just walked into my office.

"I'm so happy for you. You're going to be such a kick-ass duchess." She gave me one big squeeze, then held me at arm's length. "Do I get to come to the coronation, and where can I get some more of that soap?"

Chapter Nineteen

The sheer act of getting everyone and everything ready to travel from Philly to Saint Gilbert with my sanity intact was a feat I would not like to repeat. There were so many decisions to make and things to do before we left. Like what to do about my house. Maybe we'd be back in six months. Maybe we'd never live here again. The truth is I couldn't bear to sell it. I bought that place all by myself, and I was crazy proud of that fact. I decided the way to go was to find a renter until I had a better feel for what was going to happen. So we left it furnished, packed up our clothes and personal items, and shipped it all to Saint Gilbert.

Juliette reminded me we needed to go shopping, since none of us—least of all her—had what could be described as a wardrobe fit for a princess. Or a duchess, come to think of it. But it wasn't as easy as it sounded. There were reporters camped out across the street from our house. I'd started having my groceries delivered because I couldn't step outside without having microphones shoved in my face. Cameras followed Ceil and Roe everywhere, and the kids were getting accosted wherever they went. And just try keeping a kid in the house when the weather was great and school was out for the summer. Max, Jean-Paul, and Marcel returned to Philly to act as both security and runners and drove us into Center City and out to King of Prussia to get in some necessary shopping. They'd brought a small cadre of guards with them, several of whom accompanied my kids and my sisters wherever they went, which thrilled the kids beyond reason that they had their own security detail, but my sisters, not so much. Ceil found it cumbersome to have people trailing her whenever she left her apartment, and Roe found it annoying.

"Get used to it," I told them all. "This is nothing compared to the security you're going to have in Saint Gilbert."

Max handled a lot of the interviews early on but finally convinced me that I had to face the cameras myself at least once before leaving the country. So I did. I stood on my front steps and answered questions as best I could. It seems I wasn't the only one who'd had those princess fantasies as a little girl, because almost every woman reporter I spoke with confessed on the sly that I was living her dream.

At the last minute, I reluctantly agreed to make a few trips to New York to appear on all the morning television shows. The interviews were all easier and more pleasant than I'd expected. I really hadn't wanted to do any of them—I was nervous, and I was afraid I'd come off looking like a tongue-tied dork, but Ceil and Roe both watched and said I came across as being very relatable. Which I suppose meant almost the same thing as dorky, but okay. I tried to be as pleasant as I could, because it occurred to me that once we started marketing Saint Gilbert—and that fabulous soap—I'd want *GMA* and all the others on my side. So I went and I faked being relaxed and told the story over and over and over. Everyone wanted to hear it.

The kids were especially happy about the spread in *People* magazine because they were in it. And every interview, I talked about how beautiful Saint Gilbert was and how everyone would have to plan a visit so they could see the castle and the city and the countryside. Ceil was already planning on selling Saint Gilbert as the most romantic spot on earth for a wedding. We'd have to see how that played out, but she was pretty convincing.

Keep in mind all this happened in less than two weeks. Was it any wonder I was eager to leave once the decision was made? Not to mention the kids were antsy to get there and see everything. I suspected Juliette couldn't wait to take pictures of herself in the castle to send back home to her friends. Ralphie had cute Saint Gilbertian girls and soccer on his mind.

On the day we were to leave for Saint Gilbert, the long black car pulled up in front of the house, and this time Marcel accompanied Max to the door. Between the two of them, they managed to fit all our travel luggage into the trunk. We were traveling light since most of our things had been sent ahead, but still, there were five of us making the trip this time. We'd had a few friends over the night before to say goodbye and promised invitations to the coronation—should there be one—to everyone except Ralph Senior and his missus. Truth be told, if I never had to look at him again, I'd be happy.

He'd come into my house—invited by our son—slapped me on the back, and said, "I always thought your mother was stuck up. Now I know why."

Before I could respond, he went on. "Look, I don't mind you making Juliette into a princess—girls love that stuff, I know—but I'm not so sure I like the idea of you taking Ralphie to another country. Like, away from my influence, surrounded by a bunch of women. I don't want you turning my son into some pansy prince. Wearing tights. That kind of shit."

You should know I'd always tried to maintain a respectful attitude toward the father of my children—only because he was their father and because I never wanted them to feel torn between us. But it took me a moment to compose myself and get past the ugliness of his remark. Honest to God, who still thought like that? It's 2023! In my job and sometimes in my neighborhood I heard rough talk. Often profanity. I could deal with that. But stupid talk like that crossed my personal line between tolerance and intolerance. I was glad Ralphie was in the kitchen.

"You're an idiot, you know that, Ralph? An insensitive idiot. Our son is who he is, and I thank God he hasn't been under your influence these past few years. As a result, he's growing into a kind, caring person who doesn't judge anyone. Yes, he'll be a prince, and whether he wears tights, soccer shorts, or a tiara, I'm good with it. As I've always been good with whoever those kids are or who they choose to be."

It could have been the fire in my eyes—or maybe the growling undertone my voice takes on when I'm really pissed off—but he backed up a few steps. Then his wife—the ever-lovely Lorraine—appeared and took him by the arm and reminded him that their twelve-year-old next-door neighbor was watching their kids and the babysitter had a curfew.

"Go say goodbye to your kids, Ralph." I started to walk away. "And don't expect an invitation to the coronation."

"Really?" Lorraine looked genuinely surprised. "Huh. I thought as parent and stepparent, we'd be invited for sure."

"Not gonna happen." I had to bite my tongue to keep from making a crack about those silver Tiffany earrings she was wearing—the ones that had disappeared from my jewelry box right about the time Ralph had started dating her—but I refrained. I made my way through the crowd to the kitchen and out the back door. I needed a few minutes to myself. I was trying to remember what I had seen in Ralph that had made me want to marry him. Nothing came to mind except the reasons why I'd wanted to unmarry him. I wondered if there was a woman alive who didn't look back on that one guy who made her ask herself, *What the hell was I thinking?*

My backyard wasn't exactly what you might think of when you think *yard*. There was no grass to speak of, and the majority of the space was a concrete pad that served as a patio. I had a small table with four chairs, and that was about it. The year we moved in, I planted perennials in the few areas that had dirt—mostly around the fence—because someone told me you could stick perennials in the ground and you didn't have to do much else except water them and they'd come back every year, and that sounded like a pretty good deal to me. Maybe I was remembering the beautiful flower beds at Gran's house. But not having much of a green thumb myself, I planted some iris and a couple of peonies and some black-eyed Susans that a friend at work gave me, and that was pretty much it. It wasn't exactly a botanical garden, but it was mine.

I sat on one of the chairs and thought about what I'd done, quitting my job and going on record as the new grand duchess. I kept going back and forth between knowing I was going to kick butt in Saint Gilbert and do a lot of great things for the people there and utter despair, fearing I'd totally overstepped and would sooner or later step in it big-time and I'd be a ginormous disappointment to everyone—my kids, my sisters, the people who held my great-grandparents in such esteem. And Max, because most of all, I felt he really believed in me, in my ability to do what needed to be done. To roll up my shirtsleeves and dig in, as he'd once said.

"Second thoughts?" Ceil said as she stepped outside.

"Yes. No." I shrugged. "I don't know."

She stood behind me and massaged my shoulders. "You're going to be the best thing that happened to Saint Gilbert since our great-grandparents stashed the cash in a Swiss bank."

"Or its biggest disaster."

"Not a chance, sister. You're going to be great. Just remember where you heard it first."

I put one of my hands over hers and squeezed it. Even though I was two years older, Ceil has always been my champion, and I knew I'd never thanked her as much as I should have. I wanted to then, but the words logjammed in my mouth, and I just couldn't say what I wanted to.

But in true sisterly fashion, Ceil squeezed my hand in return and simply said, "I know." She kissed the top of my head. "I know, sis."

Then she pulled me out of my chair, saying, "Go back inside and thank everyone for coming. We have an early flight, and it's going to be hard enough to sleep with the trip tomorrow and everything."

And that's what I did. I thanked everyone and, with Ceil's help, sort of ushered them all to the front door. Which, upon opening, revealed Ralphie sitting between two girls on the front steps and two more sitting on the step below him. At each side of the bottom step stood a member of the black-clad castle guard. I wondered how they were managing to keep straight faces, just from the little bit of conversation I heard.

"It's so exciting to know a real prince," one of the girls cooed. "Do you think you'll come back for prom next year?"

"Well, since I won't be going to school with you guys, I guess not." He paused before adding, "Unless someone invites me."

Four voices piped up at the same time with an invitation.

"Sorry, girls, I hate to interrupt your prom plans, but I'm afraid I'm going to have to send you all home. The party's over, all these nice people behind me want to go home, and we have to be at the airport early." I stood on the top step, my arms crossed over my chest, so they all knew I meant business. Ralphie didn't bother to protest, so I figured he must be tired. "Say good night, Ralph."

The steps cleared and the adults left. It was nice that so many of our friends and friends of Mom took the time to stop over. I wished I'd had more time to chat with people, but I was exhausted. Ceil and the kids and I did a quick cleanup, loaded the dishwasher, took out the trash, and went to bed. Marianne had promised to come over on the weekend to get the house ready to be rented, which was just one of many reasons why I loved that woman like another sister. Plus the lease was up on her apartment in six weeks, and she said she'd move into the house if we hadn't found a renter by then.

One less thing to worry about, I thought as I pulled the light blanket up to my chin and started counting sheep. In an Alpine meadow. Next to a vineyard. On a hill just slightly below a chateau that my sister has big plans for, a hunky Saint Gilbertian by my side . . .

Chapter Twenty

How to describe what awaited us in Beauchesne? If I said everything but a marching band, would you get the picture? It was like the Mummers Parade on New Year's Day in Philly—without the Mummers. People actually lined the city streets to see our car arrive. Since there were five of us Max had arranged for a limo, so the ride got a little hairy on those tight mountain turns. The windows were tinted dark, but Ralphie— ever the ham—rolled down the one closest to him so he could wave to the crowd. His smiling face appeared on the front page of the city's only newspaper, and I swear he'd frame it and hang it on the wall if I let him. He was hoping someone would leak it to *People* magazine so everyone—meaning the girls from school—would see it. Eventually that did happen, and I'd never seen him so happy.

There was the drive through the castle gates and the kids and my sisters trying to take it all in at once, as I had done. Then the entry into the castle, where once again the staff lined up to greet us. But this time around, there were familiar faces in the crowd, and I greeted those I remembered and introduced myself to the ones I hadn't met, then I introduced my sisters and kids to everyone. There were a few curtsies here and there, but I was going to leave that conversation to Claudette. I couldn't help but notice there seemed to be more people gathered in the reception area than last time. Just like I couldn't help but notice the stars in my children's eyes.

Claudette was, as always, in control. She'd had our things taken to our rooms as they arrived. She'd made sure our rooms were all in the same hall so I could be close to my kids and my sisters. There was dinner in one of the smallish dining rooms, and while I remember thinking how delicious everything was, I was so jet-lagged and there was so much chatter, by the time our entrées were served, my head was spinning like one of my mom's old 45s. Shortly after dinner, I said good night to both kids in their rooms and I went to bed. I think the deliberations of the past month had taken a toll on me, and now that I'd made a decision and was actually here, in the castle, with my family, I just wanted to sleep.

Early the next morning, there was banging on my door. I wondered why Hans or Sebastian or whomever was on duty in the hallway was permitting it. Finally the door opened just a crack.

"Mom?"

"Yes, Juliette?" I sighed.

"Are you up?"

"I am now. Come on in."

Jules flitted into the room, already dressed in jeans and a nice top. She flopped onto the bed next to me.

"Mom, pinch me."

I gave her a tiny tweak.

"We're really here," she said, wide-eyed. "We slept all night in a castle."

"We are and we did." I pushed myself up onto my elbows. "Did you sleep well? Was your bed comfortable?"

"Like sleeping on a cloud." She snuggled next to me. "Don't you wonder if maybe this is an alternative reality? Like we're still back in Philly, doing our normal thing, and yet we're here at the same time?"

"Um, no. I barely have enough energy for one reality, and this is it." I smoothed her hair back from her face. "I'm going to get up and take a shower. Maybe you could ask whoever is at the door if he'll order a light breakfast for us. Berries, croissants, scones, coffee . . . you know."

"I can do that." She started toward the door, then glanced over her head. "I'm a princess. I can give orders."

"No, no," I corrected her. "Not *orders*. A princess never gives orders. She requests nicely. Politely. A princess would say something like, 'Good morning. Do you think perhaps we might have a light breakfast brought up for my mother and me?"

She nodded. "A princess is polite. Not rude. Doesn't order people around. Got it."

When I came out of the bathroom dressed for my day, the tray had already arrived, and my sisters had arrived as well. They were seated in front of the fireplace in the front room, and I joined them.

"I hope you don't mind that we crashed the party," Roe said. "But Ceil and I thought it might be nice to have a few minutes to catch our breath with you."

"I'm glad you're here." I noticed there were more coffee cups and plates than there would have been for just Juliette and me.

"When Aunt Roe and Aunt Ceil came in, I asked the guard if he would please request another tray," my daughter announced proudly. "I was very gracious."

"I'm so proud." I could feel the approval of Mom and Gran. I guess they understand how hard it is to raise polite kids in today's world.

I patted Jules's shoulder and sat next to her on the settee and poured myself a cup of that amazing Saint Gilbert coffee. I took a sip and sighed. "Oh, how I missed you," I murmured to my cup.

"I totally understand why," Ceil said. "The coffee, the fruit, the croissants—all delectable. You did not oversell any of it."

"I hope this place has a gym." Roe helped herself to what might have been her second scone. Maybe more than second since I was late coming to the party.

"I don't recall you ever going to a gym." I piled strawberries onto my plate along with a dollop of whipped cream. Heaven.

Roe shrugged. "I could never afford a membership."

"Well, I don't know if there's one now, but if not, maybe we can find some room in the budget to bring in some equipment."

Roe and Jules stared at me blankly. Finally, Roe said, "What budget? You're the duchess. You rule this place."

"Ah, I think we need to get a few things straight right off the bat." I poured a second cup of coffee while I got my thoughts in order. "The treasury is not my personal bank account. And I don't know that there's much in it right now. Frankly, I don't know the extent of the country's finances, but I intend to learn. Do we get an allowance? Do we own anything outright? I have no idea. In the meantime, please mind your best manners and treat everyone kindly and gently. Pretend Mom is looking over your shoulder." It wouldn't surprise me if she was. "We're not here to steamroll over the country or the people. We are here to help. Got it?"

"You sound just like Mom when we went to Gran's house," Roe muttered.

"Well, we *are* in Gran's house," I reminded her, then watched her face as that reality sank in.

"So what's on the agenda today?" Ceil asked.

"I'm going to be in meetings most of the day, so you guys can do what you want." I paused. "What would you like to do?"

All three spoke at the same time.

"Okay, let me start over. Ceil, would you like to go sightseeing? Travel around the country to see what's here?"

"Yes. I can't wait to see those chateaus and those desperately-in-need-of-rehabbing castles you told me about."

"I want to see the vineyards and the farms where the cheeses are made." Roe, ever the food-hound.

"I want to see everything." Juliette. So easy to please, my girl.

I walked to the door and asked Hans to see if he could get in touch with Claudette. Within minutes she was at the door. I explained what my daughter and sisters were wanting to do, and she nodded.

"I will arrange for a car and a guide, and I will alert Max so he can order security for the day," she told them. "In, shall we say, thirty minutes?"

"Perfect." I thanked her and walked her to the door. "And thank you for sending up breakfast for all of us. We all appreciated it."

"Of course, Your Grace. Will there be anything else?"

I hesitated. I wanted to sit down with a few advisors, but I wasn't sure who they would be.

"If I could speak with Max in about a half hour? In that small sitting room on the first floor?"

"He is at your service, as are we all." She turned to the others, who were listening from their seats near the fireplace. "Your Highnesses, perhaps we could gather in the reception area where we met yesterday when you arrived?"

It took a few seconds for it to sink in she was addressing them.

"That would be fine. Thirty minutes, then." Ceil stood and smiled. Roe and Juliette were still processing the fact that someone had called them *highness*.

"All will be ready for you." Claudette acknowledged the arrangement with a slight nod of her head before she left the room.

"So you have a half hour to get yourselves pulled together." I turned to my daughter. "You might ask your aunt Ceil to help you pick out something that makes you look more like a princess." When she started to protest, I reminded myself she was only fourteen, so I added, "Maybe one of those cute sundresses you bought, but even your denim skirt with a cute top would be more appropriate than jeans. Until we figure out the protocol, let's confine the jeans to the castle."

"Not to hammer home the obvious, but I believe we'll set the protocol." Roe paused. "Well, you will. There hasn't been a monarch here since 1941, so I think it's safe to say there's no precedent."

"Good point. But remember, people will be watching what you wear as well as what you do and what you say, so I'd like us all to dress nicely when we leave the castle grounds. Agreed?"

They all nodded. "So go. Drive through the countryside. Spend some time in the city. Poke into the shops. Talk to people. Learn as much as you can. Smile and be gracious and let people know you are happy to be here and that you want to be one of them."

"Aren't you coming with us?" Roe asked from the doorway.

I shook my head. "I'll catch up with you later."

Juliette asked, "What are you going to do while we're gone?"

"What I came here to do." I opened the door and shooed them out.

~

I dressed quickly—black dress, pretty scarf, comfortable but good heels—and grabbed my leather folder from the table. Maybe Max planned to have someone accompany me, but I wasn't waiting around. I left the room, nodded good morning at Hans as I passed. At the end of the hall, I went down the steps and right to the cozy room that I'd noticed the last time I was here. Between the large drawing room and one of the dining rooms, it was small enough to feel intimate but large enough to give me space, so it didn't feel *too* intimate. I'd decided to use it as my go-to meeting and planning room. My office, until I could arrange something better.

Max was waiting for me when I opened the door, and he stood as I entered the room.

"Your Grace." He bowed slightly at the waist. "You wished to see me."

"I did," I said. "I do."

Next to the windows that faced the lake stood a table. I dropped the folder on its top and gestured for Max to come over and take a seat, which he did after he held my chair. I sat and rested my arms on the folder.

"We have things to discuss," I told him.

"Where would you like to begin?" he asked.

"Well, I know in order to get the money released from Switzerland, I have to be crowned. So how does that happen? Crowning me, I mean."

He appeared momentarily stunned. Then, "I'm afraid I don't know what the process is. I am certain there's a protocol, a ceremony of some sort, but since I've never seen one, I can't say for sure." His mouth turned up at one side in a sort of half smile. "But we can find out. There has to be something written down. Perhaps my mother knows where."

"If you could find out what we have to do, I'd appreciate it." I took my notes from the folder. "Now, I think the first thing we need to do is look at the books."

"The books?"

"The accounts. Wherever we need to look to determine how much is in the country's treasury. And we need to know the correct manner in which to approach the Swiss bank. I want whatever belongs to Saint Gilbert to be returned as soon as possible. Does anyone know exactly how much is in that bank?"

Max was looking at me as if I'd sprouted a second head.

"What?" I stared back. "Am I going too fast for you?"

He looked slightly flustered. "I'm sorry, Your Grace, but I didn't expect you to . . . to . . . what am I trying to say?"

"Come out shooting? Hit the ground running?"

He nodded. "Like that, yes."

"I've given this a lot of thought. I decided if I were to come here, it was going to be for the best reasons. And the best reason I can see is—in your words—to get this country moving. You have no international profile because you have no businesses that deal on an international level. There is no reason for tourists to come here. You have a—pardon me—crappy infrastructure. You need new roads. Your hospital looks like it's from the Middle Ages. And what condition are your schools in? We need to make people want to come here, to visit, to stay. To invest in the country, maybe even buy a first or second home. We have something they can't get anywhere else, but we'll talk about that later."

"Everything you said is true. Sad but true." He did look sad. "All that and more."

"We'll talk about the 'more' some other time. Right now, I want to go over my agenda with you so you can tell me what my first moves need to be. I have a plan, Max. We will bring this country into the twenty-first century, and we can do it in a relatively short period of time."

He raised one questioning eyebrow.

"So tell me, where do I begin?" I asked.

"I think you should first meet with the Duke's Council. Tell them you are looking forward to your coronation. That should make it official, and plans can be made."

"And the coronation itself? How soon can we do that?"

He'd taken a pen from his jacket pocket and tapped it against the palm of his left hand. "Again, speak with my mother. If she doesn't know, she can find out. She will be more than happy to assist you in organizing the coronation and whatever that entails."

"I will do that. We clearly need an event planner, and I don't know anyone else who knows more about the monarchy than your mother." I made a note on the pad I took from my folder: talk to Claudette re. coronation. And a hairdresser. One who can tend to my roots. I'd had them done before I left Philly, but those suckers grow out fast.

"You mentioned you had an agenda. A plan . . ."

I shared the details with him—*all* the details—and when I finished, he sat back in his chair, silent for a moment. Then a smile spread across his face.

"Remarkable. Ambitious. Certainly challenging. But quite possibly all doable."

"I thought so." Yes, I did feel smug. "So let's begin. Will you ask the other dukes to meet with me?"

"Generally, the chancellor is charged with convening the council. Under the circumstances, it might be best if you handwrite a letter to him yourself and ask him to call for a meeting at the earliest possible time."

"That's Vincens?"

"Yes. One of his official duties is to be one of your chief advisors."

"Okay, then. Vincens it is." I thought for a moment. While I had—for the moment, anyway—chosen Max as my primary counsel, I had to leave the door open to consider other options should it turn out that he had an agenda of his own. Was I wrong to put my trust in one man? My gut told me I could trust him, but still, how well did I know him? He was the first person I met, and the one who'd been sent to find me and convince me to come to Saint Gilbert. I really didn't know anyone else on the council other than Vincens DellaVecchio. Could I trust him? I didn't think so, chancellor or not. Maybe in time he would prove me wrong, or someone else might step up, but right now, Max was all I had. "Could you give me a list of everyone who's on the council? Your mother mentioned names to me once, but I don't remember them."

"If you have something upon which I could write . . ."

I took a yellow legal pad from the folder and handed it to him. While Max wrote, I got up and looked out the window. The distance to the lake was at least a football field. The water was almost the same blue as the sky, and it looked so peaceful. I still couldn't believe I was here, that I was doing what I was doing. In for a dime, in for a dollar, my dad used to say. Well, I was in, all right.

Max completed the list in a remarkably short time.

I looked over his shoulder at what he'd written. "Why are there only seven people on the Duke's Council?"

"There's been attrition over the past few years. We lost several senior members due to . . . well, old age, basically. In past years, before my time, perhaps there'd been more. How many do you think there should be?"

"I don't know. More than seven, I would think." I frowned as I scanned the names.

"There had been eight, but we lost our most senior member to pneumonia earlier in the year, right after the referendum."

"So there's at least one vacancy," I noted. "Can you tell me about these people? Whatever you know? I know I've met a few, but I don't know them."

"Of course." I sat down and pulled my chair closer to his, and he ran down the list while I made notes. This one was ancient and ornery. That one was affable but not very bright. This next one argued with everyone for any reason. And so on. I had to admit, by the time he'd finished, I was uneasy. This group didn't bode well for the future I had envisioned for Saint Gilbert, but maybe I was overreacting.

"Why hasn't the deceased member been replaced?" I asked.

"There hasn't seemed to be a sense of urgency. Also, I suspect there are certain members of the council who are quite content with seven."

"Why? Wouldn't spreading around the authority make it easier to get things done?"

Max smiled. "Ah, Annaliese, you think with such logic. I'm afraid when it comes to our council members, seven is an ideal number."

I must have looked puzzled because he added, "It's an odd number. An odd number means there's never going to be a tie. When it comes time to vote, one side will always have at least one more vote."

I wrinkled my nose. Talk about stacking the deck.

"Who decides how many members should be on the council?" I asked.

He appeared to think for a moment. "I believe it may have been done by charter. If so, there should be a copy in the library. Would you like me to look?"

"I would. Thank you."

Max stood as he prepared to leave the room, but before he could take two steps, I asked, "Tell me again, why are there no women on the council?"

"Because it's the *Duke's* Council, my lady."

"That stinks. Some of the smartest people I know are women."

"Agreed, Your Grace." He paused. "But perhaps a full reading of the charter is in order. There may have been other provisions that might open the door for inclusion of a woman other than the duchess."

"We should check the document," I said.

Five minutes later, we were doing exactly that.

"Where does it deal with vacancies?" I was looking for a place where it might spell out how to replace members who died without a natural replacement.

"Ahhh, here. Article thirty-five." Max tapped the section with his index finger.

I read the paragraph several times just to be certain I understood, then sat back in my seat and smiled. I was pretty sure I knew how to get around the fact that up until now, the Duke's Council had been a men's-only club. I just needed to practice a little patience.

Chapter Twenty-One

Things moved pretty quickly after that. I wrote the letter to Vincens, and he wrote back inviting me to address the Duke's Council. Three days later, I met with them and formally announced I was accepting my role of grand duchess. I was careful to watch the faces of the men around the table when I did so, hoping to gauge the level of enthusiasm or lack thereof. But everyone appeared to think it was a swell idea, and they were all cheerfully on board. Of course, the thought of all that lovely money coming back into the country's treasury probably inspired their delight at the prospect of having a grand duchess again. Research had concluded that the ceremony itself should take place in the Church of Saint Ann, which made me happy since I figured my ancestors were right there out back and maybe would be watching somehow. As my first official act, I put Claudette in charge of the festivities.

"I am honored, Your Grace." She bowed at the waist when I asked her if she would take on that project. While she'd never attended a coronation herself, she'd heard tales from her mother and had a pretty good sense of what was proper. "Somewhere, perhaps in the library, there should be notes on past coronations."

We agreed she'd have someone search for any documentation that could be found but also that the ceremony wouldn't be crazy lavish and should focus on the country more than on me. I wanted the foreign press invited and wanted tours of the city offered to them. I wanted to reach out to the TV shows that had interviewed me recently and invite certain of their hosts to attend. We made list after list of who should receive invitations and how many events there should be. An A list to attend everything, a B list to attend the celebration Claudette said would be held in the streets of the city. What foods to serve, which tiara to wear to which event, and what activities should lead up to the actual day and what should follow, e.g., should there be a ball afterward (I nixed this, tempted though I was by thoughts of swirling around the dance floor in the arms of a certain handsome captain), a day of activities on the lake, things like that.

Claudette would definitely need an assistant. I was certain she'd have a few people in mind who could help out, but I wanted Ceil in the mix as well. And reluctantly, I conceded that Roe should be included when it came to planning what we'd be feeding the people who came to the castle.

Who knew becoming a duchess would be so exhausting?

After adding the names of a few select friends from home to the guest list, I left the details in Claudette's hands and agreed to meet every morning to go over her progress and to discuss any other issues that might arise from day to day. I did enjoy a good party—and had given a few over the years—but I'd never been to an event of this scale. Every meeting concluded with my head spinning, but Claudette was unflappable. In the archives she found an invitation to my great-great-great-grandmother's coronation, and she used that as a template. I had to admit I felt a bit of a thrill looking at the finished product. We'd decided to include a personal note of invitation from me to everyone who'd interviewed me or who'd asked for an interview. I was really starting to enjoy this.

Having everyone in my family under the same roof—especially if that roof sat atop a castle, even if it leaked in a few places—was alone worth the trip. I had breakfast with my daughter and sisters every morning—Ralphie was usually up and out by then since he'd started jogging early every day along with his personal security detail—and the five of us had dinner together every night when something official wasn't on the calendar. There were several events to introduce my children and sisters to the members of the council and their families, and I was surprised by the way my kids comported themselves. Of course, I reminded them before every dinner or party that their ancestors—especially my mother and grandmother—were watching from somewhere, so make them proud. And they did.

Claudette had given us all a quick tutorial on what was expected of us, from the order in which we should stand in the receiving line to which was the fish fork and which was the oyster fork. We made it through the first few dinners without too many screwups, so I was grateful for her help. The formal dinners were usually accompanied by music—a violinist or harpist or some soft piano playing—and the conversations were generally a bit stiff. But when it was just the five of us in the small breakfast room (we preferred it for our family dinners), it was almost like being back in Philly, with everyone talking at the same time.

"Mom, you're never going to believe what happened when I was jogging this morning." Ralphie's eyes were lit with a happy fire. "I met a guy who plays soccer and thinks we should have a team and compete with all the other national teams. He played in high school, like I did, and he knows some other guys who play. He said they're really good. But there's no stadium. Can we build a soccer stadium?"

"Oh my God, Annie, Ceil and I toured this castle today, and you would have died it was so gorgeous. Not nearly as big as this one, but it was pretty big. It belonged to . . ." Roe turned to Ceil. "Who did it belong to again?"

"It belonged to Princess Gabrielle Maria. Great-grandmother's cousin who married an Italian count. The castle was hers, though, so it stayed in the family. Our guide told us Gabrielle had three sons. Two died in a futile attempt to oust the Soviets, but the youngest survived, and he had two sons, both of whom are deceased and neither of whom left heirs. The castle needs some work, but it has elegant bones and overlooks beautiful meadows and streams, and there's an orchard and a vineyard." Ceil sighed. "It's just waiting to be rehabbed. It would make a perfect wedding venue."

"Oh, but tell her about the castle with the terraced fields and the rows of grapevines." Roe rested her elbow on the table and her chin in the palm of her hand, a faraway look in her eyes. "The wine here is spectacular, but imagine if we had a royal brand of wine. Can't you just see the label? Serafina sunning herself on one of those big rocks down near the lake with *Wines from the House of Gilberti* in script. Maybe with a falcon somewhere on the label."

"House wine indeed." I grinned. The idea appealed to me. I mentally added it to the list. Could I put Roe in charge of such a venture?

"Mom, I made a friend today," Juliette announced. "She's Claudette's granddaughter, Remy, and she's so fun. Her mom died in a car accident, so she stays with Claudette a lot. She goes to a private school just over the border in Switzerland. Mom, can I go to private school, too?"

And so it went every night. New experiences, new friends, new dreams for this new life of ours. Whether those dreams would become happy realities or haunting nightmares was anyone's guess.

Chapter Twenty-Two

The frenzy at the castle before the coronation began days before the event was to occur. The steady hum of vehicles driving up the long lane seemed to go on nonstop for hours. Imagine the biggest party you've ever been to and all the work that went into it, all the people who were involved in the preparation, and multiply that by about, oh, maybe five hundred.

I'd had trouble falling asleep the night before the big day: the clock read two fifteen the last time I'd looked at it, and I'd barely gotten three hours of sleep. I finally got out of bed and showered, taking my time to inhale the now-familiar subtle scent of the soap that always had a calming effect on me. I would forever associate that gentle scent—Gran's violets—with my first days in Saint Gilbert. I slipped into my silk robe and waited for Claudette, who'd promised to take care of everything I would need for the day. Honest to God, I don't know what I'd have done without her. She'd become like my fairy godmother, and while she directly tended only to me, she'd found and trained the appropriate personnel to tend to each member of my family. Ladies-in-waiting for my daughter and sisters and a butler for Ralphie, who might never get over having a butler of his own.

Surreal.

But then again, that entire day was like walking through a dream.

Breakfast was served with the usual crew joining me in my room as they had every morning since we'd arrived. The conversation was more subdued, though, and ran the gamut from clothes to who was to stand where when the official photographs were taken.

"How excited are you, Annie?" Ceil asked.

"About five seconds away from hyperventilating."

"You might want to get over that before we get to the church," Roe suggested.

"Yeah, Mom," Jules chimed in. "Passing out at the altar would not be a good look."

Ralphie nodded. "No way to gain the confidence of your subjects."

We all sort of half laughed.

"Speaking of your subjects," Ceil said, "people have been lining up around the church, through the park, around the square—however close they can get to the church—since yesterday."

"Like they were lining up for rock tickets," Ralph said with a grin.

"How would you know this?" I asked Ceil.

"I heard the guards talking about it in the hallway this morning. They were right outside my door."

"Were they concerned about anything in particular?" I tried to sound as nonchalant as I could. Me passing out at the altar would be far better than someone else blowing up the church.

"No. Just that they were calling in guards from other places to make sure they had enough." She nibbled a croissant. "Oh, and they were talking about the need to hire more."

More guards? Hadn't they just brought in a new class of guards? Why would they need more? I need to ask Max if something was going on I should know about.

We were all finishing up breakfast, and while I would have loved to have prolonged the time with my family on this momentous day, I knew we needed to get moving. Reading my mind, Ceil finished her coffee, stood, stretched, and said, "It's almost showtime, ladies. And Ralphie. Time for all the royal Gilbertis to prepare for the main event."

Ralphie was the first out the door, and my sisters were about to follow him when I grabbed each of them by their arms.

"Tell me the truth. Would you rather you were being crowned today instead of me?" I asked. The question had been nagging at me since the morning after I'd first met with Max and company.

"Would I still be able to renovate the castles and plan weddings there?" Ceil asked.

"Would I still be able to be the chef for Ceil's castle weddings?" This from Roe, who doesn't know that I know she's made the acquaintance of the castle chef and has ventured downstairs to cook with him on more than one occasion.

"Probably not," I told them both. "There's too much other business the duchess has to take care of."

"Then no," Ceil said.

Roe shook her head. "Me either."

"Okay," I said and kissed them each on the cheek. "I just had to ask."

"Go get gorgeous." Ceil gave me a quick hug, which was followed by a hug from Roe as they left the room.

"Mom, your gown is the most beautiful dress I have ever seen. I hope I get to wear it one day at my coronation." Jules hastily added, "I mean, when you don't want to be duchess anymore."

I hugged my daughter to me, then pushed her out the door and closed it behind her.

I maybe forgot to mention the Dress.

When it came time to discuss what we'd all be wearing for the occasion, I mentioned that I'd met the dressmaker in the city, been greatly impressed with her work, and thought she should be given an opportunity to work with us rather than bring in a foreign designer. Claudette agreed immediately and we called Gisele, who'd about fainted when we told her why we wanted to speak with her. When she realized we were serious, she asked first if photographs of any gowns from previous coronations were available. Claudette and I exchanged a smile and led the young woman to the room where clothing from other eras had been stored. After her initial shock, we left her alone to inspect and sketch. When we returned an hour later, she'd pulled out several gowns that had caught her eye.

"These are classic gowns, one a Worth, and it's beyond perfection. And perfectly preserved." Gisele gestured to three gowns, each a shade of white but different in style as befitted each era. "I could re-create any of these—with enough time, of course—or I could possibly alter one to fit you. Whatever is your pleasure, Your Grace."

I studied each dress carefully, then glanced at Claudette. She was standing still, watching me, debating, I sensed, as I was, the propriety of wearing a gown once worn by a former grand duchess as opposed to spending a bit of a fortune to have one made.

I touched the sweetheart neckline of one, the satin skirt of another, the silken bodice of a third. Any one of them could be altered to fit me. Although the Duke's Council had obtained some funds for the coronation from the Swiss bank, I didn't want to spend too much of that money on myself. There were so many other things to consider.

"Claudette, what do you think? Is it sacrilege to alter one of these historic gowns?"

"I think it would be lovely, Your Grace. Perhaps afterward we could open a small museum in the city where these vintage gowns and uniforms could be displayed. It would make a most interesting tableau to have photographs of you wearing one of these gowns hanging next to a portrait of the first duchess who wore it, whichever you choose. Tourists would love it as much as Saint Gilbertians." She hastened to add, "Of course, it's up to you."

"Perhaps Your Grace should try on all three and see if one pleases you." Gisele's suggestion was spot-on, and so that's what I did, and that's how I chose the gown I'd be coronated in.

Which did I choose? Why, the one that looked best from the back, of course. You really didn't think I'd pick a dress that made my butt look big, did you?

~

The procession from the castle to the church was led by a prancing white riderless horse decked out in colorful fashion. Why riderless, since that generally implies that someone has died? Well, of course, someone had, but that was years ago. As explained to me, the presence of the horse was the Saint Gilbertian equivalent of the Brits declaring, "The queen is dead. Long live the king." After the coronation, a member of the castle guard would ride the horse back to the castle.

Since there were no antique carriages available—no one knew what had happened to those that had once been housed in the carriage house next to the royal stables—I and my family arrived separately in white Mercedes limousines. I had no idea where those cars had come from, but there was an entire fleet of them in front of the castle when I walked out through the front doors into the glare of the morning sun. I hoped they were leased and not purchased.

As head of the castle guard and therefore my personal security—not to mention a senior member of the Duke's Council—Max accompanied me in my car, for which I was grateful beyond words. I was nervous and felt like a total imposter, or a really bad actor about to step onto the stage in front of the entire world. Max wore his uniform, replete with medals and ribbons. I was never particularly attracted to men in uniform, but damn, that man looked good. I ignored the sudden jump in my libido—*so* inappropriate under the circumstances!—and asked what the medals signified, and he took his time explaining each one, maybe to take my mind off what would come once the ride ended. Max being Max, I doubt he'd suspect the flush on my face was due to his proximity, which I told myself I could think about later because right now there were other more pressing matters.

Due to the deep curve in the road leading from the castle to the church, the long cars had to circle the city and approach Saint Ann's from the opposite direction. I was surprised to see how many people lined the streets and shouted and waved as the cars passed by. Was I supposed to wave in return?

As if he'd read my mind, Max said, "After the coronation, you might want to greet the onlookers as we drive by. But on the way to the church, the windows should remain closed."

I nodded. I'd do that. I hope someone got the word to the others, particularly my son, who we recently discovered loved few things more than an open window and a cheering crowd.

I'd checked out Ralphie and the others earlier that morning before they left for the church. It had been decided that members of the royal family would arrive at the church in a specified order, with Ceil and Roe the first to leave the castle, followed by Ralphie, then Juliette, my presumptive heir. I'd asked them all to wait in the hall outside my room before they made their way ceremoniously down the grand stairwell. Ceil and Roe both wore gowns designed by Gisele and made by her trusted seamstresses, Ceil elegant—of course—in a dark-blue satin, Roe in a similar gown of a lighter shade looking pretty regal as well. They wore jewels at their necks and in their ears and tiaras on their heads, and both looked as royal as any of our ancestors whose portraits hung on the castle walls. Juliette was the picture of a young princess in her gown of peony pink, rubies at her throat and dangling from her earlobes. On her head she wore a tiara of diamonds and rubies and on her face, a look of disbelief that this was actually happening.

But the biggest transformation was that of my son. Ralphie had been dressed in a uniform that was a near replica of one worn by my great-grandfather in one of his portraits. There were ribbons and gold braid and medals and God only knew what all on that boy's chest. He stood tall and straight and, well, *manly*, and his face appeared so serious and mature, I had to blink to make sure it was really him.

Who says clothes don't make the man?

And this only days after Juliette showed me his Twitter account, where someone had started a page called @RealSPhillyGurlz and, using the hashtag #IKissedAPrinceAndILikedIt, invited all the girls Ralphie had dated through high school to share their memories of their special time with my son. I stopped reading after I got to the part where someone suggested a rating system. There are some things a mother didn't need to know.

Anyway, we got to the church and found the doors closed and no one standing on the steps except members of the castle guard. Everyone else who was to attend the ceremony had already been escorted inside, where they awaited my arrival. I've never been comfortable being the center of attention, so the panic attack that hit me at that moment was to have been expected, I guess. In any event, it took me a while to convince myself to exit the car, climb the church steps, and go inside and just get it all over with. After today, we could control the amount of pomp and circumstance, right? I'd only have to do the things I'd taken this job to do. New roads. Better schools. A modern hospital. Build a tourist industry. You know, save the country.

I took a deep breath and with Max's assistance, I started up the steps. Several young women wearing long dresses appeared from nowhere to lift the long train on the back of my cape to keep it from sweeping the ground. Did I mention the cape? Long, red velvet, and trimmed in fur? I laughed when I first saw it—it looked like something Ceil had worn to the Halloween party we went to one year at the Victorian Room at the hall owned by the South Philly Vikings, the Mummers band. The cape Claudette had placed over my shoulders before we left the castle was real, heavy, and hot as a bitch in that mid-August heat. Oh, and they'd pinned a red satin sash onto my dress, from one shoulder to my waist. The Order of the . . . I forget what it was, but Claudette said it was mandatory that I wear it, so I did.

Did I feel like I was playing dress-up? Did I want to make nervous jokes the entire time I was being outfitted? Did I hear Bert Parks singing "There She Is, Miss America"? Yes, yes, and yes.

The doors opened at my approach and organ music began to play and everyone stood and turned. As we'd rehearsed several times over the past week, I slowly walked the aisle to the altar, hoping I wouldn't trip. It took all my willpower not to bolt just to get there as quickly as possible. But I was okay. I knew I wasn't walking alone.

I stood as the ladies-in-waiting removed my cape and carried it off. I'd rehearsed with Claudette several times—thank goodness someone knew the protocol!—so I knelt when I had to, stood when I was supposed to, bowed my head when it was indicated. Father Francisco, the local priest, assisted Bishop Guardini, who'd arrived two days ago from Italy and who'd prayed for a long time before placing the ruby-and-diamond crown on my head. That crown was beautiful beyond anything I could ever have imagined—red velvet with all those jewels on it. They told me it only weighed one and a half pounds, but sitting atop my head, it felt more like fifty. Now I know where the expression "heavy is the head that wears the crown" came from.

Imagine, if you can, being me on that day. It was as if I were playing a role in a historical drama. I mean, it was like something I'd seen in movies.

The altar had been covered in fragrant white roses, and I mean *covered*. Several times during the ceremony, a lone violin played. But there were moments I know I will never forget if I live to be a hundred: the wink of confidence from Ceil when I caught her eye; the look of pride on my son's face, the awe on my daughter's. Living in South Philly all our lives, nothing had prepared any of us for what was happening. The closest we'd ever come to any manner of pomp and circumstance was when, thanks to our father's army veteran brother who lived in Springfield, Roe was Poppy Queen at the American Legion Memorial Day Parade the year she turned ten. She rode on the float and waved to the crowd, "America the Beautiful" blasting from the speakers on the back of the truck. I remember her fingers were dyed red by the end of the day because she'd handed out so many red crepe paper flowers to the parade watchers lining the streets.

After what had seemed an eternity to me, a lone trumpet began to play, a choir of children began to sing, and the ceremony was over. It was done. I was officially the Grand Duchess Annaliese Jacqueline Terese of the Grand Duchy of Saint Gilbert. I went back down the aisle—the "no curtsy" memo apparently hadn't been widely circulated, because people actually curtsied as I passed by—and when the front doors opened, I stood on the top step as I'd been directed and waved to the cheering crowd that had gathered along the street and in the park waiting for my family to emerge. There were cameras everywhere. Television crews from various countries around the world had come to record what they'd called "a modern fairy tale come true." When my sisters and my children joined me, we stood together, all of us soaking up the good wishes along with the improbability of the moment.

The internet was awash with photos of all of us looking dignified, regal, and ready to rule. Apparently there was a worldwide fascination with this story, and it was repeated over and over in newspapers, magazines, and television reports, all basically the same story: "Middle-aged Single Philadelphia Mom Learns of Royal Heritage!" "From Divorcée to Duchess! How It Happened (see page 3)!" The Philadelphia papers were full of interviews with friends and coworkers and even, unfortunately, Ralph Senior, who at least didn't repeat the comment about my mother being snobby.

Again, it was surreal. But I welcomed the publicity because it worked along with my plans to give Saint Gilbert a higher profile. A *much* higher profile.

I should say right here that while I wasn't much for the pomp, I had to admit, I had tears in my eyes. Not for myself, but for Gran. She should have had the chance to stand there with that crown on her head; she was the Annaliese the people should have been calling for. It broke my heart to think about everything she'd been deprived of. And my mother . . . she would have been next in line after Gran. Mom would have been a kick-ass grand duchess. Those roads would have been repaired if she'd had to go out there and fill in the ruts herself or, at the very least, direct the road crews.

So I broke from the agenda, and the first thing I did was lead my immediate family through the gate into the graveyard. When we got to the place where our relatives were buried, I turned to my sisters and my kids and said, "I think it would be appropriate to say a prayer for our great-grandparents and our other relatives before the celebrations begin."

Everyone nodded silently.

We all bowed our heads and I told them I was sorry that things turned out the way they did so that my grandmother or my mother wasn't the one wearing the crown. I said I'd do the very best I could and for them not to be shy about offering advice if at all possible—like if they found a way to communicate, that would be good—and that I'd try to make them proud of me.

The rest of the day was a total blur. There was a reception in the castle organized by Claudette and her committee. Large potted plants—trees and flowering things I didn't recognize—were arranged throughout the gallery where local wines and cheeses were being served along with some very fancy goodies. There was music from a harpist. The guests consisted of Saint Gilbertian loyalists, members of the Duke's Council, those elderly friends of my grandmother, and heads of state from various countries. Every invited nation had sent dignitaries, the Brits even sending a prince, a princess, and a duke—ones I'd never heard of, but still, they were members of the royal family, albeit peripheral.

The French, Germans, and Italians had sent dukes and counts along with prime ministers and other civil representatives. I'd been schooled in protocol for greeting such visitors, but even so, the entire day had seemed so ridiculously implausible, I had moments when I couldn't believe this was actually my life. A whole contingent came from the States, including Marianne, but I didn't have much time to spend with her. We agreed she'd come back for a longer stay once everything settled down. The day was pleasant enough, but I have to say, one thing really got under my skin.

I took Ceil aside and said, "We have to talk."

"You betcha. God, you look so regal. So imposing." My sister's eyes were shining. "I can't believe we're here and all these people are—"

"Going to be leaving later to stay at a hotel in another country. We have to talk about hotels." I glanced around the room. "None of these people are staying in Saint Gilbert."

Ceil stared at me while she let that sink in. "Because there's no place for them to stay here."

"Tomorrow morning we talk about that castle you toured, the one that belonged to our great-grandmother's cousin, Gabrielle. We need to find a contractor to go out there and check it out, stem to stern."

"You're thinking hotel."

"I'm thinking it pisses me off that even if we get people to come here, they're going to be staying somewhere else unless we do something about it, and quick. This is not going to happen again."

Ceil nodded. "Right. Priorities. But . . ."

"But what?"

"I wanted that castle for the spa. You know, the place where we will wash away crow's-feet, marionette lines, and elevens."

That was important.

"Okay, there must be someplace else we could turn into a hotel. Make the spa a priority. I've already had visitors comment on the beauty of everyone's flawless, wrinkle-free skin. We need to strike while that iron is still hot."

It had been my plan to introduce those wrinkle-free ladies of a certain age to our guests who were decades younger.

"I'm finding the people of Saint Gilbert are so beautiful, so youthful," one of the ladies from the French contingent had commented. I'd judged her to be in her midsixties, and to say that time had not been kind to her skin would have been . . . kind. "Everyone I've met here has the most beautiful skin. And if you'll forgive me for mentioning it, Your Grace, you could pass easily for thirty or even less, though I've read you're . . . well, a tad bit older than that."

"Quite a few years older, yes." I smiled.

"What is your secret?" She returned the smile. "There must be a secret."

"Oh, there is." I'd leaned close to her to whisper as if sharing a strict confidence.

"Tell me," she'd begged.

"We're not ready to share, but we will, and soon. If you like, I will put your name on the list of first-to-knows."

She stared at me for a moment, then I raised an eyebrow.

She grabbed my arm. "You're serious, aren't you? There really is something . . ."

I nodded knowingly, if not smugly.

"Put my name on the very top of that list. I must be the first to know! I would be eternally grateful!"

I squeezed the hand of my new BFF and assured her I would do that.

Just as I'd assured dozens of other women with whom I'd had similar conversations. As long as all these obviously beauty-conscious aging women were here, I should take advantage of the situation, right? I mean, what else did we have to talk about after we got past the clichéd "Quite a change from your life in America, isn't it?" and "How does it feel to be royal after growing up in . . . where was it now, Baltimore?" So I decided to plant the seeds, as it were. Dangle a carrot. Ensure a certain number of people left this weekend with Saint Gilbert firmly in their minds and wondering about that secret I'd hinted at. They were going to think about Saint Gilbert every time they looked in the mirror. Of course, now that I had people interested, we'd have to deliver, but I was already working on that.

After the coronation reception, we'd moved on to a luncheon. Later there would be a tea, then a formal state dinner for select guests that would be held in the throne room. I got to sit on the throne, which I have to say, while a beautiful piece of antique furniture, was not very comfortable. I had taken a few minutes on rehearsal day to inspect the carvings of falcons, flowers, and Serafina and noticed then the presence of two chairs. Fortunately or unfortunately—depending on how you looked at the situation—this duchess had no duke to occupy the other.

Of course, we had to change clothes for every event. Now, I've never been much of a clotheshorse—honestly, I couldn't afford to be, what with the mortgage and two kids. But I had to admit, it was fun, like an all-day, all-night costume party.

I got to wear the most amazing clothes—and jewels! Dressing up at all was a new experience for me. Except for weddings and funerals and the occasional important meeting at work, I almost never wore anything fancier than a good blouse with a skirt or, if it was important, a suit. So to wear several couture-quality dresses and gowns in the same day, thanks to Gisele's clever designs and quick seamstresses, made my head spin. Ceil, Roe, and Juliette all found their wardrobes drastically changed as events were added to the agenda and proper outfitting was necessary. A tailor tended to Ralphie's needs as outlined by Claudette. It occurred to me on Monday afternoon watching the sailboats as they raced around the far end of the lake—the last of the scheduled activities that included visitors—that I hadn't seen either of my children dressed in jeans and T-shirts in almost a week.

But once the last luncheon had concluded, my family and I bid goodbye to our guests, and the gowns and jewels were put away, it was time to put on regular clothes and get down to work. I couldn't wait.

Chapter Twenty-Three

The morning after the last official event, Ceil, Roe, and I sat lazily around the table I'd had set up in my bedroom to use for small informal family meetings. We had pads of paper on the table, pens in our hands, coffee in our cups, and scones on a pretty blue plate with a raised gold crown on it. I thought we'd be all rough and ready to roll, but we were exhausted. I didn't expect to see either of my kids until later that day. So it was a drink coffee with the sisters, munch on goodies, and relax morning. I'd wanted it to feel more like an official meeting, but I was fried from the intensity of the past week. But I still wanted to feel productive.

"We need a plan," I told my sisters. "And it has to be smart, easily implemented, and not cost a fortune. And we need to start right away, while this 'fairy-tale story' is still fresh in everyone's minds. We need to put our little country on the world map, give people reasons to want to come here."

"Right. Let's start with something easy." Roe rolled her eyes.

Ignoring her, I continued. "We have to put the emphasis on what we have that no other country has. So write down 'the fountain of youth.'"

"Really? You think anyone's going to believe that the actual Fountain of Youth is located in Saint Gilbert?" Roe tapped her pen on the palm of her left hand.

"There are some who already do." I smiled smugly. "I already have a list of potential invitees, that is, ladies who are eager to know the secret of why everyone in Saint Gilbert has such beautiful skin. We're going to invite select high-profile women who could use a little facial and body magic to our spa and give them our secret treatment. It's a start."

"Wait, what spa?" Roe frowned. "What special treatment?"

"The one Ceil is going to open this fall. I understand the weather is lovely here in October and November." I turned to Ceil. "How much time do you think you'll need to get one of those castles or chateaus in shape?"

Ceil closed her eyes, and for a moment I thought she might be meditating. But it turned out she was putting the whole thing together in her head.

"Okay, we're going to need an actual spa area, a place where aestheticians can give 'facials' using the amazing soap," she said. "We'll need bedrooms for the guests with adjoining baths. A lounge or three. A pool. Patios or someplace really nice outside. A lovely dining area. Everything top of the line and luxurious."

"How long, Ceil?" I asked.

"Give me enough money, the right crew—and the right building, of course—and I'll give you your spa with five-star accommodations in maybe three months. Four at the most," she said in that cool, confident Ceil manner. "Depending, of course, on how much restoration and updating is necessary."

She paused, and I could see those wheels of hers turning.

"There's the castle that had belonged to Princess Gabrielle Maria. Oh, and the one that our great-uncle Theodore lived in—I haven't been inside, but the exterior looks pretty good. I'd have to go through it top to bottom to see if it's suitable, but it could be a contender."

I nodded. "So if our great-uncle had no heir, the ownership should have reverted to the family or the government. Either works for our purposes. I'll ask Max to check on that, but in the meantime, he can arrange for you to get inside. Do either of you have plans for the week?"

Ceil shrugged. "None. I'm available every day."

I turned to Roe. "I'd like you to go with her and check out the kitchen."

"Why?" she asked.

"Because if we're going to have people staying there, they're going to have to be fed. Which means there has to be working appliances." I sat back in my chair. "You're the only one in the family with experience cooking for a crowd, the only one who could tell me if we have what we need. If not, what do we need and how much will it cost? And then start thinking about hiring a top-notch staff. Emphasis on healthy meals."

"Oh, okay. Outfit a cooks' kitchen? Easy peasy. And I know lots of people who are really good in the kitchen." Roe's face brightened. "I can definitely do that." She paused. "Can I be the chef? I really want to be a chef."

"Fine, you can be the chef." I'd tasted her cooking and for all her faults, she really is a damned good cook.

"In that case, I'm free all week, too, so just let me know day and time and I'll be ready to go."

Ceil began making notes, as did Roe, who was making a list of things she wanted to check out in the castle's kitchen.

"So, one castle or two?" I asked. "Gabrielle's and Theodore's, or just one?"

"Both." For once, my sisters were in accord. "One for the spa, one for our first hotel."

I looked at Ceil. "You're going to have to pick one to start."

"I'll have to take a good look at both of them before I can make that decision."

"So that's step one of making Saint Gilbert a destination." I flipped to the page of notes I'd made while I was having my first cup of coffee earlier, before anyone drifted in to have breakfast with me.

"We're going to want local food and wine to be showcased when we start having tourists. We're going to need someone to oversee all that." My head began to spin, and I began to experience a rare moment of panic. I had no idea what I was doing. What in the name of God made me think I could do this? I tossed my pen on the table.

Sensing my frustration, Ceil said, "Let's just work on one thing at a time. First let's focus on getting the right building ready, get the spa up and running, and get people to come here and give them a lovely place to stay and an experience they'll never forget."

"That's not exactly one thing," I said. "And we'll still have to feed them."

"Next year we'll plan ahead and have lots of local produce. Imagine serving our guests those amazing strawberries. And we can talk to the baker in town and make sure she and her husband can produce more bread and croissants." Ceil was making a list of her own.

"And we'll need to make sure there's excellent wine to go along with all the delicious food I'm going to prepare," Roe said.

"Let's see what shape the vines are in at that chateau we passed the other day," Ceil said to Roe.

"I remember that one. It's on a hill, and the vineyard sort of flows down from it. So picturesque. We should find out who owns it. And we should look into producing our own wines." Roe repeated the thought she'd had when we first talked about the vineyards.

"Let us handle all this, Annie. The castles, the vineyards, everything. We can check in with you every week and let you know where we are, but right now, you have other things to deal with," Ceil pointed out.

"Like my meeting with the ladies who make the magic soap. Without them, there won't be any need for a spa." I closed my notebook and pushed back my chair. "And my first official meeting with the Duke's Council is Thursday morning." I blew out a long breath, making my cheeks billow the way I did when I was a kid and frustrated about something. "But first let me call Max and see what we can do about having you two get into those castles."

"I want to be with you when you speak to the soap ladies," Ceil said. "That way, I can be the point person on soap so you don't have to be."

And that's why most of the time, Ceil was my favorite sister.

~

Max knew right away who to call to help tick off a few things on the list. As soon as could be arranged, Ceil and Roe would tour the interiors of the castles in question with a man named Louis Bondersan, who owned one of the few contracting companies in Saint Gilbert. He was, Max assured me, an expert on restoring old buildings, very reliable, and his work was impeccable—he was the best the country had to offer. He also arranged for a farmer to check out the chateau Ceil had mentioned to see what shape the vineyard was in.

Later that day, Max and I were in the little room on the first floor that I liked to use as my private office and for meetings. It was cozy and filled with light, and I could picture it in the fall and winter with a nice fire going. For such an enormous building, it was filled with charming little rooms scattered throughout. I couldn't wait to see what was in the closed-off wing and show off its beauty. Maybe invite heads of state to come to Saint Gilbert and stay in the castle during their visit. I wondered how long it would take to get the castle repairs completed once the funds were available.

Which reminded me to speak with Andre DiGiacoma, who for years had been the liaison between Saint Gilbert and the Swiss bank holding our funds. I told Ceil to stay on Bondersan to get estimates as soon as they were available so I could have DiGiacoma put the request through to the bank once we decided which castle would best suit the spa. One more thing on my list.

"Perhaps it might best serve your purposes to . . ." Max had hesitated after I told him of my plans to add members to the Duke's Council and for the spa.

"To do what?"

"To slow down just a bit."

I frowned. "Slow down what?"

"Some of your efforts to—well, to take on everything at once."

"Why would I do that?" I put down the pen I'd been holding, looked him in the eye, and waited.

Finally, he said, "Because sometimes it might be better to accomplish one goal before attacking another."

"What, you think I can't walk and chew gum at the same time?" At his look of confusion, I added, "Do more than one thing at the same time."

Max sighed. "I think you are the most capable woman I've ever met, but if I may speak freely . . ."

"You already have, so you might as well just put it all out there." I crossed my arms over my chest, not sure of what he was going to say but suspecting I might not like it.

"I would hate to see you complete your research on all these many projects only to have the council not approve them."

"Why do I need their approval?"

Max shrugged. "It's always been so; the council controls the agenda."

"Only because since the Russians left, there hasn't been anyone else in charge. And it hasn't always been so. I've been reading up on the history of Saint Gilbert, Max. I've done my homework. So I have news for you and the other members of the council.

"The way the council functions today isn't the way it was intended. I understand why the council has made all the decisions for the past twenty-five years or so. There's been no duchess or duke, no head of state, since my great-grandparents. But here's the thing: originally, the

Duke's Council was established to *advise* the ruler, not to dictate to whomever was on the throne."

"Perhaps that's so, but this group has functioned for many years as the ruling body. You should be prepared for some to object to a return to the old ways." Max sighed and leaned forward. For a moment, I thought he was going to take my hands in his. "Put bluntly, the members of the council are not accustomed to having anyone tell them what to do or how to spend the country's funds, limited though they have been. Especially now with the influx of so much money from Switzerland in sight, there are some who will reject any oversight on your part, because more funds are at stake."

"I'll find a way to work around them."

We stared at each other for a long moment.

"So in other words . . ." I wasn't sure how I wanted to phrase this part, but it didn't matter. Max cut to the chase.

"Some might consider you a threat."

"Why would they vote for me in January but consider me a threat now?"

"Before they met you, some might have thought—erroneously, obviously—they could control you."

Swell. So in addition to the faction of the population who'd voted *against* bringing back the monarchy, now I had to worry about some of those who'd voted *for* the return of the old ways. Except now they were going to find out that some of the old ways weren't going to work for me, and the new ways might bring about changes they might not like. Eventually, I was going to have to come up with a way to make them want to walk my way.

I did have a few thoughts on that.

"You're saying I might have to watch my back."

Max nodded.

"But that's *your* job, right? You watch my back."

"I do. I and the members of the castle guard would lay down our lives for you."

"Take a bullet for me?" I was only half kidding.

"Without hesitation." He wasn't kidding at all.

It sounded so corny, but I knew he meant it. I felt humbled and maybe just a teensy bit scared inside. I mean, I'd be a fool to laugh off the fact that there might be some who wished that I'd stayed in Philly. The thought was sobering, not gonna lie. But I was raised by a woman whose mantra under adverse conditions was *never let them see you sweat*.

So I flashed my best smile for Max.

"Then I guess I don't have anything to worry about," I said with all the bravado I could muster, resolved to keep on the path I'd set for myself and for Saint Gilbert.

Chapter Twenty-Four

On Thursday I got up early and dressed in my I-mean-business clothes: a black linen dress and low-heeled shoes and the four strands of pearls Claudette produced and deemed necessary for what I wanted to accomplish. I spent the entire morning trying to decide which one of two bombs to set off at that afternoon's meeting of the Duke's Council. I was prepared either way, but I wanted to have my plan solid in my head before I walked through the door into that room. I was pretty sure I was going to upset more than one applecart whichever foot I led with (so to speak), so it was just a matter of me making up my mind.

When the time came, I was ready. I entered the room with a confident smile on my face.

After all the pleasantries had been exchanged, I jumped right into it. Gently, though.

"I'd like to thank each of you for the part you played in my coronation. It was a day I'll never forget, and I owe the success of it all largely to you. So thank you."

Smiles all around. Everyone likes to be acknowledged and thanked, right?

"I also want to thank the members of this council, past and present, individually and as a body, for running this country in the absence of a monarch. You've done an amazing job in the face of so many obstacles to keep the heart of Saint Gilbert beating. You and your predecessors are to be commended for the part you played in ensuring the country maintained its sovereignty. Every day I'm becoming more aware of the challenges the council faced over the years. I'd like to honor you all at a special dinner in November. You are the true heroes of Saint Gilbert."

Okay, that last part came flying out of my mouth before I'd really thought about it, but it was the right thing to do.

And the funny thing was, as I was speaking, I realized I actually meant every word. Facing the Germans, the Soviets, the political infighting, and the many factions that had tried to steer the country in a dozen different directions must have been hell at times for the men who'd had to deal with them, all to preserve the heritage their ancestors had established in this little bit of a country. Saint Gilbert was David in the face of many Goliaths, and it was important to acknowledge that struggle.

For a moment, there was silence. Then there was much chatter and congratulating each other on their successes over the years. I let them prattle on and talk about whose ancestors had sat on the council and whose ancestors had served Saint Gilbert in the dark days of occupation by two foreign countries. They'd come through it all intact, lost no territory, and had managed to keep the lights on—so to speak—and the bills paid with what little revenue they had. Yes, I did have the impression that some skimming off the top had occurred, but all things considered, that had been a small price to pay. Now the country was back on track, they had their duchess, and soon the money would flow in from Switzerland like manna from heaven.

"And now we will have all the funds we need to restore our beloved country." Vincens stood, his hands holding on to the lapels of his suit jacket.

Now the buzz began for real, everyone excitedly talking about how they were planning to spend the money. I heard everything from "buy a yacht" to "repair my villa" to "build up the army."

The vision of the bunch of them standing with their arms up as millions of euros fell into their smiling upturned faces flashed through my brain.

"I've been wanting a golf course here for years," someone was saying.

"We need the polo grounds refurbished," someone else said.

"What good are polo grounds without the horses? We need the stables rebuilt."

"And we must do something about renovating the ski lifts."

"May I remind you that it's impossible to get to the ski lifts? The roads are ridiculous, and the lodge is uninhabitable. No one's been down those slopes in years that I know of."

"Kids still go up there."

"They aren't supposed to. I doubt if it's safe. Why—"

I took this all in for a few moments, then said, "Okay, seriously? Yo. Slow your roll. A moment?"

I took a deep breath and reminded myself to be professional and duchess-like and not dis anyone, a challenge because I like to speak freely. I was having to learn to be a little more diplomatic than comes naturally. So instead of saying the first thing that came to my mind— *Golf course? Polo grounds? Yeah, those are top priorities*—I said, "A golf course and ski runs and polo grounds would be fine additions, of course. Excellent tourist attractions, to be sure. Someday." I paused to let that word sink in. "That day is not now."

Before the objections got out of hand, I continued. "You can drive only so far out of the city before the roads become rough and, in some places, impassable, as someone just pointed out. The roads are crap, so how does one get from one place to another? And where are these golfers and skiers and polo people going to stay? The players and the spectators? Right now, Saint Gilbert needs good roads and upscale accommodations for visitors, neither of which we currently have."

Blank looks were exchanged all around the table.

Finally, Vincens spoke up. "Your Grace, if I may . . . we've had no problem with our guests obtaining accommodations in Switzerland and in France, so I—"

"*I* have a problem with that. That's not going to happen again," I snapped more sharply than I'd intended, shocking him and everyone else. Possibly even me. "Why should we send our guests into another country where they will spend their money on rooms and dining and shopping and recreation? Why shouldn't we keep that money here? And think of the new jobs that would be created in and around the city and in the villages. I've heard that Saint Gilbert's children grow up and leave, to return only occasionally to visit family, because there are no jobs for them here."

More than one head nodded at this.

"Madam, surely with the money flowing into the country from the Swiss bank, we're no longer in need of funds. We can build that golf course, the polo grounds, and our visitors may stay wherever they please." Vincens made the mistake of chuckling as he looked around the room.

"Chancellor, in America, there are lotteries where you can buy a ticket and potentially win millions of dollars. Studies have shown that a good number of those lottery winners have gone bankrupt within years of winning. Why? Because they spend like drunken sailors and don't pay attention to where the money is going. They had no plan, no discipline. It was just spend, spend, spend, like the money was going to last forever." I fixed him with a stare that I hoped might make him squirm, though I saw no visible sign of that. "I do not intend for this country to be watching the funds dwindle down to nothing within a few years, and that's exactly what will happen if we are not careful handling what we have and find ways to bring new funds in. We need to invest our money cautiously." No one moved. "So yes, the funds my great-grandparents sent to Switzerland will be made available to us, and we will use them wisely. When they are made available. Eventually."

"Eventually?" someone spoke up. "Why not immediately? We've complied with the terms of the former duchess and duke, we have our duchess . . ."

"And where would those funds be sent, sir?" I asked.

"Why, to our bank, right here in Beauchesne, of course."

"Until Saint Gilbert has a financial institution stable enough to handle funds of this magnitude, I'm afraid the money will remain in Switzerland," I explained to them, as it had been explained to me earlier that morning on a call with the Swiss gentleman who'd been safeguarding our accounts. He'd clued me in on a number of things I hadn't been aware of. "We can request certain amounts to be transferred as needed, but I'm afraid until we have a trusted, experienced, competent system in place, we cannot put the entire fortune into the bank here in the city. The systems have not been updated in twenty years. It can't even handle the number of decimal points in the amount of money that will be coming our way. We need a first-rate financial consultant with a staff who knows what they're doing to set up our new system. I admit this is all beyond me. I don't know what we need, but I do know after speaking with the Swiss gentleman this morning and with the liaison between Saint Gilbert and the Swiss bankers"—I nodded in the direction of council member Andre DiGiacoma—"I became aware of certain . . . deficiencies in our systems. Sir, if you would . . . ?"

Andre nodded and stood. He was tall and thin and had a full head of bushy white hair and a beard that matched. "Her Highness is correct. As you know, as head of the state bank, I have had the privilege and the honor to serve as the liaison with our Swiss partners. I must say they have been excellent stewards of the money that had been passed to them by our late rulers. They have invested very well over the years. Our country is very sound financially. *Very* sound."

"Then what is the problem?" A visibly annoyed and frustrated Vincens spoke up.

"As Her Highness has said, our bank cannot handle the amount of money that is being held for us. There is a desperate need for the systems to be completely overhauled. I'm afraid until we have totally upgraded our technical systems and our digital capacity, the money will stay where it is."

There was an outbreak of protests—the bottom line being, *So how do we get our hands on the cash?*

"Guys, enough. Please." I turned and addressed Andre. "It's my understanding that your counterpart in Switzerland will make funds available as you request them for specific projects, correct?"

"Yes, my lady."

"So if we wanted money for our roads to be improved, say, and new roads to be built, how would we go about getting the money for that project?" I asked.

"We would submit a request for the funds, my lady."

"And just like that, they'd hand over the money?" I frowned. "So what would stop someone from requesting, say, ten million for roadwork that cost eight million and then pocketing two million for themselves?"

"Very little, madam," Andre admitted. "Only a strong moral character."

Swell. Best not to rely too heavily on that.

I cleared my throat.

"I would like to propose some safeguards. Any money that's requested should be accompanied by what in the States would be called backup. You want money for roads, submit an estimate from whoever is going to be building them showing how much it's going to cost, how much each piece of the project will cost. I worked in insurance for years, and if I wanted a bill paid, whether it was a doctor's bill or an attorney's, the request had to be submitted with the appropriate backup or it wouldn't be paid."

"Surely Her Highness isn't suggesting that our requests are broken down like grocery lists, with the cost of the milk, the bread, the meat itemized?" Vincens demanded.

"Actually, that is exactly what I'm suggesting." I turned to Andre. "Does that suit your purposes?"

"Oh yes, madam. More than enough." He nodded. "I would venture to say my counterpart in Switzerland would have no problem freeing up funds if the requests were made in such an organized, competent fashion."

"I would like to volunteer to assist Andre. As chancellor, I can surely be of service when it comes to budgeting and overseeing the transfer of funds," said Vincens the volunteer.

I wasn't sure if this would be the equivalent of putting the fox in charge of the henhouse.

I glanced at Andre, who appeared less than delighted. But Vincens was still the senior member of the council, so Andre merely nodded and said, "Of course, Chancellor. I would be honored to have you work with me."

"So that's how we're doing it." I glanced around to see if anyone was nodding now. No one was. I did see a lot of angry men who saw their plans to capitalize on the influx of funds disappear before their eyes, but I knew how to get them to walk my way.

"But our golf course . . . ," Pierre Belloque began.

"Do you have a site in mind?" I asked, clearly catching him off guard.

"We—that is, a few of us—have long thought that area to the south of the city proper would be appropriate."

"I agree." He was visibly surprised at my immediate concurrence. "Find us an expert on golf course design—someone recognized as one of the best, if not *the* best—and invite that person to come to Saint

Gilbert. If we're going to do this, we're going to have the best golf course in Europe. Have the property you have in mind assessed and see if it's feasible. If it isn't, find another site."

Belloque's face broke into a wide smile of joy. "Immediately, my lady. Thank you."

"Who owns that property, by the way?" I asked.

"Actually, my wife does," Belloque said somewhat sheepishly.

"Would she be willing to part with it at a fair price?" I asked.

"Yes, of course, madam."

"Then start the ball rolling." I smiled and pretended to be looking at something in my folder. "Oh, perhaps you could also look into the renovation of . . . what did you call it earlier, the polo grounds?"

He nodded. "They were quite popular back in the day. My grandfather played. He wore the colors of the last duchess." His chest swelled a little at this pronouncement. "People came from all over Europe to play here."

"Really?" This was news. My brain immediately added *polo grounds* to my list of things to do. "But if we're going to invite people here to enjoy recreational pursuits, we're going to need our roads repaired, so we're back to that again. And suitable accommodations." I looked directly at Vincens. "I repeat, I will not have visitors coming here and leaving for dining and overnight stays in Italy or France or wherever. If they come here, they will stay here. I am in total agreement that we need to offer a world-class golf course, for example. Anything we can do to promote the country and attract tourists should be on the table. But we cannot promote tourism until we have solid infrastructure in place. That means we will have five-star hotels with fine dining."

"Building new hotels will be an expensive proposition, my lady," Vincens reminded me. Why did he always look so damned *smug*?

"I'm aware, Chancellor. Which is why I'd like to propose that we utilize several old chateaus outside the city for this very purpose."

"Madam, with all due respect, I know for a fact that most of them lack indoor plumbing," Vincens said. "Even the Russians wouldn't stay there."

"The chancellor is correct, my lady," Dominic Altrusi spoke up. "I happen to own one of those ancient chateaus, but there are others. I've not been able to afford any of the necessary work."

"Might I then appoint you, sir, to head a committee to determine the feasibility of renovating some of those chateaus for use as hotels?" I asked Dominic as if I hadn't already thought of that. "Find out who owns them. See what it would cost for the country to buy, then renovate each one up to modern standards."

"Of course, Your Highness. I'd be pleased to," Altrusi said.

"If anyone knows of another chateau that might be considered, please let Dominic know so he can add it to his list. We would also be happy if the owners decided to renovate their properties and keep them privately owned. As long as we can count on a certain number of hotels or bed and breakfasts, I don't care who owns or runs them." I sighed deeply. "Of course, once again, there is the matter of the roads. We'll need someone to look into the possibility of having roads repaired or new ones created." I tapped my pen on my folder and waited to see if someone would step forward.

"My lady, if I may?" Jacques Gilberti stood. Up until the day of the coronation I hadn't even spoken to him, though I was told he was a distant cousin. He was an attractive gentleman in his fifties—I guessed at his age—and married to a lovely woman named Lorena. That was all I knew about him.

I nodded. "Of course."

"I would be happy to assume the responsibility of looking into the situation with our roads and our bridges. While I myself have no experience, I have a son who is an engineer. I could call upon his expertise to guide us if Your Highness agrees."

"Your son studied engineering?" I was so relieved that someone actually got my concern about the roads, I could have kissed the man right on the mouth, cousin or otherwise.

"He is a graduate of a fine school of engineering in America," Jacques said proudly. "Perhaps you have heard of the Massachusetts Institute of Technology."

I was momentarily stunned to think anyone I was related to—however distantly—got into MIT.

"Of course. Congratulations. It's one of the finest engineering schools in the world."

"So I've been told, my lady." Cousin Jacques was still beaming. "He's been working in America, but perhaps we can persuade him to come evaluate our needs."

"We'd be grateful for his input."

By the end of the meeting, every member of the council had agreed to take responsibility for something. One was going to look into what we would need to build a new hospital (his daughter was a doctor in Germany), another was going to look into promoting Saint Gilbert's products for export. Max's uncle, Emile Rossi, offered to look into ways of attracting new businesses to Saint Gilbert (once we get Operation Soap off the ground, he and I will talk). Someone else stepped forward to look into what the country's needs were as far as education was concerned. Soon I had more than half of what I mentally thought of as *Jobs to Assign* actually covered, and I hadn't had to twist one arm. I felt we were on our way to doing some serious business.

So perhaps now might be a good time to move along to step two of my agenda.

"You know . . ." I started looking thoughtfully at the contents of my folder, as if something were just occurring to me. "I'd been discouraged by everything I thought would be necessary to bring Saint Gilbert into this century, and I am so pleased that every member of this council has stepped up to offer his skills and creativity to ease some of my concerns. But I think perhaps some of these tasks are going to prove to be an eventual burden for one person to handle." I bit my bottom lip and tried to look pensive. "I did some reading up on the history of the Duke's Council." I looked across the table to my left and saw a *here we go* look cross Max's handsome face, and I inwardly smiled. "I was surprised to learn that originally, the council had many more members, and it wasn't unusual for some of those members to be women. In view of all that I and the council are tasked with doing, I think it is appropriate to add a few new members at this time. This is permitted by the charter."

There was some grumbling, not unexpected.

"Does Your Highness believe we're not up to the tasks?" someone asked with just a hint of indignation.

"I believe you are all very competent, very accomplished. And as I said earlier, the country would not have survived without your leadership. But"—here I made it a point to look every member of the council in the eye—"I'm also thinking it's unfair to ask the few of you to shoulder so many burdens. Obviously, there is much to be done, but the more people we have working on our concerns, the faster our goals will be met. There's an expression my mom used to say, something like 'many hands make light work.' Something like that. In that spirit, I want to propose that we add a few members to the council so that—"

There was more grumbling, louder this time. I let them go on for a few minutes before breaking it up.

"Sorry, but the more I've thought about it, the more I've come to understand the necessity. If you know someone you think would be a capable and hardworking addition, please speak up. You are seven now, I make eight. Let's shoot for a few more, shall we, keeping in mind that quality is more important than quantity?"

The griping immediately began anew, but Vincens spoke up over the din.

"I agree with Her Majesty. We have a huge responsibility before us. We are being tasked to rebuild this country. There is much work to be done before *all* our money is in our coffers. So in that regard, I would like to propose adding my son to the council."

Swell. I inwardly groaned. The thought of facing that leering mug once every week was enough to make me ill.

Max stood. He was wearing what I thought of as his Lord of the Castle Guard uniform, and may I say, he wore it exceptionally well. It's difficult sometimes to keep my inappropriate thoughts from getting the best of me.

"I agree, Your Grace." Max turned to the others. "The chancellor has suggested his son should join the council, and I heartily concur."

I tried to mind-meld with him from across the table. Mentally I was screaming, *Shut up! What are you doing? I can't stand that guy!*

But then Max continued. "I would be pleased to welcome Carlo DellaVecchio as the first new member of the Duke's Council."

I frowned. Carlo? Who's Carlo?

"But . . . no, no, I meant Philippe . . ." Vincens tried in vain to speak over the chorus of *yeas*.

As much as it pained me to agree to adding another DellaVecchio to our numbers, Max must have had a good reason to endorse him so readily.

I took my cue from him and said, "If there's a reason why Carlo DellaVecchio should not be invited to join the council, or if anyone feels he is unfit for any reason, now is the time to voice your objections." I glanced around the table. No nays. While Vincens clearly had preferred his other son, he could not very well say nay to the inclusion of any of his children.

"Very well, then." I turned to Vincens. "Would you care to deliver the news to your son yourself, or should we approach this in a more formal manner?"

"Perhaps a written invitation from Your Majesty . . . ," he said with some resignation.

"Consider it done." I waited a moment so Vincens could accept the congratulations from his peers.

When all the backslapping ended, I turned back to the table. "I'd like to suggest someone whose honesty and intelligence is well known to me personally, and hopefully will soon be to you as well. My sister, the Princess Cecilia Elizabet."

The room grew really quiet really quickly.

"Well, then," I said with a Cheshire-cat smile, "apparently there are no comments so we'll assume it's fine with everyone?" Heh.

Dominic Altrusi cleared his throat. "Your Grace, the princess is . . . a . . . well, she's a *woman*."

"Indeed she is, sir. As am I. Is that a problem?"

"Well, only because, well, as you know, this is the *Duke's* Council. Dukes are, traditionally, men," he said awkwardly.

"Actually, I've discovered something interesting about the council. It was established as the council the duke of the day could rely on to advise him, not necessarily a council comprised only of *dukes*, though it may have been so for years. You see the difference?"

I glanced at their confused faces.

"The council was mentioned in the charter as an advisory body to the first duke, though it was understood it would advise whomever would later sit on the throne. In the past there have been women on the council."

Deep breath, Annie, then lower the boom.

"And I should add that I also read that the members of the council serve at the pleasure of the sovereign." I waited a beat before I added, "That would be me."

Before anyone could object, Dominic said, "Her Grace is correct. It's all in the charter."

"I would most heartily welcome the princess to the council, Your Grace. It seems only fitting, does it not?" Emile Rossi looked around the table. No one was jumping up to agree with him, but no one apparently wanted to risk their position by telling me *thanks but no thanks.*

"Thank you, Emile. I'm sure she will serve the country well. Are there any objections to either of our proposed members?" The room was as quiet as a tomb. "Wonderful. We have our first new members. Anyone else want to propose someone?"

No one spoke.

"So maybe think about who you might want to see join us on the council and bring it up at next week's meeting. Otherwise, while I would really rather see twelve people, if ten is the best we can do for now, so be it." I closed my folder. "Is there anything else we need to discuss today?"

Andre stood. "There is one other thing I should perhaps mention in relation to the funds . . ."

"Yes?" I'd just picked up my pen and dropped it into my purse, ready to pull the plug on that day's meeting.

"As it had been explained to me years ago—and I confirmed anew with my liaison—before the balance of the funds can be returned, Saint Gilbert must be able to prove a means of ongoing self-sufficiency."

"Meaning what?" Jacques asked.

"We have to show that we have a sustainable economy. That this country can support itself without draining the funds once they are returned to us."

I nodded slowly and smiled. "I have a plan for that."

"And that would be?" Vincens asked.

"That would be on the agenda for next week's meeting. Thank you, Andre, for sharing that information. Will there be anything else? Anyone?"

Most of the men seated around the table looked confused. Others were busy with their phones doing whatever old men do on their phones.

"Very well, then." I channeled my best Sister Mary Camille, my tenth-grade history teacher. "Till next week."

Chapter Twenty-Five

Five men scrambled to be the first out of the room. When only Emile, Max, and I were left, I smiled. "Was it something I said?"

"I never would have believed that anyone on the council could have been persuaded to actually *work*," Emile said.

"It's the old carrot and stick thing. You want a golf course? Here's what you have to do to get it. It's amazing what people will do when the outcome is in their best interest."

"You played it perfectly, madam." Emile bent slightly at his waist. "I commend you."

"Thank you," I said just a bit smugly. "I was pretty smooth, wasn't I?"

"Indeed you were, madam." His eyes were deep brown like his nephew's, and they were smiling. "Well done."

We entered the hallway, and Emile bowed again before excusing himself, which left Max and me alone. He started walking in one direction and I in the other.

"May I ask where you are going?" he asked when he realized I was no longer beside him. "There's nothing over there except . . ."

"The library," I stage-whispered. "I love the library, and I love the idea of having a little bit of time to myself in a place where no one knows where I am when I need a break. Which means I won't have to speak to anyone or make any decisions. I can read, or I can just sit and gaze out at the lake and think my thoughts without having to share them. When I was living my old life, I drove an hour to work and an hour home, every day. That was two hours to myself to listen to music or sports talk radio, or think about something I wanted or needed to do at home, or think about the kids, or just think about myself. You know, my place in the world?

"Now my place is very different, but I still have times when I miss being alone. I've always loved libraries, and the books here!" I grinned. "Woo-hoo! Such a treasure trove of genealogy and history. And art. Did you know that at one time, Castle Blanc had collections of art that today would be worth . . . oh my God, millions. Maybe even billions. I mean, beyond the portraits of my ancestors."

"I do know that at one time there'd been an extensive collection, yes, but I don't believe it's ever been proven what happened to the paintings. My grandmother told me the story about how things disappeared, one by one, gradually, so at first no one noticed."

"How can that happen?" I frowned. "How can there be a Degas on the wall one day and not the next, but no one noticed?"

"The originals were replaced with reproductions, some of them not very good, but the eye often sees what it wants to see. By the time it was realized that only poor fakes hung on the castle walls, it was too late. They were gone, and there were no clues as to where they might have gone."

"Hmm. And here I was thinking they were sold off or something. Sounds like an inside job to me."

"Most likely, yes. But there was nothing that pointed to any one individual, so . . ." He shrugged.

"And when did this happen?"

"In the mid-1930s."

"Hmmm. Right before World War II began." I thought about that for a moment. "Almost as if someone knew what was coming. What do you think happened?" I mentally added *find the missing paintings and make whoever has them give them back* to my agenda.

Another shrug. "My best guess? Whoever took them sold them to private collectors who would agree to keep them out of sight."

"What's the purpose of having art that's out of sight? Isn't the idea that you look at it?"

"That's what normal people would do. But there are some people who like to have what no one else can. I suspect it would be people like that who ended up with our paintings."

We'd arrived at the library's double doors. "This is where you leave, my friend," I told him. "And where my hour of peace begins."

"I will have a guard posted immediately," he told me.

I made a face. "I don't need a guard. No one knows I'm here but you."

"You always need a guard and always will have one, as long as I am captain and responsible for your safety."

"But I'm the duchess, so I can overrule you."

"In all things but this, Your Highness. When it comes to your protection, I'm afraid I outrank you."

"Seriously?"

He nodded.

"That's written down somewhere, like a law?"

Another nod, this one accompanied by that half smile that makes my heart flip over backward.

"All right. Send someone. He can stand out here and guard the door. But tell him I'm to be left alone, that no one is to bother me."

"Understood, madam."

"Good. So go on, call someone." I turned to open the door, but Max reached past me, his arm grazing mine. Sigh. I didn't even want to put a name to what I felt when he was that close to me. "But I'm going to look up this 'captain of the castle guard trumps the duchess' thing."

"I would expect nothing less from you, Annaliese." His mouth was close to the side of my face, and don't think for one second that it did not occur to me that if I turned my head just a scootch, we'd be mouth to mouth. The temptation was overwhelming, and I could feel my face flush at the very thought of having that choice to make.

But he opened the doors and walked past me to turn on the lights and look around the room, no doubt to make sure there were no pirates or terrorists or other bad-deed doers lying in wait.

I went inside the large room with the tall glass windows and the two fireplaces, and I simply wandered.

"Marcel will be at the door momentarily." I could feel Max's eyes on me. "Do you have any instructions for him?"

"Yes. What I said before. No one is to bother me for the next hour."

"I'll pass that along to him. Good afternoon, Annaliese." Max left the room and closed the doors behind him.

For a moment I just stood in the middle of that grand space and soaked it in. Could there be a more wonderful dream than a library of your own? One filled with books from floor to ceiling on three sides, everything from fairy tales to history to memoirs and biographies and sciences? Oh, the joy of it! In those stacks I found books about the early rulers of Saint Gilbert, about noteworthy people who'd lived there. I read about alleged sightings of Serafina and the earliest families who settled in that corner of what had been originally part of France. Or what would now be France if it hadn't been carved out as a duchy by one of my ancestors. I met those ancestors—and others, most of whom ruled wisely, though there were a few duds in the lineage—and discovered my heritage. With all the responsibilities of being the GD (Grand Duchess), I totally appreciated that I could have one hour to myself when no one could get in my face about anything. I claimed that time as mine, and I was going to safeguard it—with a little help from Marcel.

I found a book that intrigued me and relocated a chair from next to the fireplace to the windows. I sat, kicked off my shoes, and pulled my legs up under me and opened the book and began reading about how Napoleon had made a request to my great-great-great grandparents for troops to reinforce his army, a request that apparently amused my G-threes greatly. Apparently Saint Gilbert has never had much of a military, and frankly, I'd say they'd managed to survive through the ages well enough without all that fighting other countries seemed to get off on. Even if they'd had an army with which to defend themselves in the 1930s and '40s, they'd have been no match for the Germans or the Soviets, so I guess there was some wisdom there.

There were several photos of my G-two grandfather in his uniform, the jacket of which was covered with ribbons signifying the Order of This or That and the whatever regiment and God only knows what else. Thinking about men in uniform, however, made me think of Max, and how amazing he looked in his Captain of the Castle Guard finery. Which made me think about how fine he looked in everything—his uniform, a three-piece suit, casual slacks and a shirt with the sleeves rolled to his elbows.

All of which made me think about Max in general. I knew it sounded corny, but besides being the most beautiful man it had ever been my pleasure to meet, he was also the *nicest* man I ever met. His quiet humor never failed to make me smile. He was thoughtful and kind, and he treated everyone with respect. Including his mother and me. Especially his mother and me. It made me think that his father must have been a nice guy, too, because I thought boys learned a lot from watching their fathers.

Fortunately, in the case of my son, his father wasn't around all that much during his formative years. Thank God.

I hesitated to describe Max as *nice*, because the word generally sounded so dull, so milquetoast-y, but when you really thought about it, the nice people were the ones you needed in your life. Nice was the friend who was always your port in the storm. The shoulder you cried on. The one who always told you the truth and helped you up when someone else had knocked you down.

That was Max. He was also one of those guys who could get away with being a bit of a jerk because he was so charming and sexy and handsome, but I'd never seen a sign of the jerk in him. He was always a gentleman.

Had I just called Max sexy? I did. I'd been trying really hard not to think of him in terms of sex for a number of reasons. A—I didn't know how he felt about me. B—I didn't know if he was seeing someone and couldn't bring myself to ask because I wasn't sure I wanted to know. C—maybe he was still in love with his late wife. D—and maybe most important, I was the duchess, so in a sense he worked for me—and that could be a problem.

For example, suppose I made an (ill-advised) advance and he felt pressured to comply. You know, like the movie guys used to do to young women who just wanted to act in a film and were made to feel there was a price to pay for their dreams. And that was sexual harassment, because like I said, I was the duchess and that could be seen as me coercing him into a relationship he really didn't want. I'd been on the other side of that scenario, and believe me, I would never want anyone to feel the way I was made to feel. I quit a job once because of it, and I couldn't even explain to my mother why I wanted to leave a good-paying position when I had nothing else lined up, though I knew I'd find something quickly (and I did). I know everyone doesn't have the luxury to walk out, but I was still living at home, so I didn't have to worry about being homeless or starving.

Here's the thing: I really liked Max. I would rather we never moved out of the friend zone than to have him feel he was being forced to want me *that* way. But if he ever gave me a sign he was interested, oh, mama—don't think for a minute I would . . .

My deep thoughts were interrupted by loud giggling. The library door swung open, and my daughter and two other young girls practically fell into the room.

"Excuse me? Did you not see the 'Do Not Disturb' sign on the door?" I asked.

"There's no sign on the door, Mom." Juliette was still giggling.

"Marcel is the sign. He was told not to let anyone in."

"Oh, yeah, that. He said that, but I said it wouldn't apply to me because I am your favorite child." Jules wrapped her arms around me and kissed me on the cheek.

"Not right now you're not," I grumbled. So much for me time.

"Mom, do you know Remy?" She stepped aside and pulled the taller of the two girls closer.

"Of course I know Remy." Max's daughter. Long, dark hair, beautiful long-lashed blue eyes. "I do remember her."

Remy dipped her head in acknowledgment.

"And this is Mila. I met her this morning. She goes to school with Remy."

"Your Majesty." Mila's smile was a mile wide, and she sort of half curtsied. She was shorter than Jules and Remy and carried a few extra pounds that somehow made her seem even cuter. Someone had apparently coached her on how to properly address the duchess.

"It's nice to meet you, Mila." I returned the smile, then looked up at my daughter, who was now draped over the back of my chair. "So what are you three up to this afternoon?"

"We just made a video," Jules announced proudly.

My eyes narrowed. "What kind of video, and for what purpose?"

"It's a sort of travelogue," Jules said excitedly. "I thought it would be fun to do a series of videos about Saint Gilbert and put them on YouTube? That way, my friends back home can see where I live and how beautiful the country is, and maybe they'll want to come here on vacation. You know, like you're always talking about making people want to see the country because nobody's ever heard of it?"

I thought this over for a minute. The kid might be onto something.

"Remy's helped a lot because she knows just about everything about Saint Gilbert, so she's like the travel guide." Jules nodded in the direction of Mila. "Mila's brother has lighting equipment, and he showed her how to use it so she's like our producer and camera person and technical director."

"What have you shot so far?"

"This morning we just walked through the castle—just a few rooms on the first floor. I think it would be cool to start each segment with just a little peek at the castle. And we shot it from outside, too. You know, so people can see how big and beautiful it is." The more excited Juliette got, the faster she spoke.

"People who have seen it compare it to Cinderella's castle in the books," Remy piped up.

"Then we walked into town and just showed some of the shops. The bakery. Gisele's shop. We had to tell the security guys to stay out of the picture. And tomorrow"—Jules's eyes were shining—"we're going to shoot Serafina and then walk down to the lake and tell people about the legend. That was my idea." She smiled with much self-satisfaction. "Everyone loves a good mermaid legend, right?"

"Well, I know I certainly do. And I can't wait to see what you've done. I'm intrigued." I really was. We might be able to use it when we start our big campaign vying for tourist dollars later this year.

"It's not ready for anyone to see yet," Mila spoke up. "We need to clean it up a bit."

"What needs to be cleaned up?" I felt my eyes starting to narrow again.

"Just, you know, bad lighting, or times when the camara got turned around and all you see is sky or grass. That sort of thing," she explained. "And I dropped the phone a couple of times."

"You shot it with your phone?" I asked.

Mila held up her cell. "My brother's going to show me how to upload it so I can edit it."

"Well, when you're finished doing all that, please let me be the first to see it."

Jules turned to her friends. "Mom wants to make sure there's nothing objectionable. Or that we didn't do anything stupid or that makes us look dorky."

"You make me sound like a professional critic."

"You are sometimes. You always say that it's part of your job." Jules leaned over and kissed the top of my head. "It's okay, Mom. I still love you."

"Of course you do. Now you three go. I have . . ." I glanced at my watch. "Twenty minutes left on my hour."

"Mom needs to keep one hour every day for herself," Jules told her friends. "She has to make up for the alone time she used to have when she drove to work and back every day."

I was taken aback by her insight. I didn't realize it was evident that I missed that drive time. Maybe those two hours alone had kept me sane between the people I had to deal with every day—demanding attorneys, misogynist coworkers, entitled claimants, indignant insureds—not to mention my ex. And then there was my family. If you think it's easy raising two teenagers by yourself these days, I invite you to try. It has its joys, of course—I think by now you know I would die for my kids—but I'd be lying if I said it was all fun and games. They are both pretty good, mostly, but man, they've both tested me to the limit at times. It was okay, though. We all survived.

Jules's friends said polite goodbyes, and my daughter led them out of the room. I tried to get back into the frame of mind I'd been in before the interruption, but my brain was soaring around in a dozen directions. I knew that popular videos could get a gazillion views and that the makers of those little gems could become quite influential. Did I want my daughter to become a media influencer? Not really. But what harm could it do if she and her friends spent some of their time introducing people to the beauty of this little country? So I mentally gave them my blessings and thought of a few more things they could video.

Ceil should take them to the castle she's going to be working on. It could be the first step in laying the groundwork for our spa. I leaned back and closed my eyes and imagined all those teenage girls showing their middle-aged mothers and older grandmothers the magical place where they could spend two weeks and leave their wrinkles behind. I was still toying with the idea of whether to use a reference to the fountain of youth when my phone's alarm told me my hour was up. I tucked my book back onto the shelf and went to my office to confirm that the plans were in place for me to sit down with the entire group of soap makers on the following day. I couldn't wait.

Chapter Twenty-Six

At breakfast the following morning, Jules showed off her finished video to me, her aunts, and her brother, who stopped in to see if we had eaten all our chocolate croissants (we had, to his disappointment). I had to admit those young girls did a damned fine job. If I didn't know better, I'd have thought I was looking at a professional production. While Juliette and Remy did get a little giggly at times, it was just enough to add a touch of sweet girlish charm.

The video started with Juliette standing in front of a portrait of my grandmother that hung in the upstairs hallway. She and Remy were both dressed in short black skirts and white button-down blouses, the sleeves rolled to the elbows, and looked like tour guides. Which, now that I think about it, was probably the intent.

"Hi," Juliette said brightly. "My name is Princess Juliette Elizabet Terese of the Grand Duchy of Saint Gilbert. Yes, I am a real princess." Eyes wide. Giggles. "Is that crazy cool or what? And this is my friend Remy," she said as Remy stepped into view. "She's not a princess, but her father *is* a duke. Remy grew up here in Saint Gilbert, and she knows all the cool places. So I thought it would be fun if we could show my friends back in my hometown of Philadelphia my new home and tell you all about the country that my mom inherited from her grand-mother. My mom's the grand duchess, which is sorta like queen if they had a queen here." Here she grinned. "I know, right? I wouldn't believe it myself if I didn't know for a fact it's all true! I mean, I'm living it!"

Another giggle.

"Oh, and you don't have to be from Philadelphia or one of my friends to take the tour with us. You just have to love a good fairy tale." She appeared to be thinking this over. "Or maybe you just want to learn about a beautiful place you've maybe never heard of."

Juliette stepped aside and pointed to the portrait she'd been standing in front of. "This is my great-grandmother. My grandma's mom. Her name was Her Royal Highness, Grand Duchess Annaliese Emelie Sophia Elizabet of the Grand Duchy of Saint Gilbert. She was twelve when this painting was made. Wasn't she beautiful? She was fifteen when she was forced to leave the country when . . . well, I'm saving *that* story for another day, but it's dramatic and scary and maybe just a little bit romantic. Well, just the part about how she met my great-granddad in London. It's so cool. Oh, and it's real history, like, the Second World War history? So it's educational! You'll love it, I promise . . ."

And so went the video. At the end, once more standing in front of the castle, she smiled for the camera and said, "Come back next time and you'll see more of the castle we live in. It's called Castle Blanc because it's white, and *blanc* is French for 'white.' See you!"

When it was over, I got up and gave her a hug. "That was amazing, sweetie. You did a great job leading the narration. I'm really impressed."

"Way to go, Juliette. You were adorable." Ceil, who'd been hanging over my shoulder, applauded. "The castle looks magical, and I love the way the shops all look like they're from another world."

"Well, they sort of are, Aunt Ceil," a beaming Jules told her. "They're, like, a thousand years old."

"Not quite a thousand, but they are pretty old," I pointed out.

Roe grabbed the phone and studied the images for a moment. "It sort of reminds me of Society Hill back in Philly."

"Yeah, if Society Hill had been built when Tudor architecture was the latest thing. Like, in the fifteen hundreds." I got up and tugged on a strand of my daughter's hair. I really was proud of her. When your teenager tells you she's made a YouTube video, you're at the mercy of the gods, so I'd been holding my breath until I'd seen what the girls had produced. "You and Remy nailed it on your first try. I hope you get a million hits."

"I love the flute music in the background," Ceil added.

"That's actually Remy playing the flute. It's from a recital she did at school last year. Her dad bought the video and we lifted the sound. Pretty cool, huh? It was my idea to add music." Jules was delighted with herself, the way almost-fifteen-year-olds are when they do something new and they are perfect the first time out.

"It almost looks professionally done," Roe said as she handed the phone back to Jules. "Like there are no stumbles or anything."

"That's 'cause Mila's brother edited it for us last night," Jules explained. "He's really good at that sort of thing. He's going to be a filmmaker."

"Let me see that." Ralphie reached for the phone. "What's your friend's brother's name? The guy I play soccer with in the afternoons is studying film."

"His name's Henri." Juliette turned to me. "Isn't that the coolest name? It's spelled like Henry but with an *I* instead of a *y* at the end, but they pronounce it like *On-ree*. Emphasis on the *ree*."

"Gotta be the same guy. Yeah, he's a cool dude. Good soccer player, too." Ralphie turned to face me. "He's the guy I told you wants to put together a team and maybe find someplace to make a field."

"I gotta go. I'm meeting Remy and Mila in an hour, and I have to get dressed." Juliette put out her hand, and her brother put her phone into her palm. "Thanks for letting me share your breakfast again, Mom."

"You're welcome. I love starting the morning with you." I stood and stretched, wondering if there was ever a day in my life when it took me a full hour to get dressed. My coronation maybe. I know I didn't take that long to dress for my wedding.

"A soccer team. That would be good." It was on my list, but now I started thinking about it for real. All the European nations have soccer teams, right? It's like the big sport, except they call it football. Which is not what people in the States think of when they think *football*. Still, soccer is pretty popular in the US. Ralphie and Jules both played from the time they were little. Jules dropped it in high school—lacrosse and field hockey are the "in" sports for girls at her school—but Ralphie was really good.

"Maybe you could put that on that list of things to do you're always talking about. I mean, you're the duchess. That should count for something." That son of mine. He's a study in subtlety.

"It's already there." When he started to pump his fist, I hastened to add, "Not at the top of the list, but it's on there."

"Wait till I tell Henri." Ralphie started toward the door.

"Nope. Not yet. I'll let you know when." He gave me a thumbs-up, which means he heard me but he wasn't making any promises. "Not kidding, Ralphie. Not for public consumption." But the door was already closing behind him. "And if you're going jogging, don't forget to tell your security people."

Not that the guards at the front door would let him leave the castle without someone with him.

"Good talk, son," I muttered. "Well, this has been a pleasant way to start the day, as always, but we all have things to do, places to go. I'm meeting with the soap ladies—"

"Don't leave without me. I'm coming along." Ceil drained her coffee cup and set it on the tray.

"I thought you were touring castles today."

"We'd hoped to. The contractor was busy, but he said he'd free up tomorrow for us. Of course he immediately offered to put off his work today to accommodate us, but I didn't want him to do that. I remember how pissed I'd get when a contractor I was working with didn't show up and set my entire job back, so I told him tomorrow was soon enough."

"Nice, Ceil." My sister always put herself in the other guy's shoes. I admire her for that. It was something I didn't always remember to do. I made a mental note: be more like Ceil.

"And Roe—what's on your agenda?" I finished the very last of my coffee.

"I thought I'd drive around and see a little more of the country," she told us. "Check out a few farms, see what's growing. That sort of thing."

"I'll ask Max to arrange for a driver." I searched my bag for my phone.

"Just a car. I can drive myself," Roe said.

"Um, no. They drive on the opposite side of the road here."

"So?" She was scrolling through her phone, smiling at something.

"So when was the last time you drove a car?"

Roe shrugged. "I dunno. Last year, maybe?"

"It was the week before Christmas, and you borrowed my car and you took out the trash cans Mrs. Girardi used to save her parking spot."

It's a South Philly thing. Parking on those narrow streets is a bitch. All those row houses, no garages, so little room out front to park a car. Residents will put anything out in the street in front of their houses— trash cans, folding beach chairs, whatever they can find—to mark their territory to reserve what they believe is their personal parking space. It's South Philly for *don't even think about parking here.* It's not legal, and the city's cracked down on it, but it still happens.

"I paid to replace them," she said archly.

"The dent in the front of my car is still there," I reminded her.

"Not my fault your insurance has a high deductible." She made a face at me. So mature.

"In any case, Annie's right, Roe," Ceil chimed in. "Back home, you can barely drive on the right side of the road. You're not driving here. Besides, I thought you said you wanted to see more of the countryside.

Which you cannot do if you're desperately trying to keep the car on the road."

Before Roe could argue the point further, I said, "Ceil's right. You can't drive and sightsee at the same time. Plus you can't leave the castle without security."

"Still not sure I see the point of that, but okay." Roe nodded. "See if you can get someone to drive me around and keep me safe. Let me know."

Ceil shoved our sister out the door. "I'll be back in twenty minutes to go meet the soap ladies," she said over her shoulder.

"Ceil," I called to her before she closed the door. "You said *back home.*"

"I did?"

"Yeah, you did. Do you think you'll ever feel like Saint Gilbert is really your home?"

She paused, and I could tell she was thinking. Finally, she said, "I don't know. I hope so. I want to. It's different, but it's a good place. I feel comfortable here. You?"

"Same."

"Do you ever miss the States? Philly? Your old life?" she asked, one hand on the elaborate brass doorknob.

"Yeah. Oh, yeah, I do sometimes. There's no place like home, Ceil."

"And yet, here we are."

I shrugged. "I think this is where we're supposed to be."

"Do you think you'll ever go back?"

"Definitely to visit. But to stay? I don't know. I kind of feel torn. I love the US of A. But I'm loving Saint Gilbert, too."

"We can have dual citizenship, though, right?"

"I'm pretty sure. I wouldn't give up my US citizenship."

She left the room, closing the door softly behind her. I sat for a moment, thinking about all that I'd left behind. My house, my friends, my neighborhood, my job, my coworkers. My old life, my old city. I was feeling a little nostalgic for Philly, to tell you the truth. It's a very unique place, Philly is. Oh, I know all the negative things people say about it, but it's not that bad.

Well, okay, sometimes it is. But I was born and raised there, had my kids there, worked hard to buy us a home there. It would make me very sad if I never saw the city again.

But right now there was another city on my mind, and I needed to get myself pulled together to deal with the needs of Beauchesne and the surrounding villages.

~

Roe was off and running with her driver and her guards by the time Max had our car waiting exactly at ten. Ceil and I left the castle with our little entourage of security. I likened them to the Secret Service but much lower key, though they did all dress in black. They accompanied me everywhere outside the castle walls. I still didn't see the need, but Max insisted, and since protecting me was his primary official function, I'd stopped questioning the need for the car in front and the car behind the one I rode in.

"This is so exciting," Ceil whispered as we both settled into the back seat of the car. "Aren't you excited, Annie? We're going to meet the ladies who make that lovely soap and see if we can talk them into making more and being part of our efforts to bring . . ." She paused. "What?"

"What what?"

"What are you thinking about? You're a zillion miles away and thinking about something else when you should be thinking about soap. What's going on?"

"There's something I've been needing to talk to you about, but I needed to wait until we were alone for more than five minutes, so I guess now's as good a time as any," I said.

Ceil poked me and drew my attention to her left hand, where her index finger pointed like a little arrow to the front seat, where Max sat behind the wheel.

"Not exactly alone," she whispered.

"Oh, Max already knows." I met his eyes in the rearview mirror, and for a moment I forgot what I'd wanted to discuss with her.

"He does?" Ceil frowned.

Might as well just toss it out there. "Ceil, I suggested to the Duke's Council that you be brought on as another member."

"What?" Her eyes went wide. "Why? I'm not a duke, and I'm not a man."

"True, but you don't have to be either." I explained to her what I'd found about the council through my research. "We need more responsible people tackling the problems we have to resolve, Ceil. I need someone I trust with my whole heart. Someone I know is smart and hardworking and . . ."

Ceil laughed. "Don't overplay your hand. I'm in if you need me."

As if there was ever a doubt. "Thank you. You're the best sister ever."

"Are you adding Roe as well?"

I shook my head. "I'm thinking two Gilberti women are all they're going to be able to handle. Besides, I don't think Roe's the council type."

"Don't sell her short. Granted, she's different in a lot of ways, but she's smart in her own right, and if you give her free rein with the kitchens for the castles and the chateaus, you will congratulate yourself for your brilliance. She's an amazing cook. I'm happy that she's going to have the chance to come into her own."

"All the more reason for letting her do her thing while we do ours." It wasn't so much that I doubted Roe's abilities or her intelligence or her work ethic. It was just that sometimes, I couldn't deal with the baggage, the drama, that Roe always seemed to drag around with her. In the end, though, she was my sister, and I did love her. Most of the time.

"Yeah, I know she can be tough." Ceil patted my hand.

"Right," I agreed. I mentally checked off *Ceil to council*. Which left about eight hundred other things to resolve by the end of the day. It was a depressing thought, and it was weighing me down. Most days I'm okay with all the responsibility—I actually *like* it, and I love being in charge. But some days—like today—I feel like I'm floating in a sea of giant cotton balls, getting nowhere and fighting off suffocation.

When I didn't say more, Ceil poked me again.

"What's going on with you?" she asked. I could feel her studying my face. A moment later, she said softly, "You're losing your mojo, Annie."

I shook my head. Suddenly even the thought of explaining how I felt exhausted me.

"I'm not going to stop asking, so you might as well spill."

"You know, like when you have one of those days when all of a sudden, it all seems like too much? Like, thinking about one more thing will make your head explode?" I forced a smile. "I'm sure it's only temporary."

"No, it's Annie syndrome. Must do all things. Must be all things to all people. High-achiever syndrome." She sighed. "It's a lifelong affliction for you. You're a people pleaser and a doer, a combination which could end up making you empress of the world or hiding in a small room somewhere clutching your blankie."

"Or the grand duchess of Saint Gilbert."

"There is that for real." Ceil took my hand. "What do you need, Annie? Let's figure this out. Your shine is slipping."

I gazed out the window and thought about that. What did I need? Finally, I whispered, "I need help."

"Okay."

"I have so much going on inside my head right now. All the things we need to accomplish. Everything that has to be done." I felt tears building behind my eyes, and I tried to hold them in. "It's overwhelming. I want it all and I want it all done right."

"And you want it all done right right now." Ceil knew me all too well. "So let's look at where we can get help. Maybe it's not necessary to do it all."

I shook my head again. "I've set out this whole agenda and committed to it, and now I have to do it. Fix it all. The roads to nowhere and the schools that don't function and having to go to Switzerland or France or Italy for everything we don't have here and that's most everything. I have to do it. All of it, or I've failed."

"That's ridiculous." Ceil swatted away the thought with her right hand. "You're trying to resurrect a country that's been dormant for years. Just the thought that you would attempt such a thing is mind-blowing."

"It's what I came here to do."

"And you've already set the wheels in motion for so much to happen. There is no failure here, girl. Especially on your part." She paused. "Want my advice?"

"Of course."

"Bring in people you trust to handle some of the load."

"Other than you, and sometimes Roe, I don't have anyone." I thought that over. "I have Max, and I have Claudette, both of whom are already overloaded with responsibilities."

"Who do you trust most in your life? Other than us."

I didn't have to think twice. "Marianne."

Ceil pulled my phone from my bag. "Call her. Right now. Offer her whatever she needs to come here and be your right hand."

I stared at the phone.

"You need a right hand," she told me.

"I have you."

"I have my own responsibilities here, Annie," Ceil said softly.

She was right. She has a whole spa / wedding destination / luxury stay-in-a-castle getaway industry to create, castles and chateaus to renovate and decorate, a PR plan for the country, marketing for the spa. I did need a right hand, but it couldn't be her.

"I'll call Marianne this afternoon when we get back. Maybe she'll consider it."

Ceil laughed. "Please. 'Come live in my castle and we'll do stuff together.' She'll be on the next plane."

I smiled. "She'll clear her decks and then she'll come. I don't know why I didn't think of it. Thanks, sis."

"Of course. That's why I'm here. To help you think."

We both laughed lightly. I did feel better. Ceil was spot-on, as always. I needed help, and I was too bogged down to realize that all I had to do was ask. There was no doubt in my mind that Marianne would be here by the end of the month.

"So does that about cover it?" Ceil asked.

I nodded. "Pretty much. Except for the apple thing."

Ceil frowned. "What apple thing?"

"Someone was telling me last night that in the southwest corner of Saint Gilbert, there's an orchard where they're growing heirloom apples. Some of the varieties are so rare, there's only one tree of its kind left. Can you imagine? How sad is that? One tree before that kind of apple disappears forever. So I need to . . ."

"No, you don't. Appoint someone minister of agriculture and turn it over." Ceil looked to the front seat. "Max, I'll bet you know someone who is really into agriculture who would love to take on such a project."

He nodded. "I do, indeed, Princess. Should I make a call?"

Ceil answered before I could open my mouth. "Yes, please."

"Consider it done, Princess." His smile lit up the mirror.

Ceil turned to me. "And that is how you handle the fate of the lone heirloom apple tree."

"Thanks, Ceil." I felt more than a little foolish for having forgotten how capable my sister is. I've always said she should have been the first-born. She's more like the older sister than the middle.

"Max," Ceil said to the face in the mirror. "What do you call my sister when you're alone, like, talking casually?"

He paused. "At her insistence, I call her Annaliese."

"At my insistence, under the same circumstances, please call me Ceil. Or Cecilia."

"As you wish."

Max followed the car in front of us as it made a right turn onto a lane that led to a pretty white building that had masses of flowers planted around the steps. It reminded me a little of the villas you see dotted through Southern Italy. Ceil leaned close to the window and gazed out. "Oh. Are we here?"

"Max?" I asked.

"Yes, Your Grace. This is where the soap makers' guild meets." He parked the car behind the first one, whose passengers had gotten out and headed up the steps into the building. Moments later they returned and signaled Max. Very James Bond. I'd gotten so used to it that I barely noticed them, but it was clear Ceil was intrigued.

I answered her unspoken question. "I don't know what they're doing, but it's what Max wants, and he's the chief."

"Captain," he good-naturedly corrected from the front seat as he opened the driver's side door and stepped out. "And it's just a precaution, Your Grace. We take the security of all our royals very seriously."

Chapter Twenty-Seven

The ladies of the guild—and yes, they were all ladies—were gathered in little clusters here and there throughout a large reception area. They were chattering when we entered the room, but our entrance caused a bit of a stir. I greeted the members I'd already met by name, and there were many of them, but I was surprised at just how many women in this twenty-first century were still making their own soap. I said as much after Ceil and I were formally introduced by the head of the guild, Louisa Allard, whom I'd met several times in the past. I took a few moments to explain why I was there, our thoughts about the soap, our plan to market it right there in Saint Gilbert, and how I thought the soap would be the *it* factor to put the country on the world stage. Where, I said with conviction as I closed, Saint Gilbert belonged.

There was silence. Then there was applause. Wild, happy applause.

"Your Highness, I believe you can see with your own eyes how delighted we are with your recognition of our humble product," Louisa began once the room began to settle. "We are deeply grateful for the opportunity to play so important a role in your strategy to improve the lives of the people of our country, and we are honored that you chose the women of Saint Gilbert to lead the way." She smiled broadly. "Because it is the women—only the women—who make the soap."

"I'd wondered about that when I realized there were no men in the room," I said, and light laughter followed.

"The men have always believed soapmaking is beneath them," someone said.

"It's the soap that will save Saint Gilbert," I told them, and I meant it. The golf courses and the ski slopes were all going to be solid tourist draws, but the salvation of Saint Gilbert would be the soap. Because if there was a woman alive who at fifty or sixty or seventy wouldn't love to shave a decade or three off her face, I haven't met her. Not that everyone had to look like they're twenty-five. My philosophy was you do you. But I know a lot of women don't like what they see in the mirror, and if something as natural as soap could make those ladies a little happier, why not? I say no judgment either way.

"The women have always been the backbone of this country." I knew that voice. It belonged to a woman I'd met during my first visit. Her name was Marguerite, and she was a contemporary of my grandmother's and her second cousin. She'd told me once that her mother had been an attendant of my great-grandmother. How's that for a legacy?

"Our times of greatest prosperity were those times a grand duchess sat on the throne. Our greatest monarchs were women." Turning to me, she continued. "It was your great-grandmother who devised the scheme to send our treasure to the Swiss for safekeeping. It was she who insisted that your grandmother be crowned and swept from the country even as the invaders were at our door and she knew for certain that her own death was but hours away. Even so, she kept a cool head and ensured the monarchy would continue, and with the monarchy would come prosperity once again. It has always been so." She smiled. "You are a worthy successor. We are fortunate that you have come home to us."

Well, choke me seven ways to Sunday. I had a lump in my throat the size of the Liberty Bell. Honestly, you want to shut me up, say something like that. Compare me to the women in my family who were heroes in their own right—call to mind the bravery of my grandmother, the wisdom and forethought of my great-grandmother—and I'm a puddle. It gets me every time.

"You are most gracious. Thank you for your kind words," I heard Ceil say when I'd fallen silent. "I speak for my sister—for both my sisters—when I tell you we are blessed to be here. We want nothing more than to see this country thrive. And to that end, let us get down to work. The duchess has told you what we're planning. Tell us what you will need to make those plans a reality. We need to speak specifically, ladies. What raw materials will you need, how much, and where will they come from? How much soap do you produce now? What could we count on to be produced in the future?"

And the excited chatter began again. I breathed a sigh of relief, stepped back, and let Ceil do her thing.

"What can I get you, Your Grace?" Claudette appeared out of nowhere as she sometimes seemed to do. "A coffee, perhaps?"

"I would kill for a cup, yes, thank you."

"No need to go to that extreme." Smiling, she led me to a settee near the front of the room, where I could watch and listen but not intrude upon the magic my sister was weaving among the ladies of the guild. With a gesture, Claudette had a tray holding several cups, a carafe, a sugar bowl, and a small pitcher set up before me on a small table.

I glanced up at Claudette. "You know me too well."

Still smiling, she poured a cup for me. "I know you often enjoy a little midmorning 'pick me up,' I believe you call it."

"I do. Thank you." I sipped the delicious liquid and sighed. The day was unfolding better than it had begun. I was happy for a few moments to sit back and listen to Ceil asking questions and discussing the viability of the type of spa she had in mind. It was a great relief to have someone else take the reins, and after all, the spa would be her baby.

That lasted for about five minutes. When I heard the word *lye* bandied about, I had to interject.

"Lye?" I stood, cup still in hand. "Did you say lye? You aren't talking about putting lye into the soap, are you? It's corrosive. It'll burn the skin right off your face."

"All soap contains lye, madam," Louisa explained kindly. "Soap is made when a fat—such as olive oil or coconut oil or lard—is combined with an alkaline, such as lye. A chemical reaction called saponification occurs. It takes time for the process to work, but through it, the lye is naturally removed from the mix, and what remains is ready to be worked into soap. I invite you both to watch the process sometime. You must take precautions, of course—protect your skin and eyes and clothing from the lye, which is in a flaky form—but the process is very safe when you adhere to the guidelines."

"When does the goat milk go in?" I asked.

"Ah, that is a different part of the process. We freeze the goat milk, add the lye to it, stir it until the lye has melted the frozen milk. Then we add the oil . . ."

"Do you use olive oil or . . ."

"Olive, sometimes, yes. Our climate is not suitable to grow the fruit, but my sister has a grove in Italy, and she sells only to us," someone said.

What followed was a lively discussion of who preferred one fat over another and why. Apparently there was no one way, no set recipe for the soap. So what was the magic ingredient that kept the skin of everyone who used it looking so many years younger?

I asked, and the room fell silent. I looked around at all the faces, waiting for someone. Anyone.

"If you don't all use the same recipe, why is the end effect always the same?" I asked. Still nothing.

Finally, I asked, "What are the common ingredients?"

"Goat milk," someone said.

"Violet petals," someone else offered.

"There are many soaps that smell of violets, some artificially, though. And there are lots of soaps on the market in America that contain goat milk," I told them. "None of them have the effect on the skin that yours does. Why is that? What's the difference between the goat milk in Saint Gilbert and everywhere else?"

Again, no response.

"Maybe there's something in the grass the goats eat," Ceil suggested.

"They eat other vegetation as well," someone noted. "Maybe there's something in the vines or the flowers. Goats eat what they eat. They're not very discriminating."

"Maybe it's in the water," Louisa suggested. " Forgive us for not having a definitive answer. None of us really thought about how the soap affected our skin until you began inquiring. It's simply been the way we've made soap in this country for hundreds of years. No one's questioned it before."

"It could be something in the water," Ceil agreed. "The water here is partly glacial runoff." She turned to me. "I read that somewhere."

"So it could be a mineral in the soil, or in the water, or in some way the goats metabolize whatever they eat or drink. Or somehow a combination of the water and the—whatever it is the goats are eating." I thought for a moment. "Are these everyday, common, anyone-can-buy-them-anywhere goats? Or are they special to Saint Gilbert?" Thinking about heirloom apples has a way of making your brain expand into other territories. Like heirloom goats.

"They're just goats, Duchess," a voice from the back volunteered. "The only kind of goats we've ever had."

Hmmm. I looked at Ceil and she looked at me. Maybe these were special goats that produce magic milk? We shrugged at each other. Maybe someone in the country knew, but it was clear no one in this room did.

Mental note to self: Where did the goats come from originally?

Then we talked about infusing the soaps with scent and adding flower petals to make it pretty. Everyone seemed to have their own idea of how the flowers should be prepared before dropping them into the soap, when, and how much. We spent an enlightening few hours with the ladies of the soap guild, including a delicious lunch prepared back at the castle and delivered and supervised by Claudette and her staff. Which explained why Claudette was there, but not why her staff was larger than mine.

I brought this up to Ceil when we arrived back at the castle, gift bars of soap in hand.

"Claudette is the most together person I've ever known," Ceil said. "She just figures out what has to happen and then she makes it work. What exactly is her position here?"

I had to think that over for a moment. "She's sort of like the major-domo, the person in charge of the castle."

"With your blessing?"

"Absolutely. No one—I mean, no one—knows this country or this castle the way that woman does. She's been in charge since the day I first set foot in Saint Gilbert, and I couldn't function without her. She has this network . . ." I shook my head in wonder at just how vast that network must be. "She knows everyone in the country, and she knows where to go to get what we need and who best to do whatever. I think she's been planning for this—the return of the duchess—her entire life." I pondered that thought. "She did say that her mother had been the head lady-in-waiting for our great-grandmother, so I guess she learned protocol and everything from her mother. I think they all thought that Gran would come back someday and she'd be the grand duchess and life would return to normal. So maybe Claudette's mother was training her so that when that happened, she'd know what to do."

I thought about what I'd just said. "So of course, she'd be the person for me to go to, to help develop a staff that could lighten the load. Someone to handle communications, someone to keep a calendar for me."

"Excellent idea," Ceil said. "Especially since there are days when you don't know what day it actually is."

"Right." I could see this working out for me.

"And someone to help you with your clothes," she added.

I felt my face draw into a frown. "What about my clothes?"

"You spend twenty minutes every morning standing in the closet, trying to remember where you're going that day, who you're going to meet, what you're going to do, and what you should wear to cover all the bases. And then you end up wearing one of your black dresses anyway."

"I like my black dresses," I muttered.

"Well, some events call for a little more pizazz. You could have someone who knows your schedule, knows what you need to wear, and has it ready for you."

When I started to protest, she talked right over me.

"And there are days when you have to change from something casual to more formal for a different meeting or whatever, and you waste another twenty minutes or so in the closet trying to decide what to change into. Someone else could have that change ready for you."

"I haven't needed anyone to dress me since I was three. It all sounds ridiculously indulgent, Ceil."

"It would be if you didn't have an image to create and maintain. You are now the face of this country, kiddo. You need to play the part. You shouldn't be wasting time trying to figure it out, and you shouldn't show up everywhere in the same dress."

Hmmm. As much as I hated to admit it, Ceil was right. I spent a lot of time trying to figure these things out. "Maybe I'll talk to Claudette."

Ceil held up her hands. "My work here is done. Look how much we've accomplished already today. Soap guild—check. Annie's agenda—check. New staffing—check." She nudged me with her shoulder. "Help is on the way, sister. Just hang in there."

"First thing when we get back to the castle, I'm calling Marianne," I told her. "Then I'm going to set a meeting with Claudette and figure out the rest of it."

By the end of the day, Marianne had promised to be here by next week at the earliest, the end of the month at the latest. As predicted, she was over the moon about joining us and said she'd been secretly hoping I'd need her. She was going to be the royal secretary—keeper of my calendar and scheduler, for starters. Claudette had offered to have Marianne more or less shadow her for the first few weeks after she arrived so she could see how the castle was run, and she'd also gone over official castle functions pertaining directly to me and offered her suggestions on not only positions but personnel to fill them ("For Her Grace's mistress of the wardrobe, I'd suggest Elaina Montrose. She has an excellent sense of style and protocol for one so young . . ."). And before the sun had set, we had a candidate for minister of agriculture. Max had personally suggested Carlo DellaVecchio, a name that sat uneasily with me, but Max had faith in him, and I was going to have to trust him.

Besides, Max had told me he believed Carlo would work very well with Ceil, and while I wasn't sure exactly what that meant—for Ceil or for the soap industry or for the goats we were going to try to track down—I gave Max the green light to offer the new position to Carlo. I could only hope it didn't turn out to bite me in the butt. I still hadn't met a DellaVecchio I trusted.

Chapter Twenty-Eight

With Ceil and Rosalie off early to check out possible spa venues with the contractors—in the end, Max had arranged for two: one who specialized in exteriors, the other interiors—I had a fairly quiet day. I suppose at some point, after all the repairs on Castle Blanc had been completed, we would be hosting social events, but right now weekends are low key. I spent most of the day in the little room I'd claimed as my own, located within the suite we'd designated as the castle offices. So far, mine was the only office in use other than the larger space I'd offered to Claudette, who, as our driving force, needed the most room. I was still writing thank-you notes to the visitors who'd attended the coronation, many of whom had brought gifts from their respective countries. My mom had always insisted on handwritten thank-yous, so I'd had plenty of practice over the years. At my request, Claudette had a list of visitors and gifts and their donors left on my desk so I didn't miss anyone. I especially enjoyed writing notes to the ladies who'd been so intrigued by the flawless, wrinkle-free faces of the people of Saint Gilbert. For them, I tossed out a cryptic line: I'll be in touch soon regarding your possible return to Saint Gilbert. Heh.

Sometime in the midafternoon, I thought I heard voices—lots of voices—coming from the front of the castle. I left the office and greeted the guard who was always stationed outside any room I was in, but as

I passed him, I realized I was not alone. Two guards accompanied me, silently falling into place, one on either side.

"I'm good," I assured them. "You don't need to walk me to the front door. I know the way, but thank you."

"Captain's orders, Your Grace."

"All righty, then." I didn't see the need, but there was no use protesting. These guys answered only to Max. I pointed toward the end of the hall and the front entrance to the castle. "Onward."

Of course there were uniformed guards to open the castle door, and our little trio walked out into the courtyard where what appeared to be a battalion of guards were assembled. At the front of the troop, Max stood in full uniform, speaking softly enough that those in the back had to lean forward to hear. All in all there were probably close to sixty or seventy, mostly men, but I was glad to see several young women in the group. As I and my two new best friends made our way across the wide courtyard, heads began to turn in our direction. When Max saw us, he said something I could not hear to the assembly before him and strode toward us.

"Your Grace," he said, stiffly half bowing from his waist.

"Captain Belleme," I said with more formality than usual. "What's going on here?"

"I was having an informal chat with our newest recruits," he said.

"Why are you recruiting more guards? You just added more right before the coronation. Is there something I should know?"

His hesitation was brief but still, I caught it. "Only that with the increase in the number of people coming and going from the castle every day and the efforts we know will be made to bring tourists into our country, it was thought best to prepare now for a time when we might better guard our castle, our city, the villages. And of course, our duchess and her family."

"How many new recruits are there?"

"Counting these, perhaps a hundred or more."

I felt an eyebrow raise. "To guard a castle in a country as small as this?"

"I believe in being prepared for any and all . . . situations, Your Grace."

"I think I'd like to hear more about those *situations*. Let's take a walk." I nodded in the direction of my two personal guards. "I don't think we need the extras."

Max dismissed the two guards, then gestured to another of his officers, who apparently picked up where Max had left off in his address to the recruits.

I wandered toward the far side of the castle in the direction of the lake, and Max followed, his hands clasped behind his back, his expression thoughtful. We walked in silence until we arrived at the grassy area that led down to the water. It was a beautiful afternoon, sunny, a clear blue sky and a soft breeze, and the lake sparkled. I'd have loved to kick off my shoes, grab Max by the hand, run down to the water's edge, and wade into the lake, but I felt eyes on me from every direction and figured it might not be cool if anyone took a picture. So unduchess-like. Then again, it would make me happy. Still, I reined myself in. I was curious about this effort to add to the number of castle guards. Max wasn't one to act without good cause.

"What's really going on, Max?" We'd reached the stone wall surrounding the lake, and I leaned against it. "What's with the troops?"

"Information has come my way relative to some rumors that are drifting around the city. No one seems to know where they're coming from."

"Rumors?" I couldn't help it. I rolled my eyes. "Rumors have you concerned enough to recruit additional guards?"

"You are aware there is a faction of the population who . . ."

"Right. Didn't want the monarchy returned. Wanted something else." I paused. "What do they want? Besides maybe or maybe not wanting to shoot me."

"They've not been very active lately, so we're still trying to determine that."

"They didn't want the monarchy back in January, so they probably still don't want it." I was trying hard not to pout. No one likes to hear that they are unpopular or unwanted, even if it's only by a small segment of the population. "Are these people credible? I mean, are they just rabble-rousers or do they have a point? Small group? Big group? Are there active protests?"

"Most likely a small faction, since they haven't been heard from since your coronation. Credible? I don't know."

"Why the concern now if you've known about them all year?"

"Someone's been chatting up people in the cafés and on the street, but we don't know if it's the same group. But that someone's been starting conversations with something along the lines of 'Who is Annaliese Gilberti?'"

"Seriously? Who *am* I?" I laughed out loud. "What is that supposed to mean?"

"That's one of the things we're trying to find out."

"Is this the first you heard about this?"

"I have only been recently informed," he said cryptically.

"Informed by whom?" I stopped and recalled something he'd said a moment ago. "And this information that 'came your way'? Where did it come from?"

He shrugged. "There are eyes and ears."

"Eyes and ears?" I grinned in spite of the seriousness of the conversation. "You mean, like *spies*?" Intrigued, I leaned a little closer and lowered my voice. "Are you telling me the captain of the castle guard has *spies*?"

He cleared his throat. "The castle guard is charged with protecting the realm in any way necessary. That often requires information to be gathered by whatever means is available."

"We have *spies*." I couldn't help it. The latent James Bond in me was tickled at the very idea of a network of spies operating in my castle. Yes, it may have been a little childish, but come on, it was just another part of the fairy tale I was living. "So do they have a name? Like MI6? CIA? KGB?"

He looked skyward. "I never should have said 'eyes and ears.'"

"Oh, come on. Don't stop now." I moved closer. "Max, are you the spymaster?" An image of Varys, the Master of Whisperers, the Spider from *Game of Thrones*, popped into my head.

"You are making entirely too much of this, Annaliese." It seemed he was trying to sound a little stern, but when you were Max, it was hard to pull off. His half smile was always the tell. "Suffice it to say that there are a few individuals in key places who keep their ears to the ground. And that is all I will say about that."

"Not even to tell me who . . ."

"No."

I sighed, and Varys disappeared in a cloud of smoke. "So where do we go from here?"

"We wait to see what the intelligence shows. And we will continue to search for the leader of the January opposition to see if they are involved."

I brushed off the back of my skirt where I'd been leaning against the wall. "Is there any danger right now?"

"None that I can see," Max assured me. "I would certainly alert you if I thought there was an imminent threat."

"Good. Because right now, my sisters are off somewhere with a couple of contractors looking at old buildings."

"A couple of contractors and a good number of guards, who have gone through each of those properties prior to the princesses arriving and have been stationed there while the chateaus are being evaluated."

"Thank you."

Max nodded, and together we started to make our way back up to the castle. Several times the backs of our hands glanced off each other, and I wanted nothing more than to take his hand and walk the rest of the way holding it. But I couldn't bring myself to do it. What if he pulled away? How embarrassing would that be? I've never been shy about approaching a man I was interested in, but this was different from flirting with a guy at a club in Philly. There was so much more at stake than whether he was going to buy me a drink or ask for my number and whether he'd turn out to be a nice guy or a jerk. This man literally held my life and that of my family in his hands. But even more important, I was afraid any overt action on my part that turned out to be unwanted might change our relationship—not in a good way—and I could not bear to have that happen. So I merely continued to let my hand brush against his a few more times all the way back to the castle.

~

If Saturdays at Castle Blanc were just another day at the office, the nights were no more exciting. We'd fallen into the habit of having a family dinner together in one of the small informal dining rooms, and we'd talk about the same sort of things we used to talk about at the table in Philly. News from the old neighborhood. What the kids' next year of school might look like. What everyone had planned for the coming week. Yes, of course, the details differed wildly from the past, but the essence remained the same. We were just a family talking about our lives. Then the kids would go up to the room on the second floor that we'd designated as a theater—really just a TV with a massive screen and some comfy chairs—so they could watch a movie. This weekend Juliette had asked if she could have Mila and Remy come to watch some favorite movies, so of course I said sure. The girls were going to spend the night, so Jules was looking forward to her first real sleepover since we moved to Saint Gilbert. I knew she missed having the kind of close friendships she had back in Philly, and I hoped these two girls would be the same kind of loyal and true friends as those she'd left behind. I knew she loved being here and loved being a princess, but I also knew she'd sacrificed a lot, as all of us had.

I went back to my office after dinner and rooted through my trash can—what, like you never did?—searching for that morning's newspaper. I found it under a bunch of discarded notes I'd made while I was writing thank-yous earlier in the day. I spread the paper out on my desk and started with the first page. The story I was looking for was on page 3:

Castle Guard Calling for Recruits

It sounded nonthreatening, and certainly gave no hint of an emergency. Just a callout to add to the numbers of guards charged with protecting Castle Blanc and the royal family. A list of requirements, age limits, who to contact, what to bring with you if you are called for an interview, what the training would consist of, what benefits were attached to the positions. I could see where some of the younger people in the city and the villages would respond favorably. At present, there were not a lot of options for employment. That would change in the coming months, but most of the population was unaware of what we were planning. Which made me think we should do a better job letting people know what we were going to be rolling out soon. I'll have to take that up with the council.

I turned off the light and closed up the suite of offices. A guard was outside in the hallway, and I noted he remained there even after the two others appeared to walk me to the second floor. I have no idea how they knew I was on the move, but they popped up like fly balls at Citizens Bank Park. When we reached the second-floor wing where I and my family had our private rooms, I noticed a little more activity than usual. There were two guards posted at the entrance to the wing, and two outside each of our rooms. The two who escorted me returned to the mouth of the wing and stood with the others. Max was being overly cautious, I was sure.

Chapter Twenty-Nine

Once in my suite, I toed off my shoes and called Ceil to tell her to come to my room when she and Roe got back. Over breakfast, we'd agreed to have a sisters' night like the ones we used to have in Philly on those Saturday nights when no one had a date (which was practically every weekend) or had to work late (mostly Roe, but sometimes Ceil was pushing to finish up a job). We planned on wine, snacks, and maybe a showing of our favorite movie, *A League of Their Own*. I took a shower—I loved that shower niche every time I stepped into it and couldn't get enough of that delicious soap (our spa-goers were in for a treat)—and by the time I'd dried my hair, my sisters had already made themselves comfortable in front of the fireplace in my cozy sitting room. Ceil wore a three-piece knit lounging set that could pass for daywear—long pants, a tank, and a cardigan that matched the pants. Roe wore Snoopy pj's and fluffy slippers.

"Did the guards have trouble keeping a straight face when you emerged from your room dressed like that?" I couldn't help but ask Roe.

In typical Roe fashion, she shrugged. "I didn't notice."

And I was certain she hadn't. I'd never known anyone who was less self-aware than my sister Rosalie. I can't remember her ever really caring about what anyone thought of her.

"So I want to hear all about these places you saw today," I said. "Between Ralphie and Jules chatting away at dinner about who they'd been texting from Philly—mostly Jules running on about who watched her video and who wanted to come to Saint Gilbert—I didn't get a chance to grill either one of you."

"So unlike you to miss an opportunity," Roe said.

"I know. Doesn't seem right." I sat on the settee next to her and eyed the tray of goodies that had been delivered while I was in the shower. A beautiful display of cheese, fruit, crackers, and some little pastries had been set up on a table near the fireplace. "So tell me everything."

Ceil spoke up enthusiastically. "Both contractors are terrific. I've worked with my share, and these two know their stuff. The exteriors of both the castle—that would be Gabrielle's—and the one belonging to our great-uncle Theodore are in good shape. His is actually more of a chateau than a castle—not fancy, no turrets or anything. Maybe add some downspouts to one, redo a patio on the other, some plaster repair, but for the most part, things look very good. We will need accessibility ramps added to both, and I'd like to see a terrace off the back of the chateau, but I've been told both are easy additions."

"And inside?" I asked.

"More work in there. First of all, we need all modern plumbing. All new electric systems. And I sketched out the interiors to show Gaspard—Gaspard Gauthier—where I wanted the actual spa area and how I wanted the private rooms set up. We also talked about a common room, which I doubt will get a whole lot of use—most of our ladies aren't going to be coming here to socialize with each other—but at the same time, we don't want to give the impression that we expect them to hide away the entire two weeks they're here, as if there's something wrong with going to a spa that's going to take years off your face and body."

"How long will all this take?" My stomach took a dip. It sounded like a lot of work. I'd wanted it all done *now now now* because I couldn't wait to get started and show off what we, as a country, had to offer. I was certain we would be the destination of the rich and famous (at least, the aging among the rich and famous) once the rest of the world caught up.

"When did you want it done?" Ceil asked, and I laughed.

"Is next weekend too soon?" I said.

"Realistically. And keep in mind I couldn't even get the promo ready by next weekend." She tapped the side of her wineglass. "However, I think a lot could be done in, oh, six or seven weeks."

"Mom always said it's not nice to tease." I gestured for her to pour some wine for me.

"Not teasing." She grabbed my glass by the stem and proceeded to pour. "The work inside is mostly cosmetic. Well, except for the plumbing and the electric work. Oh, and bathrooms, but the contractor said if he had free rein to hire he could get it done."

"Did he give you an estimate?"

"Just a ballpark." She sipped her wine, calm as always. "It's a big number. Stunning, actually. Guaranteed to get bigger if we give him 'free rein.'"

"Did you get it in writing?" I asked.

Ceil shook her head. "Not yet, but it's coming. He promised to have it to me no later than Tuesday. He has to check some prices first."

"A really big number?" I winced at the thought.

"Yup." Ceil smiled. "But if we want it done both fast and right, we don't have a lot of options."

"True enough. Give me a copy of the estimate as soon as you get it." I sipped my wine for a moment while I thought this over. I figured it would cost us a lot to renovate a couple of castles. "Tell him to make sure he gives us separate estimates for the two buildings."

"I already did. I figured if the number makes us gag, we do one building at a time." Before I could ask, Ceil added, "I'd go with Gabrielle's castle first. It needs the least amount of interior work."

"How do we know we can trust this guy?"

"Max suggested him, so he must know him. Ask him what he knows about his reputation. Though I have to say, going on my own experience with contractors, he did know what he was talking about. But oh—I almost forgot the most exciting part! The place is furnished! All this glorious furniture we can use! Someone had the foresight to cover everything so there's no dust, no fading fabric—thought that could be cool, you know, to give things an authentic antique vibe. But it's all there. You could almost believe someone was still living there."

"How is that possible? We know that during the occupations, furniture was stolen or destroyed."

"The story I heard from the guide who took us through was that Gabrielle fled the country right before the Germans arrived," Ceil said. "Remember, she was the first cousin of our great-grandmother, so she would have been aware of what had happened to the duchess and her family. Maybe when she fled Saint Gilbert, she managed to take some things with her, or bought a lot of stuff before she returned after the Soviets left. It's going to save us thousands."

"I wonder where she spent those years." I did wonder. So much of Europe was under German occupation during the 1940s.

"Maybe Switzerland? Maybe Italy, because she was married to an Italian count? They had a few kids, but the guide said there are no heirs, which is why we are able to get our hands on the castle. It belongs to the state now," Ceil reminded me. "I bet Claudette knows the whole story, though."

"The kitchens are going to kick ass." Roe hopped in the second Ceil paused for a breath. "Everything shiny and geared toward taking care of a crowd of pampered guests. Lots of refrigeration space for all the cheese and fruits and salads. It's going to be *gorgeous*. Our visitors are going to leave Saint Gilbert looking better and feeling better than they did when they arrived. The meals alone are going to be worth the price of the spa experience."

"We'll have to take that into consideration when it comes time to decide what we're going to be charging," I told them, even as I debated whether to tell my sisters about my conversation with Max that afternoon. Would they feel threatened? Frightened?

"Roe's drawn up a design for the tableware, and it's perfect," Ceil interjected. "Simple, elegant plates and cups and saucers—creamy white porcelain with only a sketch of the crown at the top. It all screams—albeit quietly—we're expensive and exclusive. Of course, they're pricey, too. We're thinking the promo should say something like, *You deserve to be treated like royalty. Come to Saint Gilbert and let the magic happen.*"

"I like it." I tapped Roe on the knee. "Good job."

"What, the dishes? Ha. The mere tip of my brilliance. Wait till you see the menus I'm drawing up. Oh, and Roberto was at the chateau checking his vines. He's working on a special wine that will be available only to the castle, but I'm thinking one special to the spa might be the way to go. Like, our visitors could take home a bottle or two, but it would only be available to those who have been 'guests' of the spa. And Roberto has the most amazing garden with a greenhouse where he can start vegetables early in the spring and keep the growing season going well into the fall."

"And Roberto is . . . ?" I leaned back and watched my youngest sister come to life.

"He's the son of the head gardener here at the castle—also Roberto—and he has the most amazing vision," she said, eyes shining. Not sure if the glow was there because of Roberto himself or his "vision," whatever that might be. "He's going to work with me to plant what I want to serve not only at the spa but here at home." She looked smug for a few seconds, then said, "Oh. I said *home.*"

"I guess you're feeling it," I said.

"I am, for sure. Oh, and you know, there should be a gift shop at the spa." Roe's eyes lit as inspiration struck. "We could sell the robes—Ceil and I were thinking dense white terry with the crown logo on the pocket—and the soap. Maybe the wine . . ."

"I don't think we should sell the soap for people to take with them," Ceil pointed out. "Maybe when they leave, a gift basket with a few bars to keep the magic going, but if we start selling the soap, won't it be easy for someone to analyze it and make it somewhere else and poof! So much for exclusivity."

"I don't think it would be that easy to re-create this stuff outside Saint Gilbert. I mean, we don't even know what's in it." I reminded them, "The ladies in the guild don't know what's in it and why it works the way it does. I'm not too worried, but I definitely would not want it sold outside Saint Gilbert. Giving our spa-goers a little parting gift is one thing. Letting someone else sell it alongside bars of Dove and Ivory in the supermarkets is something else." Thinking of protecting our exclusivity brought to mind something else. "And we need to make sure those goats don't leave the country."

"Right. We'll anoint them national treasures and make it a crime to sell the goats to anyone outside Saint Gilbert," Roe said.

I added, "A to-be-determined stay in the castle dungeon if you're caught."

"I agree," Ceil said, and Roe nodded her agreement just as there was a knock on the door.

Roe jumped up. "I'll get it."

Ceil was busy opening a bottle of wine, and I was scooping up some brie-like cheese onto a cracker that by itself was delicious. No wonder Roe was happy and felt so at home here. Saint Gilbert was foodie heaven, and, I realized, all her life, Roe had been all about the food.

"Here, I can take that. No, no, it's no trouble at all. Thank you so much for making this. We appreciate it."

I heard the door close and turned to see Rosalie carrying a large tray with a silver dome in the center.

"What in the world . . . ?" Ceil glanced up just as she was about to pour wine in each of our glasses.

"Nachos." Roe sat the tray on the ottoman in front of the chair Ceil was sitting in.

"Nachos?" Ceil and I said at the same time.

"In Saint Gilbert?" I leaned over and lifted the dome. "Those are sure enough nachos."

"I taught Emmeline, one of the cooks, how to make them. I thought the kids would like them, but I wanted us to try them first." The smug, happy smile was still on Roe's face.

The three of us dug in. For a few moments, the only sound in the room was the crunch of the tortilla chips and the occasional moan of joy as we indulged in salsa, guacamole, savory beef, sour cream, sharp cheddar . . . ahhhh.

"Am I the only one who's finding this"—I gestured at the plate of nachos—"almost sacrilegious? I mean, here we are in this luxurious room in this beautiful centuries-old castle, where since we arrived we've been served only the most elegant, sophisticated, glorious food . . . and we're eating nachos."

"Yes, and I'm happy for it." Roe scooped up another chip and bit into it. "The jalapeños aren't as hot as the ones back home, but these aren't bad."

Ceil nodded. "It did cross my mind to object on general principle, but the need for nachos has overwhelmed my better judgment and I can't help myself. But it is funny, now that you mention it, that we really haven't seen any junk food since we arrived."

"This is a country that understands food," Roe said between bites. "Even their snacks are beautiful and healthy and delicious. I don't understand why everyone here doesn't weigh about a thousand pounds, what with all the cheese and the sublime chocolate and the tortes. All of which make me deliriously happy, but still. Every once in a while, you need a little street food."

"Amen." I scooped up another beefy, cheesy chip, still trying to decide if I should tell them about my conversation with Max, when Roe piped up.

"We had double guards today," she said nonchalantly. "Because there's someone who's spreading rumors about us and what to do about us, I guess. Shoot us? Send us packing? Whatever."

My jaw dropped.

"Yeah, they're doubling security," Ceil added. "But I'm sure you know about that, Annie."

"Well, yeah." I tried to match their easy tone. "But who told you?"

"We overheard the guards talking when we were touring the castle. I asked them if they thought we were in any danger, and they said no, that they were there as a precaution." Ceil turned to me. "Were they right? There's no real danger?"

"That's what Max said, so I guess it's under control."

"Good, because we're having too damned much fun right now to have to worry about some yahoo trying to upend all this." Ceil took a sip of wine. "They did say that a bunch of new guards were being trained, so I guess that's a good thing, but I'm telling you, God help the yokel who tries to get between me and my castle. I have big plans for that place, and no malcontent had better get in my way."

"Are you sure you wouldn't want that place for your own? You don't have to spend the rest of your life living here, you know," I told her.

"I know. And I will find a place to call home. Right now, I can't focus on anything but getting the spa up and running. There are plenty of places in and around the city that I could happily live in. I'm in no hurry." She shrugged nonchalantly. "I'll know the right place when I see it. Gabrielle's castle doesn't feel like home to me."

I watched Ceil pick through the nachos in search of one with a lot of cheese and wondered why we'd reacted so differently to the same situation. Ceil was ready to kick anyone to the curb who got in the way of her fulfilling a lifetime dream of actually making over a castle.

I was seriously concerned about even a hint of unrest. Was it because I was the one who was being named in those rumors, questioning who I am, while she was the one having the time of her life, orchestrating a makeover of a beautiful and classic three-hundred-year-old building? After all, it was there that her responsibility ended. Or was it because, as the mom of two kids who at any given time could be anywhere in the country and therefore possibly at risk from a malcontent, I had a different stake in the stability of Saint Gilbert?

And then there was Roe, who seemed to totally dismiss the very thought of any threat. She had gardens to plan, exquisite dishes to concoct, and whole menus to write, and bless her heart, neither hell, high water, nor rebel factions were going to rock her world.

Wait—what? This behavior was so un-Roe-like. Who was this woman, and what had she done with my little sister? This woman was all dreams and joy for the moment. Her eyes sparkled as she spoke of her plans to create the most wonderful food on the planet.

Oh, she looked like Rosalie. Sounded like Rosalie. But I hadn't heard one negative word in . . . I couldn't remember the last time I'd heard her complain about anything. Maybe when we told her she couldn't drive in Saint Gilbert. But not so much as a contrary word since.

Huh.

Roe was seated on the floor, leaning back against the sofa. I poked her with my foot.

"What?" she asked without looking at me.

"You're in a pretty good mood," I said.

"Why wouldn't I be?"

"Nothing to complain about? Nothing to whine about?"

Roe shrugged but didn't respond. Ceil looked from me to Roe, then back again to me.

"Annie's got a point," Ceil said. "It's not like you to not find fault with something."

"What's to find fault with?" Roe picked up two of the last chips from the plate and took a sharp bite out of one of them.

"You usually find something." There. I said it. "And we're both wondering what's changed to make you so . . . oh, mellow might be the right word."

Roe ate the chips. Ceil and I waited for a response.

Finally, Roe said, "For the first time since Nonna Rose died, I don't feel as if I need to explain myself."

Huh?

"Roe, Nonna Rose died when you were . . ." I quickly calculated. I'd been eighteen, so Ceil had been sixteen. "You were fourteen when she died."

Roe nodded but didn't look at either of us. "November 9. Right after my fourteenth birthday."

"So I don't understand what you're saying."

Roe sighed a long, drawn-out sigh. "Nonna always made me feel . . . crap, I hate using 'hip' expressions, you know? Like, new clichés? But she always made me feel *seen*. Like she knew me and understood who I was. I never had to be anyone else when I was with her."

"Why did you ever feel you needed to be someone else?" I slid down to the floor to sit next to her.

"You're kidding, right?" She scoffed. "Daughter number three, coming in a distant third to you two." When I started to protest, she talked over me. "Sister number one, the pretty one, who also happened to be the smartest kid in her class. Sister number two, also pretty, athletic, smart, artistic. Where did that leave sister number three, who was neither pretty nor particularly smart compared to the first two. Not athletic, not artistic. Just—*average* in every way. Mom and Dad were always bragging about the two of you. Me? There was never anything to brag about. Average grades. Always picked last for games on the playground. Usually the last one called on in class if I actually knew something and got up the nerve to raise my hand."

"Aww, honey . . ." I put my arm around her shoulders. Closer to her, I could see tears in the corners of her eyes.

"But Nonna—she gave me something of my own. She taught me how to cook. By the time I was ten, I knew all her recipes by heart. She taught me everything I know about food and flavor and how to combine textures to perfection. The weekends I spent at her house were the best times of my childhood. When she died, I thought my life was over."

"Sweetie, I had no idea . . ." Ceil sat on Roe's other side. "Why didn't you say something?"

"Like what? What does a kid say when they're in pain and no one seems to notice?" She dug into her pocket and pulled out a tissue and blew her nose, then wiped her face with the tail of her shirt. "Anyway, she was my guiding star, my whole life." She blew her nose again. "Do either of you remember the night Nonna died?"

Ceil and I both nodded.

"The nurse had called and told Dad he should come over to the house, but she didn't tell him how bad things were. It was late when Mom and Dad returned home, and they both had red eyes from crying."

Roe nodded. "Dad came into my room and put something on my dresser. He was trying to be quiet. I woke up, but I didn't say anything. After he was gone and had closed the door behind him, I got out of bed and went to see what he'd left there. It was Nonna's recipe box. All her recipes, written in her hand, some of them in Italian, some in Italian and English. I knew without being told that she was gone." She fell silent for a moment, then added—as if we didn't already know—"That box and its handwritten notes are my treasures." Roe looked up at me. "Nonna knew me—saw me—in ways the rest of you didn't. I'm not blaming you. I was the pesky little sister and you two were so close, there wasn't any room for me."

"I'm so sorry," I said.

"Me too," Ceil told her. "I had no idea you felt that way."

"Neither did I." I swallowed back tears.

"It's okay. Really. But if you're wondering why I always saw myself through a lens that seemed a little dark, it's because I never felt I measured up, and when the one person who thought I was the best thing since sliced bread died, I felt like the lights went out and no one could see me. So yeah, everything in my life seemed to dim after that. What was there to be happy about? But coming here—I feel energized. I feel worthy of everything Nonna taught me. Everything she gave me. I feel like I've found my place, maybe even like she's here with me." Roe looked at me, then at Ceil. "I'm happy. For the first time since Nonna died, I feel like I'm in the right place."

"Come here, little sister." I went to hug her, but she pushed me away. At least she was laughing.

"Oh yeah. Sister hug." Ceil leaned in on Roe's other side. "Big one. All in."

"Stop! Go away!" Roe started to laugh. "Okay, fine. One hug. Then nachos."

"The nachos are gone," I told her as I pulled her closer. "But I know how to get more."

"In that case, you can both hug me." Roe was smiling, somewhat smugly, I thought, but it was okay.

Ceil and I both hugged her, and the three of us stayed in our group hug until the second round of nachos arrived. All in all, it had been a very good sisters' night, just like the ones we used to have back in Philly, but better. Roe was happy, and Ceil and I could see her very clearly.

Chapter Thirty

Breakfast the next morning was more subdued than usual. Roe begged off (wine headache), and Juliette was having breakfast in her suite with her friends, so it was Ceil and me for a while, then Ralphie showed up looking for leftovers.

"And how did the prince of the kingdom—er, duchy—spend his Saturday night?" I asked.

"My friend Henri stopped over and we watched a movie. He's Mila's brother, so he drove her over and stayed for a while." Ralphie ate a croissant or three before polishing off the last of the strawberries.

"What movie did you watch?" Ceil asked.

"A great American Christmas classic," Ralphie said. "*Die Hard*. Bruce Willis at his best."

Ceil snorted. "I'm sure that's not a Christmas movie."

"It takes place at Christmastime. It's a Christmas movie. Best. Ever."

"Jerk." Jules blew into the room. No Christmas spirit there.

"Good morning to you, too." I glanced behind her. "Where are your friends?"

"Remy's doing something with her grandmother, and Mila had to go to some family birthday thing," Juliette muttered.

"Her uncle's birthday party. Henri had to go, too," Ralphie said.

"Shut up. I hate you." Jules sat down in a huff.

"Whoa, what's going on?" It had been so long since the two of them had this sort of exchange, I'd thought she was kidding at first. But the look on her face told a different story.

"Okay, so me, Remy, and Mila were all set to watch our favorite movie, *Legally Blonde*, which stars Reese Witherspoon, only the best and coolest actress ever in the best movie in the entire history of movies and we know all the best lines and were psyched to watch it together? Then jerk-face and Henri came in and took off *our* movie and put on theirs." She was really getting into it. "I hate you."

"Hey, bros before ho—"

I jumped up and clapped my hand over his mouth. "Don't you even say it. Not one more word. Especially *that* word. I never want to hear that word come out of your mouth ever."

"Mom, it was just a joke." My son, who is almost six feet, two inches tall, tried to wiggle away from me, but I have an iron grip when I need one. I may be small, but I'm mighty.

"Really? And how was that funny? Explain to me the funny part, because it went over my head." I—as Mom and defender of my gender, and my daughter—was seeing red.

Juliette froze—she'd never seen me react like this before.

"Mom, everyone says—" Ralphie protested.

"You are not *everyone*. You are a *prince*. You're supposed to set an example." I loosened my grip but pushed him into the nearest chair. I had only begun to lecture. "You are not back in South Philly with your old friends, Ralphie. You're in a whole nother place now. You're an adult—well, almost. You have to decide who you are and who you want to be. You can be a smart-mouthed guy who thinks it's cool to hang out on a street corner for the rest of your life, or you can be something more. You can be the prince of the Grand Duchy of Saint Gilbert. But if you choose to be a prince, you'd better be worthy of it. You decide."

"Mom, I'm sorry." My son was ashen at this point. I guess maybe I'd gotten my point across. "I wasn't thinking about all that."

"Well, I hate to be the one to tell you, but from now on, you will have to be thinking about 'all that.' What you say and how you say it. There are a lot of little boys in this country who will learn from you either way. For better or for worse, they will look up to you and emulate you, their prince. Are you going to show them how to be a goof, a jerk, or a thoughtful young man?"

He paused. "Is this a trick question?"

I fought an urge to smack him. Not very royal on my part, but he knows better than to poke the bear. That would be me.

We stared at each other.

Finally, he said softly, "I get it, Mom."

"I hope so. Oh, I know everyone loves you right now. You leave the castle and people follow you and want to take their pictures with you. You visit a shop today and tomorrow there will be a photo in the newspaper along with an interview with the shopkeeper. 'What did he buy? What's he like?' The people of Saint Gilbert adore you. But they need to respect you as well. They need to see a solid example of a fine young man growing into adulthood, a young man worthy to represent their country." Okay, so I might have laid it on a little thick, but I was on a roll. Besides, desperate times, desperate measures. "You can do this through soccer, or by deciding on a career, or . . ."

"I thought my career was being a prince."

"A prince has to stand for something. He can't be a playboy. He can be a source of national pride or national embarrassment. He has to serve his country, earn his keep."

"So what are my choices?"

"Open your eyes. Look around, see what the country needs that you could help fulfill."

He pointed to his sister. "What's she fulfilling?"

"Juliette's videos already have gone viral. She's helping to build up what we hope will be a flourishing tourist industry. She's spreading the word to girls all over the world, and a lot of those young girls are showing their mamas those videos. They're going to want to come visit the country because Juliette is showcasing the highlights. They—and their mamas—could end up pumping some serious euros, not to mention American dollars, into the country's treasury."

Jules stuck her tongue out at her brother. He raised his middle finger in reply. Some things never changed.

I smacked his hand. "Knock it off, both of you."

I stared at Ralphie so he'd know I was still waiting for a response from him.

He finally caught on. "Can I choose soccer?"

"You can choose whatever you like, as long as it benefits the country in a positive way. Actually, soccer might be perfect. You could start up little soccer clubs in the villages and . . ." It really could be his niche.

"Organize tournaments." He nodded slowly. "Soccer for little guys. And girls, the girls can play, too."

"Raise money for a stadium," Ceil broke her silence and chimed in.

"I can do those things." Ralphie looked pensive. "I hope it's not going to be a problem that I can't remember to call it *football* here. It almost seems like a sacrilege."

"Understood," I said, because as a lifelong fan of the Philadelphia Eagles, this was tough for me, too. "You need to go to school, Ralphie. We haven't talked about school in a while, and you still have one more year of high school. You have to think about where you want to go."

"This could be my gap year. Then I could go to Switzerland for my twelfth year, or back to the States. Then I can go to college somewhere and get a degree in . . ." He paused and mulled it over.

"Maybe something like economics would be useful here in Saint Gilbert," I suggested.

"Economics sounds really hard, Mom. Maybe something easy. Like something to do with sports."

"Perfect." I knew if I knocked on that hard head of his long enough, something would get through.

"Oh, and by the way, Dad texted me. He wants me to come back to the States for a while." He tossed this out nonchalantly.

"Not a chance."

"That's what I told him," he said smugly and got up to leave the room.

"Whoa. Don't you have something to say?" I stopped him with a few pointed words.

"To who?" He looked surprised.

"To your sister, that's to *whom*," I said.

He looked at Juliette, who was once again glaring at him.

"I'm sorry, Jules. It won't happen again." He was trying to look contrite, but his sister wasn't buying it.

"Yeah, till the next time." She did know her brother well.

"Say it like you mean it, Ralphie," I told him. "And mean it this time."

"Jules, I am sorry."

"You ruined my first sleepover with my friends, Ralphie. They think I have the world's worst brother." She didn't say it, but the implied *and I do* was loud and clear.

"I'm *sorry*. You think of something I can do to make up for it, and I'll do it," he told her.

A slow smile spread across her lips. "Anything?"

"Okay," he agreed, but I could tell he wished he'd left that part out of his apology.

"So if I had my friends back again, you'll let us watch whatever movie we want?"

"Yeah."

"And you won't bother us except to make us popcorn and bring us snacks?"

He paused, then nodded. "Okay. I'll be your snack man for the night."

"Promise?" Juliette sat up. "Pinkie promise?"

"That's for little kids," he protested.

"Pinkie promise, Ralphie," she insisted.

"All right. Pinkie promise." He held out the pinkie of his left hand.

Jules shook her head. "Uh-uh. *Right*-hand pinkie. Everyone knows the left pinkie is for liars."

"Geez," he muttered as he grasped her right pinkie with his. "Right-hand pinkie promise."

"I forgive you for being such a jerk." Juliette dropped his finger and immediately turned her attention from her brother to the breakfast tray Ceil and I had shared, the same one Ralphie had plundered. "You guys ate all the croissants *and* all the strawberries?"

Ralphie had one hand on the doorknob. He looked at me, smiled, then channeled his best Diana Rigg as Olenna Tyrell in *Game of Thrones*. "Tell Juliette. I want her to know it was me."

Juliette tried to roll up a napkin to throw at him, but it was heavy linen so she didn't get much mileage out of it. Ralphie laughed and started through the door.

"Get dressed for church and meet us downstairs," I called to my son, then turned to my daughter and sister. "And you both should get moving as well. I'll meet you all in exactly thirty minutes at the front door."

"Mom, we went last week," Jules said.

"What did you promise your grandmother before she died?" I asked.

Grumble grumble, groan groan, but they were ready and waiting when Ceil and I arrived downstairs.

I had discovered there is a chapel in the castle. It's lovely and peaceful, and Claudette told me if I wanted to have the priest come there, he'd be happy to do that. But I liked going to the services at that sweet church in the city where generations of my family had worshipped. It really did make me feel that I was part of something so much bigger than myself. The royal family had a section off to the left side of the altar that reminded me of the box seats at the old Spectrum arena in Philly.

I'd been in one once when I was eighteen and won a contest the local sports radio station ran: be the sixth caller to name three of the Philadelphia Flyers who helped the team earn the nickname the Broad Street Bullies in the 1970s (Saleski, Schultz, Dupont). I took my dad to the game as my guest and we sat in a private box and it was the best night I ever had with my father. I think my love for Philadelphia sports was born that night.

Anyway. We went into the church through a special door in the back and filed into our seats. There was a fancy French-looking uphol-stered chair and an individual kneeler for each of us. The priest, Father Francisco, always seemed happy to see us and always asked the members of the congregation to pray for us, which I greatly appreciated. After the services, we went as a family to say a prayer at the graves of our ancestors in the cemetery behind the church before we left, something else that made me feel good.

Chapter Thirty-One

When we arrived back at the castle, Max was waiting in the reception area. After exchanging some pleasantries, he asked if I had plans for the afternoon. When I said I'd planned on working for a while—those remaining thank-you notes weren't going to write themselves—he suggested I change into something more casual and meet him out in the back courtyard after lunch. He wouldn't give me a hint of why, but since I'd meet him anywhere, at any time, for any reason, it didn't really matter.

So after lunch with my family, I changed into a pair of linen pants, a long blue tunic, and my ever-comfy white Keds. Escorted as usual by my two stoic guards—Sergei and Yves—I arrived at the grassy courtyard around two in the afternoon. I always loved coming out those wide French doors and stepping outside because the flower gardens were spectacular, colorful, and fragrant, the beds artfully placed. Whoever had designed them should be given a medal. I added that to my list of things to think about.

I saw Max standing midway between the castle and the lake with another man I didn't recognize. When they heard me approach, they both turned.

"Your Grace, may I introduce you to Fergus Taggart, who recently joined the castle staff as royal falconer." Max was smiling.

"Nice to meet—wait. We have a falconer?" My eyes grew wide at the thought. I'd been intrigued by the birds and the stories I'd heard about the falcon being my family's spirit animal. All the paintings and carvings throughout the castle had reinforced the tales.

"You have one now, madam. It's my pleasure to meet you." Fergus did a head bow.

"Fergus has come from Scotland, where he was a master falconer. He's agreed to reestablish the birds here in Saint Gilbert." Max said.

"Come and meet Sasha." Fergus gestured toward the old stables.

"Who's Sasha?" I fell into step next to him.

"She's the falcon I've been training for you," he said. "Let's hope you get along."

"You trained a falcon just for me?" I stopped midstep.

"I did, madam," Fergus replied in his rich brogue.

I had my own falcon! I could barely contain my excitement. I couldn't wait to see her and watch her fly.

I spent much of the afternoon getting to know Sasha and learning how to handle her. Watching her hunt on her own, seeing her soar off above the field and over the castle, I'd pray she'd come back to me and land on my leather glove–covered left hand and arm. She always did. It was exhilarating, watching that majestic bird catch the updraft and take to the sky, then seeming to float overhead before going into a lightning-quick dive. She was magnificent, and it was a thrill to watch. It was the single most fun I'd had since I arrived in Saint Gilbert, and I told Fergus so as he was returning Sasha to her cage.

"I can't thank you enough," I said. "This is the most wonderful gift. You've no idea how much I enjoyed these past few hours."

"You honor me, Your Grace, but thank your captain." Fergus nodded at Max. "He sought me out and lured me to Saint Gilbert with tales of how the monarchy and the royal falcons were linked. It's been my pleasure to train her. I hope you'll be back soon. The more you work with her, the more she will relate to you."

"I'll be back tomorrow," I promised.

"Sasha will be waiting." Fergus coaxed the bird onto a perch and replaced her hood.

"Thank you again." I looped my arm through Max's and we started back toward the castle. The terrain was slightly uneven, so I had a good excuse. "So you did this?"

"You'd expressed an interest," he reminded me. "I thought if we were going to bring back the falcons, we needed to find the best man for the task. I believe we did."

I wanted to put my arms around him and plant one big loving kiss right on his lips, but of course, I couldn't do that. Instead, I said, "Thank you. It was so thoughtful of you to find him and bring him here. I can't believe you kept this a secret. Sasha's the best gift ever."

"Well, we know that every grand duchess has had her own falcon. It seemed only right that you should have one, too."

"I'm going to come out here every chance I get and work with her. I'm going to become a real falconer."

"I have no doubt that you will. I think you can do anything you set your mind to."

We walked the rest of the way to the castle, the sun just starting to drop below the tree line. It was going to be a gorgeous sunset here in Beauchesne. As we drew closer and the ground flattened, I dropped my arm lest anyone see us and start rumors. It made me sad to know I had to be aware of such things, but it was for both our sakes. We reached the courtyard, and as we approached the back doors, two guards stepped out. They saluted Max, and he nodded in return.

"Which way, Annaliese?" Max asked once we were inside.

"My office," I said.

He escorted me to the door flanked by two guards, but before leaving, he went inside the suite with me. After looking around and deciding that no one had breached the security here, he turned to leave.

"Thank you again, Max."

"It was my pleasure."

"Same time tomorrow?" I asked.

"If your schedule permits."

I nodded. "We'll make it permit."

I turned on the light in my little office, and Max turned to go.

"Max, do you have a woman in your life?" I heard myself ask.

He smiled. "Several, Your Grace."

Of course he did. I should have assumed that. Why did I even ask? He was handsome and kind, he had a great sense of humor, he was honest, and damn it, if things were different, if I weren't the duchess and just Annaliese Gilberti and I was still living in South Philly, I'd have sent the kids to Ceil's house for the weekend and invited Max for dinner and whatever might happen after that. An image of the two of us flashed before my eyes. We were seated at the dining table at my little row house, enjoying a fabulous meal I'd cooked from scratch (so you know this is obviously a fantasy), sipping a nice wine and laughing at something he'd said. I'd put the flowers he'd brought me in my mother's favorite blue vase, and . . .

"Annaliese?" Max's voice broke through the vision. "Is there anything else I can do for you this afternoon?"

"No, thank you." I sat at my desk and pretended to go through some papers that I'd left the day before. "And thanks again for luring Fergus here."

Max smiled and left the room. I heard him speaking with the guards at the door for several minutes, then the hall fell as silent as the office. I tried to conjure up the dinner scene again, but the moment had passed and I couldn't seem to get it back. I picked up my pen and started in on another batch of thank-you notes.

I wish I hadn't asked about his love life. Competing with one surely gorgeous woman was one thing. (Would a man like him be romantically interested in anything less?) Competing with "several" was impossible.

Chapter Thirty-Two

It was late on Tuesday—so late I was thinking about dinner—when I heard someone in the outer office. Before I could get up from my desk to check it out, there was a soft rap on the door.

"Come in." Most likely it was Max or one of my kids, or my sisters.

I was surprised to see our chancellor step into the room.

"I apologize for coming without an appointment, but I saw the light from your office and . . ."

"My door is always open to you, Chancellor. Please, sit." I tried to sound gracious, like I always told my kids to be. "What brings you to my office today? I don't recall a visit from you in the past."

"In the past, there'd been no cause, but something's happened that I feel you must be advised of." He paused as he tried to catch his breath. "We should probably call Captain Belleme as well. He needs to be alerted to this situation."

I picked up my phone and sent Max a text. **My office please. I have company.**

"The captain will be along shortly. In the meantime, tell me what has you concerned."

"I hardly know where to begin." He shifted nervously in the chair. "I am hearing rumors, most disturbing rumors questioning . . . I hesitate to say this, Your Grace, but questioning your legitimacy."

"My legitimacy?" I frowned. As far as I knew, my parents were married for several years before I was born.

"Your legitimacy to have inherited the crown," he explained, his eyes down. "The latest 'question' being circulated is, who is the true heir?"

It took that a moment to sink in.

"What are you talking about? My grandmother . . ."

"Oh, madam, please, do not misunderstand. I am not the one asking the question. I know exactly who you are, who your mother was, who your grandmother was. I was part of the committee who searched for the rightful heir to the throne. We were very diligent. There was no one else."

"Then why would someone . . . ?" I really felt confused.

"I do not know, other than to wonder if perhaps there is someone else who feels she—or he—had a claim as well. No such person—man, woman, or child—was revealed by our efforts, I assure you. No one stepped forward even after we sent out a call for anyone who thought they might have a case, even though we'd known about you since the day you were born."

I forced a smile. "There was a time when I wondered if perhaps you felt you had a claim to the throne."

Vincens's smile was more sincere than mine. "There was no real threat from me or my family. We know that the crown was to be passed within the family of the duchess. The duke's side of your family had no standing."

"Do you have any idea who might be behind this?"

"I have been pondering this for several days. Could it be a hoax, someone who simply likes to stir up controversy? I do not have a clue." Vincens held out his hands, palms up.

"Nor do I," Max said as he strode purposefully into the office.

"The chancellor was just telling me that he has heard the latest rumor. 'Who is Annaliese Gilberti?' is now being followed with, 'Who is the true heir?'"

Max pulled a nearby chair closer to the desk. "We've located the leader of the January protests, Joseph Andretti. We spoke earlier today. He swears his group is not behind any efforts to delegitimize you. He's taking the position that since the majority of his fellow countrymen had voted in favor of the monarchy, their votes must be respected and that any protests he might attempt to mount would be a waste of time. After the coronation, his group disbanded."

"A wise move on their part," Vincens said.

"But he did tell me this: a few weeks ago, there was a message left on his phone." Max was frowning, which told me he was more concerned than he was letting on. "The person calling did not identify himself, but he said plans were underway to reveal Annaliese Gilberti as a fraud, and if he were a true patriot, he'd join in the effort to return the rightful heir to the throne."

"Did Andretti tell you who the caller believed was the true heir?" I asked.

"He did not. He told Andretti to call him the Royal Watchdog. Andretti dismissed it as a hoax and pretty much forgot about it until I contacted him."

"Your Grace, I assure you, the captain and I were both generational members of the council who followed your grandmother—later your mother, then you—so that when the time came, no time would be wasted in bringing our duchess home to Saint Gilbert." I had to admit that Vincens, while annoying in other ways, apparently was sincere in this. This situation has shown me a different side of him.

"Generational?" I asked.

"The sacred duty, the responsibility, to protect the duchy fell first to our grandfathers, then our fathers, then to us," Max explained.

"I see." I knew the part Max's grandfather played in getting my grandmother out of the country when the Germans were at the door, but I had not been aware that Vincens had also inherited a 'sacred duty' to protect the monarchy. Who knew?

"So what do we do? How do we find this guy?" The thought of someone running around the country besmirching my name and accusing me of being anything other than legitimate made me see red. I wanted to find this guy and set him straight myself.

"We will of course be searching for him, but with no clues as to his identity, we can only hope he will come to us," Max said.

I felt myself frowning again. "Why would he do that?"

"Perhaps eventually he will realize he needs some help from the inside if his case is to be taken seriously." Max and Vincens stared at each other.

"Perhaps we should give him a nudge in the right direction," Vincens said, still looking at Max. There seemed to be some sort of unspoken agreement, sort of like a Vulcan mind meld going on.

Vincens reached for the pad of legal paper on my desk. "May I?"

"Of course."

He began to write, and while he did, Max and I tried not to stare too hard at each other. I was thinking that we had to get to the bottom of this nonsense as soon as possible, sooner if it turned out not to be nonsense. I had no intentions of going back to Philly, my tail between my legs, for the entire world to see. My lineage was well known to everyone. But if in fact there is someone out there with a stronger claim than mine, the council had better figure out how this person was missed while the vetting process was going on.

What if I really was illegitimately sitting on the throne?

But no, it wasn't possible. I knew the story by heart. *Everyone* knew the story and knew it to be true. There was no question that my grandmother was exactly who she and everyone else said she was. And if she was really who she claimed to be, then it followed that I was as well.

So who was this person stirring up doubt, and why now? Why not before I was coronated, like, during the week I visited here? Or when my family and I moved here? Why wasn't something said then?

Vincens put down his pen. "This statement can be sent to the TV stations, the newspapers, and all the social media platforms."

He cleared his throat.

"This statement is being issued directly by a spokesman from the Duke's Council: While we unanimously stand behind Her Royal Highness, Grand Duchess Annaliese Jacqueline Terese Gilberti, we request whoever may believe there is another potential heir to the throne to step forward now in order that we might evaluate their claim." He looked up from the paper. "If there is no objection from you, Your Highness, I'm going to call an emergency session of the council for tomorrow morning. I agree—the earlier we identify this person the sooner we can shut down the innuendos. It is not in the best interest of the country to have such baseless allegations made. We need to have them shown as being without merit, the sooner the better." He looked from me to Max, then back again. "But only if you agree, madam."

Before I could respond, Max said, "I'm not so sure I want to give this person a sense of legitimacy without knowing who he is or what he wants."

I shook my head. "I agree with the chancellor. I think this needs to go out there as soon as possible. I'd prefer to flush him out rather than sit around waiting for him to show his hand."

Max remained unconvinced. "Right now, he is a gnat. Give him legitimacy, and he becomes a wasp."

"Excuse me, but I spent a good many summers at the Jersey Shore. I know how to swat a gnat, and I know how to slap down a wasp. If someone is spreading untrue rumors, let him look me in the eye and say it to my face."

"Let's see how the other members of the council feel about this plan," Max suggested. I could tell by the set of his jaw what he was hoping the other council members would say.

I turned to Vincens. "Go ahead and contact the others. Tell them we'll meet at nine tomorrow morning."

"As you wish, madam."

"Anything else?" I looked at Max, and he shook his head. "Then I guess I'll see you both tomorrow morning."

Max and Vincens left me alone in my office. I wanted to just take a deep breath and continue on with what I'd been doing before Vincens knocked on my door. But the truth was, I was uneasy, not knowing where this anonymous person was going to take this campaign of his. Were his stupid little innuendos a prelude to something else? Did he have others behind him who were ready to, I don't know, mount a coup? I tried telling myself that I was in good hands, that Max would never, ever let things get that far out of hand, but I still felt the need to put a brown paper bag over my mouth and breathe into it to stop me from hyperventilating.

For the first time in my life, I knew what it was like to think like Roe.

Chapter Thirty-Three

I could barely wait to get to the council meeting. Since the rumors had started circulating, had one of the members suddenly remembered someone who could conceivably have a better claim to the throne than me? For all their vetting, stranger things had happened, right? Or maybe one of the dukes had heard something connecting someone to the rumors. I went into the meeting hoping we could get a handle on what was behind the rumors and soon. I had no time for something like this. There was serious work to do—roads to fix, soap to make and a spa to open, tourists to attract—and this was an unneeded distraction. At least, I hoped that was all it was.

Just as I was about to step into the council room, I noticed Ceil about ten feet away totally engaged in a quiet conversation with a man who looked vaguely familiar but I couldn't place. He was a few inches taller than Ceil and very good-looking in a professorial sort of way, with his tweed jacket and glasses. He had dark curly hair and a pleasant smile, and he appeared to be as absorbed by what she was saying as she was by him. Like, people were walking around them and neither seemed to notice. Hmmm. So un-Ceil-like. We'd skipped breakfast this morning because we both needed to get ready for this early meeting, so I hadn't seen her yet today, but I was going to get the scoop on this guy.

"Ceil," I called to her. "The meeting . . . ?"

She nodded, and I expected her to follow me into the conference room. Instead, she followed him in. Did he not know this was a closed meeting?

Before I could point this out, Ceil caught my arm, turned me partway around, and said, "Annie, have you met Carlo DellaVecchio? He's new on the council as well."

"Your Grace, we met briefly at your coronation but didn't have an opportunity to speak more than a greeting," he said.

"Oh. Yes. Carlo. The chancellor's son." Of course. That's why he looked familiar.

Vincens had introduced me to several members of his family that day, but honestly, I didn't remember many of them. I met hundreds of people. I couldn't say I was pleased that the man who was giving my sister a happy glow was a DellaVecchio—I mean, his brother was a lecher as far as I was concerned, and his father had been the occasional pain in my butt since the day I arrived. I know it wasn't fair to judge someone on the basis of their relatives—would I want my kids to be judged by the character of their father?

Gosh, that's a tough one. No.

Then again, last night Vincens had come directly to me with his concerns about the whole rumor thing. That, and his "sacred duty" to the crown speech, had come as a big surprise, but he'd seemed sincere. So I should keep an open mind about Carlo, right? And Max liked him and had been the one to nominate him for the council in the first place, so we'll see.

"Carlo." Max came up behind us and gave Carlo a friendly slap on the back. "Glad to see you accepted the opportunity to join the council."

"As am I." At this, he looked directly at Ceil, who blushed.

Blushed. Ceil the unflappable actually blushed.

"Carlo is researching the origin of the goats," Ceil said.

He laughed good-naturedly. "My first official duty as minister of agriculture: find out where the goats came from. It's not as simple as it sounds, but I've been told there are some men in one of the villages who might know. I'll be meeting with them this afternoon."

I have to admit, that did impress me. "Thank you for acting quickly, Carlo. It may sound funny, but the goats are a big part of our plan."

"Princess Cecilia has been explaining the overall strategy to me, and I think it's going to be the key to turning around our economy," he said as we began to move into the room. "Who would have guessed, all these years, that it would be our soap that saved us?"

Other members of the council came in and we took our seats, the two new members seated together at the end of the table. The chancellor called the meeting to order and outlined the reason for the emergency session.

"I trust you all have heard the rumors," he said.

"Regarding the legitimacy of our duchess?" Emile Rossi shook his head. "What nonsense. Every man in this room will recall the efforts we made to ensure that the proper heir was named." He turned to address me. "I hope Your Highness has not been overly concerned. I would hate to think you've been upset by someone's idea of a prank."

"Is it a prank? Or is it something more? Perhaps someone who believes he is rightfully the heir, whether or not he is. I think we need to shake my family tree a little harder and see who falls out. For example, did my great-uncle Theodore have children? I know my mother's brother has a daughter, but . . ."

"But she is—not to malign your family, madam—wholly unsuitable," Andre DiGiacoma pointed out.

"She does have a prison record, as I recall," Jacques Gilberti said.

"I was told that was all a misunderstanding." I felt I should toss this in, in defense of the family. But since it had been her father relating the story in a Facebook post—maybe not so much a misunderstanding as wishful thinking.

"In any case, we know that none of your great-grandparents' children had issue other than your grandmother and her siblings. We know who our duchess is," Vincens said. "What we don't know is who is behind these rumors and what their endgame might be, but we have to find out. This insult to the crown cannot be permitted to continue. I have discussed this matter with Her Highness, and with her permission, I will read a statement I prepared last night." He looked across the table at me, and I nodded.

When he was finished reading, there was silence.

"You're asking someone to meet with you?" Andre sounded as skeptical as Max had the night before. "How do you know this person isn't unhinged? He may be dangerous."

"I will not be meeting alone with him," Vincens replied. "I assume Captain Belleme will provide ample protection?"

"Of course," Max said, "though I'm still concerned that we are giving this person an even larger platform than the one he's making for himself."

"If there's a better way to find out what's behind this, I'd like to hear it. Otherwise, I agree with the chancellor." I looked around the table. "I propose we vote. All in agreement with releasing the chancellor's statement, say aye."

Seven ayes.

"Since there are ten of us, and seven have voted to release the statement, there's no point in asking for the nays." I turned to Vincens. "I would like you to send your statement to every newspaper, television, radio, and social media outlet in the country. Let's see if anyone speaks up. Until then, I suggest we continue on with our business of running this country."

From there, I proceeded to bring the council up to date on the plans to renovate one of the unoccupied castles to use as a spa and the part it—and the soap—would play in the overall resurgence of the country. I turned to Ceil and asked her to tell the others what she'd found, what she'd planned to do, and what we hoped would be the outcome. Since none of this involved golf, polo, or race cars, most of them merely nodded their agreement to what was being proposed while they checked their phones.

"Excellent idea. The ladies will come to the spa, and their men can play golf," Dominic Altrusi commented, after which the other men on the council seemed to wake up.

"Or," I said pointedly, "the ladies can play golf while their significant others can go to the spa."

"Yes, yes, of course," someone said as they discussed their plans for the golf course with much more enthusiasm than they'd shown for the spa. But they did have a point. Spa plus golf equaled more tourists.

The council was dismissed, and a few minutes later, I was back in my office, seated at my desk, hoping that Vincens's statement would encourage someone to show their hand sooner rather than later. I hated the feeling that there was a large question mark hanging over my head, like one of those big cartoon balloons in the annual Macy's Thanksgiving Day Parade. Like everywhere I went, that question mark was going to be bobbing along, following me.

Around eleven in the morning, Claudette poked her head into my office.

"Madam, there is someone here to see you."

She barely got the words out when Marianne literally ran into the room. I couldn't remember the last time I was that happy to see someone. I grabbed her and hugged her and held on.

"I thought you weren't coming for another week."

"I got your house rented sooner than I expected, so I decided to surprise you. My cousin Kevin—You know, the cop? He used to date Claire Murphy?—was looking for a small house to rent. I called him, he came down to look at your place, loved it, agreed to a one-year rental on the spot." Marianne was still hugging me, and I realized we were jumping up and down like a couple of five-year-olds on the playground.

"So I handed him the key, packed my bags, changed my flights, and here I am."

"How'd your boss take it?"

"Not well. It means he actually has to do some work until he can replace me."

"No one can replace you, Mare." I released my grip on her after giving her another quick hug.

"True." One of the things I liked about her was the fact that she had always been aware of her own worth.

"The castle seems so much bigger without so many people milling around," she noted. "That great hall where you first come in? It was crowded when I was here for your coronation, but it looks absolutely cavernous now."

I nodded, wondering why I had never thought to refer to that area inside the front entry as "the great hall." I'd try to remember to do so from now on.

"So tell me everything that's been happening," we both said at the same time, and we laughed. We'd been doing that all our lives, almost as if we simultaneously had the same thought.

We had a lot to catch up on. I closed up my office and took the arm of my longtime bestie to take her on a tour of the castle's first floor. Then I wanted to show her to her suite of rooms (across the hall from mine) and settle in for some long overdue gossip.

"So bring me up to date," I said as we prepared to eat lunch in my private sitting room.

"Same old, really." Marianne was still googly-eyed from her tour of her own suite of rooms—smaller than mine, naturally, but still, spacious and beautifully appointed. "Oh my God, look at those strawberries!"

"I know, right? They grow them in the garden right here on the castle grounds," I said with no small amount of pride.

"You said the food here was fabulous, and everything they served over the week of your coronation was delicious. I'm going to love being here." Marianne was grinning from ear to ear. She always was the first person in line at the buffet. "So tell me what I'm going to be doing now that I'm here."

I explained that she'd be more or less interning with Claudette while she learned her way around the castle and who was who but that mostly she'd be my assistant. Answer my mail, remind me of where I had to be and when, handle my social media platforms, that sort of thing.

"You have social media?" she asked.

"Just general stuff. Like, 'Good morning, Saint Gilbert. It's a beautiful day in the duchy.' Like that. No personal stuff. Just to, you know, make people feel like I'm in touch."

"I can do that." Marianne was a great schmoozer, so I knew she'd do a good job there. "Love Juliette's videos, by the way. The girl's a natural. She's going to grow up to be a TV anchor. The next, you know, what's her name. Gilda Radner used to be her on *Saturday Night Live*."

"Barbara Walters." I nodded. I could see my daughter doing important interviews and things like that. Once she outgrew the giggle, of course.

That's how the day went. Catching up with my friend and feeling happy to connect with her in person. We had dinner with my family, and everyone was happy to see her. Afterward, Ceil and Roe filled her in on the plans for the spa and promised to take her to see the castle. We talked about "the rumor," and she predictably expressed her indignation and placed an Irish curse on the perpetrator. When we finally called it a night and everyone retired to their own rooms and I crawled into my bed, all the apprehension I'd felt earlier had slipped away, and I knew that whoever was out there trying to steal my thunder was not going to succeed. I felt like we'd called out the cavalry, and it had shown up wearing yoga pants, an oversize sweater, slightly teased hair, stiletto heels, and plenty of attitude.

Chapter Thirty-Four

I was still in a good mood the next morning, still relaxed, still happy. I shared breakfast with my sisters, my best friend, my daughter, and my son. My heart was full, believe me, to have all the people I loved there with me.

Ceil was once again describing her plans for the castle spa I could tell had become her pet project.

"I'd love to see it," Marianne told her. "When can I see it?"

"Is there anything going on today I should know about?" Ceil asked me.

"Not a thing," I replied.

"Then today's a good day," Ceil said. "The weather is perfect for a ride out into the countryside." She turned to me. "Unless you have something pressing, you should come, too."

"You haven't seen it yet?" Marianne asked, and I shook my head.

"Only in pictures that Ceil took," I said.

"Then you have to come with us."

Marianne was right. I should go. I should see this place where our country's fortune was going to be made. So far I'd left it all in Ceil's hands, and while I knew when it came to renovating houses and decorating them she needs no help from me or anyone other than a good contractor, I should be more than a casual observer.

"All right. We'll all go," I announced.

"Count me out," Ralphie said. "I'm playing soccer with Henri and some guys he knows. I'll see you all later." And with that, he was gone.

"Annie, wait till you see the grounds. The vineyards and the gardens." Roe stood, eager to get going. "Well, they don't look like much right now, but when Roberto gets finished with them, they're going to be fabulous. Our spa ladies will sit on that beautiful patio and look out over colorful flower beds and beyond to the grapevines." Roe sighed.

"Oh, that sounds glorious." Marianne was already on her way to the door. "I'll be back in a jiff."

"I think it's the lure of maybe finding the fountain of youth that's going to sell it, but yeah, the beautiful surroundings will be the icing. Losing the marionette lines will be the cake." I stood.

"Count me out, Mom," Jules said. "We're filming again. Today I want to talk about Serafina."

On her way out of the room, she paused for a nanosec to kiss my cheek, then she was gone.

"Hurricane Juliette." Ceil laughed. "Don't get in her way."

"I wouldn't think of it. Now you two go, change into something casual enough for the country but nice enough in case there's someone around taking pictures."

~

The drive from castle to castle was just beautiful. We passed field after field, some where goats and sheep grazed, some with cows, some with crops now reaching the end of their growing season, and some fields of wildflowers. We drove through villages of no more than a dozen houses that appeared to have been built centuries ago (which they probably were). There were vineyards where the grapes had been picked, and others where the vines were still laden with fruit. It was a perfect day to sightsee, clear blue skies and bright sun.

"I can see why you love Saint Gilbert so much," Marianne said after we'd driven through a picturesque village. "It's beautiful. We haven't passed by one house I wouldn't love to live in."

Before I could respond, Max pointed out that we were approaching our destination. "If you look off to the right, you can see the castle."

Marianne leaned forward. "Oh my God, I see it! It looks like a fairy-tale castle. Not as much as yours—I mean, your castle is straight out of a fantasy—but it sorta looks a little like yours only smaller and there are no turrets."

"It's perfect." Ceil was clearly in love with the place. "It's just the right size for what we want to do. Wait till you see inside, Annie. You're going to want to start the promo for the spa like, tomorrow, if not sooner."

"I can help you with that. I'm very good at writing promo," Marianne told her. "I did all the print promo for the insurance company Annie and I worked for. Of course, my boss took credit for it—he always said he just took my ideas but had to heavily edit them. Edit, my butt. He never changed a word. I know what I wrote."

"I'd forgotten all that."

"I didn't. Which is why it gave me immense satisfaction to give him notice I was leaving immediately. I spent the rest of the afternoon cleaning out my desk and saying goodbye to my friends, and there wasn't anything he could say that would change my mind. He threatened to tell any future employer that I was totally unreliable and had a bad attitude."

"Please. I've known about your attitude since we were in kindergarten. It's one of your finest qualities."

I could see Max's smirk in the rearview mirror, and I smiled when we made eye contact. I loved those quiet, secret moments when we seemed to be on the same wavelength. I just wished we could do something more than smile.

The castle came into full view as we rounded a curve. It sat on a rise overlooking the vineyards Roe had talked about and was as white as Castle Blanc.

"It looks so elegant," I said.

"Wait till you see the inside," Ceil said. "It's absolutely lovely."

As we drew closer, it became apparent the exterior could use a little work. Nothing major, just some touch-up here and there, and it needed some landscaping. Weeds were growing between the boxwood shrubs, and flowers popped up in random places. But those minor flaws did not detract from the simplistic beauty of the structure. Where it could have been embellished, it was restrained and sophisticated. I could imagine pulling up in front, two weeks of spa treatments already booked, and seeing this lovely building. I would definitely be impressed, no matter where I came from.

Max drove slowly to ease between two of those ubiquitous black cars. I guess our Bond team had arrived before us and were, assumedly, checking the interior for someone who wants to send me back to Philly.

"How many rooms, Ceil?" I asked.

"I think there are forty-five, thereabouts." Ceil was gathering up her bag, preparing to hop out of the car the second it stopped.

"Forty-five rooms?" Marianne's jaw dropped. "Definitely not in Kansas anymore."

Max stopped the car and, yup—off went Ceil as if she were racing someone unseen to be first inside. The rest of us got out and stood quietly admiring the castle and the setting.

"Roberto has been pruning the vines," Roe said. "He thinks we'll have grapes next year because the plants are well established. They just needed some cleaning up. Clip off the suckers, trim back the vines, that sort of thing. And then we can start making wine here, special for the spa." Roe closed her eyes and from the smile on her face, she was picturing the labels just as she'd once described to me.

"My little sister, the winemaker." I grabbed her arm and turned her in the direction of the front door. "Walk. We'll do the outside later."

She walked, and Marianne, Max, and I followed. Ceil was already somewhere inside. It was a warm day, but the castle was cool inside. The large windows let in lots of natural light, giving the marble tile in the entrance hall a glow. The ceilings were high and the chandeliers dripping with crystals.

"In here," Ceil called to us, and we followed the sound of her voice.

"This is what I'm assuming was used as a reception room. I'm thinking it should serve the same purpose now. You know, you arrive, you're welcomed at the door. There will be a huge arrangement of flowers on a table. Someone takes your bags up to your room, and you're led in here to have a glass of wine, maybe some cheese and some fruit. You sit and chat for a bit with the hostess." Ceil was drawing such a clear picture, I could almost get a whiff of that wine. "And then you're taken to your elegant room—your home away from home for the next two weeks—where a welcome basket is waiting for you."

"Oh, I can help with those," Marianne told Ceil. "I always did the gift baskets for our big clients at holiday times. Big baskets filled with goodies. Oh, you could do such fun souvenirs. You have that mermaid, right?" Marianne had been fascinated when I told her about Serafina after my first trip to Saint Gilbert. "You could do cute things with her as a logo."

"I'll definitely get back to you when we get closer to opening day," Ceil told her, but I couldn't tell if she was humoring Mare or if she really was intrigued at the thought of putting Serafina on souvenirs. With Ceil, you couldn't always tell.

"And check this out." Ceil lifted the covering from a settee, then stood back to show off its delicate white legs and rose-and-white-striped fabric. I ran a hand over the seat, and it sure felt like silk to me.

"Wow. It's beautiful." I went from one covered piece of furniture to another, peeking underneath the sheets, and I couldn't help but marvel at the treasures. "Ceil, any idea how long this stuff has been here? It's all in perfect condition. I can't believe someone didn't just come in and help themselves."

Marianne looked around the room. "Yeah, like, no graffiti or anything rude written on the walls. Back in Philly, a place like this would be trashed the minute someone left."

"I guess it would have fared the same in any city," Roe said.

I looked at Max, who was leaning against the doorway looking amused—one of my favorite looks for him. "Any thoughts on that?" I asked.

Max shook his head. "None, Your Grace."

I shot him a look and mouthed *Annaliese*. He nodded, but I knew in front of a group he was going to keep to formalities. We heard the sound of footsteps on the stairs, and he went to investigate.

"So how long do you think?" Mare asked. I peeked into the hall to see who'd come downstairs and saw a small band of Max's guards in quiet conference with him. He motioned to the room we were in, and four of the guards moved to stand in the doorway. Max followed several of the others up the steps.

"... so who knows?" Ceil was saying when I tuned back in. "I asked Claudette what she knew about Gabrielle. She told me that Gabrielle and her family moved to Switzerland to sit out the war, and they took everything with them. Sometime in the late 1990s or the early 2000s, things were brought back by Gabrielle's grandson. Great-grandson? He died in 2017. Never married. No children."

I nodded as if I'd been listening all along when in fact, I was trying to figure out what had sent Max up the steps so quickly.

"Now, come into the dining room," Ceil was saying. "It's extraordinary." She continued talking as she led us on through the house. "Look at that chandelier! I've never seen one that big or that beautiful. The scrollwork around the top piece was all hand-painted. And check out this table! I feel like all these lovely things have been waiting for me to find them and bring life back into this place."

And so it went, room to room, Ceil calling our attention to this piece or that, all the time marveling at the artwork and the furniture, the rugs, and the many little things that had been sitting idle for years. Ceil clearly had hit the decorator's lottery. She showed us where she thought the spa should be located, where the aestheticians would do their thing, lathering up the faces and necks of the women—and of course the occasional man—who would come here seeking a new lease on life. Then we went upstairs and she showed off the bedroom suites where our future spa-goers would stay. Some had balconies; all had private baths and large closets and gorgeous views. The spa at Saint Gilbert was going to be like nothing else in the world. The very thought of such success made my head spin. This was going to happen.

"Ceil, we're going to need a timetable from the contractors. And a professional photographer. And some really effective ad copy. Mare"—I turned to her—"work with Ceil on that, and we'll see if what you come up with is . . . well, *good enough* won't be good enough. Not to be critical, but we have a lot at stake here. The copy has to have zing."

Marianne rolled her eyes. "Oh, please. Zing is my middle name."

"Then now's the time to bring it." I watched her and Ceil wink at each other, a good sign they'd work together to make our initial promotion a success. I had no doubt after the first wave or two of spa-goers, we wouldn't need as much promo. Word of mouth and unretouched photographs were going to sell this place.

I stood in the center of the second-floor landing—almost as large as the foyer below—and wondered where Max had disappeared. Except for the four of us chattering away, the rest of the house was silent.

"What's upstairs?" I asked.

"The ballroom and a few drawing rooms, a small private dining room. It's gorgeous, but I have no idea what we'd use it for. Then on the fourth floor, there are more bedrooms, smaller than these, though.

They probably used those originally for their live-in help. I'm sure they had a large staff of maids and cooks and whoever else a castle required to function. I'm not sure we would use those rooms. I wouldn't want anyone to feel as if they are second-class citizens."

"Good point." I looked up at the staircase.

"The fourth floor also has several large storage rooms. A trunk room with some of the old trunks still in there. They might be fun for Juliette and her friends to go through. Maybe there are some old dresses and hats. Remember how much we loved playing dress-up when we were little?"

"I do. I'll definitely tell Jules to check it out. That could be one of their videos." I was picturing the girls dressing up in old fashions. I was also thinking about going up and checking out those trunks myself when Roe grabbed my arm.

"Can I please show you the kitchen now?" She was almost pleading.

"I can't wait to see it, Roe." Actually, I could—I was more intrigued by the thought of finding fun things in the trunk room—but I knew the kitchen was all Roe's, and she was excited about the things she planned to do there.

We all went back down the wide staircase and through a hallway into a large open space in the back of the house.

"This is it." Roe's eyes were shining. "Okay, picture a huge stove right here, a second one right next to it. Then an enormous refrigerator over there, a double sink under the windows, and two extra-large dishwashers right alongside the sink." She spread her arms expansively and grinned as she described her vision. "I know we won't need double everything when we first start up, but down the road, we will. A mile of counter space for prep work. There's a butler's pantry behind that door." She walked across the room to show it off. "Come look at all the shelves. I can store a lot of stuff in here. Isn't it all just perfect?"

We all dutifully looked and oohed and ahhed for her sake.

"It is perfect," I agreed. If she was happy—and it was clear she was—I was happy. Plus her happiness would spill over into the food she made for our patrons, and that did make me happy.

"Oh, Roberto's here." Roe had glanced out the window, then she lit up like it was Christmas morning. "Looks like he's working on something in the orchard."

Roe sped off in the direction of the orchard, and we didn't see her again for a good half hour.

We were halfway through our tour of the grounds when Roe joined us. She had a goofy smile and didn't even chide us for starting off without her.

"Roberto's pruning the apple and cherry trees today. Tomorrow, he'll work on the fig trees. When I think of what I could do with a big crop of figs . . ."

"I think you're imagining what you could do with Roberto," Ceil said.

"Funny. I was thinking the same thing," I chimed in.

Roe nodded without hesitation. "Oh yeah. That too."

"The grounds here are gorgeous," Marianne noted. "That back patio would make a perfect little café-like spot." She looked over the vast lawn leading to a reflection pool. "There's no end to what you could do with a property like this."

"I think right now we have more ideas than we know what to do with," I said. "We should write them all down and then go through them and see what makes the most sense to begin with."

"Speaking of much to do," Ceil began slowly. "Remember how we talked about using one of the castles or chateaus—not sure which is the proper term—"

"I think chateau might be French for little castle," Roe said.

"Whatever we want to call them. Uncle Theodore's place would be perfect for a wedding venue, like we talked about. It has such a grand staircase, and it also has a ballroom. I think maybe twenty bedrooms and baths—I meant to count but I forgot. And the grounds are so pretty. There's actually a small lake behind the castle. You can't see it from the back of the building because there are so many trees in the way. The place is empty—we'd need to furnish that one—but it could be a real moneymaker. We could also use it as a hotel."

"We could sell a package—a week before the wedding at the spa for the mother of the bride and/or groom, then the wedding at the castle," I mused.

"Don't forget the older brides," Marianne noted. "I'll bet there are a lot of older women getting married who'd love to wash a few years off."

"Or we could offer a discount for the older bride and groom together," Roe said. "We could call it the Senior Special."

We all chuckled, but Mare and Roe were both onto something that we should explore at some point. Just not today. Today we were all relaxed, and for a while it was just like old times when Marianne would come over to our house and the four of us would just sit and talk about *stuff*. But soon enough, Max appeared and announced it was time to leave.

Mare and Roe both fell asleep on the way home, but Ceil and I were wide awake with our thoughts, she thinking about her castle renovation, me wondering where Max and some of the other guards had disappeared for over an hour. When we returned to the castle, he excused himself, then took off as soon as we got out of the car, leaving us in the care of the four guards who'd been with us at the castle, and me wondering where he'd gone in such a hurry.

Chapter Thirty-Five

By breakfast the next morning, I thought I knew what had put the bee in Max's bonnet. A new full-page announcement in yesterday's local paper—and apparently in all the papers in the country as well as on the social media accounts of someone who called himself the Royal Watchdog—asked, *Why does a foreigner sit on our throne?* I would have missed it completely if I hadn't left the paper on the table next to the love seat in my sitting room. I hadn't had time to look through it in the morning, so I'd left it to read when I got back from our outing but forgot about it until this morning.

Why does a foreigner sit on our throne?

Well, I suppose that was food for thought, but what exactly did he—Andretti had confirmed a male voice had left the message on his phone—want? Was he expecting me to quietly leave Saint Gilbert?

Don't hold your breath.

I tried not to think about it too much. I had a meeting with Jacques Gilberti and his son, Alaine, the engineer, who'd flown in earlier in the week to evaluate our existing roads and to see where new roads might be most efficiently built. I wanted to give them my undistracted attention because the roads were a big deal. That took most of the day, since we talked at length, then had lunch, then had taken a drive to see where Alaine had suggested repairs and where he thought new roads would most logically be cut in. At the end of the day, I was optimistic, because there was little we could really do to lift up this country if we couldn't get around in it. I told Alaine I'd like him to address the council directly, which he agreed to do if we could schedule that within the next week.

After dinner and a short visit with my family, we all agreed to turn in a bit early. The last few days had been busy, and we were all tired. Then I turned on the TV in my sitting room and bam! The city's major television station was covering the "who is Annie and why is she on our throne" story. At first, both the anchors appeared to be treating it as a joke. But toward the end of their banter, one said to the other, "I do recall the Duke's Council's announcement that the heir to the throne had been located in Philadelphia in the United States and that a contingent had been sent to discuss with her the possibility of returning to Saint Gilbert to take over where her great-grandmother had left off. As I recall, everyone was pretty happy about it."

"Right," newsperson number two agreed. "A spokesman described in detail how, through the years, members of the council had been in touch with the exiled former duchess and how they'd searched every inch of the Gilberti family tree and were one hundred percent positive that Annaliese Gilberti was in fact the rightful heir. The *only* rightful heir. So what's the point in starting these rumors when we all know the truth? Who do you think is behind it?"

The first anchor shook his head. "I have no idea. I think it's silliness, frankly, and a waste of our time to even talk about it. But there's one rumor I hope proves true: I heard there are plans to repair the roads between Beauchesne and the ski slopes."

"I hope it's more than a rumor. The slopes have been off limits since I was a child because the roads are a mess and the lifts are unsafe and . . ."

I turned off the TV and sat on the love seat, staring at the wall. I could probably have overlooked *Who is Annaliese Gilberti?* if everyone else had let it drop. I mean, it could have been some promo for a hastily written book, right? Even "who is the true heir?" didn't get under my skin the way this latest did. This felt different. It felt mean and personal, and its intent seemed to be to get people to talk about that very thing: Why was I, born in the USA, ruling their country? Everyone knew the story and seemed to be fine with it—except this one person. So the real question was, who is this person?

I know Max and his "eyes and ears" were on high alert, and I believe even Vincens was making an honest effort to find out who and why. But the more I thought about it, the crazier it was going to make me. The best thing I could do for myself right now would be to go to sleep.

Just as I was about to change into a nightgown—I'd purposely tossed my old nightshirts because if something happened in the middle of the night and I had to leave my room, how embarrassing it would be for me to appear in the hall wearing a long, faded *Nutcracker* T-shirt— my phone rang. Max. Calling no doubt to see if I was up for some fun in the moonlight.

A girl can dream, can't she?

So I answered the phone, and before I could speak, Max said, "I think we should talk."

"Now?"

"Yes."

"Did something happen? Did our anonymous friend respond to the chancellor's invitation?"

"Not to my knowledge. But I do need to speak with you."

I looked down at my bare feet and thought about finding my flats or my slippers, then figured the hell with it.

"You're going to have to come up here," I said. "I'm too tired to make myself presentable."

He hesitated for a moment.

"If you're worried that someone will start a rumor about you coming into my room at night, you're just going to have to live with it."

"I'll be there in a few minutes."

"I'll have coffee waiting." I went into the bathroom and checked my appearance in the full-length mirror. There was no time to do anything more than put on a minimal amount of makeup—mascara and maybe a little blush.

"Thank you. That would be appreciated."

We hung up and I called the kitchen. After apologizing for the late call, I told the person who answered the phone what I would like brought up. I knew from experience that when I requested something, it showed up in the snap of my fingers. Tonight was no different. While I was speedy with a mascara wand and a blush brush, the kitchen was just as quick. A tray with coffee and the ham biscuits, pastries, and fruit I'd asked for arrived at almost the same time as I turned off the bathroom light. Max was at my door minutes after the tray arrived. The timing all around was perfect.

"Please sit," I told him. "You look exhausted."

He nodded and sat on the settee in the bedroom. "It's been a long day."

I poured coffee for both of us and handed him a cup.

"You've no idea how welcome this is." He took a few sips.

"Did you have time to eat today?"

He shook his head, no.

"I suspected as much." I uncovered the plate of sandwiches and told him to help himself.

"We need to talk first," he protested.

"I want to make sure you don't pass out from hunger or fatigue in the middle of the telling." I pointed to the plate of biscuits, and he put two on a small plate.

While he ate, I talked, and he responded.

"Max, where do you live? You don't live here in the castle, do you?" It occurred to me to ask since he seemed to be just minutes away at all times.

"I have a home, a small chateau, outside the city," he said.

"Does Claudette live with you?"

"She has a town house here in Beauchesne, but when I have things to do at night, she will stay with Remy either at my place or at hers. Sometimes my daughter prefers to be in the city, closer to her friends."

I admit to being really curious about the things he did at night, but I didn't have the nerve to ask. Someone once told me to never ask a question if I wasn't sure I'd like the answer. Words to live by.

"Has Remy shown you the video she and Juliette made?"

He finished chewing a bite. "It's surprisingly good. I didn't know what to expect when she told me what they were doing. But I must say, I'm impressed with what I've seen."

"It's the perfect promotion piece for Saint Gilbert right now, an excellent introduction to the country. They're gaining thousands of watchers every day."

He finished both biscuits and took a few more sips of coffee before returning the cup to the saucer. "Thank you, Annaliese. That was very thoughtful of you."

"You're welcome. Now, what's so important it couldn't wait until the morning?" I asked. Not that I objected to having him there.

Max leaned forward a bit toward the table, his forearms resting on his thighs. On the opposite side of the table, I did the same. Another foot and we'd have been forehead to forehead. I wished.

"Calls have been made to the castle regarding the identity of the person who's planted the rumors. This self-proclaimed Royal Watchdog."

"You have a name?" My heart sped up. Oh, how I wanted to have my turn interrogating this guy.

"Not yet. But several of the callers have described the same person. A man a few inches less than six feet tall, slender build, dark hair, slightly receding hairline, between the ages of forty and fifty. He's been in some of the local pubs over the past week talking to whomever will listen."

"Talking about . . . ?"

"You. All the callers say he seems obsessed with you and your family. He thinks the council was hasty in accepting you, talks about how there is someone more deserving to be in your place, that sort of thing."

"Do you have a list of the callers? Can you bring them in so we can talk to them?" I remembered my old claim adjuster days, how sometimes stories changed when you sat down and looked a witness in the eye. Sometimes a casual conversation could help bring to light things they'd forgotten.

"We have their names and numbers recorded on the castle line. We will spend tomorrow tracking them down. In the meantime, I have guards in plain clothes in all the pubs this man has been known to frequent."

"I want to be in on any conversations you have with anyone he's talked to," I told him.

"Of course."

"He's saying someone else is more deserving but he's not saying who?" Curious, I thought. Why not just put it out there?

"Not yet, but I suspect that's coming."

"So we won't know until he tells us, or until he's found." I'd been hoping for more definitive news, but okay, this was something we didn't have this morning. "So, about yesterday. At Gabrielle's castle. Where'd you disappear to?" I think he believed I hadn't noticed.

"Hmmm. I do not recall disappearing."

"Yes you do. You took off up the steps to the upper floors like a rocket. What was up there?" I narrowed my eyes, hoping he understood that meant I knew he was withholding something and I wasn't going to let him get away with it.

He sighed. "In checking the castle before you and your family arrived, the guards found that someone has been sleeping in one of the third-floor bedrooms. Now, it could be a vagrant, it could be young people who think they've found a place to be alone, a safe lovers' rendezvous, perhaps. Or it could be something else. We're not sure. But there was a glass in one of the bathrooms that we took to have tested for . . ."

"DNA." Of course Max would jump on that. "Which would only be useful if that person's DNA was on record somewhere where he could be identified, or if it matched someone else. If you're looking to match someone in the Gilberti line, of course, you're going to start with me. That's the thinking, right? This person is related to me?" I started pacing, forgetting my bare feet. "Isn't that most logical? Who would even think of questioning my right other than someone who felt they were more entitled? The underlying message from this guy seems to be that the council picked the wrong person, even though you all were certain there was no one else. I know you must be wondering if you looked hard enough."

"I don't know where else—how else—we could have searched. We went through every branch of your family, generation after generation. We were—we still are—positive we got it right." Max was adamant, certain they had not made an error.

"And yet someone is convinced you got it wrong."

"So it would seem."

"So you test that glass for DNA and you compare it to mine—I'm available for swabbing anytime—and see if we're related. It won't tell us who he is, but at least we'll have a better idea what we're dealing with." I thought for a moment. "It can't be a coincidence that someone's staying in Gabrielle's castle at the same time all these rumors have started. Are we certain that none of her descendants are still alive?"

"We saw the death certificates of all three of her children. The last of her line died in 2017. It's well documented."

"Could someone have fallen through the cracks? Maybe she had another child after she and her family moved to Switzerland."

"I can't believe no one would have known. Surely a record would have been made. But it wouldn't have made any difference. Gabrielle's mother was never in line for the throne, nor was she. Therefore, none of her descendants would be. Your great-grandmother was always destined to become the grand duchess. The crown rightfully passed to your grandmother even though she never had a chance to wear it after her mother's hasty abdication."

"Maybe someone doesn't know that Gabrielle was never in the queue."

"If someone believed they were the legitimate heir, why would they have waited this long to make their case? And why not bring the matter directly to the Duke's Council if you believe you have a case? Why all this nonsense?" Max rubbed the back of his neck.

"I don't know. Maybe he believes if he gets people to thinking about me not being the real duchess, they'll be more amenable to accepting someone else. Then where does he think he could go from there? Stir up a revolution, then reveal himself as the real deal so he can step into my place?"

"We'll have to find him before he can make any of that happen. But we will find him." Max stood. "It's late. I should go and let you get some sleep. Thank you for seeing me at this hour. I wanted you to hear directly from me what was transpiring."

"Thank you, Max. Anytime." And I meant that. *Any* time.

There were voices in the hall outside my door, and I startled.

"It's just the changing of the guard," Max explained. "It's midnight. But . . ."

"But . . . ?"

"It's a bit awkward with the two of them out there and me in here."

"You can wait it out, if you want. Stay as long as you want." I was trying not to be too blatant.

He smiled, and I thought, *Yes!*

Then he said, "I should have thought of it sooner. Your sitting room is through that door?" He pointed.

"Yes . . . ?" Was he thinking about bunking in on the love seat? Nowhere near big enough for a man as tall as he is.

"Come with me." He grabbed my hand, and my hopes started to rise as he led me into the sitting room.

Then he dropped my hand and began to feel his way along the molding next to the fireplace.

What the hell?

"Max, what are you doing?" I turned on a lamp.

"There should be a . . . ah yes, here it is." He looked over his shoulder at me, and I thought I saw a gleam of mischief there, right at the same time a panel slid away and disappeared behind the fireplace.

"A secret passage?" I momentarily forgot my disappointment. "There's a secret passage in my room? Oh, I wonder who built it. Who used it?" I raised my eyebrows.

"The passages, like the secret rooms, were built in when the castle was first designed. Now, for what purpose?" He shrugged. "Maybe it was an escape route in case the castle was attacked."

"Maybe it was intended to keep secrets," I offered.

"Maybe. But tonight, it will serve to deflect any rumors that might start if someone saw me leaving your room at midnight." He stepped halfway into the opening. "I'll see you tomorrow."

"Max, are we in danger from this guy?"

He shook his head. "He will never get near you, Annaliese. Every man and woman in the castle guard would lay down their lives for you."

"Would you?"

He responded without hesitation. "Without question."

Without thinking, I stepped forward and raised my hand to touch the side of his face, and oh my God, it was just like a scene from a movie, only better, because it was real. We stared into each other's eyes, and I went up on my tippy-toes to kiss him, but he beat me to it. He kissed me. Max Belleme kissed me. And oh, mama, what a kiss it was! It was hot and sweet at the same time, and may I say, I know more than a few men who could take lessons from the captain. (Let's be real—I've been divorced for a long time and during those years, this duchess has kissed her share of toads.) Honest to God, I thought my heart was going to burst right out of my chest, it was beating so fast. Max wrapped those arms around me—like iron bands, he is one strong guy—and I just about melted into a puddle. As kisses go, this was an A-plus-plus-plus. When we finally broke apart—neither my idea nor my move—we just looked at each other.

I said, "If you are thinking about apologizing, so help me God, I will have you locked in the dungeon and chained to the wall."

He gently touched the side of my face, then bam! He disappeared into the dark passage.

I stood alone in the sitting room for a long time, just savoring the moment. I'd wanted to kiss that man since . . . well, practically the first time I met him. Was it worth the wait? Oh yeah.

My only regret was that it had to end.

Chapter Thirty-Six

I was still feeling a little swoony the next morning. I'd been awake half the night thinking about it, and I woke up, not exactly singing, but I could have. For a short time, I forgot about the mystery man—the Royal Watchdog—and his rumors and just wanted to sit with my legs curled under me, a cup of the divine castle coffee in my hand, and relive that moment when I kissed Max and he kissed me back. Or had he kissed me and I kissed him back? In any case, he hadn't pushed me away or looked as if he wished I hadn't done it. Frankly, he looked pretty pleased with himself. However, family members were gathering for breakfast and there was work to do.

I dressed quickly and joined the others, who were already chowing down on soft-boiled eggs, croissants, and pastries filled with cream cheese and blackberries. I followed the banter without chiming in for several minutes before Marianne tapped me on the knee.

"So what's with you this morning? You're awfully quiet," she noted.

"Tough to get a word in, the way you guys go on," I said.

"And in the past, that had stopped you . . . when?" Ceil asked.

"I guess I just have a lot on my mind." I couldn't bring myself to announce *I kissed a duke and I liked it.*

"Well, you do, what with everything you're trying to do—that list of yours is as long as Mrs. Rinaldi's grocery lists. Remember her?" Ceil, who sat next to me on the settee, nudged me, and we both laughed.

"Who's Mrs. Rinaldi?" Marianne asked.

"She lived across the street from us when we were growing up. She used to give Ceil and me a dollar each to go to the market for her. She'd give us a list with everything she wanted and enough money to pay for it all, down to the penny."

Ceil bit off the last bit of the blackberry pastry. "This is so good. Honestly, the pastry chef here could work anywhere in the world. She is that good."

"Yeah, but don't tell her. I'd hate for her to leave us for some fancy restaurant somewhere." Marianne sighed. "Keep feeding me like this, and I'll never go back to Philly."

"That's sort of the idea," I said. "Since I've made up mine that I'm never leaving. I can't remember when I've ever been happier. I really have grown to love this country."

"I have to admit, I'm pretty happy myself," Ceil said. "When would I ever get a chance to do over a freaking castle? I'm not going anywhere."

"Chef for life here." Roe pointed to herself. "I'm not leaving, either."

"I am," Juliette announced. When the adults in the room all turned to stare at her, she added, "Well, not right now. Mom, do you think we could get a tutor for me this year? I wanted to go to school in Switzerland with my friends, but you have to speak French fluently to get in, and I don't speak a word other than, like, you know, *croissant* and *merci* and *bonjour*."

"Well, they're three words less you'll have to learn." I stood and stretched. "We'll look into a tutor. Right now, it's time to get moving. I have a meeting at nine with Andre DiGiacoma about money. What are the rest of you doing today?"

"I'm working in the greenhouse with Roberto," Roe said, a silly grin on her face. "I told him I was going to want microgreens for salads for the castle and for the spa kitchen, so he told me I should learn to grow them myself. I'm excited."

"As anyone would be," Ceil deadpanned.

"You'll thank me when your salads are bursting with nutritious sprouts."

Ceil nodded. "I'll be sure to do that."

"And what does the day hold for Cecilia?" I asked.

"Looking at fabric with Gisele. I don't know anyone else in the city who has a direct line to fabric manufacturers, so I thought I'd go over our spa needs with her. You know, upholstery and drapes and such. Oh, and I thought I'd talk to the wool lady."

"The wool lady?" *We have a wool lady?*

"The woman who owns the yarn shop. She's the one the sheep farmers bring their wool to, and she cleans it and does whatever it is you do with raw wool to turn it into yarn. She has blankets knitted from that yarn that Gisele tells me are heavenly. I thought we'd look into having her make some throws for the spa."

"Great idea. Maybe use the colors from the flag. You know, that pretty blue and the white."

"That's the idea," Ceil said.

"I'm making a video with Remy," Juliette announced.

"Where?" I asked.

"Not sure. We have a few ideas."

I thought about the nameless guy chatting up strangers in the pubs. Regardless of how many guards Max might have, I still felt uneasy.

"Stick close to home today, okay?" I thought about the Royal Watchdog and wondered if he was watching anyone besides me. "But if you feel it necessary to leave the castle grounds, take your guards. Maybe an extra one or two."

She blew me a kiss and was gone that fast.

"Don't go anywhere without your guards, Jules." Too late. She was already gone. But I needn't worry. The guards would never let her leave the castle alone. Just like they never let Ralphie take off on his morning run or for his afternoon pickup soccer games without at least two guards. "That goes for everyone else, too. If you have to leave the castle, you have extra guards."

I'd been skeptical when Max first told me he was expanding the castle guard, but now I was grateful for the protection.

"I need to go, too. I'm supposed to get together with Claudette in her office." Marianne drained her coffee cup, then stood. "Today she's going to take me through every room in the castle."

I gave her a thumbs-up. "Wear comfy shoes. This place has miles of hallways."

She stopped on her way to the door to hold up a sneakered foot. "Already figured that out."

A few minutes later, Ceil and Roe left as well. I dressed for my meeting—a black (natch) dress with short sleeves and a modest neckline that was just right for a modest strand of pearls. I looked at myself in the mirror and thought I looked pretty good for going on forty-five. I pushed my hair back behind my ears, popped some pearl earrings in my lobes, grabbed my bag, and out I went.

I walked down the steps flanked by two guards. They escorted me to the suite of first-floor offices and took up their places outside the door. I went inside to the waiting room and through to Claudette's office, which was empty. Once in my office, I turned on the light and lifted my laptop out of a desk drawer. I had just started scrolling through emails when I heard first Claudette, then Marianne, talking in the front office. Moments later Andre arrived and was shown in to me.

"Right on time," I said as I closed the laptop.

"It wouldn't do to keep our duchess waiting," he said as he sat in a side chair, then opened his own laptop and held it on his lap until I pointed to the end of the desk, indicating he should set it there. "We've got so much good news this morning, I don't know where to start."

"Really? I could use some good news right about now."

"I hope Your Grace hasn't been disturbed by the . . . the . . ."

"Rumors about me not being the rightful duchess?" I finished his sentence since he seemed reluctant to do so. "I admit I've been a bit distracted, but that has nothing to do with what you and I have to discuss, so we'll put it aside for now and we'll talk about something much more pleasant. Money."

"Specifically, money the Swiss overseer has agreed to send us to fund the roads once the estimates and the engineer's report has been received," he said. "Now, I understand that Alaine Gilberti is at the moment writing his report and will enclose it with the estimate he's going to be getting from the paving company he contacted. That company is in France, but the owner is to meet with Alaine and his father on Wednesday. Alaine has given us a ballpark figure, and that is the amount the Swiss will send us without waiting for the official estimate. They have been warned it will be a large amount. Alaine will impress upon the contractor the urgency of not only having the full, itemized estimate prepared as soon as humanly possible but scheduling the work as well. We need those roads before we can accomplish the other goals we have set."

"Exactly what I've been saying." We spent the next half hour discussing Ceil's plans for the spa and the castle renovations, then the possibility of having Louis Bondersan, the contactor she was working with, look at several smaller chateaus that had been proposed as future hotels.

"Your Grace, if I may say so, you coming to Saint Gilbert—bringing your enthusiasm and your ideas and foresight—has breathed new life into this country. Everyone will benefit from the projects you have proposed. We have been honored by your acceptance of your heritage."

"Thank you, Andre. I appreciate that more than you know." I meant that. I don't think of myself as a needy person, but right now, words like the ones he'd just spoken made me feel more confident that we would put out this fire the Royal Watchdog had started.

We discussed the efforts he was making to modernize our banking system and the search for someone who was experienced with the technical aspects of setting up the new system, and the possibility of a rail system. While the country was small, a railroad that went north to south from Switzerland to Italy with stops in between would complete the picture. I promised to support his proposal to the council whenever he felt ready to bring it up. By the time our meeting ended and I'd seen him out, I was positive we were going to accomplish everything I'd set out to do. We were going to turn this country around in less time than anyone would have given us credit for. With the right people and the funding, we could do anything.

So far the day had gone well. Combined with what I hoped was a turned corner in my relationship with Max, I was pretty much walking on clouds. I celebrated by spending an hour with Sasha in the meadow, where we both enjoyed the sunshine and the gentle breezes. I was afraid the security detail, which now numbered six, might spook her, but most of the guards made an effort to blend in with the scenery, so I shouldn't have worried. Plus, Sasha, being the sassy little thing she was, seemed to be barely aware of them at all, as if they were beneath her notice. Watching my hawk grow bolder in her hunting and her flights gave me joy. The fact that she always returned to my arm when I signaled her made me feel even more connected to my Gilberti ancestors and appreciate the heritage we shared.

I returned to the castle with a happy heart—and my security detail, which had somehow grown to eight. When had that happened? Something must be afoot. I rang for Max as soon as I got into my office.

"What's up?" I asked as I sorted through a pile of phone messages Marianne had left for me in three piles: Return Call, Call Sometime, Ignore/Trash. I put them all in the Call Sometime stack.

"The Royal Watchdog is back in the news. Literally, in the news." He sounded exasperated with the whole thing. "He sent a video to all the news outlets explaining why you are not the rightful heir and chastising the Duke's Council for having done such a shoddy job of researching the lineage."

"He sent a video? So you know what he looks like and you can . . ."

"Would that it could be that easy. He blacked himself out. All you can see is the dark outline of a man seated in a chair. He made no effort to disguise his voice, however."

"Wait—he said your research was 'shoddy'?"

"He also said we were lazy, unprofessional, and unworthy to participate in the functioning of the government. That as we had predetermined our selection, we therefore made no effort to look beyond who we perceived as the obvious choice, and therefore the entire Duke's Council has to be removed and replaced with only the lawful heir." He paused. "There may have been more, but you get the picture."

"Sounds as if the Royal Watchdog is an autocrat at heart."

"Autocrat or dictator. There's a fine line between the two, but in any case, it appears he wants to be solely in charge."

"Saint Gilbertians would never allow such a thing," I said. "Would they?"

"No. There's a reason the Duke's Council has survived for hundreds of years. The council keeps a check on the monarch, and the monarch keeps a check on the council. It's worked since the sixteen hundreds. It isn't going to change now."

"And yet you're annoyed anyway." I could hear it in his voice.

"Of course I'm annoyed. The people of this country have been without their duchess for *eighty-two years*, Annaliese. We finally have you here, finally have plans in place to lift this country up and restore it to its place on the world stage, and now we have to deal with this? We have no time for such distractions."

"I agree," I said calmly. "So you do your thing and find him as quickly as possible, and let's hear his case."

"I would rather we, in America I think they say, feed him to the fishes."

I laughed out loud. "Now who's sounding like an autocrat?"

"Apologies. You're right, of course. We just need to find him and shut this down."

"I guess he didn't bother to explain who he thinks is the legitimate heir."

"That would make this all too easy. I'm beginning to think he's some deluded individual whose family history repeats some myth about them being a direct descendant of the first duke and duchess."

"Right. Like the way every other person with Scottish blood says they're a direct descendant of Mary, Queen of Scots."

Now he did laugh. "Yes, like that."

"Maybe we should have Vincens issue another invitation to this person to meet with him."

"That's an excellent idea. He should respond in video form as well so everyone can see him. The chancellor can do *sincere* very well. And by him doing that, it shows we have nothing to hide."

"So go do your thing, big guy." I paused, wanting to say more, something like, *So, can I look forward to another midnight visit?* "Call the chancellor."

"I'll be in touch." And like that—gone, and I'd missed my chance to issue a loaded invitation.

I called Marianne and asked her to go to my suite and bring both my sisters with her. I went upstairs accompanied by my now constant companions, who I left at the door. Ceil, Mare, and Roe were already waiting in the front room.

"You saw it," Ceil said glumly. "I was hoping you hadn't seen it yet. You were in such a good mood this morning."

"No, I haven't seen it, though judging from your faces, the three of you have." I sat on the love seat and toed off my shoes. "Max told me."

"What are you going to do?"

"Max is trying to find him, and Vincens is going to make a video inviting him to meet with him or the council or whomever this guy wants to meet with. Me if he wants. We just need to shut him down."

"He sounds a bit unhinged," Marianne said.

"Max thinks so, too. He thinks he's deluded. Which means he may or may not be dangerous." I leaned back. "Which means we all are going to take this as a serious threat, so no one goes anywhere without guards." I thought about the additional detail I'd had today. "Extra guards for everyone, got it?"

They all did. I would remind the kids at dinner, and again at breakfast the next morning.

And I did.

"Ralph, when you run this morning . . . ," I began.

He nodded. "Right. Extra guards." He bit a croissant in half and chewed what he'd bitten off. "I saw the news. Some crazy guy sent a video to the TV stations. He thinks we should be sent home." He swallowed what was in his mouth, then grinned. "But we are home, and we're not going anywhere."

"Spoken like a true Gilberti," Ceil told him, and he beamed.

"That was . . . very . . . *princely* of you," I said.

"I thought so." He grabbed the last chocolate croissant and a couple of berries and took off.

"Where's your sister?" I called after him.

"Don't know. Haven't seen her today." The door closed behind him.

Juliette strolled in, yawning, a few minutes later.

"Late night?"

"I'm learning how to edit the videos so I can do it myself after Mila goes back to school." She helped herself to breakfast, in between bites telling us what they'd filmed yesterday and how she was certain everyone who saw it would be *dying* to come to Saint Gilbert.

And that was pretty much the way it went for the rest of the week. The Royal Watchdog's video was played over and over on every news broadcast, the speculation and controversy taking on a life of its own. There were debates on talk shows where those with opposing views faced off.

"If the Duke's Council had made a mistake, shouldn't we know?" versus "The search played out before our eyes. Everyone knows the rightful heir has been crowned, and from all I've heard, she's doing a remarkable job."

By the end of the week, the story began to lose some of its steam. While still in the news, the televised segments became shorter and shorter, and the calls into the castle were fewer and more vague. We kept one eye on the Royal Watchdog but gradually turned our focus to other things.

But there were more ups and downs still to come. The clouds didn't begin to darken until we all met in the family dining room for dinner at six the following Monday evening.

After everyone had arrived and taken their seats, I realized someone was missing.

"Where is Juliette?"

Chapter Thirty-Seven

"Where's Juliette?" I repeated.

Everyone looked at each other but no one responded.

Finally, Ceil said, "Maybe she's still in her room doing something with her latest video and she's lost track of time. I'll run up and check."

"No, I'll go." If she was up there with her nose in her phone, I would chastise her for being late to the table. If she wasn't there, I'd . . .

I didn't know what I'd do. She knew the rules. Six o'clock sharp in the dining room. The cooks went to great lengths to make our amazing meals, and they deserved the courtesy of us being there on time to enjoy them as they were brought from the kitchen, not ten or fifteen minutes later. Not even five. Anything less was disrespectful to the people who served us so well.

I left the dining room and started down the hall so quickly my guards had to hustle to keep up. I climbed the stairs like a demon and practically ran to her room, pausing only to ask the guards if they'd seen her.

"No, my lady."

I opened the door to her suite and called her. Three times. Four. But the room was empty and silent. I looked around for her bag, her phone, anything to show she was around somewhere, but her bag and her phone were gone. I went back into the hall and told the guard to let me know immediately if she arrived. I cannot explain the sense of dread that began to wash over me.

I went into my own room and sat on the settee and called Max.

My hands were shaking so hard I could barely tap out his number.

"I can't find Juliette," I said when he answered.

"What?"

"I said I can't find Juliette. She hasn't shown up for dinner and she's not in her room."

"Maybe she's just running late, or . . ."

"No. Something's happened to her. I can feel it."

"Where are you?" I could hear him starting to move.

"In my room."

"Go back to the dining room. Maybe she's there now."

"Will you meet me there?"

"I'm already on my way."

The second I walked into the dining room, Marianne asked, "Annie, what the hell is going on? You're shaking."

"I don't know where Juliette is. She should be here and she isn't and she isn't upstairs."

"Maybe she's with Remy," Ralphie offered.

Max came into the room. "I just checked with my mother. Remy hasn't come home yet, either."

"I'm sure there's a good explanation." Ceil, ever wise and rational, remained calm while I was starting to disintegrate. "Why are you getting so upset because she's late to dinner?"

I couldn't put words to the feeling I had. It was as if I knew—*I just knew*—something had happened to her and it wasn't good. I felt fear—a deep, heavy, clawed-into-my-gut fear. It was the fear a parent knows when they can't find their child.

Like the time I lost Juliette in the Springfield Mall when she was four. A friend at work was doing a charity fashion show and asked Jules to be one of the kid models. We went into the store where the clothes were being tried on, and I turned my back for, honest to God, no more than twenty seconds, and when I turned back she was gone. We looked all around the store, even the dressing rooms, thinking she'd followed a friend, but she wasn't there. I went out into the mall and called her, but she wasn't in front of the store, either. I had never in my life felt so helpless. I dashed down the mall frantically calling her name, and finally, I saw her way ahead of me, by the fountain, leaning over the edge staring into the water. When I reached her, she nonchalantly pointed to the bottom of the pool and said, "Mommy, someone lost their pennies."

I had damn near collapsed. The depth of my fear had exhausted me. Yes, that time I had found her. This time, I knew it was different than a four-year-old taking off to see what she could see.

"Juliette said they were going to shoot a video today." My spinning brain recalled that much.

Ralphie stood up, his face white. "I was going to go with them because . . . because I think Mila is cute and I wanted to get to know her. But then something came up and Jules said Mila wasn't going, so I didn't go."

"Did she say where they were going?"

"I guess. I wasn't really paying much attention." He looked away for a second, a guilty look crossing his face. "Mom, I'm sorry. I should have."

Max was on the phone. He'd turned his back and had taken a few steps away and lowered his voice. I was practically bent in half trying to eavesdrop.

"Mom," Ralphie said, but I shushed him. "Mom."

Finally he waved a hand in front of my face. "Mom! I just remembered. I think she said something about the woods."

I grabbed his arm. "What woods?"

"The woods across the lake."

"Where the assassinations took place?"

"Maybe. I don't remember."

I waved to Max, and he finished his call quickly. I had Ralphie repeat what he'd told me.

"Where are the guards who'd have gone with them?" Ceil asked.

"We're going to find that out." Max's jaw was solidly set. "I'll have a detail dispatched to the woods immediately. I'll meet them there. If the girls are there, we'll find them."

"I'm going with you." Ralphie went to the door.

"You are not," I told him.

He shook his head. "If I'd listened to her, I'd know what her plans were. I'd know where they are."

"Honey, you're not responsible for . . ." I couldn't even say what.

"She's my little sister. I have to go." He looked at Max and said, "After you, Captain."

Max waited for me to approve or not. As much as I hated the thought of both my kids out there in the night, I saw how distraught my son was at the thought of something possibly having happened to his sister. I nodded to Max, and we held each other's gaze before he turned and left the room, Ralphie at his heels.

Despite my fear, I felt as if I were watching my son grow up in front of my eyes.

Ceil got up and guided me to my chair. "Come sit." She handed me a glass of water.

"I can't sit," I protested.

"Just for a minute." She practically pushed me into the chair.

"Why would she choose the place where our ancestors were murdered?" I asked, the very idea macabre as far as I was concerned.

"Maybe as part of her tour of Saint Gilbert, her retelling of the history of the country," Roe suggested. "She did say she was going to talk about the war and what had happened here, remember?"

I nodded. She'd touched on that in her first video.

"How would they have gotten across the lake?" I asked.

"The guards would have had to row them," Marianne pointed out. "The girls wouldn't have done that on their own. Rowing is tough when you don't know what you're doing."

"I'm sure there's a very simple, innocent reason why she's not here." Ceil maintained her position as the voice of reason.

"Yeah, look at you being negative. That's what you always accuse me of doing," Roe pointed out.

"I don't know how to explain it." I felt fat tears begin to roll down my face. "I have this feeling . . . like I know even though I don't know."

"Well, that explains it." I know Roe was trying to be funny, but I was not in the mood.

"Stop. Annie's really worried." Ceil sat in the chair next to me and took my hands and just waited for me to speak.

"I know it sounds crazy, but I can feel it in every part of me that something is terribly wrong. I can't explain how I know. I just *know*."

"Mom used to get like that sometimes," Ceil said quietly. "Like the time Dad . . ."

She paused, so I finished the sentence for her.

"The time Dad didn't come home because he'd had a heart attack."

"Oh, Annie, I didn't mean . . . this isn't like that. I just meant that Mom got feelings about things."

I leaned back in my chair. There had been times over the years when I'd "just known" things—sometimes things that were good, sometimes not so good. Granted, I hadn't seen this whole duchess thing coming, but I had known before Mom did that she had cancer. And I'd known that Ralph Senior had been cheating on me, but then again, he hadn't been real subtle, so maybe that shouldn't count. There were other times, not a whole lot but enough to make me wonder. Then again, there was never a pattern to it, so I couldn't claim to be psychic.

"Wherever Juliette is, right now, she's scared," I told them.

"Naw. She and Remy are probably filming the whole thing to add to their video," Roe chimed in. "She's fourteen, Annie. She's going to make the most of any opportunity for a little drama."

"Under other circumstances, that would be a reasonable suggestion," I told her.

"What other circumstances?" Marianne moved to the chair on my other side.

"If my gut wasn't telling me otherwise." Now the tears were really flowing, and both Ceil and Marianne put an arm over my back.

"Let's just not get too far ahead of ourselves," Ceil said. "Let's wait until we hear from Max, okay? Maybe the girls were there, and he'll be bringing them back before you know it."

"He would have called." I tried to focus on my daughter, tried to get a feel for where she might be. If I were truly psychic, I'd pick up something, right? Except nothing came to me but feelings of dread and fear. I had to admit to myself that the fear I was experiencing could be mine and not Juliette's.

Claudette called to see if we'd heard anything and offered to come to the castle to wait with us, but I told her to stay where she was in case Remy came home. The dinner the kitchen staff had prepared for us sat untouched on the table, and we dismissed the servers. We all just sat where we were, mostly not talking, just sitting inside our own heads.

∼

By the time another hour had passed, I wasn't the only one who was worried. Ceil had gotten up and started to pace around the room, making a show of looking at something on the sideboard, or studying a painting, but it was all to cover up her growing anxiety. Roe and Marianne opened a bottle of wine and kept topping off their glasses. Finally, my phone rang, loud and harsh in the quiet room, and we all jumped. I answered before it could ring a second time and held my breath.

"Max, did you find them?"

"We found Remy alone on the opposite side of the lake. She said Juliette was tired of being followed by guards every time she poked her head out of the castle, so they decided to sneak out this morning through one of the back doors. They ran around the lake and rented a boat. But since neither of them knew what to do with the oars, they didn't get very far."

I could picture them, each with an oar they couldn't control, at first laughing as the boat went around in circles. After a while, their arms and backs aching, it wouldn't have been quite as funny.

"There was a man near the boats, watching them," Max said, "and after a few minutes, he was telling them how to row, but they just couldn't get the rhythm. When he offered to row them across, they were delighted. They said he was very nice and promised to come back for them later."

I covered my face with my hands.

"He did come back, but in a smaller boat. He said he could only take one girl at a time, so of course, he took the princess first."

"And never came back for Remy." I said what he did not.

"She had no cell phone reception there, so all she could do was wait for someone to realize she hadn't come home."

"Poor Remy. I can't even begin to imagine what must have been going through her mind."

"She knew I'd find her eventually, but she was very worried about the princess. She said she knew after waiting ten or fifteen minutes that something bad had happened." I heard the dread in his voice as clearly as I heard it in my own. "We have men searching the woods and the city. She gave us a very good description of the man. It matches the description of the rumormonger from the pubs. I have men searching the city for anyone who might have seen him at the lake today."

"Max . . ." I couldn't seem to voice another word.

"Just stay there and I'll get back to you." His voice was soft, but the underlying ice was unmistakable. "We will find her, Annaliese. Trust me."

"Okay." No, I didn't think everything was okay, but what else could I say? The call ended, and I put the phone on the table.

I looked around at the others in the room and told them, "They're still looking."

"I'm sure Max will have the guards and the city police force scour every inch of the entire city," Marianne said.

Ceil poured two glasses of wine and handed one to me.

"No, thanks," I said. "If I start drinking, I'll pass out."

"That could be a blessing. At least you won't be giving yourself agita while we wait." She took a long sip of hers and nudged my glass closer. "You know, I've always said the answer is rarely in wine, but tonight, I make an exception."

"You have a point." I picked up the glass and took a drink. The wine was delicious, so I took another.

"We're going to have to open another bottle." Roe got up and went to the kitchen to see what she could find. Moments later she came back to the dining room, a bottle in each hand. "If we're going to drink, we might as well drink the good stuff."

She opened one of the bottles. "Who's ready?"

Marianne held up her glass and Roe filled it, then filled her own. I waved her away. "You know, you don't have to sit here with me. You can go to bed, or go watch TV, or whatever."

"I'm not going anywhere," Ceil announced.

"Me either." Marianne raised her glass in a toast. "Tonight we are one."

I didn't bother to ask how much wine she'd consumed, having watched her and Roe for the past hour, but it was all right. We were each trying to get through the wait in our own way. Ceil paced. Roe and Marianne drank. I cried and prayed that my daughter was found unharmed and soon before I lost it completely.

I put my head back against the chair and closed my eyes. I had a headache, and my eyes hurt from crying. In my mind's eye, I was seeing Jules as a tiny girl, standing on the edge of the pool at the Y where I'd taken her for swimming lessons. You know how there are people who like to dive right in and others who have to ease their way? Jules was an *easer*. She'd sit at the edge of the pool and put in first one foot, then the other. She grew to love water and love swimming, but she never did learn to dive in without testing the water first.

For a second, I could swear I smelled water.

I sat bolt upright and grabbed my phone, speed-dialing Max.

"I think she must still be near the lake somewhere," I told him when he answered. "Did you check all around the entire lake?"

"Yes. We found nothing." He hesitated. "Why do you think . . . ?"

"I smelled water," I said.

"You smelled water?" I could hear confusion in his voice. "Water doesn't really have much of a smell, Annaliese."

"She's near water," I insisted. "Check the area around the lake again. Please, Max."

"Of course. I'll have some guards go back immediately."

"It's him, isn't it. The Royal Watchdog, whoever that is." I knew it without him telling me.

"It would appear so. We're tracing every possible lead. We have people in the pubs right now, and we have others knocking on the doors of the callers who'd alerted the castle about the man they'd seen. So far, no one has a name or any information that would help us find him. The only thing we know right now is that he hasn't been seen in any of his usual haunts. But we've got men and women in all those places in case he shows up."

"Keep in touch," I said before I clicked off.

I walked down to the gallery, barely seeing the portraits I passed. Through the tall arched windows, I could see faint spots of light in the woods beyond the lake. Members of the castle guard, no doubt, still searching. I stood there a long time and watched as the lights moved around the lake, shining into the coves and along the beaches at the edge of the water. None stopped. The lights continued to move, growing fainter as they moved farther away from where they'd started. I hadn't realized how big that lake was.

I thought about my mom and how much I missed her. How I wished she were here. She'd know what to do.

"Mom," I whispered, "we could use a little help. Maybe ask Gran where we should look. Maybe she has some insight we don't have since she was born here. I'm sorry you never got to come here, Mom. You'd have loved it."

I went back to the dining room where Ceil was pacing again and Roe and Marianne were just about lights-out and the second bottle of wine was empty.

"Nothing yet?" Ceil's eyes were red. She'd been crying, too.

I shook my head. "They're going to look all around the perimeter of the lake again. You know, there are lots of coves there, and a few beaches. Maybe . . ." I shrugged. I didn't know *maybe* what.

But still—there'd been that scent of water . . .

I don't know why I didn't think of it before.

I called Max back. "Gabrielle's castle. There's a pond there, behind the trees, remember? There's an overgrown woods, then the pond."

"Annaliese, we're already there. Not at the pond, but at the castle. There's no one here."

"Check the pond," I insisted.

"On my way."

That's one thing I loved about that man. He got me. He didn't argue with me, he just . . .

Uh-oh. I said *love*. I can't even think about what that might mean right now.

I went upstairs and changed into a pair of jeans and a sweater, then searched the closet for my old Keds. So unroyal, I know, but right now I was a mama, not a duchess, and I was off in search of my babe. I grabbed my bag, left the room, and looked at the two guards standing outside the door.

"Which one of you knows where the car keys are kept?"

It turned out that Yves had his own car, and over his protests and after telling Ceil and the others to stay there in case Jules came back to the castle, I had him drive the three of us—Sergei being the other guard—to Gabrielle's castle. Yves knew exactly where I wanted to go, and twenty minutes later, I was jumping out of the car and running up the steps of the castle.

Max saw me coming and stood in the front door like the goalie on a World Cup team.

"Annaliese, what are you doing here?"

"I couldn't just sit around and wait any longer," I told him. I was out of shape and slightly winded from running from the car. I wanted to put my arms around him and have him hold on to me, but I knew that wasn't going to happen.

He did take my hands, though, and simply held them for a moment or two.

"We just finished searching the pond," he said. "There's no trace of her."

I pointed to the outbuildings off to one side of the castle. "And you looked in all those?"

"Yes, of course. The stables, the barns . . . everywhere. If she's here, she's very well hidden."

I felt totally deflated. I sat on the top step and pulled Max down with me and draped his arm around my shoulders, and I didn't care who saw us. I put my head on his shoulder and cried.

After I was cried out, I said, "What do we do now?"

"Now, we are going to assume the person who kidnapped her wants something, and we're going to have to wait to see who that someone is, and what it is that they want."

"And then?"

"Then we will know what we are dealing with, and how to get your daughter back."

Chapter Thirty-Eight

I got back to the castle around two in the morning and went straight up to my room. I took my phone into the bathroom while I showered—my skin felt old and tired. There was plenty of battery left on the phone, but I put it on the charger anyway, just in case. I curled up atop the blankets on my bed and prayed that Juliette, wherever she was, knew I'd walk over hot coals for her, that I would move heaven and earth for her, if only I knew where to look. I went to the little chapel in the castle and knelt down and prayed she was okay and that she knew Max and I were searching for her. Well, Max was. Mostly I was crying and wishing I was in fact psychic, but I was lost. Dazed and confused, as the song went. The more hours that passed, the more helpless I felt. Not hopeless, though. I knew in my heart Max would turn this country upside down to find her.

At the same time, I was scared out of my mind that something terrible would happen to her before she was found.

Juliette's birthday was in a few weeks. I remembered when she was born, thinking that inside my child—inside every child—was a mystery. Who they were and who they'd become. What kind of person would they be, what would hurt them and what would bring them joy, who they would love. Like every mother, I wanted my daughter to have a wonderful, happy life, and I couldn't stand the thought of anything changing what her life should be. Then I thought of the forces that had prevented my grandmother from having the life she should have had, and I felt sick all over again.

I went back to my room and lay across the bed, tissue box close at hand. I must have fallen asleep at some point because the next thing I was aware of was Ceil shaking me. Claudette came into the room, and Ralphie was right behind her. Ceil pulled me from the bed and handed me a phone.

"He's been calling the castle for the past ten minutes, but he'll only speak with you."

"Who . . . ?"

"The Royal Watchdog, that's who."

I grabbed the phone with both hands. "Hello?"

"Who is this?" the voice demanded.

"Annaliese Gilberti. Who is this?"

"You will call me back at this number on the See-Me-Now app on your phone. I assume you have that function?"

"Of course. Give me a second to . . ."

"Thirty seconds, Ms. Gilberti." He hung up.

"Call Max," I told Ceil as I jumped off the bed. With shaking hands, I opened the app on my phone and called the number. The jerk let it ring almost ten times before he answered, no doubt trying to make me more anxious than I already felt.

But I had my first look at him, this man who was terrorizing my family. He was seated, so it was hard to tell how tall he was, but his shoulders were slender and his hairline receding. His eyes were small and his face round and his complexion ruddy—exactly as the callers had reported.

"Ah, there you are, Annaliese. I may call you Annaliese?"

I nodded. "And what do I call you?"

"You may call me cousin."

"I was told I had no cousins." I thought of Beth the embezzler, but I was pretty sure this had nothing to do with her.

"You were misled."

"You know my name. What's yours?"

"Alberto Mathias Gilberti," he said proudly. "But you may call me 'Your Highness' since I am the rightful heir to the throne you have stolen from me."

"And you have stolen something from me, haven't you?"

"Indeed I have." He stepped out of the frame and swept the camera to his left. Juliette sat motionless on a small sofa. Oddly enough, she didn't look as frightened as I thought she would.

"Jules—"

He reappeared. "No, no, there will be none of that. We have yet to come to a deal."

I wanted to scream, *Yes! Anything!* But I tried to remain outwardly calm. Something told me the more fear I showed him, the longer he would drag this out.

"What is it you want?" I asked, as if we were talking about something inconsequential instead of my heart.

"A trade." He smiled with obvious satisfaction, drawing out the moment, not offering details. He would make me ask, so I did.

"What are we trading, cousin?" Of course I knew what we were to trade. And of course he knew I'd agree to it.

Ah, he liked that. He smiled, but his eyes narrowed, and I knew without question this man was not rational.

Swell.

"Thank you for acknowledging the relationship. I appreciate that. But I have to say, after hearing the Duke's Council tout your intelligence, I'm surprised that you have not figured out the nature of our relationship."

"You said we were cousins, and I know you've been staying in Gabrielle's castle, so I'm assuming you're descended from her."

"Gabrielle was a cousin to *both* our great-grandparents. She did play a small role, however, in the story. Think, Annaliese. Who else was there?"

I had to think. My great-grandmother had three daughters: Jacqueline, who died with her, Gran, and her sister Amelia.

"I was told Amelia had no children," I said thoughtfully.

"Not Amelia!" he snapped.

"I'm sorry, I don't know who else . . ." I paused. "Gran had a brother, Theodore . . ."

"Bingo." He rolled his eyes. "It took you long enough."

"I was told Theodore never married, that he died with his parents and his sister." I really was confused.

"But not before fathering a child with the mistress he kept at his castle, one your sisters can't wait to get their hands on."

"Why . . ." I had so many questions I didn't even know where to begin.

"Why didn't the duke's 'thorough and meticulous' search find me? Because they were looking only on one side of the sheets, shall we say. That one of their grand dukes may have produced a child out of wedlock never occurred to them."

"Why did you wait so long? Where have you been? Why didn't you speak up if you thought you were . . ."

"So many questions."

He sighed a fake sigh. Like he was humoring me. It pissed me off, to tell you the truth. Add that to the anger I already felt. There would be a reckoning.

But there was nothing I could do but act like I was interested and that I cared about his story. Trust me, I did not, other than some small degree of curiosity. All I really cared about was getting Juliette home safely.

"I've been right here, in Saint Gilbert all my life. While you were in America, I was here, going to our schools and working in our vineyards. And then there was a vote to restore the monarchy, and the next thing we knew, here was this woman from a foreign country stepping into the spotlight."

"I did not ask for that."

"It doesn't matter. The Duke's Council anointed you. I didn't know then what I know now."

"Which is?"

"My grandfather, who died a month ago, talked of all sorts of things in his last days. After watching your coronation on TV, he told me that the new duchess was my cousin. He said his father had told him that his father—my great-grandfather—was Grand Duke Theodore, who died before he could marry my great-grandmother in the church. He said there may have been some written proof of this, but he didn't know where, that if I had any interest now that the monarchy was brought back to Saint Gilbert, I should find whatever proof there might be."

I nodded. "And did you?"

"It took me a while, but what I found was that when Gabrielle's things were brought back from Switzerland, all the books were placed in the library in her castle—including her diary. I found that diary. It took me weeks, but I found what I needed."

"You were staying in Gabrielle's castle?"

"While I looked through her things hoping to find her diary. But once I read it, I knew. I knew my grandfather was right. Gabrielle wrote about how the woman Theodore had intended to marry had a child before they could be wed, and that tragically, he was murdered before the wedding could take place. That she—Gabrielle—had taken the woman and the child to Switzerland with her." He sat up a little straighter. "I am the descendant of that child—and rightful heir."

"I was told the oldest daughter was always the rightful heir."

"You were told wrong." Unexpectedly, he stood and shouted. "My great-grandfather was the *first*born child of the grand duchess. His son should have been crowned, not your grandmother."

"Of course," I said soothingly, even knowing how wrong he was. "Why didn't you simply go to the council and show them Gabrielle's diary? Why bother to spread rumors? Why didn't you just speak up?"

"I had to lay the groundwork, don't you see? So the people would start to question who you were so they'd be receptive to me. You'd already been crowned. The Duke's Council had announced that you were the duchess, and everyone believed them and accepted you. The council members never would have admitted they'd made a mistake." He shook his head stubbornly. "Annaliese, you have to stand up in front of everyone and say that I am the rightful one. Don't you see? You have to be the one to proclaim it. The council will have to agree. And then they will have to resign as well for their incompetency. How could I rule with those fools on the council? Who could I trust to advise me? No, no. They have to go as well."

So much crazy talk, and he was becoming agitated. I didn't like what that might mean for my daughter.

"What is it you want from me, Cousin Alberto?"

"I want you to go to the Duke's Council and relinquish all claim to the crown," he said fiercely. "Then I want you to publicly announce that I am the true heir and that you are abdicating in my favor. The Duke's Council will have to admit their error, and you and your son and your sisters will leave the country."

"And my daughter?"

"She will be released once you have left Saint Gilbert. When you are back in America."

I shook my head adamantly. No way was I leaving the country without Juliette. "She goes with me."

"This isn't negotiable. You must do it my way or you will not see her again." He smiled again. God, I hated that smile.

Now I really was panicking. I tried to think of some other way to appease him that would not require me leaving my girl behind where any number of things could happen to her. But I had to think fast.

Then I remembered who I was, and I asked myself the question of the day: Who was the best settlement negotiator in the entire history of the Philadelphia Fire, Casualty, and Liability Insurance Company?

I was. Damn right I was.

"I will submit my resignation to the Duke's Council, and I will publicly announce that an error had been made and that you are the true heir. But I will not leave without my daughter. You can meet me at the airport in Switzerland, and she will get on the plane with me. You can watch it take off. When we are gone, you may do whatever you want. I do not care."

He frowned. "That was not my plan."

"Plans can change. Besides, Alberto, think of the good publicity for you. The entire country will know that you were so kind to come to see us off. They will applaud the way you handled what could have been an awkward and uncomfortable situation. Everyone will see that you are gracious and worthy to be the grand duke."

He nodded his head as if considering some weighty problem. Finally, he said, "That could work. Yes. They will all see me for the kind and caring man I am, seeing my dear cousins off to return to their lives in Pennsylvania." Then he chuckled, and I decided if I ever got close enough to do him bodily harm in some way, I would do it.

"I will call the Duke's Council for an emergency meeting immediately." I couldn't make this happen soon enough.

"You will have to do this publicly. Not behind closed doors."

"The Duke's Council is always closed to outsiders, so if you expect them to welcome you and accept you, you will have to respect their rules. We will video my address to the council and their admission of error. The video of me abdicating in your favor will be shown immediately on every television station in the country. Then I and my family will leave the castle and we will drive straight to the airport. You will meet us there with Juliette. The video of the council accepting my resignation and apologizing to you and naming you the new grand duke will be telecast once we are on the plane. You get what you want, I get what I want. However, if you arrive at the airport without my daughter, all bets are off."

Cousin Alberto—ugh—stared into the camera. I could see he was calculating how much to give in, and whether he could trust me. I had to push him a bit.

"Please, Your Grace." Gag. "I don't care about being the duchess. I just want my daughter."

He was still thinking.

"I would not want to wear a crown I'm not entitled to," I added softly and with as much sincerity as I could muster. "And no throne means as much to me as my children."

I could lay it on really thick when I needed to.

He nodded slowly.

"Go ahead and call the council. When I see the video of you stepping down and then getting into the car that will take you out of the country, I will leave the city with your daughter. If I arrive at the airport and I sense something is amiss, I will turn around and come back to Saint Gilbert, and you will never see your daughter again. No castle guards. No police. Understood?"

"Of course."

"I will watch for your video to be televised, Annaliese. Do not disappoint me."

"You can trust me, cousin." I gave him my most sincere smile, then piled it as high as I possibly could. "I would not want to keep what is rightfully yours."

I disconnected the call and realized that Max had come into the room. "Get dressed as if you're going on a long trip," I told my sisters and my son. "Bring some suitcases with you."

"There's not enough time to pack everything," Roe protested.

"I didn't say *pack* the suitcases, I just said *bring* them." I tossed my phone on the bed. "Now get moving, and get out. I need to talk to Max."

"Annie, I can't believe you're going along with this guy. How do you know he's who he says he is?" Roe asked. "I mean, you didn't even ask him for proof. Why didn't you even ask him to show you something, a birth certificate or . . ."

"Because I don't care who he is, Rosalie. It doesn't *matter* who he is. He could be the reincarnation of Freddie Mercury and I wouldn't care. All that matters is that he believes he's the true grand duke and he's been robbed of his throne, and I'm the only person who can give it to him. And the only thing I really care about is getting Juliette back safely. So if I have to play his game to make that happen, that's what I'll do."

Ceil crossed her arms over her chest and grinned.

"You're going to double-cross the little bastard, aren't you?"

That Ceil. She knew me so well.

Chapter Thirty-Nine

"Her Highness has called this special meeting of the council to discuss a matter of the greatest import and urgency," the chancellor led off once all the members of the council had taken their seats.

While I was preparing my speech, Max had filled Vincens in on what had transpired and what we were planning to do. He was incensed at Alberto's audacity—aghast that he'd been so bold as to kidnap the royal princess!—but understood what was at stake and agreed to taking his part and sticking to the agenda.

Had Vincens alerted the others in so short a time? I guess we would find out.

I cleared my throat, then nodded to Yves, who'd been enlisted to video my announcement. I'd worn a plain black dress and no jewelry. I rose from my seat and stood unadorned except for the crown, which I'd had taken from its safe and which now sat upon my head. My statement was brief and to the point, and in accordance with what I had promised Alberto.

"It has come to my attention that one more deserving than I to sit upon the throne of Saint Gilbert has stepped forward. In order that the rightful heir may be crowned, I am immediately relinquishing any and all claims I might have and hereby abdicate the throne in favor of my cousin, Alberto Mathias Gilberti, a true descendant of Grand Duke Theodore Philippe Emile. I wish to thank the members of the council for their faith in me, and for allowing me the opportunity to serve the people of Saint Gilbert."

And with that, I removed the crown from my head and placed it on the table, then left the room amid the many gasps and assorted exclamations: "What did she say?" (no doubt that was Pierre Belloque, who I'd noticed was a bit hard of hearing) and "No, no!" and "What nonsense is this?" and "Grand duke? What grand duke? What is she talking about?"

Yves knew exactly what to do with the video, and I trusted him to carry out his instructions. I couldn't afford a single snag when my daughter's safety—and possibly her life—was at stake. Clearly Alberto was deranged, but no one knew just how dangerous he might be. Kidnapping is one thing. What his next step might be—well, I had no desire to test him. I would uphold my part of the bargain—to a point, of course—and hoped he would deliver Jules to the airport.

I went to the front door and ran to the waiting car, which already held my sisters, my son, and Marianne, with Sergei at the wheel. Max and some others were already on their way and knew what to do when they arrived at the small private airport just over the border with Switzerland. I swear every minute of that ride felt like an hour, and I was more convinced than ever we really needed those roads repaired. But soon enough, we were there, and as arranged, Sergei drove onto the tarmac and parked next to the waiting plane. Everyone boarded except me. I remained in the car and tried to will myself not to sweat. I kept watching the time. Alberto should have been there by now. What was keeping him?

Just as I started to panic, I noticed an older-model Peugeot slowly crossing the tarmac. Thanks to Max, all flights had been halted, and his men had been moved into positions as pilots and mechanics working on the other planes, where they could spot Alberto's car when he arrived. One of the castle guards—er, airport employees—would offer to escort Alberto to the runway, an offer my "cousin" would undoubtedly accept. We would know immediately if Juliette was in the car.

Alberto drove up next to the plane and stopped the car. He got out first and walked toward me. The guard remained with the car, standing next to the rear passenger door like a sentinel, which made me think Jules was in the back seat.

"Where's my daughter?" I called to him.

"Patience. She's here. I just needed to see you face-to-face."

"You see me. Now release my daughter."

"And here I was trying to be friendly."

"I don't want your friendship. I want my daughter and I want to get out of here."

"Fair enough, then." He walked back to his car, and the guard opened the back door. Juliette hopped out and ran to me. She nearly knocked me over, but I was okay with that. She was safe and back where she belonged.

I looked into my daughter's beautiful face and said, "I'm sorry. Sweetie, I'm so sorry."

Jules, who having been rescued was now as cool and calm as could be, pulled back and looked up at me. "I bet you were more worried than I was."

"I don't know if more than you, but I was worried sick."

"I knew you'd think of something. You always do."

Ah, if only she would always have such faith in me. But I knew the "best" of her teen years were still ahead of us, so I didn't waste time patting myself on the back.

"Did he hurt you at all?"

Jules shot Alberto a dirty look. "He just fed me crap food, and I was cold all night last night. But I'm okay."

Alberto looked amused at this, but I could see he was eager to get to the castle, where he probably imagined he'd be welcomed with open arms.

"I'll see you leave before I go," he told me. "Get onto the plane. Now."

Before I could take two steps, Max crept behind Alberto and grabbed him by the back of his neck. He forced him to his knees—with one hand, mind you—and the would-be ruler of Saint Gilbert was yelling and cursing as his hands were secured behind him. In the blink of an eye, the castle guards who'd been "working" on the other planes had hauled him to his feet.

"You promised!" Alberto sputtered as he watched my family rush from the plane to welcome Juliette back into the fold.

I shrugged. "I did what I said I would do. Well, all but, you know, actually leaving."

"You won't get away with this. Everyone now knows I'm the rightful one. The Duke's Council released a statement accepting your abdication. The whole country knows by now that by your own admission, you are not the rightful heir." He was fighting the restraints, trying to get away from the two guards Max had handed him over to. "You lied to me! Everyone will know you're a liar!"

"Did you really think I'd go quietly? And seriously, did you think for one minute I'd feel any remorse at having lied to a man who would *kidnap my daughter*?" I lowered my voice. "You do not come between a bear and her cub, Alberto. It never ends well."

He was led away, still yelling and cursing, but I can't say I didn't enjoy the moment.

I turned to Max. "Where are they taking him?"

"Where would you like him to go, madam?"

I smiled. "I would like him taken to the castle dungeon. Chain him to the wall."

"I believe the orders were to take him to the police station in Beauchesne, but perhaps I can catch up with them."

"I'd like that. Thank you."

He leaned closer. "You played it brilliantly. Some of the members of the council are still in shock."

"Vincens hasn't told them yet?"

"He's waiting for me to confirm that all is well. Then he will issue a statement and explain everything. I suppose you should think about addressing the country yourself."

I nodded. He was right. I should do that. And first thing in the morning, I would. Right now I wanted to be with my daughter and just be grateful that I can be.

"We will talk tomorrow."

"We will. Thank you, Max." It was all I could do not to kiss him, right there in front of everyone.

I waved to my family, who'd gathered at the bottom of the plane's steps.

"Let's go home," I called to them.

"And hallelujah!" Ceil raised her arm in triumph. "Home is still the castle."

~

When we returned to the castle, I expected it to be dark because it was very late. I figured everyone had gone to bed. But as soon as we neared the city, we could see the castle ablaze with light. As we drove up the long lane leading to the front entrance, the doors opened and what looked like the entire staff spilled out onto the courtyard. When we got out of the car, they applauded.

I would like to say I pulled up those royal panties of mine and acted like a grown woman, but I cried. I couldn't hold it back. These wonderful people who served us and assisted us every day had waited for us through this ordeal—the story apparently had spread through the castle—and they cheered us on our return. There were no words to tell how that outpouring of loyalty and love made me feel: that despite what we'd just gone through, being the grand duchess of the Duchy of Saint Gilbert was probably the best job in the world.

I still had a thousand questions for my daughter, but I thought I should wait till the morning. You know, give her some space from the ordeal. But as Roe had reminded me earlier, Juliette was fourteen and therefore thrived on drama.

"Mom, I know you always tell us not to talk to strangers, but this guy was standing there on the shore while we were trying to figure out how to row that boat. If we got it to move at all, it just went around in circles! We were laughing, and he was laughing with us. He seemed so nice. When he saw we weren't going to make it across the lake, he offered to row the boat for us. He even said he'd come back in an hour or two to bring us back. We never thought he was someone bad or that he'd do something to us. I mean, I'm the *princess* and Remy is the daughter of a *duke*—the captain of the castle guard!—and everyone in the country knows us."

"How did he get you to go with him?" We were seated on my bed drinking milkshakes the kitchen had sent up because they knew she loved them. Okay, I loved them, too, so they sent one for me as well.

"He was so smart." She sat cross-legged atop the puffy comforter. "He came back for us in a smaller boat. Like a two-person rowboat? He said it was the only one left to rent so he'd have to take us one at a time but he should take me first, because I was the princess. So okay, I get in the boat, and he's rowing, and we're talking and he seemed really nice. He said he'd grown up in Saint Gilbert and how did I like living here and that sort of thing. When we got to the other side of the lake, I said I should maybe call someone to come and get me because it was getting late and if I wasn't at dinner by six, my mom was going to read me the riot act. That's what Gramma always said when she was really mad. Anyway, he said he'd drive me, to get into his car. Well, I did, and then I remembered that Remy was still over in the woods. He got into the car and I said, 'But my friend is still over there.' And he said he'd call someone to come for her. But he drove really fast past the castle and started to drive out of the city and my car door wouldn't open, and

I knew something bad was happening and I started to yell at him. He told me if I made a fuss, he wouldn't tell anyone where Remy was and she'd be stuck over there all night in the dark. So I stopped yelling." She paused. "He didn't send anyone to get her, did he?"

"No, honey. He didn't. Captain Belleme found her and took her home. She's fine."

"That's good." Juliette finished the last of her milkshake, and I took the glass from her hand. She yawned and lay down next to me. The adrenaline from all the excitement was beginning to wear off, and she was starting to fade.

I grabbed a warm throw from the bottom of the bed and covered her. I thought she was falling asleep, but she kept talking. Definitely her mother's daughter.

"I kept thinking about her all night and hoping she wasn't alone in the woods in the dark."

"She wasn't alone for long," I assured her.

"Good."

"I'm sorry you were alone."

"I wasn't alone. Gramma was with me. After she came, I wasn't even scared anymore. I knew she'd never let anything happen to me."

"Jules, who are you talking about?"

She yawned. "Gramma."

"You don't mean my mother?"

"Yeah. I couldn't see her—you know, because of the blindfold?—but I could smell her perfume. You know, the one she used to wear all the time?"

I did know. Dior's Poison.

"Did she speak to you?"

Jules shook her head. "No. But she didn't have to. I knew she was there, and I knew I was going to be all right. I knew you'd figure out how to make him let me come home."

I was stunned. My mother—I couldn't even put my thoughts together.

Juliette smiled a sleepy smile. "I know it sounds weird, Mom, but I know she was there."

Then she closed her eyes again and nodded off, leaving me with a lot to think about.

Like had my mother really shown up in Saint Gilbert to keep her granddaughter company and keep her from harm, or had that been Juliette's imagination, maybe wishful thinking? Mom and Jules had been very close, so I guess stranger things have happened. And after all, I had called on my mother last night to watch over Jules, so who knows?

Chapter Forty

The next morning I awoke still on top of the comforter, my daughter still wrapped in the blanket I'd put over her the night before. I was overwhelmed with a feeling of gratitude so strong that I could barely contain it. The sun was shining through the open windows, and I could hear a hawk calling from out near the woods. I got up slowly so as not to disturb Jules and peered out the window. Fergus was working a new falcon, and I wondered who this one was intended for. I watched for a few minutes as the falconer taught the bird how to come when it was called. Then from the corner of my eye, I saw my son walking from the back of the castle to the field, where he stopped and spoke to Fergus. Ralphie took a large black glove from the pocket of his jacket and slipped it on his left arm. I guess he'd decided to go full-on Gilberti and do something besides play soccer. The thought of it cheered me.

Breakfast was a quiet affair, at least for a few minutes. Jules got up to join me, then Ceil tapped tentatively on my door. Roe and Marianne followed not too long after. Soon we were all sitting there drinking coffee and eating scones and fruit. Did our menu ever vary? Other than the occasional egg, no, though it could have. We've never been big breakfast people in our family, so the fare provided by the castle was just right. We could have had eggs and sausage and toast and that sort of thing every morning, but it just wasn't our style. Maybe not the healthiest breakfast in some people's minds, but it made us feel like we started every day with a party.

"So how's my favorite niece feeling this morning?" Ceil asked Jules.

"I'm your only niece, and I'm good." Jules nodded as if she hadn't spent the previous day and night in the company of a deranged kidnapper. "I'm fine." She spread a scone with strawberry jam and took a big bite, sending some jam down the front of the shirt she'd slept in the night before. I handed her a napkin but didn't bother to say a word. For a while I feared we'd lost her, so today she was getting a pass on just about everything.

"Jules, you know you're going to have to talk to the police and Captain Belleme about what happened, right?"

"Good. I want to talk to them. I want to tell them what a whack job that guy—Alberto—is."

"Perhaps a different term might be more appropriate," I suggested.

"Mom, he is definitely deluded."

"Then maybe use that word instead of *whack job*."

Juliette shrugged. "They mean pretty much the same thing, but okay. I mean, he kept talking about what a fraud you were, which ticked me off a lot. Maybe that's why Gramma came to be with me. She probably didn't like hearing him talk about you like that."

Ceil and Roe exchanged long looks.

"Tell me about Gramma coming to see you," Ceil said.

Juliette did. Roe and Ceil accepted it without question, so I silently apologized to my mother for my skepticism and thanked her for taking care of Jules.

"Where did he take you?" Ceil asked.

"I don't know where I was, but it was someplace near water. I could hear things splashing during the night, like, you know, the way frogs plop into a pond? Like that."

"Do you remember anything else?" I asked.

"Yeah, I slept on the floor because the place we were in had no furniture. It got cold overnight."

"Theodore's castle," Ceil said. "There's a little pond in a garden right off the terrace, and there's no furniture in the place. Which is why Alberto was sleeping at Gabrielle's."

"He talked about her. Gabrielle. He had her diary, and he let me read a few pages when I said I didn't believe he was related to us."

My ears perked up. "You saw Gabrielle's diary?"

"Yup. See, Gabrielle was this guy Theodore's cousin, and they were like the same age and best friends. When she heard the country was going to be invaded, she packed all her stuff and was going to take her family to Switzerland. Before they left, Theodore asked her to take his girlfriend, so Gabrielle did, and she had a baby boy while they were there. Alberto said he was descended from her baby. The girlfriend had a baby, not Gabrielle. But Theodore never got to see the baby or marry his girlfriend because the Germans came here and killed him and his parents and his sister." She turned to me. "That's the story we were going to tell out in the woods by the marker where those murders took place, not the part about the girlfriend and the baby, but that might make a good story to add on. It's sad, isn't it? I guess that's why Alberto is so messed up."

"Did the diary say what the girlfriend's name was?"

"Uh-huh." She raised her arms to pull her hair back into a ponytail. "It was Isabella. Isabella DellaVecchio."

~

Later in the day, news reporters from the local TV stations and newspapers had been summoned to the castle, and I reiterated everything that had happened since the day before. Afterward I answered questions for what seemed to be hours, but I didn't mind. The people in Saint

Gilbert had the right to know what had happened. Everything was fine until someone asked, "So, are you okay with this cousin of yours now?"

I just about snapped. "How okay would you be with someone who'd kidnapped your daughter?"

That was the end of the Q and A for the day.

Max walked me back to my office.

"Come in and have coffee with me?" I asked.

"I would like that, yes." As we passed through Claudette's office, I paused to ask Madeleine to have a tray sent in. One of the duties she was learning was how to anticipate my needs. She brought in coffee, then discreetly closed the door behind her.

"So how is the princess this morning?" he asked.

"She's fine. Now that she's safe and home, she and the girls are planning a video about the entire experience."

Max laughed. "So that's what Remy was talking about this morning on her phone. They don't understand how quickly that might have turned ugly."

"Wait, I thought you said there was no real danger."

"Did I say that? In any case, she's fine, Remy's fine. You're fine." He took one of my hands. "You are fine, aren't you?"

"I am now, but I was terrified, Max."

"Of course you were, and I'm so sorry. I feel responsible. I was part of the council that was so sure, so certain, there wasn't anyone else who could even challenge you. The situation with Alberto was exactly what we'd wanted to avoid. We'd spent months filling out every line's family tree. We never saw him coming."

"It's not your fault, not the council's fault. If anything, I owe you thanks for helping me set up the trap. For bringing out the full force of the castle guard to make sure he did not get away with his scheme." I was very much aware of the light pressure of his fingers as they moved back and forth across my hand. "And without you, Max, I never would have known the castle had hidden passages."

He smiled. "You might like to explore those passages sometime, Annaliese. You might be surprised where they could lead."

"Why, Captain Belleme. Is that an invitation to explore those hidden places with you?"

"It is if it suits Your Grace." Ahh, that half smile. Gets me every time. But first, there was something that needed to be cleared up. "You should know, I don't like to share. I asked you once if you had a woman in your life, and you said several. So tell me, how many women are in your life these days?"

"The same, my lady."

"Well, that's a mood killer."

Max laughed. "There's my daughter, my sisters, my mother. And of course, there's my duchess." He raised my hand to his lips and kissed the palm. "There hasn't been anyone else since the first time I saw you in that market in Philadelphia."

I might have sighed out loud.

"So those hidden places you mentioned—would tonight be too soon?"

I'd like to say that we spent several hours winding our way through the castle's innards, led by a flashlight, where we'd have been wiping away cobwebs and probably scaring the mice. But it didn't happen that way.

Around ten thirty I shooed everyone out of my room and took a quick shower. I'd just finished drying my hair and I'd slipped into my robe—the silk one that had belonged to my great-grandmother. Believe me, few things made you feel sexier than heirloom silk, just saying.

Anyway, I'd just gone back into my bedroom when I heard the swoosh of the panel sliding open in the drawing room. I had a choice right then—I could ask Max to wait there until I could get dressed, or I could step right into the drawing room in that sexy, silky robe.

Reader, I seduced him.

Okay, not exactly, but the opening was there, and I couldn't resist it.

Let me just say that Max took one look at me and smiled. I smiled back.

"So is this how the royals dress for exploring?" he asked.

"Yes." I held my hand out to him and tugged him closer. I wanted him to kiss me the way he'd kissed me the other night, but I didn't want it to feel like an order from the duchess.

I needn't have worried. Max didn't wait for instructions.

You should know I'm not one to kiss and tell, so let's just say that it had been a very, *very* long, lonely drought for this duchess, but by the time the sun came up, the dry spell was over.

And that's all I'm going to say about that.

Chapter Forty-One

The spa actually opened ahead of time.

Ceil is probably the most savvy person on the planet. She showed up at the worksite every single day so the contractors and their subs all knew she was present. But she did more than just make them feel as if she were the watchdog. She asked questions so they all got to know her. After a while she wasn't just the princess to them—she was the boss. Some days she brought them coffee and pastries from the castle, so they'd have a little break and she'd eat with them. On days when it was warm or the job was particularly dusty, she brought water in a cooler.

Later, after the kitchen was finished, Ceil got Roe into the act. Rosalie would spend the morning in the kitchen, then right around noon, she'd invite the guys to sample what she'd made.

"Hey," she'd tell them, "I just tried out a new recipe. Who wants to be my guinea pig?"

Of course, they all did.

As a result, absenteeism on the job was practically nonexistent, which meant the job was finished early. Another result? Every one of the subs asked to work on Ceil's next project. The guys loved her.

Marianne worked with Ceil on the promo, and I must say, my bestie hit that out of the park. For the letters to our targeted demographic, they chose a gorgeous heavy vellum paper. A golden crown sat at the top of the page, and the letter itself was handwritten in royal blue with a fountain pen, though not by me. My penmanship was abominable. Marianne's, on the other hand, was gorgeous. She even calligraphed the addresses. The result was splendid—understated elegance, which was exactly how Ceil envisioned the entire project.

I gave Mare the list of ladies who'd been intrigued by the "secret" and who'd wanted to be among the first to know when we were ready to share, along with a list of media personalities who'd interviewed me before I moved to Saint Gilbert. To accompany the letter—or the invitation, as we liked to call it—Mare had designed a color brochure with photographs of the countryside as well as Gabrielle's castle. "Come to the castle and allow us to treat you like royalty" was the slogan she and Ceil were trying out, and it must have hit home, because we sold out the first two weeks, then another, and then another.

By the time the first session had ended, we were sold out through the New Year. We had to hire a new IT tech to create a website for the spa separate from the one we had for the country. That site kept crashing once word about the spa began to spread. We hired more and more people to make soap, and more and more people to work at the spa. Ceil finally brought in a few aestheticians from France to train some young Saint Gilbertian women who wanted to work at the spa but who lacked all the full-service skills we were offering.

Gotta love those Saint Gilbert goats. The first of which, by the way, Carlo had determined had accompanied the first Gilberti duchess who'd inherited from her father the wedge of land that became this country. Unfortunately, Carlo'd been unable to trace them back further than that, though he did learn from an old farmer that the goats had never been bred to a different breed. So maybe the magical qualities in the soap were the result of something to do with these goats that had been purely bred for hundreds of years. Or maybe not. We still don't know.

At this point, as long as the goat milk soap continued to perform miracles, I guess we stopped caring where the goats came from.

Our wines were so popular and so well received we had to start taking orders for next year because we sold out of what we'd allotted for the spa, and I wasn't about to tap into the castle's allotment. I wasn't crazy. Besides, as word about the country's beauty began to spread, we found ourselves entertaining at the castle more and more frequently. That might have had something to do with the fact that I'd asked the chancellor to draw up a list of his recommendations for ambassadors to other countries. I'd pretty much given him free rein in the appointments, though I did have Max look them over before they were announced. He knew everyone much better than I did. So we soon had ambassadors from other countries wanting to come to Saint Gilbert, which I was starting to enjoy.

Jacques Gilberti's son, Alaine, quit his job in the States and moved with his family to Beauchesne to oversee the building of the roads. We're now getting bids for the proposed golf course, which really was a brilliant move. When Ceil finishes her next project, there will be a newly renovated chateau to serve as our first grand hotel.

If I said I wasn't excited about all this, I'd be lying through my teeth. This was my vision when I first came here, and I am so happy—grateful happy—I am here to see it through.

Juliette's ordeal didn't seem to have had any lingering adverse effect on her. I mean, to the extent that she was telling people about her abduction as if it were a badge of honor. I heard her tell Mila it meant she was still South Philly tough. I'm not sure what that meant in Saint Gilbert terms, but there it is.

But then one day about three weeks after it was over, she came into the library during my afternoon time-out. She sat on a chair facing me, so I knew she wanted to talk.

"Mom, would you really have given all this up for me?" she'd asked. "I mean, when Alberto said for you to tell everyone you were a bogus duchess and he was the real deal or you wouldn't see me again, how long did you think about it?"

"I didn't have to think about it at all, Jules." I'd closed the book I was reading.

"You really would do that? Give up being the duchess?"

"Of course. You're my girl. I could always go back to my life in Philly and find another job if I had to, but I couldn't make another you. You're irreplaceable."

"So are you, Mom."

Ah, my heart just melted. Warm fuzzies are so rare when you have a teenager.

"Thanks, sweetie."

"Wouldn't you miss living in this castle and having people cooking your food and doing stuff for you? Wouldn't you miss Claudette and Madeleine and everyone? I know you'd miss Max," she'd teased.

"I'd miss everyone and everything about this country. But I'd still trade it for you if I had to."

"Wow. I guess you must love me a lot."

"Wow," I'd said. "I guess I really do."

"Thanks, Mom." She'd kissed me on the cheek, and with that, she'd bounded out of the room. I could hear her laughing with the guard outside the door for a few moments, then all was quiet again.

My "me hour" was almost up. I closed my eyes and rested my head against the back of the chair, and I thought about how I really would have felt if things had gone differently with Alberto. What if he had been determined to be the rightful heir, or I had gotten on the plane with my family and flown home, leaving the Duke's Council to deal with him? Would I have regretted leaving Saint Gilbert? Damn right I would have. Don't misunderstand—I would always choose my children over anything else. Hands down, no contest. But I would miss my sunny private room on the second floor, not so totally private now that Max was a steady overnight visitor, but they were still mine—though I did enjoy the benefits of sharing. I'd miss the work I'd set out for myself, the people in this castle who do so much for me, the city of Beauchesne, the church where I was coronated, and the serene cemetery behind its gates where my ancestors lay. I'd miss the lake and I'd miss Serafina. And oh, I'd miss Sasha. I wondered if she'd miss me or if she'd be just as happy taking off from someone else's outstretched arm.

I've planned a trip to the States for the spring. It would be my first time back and would mark almost a year to the day when I first saw Max on Ninth Street. I thought he was a beautiful man then, but I had no idea of just how beautiful, through and through. I pinch myself every now and then. When I came here, love was the last thing I thought I'd find, but there it is. We haven't talked about the future too much, just enough that I know that we'll be together, and that's fine for now. People in the castle know we're a couple, and as far as I can see, everyone's happy for both of us. I know his mother is over the moon, and that makes me happy. She has been like a mother to me from day one in the castle.

I'm still totally focused on all the things I want to accomplish for the people of Saint Gilbert. They've accepted me and grown to love my family, and I couldn't ask for more from them than that.

Of course, the kids went back to see their father. They traveled (with guards) for the long Thanksgiving weekend. They both said the visit was fine, but they felt out of place. Ralph Senior and Lorraine were expecting another baby, and that was all they talked about. The one night the kids thought they'd have their dad to themselves, he took Lorraine out to dinner and left Ralphie and Jules to babysit their half brother and sister.

As Jules said, "Mom, it was a very uncool thing for them to do. Not that we don't like their kids, but it just wasn't cool. So when Dad complains that he never sees us, please remind him that we were there, and he wasn't."

Given the way I feel about my ex, you'd think I'd feel pretty smug about this, but I don't. I've never talked him down—though he's given me tons of material—and I've never tried to put the kids between us. It makes me sad that he isn't trying as hard as he should. Maybe he thinks they've chosen me over him, but if he were being logical, he'd be pleased that his kids were having such amazing experiences here and yet still want to go back to see him. I just wish he'd taken advantage of that time with them instead of using them as babysitters.

Anyway, Max is coming with us in the spring. I want him to see the Philly I know. I always said, if you want to know someone, know where they're from. The last time he was in Philly, it was all business. This time it will be for pleasure. The kids are looking forward to seeing their old friends—they hadn't made plans with anyone over Thanksgiving because they'd planned to spend the time with their dad. Ralphie has a prom date lined up with a girl he's known since kindergarten, and Juliette's friends planned a sleepover while she's there.

I'll be taking Max to see all the historic sites—the Liberty Bell, Independence Hall, McGillin's Old Ale House (the oldest continuously operated tavern in Philly, established in 1860), the old graveyards where the likes of Benjamin Franklin and other signers of the Declaration of Independence are buried. Maybe the one thing I'm most looking forward to is taking him and the kids to a Phillies game. I don't even care who they play.

Ceil and Roe opted out of the trip. Ceil said she's too busy with renovations and ordering furniture and yada yada yada. Yes, she's busy—busy with Carlo DellaVecchio, but no judgments here. (We still haven't told his father that Alberto's mother was a relative of his—not sure how we'll handle that going forward. That's the kind of news no one wants.) Roe's busy planting grapevines and learning how to graft heirloom apple trees with Roberto. He's a bit older than her—older than me, even—but they get along really well. He's an interesting guy, tall and broad and looks like he'd be able to play on the Eagles offensive line. Yeah, big like that. But he's quiet, doesn't talk much (which is okay, I guess, since Roe talks enough for both of them), and he seems to be a bit sweet on her, so we'll see where that goes, if anywhere. But he's teaching her all sorts of things about gardening and farming, and she's loving it, so that's a good thing.

Ralphie is still planning on that soccer stadium, but right now, he and his friends who've formed a team have to be content with a field to practice on. People who know (read: Max) say he's very good and could play on a national team if we had one. Max is looking into that, not just for Ralphie but for the other boys who love the sport (Max has to keep reminding me that over here, it's *football*). It would be a huge boost for the country if we had a team that could compete, so it's being taken seriously. We're even looking for a coach. Anything that raises the profile of Saint Gilbert is good for everyone, right? Oh, and Ralphie is taking French lessons along with his sister, who's being homeschooled (she calls it castle-schooled), and he's doing well with it, though I don't know if it's because he likes the language or because the tutor is a very pretty young mademoiselle.

There are signs that we're starting to develop a real tourist trade. I've walked into the city on several occasions—well guarded, of course—and I've seen people in the shops. I always stop and chat. Recently I've spoken with visitors from France, Italy, Germany, Belgium, the Netherlands, the UK, Switzerland, and—Michigan. Hopefully our reputation will grow beyond Europe and the States, but I'm proud of what we've accomplished in a very short time. A new gift shop in the city is selling souvenirs. T-shirts with Serafina on them, little metal statues of the mermaid. Refrigerator magnets with Castle Blanc, others with a scene of the lake. Hastily written guidebooks and bottles of wine. But no soap.

The other day I started looking through the books in the library hoping to find some information about all those stolen paintings I'd heard about. It's been bugging me since Max told me the story of how someone in the castle had been making forgeries—and bad ones at that—and selling the originals, none of which have ever shown up on the open market. At least, none that we know about. So I'm thinking that could be my personal project for the coming year. I'd love to find out who took them, who painted the forgeries, and who the originals were sold to. And then I'm going to get them back. Sounds like fun, doesn't it? Every girl needs a hobby.

Once upon a time, not so very long ago, I was a single mother with a mortgage and a job I was good at but one that didn't bring me joy. I was raising my kids mostly by myself, and I knew nothing about my mother's family. I went to sleep every night alone, and lonely.

Now, thanks to a twist of fate I never saw coming—so much for psychic abilities—my life is beyond anything I could ever have dreamed. I live in a castle with my family; I have a job that makes me happy every day (Jules's kidnapping aside). I'm surrounded by beautiful countryside in this place where my ancestors lived and loved and ruled. I've been able to fill in so many blanks about my family.

I know now who my grandmother really was, and who her mother had been—women of courage and determination, and so much more. I know and appreciate their stories, and I'm still learning. I understand the legacy that's been passed to me, and I'm hoping to pass that legacy to my daughter so that one day, she'll rule this country with the same wisdom as my great-grandmother, Grand Duchess Elizabet Maria Jacqueline.

I want to make sure my children and my grandchildren never forget the sacrifices that brave woman made for this country, and how, in sending away its wealth—and her daughter—she saved both and, in the end, helped restore Saint Gilbert. I want them to know my gran as I knew her, not as the dignified, quiet old lady who lived in the small castle-like house in a Philadelphia suburb but as a woman who did her best to keep alive what was important, even though death cut short her efforts.

But I remember, Gran, and I am proud to have been part of your journey. I hope you're proud to be part of mine.

Oh, there was one other surprise awaiting me in Saint Gilbert.

I found the love of my life, a man who loves me as much as I love him. Maybe not a prince, but a duke, and that's more than good enough for this duchess.

And I never go to sleep alone.

Friends, if that's not a fairy-tale ending, I'm not Her Royal Highness, Grand Duchess Annaliese Jacqueline Terese of the Duchy of Saint Gilbert.

ACKNOWLEDGMENTS

I started writing this book for my own amusement several years ago, never intending for it to be released into the wild. But then we went into lockdown / the pandemic, and some of us were starting to get a bit bored, so I played with it a little more. The more I played, the more the characters came to life. I mentioned this story-not-to-be-a-book to a writer friend who—also bored—wanted to read it. I emailed what I had to her, and she loved it. Loved it enough to want more. So I kept writing, and before I knew it, these characters had taken over and had given me an entire book, which my friend still loved. Long story short, I sent it to my agent, who also loved it. He sent it to my editor, who loved it. And now it's in your hands, and I'm hoping you love it, too!

One of the best things about being a writer is meeting and getting to know other writers. Some of them become your tribe and as such, your greatest cheerleaders, or when necessary, your biggest critics. Robyn Carr, I can't thank you enough for all your encouragement—I don't think I'd have gotten serious about finishing this book if you hadn't sworn to love it so much. Thanks for being such a good friend, and for egging me on when I needed a nudge or five. I didn't give up because you didn't give up.

Thanks also to my agent, Nick Mullendore, at Vertical Ink Agency, for insisting that we put this book out there before it was finished. It's the least of the things I thank you for.

Maureen Downey, thanks for being my right hand and doing all the things. Seriously. ALL the things. I don't know if I could function without you! You are the very best.

The Montlake team is phenomenal, and I'm so grateful to be working with them. Huge thanks to my editor, Maria Gomez, for loving this story. Anh Schluep, Jillian Kline, Karah Nichols, Alex Levenburg, Laura Stahl—thanks so much for all you do to take that first draft, wrestle it to the ground, and turn it into a book! Many thanks to the marketing team at Montlake and the art department for giving me the most beautiful covers. Angela James, my developmental editor, you did a yeoman's job and I thank you for your insights and suggestions. *The Head That Wears The Crown* is definitely better for having your hands in it!

Many thanks to Helen Egner for many years of friendship, and for her early read of this book, and for her encouragement, which never wavers, and that killer sense of humor. Jo Ellen Grossman, thanks for those Tuesday-morning chats, and for way-too-many-to-count years of friendship (we can count them—we just don't like publicly acknowledging how many years have gone by since we met in kindergarten!).

To my readers—the ones who started out with me on this journey when my first book was published in 1995, and those who have just discovered my books for the first time—thank you for spending some time with my characters. To my FB family and friends—you all know who you are—thanks for hanging out with me online and sharing this journey with me.

And to my family—my husband, Bill, who's been through the fire these past few years, our daughters Kate and Rebecca, and their merry offspring—Cole, Jack, Robb, Camryn, Charlotte, and Gethin. I love you and am grateful to my soul that you're part of my life, and of me.

ABOUT THE AUTHOR

Mariah Stewart is the *New York Times*, *Publishers Weekly*, and *USA Today* bestselling author of several series, including Wyndham Beach, the Chesapeake Diaries, and the Hudson Sisters, as well as stand-alone novels, novellas, and short stories. A native of Hightstown, New Jersey, she lives with her husband and one sleepy rescued black-and-tan coonhound amid the rolling hills of Chester County, Pennsylvania, where she savors country life, tends her gardens, and works on her next novel. She's the proud mama of two fabulous daughters and six adorable (and, yes, fabulous) granddarlings. For more information, visit www.mariahstewart.com.

Small Worlds, Large Questions

Explorations in Early American Social History, 1600–1850

OTHER BOOKS BY DARRETT B. RUTMAN

A Place in Time: Middlesex County, Virginia, 1650–1750
    (with Anita H. Rutman)
A Place in Time: Explicatus (with Anita H. Rutman)
John Winthrop's Decision for America
The Morning of America
The Great Awakening: Event and Exegesis (editor)
American Puritanism: Faith and Practice
Husbandmen of Plymouth: Farms and Villages of the Old Colony, 1620–1692
Winthrop's Boston: Portrait of a Puritan Town, 1630–1649
The Old Dominion: Essays for Thomas Perkins Abernethy (editor)
A Militant New World, 1607–1640

Small Worlds, Large Questions

Explorations in Early American

Social History, 1600–1850

Darrett B. Rutman
with
Anita H. Rutman

University Press of Virginia
Charlottesville and London

THE UNIVERSITY PRESS OF VIRGINIA
Copyright © 1994 by the Rector and Visitors
of the University of Virginia

First published 1994

Library of Congress Cataloging-in-Publication Data
Rutman, Darrett Bruce.
    Small worlds, large questions : explorations in early American
social history, 1600–1850 / Darrett B. Rutman with Anita H. Rutman.
        p.   cm.
    Includes bibliographical references and index.
    ISBN 0–8139–1529–5. — ISBN 0–8139–1530–9 (pbk.)
    1. United States — Social conditions — To 1865.   I. Rutman, Anita
H.   II. Title.
HN57.R795   1994
306'.0973 — dc20
                                                            94–7440
                                                            CIP

Printed in the United States of America

In memoriam

Hari Seldon

Contents

Preface

This is an intensely personal volume. It may immediately strike some readers as strange that the product of a long collaboration should be called "personal," but the choice — as with so much over the course of our forty-year marriage and scholarly partnership — is Anita's. By inclination she prefers the role of éminence grise and refused for years to have her name appear alongside mine. Only in the 1970s when, in the course of our work on the Chesapeake, the possibility arose of adverse tax implications did she relent. Her attitude is perhaps best demonstrated by what happened at the Organization of American Historians meeting in Philadelphia in 1982. We had won the Douglass Adair Memorial Award for "Of Agues and Fevers: Malaria in the Early Chesapeake," and Trevor Colbourn, who was to present the award, asked to whom he should hand it. "Give the medal to Darrett," Anita answered at once; "I'll take the check."

This, then, is an intensely personal volume. In 1959, after three years as a newspaperman, two years in the army, and four years of graduate school at the University of Virginia, I began practicing the art of the historian as the public face of a collaboration. By accident and not by virtue of training I became a social historian. Indeed, in 1959 there was no "social history" as we know it today. That genre was born in the enthusiasm of the 1960s, and I was swept up in it. Having completed a traditional dissertation on the transit of the English militia system to the American settlements in the first three decades of their existence, I had decided to do a multivolume biography of John Winthrop, the leading force and longtime governor of the Massachusetts Bay colony. Henry Adams's study of *The Administrations of Thomas Jefferson and James Madison*, with its introductory chapters on the social and cultural life of the early republic, was still something of a model for young historians in those days; hence I envisioned the early chapters of my *Winthrop* as a social and cultural exploration of Winthrop's Boston. But, alas, I was waylaid. It soon dawned on me that Edmund S. Morgan had said in a slim volume of two hundred pages as much as (if not far more than) I planned to say in several thousand. More to the point, I became less intrigued with the man Winthrop and more with the town in which he lived, with Boston, and particularly with the disjuncture I came to sense between life as lived in this "Puritan" town and the "Puritanism" that intellectual historians — under the influence of Harvard's Perry Miller — were then describing.

All of the essays in this volume flow from that early perception of a disjuncture between the broad conceptualizations that historians devise to order an essentially disorganized past — what I term "megatheories" — and the past as observed apart from the megatheory of the moment, that is to say, when one consciously ceases to use megatheory to order the data (to use that too modern word for our rummagings in the detritus of the past) and instead uses data to test the viability of the megatheory. In the 1960s — in my mind — an overly intellectualized "Puritanism" was the concept at issue; in the 1970s it was the megatheories applied to, and thereby serving to describe the nature of, early Chesapeake society; and most recently a series of interconnected megatheories that have for long determined the way historians have depicted the antebellum South in general have dominated my thought. Brought together, the essays form an intellectual autobiography, the story of a young historian grown old in an attempt to come to grips not only with his subject matter — be it a Puritan town, the tobacco society of the Chesapeake, or town life in antebellum Georgia — but the very nature of the discipline of history. But they also constitute in toto a single argument. Megatheories are powerful instruments in that they so readily frame our thinking and consequently the past we pretend to depict. Yet megatheories are our inventions, our tools, and should be subject to regular reexamination. My argument is simply that we should constantly be suspicious of the paradigms that rule us. It is perhaps a futile argument. Paradigms — megatheories — are comfortable things, tending on the one hand to substitute for thought and on the other to protect us from criticism. (One is always safer running with the crowd.) Still, having made the argument for so many years, I cannot abandon it.

Let me speak very plainly here, full well knowing that in so doing I will only enhance an existing reputation for abrasiveness. Were I a physician trying to make my mark as a revisionist by arguing that genes were unimportant and we should look anew at the "humours" as influencing human behavior, I would be laughed out of the hall. Yet what I have seen over the course of my career in history is exactly such behavior, the recycling in atavistic fashion — every score of years or so — of a slightly modified version of the past dressed up in, or serving the purposes of, an overarching scheme. Others see the same behavior but seem to glory in it, such as the editor of the *William and Mary Quarterly*, the preeminent journal in the field, who wrote by way of celebrating the fiftieth anniversary of the *Quarterly*'s third series that with contemporary "studies of 'consciousness'" we have come full circle and returned in tone if not in conclusions to "Miller's examination of the Puritan mind" of a generation ago.[1] For a little while that fortunately coincided with my early years in the profession there seemed to arise something different—a recognition that to be anything more than propaganda or airy opinion, history ought to attempt to be cumulative and contributory to an understanding of what is to be part of the species *Homo sapiens*. Theories of the past ought to be viewed as hypotheses to be tested (hence testable), modified when appropriate, and dismissed when failing tests. The advent of the computer was fortuitous not simply for quantification but, far more importantly, because it encouraged—demanded!—the honing of reasoning. Unfortunately, it also required mastering new skills and the power of thinking rigorously, just at a time when universities and doctoral programs were exploding in size and simultaneously declining in quality. As I come to the final years of my career, I take little comfort—and suspect that like-minded colleagues are similarly dismayed—that so many of the profession have neither the classical training of those who were senior when I entered the profession nor the logical reasoning that the computer imposes. The contemporary vogue for a flaccid language of "voices," "text," "class," "empowerment," and "agency" is an adequate substitute for neither. But perhaps another score of years will see the cycle come round again.

A word about the organization of these essays and the terminal dates (1600–1850) that surround them. The dates reflect a general tendency in early American history to enlarge the boundaries of the field. To use 1600 reminds us (as David Hackett Fischer, among others, has insisted we remember) that our American history begins amidst the fields and villages and towns of England, while 1850 reflects an emerging trend to span the American Revolution, to consider it less a punctuation mark—a period ending an era—and more an event in the ongoing evolution of our society. Where "early American history" properly ends is uncertain at the moment. For my part, I have opted to use a particular phenomenon, "the coming of the mills," a shorthand way of pointing to the enormous social changes that followed upon equally enormous changes in the organization of capital, production, and labor that, if they did not begin in the early nineteenth century, certainly became most obvious then. Applied to New England, "the coming of the mills" might mean the 1820s; applied to the South it certainly sends the early American historian into the 1840s and 1850s.

The organization of the essays, for its part, conforms to my own insistence that the historian ought to shift voices. Traditionally we sound to

---

1. Michael McGiffert, *In Search of Early America: The William and Mary Quarterly, 1943–1993* (Williamsburg, Va., 1993), x.

our readers like omniscient, God-like speakers from the clouds pronouncing "facts" and "truths"; "this is the case, and such is the cause." Seldom do we admit publicly to the real truth — that we are inventing our story as we go, reconstructing, on the basis of always dubious evidence, what we think happened and why. In the inner sancta of the profession, of course — in our conferences and seminars — we readily admit that we are dealing with inventions, that our inventions vary widely with historians putting forth (and arguing about) different stories, and that such variance is very much a consequence of our different views as to human nature and social processes in general and, quite specifically, of the different "rules" we individually adopt in our fabrications of the past. But the tendency to hide the nature of history from those outside our ranks who consume (read) our product is, I think, unfortunate. It makes us appear as moribund as the past we write about, mere purveyors of stories of the long ago, interesting to some, misleading to others, unimportant to most. For my part, I prefer to engage the reader, if I can, in the exciting doing of history and not simply in history done. The organization of these essays proceeds from this preference. Part I sketches my "faith" in how to do history, its three pieces arranged pyramidally and proceeding from large assumptions about the human condition that have guided the work to the small techniques of "place-oriented" research or "community study" that have been used to produce results. Both assumptions and techniques are associated with the advent in the 1960s of what some still refer to as the "new social history," and in one of the pieces included in this section I have outlined my understanding of the historiographic "revolution" in which this new sort of history took shape. Part II illustrates in practice the faith and techniques of its predecessor. Part III extends the totality of this research to a number of large questions involving, in the first instance, our prevailing views of the antebellum South and the consequent isolation of southern studies from national questions and, in the second, the very nature and force of that overused word *community* in our history.

Earlier I referred to these essays as summing to an intellectual autobiography, and so they do. Quite consciously I have selected the essays of the middle section of the volume (Part II) to span the three areas in which, over the years, I have worked: New England in the early seventeenth century in the 1960s; the Chesapeake from mid-seventeenth to mid-eighteenth century in the 1970s and early 1980s; and, currently, the Lower South in the late eighteenth and early nineteenth century. To some extent this personal progression echoes the more general progression of the "new social history" through the field from north to south. But one consequence is that some of the essays, particularly those of the 1960s, might seem to have more historical than historiographic value. Indeed, a young scholar of the 1990s, on reading "The Mirror of Puritan Authority," might well ask what all the fuss is about. We are today well past the time when ideas ruled behavior and the historian could dismiss "the rank and file" as irrelevant to the New England (or American) mind. I would, however, argue otherwise. If, indeed, we have come full circle with "studies of 'consciousness'" and returned to Miller — and I believe we have — then the problem addressed in both "The Mirror" and the subsequent "Children of the Fellowship" remains very current. How do we relate — other than by simply asserting a relationship — "consciousness" and conduct? How, as historians, do we move between evidence of the former — however enlarged it is from the ministerial writings which Miller once used and called "Puritanism" — and evidence of the doings of ordinary men and women? The problem dangles awkwardly in New England studies. But it also dangles in American history in general. The "transition to capitalism" is the megatheory of the moment, yet the transition is written of as more than a matter of economic and social structure, more even than a change in the "mode of production." The paradigm asserts a transition of mind, of *mentalité*. To re-create a pretransition mind, however, we must somehow come to grips with very market-oriented, even capitalistic-looking, behavior — that, for example, displayed by the men of Massachusetts in the 1640s as depicted in "Governor Winthrop's Garden Crop" and by the townsmen of Georgia in the mid-nineteenth century ("The Village South"). The problem dangles even in studies of the early years of Chesapeake development, but in ironic fashion. Rescued from neglect with the "new social history's" movement southward from New England, the region can boast a series of splendid studies of social behavior but virtually no studies of a concomitant mind. The juxtaposition of mind (religiosity broadly defined) and social behavior (the institutional force inherent in the notion of "church") attempted in "Magic, Christianity, and Church in Early Virginia" is an example. It stands in isolation in the literature — a good beginning to a subject, but far short of what is needed.

Of the fourteen essays included in this volume, nine have been previously published in English, one only in Russian (a consequence of my having spent a semester in 1988 teaching at Moscow State University), and four were presented in one forum or another over the past few years but not published. All of the essays appear here revised and expanded to a greater or lesser degree. For the most part, however, I have not updated the original annotation, adding only here and there a reference to a particularly vital article or book. In footnotes and text, all dates before 1752 are given in the original (Julian) form with the year adjusted to make January 1 a consistent New Year's Day.

A hundred-odd acknowledgments are sprinkled through the prefaces and initial footnotes of the books and articles from which the majority of these essays are taken. I cannot repeat them here, but I often remember the helpers I have had, particularly the graduate students at three different institutions who have, over the years, suffered not only my ideas but my insistence that they be critical of them! A number of Muscovites demand acknowledgment: Eugene Yazkov, Yurii Rogoulev, and Victor Terekhov of Moscow State University, who were so enthusiastic about my attempts to explain the "new social history" and where it came from as to insist I formalize my thoughts for their *Novaia i Noveishaia Istoriia*, and Marina Vlasova of the Russian Institute of General History, who offered me a podium from which to speak on historical synthesis and thereby inspired "Myths, Moralities, and Megatheories." David Colburn of the University of Florida offered me podiums on two occasions; "An Empiricist in a Marxist Den" and "A Sunny Little Dream" were the results. The enthusiasm of Nancy Essig of the University Press of Virginia encouraged me (to a degree she does not realize) to put the volume together, while the comments of a number of people who read the initial draft—including the Press's "blind" reviewers—were invaluable. The maps were prepared by Jan Coyne, Department of Geography, University of Florida. Charles Wetherell of the University of California, Riverside and my Florida colleagues, Ronald P. Formisano and Jeffrey S. Adler, will note immediately the advices I did not follow. I probably should have.

DBR

Gainesville, Florida
October 1993

I

FAITH

By Way of Prologue:
Historians' Imperatives,
or An Empiricist in a Marxist Den

I

What follows is the first public talk I gave at the University of Florida, which I joined in 1984. It was in a very real sense my attempt to introduce myself and my way of thinking to my future colleagues. I insert it here for the same reason, that is, as an introduction to the body of more formal essays. In keeping with its informality, I have held annotation to a minimum.

I have, you will note, given this short talk an overly grandiose title, "Historians' Imperatives," a conscious play on David Hackett Fischer's title of some years ago, *Historians' Fallacies*.[1] I had hoped to rescue myself from pomposity by attaching a subtitle, something along the lines of "Historians' Imperatives, or, Dudley Doright and the Redcoats." But nothing that was flippant enough made much sense, and nothing that made sense was flippant enough. The subtitle as it stands, therefore — "An Empiricist in a Marxist Den" — is simply descriptive.

In any event, Fischer's book, as I am sure you recall, involved a listing of the logical errors that historians make, the flaws in their thinking. The implication of my twisting his title in the way I have is that I intend a switch from Fischer's negatives (what historians do wrong) to positives (what they ought to do right). Admitting immediately the audacious egotism involved, I confirm the implication. I do, indeed, intend to speak on what I think historians ought to be doing.

First, however, a bit of history about these remarks — enough so that you will understand (although perhaps not excuse) my audacity.

I am a social historian interested in general in the way people in the past have lived, but most particularly in their relationships to one another and in the configurations which those relationships form in various circum-

Originally presented before the faculty and graduate students in history at the University of Florida, January 1984.

1. Fischer, *Historians' Fallacies: Toward a Logic of Historical Thought* (New York, 1970).

stances. I have looked at Boston in the early seventeenth century, trying to make sense of relationships defined, on the one hand, by an articulate communalism (Puritanism) and, on the other, by great individual opportunity, more often than not described as the antithesis of community.[2] More recently, with my collaborator, Anita H. Rutman, I have completed more than a decade of near-stygian labors trying to understand the evolving web of relationships in a single Chesapeake county over a hundred-year period.[3] Such works are, of course, simply part of a genre — a general type — in history, the community study, the object of which is to try to discover on the very small stage of a single place the details of everyday life that are inevitably missed when one tackles history on a larger scale. In time, the devotees of the genre hope, the many small studies will form the basis of large-scale synthesis — the real pay-off of the effort. That, it seems, is still in the future.

But to get on with the story. I am a social historian; my subject matter is the community — the place writ small. In the aftermath of completing this latest work, with the manuscript of the book safely off to its publisher, I took to the lecture circuit. This is a customary ploy for the historian. You finish a manuscript, then go about the country hinting at its contents, building up a feverish interest so that when the book is finally in print, all your colleagues will rush out and buy a copy, order other copies for their university libraries, perhaps even assign the book to be bought and read by vast numbers of undergraduates. At one stop in the lecture tour, however, after speaking to a group such as this, I found to my chagrin that the audience was not applauding my erudition. Rather, they were asking hostile-sounding questions:

What was the class structure of my county? one asked. I patiently explained that while the county evidenced stratification, "class," with its overtones of inevitable conflict, was inappropriate. The answer did not serve.

"Well, what about power relations?" somebody else asked. "Who made decisions?"

Again, inappropriate! Who made a decision depended upon the decision to be made.

"How were relationships prioritized?"

The word *prioritized* grated. I still am not sure that it is really English. But I answered: The paramountcy of a relationship depended upon the immediate circumstances. If a man needed a wagon to bring in his hay,

2. Rutman, *Winthrop's Boston: Portrait of a Puritan Town, 1630–1649* (Chapel Hill, N.C., 1965).

3. Rutman and Rutman, *A Place in Time: Middlesex County, Virginia, 1650–1750* and *A Place in Time: Explicatus* (New York, 1984).

friendship relationships were momentarily paramount. Only from a friend could he borrow the wagon he needed. If, on the other hand, he needed some manner of protection — say, from a creditor — a patron-client relationship momentarily loomed largest.

The questioning continued, verging toward heated argument. Perhaps I was tired, perhaps made dense by my concern for accurate detail. In any event, it only gradually dawned on me what the problem really was. I was, if you will excuse the phrase, in a den of academic Marxists. They were not interested in my reconstruction of the past, only in how to fit it into their theory of the past.

With the realization, I cut the emerging argument short: "You cannot," I said — shouted is the better word — "you cannot apply categorizations from the nineteenth century to the seventeenth and eighteenth centuries. The categories were not yet invented!" This was unfair of me, I know; historians do — must — categorize and are free to define their categories as they will; hence my outburst begged the point. It even involved one of Fischer's fallacies. And, of course, it did not satisfy my critics. But it got me out of the room.

Later that night in my motel room, I jotted down some notes to myself — very much in the way of losing an argument, then going home and telling yourself what it is you ought to have said. Those notes were in the form of imperatives — a list of those things with which, I believe, historians ought to concern themselves.

Do not take my story wrongly! I am not at all what one can call a "knee-jerk anti-Marxist," that is to say, a person who at the mention of Marx conjures up all sorts of images of a red menace which must be resisted at all costs.[4] Neither am I dismissive of any and all scholarship informed by Marx. The very opposite is the case. On the very broadest level, Darwin, Marx, and Freud are certainly basic to modern thought. On a more personal level, my own view of the starting point for the historian mirrors Marx and Engels when they wrote in reaction to the prevailing idealism of their time. Some snippets:

> Man [we would, of course, add "and woman"] is in the most literal sense of the word a *zoon politikon*, not only a social animal, but an animal which can develop into an individual only in society.[5]

4. Recall that this was originally delivered in 1984.

5. As a convenience all citations to Karl Marx and Friedrich Engels include simply the title and, in parentheses, the date of composition of the work (not publication, which in many cases is relatively meaningless); with the one exception noted, page numbers refer to the version to be found in Marx, *Selected Writings*, ed. David McLellan (Oxford, 1977), an

We must begin by stating the first premise of all human existence and, therefore, of all history, the premise namely, that men
must be in a position to live in order to be able to "make history." But life involves before everything else eating and drinking, a habitation, clothing.[6]

History is *nothing but* the activity of man pursuing his aims.[7]

We do not set out from what men say, imagine, conceive, nor
from men as narrated, thought of, imagined, conceived, in order
to arrive at men in the flesh. We set out from real, active men,
and on the basis of their real-life process we demonstrate the
development of the ideological reflexes and echoes of this life-
process.[8]

The social history of men is never anything but the history of
their individual development, whether they are conscious of it
or not.[9]

It is not the consciousness of men that determines their being,
but, on the contrary, their social being that determines their
consciousness.[10]

No contemporary social historian, I suggest, would argue with these
elementary postulates. For the problem is not the elemental Marx, not
even to any great extent the historian Marx. Problems arise only when we
move to the polemical Marx, to the Marx who, as a nineteenth-century
revolutionary, divided his present into the producing many and the exploiting few, associated the latter with the world's powerful — the rulers —
and the former with the powerless and ruled, and, extrapolating from his
present into the past, argued social conflict as the social norm.[11] Conjur-

---

excellent and readily available one-volume compilation. Thus this quote is from *Grundrisse*
(ca. 1857–58), 346.

   6. *The German Ideology* (1846), 165.

   7. *The Holy Family* (1844–45), in Marx and Engels, *Collected Works* (New York, 1975),
4:93.

   8. *The German Ideology* (1846), 164. This is a postulate of the original Marx ignored by too
many Marxists, who "set out" from "men as narrated" by Marx.

   9. Letter to Annenkov (1846), 192.

   10. *A Critique of Political Economy* (1859), 389.

   11. Most overtly, of course, in the opening line of *The Communist Manifesto* (1848), 222:
"The history of all hitherto existing society is the history of class struggle." But conflict is
pervasive in the materialistic historiography for which Marx argued — in, for example, *The
German Ideology* (1846), 168, where "the division of labour implies the possibility, nay the

ing his dichotomies, the polemical Marx swept aside all details, all exceptions, with an airy wave of his hand. Hear him, for example, when describing the "classes" of nineteenth-century England—undefined as categories, I add, simply recognized by Marx as existing entities: "In England, modern society is indisputably most highly and classically developed in economic structure. Nevertheless, even here the stratification of classes does not appear in its pure form. Middle and intermediate strata even here obliterate lines of demarcation everywhere. . . . However, this is immaterial for our analysis."[12] Immaterial? But are not these "middle and intermediate strata" populated by men and women pursuing their aims—the proper beginning point of history? Does not their presence imply a nuanced rather than dichotomized social structure and social processes somewhat more complex than perpetual "class struggle"? Yes, for Marx the historian. Unimportant for Marx the revolutionary.

Now I have no argument—at least none here and now—with the polemical Marx. As my grandmother would say of the dead—both saint and sinner—"God rest his soul." But nineteenth-century polemics carried baldly and ahistorically into the work of late twentieth-century social history makes for patent absurdities. One example, drawn from a work published recently: "An unambiguous and sharp gulf developed between the laboring classes who produced the wealth of society—but who lost all power to control either how they labored, what they produced, or how their product was disposed as well as control over other aspects of society—and an owning and ruling class which lived a luxurious life-style on the basis of the exploitation of the laboring classes. . . . However, typically, details of production were left in the hands of local villages, which still pretty much ran their own affairs."[13] The first part of the quotation accords with the polemical Marx and offers the necessary dichotomy be-

---

fact, that intellectual and material activity—enjoyment and labor, production and consumption—devolve on different individuals, and that the only possibility of their not coming into contradiction lies in the negation in its turn of the division of labour." It is precisely on this point that social historians of a "Marxist" and "non-Marxist" persuasion—equally "materialistic" in their fundamental outlook—divide. For a very recent example, note Allan Kulikoff's criticism of Winifred Rothenberg in his *The Agrarian Origins of American Capitalism* (Charlottesville, Va., 1992), 22–23: "Where a student influenced" by Marx "sees a 'transition to capitalism' that entailed great class struggle, a market historian" such as Rothenberg "searches for structural economic change" and "sees little struggle in the development of . . . markets." See also Britain's E. P. Thompson, *Customs in Common* (New York, 1991), 18–19, who clings to terms such as "feudal," "capitalist," and "bourgeois" as directing attention "to conflict or tension within the social process" and rejects "pre-industrial," "traditional," and "modernization" as purveying "specious scientism" in order to depict "society in terms of a self-regulating sociological order."

12. *Capital*, 3 (1864): 506.

13. Albert Szymanski, *Class Structure: A Critical Perspective* (New York, 1983), 27.

tween the powerless producer on the one hand and the all-powerful, ruling, decision-making exploiter on the other. Reality—or at least the empirical research into realities of the past dozen-odd years—demands the second and contradictory part, the casual acknowledgment of a full, rich-textured village life, quite apart from the dichotomous class structure that is the subject of the author's book. We should be thankful, however, that—at least in this case—the historian felt compelled to make the acknowledgment, albeit the result is a paragraph which can only leave the careful reader wondering which side is up.

By way of contrast, in the area of early American history that has engaged my attention most recently—specifically, in the social history of the pre-Revolutionary South—there is to date little empirical research into local life to be acknowledged. As a consequence, authors such as James A. Henretta, Rhys Isaac, and Allan Kulikoff have felt free to lump all slaveholders into the class "exploiting rulers" and the nonslaveholding whites in with the slaves as "oppressed laborers" and to proceed to contemplate the obvious questions: If dichotomous classes existed à la Marx, why no overt conflict? Why no visible signs of class antagonism? Introductory Social Psychology—Psych. 104 in the college catalog—supplies the answer. To quote Henretta: "The strength and pervasiveness of . . . role expectations . . . worked constantly to inhibit any wide-spread intellectual or personal challenge to the existing system. They became, in a very real sense, the social chains which bound this stratified society together. The shackles of psychological dependence and subordination" bound "the minds of poor whites as tightly as iron chains bound the limbs of blacks."[14] Marx is not abandoned with this dip into psychology, only rescued from a minor difficulty by Freud's descendants. The antithetical class existed— the lower order, the oppressed. But it was, in pure Marxian terms, a "class *in itself*," not a "class *for itself*," a distinction used to cover the case of what are categorized as classes remaining unconscious of their own identity and incapable of voicing—let alone striving for—their own interest.[15]

14. Henretta, *The Evolution of American Society, 1700–1815: An Interdisciplinary Analysis* (Lexington, Mass., 1973), 94–95. The paragraph disappeared as the original work metamorphosed into Henretta and Gregory H. Nobles, *Evolution and Revolution: American Society, 1600–1820* (Lexington, Mass., 1987), replaced by the more subtle argument for cultural hegemony put forth in Isaac, *The Transformation of Virginia, 1740–1790* (Chapel Hill, N.C., 1982). See also Kulikoff, *Tobacco and Slaves: The Development of Southern Cultures in the Chesapeake, 1680–1800* (Chapel Hill, N.C., 1986).

15. See, e. g., James Russell, *Marx-Engels Dictionary* (Westport, Conn., 1980), 16. The distinction is drawn from Marx's description of the French peasantry in *The Eighteenth Brumaire of Louis Bonaparte* (1852), 317–18: "In so far as millions of families live under economic conditions of existence that separate their mode of life, their interest, and their culture from those of the other classes, and put them in hostile opposition to the latter, they

Enough of Marx for the moment. Let me turn to my imperatives.

First, I think it imperative to keep in mind that history is description and that it is first and foremost an empirical craft. I lay this down as a first imperative full well knowing all the difficulties involved. Human affairs — the thing we describe — are almost infinitely complex. We are not firsthand witnesses but must depend upon the remnants of past times, bits and pieces, more often than not dubious in meaning, often of suspicious origin. And even if we were — via some yet-to-be-invented time machine — able to witness at first hand, we could neither witness enough nor comprehend enough to describe fully and accurately what we see, let alone describe causes and motives. Any who doubt this last observation should read some anthropology or sociology and watch scholars who are, indeed, actual witnesses struggle to make sense of what they see.

Which immediately suggests my second imperative: We must enter the past (or, rather, the materials of the past) with precise and well-formed questions, else drown in its swirling, kaleidoscopic confusion. Consider for a moment that classic ploy in law school. A class of would-be lawyers is suddenly interrupted as two figures rush into the room, shouting at each other; they struggle; a gun goes off; one figure falls to the floor. The instructor then passes out a quiz with a series of questions about the scene. Average grade: F. Forearmed with the questions to be asked, however, the members of the class filter out the confusion of the scene and fasten on those aspects which offer the answers. Average grade: A. Just so in history. Forearmed with precise questions, we have a relatively good chance of arriving at fairly accurate answers.

But where do the questions come from, you ask? From theory, of course. Realize, however, that (third imperative) theory forms questions; it does not offer answers. This is, in my mind, the essential flaw in the sort of Marxist history represented by my academic hecklers. The polemical Marxism from which they proceed presupposes the course and cause of events; the historian only fills in details. In effect, a Marxist outlook tends to set up a situation akin to a child's coloring book. The child has no control over the picture of the bunny. A bunny is a bunny is a bunny — only now (in the child's hands) it becomes a blue bunny, now a red bunny, now a green one. This may well be a fine exercise for children, teaching them about colors and developing hand-eye coordination. When you think about it, however, it is a rather silly thing for an adult historian to do.

---

form a class. In so far as there is merely a local interconnection among these small-holding peasants, and the identity of their interests begets no community, no national bond, and no political organization among them, they do not form a class. They are consequently incapable of enforcing their class interest in their own name."

If every society is a polarity, every relationship a matter of power, every exchange oppression, every revolution class conflict, every war imperialism, why bother telling and retelling the same old story?

But it is not simply polemical Marxism — one of the large theories, the megatheories, of human evolution. What I am saying applies equally to middle-level theories as well, particularly middle-level theories as used by so many of our contemporary social historians. Some examples from the sorts of things in which I am involved:

Theory: Modernization has been accompanied by the decline of community. Result: Book after book painting a picture of a declining community.

Theory: The governing engine of Chesapeake society in the seventeenth and eighteenth centuries was a classic "boom and bust" cycle in tobacco prices. Prices went up, Chesapeake planters expanded production, immigration rose, et cetera. Prices then dropped, production contracted, immigration declined — again, et cetera. Result: Books and articles galore depicting boom and bust cycles in everything from politics to family life, all related to the boom and bust cycles in tobacco prices.

Consider a demographic theory: Women live longer than men. Now, it is true that for a while the theory led historians of the seventeenth-century Chesapeake to describe women as living longer (the theory passing for answer) and spinning all sorts of consequences from the description. Women, for example, were more often than not left as widows, thereby gaining economic and familial power. But no demographer would proceed in this fashion. For the demographer (and for the historians when they eventually caught up with the demographers from whom they had the theory in the first place) the theory simply framed a question: How long relative to each other did men and women live? When the answer turned out to be "women were dying on average younger than men," the contravention of theory led to other questions: Why? Is the theory wrong? No. It has held good too often in other times and places. Then what in the conditions of life in this particular time and place led to the apparent anomaly?[16] Note that theory used as answer in this instance led to logical-sounding fairy tales; theory directing questions cumulated answers (and understanding).

16. The anomaly was first presented at a conference on the seventeenth-century Chesapeake held in 1974 at the University of Maryland, College Park, and St. Mary's, Maryland; the resolution was presented at a conference on early American social history held the next year at the State University of New York at Stony Brook. Published versions of these papers are included here as chapters 10 and 9 respectively, but see also the appendixes to the former in *The Chesapeake in the Seventeenth Century: Essays on Anglo-American Society*, ed. Thad W. Tate and David L. Ammerman (Chapel Hill, N.C., 1979), 175–82.

Moving backward through the examples I have offered, the various theories — including Marxism as a megatheory — suggest similarly precise questions. Did tobacco prices actually conform to the economists' cyclic model? (This one has recently been asked. Answer: No! A half decade of interpretation of Chesapeake society falls under suspicion.)[17] Has the form of community actually changed over the years, and does the change correlate in some ways with what we define as modernization? (In part these are the questions I am currently asking.) Are oppression and class conflict inevitable consequents of a particular exchange system?

Note the words I have used here: *community, modernization, oppression, class. particular exchange system.* The very fact of my using them suggests a fourth imperative. Again, it is in the form of something for the historian to keep in mind while working. The historian's descriptions inevitably involve categorizations. In the vernacular: We describe by sticking labels on things. Indeed, labeling runs the grammatical gamut. Consider: "The Puritan Mind." (Both adjective and noun are labels.) "Traditional communities declined." (Adjective, noun, verb — all are labels.) But I choose the formal word *categorization* rather than *label* as a better word inasmuch as from it we can draw a whole sequence of subordinate postulates developed by statisticians, the masters of categorization. Categories require finite definition. Categories must be mutually exclusive. Most categorization implies internal distribution; that is to say, within the category there is dispersion — a phenomenon which lies behind the statisticians' disciplined games with such fanciful terms as *sum-of-squares-within* and *sum-of-squares-between.*

I cite the statisticians here not to make the point that we all ought to move in the direction of what, in a less sensitive age, was once called "the bitch goddess" quantification. Even in these enlightened days I would be properly tarred, feathered, and ridden out on a rail by my colleagues if I proposed that. No, it is simply the statisticians' logic to which I point, and their usually clear-eyed view of what they are about. As historians, we do categorize. The imperative is to keep in mind the logic of categorization.

And one element of that logic stands out above all others: Categorizations are artificial constructs of the observer, in our case, of the historian. They are not implicit in the things being described.[18] As a consequence,

17. Charles Wetherell, "'Boom and Bust' in the Colonial Chesapeake Economy," *Journal of Interdisciplinary History* 15 (1984): 185–210.

18. Marxist historians would disagree, of course, arguing that "class" is, indeed, a reality — a feeling analytically akin to "love" according to E. P. Thompson, *The Making of the English Working Class* (New York, 1963), 9 — but the inevitable tendency is to attribute the feeling to a group tautologically defined as sharing the feeling, then treat the group as a category.

they cannot be part of a causal chain. If I may return to my den of academic Marxists for a moment: I ought to have cited this imperative to them, and told them in so many words:

Okay, you want to categorize by class? Fine!

You want dichotomous classes — producers and nonproducers, powerless and powerful — equally fine. It makes little sense to me. Indeed, it strikes me as equivalent to categorizing birds into the colorful and drab, losing sight in the doing of all the intermediate hues.

But you cannot then turn around and make your categories instrumentalities in past events.

You cannot, in other words, categorize people into one or the other of your two classes, then argue that because people were so divided, such and such happened. Such and such may indeed have happened, but the classes (being the historian's invention) cannot logically be the cause.

And in my own field, I should answer Henretta in the same way. It is ludicrous to categorize the early South into two and only two classes and then go on at length to explain (with role psychology or theories of cultural hegemony) why something which should have happened as a result of the categories imposed did not happen. What Henretta did in this instance is exactly akin to a modern householder who thinks of his automobile in terms of horsepower and puzzles over why his driveway is not littered with droppings!

History is description. Particular descriptions are answers to precise questions. Questions (not answers) flow from theory. And answers take the form of artificial categorizations. Four rather simple imperatives for the historian to keep in mind. Here is my fifth and last: The whole of the historical venture must be consciously recognized as reflecting the historian's essential view of humankind. The theories that underlie the questions which prompt the descriptions in the form of categorizations must themselves be chosen on some basis, and there is no other basis than the historian's own overarching view of human nature and the human condition. Historians cannot be lazy in this matter. They cannot immerse themselves in dusty archives, pretend that they are dispassionately and objectively investigating "ye olden times," and leave philosophizing about humankind to others. They cannot because in the end they escape philosophizing only by adopting, all too often unconsciously, someone else's philosophy — Marx's perhaps. To do their own work, therefore, they must think through the human condition on their own, arrive at a position, and bring that position out in the open, make it a conscious thing. It need not be elaborate or esoteric. Indeed, I suggest simplicity. But it must be consciously held and consciously displayed to the reader.

In my own case, my view of human nature and the human condition is simplicity itself. The human is an animal — perhaps one with an immortal soul, perhaps one with some ultimate destiny (these things might or might not be, but are, in any event, beyond my ken); certainly one with a genetic heritage, a biological nature, and a primordial urge to survive. Biology dictates the bare necessities for individual survival. We need Marx's "eating and drinking, a habitation, clothing." Genetics have framed the setting in which we attempt to meet these needs. We are social beings, "*obliged by nature*," as Gerhard E. Lenski put it, "*to live with others as members of society.*" [19] Genetically, too, we are sentient, hence can imagine, and somehow we have imagined our way into an enormous number of wants — always transmuted by the human into needs — some of them physical (the creature comforts), some social (status, prestige), and some even psychological (identity, self-esteem). We are selfish. Lenski again: "When men are confronted with important decisions where they are obliged to choose between their own, or their group's, interests and the interests of others, they nearly always choose the former." [20] The things we want (need) — certainly the physical things and most of the social things — are in short supply. Hence we compete, and in the competition we divide. Our groups become complexes of interwoven layers, antipathetical and cooperative at one and the same time, ever in need of a more and more elaborate organizational structure to hold the whole together. Some who think about the human condition are likely to bemoan this line of development and link — as does Michael B. Katz — "inequality, exploitation, bureaucracy, and the pain and contradictions of private life" as a preliminary to imagining something better. [21] But if, as is frequently argued by way of introducing an alternative model, the hunter-gatherers of humanity's beginning constituted happy, egalitarian societies, that notion simply suggests that we either return to hunting and gathering or accept and try to understand the reality of complexity, structure, and hierarchy. We are, at least for the moment, what we have become.

For me, as a social historian, it is this "becoming" which is so fascinating, which sends me to theories that suggest questions, the answers to which constitute my descriptions and categorizations. Our wants (again, read needs) on the one hand and the nature of the groups within which we attempt to satisfy those wants on the other are variables, not constants. What is the pattern of their variance? Why have they varied in the ways they have? How are these two prime variables related? And what other variables are involved?

The questions are enormous, but the beauty is that they can be ad-

19. Lenski, *Power and Privilege: A Theory of Social Stratification* (New York, 1966), 25.
20. Ibid., 30.
21. Katz, Michael J. Doucet, and Mark J. Stern, *The Social Organization of Early Industrial Capitalism* (Cambridge, Mass., 1982), 41.

dressed on any size stage and in any period. I look at small places — communities — at particular moments in time. Halfway through the hundred years of my Chesapeake county, for example, the society switched from white indentured labor to black slavery. What effect did the switch have on the nature of the group and the desires of its individual members? The answer is appropriate to what we are talking about today. There was, indeed, polarization as measured in the customary ways. The microeconomics and demography of slavery were such as to make the purchase of slaves a stable and secure investment for those who could buy in quantity and a highly risky investment for those who could buy only a few. Slavery was, in effect, a rich man's game, and the rich got richer. I could, undoubtedly, have left it at that and so contributed my mite to Henretta's interpretation. But my interest was not simply in the structure of the group — certainly not simply in the wealth structure — but in the juxtaposition of changing structure and changing desires. The onset of slavery was accompanied by the phenomenon of the slave becoming an object desired by all, a felt need. Far from becoming divided, the group (the whole society) seemed more united by virtue of having a common thing for which to strive and a common measure for success.

Mine is not the only way to address such questions, of course. Another historian might well address another theme, perhaps even a highly technical theme such as conscious family limitation. To not have more children is by any definition a desire, a want, a need, albeit a negative one. What in the nature of the group calls forth this negative, and, resolved en masse, what consequences follow for the group?

Still another example. Not too long ago in my peregrinations I was talking to a graduate student at another institution. She was very involved in what — she assured me with not a little embarrassment — was an inconsequential bit of trivia: theater in Baltimore in the early nineteenth century. But as we talked it became clear that the subject was not at all inconsequential. What was being offered from the Baltimore stage and the nature of the audience there were changing over time, but each was apparently changing in complex and shifting relationship with the other. Sometimes changes in the theater — the price of admission lowered, the performance more slapstick — seemed to provoke changes in the audience, the latter growing and encompassing more of the population, drawing in people who had not previously been to the theater. Sometimes changes in the audience appeared to provoke changes in the theater: the performers catering to the changed audience or, conversely, sensing an audience declining in cultural proclivities, trying to uplift it by better, more highbrow offerings, which in turn effected a further change in the audience, with Baltimore's cultural lowbrows turned off and the city's highbrows turned on. In this subtle and near-interminable interplay I for one saw in microcosm the whole problem of the relationship of shifting structure (the theater itself) and shifting wants (the changing audience). I am happy to report that the student saw it as well.

As far as I am concerned, this young student was practicing social history at its very best. I do not think my Marxist hecklers would have agreed. For the student (and for me) the dynamic in history is the interplay of structural change and changing wants, all to the point of the former constantly resolving the latter. There is tension in this process, sometimes conflict, but essentially it is merely ongoing and peaceful. This conceptualization is poles apart from that of the Marxist historian who substitutes frustration for resolution and insists that incipient or overt conflict is the way of the world. So be it. We are poles apart.

But, of course, they — my Marxist hecklers — will have the last word. In the scattered, diffuse writings of the bearded gentleman of the British Museum there seems always a last word. In this case it comes from Marx and Engels's *The German Ideology*: "The class which has the means of material production at its disposal, has control at the same time over the means of mental production, so that thereby, generally speaking, the ideas of those who lack the means of material production are subject to it. The ruling ideas are nothing more than the ideal expression of the dominant material relationships."[22] By this postulate I am either among the rulers (hardly!), or I have been psychologically shackled — Henretta's phrase — to the service of the rulers. When this occurred to me in my motel room that night, I could only shake my head in bemusement.

Blue bunnies, red bunnies, green bunnies! What a curious way to look at the world.

22. *The German Ideology* (1846), 176.

2 The "New Social History" in America

In 1988 I was invited to spend a semester with the American Studies program at Moscow State University in the former Soviet Union. Traditionally the program there has accentuated the American political process; indeed, I was the first social historian — new or old — to hold the Fulbright Distinguished Professorship associated with the program. The first version of this essay was written early during my stay and presented before the faculty and students of the "chair" (we would say department) of modern and contemporary history. With my books and materials almost six thousand miles away, quotations were perforce paraphrases, citations were drawn from memory, and the tone of personal recollection was the only possible one. Revised on my return home at the urging of my Russian hosts, it was subsequently published in their equivalent of our American Historical Review.

Over the past three decades a "revolution" has taken place in America, a bloodless intellectual revolution which has transformed the writing of history in and about the United States. In brief, all of the grand old shibboleths (some call them "interpretations" or "organizing principles," others call them "lies") have been done away with, replaced, it seems, by a plethora of "new" histories — a "new political history," a "new economic history," a "new urban history," a "new social history" — new histories rich in methodological advances but essentially unrelated to each other and (in the view of many American historians) impoverished and therefore failing in terms of new, wide-sweeping generalizations. What

Originally presented as the fifteenth annual Fulbright Lecture in Modern and Contemporary History, February 1988, and subsequently published in Russian in *Novaia i Noveishaia Istoriia* [Modern and Contemporary History] 34 (1990): 66–80. Copyright © 1990 by the Department of History, Academy of Sciences, U.S.S.R. Reprinted with the permission of the board and editors.

follows focuses on but one of these "new" histories, the "new social history" — What is it? Where did it come from? What has it accomplished? Where is it going? — a commentary, if you will, by a participant in America's historiographic revolution, a "brash young social historian" of the 1960s (the quoted words are those of a retrospective reviewer) who, living on in the world of history fashioned by the event, would declare himself in 1984 "an unreconstructed rebel."[1]

What is America's "new social history?" The question comes easily; the answer does not, for the "new social history" is not and has never been a single movement. James A. Henretta put the matter succinctly in the late 1970s: "There are," he wrote, "many practitioners . . . but few theorists or philosophers. No manifesto marked its advent, and no single handbook or work of scholarship decisively shaped its development. . . . Instruction has been by example, not by precept. . . . [Hence] the 'new social history' in the United States does not resemble a coherent subdiscipline but rather a congeries of groups — cliometricians, interdisciplinary social theorists, and critically minded social democrats."[2] There is, in effect, no single leader to quote, no dominant voice, no research model that others invariably follow, no Braudel, in other words, although Fernand Braudel and a whole host of French and British scholars have had an impact. Neither has the "new social history" a single organization, no central committee to define who is "new" and who not. And no single journal holds the movement — to use the word in its broadest sense — together. To the contrary, journals (plural) have been a consequence of diversity: *Historical Methods*, established originally as a newsletter in 1967, the *Journal of Social History* in 1968, the *Journal of Interdisciplinary History* in 1970, the *Journal of Family History* in 1972, *Social Science History* in 1976, to stipulate a by-no-means exhaustive list.

This lack of a central focus flows inevitably from the fact that, like everything else, the "new social history" itself has a history, albeit still unwritten. Most commonly its origins in terms of the writing of the history of the United States are said to lie in a reaction against the sort of history which, while originating in the 1930s, came into vogue in the years immediately after World War II. And there is certainly merit in the argu-

---

1. Gene Wise, "The Contemporary Crisis in Intellectual History Studies," *Clio* 5 (1975): 65; Rutman, "New England as Idea and Society Revisited," *William and Mary Quarterly*, 3d ser., 41 (1984): 59. A commentary by a participant is inevitably a personal statement and hence to a degree biased, while an historiographic comment cannot help but be focused on the particular subfield of the author, in my case American history to circa the 1850s. Conscious of bias, however, I have attempted (not always successfully, I fear) to curb it; conscious of my narrow focus, I have tried to use the evolving early American field to represent what I take to be a general evolution.

2. Henretta, "Social History as Lived and Written," *American Historical Review* 84 (1979): 1293–95.

ment. Entering into the world of American history in the late 1950s, I found it neat, well-ordered, but ultimately stifling. "Intellectual history," that is, the study of ideas as the guiding force in social evolution, had gained a paramount position in American scholarship during the 1930s and 1940s, replacing older concerns with institutional developments, political narrative, and the influence of "the frontier" — indeed, Frederick Jackson Turner's "frontier" had itself become only an idea! Paramount, too, was the notion that there was a single American "mind" or "character," the product of our unique history and hence the most appropriate subject for historical inquiry; the clash of interests and classes that had marked our historiography before the Second World War — in, for example, the work of Charles A. Beard — had been banished and replaced by an accent on continuity, contentment, and "consensus."[3] The interplay of the two — intellectual history as a mode of inquiry and consensus as a finding — is well illustrated at one point in Oscar Handlin's *Boston's Immigrants: A Study in Acculturation* of 1941. To Handlin, Boston in 1845 was "a comfortable and well-to-do city in which the people managed to lead contented and healthy lives," and he had only to quote Ralph Waldo Emerson to indicate "the fundamental ideas and basic assumptions permeating the social and economic structure of the society."[4]

For its part, my chosen field of early American history — the period from settlement in the early seventeenth century to the beginning of industrialization in the early nineteenth — was dominated by studies of New England and its Puritanism, and in particular by Perry Miller, a giant of a scholar whose two volumes on *The New England Mind* established both the essential method of intellectual history ("'Mind,'" he wrote in the preface to the second of these volumes, "means what was said and done publicly. Therefore I have made sparing use of diaries or private

3. See John Higham, "American Intellectual History: A Critical Appraisal," *American Quarterly* 13 (1961): 232: "To understand the encounter of ideas with action in a massive way, we need a systematic view of the ideas." Higham, "The Rise of American Intellectual History," *American Historical Review* 56 (1951): 471: "Given interpretive imagination, a thorough awareness of methods and techniques, and a defiance of the institutional pressures toward specialization, scholars may well hope for a deeper understanding of 'the American mind.'" Higham, "The Cult of the 'American Consensus': Homogenizing Our History," *Commentary* 27 (1959): 93–100, a critique of the tendency. It is important to understand the distinction between intellectual history as practiced in Europe — that is *histoire des idées, Geistesgeschichte, storia della filosofia* — and in America. Robert Darnton, "Intellectual and Cultural History," in *The Past before Us: Contemporary Historical Writing in the United States*, ed. Michael Kammen (Ithaca, N.Y., 1980), 330n, makes the point well. He quotes the catalog description of a Harvard course in intellectual history popular in the 1950s and 1960s: "An examination of changes brought about in the sentiments and theories of ordinary Western Europeans in the centuries which witnessed the American, the French, and the Industrial Revolutions. Not primarily a history of formal thought; rather concerned with the penetration downward into the crowd of the theories professed by formal thinkers."

4. Quoting the revised edition (Boston, 1968), 20–21.

papers, and have . . . taken my illustrations indifferently from whichever writer seemed most to the point") and the central paradigm within which all interpretations were to fit ("The first three generations in New England paid almost unbroken allegiance to a unified body of thought, . . . individual differences among particular writers or theorists were merely minor variations within a general frame").[5] In this atmosphere what society's leaders wrote meant everything, what everyday people did meant nothing. "All scholars agree," wrote one commentator in 1962, "that it was the Puritan leaders who shaped the culture of New England, whatever the rank and file may have wanted. Government, religion, Church-State relations, education and learning, literature and the arts, family life, customs, morality, and the philosophical assumptions of the whole culture," all bore the hallmark of Puritan theorists.[6]

For someone interested (as I was) in the ways in which the rank and file ordered their lives under the particular conditions attendant upon removal from an old to a new world, this was an impossible stance, particularly when my research in the records of towns and counties rather than published tracts and treatises seemed to indicate that the behavior of the many bore only a tangential relationship to the expressed ideas of the few. And, perhaps too stridently, I said so, earning the sobriquet "brash young social historian" quoted in the opening: "The view of society discernible in the New England community is quite different from that expounded by intellectual historians who have turned to the writings of the articulate few — and little else — as their mirror of New England's mind." "What are we to describe as 'Puritan,' the ideals of the articulate few which, relative to society and authority, were neither unique nor pervasive, or the actuality of the man in the street — more accurately, the man in the village lane — which does not fit the ideals? The very fact that such a question can be asked would seem to imply that the description of New England in terms of Puritanism, or of Puritanism in terms of New England, is erroneous."[7]

And yet, if this is the most common interpretation — that the new social history emerged as a reaction to an old intellectual and consensus history — it seems curiously incomplete. Somehow it ignores the subtle (and sometimes not so subtle) questioning of the craft of history itself that can be found in the writings of such scholars as M. M. Postan (a British economic historian), William O. Aydelotte (an American historian of British nineteenth-century politics), Lee Benson (an American historian

---

5. Miller, *The New England Mind: From Colony to Province* (Cambridge, Mass., 1953), x; Miller, *The New England Mind: The Seventeenth Century* (New York, 1939), vii.

6. Richard Schlatter, "The Puritan Strain," in *The Reconstruction of American History*, ed. John Higham (New York, 1962), 26.

7. Rutman, "The Mirror of Puritan Authority," in *Selected Essays: Law and Authority in Colonial America*, ed. George Athan Billias (Barre, Mass., 1965), 163–64 [chap. 4 below].

of nineteenth-century American politics), Charles Tilly (a sociologist turned part-time European historian), Murray G. Murphey (an American historian of philosophy), and Robert F. Berkhofer, Jr. (an Americanist and self-professed "generalist").[8] What is history? and Why do it? were questions very much in the air in the late 1950s and 1960s. Was it an art meant to amuse? A humanistic venture from which to moralize upon the good (and bad) in humankind? Or was it in some way a "science" intending an explication of human interrelationships over time and hence a contributor to an emerging "science of society"? And how was one to do history? What was the relationship of evidence to "fact," of diverse facts to generalizations, and of the whole venture to social theory? In the eighteenth century Giambattista Vico had entered the past by "immersing" himself in its remnants and self-consciously distilling from those remnants the "essence" of past times and places; in the nineteenth century Johann Gottfried Herder, the father of German historicism, had argued that the historian had to "envelop himself" in the past, "empathize with it, become so absorbed in it that he understood it as he understood himself. . . . The ultimate test of evidence was in his identifying with the subject and feeling the truth of the fact." And in the 1960s a handbook on "method" still exalted "the power of meditating upon a series of separate facts and forming a general opinion on them. . . . When it is well developed in an historian it is called the 'historical imagination,' that is the power of imagining the conditions, the men, the actions of a past period as a convincing whole distilled from the disparate evidence available. . . . No accumulation of detail however massive, no mathematical procedures however ingenious, can alone produce the general picture of a group, a situation or a man."[9] Nonsense! said Aydelotte, a pioneer in quantification and careful "fact" making, in a famous exchange of letters with J. H. Hexter which seemed to set the terms of a portentous debate: "I wish that historians in general were more thoughtful, careful and responsible in regard to (a) analysis and theory and (b) the verification of general statements. . . . The general statements that historians make are often rather free-wheeling. I object when a historian, who has checked his detailed data carefully and makes scrupulously limited claims about it, goes on to talk like God and the prophets. . . . They should play fair with the reader by distinguishing

8. See Postan, *Fact and Relevance: Essays on Historical Method* (Cambridge, 1971); Aydelotte's essays in his *Quantification in History* (Reading, Mass., 1971); Benson, *Toward the Scientific Study of History: Selected Essays* (Philadelphia, 1972); David S. Landes and Tilly, eds., *History as Social Science* (Englewood Cliffs, N.J., 1971); Murphey, *Our Knowledge of the Historical Past* (Indianapolis, 1973); Berkhofer, *A Behavioral Approach to Historical Analysis* (New York, 1969).

9. Quoting from my "Notes to the Underground: Historiography," *Journal of Interdisciplinary History* 3 (1972): 374–75.

between statements they are fairly sure of and statements they are less sure of." For his part Hexter dismissed methodology ("What a pretentious term!" he wrote) and confessed he had none. "I do not think I have ever formulated it very systematically. I suppose it would come to a sort of gross loose-minded eclecticism . . . that will grab at whatever at the moment looks like the handiest tool for dealing with each historical problem as it emerges in my mind" — the very looseness which Aydelotte had complained of to start with![10]

The portentous debate, however — one that might ultimately have given the "new social history" finite definition — never developed.[11] Events beyond the academy overtook and swamped it. Quantification — seriously begun by such as Aydelotte and Benson — took hold in the sense that more and more historians began to count and correlate. Attitudes and methods developed in France and Britain crossed the ocean. In a wide-sweeping review essay in 1967, for example, Philip J. Greven, Jr., formally introduced early Americanists to British and French historical demography and the microstudy of macroquestions, that is to say, "community studies," and Peter Laslett, E. A. Wrigley, D. E. C. Eversley, "The Cambridge Group for the History of Population and Social Structure," W. G. Hoskins and W. M. Williams, Etienne Gautier, Louis Henry, Pierre Goubert, and beyond them the *Annalistes* moved into their consciousness.[12] And intellectual history as the dominant mode of American historical inquiry tottered and finally fell in 1970, succumbing specifically to four books on early New England — not the least of which was Greven's own — which seemed to suggest that one could address the fundamental social history of the region without recourse to Miller's "New England mind."[13]

10. Aydelotte to Hexter, 29 Mar., 14 June 1967, Hexter to Aydelotte, 19 Jan. 1970, in Aydelotte, *Quantification in History*, 158, 160–61, 165, 167, 168.

11. Echoes of the old debate linger in, for example, Robert W. Fogel and G. R. Elton, *Which Road to the Past? Two Views of History* (New Haven, 1983), but to all intents and purposes it has given way to a rancorous diatribe against the "new social history" by American Marxists and a general complaint that the new histories have produced no new grand generalizations, both points developed infra. Robert F. Berkhofer, Jr., "The Two New Histories: Competing Paradigms for Interpreting the American Past," *O.A.H. [Organization of American Historians] Newsletter* 2 (May 1983): 9–12, comments on the first; Samuel P. Hayes, "Scientific versus Traditional History: The Limitations of the Current Debate," *Historical Methods* 17 (1984): 75–78 — an extended review of the Fogel and Elton volume — exemplifies the latter.

12. Greven, "Historical Demography and Colonial America: A Review Article," *William and Mary Quarterly*, 3d ser., 24 (1967): 438–54.

13. Greven, *Four Generations: Population, Land, and Family in Colonial Andover, Massachusetts* (Ithaca, N.Y., 1970); John Demos, *A Little Commonwealth: Family Life in Plymouth Colony* (New York, 1970); Kenneth A. Lockridge, *A New England Town, the First Hundred Years: Dedham, Massachusetts, 1636–1736* (New York, 1970); and Michael Zuckerman, *Peaceable Kingdoms: New England Towns in the Eighteenth Century* (New York, 1970). The inter-

But America in the 1960s and early 1970s was, recall, a time of challenge and debate: civil rights, the Vietnam War, Berkeley's "free speech" movement, campus sit-ins and riots, the specter of four students shot to death on a quiet green sward at Kent State University in Ohio. Such things could not help but have their effect on scholarship. Consensus history crashed when the streets displayed so obviously the lack of an American consensus. The notion of an American character gave way to a cultural pluralism in which the way of the WASP (the white Anglo-Saxon Protestant) was only one of many ways. The "melting pot" became a mosaic and *ethnicity* a more popular word than *acculturation*. But then, there were many new words and phrases: "Alternative lifestyles" (the "hippies" of San Francisco's Haight-Ashbury district and the communes), "raising consciousness" (the byword of militant feminism). And, of course, all of the different ways and lifestyles, all of the groups defined by ethnicity, race, and gender, perforce must be recognized as having their own histories.

In this situation two things happened to the inchoate "new social history." The first—and more easily stated—is that it lost any chance of emerging with a coherent subject for analysis. From its very beginning there had been an inner tension among practitioners between the study of a total society (however defined) and some small aspect of that totality—a distinction drawn early by E. J. Hobsbawm when he wrote of "social history" vis-à-vis the "history of society."[14] Of the four books mentioned as bringing down intellectual history in 1970, for example, three were lauded as "community studies," but only one (Kenneth A. Lockridge's) was the study of a total community, while two others (Greven's and John Demos's) were simply studies of family life within communities. But now the situation was aggravated. All of the new histories emerging—of the black, the

---

disciplinary and statistical nature of these works, particularly Lockridge's use of the anthropological concept of "peasant" and Greven's reliance upon a limited and heavily biased sample, seem rudimentary today, but that does not take away from their effect then. For the implications of these studies as seen at the moment, see Richard S. Dunn, "The Social History of Early New England," *American Quarterly* 24 (1972): 661–79, and John M. Murrin, "Review Essay," *History and Theory* 11 (1972): 226–75. For the link between their publication in 1970 and the collapse of intellectual history, see John Higham's introduction to *New Directions in American Intellectual History*, ed. Higham and Paul K. Conkin (Baltimore, 1979), xiii; the volume was an extended mea culpa by the leading intellectual historians of the moment. Here Higham notes that "the full force" of the attack upon intellectual history did not dawn upon him until Gene Wise's appearance at the 1974 Organization of American Historians annual meeting; at that meeting Wise delivered an early version of his "Contemporary Crisis in Intellectual History," which highlighted the 1970 volumes.

14. Hobsbawm, "From Social History to the History of Society," *Daedalus: Journal of the American Academy of Arts and Sciences* 100 (1971): 20–45. For the distinction specifically in community study see Darrett B. Rutman, "Community Study," *Historical Methods* 13 (1980): 29–41 [chap. 3 below].

Indian, of women, of ethnics — although their practitioners tried (and are still trying) to maintain their independence on the basis of subject matter, were inevitably subsumed in social history, and social history in America to a large extent became accepted as the history of women, of blacks, of ethnics, in sum, of the parts of a pluralistic society rather than of the society itself.

Second — and not at all easily stated — the "new social history" in America took on a radical hue. Intellectual history as a mode and the American consensus as a finding clearly dominated America's postwar historiography. So much has been said. But dominance is not monopolization, and a minor, nonintellectual, nonconsensus history persisted, represented at its extreme edge by such American Marxists as Herbert Aptheker and Philip Foner. In the tumultuous days of the 1960s, in the guise of the "New Left," young, programmatic activists in search, historically, of "a usable past" bubbled to the surface. Intellectually they presented a reassessment (and denigration) of American foreign policy and of twentieth-century reform movements while making heroes out of the social rebels of the nineteenth century; institutionally they attempted to force the staid American Historical Association to join the political denunciation of Lyndon Johnson and his war. More to the point here, they touched upon the evolving "new social history" by usurping the attack upon intellectual history and its practitioners, "elitist" historians who, the young men of the left said, drew only from the elitist writings of a past time to concoct pabulum for their own time. "New Left" titles became catch phrases — Jesse Lemisch's "history from the bottom up," for example, and "listening to the inarticulate." Social historians could hardly dispute the phrases; indeed, my own "man in the village lane" of four years earlier was just such an "inarticulate" as Lemisch was urging us to hear.[15] But the result was to confuse the line between the "new social history" that had been developing and a left, or radical, history firmly lodged in a Marxist tradition.[16] The poor, the impoverished, the dispossessed, the tenant, and the

15. Lemisch, "The American Revolution Seen from the Bottom Up," in *Towards a New Past: Dissenting Essays in American History*, ed. Barton J. Bernstein (New York, 1968), 3–45; Lemisch, "Listening to the 'Inarticulate': William Widger's Dream and the Loyalties of American Revolutionary Seamen in British Prisons," *Journal of Social History* 3 (1969): 1–29. See, in general, Irwin Unger, "The 'New Left' and American History: Some Recent Trends in United States Historiography," *American Historical Review* 72 (1967): 1237–63.

16. Note how facilely Henretta, "Social History," 1293, includes Lemisch with Aydelotte, Benson, and Berkhofer among the theoreticians of the "new social history." Note, too, the usurpation of the adjective *social* by Allan Kulikoff, first in his "The Transition to Capitalism in Rural America," *William and Mary Quarterly*, 3d ser., 46 (1989): 120–44, and most recently in *The Agrarian Origins of American Capitalism* (Charlottesville, Va., 1992); for Kulikoff "social history" and "Marxian history" are synonyms. See also Daniel T. Rodgers, "Republicanism: The Career of a Concept," *Journal of American History* 79 (1992): 25, where social history and "neo-Marxian" history are hopelessly confused. Laurence Veysey had the

renter became prime subjects for scrutiny, again to the detriment of studies of the total society that included the poor. And a vague language of "class" — usually only two, an exploited "underclass" and a dominant "elite" — crept into our prose, calculatedly in the hands of some, thoughtlessly in the hands of most.[17]

One final twist in this narrative of America's "new social history" was the reinvigoration of intellectual history — or at least the study of "mind" — under the guise of an interdisciplinary "cultural" history.

By the mid-1970s American intellectual history stood revealed as simply the history of "the discourse of communities of intellectuals" (the words are from the report on a conference of the battered practitioners held at Racine, Wisconsin, in December 1977) with problematic, not certain, implications for the larger society under scrutiny, hardly a comfortable position for scholars used to exploring "the American mind." In effect, intellectual historians were left with the problem of connecting the ideas of a past society — that is to say, their exegeses of the discourse of intellectuals that nobody had effectively challenged (Miller, for example, remains the standard starting place for any study of Puritan ideas) — with behavior in the everyday world.[18]

At the same time the social historians were displaying a barren side. To put the matter in terms of early American history: In counterposing behavior (the doings of "the man in the village lane") and ideas (the words set down by the minister in his study), social historians at first simply accentuated the one and threw out the other. As Gene Wise wrote of my own work: "If intellectual historians before [Rutman] would claim that ideas clothe the American reality with meaning and give it dynamic energy, Rutman in 1965 would simply reverse the order" and "contend that the real story . . . lies not in . . . ideas" but in the "pragmatic adjustment to environmental imperatives. . . . He would ask the question, 'How did these people live?,' not 'What did these Puritans think?' "[19] The criticism was apt, for obviously how people live and what they think are clearly

---

relationship right in "The 'New' Social History in the Context of American Historical Writing," *Reviews in American History* 7 (1979): 4: "The 'new' social history emerged in the 1960s quite separately from Marxist history, though riding the climate of engaged interest in the nonelite population." See also Peter Novock, *That Noble Dream: The "Objectivity Question" and the American Historical Profession* (Cambridge, 1988), 418.

17. See Michael Zuckerman, "Myth and Method: The Current Crisis in American Historical Writing," *History Teacher* 17 (1984): 236–37: "Scholars . . . bound together . . . by the earnestness of their experience of the sixties . . . may or may not have been partisans of the New Left, but they have absorbed its outlook and accepted its problematic."

18. David Hollinger, "Historians and the Discourse of Intellectuals," in *New Directions in American Intellectual History*, ed. Higham and Conkin, 42.

19. Wise, "Contemporary Crisis in Intellectual History," 65. I use Wise's criticism of me as a diplomatic gesture toward my friends, but the criticism is generally applicable.

interrelated. But how are we to enter the world of thought? How read the minds of past men and women? Social historians, in effect, faced the exact problem confronting the intellectual historians, only framed in reverse: How to relate behavior (as observed and now more often than not counted) with the discourse of ideas?

One way out for the social historian was to assume that thought — "mind" — was somehow implicit in behavior and proceed accordingly to read the former by observing the latter. A kinship problem exemplifies. A particular form of bedtime behavior between two brothers and their respective wives might ultimately produce an observable phenomenon — cousinship. But did the cousins think of themselves as bearing any special relationship to each other? We could follow them through their lives, marking those incidents in which they, as individuals, had to rely upon someone other than themselves — naming a godfather for a child, for example, or recruiting someone to stand surety in a court proceeding or to serve as executor of their estate; if the cousins largely called upon each other rather than upon noncousins, then we might infer that a particular "trust" existed in the minds of each toward the other, and "cousinship" would be given substance as a prevailing idea or attitude. In much the same fashion, we could observe the behavior of a minister's congregation vis-à-vis the words addressed to it by the minister in the pulpit. If behavior among the members of the congregation shifted in the direction of the ideas expressed, then we might conclude the social efficacy of those ideas; they were now (although perhaps in an amended form) in the minds of the minister's hearers.[20]

Approaching the intersection of ideas and behavior in such a fashion, however, was fraught with at least perceived difficulties. Sometimes the idea for which the historian desired to probe seemed to emanate in behavior difficult if not impossible to observe, let alone count. But even when observation and counting were possible, they were inevitably seen as arduous and — above all in the impatient world of American scholarship where tenure and promotion are largely dependent upon publication — time-consuming. Equally to the point, it was soon clear (and it is even clearer today) that inferring anything, let alone attitudes and ideas, from what is counted requires exquisite technical expertise in formal statistics. Pioneers were dismayed. Henretta in 1977 deplored the fact that "it takes

---

20. This was the basis of a "transactional" view of Puritanism I sketched in *American Puritanism: Faith and Practice* (Philadelphia, 1970). The approach has seldom been overtly used in the context of Puritan studies, but see George Selement, "The Meeting of Elite and Popular Minds at Cambridge, New England, 1638–1645," *William and Mary Quarterly*, 3d ser., 41 (1984): 32–48. More generally on the problem of relating ideas and behavior, see Adrian Wilson, "Inferring Attitudes from Behavior," *Historical Methods* 14 (1981): 143–44, a brief theoretical statement, and James A. Henretta, "Families and Farms: *Mentalité* in Pre-Industrial America," *William and Mary Quarterly*, 3d ser., 35 (1978): 3–32, a valiant effort.

months — even years — of laborious and painstaking work to assemble . . . even a few pieces" of data. "The hours or days which might have been spent in reading diaries, newspapers, or letters — in discovering and then pondering the felt *meaning* of the lives and cultural values of the historical actors — are consumed instead by a quest for technical exactness and statistical finesse. . . . Consciousness and meaning have been usurped by data and diagrams."[21] And some abandoned the effort altogether — Benson, Lockridge, Lawrence Stone.[22]

In the mid to late 1970s, then, the combatants of the sixties confronted essentially the same sphinx. Whichever way you looked at society — from the standpoint of ideas and attitudes or from the standpoint of behavior — it was a single, enigmatic animal. For some — on both sides — resolution came via a deus ex machina: the discovery of "culture."

The whole tumultuous period that saw the rise of the "new social history" saw, too, the education of the American historian to a world of scholarship which extended far beyond the boundaries of any particular field or subfield. American historians in general and early Americanists in particular became far more widely read than any of their predecessors had ever been. Their reading ultimately took them into ethnology and anthropology and, in particular, to a soft approach to culture represented by Clifford Geertz, Victor Turner, Peter Berger, and Mary Douglas but ultimately traceable to a French intellectual tradition extending back to the nineteenth century, one which, on the surface, solved the enigma for many on both sides. Here "culture," "popular culture," "collective mentality," *mentalité* — rough synonyms, as historians use them — were presented as a pervasive framework delimiting and defining both ideas and behavior. For the intellectual historian the discovery was reinvigorating. It broadened the scope of the field to include ideas expressed both formally and informally — the minister's sermon, on the one hand, and a printer's almanac on the other. It restored confidence to a shattered psyche, for no longer was the intellectual historian an "elitist" dealing only with "elite" ideas. Ideas, wherever found, were all part of a single "collective mentality," the description of which could be accomplished by an exegetical analysis of the ideas themselves. And it ensured the relevance of the work to the study of the larger society, for behavior was inevitably constrained by (and understood through) the single encompassing cul-

21. Henretta, "The Study of Social Mobility: Ideological Assumptions and Conceptual Bias," *Labor History* 18 (1977): 167.

22. See Stone's "The Revival of Narrative: Reflections on a New Old History," *Past and Present* 85 (1979): 3–24; Benson's "The Mistransference Fallacy in Explanations of Human Behavior," *Historical Methods* 17 (1984): 118–31; and the essays by Stone and Lockridge in *The Future of History*, ed. Charles Delzell (Nashville, 1977), the latter read in the light of Lockridge's *The Diary, and Life, of William Byrd II of Virginia, 1674–1744* (Chapel Hill, N.C., 1987), an attempt to enter the mind of the past via psychobiography.

tural framework.[23] Some social historians, for their part, discovered in such as Geertz and Berger that one need not spend months and years gathering the data necessary to explore particular phenomena for particular attitudes or ideas. One or two detailed vignettes subjected to what Geertz called "thick description" were enough. For if Geertz could depict the depths and sinews of Balinese culture by analyzing a cockfight, historians could (for example) explore the dynamics of gentry and church in colonial Virginia by analyzing in similar fashion a confrontation between a gentleman and a preacher.[24] With the riddle of the sphinx solved, at least to the satisfaction of some, the chasm between American intellectual and social historians narrowed, and the "new social history" perforce took on still another — an ethnographic — dimension.[25]

Long as this digression into the evolution of America's "new social history" has been, it returns us to the initial point. The product of its own history, the "new social history" displays, on the surface, a geometry of many dimensions, not just one. Its subject is diverse. The family and community, women and blacks, the poor and (occasionally) the prosperous, mortality and wealth distribution, class, status, power relationships, and village festivals — any, all, and more are grist for its mill. It is quantitative and ethnographic (in the sense of Geertzian "thick descriptions").[26] Its mode of presentation is both statistical and impressionistic. It

23. See Darnton, "Intellectual and Cultural History," 327–54. David Hall is the best representative in early American history. See particularly his "The World of Print and Collective Mentality in Seventeenth-Century New England," in *New Directions in American Intellectual History*, ed. Higham and Conkin, 166–80; "The Mental World of Samuel Sewall," Massachusetts Historical Society, *Proceedings* 92 (1980): 21–44; "Toward a History of Popular Religion in Early New England," *William and Mary Quarterly*, 3d ser., 41 (1984): 49–55; and *Worlds of Wonder, Days of Judgment: Popular Religious Belief in Early New England* (New York, 1989).

24. Geertz, *The Interpretation of Cultures: Selected Essays* (New York, 1973). Note particularly "Thick Description: Toward an Interpretive Theory of Culture," pp. 3–30, and "Deep Play: Notes on the Balinese Cockfight," pp. 412–53. Rhys Isaac's *The Transformation of Virginia, 1740–1790* (Chapel Hill, N.C., 1982) is the preeminent example in early American history. For criticism of the historian's use of anthropology in this way, see John W. Adams (an anthropologist) on "Consensus, Community, and Exoticism," *Journal of Interdisciplinary History* 12 (1981): 253–65; Ronald G. Walters, "Signs of the Times: Clifford Geertz and Historians," *Social Research* 47 (1980): 537–56; and my own "Encounter with Ethnography: A Review of Isaac's *Transformation of Virginia*," *Historical Methods* 16 (1983): 82–86, and "History and Anthropology: Clio's Dalliances," ibid., 19 (1986): 120–23.

25. It is ironic that the Racine conference of American intellectual historians noted in the text — where so many of the practitioners in effect announced their conversion to Geertz and culture — was separated by only a few months from a conference of early American social historians in Chicago at which Isaac announced his ethnographic method. The proceedings of the latter conference were published in part in *Historical Methods* 13 (1980): 1–74.

26. There is, of course, considerably more to the intermixture of social history and anthropology than the "ethnographic connection." See, for example, Andrejs Plakans, *Kinship in the Past: An Anthropology of European Family Life, 1500–1900* (Oxford, 1984), a volume

is, in sum, no one thing, no "movement" in the regular sense of the word. At its worst, it is what critics have called it: "mindless empiricism" applied to any subject which in some way can be designated "social." In this sense it is the fulfillment of Auguste Comte's prophecy for history as a whole: an "irrational spirit of specialization" leading ultimately to the "vain accumulation of unrelated monographs" in which "all idea of the real and simultaneous connection between diverse human events" is "lost in the midst of the sterile encumbrances of . . . confused descriptions."[27] At its best, however—and I insist there is a "best" side—it seems to me to be a particular attitude toward the doing of history which involves three things: the subject of the work, the method, and theory.

Subject first: Very simply, the American social historian deals with past societies, his own if he is a "new social historian" of the United States. The total society evolving in time is ultimately at issue, of course; but whole societies, let alone ever-changing societies, are complex, pattern-streaked affairs, resistant to analyses. Whole societies, however, if larger than the sum of their parts (and most would say they are), are at least equal to the sum. Hence there is a tendency to concentrate on the parts as manageable affairs rather than on the difficult whole, first to determine the variables on which the whole seems appropriately broken into parts meaningful for the particular time (gender, age, kinship, wealth and income, power, status, occupation and profession, ethnicity, geography, and more); then to analyze the parts themselves (families and kin groups, status groups) and their perception of themselves vis-à-vis their material and social surroundings; finally, to analyze the relationship of one part to others. Always there is at least the ideal of the work somehow bearing upon the totality of relationships between the individuals grouped in parts (however those parts are defined) and among the parts themselves—that is to say, on the

---

drawing upon a British social anthropological tradition and unmatched in American history despite the enormous literature on the American family. But the ethnographic historians have very largely defined anthropology for American historians. See Kammen in his introduction to *The Past before Us*, ed. Kammen, 41, and Daniel Scott Smith, "Early American Historiography and Social Science History," *Social Science History* 6 (1982): 284; Smith cites Isaac when declaring that "the anthropological method" is "the best hope for actually writing the history of the inarticulate." Cf. Adams, "Consensus, Community, and Exoticism," 253–54. Adams points to Marvin Harris as representing a materialist position in anthropology which considers "demography, ecology, and the economy" to be "more fundamental than such superstructural ideas as the sacredness of cows." Most social historians, however, have gravitated to the cows in ignorance of an anthropological tradition which has produced such works as Harris's *Cows, Pigs, Wars, and Witches: The Riddles of Culture* (New York, 1974), *Cultural Materialism: The Struggle for a Science of Culture* (New York, 1979), and his massive review of the various anthropological traditions in *The Rise of Anthropological Theory: A History of Theories of Culture* (New York, 1968).

27. Quoted in my "The New Social History: Enthusiasm Revisited and Found Wanting," *NEHA News: The Newsletter of the New England Historical Association* 9 (1982): 4.

nature of the whole society, an ideal which seems to explain, to some extent at least, the popularity of local or community studies among our "new social historians". Small, delimited societies obviously are more readily encompassed as total entities than are larger, more spacious societies such as nation-states, while there seems at least the possibility that the form of the larger society can be glimpsed through many studies of its smallest geographic parts.[28] And always there is an awareness of time, and with it a concern for the potential for change in the variables being used, in the constituencies and self-perceptions of the parts as defined by those variables, and in the relationships between parts. We would hardly be historians without this awareness of time and change. In brief, the subject of the best of our "new social history" is the ever-changing social and (to the extent we feel we can enter into them) mental systems of the past.

Why social historians choose this as a subject is, I think, an individual affair. In some instances, of course, it is little more than the fact that a particular historian finds a particular society or societal part interesting. The work, in effect, is fun; it satisfies a curiosity. For others, the work is perhaps an expiation of past sins (his ancestors having emasculated the black and deprived him of his culture, the white historian makes amends by creating a black past) or in anticipation of future politics (the demonstration of the "maldistribution" of wealth in past times in some fashion is seen as paving the way for the redistribution of wealth in some future time). And a very few (myself included) still dream vaguely of some kind of "science of society" and search for constants of human social behavior that can be applied, perhaps, to some future social planning. Such motives tend to direct our individual work, even color it at times and hence provoke argument. But essentially motive is irrelevant to the subject of the venture that all share. The "new social historian" in America studies total societies over time, normally in terms of parts and the interrelationships between parts.

Second, method — or, better put, a concern for method — is a mark of our "new social history." By this I obviously do not mean that all use the same tools in the work, that all are "quantifiers," for example (although quantification is certainly a strong suit), or that all are Geertzian ethnologists. My point, rather, is that there is, in the best of our "new social

28. See, e.g., Kathleen Neils Conzen, "Community Studies, Urban History, and American Local History," in *The Past before Us*, ed. Kammen, 270–91; Darrett B. Rutman, "Assessing the Little Communities of Early America," *William and Mary Quarterly*, 3d ser., 43 (1986): 163–78; Richard R. Beeman, "The New Social History and the Search for 'Community' in Colonial America," *American Quarterly* 29 (1977): 422–43; Robert R. Dykstra and William Silag, "Doing Local History: Monographic Approaches to the Smaller Community," ibid., 37 (1985): 411–25; Clyde Griffen, "Community Studies and the Investigation of Nineteenth-Century Social Relations," *Social Science History* 10 (1986): 315–38.

history," a consistent and overt concern for the relationships between the questions asked, the materials to which questions are addressed, the answers which the materials offer, and, above all, the relationship of answers to a past reality. The last is the most important for it is a given — that is to say, a primary axiom — that there are no pure and absolute truths out there patiently awaiting some historian's discovery. History is acknowledged to be a manufactured product, something made by the historian out of the detritus of past lives and bearing only a probabilistic relationship to the reality of those lives. Our facts and theses, in other words, are not truths but probability statements, some, by virtue of the simplicity or parsimoniousness of the statement and the weight of evidence, bearing little chance of error ("Columbus sailed . . ."), others so broad and tangentially drawn from evidence as to have little more than a random chance at truth ("Americans felt . . ."). In this light, a concern for method is a concern for the way the detritus is mined to produce not an unattainable absolute but a most probable estimate.

By way of a simple example: Our quantifiers have produced innumerable Lorenz diagrams of the distribution of wealth, complete with a variety of summary indices — Gini, Schutz, SSTT (Size Share of the Top Ten percent) — which enable ready comparison across time and place. But all know that these are only approximations of a reality; all know, too, that they are more often than not based upon partial data, and that what is missing can as easily bias the result as not. In the case of early American history, such diagrams and statistics are based on a particular class of records — probate — and in particular on an aggregate analysis of inventories of the estates of deceased individuals completed in the weeks or months following their deaths. But do the inventories reflect true values? We know that those doing the inventories were laymen drafted by the community to do the work. Did they consistently do it well or carelessly? Did they know or simply guess at the value of things, and if the latter, did they consistently guess high, or low, or randomly? Equally to the point, for what percentage of deaths do we have inventories? Is this percentage equal across age and sex groups? Across wealth groups? On the answers to such questions depends our ability to extrapolate from the distribution of wealth indicated by the inventories to the most probable distribution of wealth for the living population. What has happened, actually, is that an old nineteenth-century habit of textual or internal criticism — Who wrote this document? What is the bias of the author? How might the author's bias affect a conclusion drawn from it? — has been revived and applied generally to the classes of documents used by our quantifiers.[29] But it is

---

29. See, e.g., Daniel Scott Smith, "Underregistration and Bias in Probate Records: An Analysis of Data from Eighteenth-Century Hingham, Massachusetts," *William and Mary*

not just the quantifiers. Another example is to be found in Robert Darn-ton's attempt to depict the *mentalité* of the eighteenth-century French peasantry by analysis of their fairy tales. Whether in the end Darnton succeeds or (as many believe) fails is beside the point. Darnton displays a "new social history" stance by opening the study not with a finding but with an analysis of the fairy tales themselves—What are they? What is their relationship to the peasantry? How (if at all) can we extrapolate from the plots and language of the tales to the peasant *mentalité*?[30]

A common subject and a common concern for the interrelationship of questions, materials, and answers: these are two marks of the best of our "new social history." A third is a common rejection of all the grand gener-alizations or historical megatheories. Born in a rejection of megatheory— the intellectual history consensus of the 1950s—the genre has been im-pervious over the years to the development or imposition of any new grand synthesis. In the case of most practitioners the rejection is implicit; they present their findings relative to this or that phenomenon—the fam-ily, for example, or wealth distribution, or an all-encompassing study of a single community—only in terms of the evolving literature concerned with the subject itself, all the while constructing, testing, or merely using (sometimes impressionistically rather than systematically) low- and middle-level theories about the subject drawn from or applicable to the other social sciences but ignoring the potential for incorporating findings into the overarching grand scheme of a Turner, a Marx, or a Weber. A few, however, consciously reject megatheory as conducive to false questions and easy, deductive answers. A Turnerian, for example, would ask, How did the fact of a frontier affect the population of a newly settled area?— assuming in advance that "frontier" has, on the one hand, an intrinsic meaning and, on the other, that it axiomatically had an effect. The best of our social historians ask, Did a new material environment have an effect on the entering population? and even reverse the question to ask whether the incoming population had an effect upon the environment and whether there was a looping effect of the changed environment back upon the population. For his part, a Weberian might ask, In what way did the Puritan ministry of New England embody capitalism? rather than, What sort of economic attitudes did the ministry express, and how did these attitudes relate to the economy of the moment? And an American Marxist,

---

Quarterly, 3d ser., 32 (1975): 100–110, and the work of Gloria L. Main, including "Probate Records as a Source for Early American History," ibid., 89–99; "The Correction of Biases in Colonial American Probate Records," *Historical Methods* 8 (1974): 10–28, and *Tobacco Colony: Life in Early Maryland, 1650–1720* (Princeton, N.J., 1982), Appendix C, "Probate Records as a Source for Historical Investigation."

30. Darnton, *The Great Cat Massacre and Other Episodes in French Cultural History* (New York, 1984), 9–72.

assuming the general appropriateness of "class" as a categorical scheme and "class conflict" as the moving force in history, will ask (almost plaintively), Why don't Americans "think" in class terms? in contrast to the social historian who sets "class" aside and seeks simply the categorical and causal scheme that best fits the data at hand.

It is no understatement to say that this rejection of large generalization is, in the United States, the most obvious and the most criticized feature of the "new social history," now grown at least mature, if not old. No critic has faulted the quantum leap (both in kind and extent) in historical knowledge of the past three decades. The new social historian has peered into bedrooms to study conception cycles, sat by sickbeds to explore the social effects of disease, peered over the storekeeper's shoulder as he entered items in his ledger to get a sense of the kind and extent of debt networks. The historian — or rather his computer — has absorbed volume after volume of vital records, censuses, city directories, and the like, counting, categorizing, and correlating the number of children, kin, households, families, occupations, mills, and mill hands. Who was literate and who not? Who black, who white? Who moved (socially, economically, spatially) and who stayed put? Who had electricity (and when?) and who had none? An old newspaperman's motto — "Who did what? When? And where?" — has taken form in myriad graphs and tables.

All this is well and good, say the critics; new knowledge, new insights, even into small affairs, are certainly welcome. But history per se — or at least the American Clio — stands disheveled. "Monographs fly about in hopeless disarray," one critic complained; "there is no coherence, there are no central organizing principles, no themes or stories — no narratives — to hold the pieces together." Wrote another: "At this point in the history of American historiography, we have lost any overall approach to the framework of American history." Still another: The new scholarship "affords us merely a melange of isolated, unconnected truths. It seems almost untouched by any evident passion for grander patterns of truth that might vivify lifeless local truths, and unaffected" — here one senses the critic's tear for the old consensus history that the new had overturned — "by the faith that fired the persisting quest of earlier annalists for the national character."[31] But from no quarter is the criticism more shrill than from American Marxists. Having emerged from near oblivion in American historiography in the 1960s and early 1970s — in tandem with the "new social history," recall — they turned almost immediately upon any and every social analysis which did not share their own overarching

31. Gordon Wood, "Star-Spangled History," *New York Review of Books* (12 Aug. 1982): 6; Robert F. Berkhofer, Jr., "The Organizational Interpretation of American History: A New Synthesis," *Prospects* 4 (1979): 611; Zuckerman, "Myth and Method," 221.

conceptualization; for them, non-Marxist social history in general and quantitative social history in particular not only has no point but is based upon "inadequate assumptions about how the world works," is "wedded to Western bourgeois liberalism in ways that cleverly mask as 'science' some very important myths that act as agents of stability," and uses statistics (ignorantly and inappropriately) at the cost of the depth and richness of the human experience. Class consciousness, after all, "is not susceptible to the same kind of measurement as other features of individual or group life."[32]

And yet all of this criticism misses the point of America's "new social history." True, it is empirical, but not mindlessly so, or out of some naive belief in an old-fashioned "scientific" realism, a charge frequently made.[33] The only reality recognized consists of the material remnants of an otherwise mute past — for the most part bits of paper inscribed with words of uncertain meaning — and, as noted, the best of its practitioners attempt to reconstruct only a "most probable" past from these remnants. True, too, it is antipathetical to any and all grand megatheories that define in the abstract how the world operates and hence direct their devotees in the act of reconstruction. But this by no means implies a lack of theory. The "new social historians" proceed inductively rather than deductively, upward from small observations and small theories (replete in our small studies, for those who care to look) toward and eventually to middle- and higher-level theories. And they proceed parsimoniously, seeking to make connections as directly and with as few assumptions as possible. They are, in brief, akin to the inchworms patiently working their way among the leaves; frequently retracing their steps — as witness the incessant arguments among the practitioners of this kind of history — they are as critical of each other as others are of them, bemused but not confounded by the butterflies who condemn their slow progress. True, finally, the "new social historians" in America are cautious. In essence, this seems the gist of much of the criticism that we have neither developed nor adopted a grand synthesis or theory. But humankind — of the American or any breed — is a difficult animal to comprehend, and human society (we are told time and again by philosophers) more complex even than the universe. Given this, the caution that today so marks America's "new social history" — and, indeed, all those aspects of American historiography touched by the intellectual revolution of the past three decades — seems far more appropriate than any precipitous rush to grand generalization.

32. Nancy Fitch, "Statistical Fantasies and Historical Facts: History in Crisis and Its Methodological Implications," *Historical Methods* 17 (1984): 248–49; Katherine A. Lynch, "The Use of Quantitative Data in the Historical Analysis of Social Classes," ibid., 234.

33. See, for example, Fitch, "Statistical Fantasies," 240.

3 Community Study

*I have twice attempted to define the nature of historical commu-
nity studies, the "small worlds" of my title, once in a lengthy chapter published in
1973, again in a paper delivered to a conference on "Strategies and Approaches in
Early American History" held at the Newberry Library in Chicago in October
1977 and subsequently published in* Historical Methods. *A great deal of thought
about the approach intervened between attempts. The second (and I believe better)
is included here, sans only a brief, technical appendix on network analysis.*

Clearly the community study has become, over the past decade and a
half, a distinct and popular research strategy in early American history. So indefatigable has been the onslaught on local records, so lengthy
has the list of locally oriented books, theses, and articles become, that
John J. Waters has been led to comment, only partly tongue-in-cheek, on
an academic revivalism akin to the Great Awakening.[1] Yet what is it that
we study when we study "community," and how is it to be studied?

Two cardinal distinctions are immediately in order. The first is commonly accepted in sociology and anthropology but too frequently unrec-
ognized in history. It is that between studies of a particular phenomenon
(or of particular phenomena) which are simply sited in a single locale and
studies in which community per se, either as an abstract concept or with
the locale as a particular example of that concept, is the actual subject
under scrutiny.

Philip J. Greven, Jr.'s study of Andover is certainly the first type. The

Originally published in *Historical Methods* 13:1 (1980): 29–41. Reprinted with permission of
the Helen Dwight Reid Educational Foundation. Published by Heldref Publications, 1319
18th Street N.W., Washington, D.C. 20036–1802. Copyright © 1980 by the Helen Dwight
Reid Educational Foundation.

1. Waters, "Patrimony, Succession, and Social Stability: Guilford, Connecticut, in the
Eighteenth Century," *Perspectives in American History* 10 (1976): 131.

subject of his work was not community in the abstract, nor even the community of Andover, but rather "the character of family life in an agrarian society." The town itself was no more than a convenient universe in which to investigate the subject. Locally based historical demography as a genre falls into this first category, too. When, for example, Daniel Scott Smith approached the records of Hingham, Massachusetts, or Daniel Blake Smith tested demographic conclusions about early Chesapeake society in Charles Parish, Virginia, or John Demos used a Bristol, Rhode Island, census, they were investigating neither community as a concept nor particular communities.[2] All of these studies, and more — studies of mobility and persistence, of equality and inequality, of politics in towns and counties, most recently of *mentalité* — are manifestations in history of what one sociologist has distinguished in that sister discipline as "studies of *life in communities* . . . not really studies of communities as such, but of social life which happens to take place and be studied within community settings."[3]

In early American history relatively few studies have assumed community itself as the subject. Overwhelmingly these few have dealt with New England and are extensions of Puritan studies. They involve the definition in terms of community and communalism of "the world we have lost" and, conversely, the transition into the world we have gained. Community is something which existed at a point in time and either does not exist today or exists in a very much diluted form; hence it is something whose disappearance or decline is a historical event to be explored. Kenneth A. Lockridge's *A New England Town* is a prime example, the story of "a Utopian Commune" collapsing into "A Provincial Town" well worth the telling, according to its author, because from it "emerges the certainty that the village community had physically disintegrated, [and] the probability that a society more accustomed to social diversity and political dissent had begun to evolve." But the locus for such studies has not always been the single community. Michael Zuckerman spanned fifteen Massachusetts towns to depict "a broadly diffused desire for consensual communalism as the operative premise of group life." John J. Waters used the towns of one Mas-

2. Greven, *Four Generations: Population, Land, and Family in Colonial Andover, Massachusetts* (Ithaca, N.Y., 1970), 1; D. S. Smith, "The Demographic History of Colonial New England," *Journal of Economic History* 32 (1972): 165–83; D. B. Smith, "Mortality and Family in the Colonial Chesapeake," *Journal of Interdisciplinary History* 8 (1978): 403–27; Demos, "Families in Colonial Bristol, Rhode Island: An Exercise in Historical Demography," *William and Mary Quarterly*, 3d ser., 25 (1968): 40–57.

3. Richard L. Simpson, "Sociology of the Community: Current Status and Prospects," *Rural Sociology* 30 (1965): 127. See also Conrad M. Arensberg and Solon T. Kimball, "Community Study: Retrospect and Prospect," in *The Sociology of Community*, ed. Colin Bell and Howard Newby (London, 1974), 339.

sachusetts county to depict "an old model" of community with "peaceful, consensual, and participatory peasant villages." Richard L. Bushman took all of Connecticut as his laboratory in demonstrating the end between 1690 and 1765 of "the close-knit, tightly controlled, homogeneous community" of a past time and the appearance of a new, open, pluralistic, and voluntaristic social order.[4] What holds such studies together is the exploration of community as a reality of the past (but probably not of the American present) involving specific values and behavior patterns.[5]

The second distinction to be made in community studies is that between community as an ideal (either the historical actor's idealization or the historian's) and the community as simply a field of social interaction. A modern glossary of terms makes the distinction clear when it defines *community* in two separate and distinct ways: (1) "A group of people living together in some identifiable territory and sharing a set of interests embracing their lifeways" and (2) "that mythical state of social wholeness in which each member has his place and in which life is regulated by cooperation rather than by competition. It . . . always seems to be in decline at any given historical present. Thus community is that which each generation feels it must rediscover and re-create."[6] We can restate the distinction in terms of historical situations. When, for example, John Winthrop of Massachusetts spoke of the necessity of the settlers being "knitt together . . . as one man," he was reflecting an ideal of community; when he entered Robert Keayne's Boston store to buy a plow for his farm or sought a wife among the widows of the town after the death of his beloved Margaret, he was interacting socially within a communal setting whether that community met the terms of his ideals or not. When Virginia's Roger Green complained of the "dispersed manner of planting" in that colony, he was reflecting his ideal of community, one very much akin to Winthrop's. When, however, he mounted the pulpit to speak to the scattered planters now assembled in church, he was taking part in a communal rite of some

4. Lockridge, *A New England Town, the First Hundred Years: Dedham, Massachusetts, 1636–1736* (New York, 1970), 91; Zuckerman, *Peaceable Kingdoms: New England Towns in the Eighteenth Century* (New York, 1970), 4; Waters, "The Traditional World of the New England Peasants: A View from Seventeenth-Century Barnstable," *New England Historical and Genealogical Register* 130 (1976): 21; Bushman, *From Puritan to Yankee: Character and the Social Order in Connecticut, 1690–1765* (Cambridge, Mass., 1967), ix-x.

5. Zuckerman is something of an exception. In *Peaceable Kingdoms*, 256–57, communalism survives into our modern America and "belies the belief that we are a liberal society which . . . has always known 'the reality of atomistic social freedom.'" In "The Fabrication of Identity in Early America," *William and Mary Quarterly*, 3d ser., 34 (1977): 183–214, atomism and communalism (or "self and society") are in antagonistic juxtaposition from early modern Europe to modern America.

6. Charles Abrams, *The Language of Cities: A Glossary of Terms* (New York, 1971), 59–60.

kind even though the community was so far removed from his ideal that he could deny its very existence.[7] Similarly, when the student of community idealizes the concept in terms of particular values or behavior patterns — peaceful, consensual, tight-knit — the subjects within his locale will be interacting socially on a local (or communal) scale whether reflecting the scholar's idealization or not.

Obviously the ideal of community at particular times and places is an appropriate subject for investigation. The difference (or lack of difference, if that should prove to be the case) between the idealized community and the reality of the local society is similarly appropriate. But the confusion of the communal ideal and the operative community, the failure to disentangle the two, has long bedeviled community studies.

More often than not the damaging ideal has been lodged in the investigator's mind with the result that the community has been both something of value and something to be subjected to dispassionate analysis. The impossible duality was present at the birth of community as an analytic concept, when Ferdinand Tönnies first dichotomized *Gemeinschaft* (community) and *Gesellschaft* (society or association). Community involved an old, warm, personal, and friendly way of village life which Tönnies viewed with sadness as disappearing from late nineteenth-century Germany; society involved the cold, impersonal, fragmented, urban life emerging. "In community with one's family, one lives from birth on, bound to it in weal and woe," Tönnies wrote. But "one goes into society as one goes into a strange country. A young man is warned against bad society, but the expression bad community violates the meaning of the word." "Community is old; society is new as a name as well as phenomenon."[8] The same duality was transmuted into the anthropologists' folk-urban continuum. Robert Redfield's folk village had "a Rousseauean quality," wrote his most vigorous critic, an "homogeneous, isolated, smoothly functioning and well-integrated society made up of a contented and well adjusted people" more the product of the scholar's values than a reflection

---

7. Winthrop, "A Modell of Christian Charity" (1630), in Massachusetts Historical Society, *Winthrop Papers* (Boston, 1929–47), 2:294; R[oger] G[reen], *Virginia's Cure: or, An Advisive Narrative concerning Virginia* (1662), in Peter Force, comp., *Tracts and Other Papers, Relating Principally to the . . . Colonies in North America* (Washington, D.C., 1836–47), vol. 3, tract 15:5.

8. Tönnies, *Community and Society* (1887), trans. Charles P. Loomis (East Lansing, Mich., 1957), 33–34. I have taken the liberty of translating "community" and "society" in the quotations. Writes Alan Macfarlane, "History, Anthropology, and the Study of Communities," *Social History* 5 (1977): 632, of Tönnies's gemeinschaft: "The belief in such 'communities' is one of the most powerful myths in industrial society, shaping not only policy and government . . . but also affecting thought and research. Expecting to find 'communities' the prophecy fulfilled itself and communities were found."

of reality. Redfield could only agree. His Tepotztlan as restudied by another scholar was indeed far from the idyllic community of his own work. And "the greater part of the explanation for the difference," he wrote, "is to be found in differences between the two investigators. . . . Without benefit of any well-considered scheme or theoretical idea at all, I looked at certain aspects of . . . life because they both interested me and pleased me."[9] Transmuted into still newer dichotomies (peasant villager and commercial farmer, the world of tradition and the modernized world, "the world we have lost" and the world we have gained), the duality persists. Somehow that which is passing is better. So it is, for example, in Lockridge's Dedham. The descriptive words and phrases ring with values. "Simplicity," "stability," "tranquility" describe the passing "Closed Corporate Peasant [and Puritan] Community," and that passing involves disintegration before "powerful divisive forces" as men "heeded the voice of mere convenience" and "abandoned" their villages for isolated farmsteads and profit.[10]

Contemporary sociologists and anthropologists are well aware of the damage done by the failure to separate community as an ideal from community as simply a field of social action. A recent survey of sociological community studies described the literature as "some of the most appealing and infuriating products of modern sociology." "They are," the writers continued, "appealing because they present in an easily accessible and readable way, descriptions and analyses of the very stuff of sociology, the social organization of human beings; and infuriating because they are so idiosyncratic and diverse as to steadfastly resist most attempts to synthesize their findings." Historians, too, for much the same reason, are beginning to question the validity of community studies. Edward M. Cook, with reference to works on New England towns, has noted that although they would fill a sizable bookshelf, "the interpretative advances hardly seem proportional to the effort invested." Richard R. Beeman has written that their "glimpse into the diversity of colonial America" has discovered

9. Oscar Lewis, *Life in a Mexican Village: Tepotztlan Restudied* (Urbana, Ill., 1951), 428; Redfield, *The Little Community* (Chicago, 1960), 134–35.

10. Lockridge, *A New England Town*, 18, 167–68, 172–73. Parenthetically, the application of a peasant model to New England by Lockridge and others who followed his lead — including Waters in "Traditional World of the New England Peasants," 3–21, and Darrett B. Rutman in *American Puritanism: Faith and Practice* (Philadelphia, 1970), 77–78 — misses completely the dynamic quality of both leading peasant models in anthropology, Eric R. Wolf's *Peasants* (Englewood Cliffs, N.J., 1966) and Robert Redfield's *Peasant Society and Culture* (Chicago, 1956). Wolf's peasant is constantly adjusting his strategy as he deals with economic demands upon his production. Redfield's peasant is regularly incorporating elements of the external "great tradition" into his local "little tradition." Wolf's words (p. 17) apply to both conceptualizations: "Literary clichés about the immovable peasantry to the contrary, a peasantry is always in a dynamic state."

"a particularism . . . which makes it hazardous to advance almost any generalization." And Robert F. Berkhofer, Jr., has commented that "while the proliferation of community studies in all periods of American history attests to their relative ease of accomplishment . . . they all too frequently fail to enhance the historical understanding of American society at any one time or over time."[11]

In sociology, too, the associated sins of "pronouncement" and "expropriation" have been isolated — the scholar pronouncing what values and behavior patterns ought to constitute community and expropriating as community that which meets the test pronounced.[12] In history, the variety of pronouncements and expropriations over the past few years has made us appear to be classic absent-minded professors regularly losing our valuables. Robert Wiebe depicted the loss in America between 1877 and 1920 of what he pronounced to be community. Stephan Thernstrom and Michael H. Frisch independently lost community in the early nineteenth century; Bushman lost it in the eighteenth; Lockridge lost it around 1690; and some have said Rutman lost it when he disembarked John Winthrop from the *Arbella* in 1630.[13]

And sociologists are currently attempting the rescue of the genre by consciously divorcing community from any and every particular set of values and behavior. Community is being considered simply an inevitable concomitant of the fact that people live and associate territorially; hence the nature of associations within territories and, because no group is ever completely isolated, between those within and those without can be studied on the level of territory. Community is real — the concurrence of

11. Bell and Newby, "Introduction," in *Sociology of Community*, xliii, and in their *Community Studies: An Introduction to the Sociology of the Local Community* (London, 1971), 13; Cook, *The Fathers of the Towns: Leadership and Community Structure in Eighteenth-Century New England* (Baltimore, 1976), xi; Beeman, "The New Social History and the Search for 'Community' in Colonial America," *American Quarterly* 29 (1977): 426; Berkhofer, "From Colonial Communities to Modern Mass Society: A Social Evolutionary Model of American History" (Paper read before the American Historical Association, Washington, D.C., Dec. 1976).

12. George A. Hillery, Jr., *Communal Organizations: A Study of Local Societies* (Chicago, 1968), 4. In his "Definitions of Community: Areas of Agreement," *Rural Sociology* 20 (1955): 111–23, Hillery isolated ninety-four separate definitions of community "pronounced" by various scholars.

13. Wiebe, *The Search for Order, 1877–1920* (New York, 1967); Thernstrom, *Poverty and Progress: Social Mobility in a Nineteenth-Century City* (Cambridge, Mass., 1964); Frisch, *Town into City: Springfield, Massachusetts, and the Meaning of Community, 1840–1880* (Cambridge, Mass., 1972); Bushman, *Puritan to Yankee*; Lockridge, *A New England Town*; Rutman, *Winthrop's Boston: Portrait of a Puritan Town, 1630–1649* (Chapel Hill, N.C., 1965). Berkhofer, "Colonial Communities to Modern Mass Society," makes the point of this recurrent loss of community, as does Zuckerman, "Fabrication of Identity," 183–84, and Thomas Bender, *Community and Social Change in America* (New Brunswick, N.J., 1978), 46–53.

group and place — but so diverse a social phenomenon as to defy every attempt to define it in terms of specific behavioral characteristics or values. It is, to use Talcott Parsons's definition, merely "that aspect of the structure of social systems . . . observable and analysable with reference to location as a focus of attention."[14] If history is not to produce in the end the same sort of community study literature — appealing yet infuriating, filled with the stuff of history but so idiosyncratic as to defy comparison and generalization — it will have to adopt just this sort of pragmatic, neutral approach.[15]

To return to the question with which we opened: What is it that we study when we study "community"? As a matter of strategy, we conceive the subject to be simply the people of any particular locale, the pattern of their associations among themselves and with others beyond the locale, and, over time, the changes in those patterns. No assumptions are made as to particular ideas, values, or behavior patterns that are, or are not, to be associated with community, no antecedent thought as to the strength of community bonds or community sentiments. Perhaps, in a given place at a given time, the ideas, values, and patterns underlying interpersonal relations will be found to be such as to be capable of categorization as village, folk, peasant, or traditional. But at best these are adjectives to be attached as a result of study, not attributes inherent in the very concept of community and carried into the study. At other times or in other places we must be ready to find open-country communities, urban communities, farm communities, and the "communities of limited liability" of our modern world.[16] Indeed, one goal of community studies ought to be the refinement of these and other yet-uncoined adjectives and phrases and in the doing contribute to the development of a typology of community types.

How does one go about such a study? What follows sketches a single research model predicated upon a series of informing assumptions, the first of which is a truism needing expression only because of an American tendency to exalt individualism. Simply put, it is the assumption that people inevitably associate in groups, that with regard to humankind nature abhors the solitary individual. As sociologist Gerhard E. Lenski put it, "The starting point . . . is the deceptively simple assertion that *man is a*

14. Parsons, "The Principal Structures of Community," in *Community*, ed. Carl J. Friedrich (New York, 1959), 250.

15. A case in point is the tendency in American history to equate community and the New England town. In addition to the studies already cited, see Page Smith, *As a City upon a Hill: The Town in American History* (New York, 1966), and David J. Russo, *Families and Communities: A New View of American History* (Nashville, 1974). The tendency inevitably leads either to the proposition that other areas (e.g., the early Chesapeake) were devoid of community or to new definitions of community that can be applied to those areas. In either event the ability to compare and generalize is lost.

16. Gerald D. Suttles, *The Social Construction of Communities* (Chicago, 1972), 47–48.

social being obliged by nature to live with others as members of society." John Donne was more lyrical: "No man is an *Iland*, intire of it selfe."[17]

Second, the associations which link people within society are not chaotic but ordered in the sense that people tend to relate to each other in and through certain well-defined nodal points. For personal and group purposes — and the two cannot really be separated — people come together at particular locations and in particular institutions to act together in formal and informal ways. The workplace and shopping center, a bar — Boston's fictional "Cheers" — a parent-teacher association are all readily identifiable as contemporary nodes, but obviously past societies might have different sets.

Third, associations between individuals are to some extent related to landform, distance, and technology. The assumption is taken from geography and can again be summed up in truisms. People living on opposite sides of a milewide river will associate less than people living on the same side. And people constrained by the level of their technology to walking or riding horseback will have a more limited geographical circle of active relationships than those who drive cars or ride Boeing jumbo jets. The river is a "barrier" to relationships between those on either side or, from the vantage point of one group, a "boundary" separating it from that on the opposite side. Distance relative to technology is "friction."[18]

Fourth, just as associations are related to the physical topography of the locale, they are related to the social topography. We can, in other words, presume the existence of social friction as summed up, again, in a truism: The scullery maid has little occasion to meet and marry the king. And just as spatial fiction is dependent upon technology, social friction is dependent upon the extent to which a hierarchical ordering, or other differentiation, is accepted within the locale.

Finally, interpersonal relationships form networks among people. To put the matter simply, any single individual lives in some relationship with other individuals, and these others with still others, some of whom live in relationship with the first, some not. In the abstract one could start tracing these relationships with a single individual and proceed infinitely in time and space; in this sense the "human community" is boundless. In the abstract, too, the nature of the relationship being considered can be defined in such a way as to make viable such terms as "community of scholars" and "the Christian community." But in the reality of community study, a venture which begins with the notion of locale, the student at one and the same time isolates a geographic segment of the human commu-

17. Lenski, *Power and Privilege: A Theory of Social Stratification* (New York, 1966), 25; Donne, *Devotions upon Emergent Ocasions* (1624), ed. John Sparrow (Cambridge, 1923), 98.

18. See Ronald Abler et al., *Spatial Organization* (Englewood Cliffs, N.J., 1971), chaps. 8, 10, 11, for a general discussion of these basic concepts.

nity and attempts to deal with the totality of the isolate, scholars, Christians, and all.[19]

The assumption as to interpersonal relationships forming networks among people opens for the researcher a formal mode of analysis developed first in geography and subsequently applied in anthropology and sociology.[20] Figure 3.1 exemplifies the analysis. Each point symbolizes an individual within a spatial or social context; each line between points depicts the existence of a defined (but for purposes of illustration unspecified) relationship; and the whole complex is considered to constitute a single network. An attendant — but by no means complex — mathematics allows a finite description of the network. The mean number of linkages that members of any network have with each other defines the "degree" of embeddedness of the network. Among any given number of network members there is a maximum number of possible linkages; the percentage of all such possibilities actually existing defines the "density" of the network, a number representing the probability of a member chosen at random being linked to another also chosen at random. The clustering that we intuitively sense in figure 3.1 — the fact that the members form two groups — can be tested by comparing the density of the whole network with that for each cluster. In this oversimplified case, all possible relationships within the clusters considered independently are active, hence each has a density of 100 percent. The density of the network as a whole is 46 percent. The clustering might well reflect the presence of a boundary or barrier between the groups, perhaps a physical obstacle, or the fact of spatial or social friction between groups, or the centripetal effect of nodes within each that create a proclivity toward relationships within (in contrast to barriers that act as constraints to relationships without). Obviously the logic of the analysis is reversible. If demonstrable clustering (as in fig. 3.1) suggests the possibility of barriers, friction, and nodes, then the demonstration that barriers, friction, and nodes do indeed exist at a particular time and place ought to suggest the possibility that social relationships are clustered. The historian, although unable to undertake the formal mathematical analysis in every instance, can still be guided by the theoretical framework underlying the mathematics.

A network approach to community study, moreover, opens the way for a researcher to catch the linkages that bind the locale to the broader

---

19. Macfarlane, "History, Anthropology and the Study of Communities," 649.

20. For a brief introduction to the theory and practice of network analysis, see the appendix to the version of this essay published in *Historical Methods* 13 (1980): 37–39. For a far fuller view and a comprehensive bibliography of the sociological literature, see Barry Wellman and S. D. Berkowitz, eds., *Social Structures: A Network Approach* (New York, 1988), particularly chap. 2 (Wellman's "Structural Analysis: From Method and Metaphor to Theory and Substance") and part 2 ("Communities").

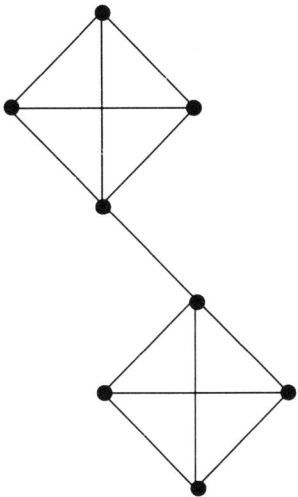

Fig. 3.1. A hypothetical network with two clusters

society. We study isolates, places, small worlds, but in the firm knowledge that places are not, in reality, isolated but parts of larger worlds. In an earlier grappling with this elusive notion of community I put the point in terms of the people of an early American locale, for the most part looking "inward toward the community itself, their activities and their contemplations confined, localized," but with a few here and there "whose activities and thoughts" went beyond the locale:

> The storekeeper who takes in the surplus agricultural commodities raised by his neighbors, passes the surplus into channels of commerce, receiving back articles which the community cannot produce for itself. . . . The minister, on the one hand shepherd of his local flock, on the other drawn irresistibly into association with his compeers throughout the area. . . . Those who, by virtue of their offices, are part of an elaborate political web stretching from the lowly poundkeeper obliged to enforce the colony laws relative to stray animals, through the leadership in the colonial capital, to the officers of the Crown in London.[21]

We can, in essence, think of community study as involving the exploration of relational networks sketched on two planes, one horizontal and (to use Parsons's words again) "analysable with reference to location," the other

21. Rutman, "The Social Web: A Prospectus for the Study of the Early American Community," in *Insights and Parallels: Problems and Issues of American Social History*, ed. William L. O'Neill (Minneapolis, 1973), 77–78.

vertical, bisecting our location and extending upward and downward, bisecting countless other locations in turn. Thus figure 3.1 might depict horizontal networks within two geographically bounded locales linked by an element of a vertical network — that relationship drawn between the apex of the lower diamond and the nadir of the upper.

Carried into the materials of the study, the five assumptions frame essential questions as to the physical, cultural, social, and institutional terrain. How were the individuals and families of the locale distributed spatially and socially? What features of the land, of technology, of social thought, or economics divided them or threw them together? With whom did particular individuals associate, and what configurations did their networks assume? What vertical networks linked the locale to the wider world? A hypothetical and much-truncated reconstruction of a locale at the turn of the eighteenth century based upon a study of Middlesex County, Virginia — summarized in the diagrams of figure 3.2 — exemplifies a network approach to these questions.[22]

The locale is a roughly rectangular Chesapeake county, approximately twenty miles long and averaging five miles in width. To the north it is bounded by a milewide river, to the south by a narrow stream and swamp, to the east by Chesapeake Bay. Only to the west is there an unobstructed political boundary. One road winds down the spine of the county from west to east; another branches from the main road near the center and leads across a bridge into the county to the south. In the first diagram of figure 3.2, we have located upon the land a sample of the white families of the county at a particular point in time and indicated the location of the county courthouse and the three churches, an Anglican parish church and its two chapels. In the second we have indicated consanguineous and affinal relationships among these families. Where a family is related to one beyond the county, the linkage is indicated as crossing the appropriate boundary.[23] In the third we have plotted economic transactions between heads-of-family over a given period, while in the fourth we have plotted those heads-of-family whose infants were christened in the western and eastern chapels during a two-year span and those attending court (as justices, jurymen, witnesses, plaintiffs, and defendants) on a particular day.

22. The larger study of community organization and lifestyle on which this hypothetical illustration is based was undertaken with Anita H. Rutman and published as *A Place in Time: Middlesex County, Virginia, 1650–1750* (New York, 1984) and *A Place in Time: Explicatus* (New York, 1984).

23. For purposes of illustration we have confined cross-boundary linkages to the next-adjacent counties. Note also that in network analysis air distance is as adequate a measure as road distance. See D. W. Crumpacker et al., "Air Distance versus Road Distance as a Geographical Measure for Studies on Human Population Structure," *Geographical Analysis* 8 (1976): 215–23.

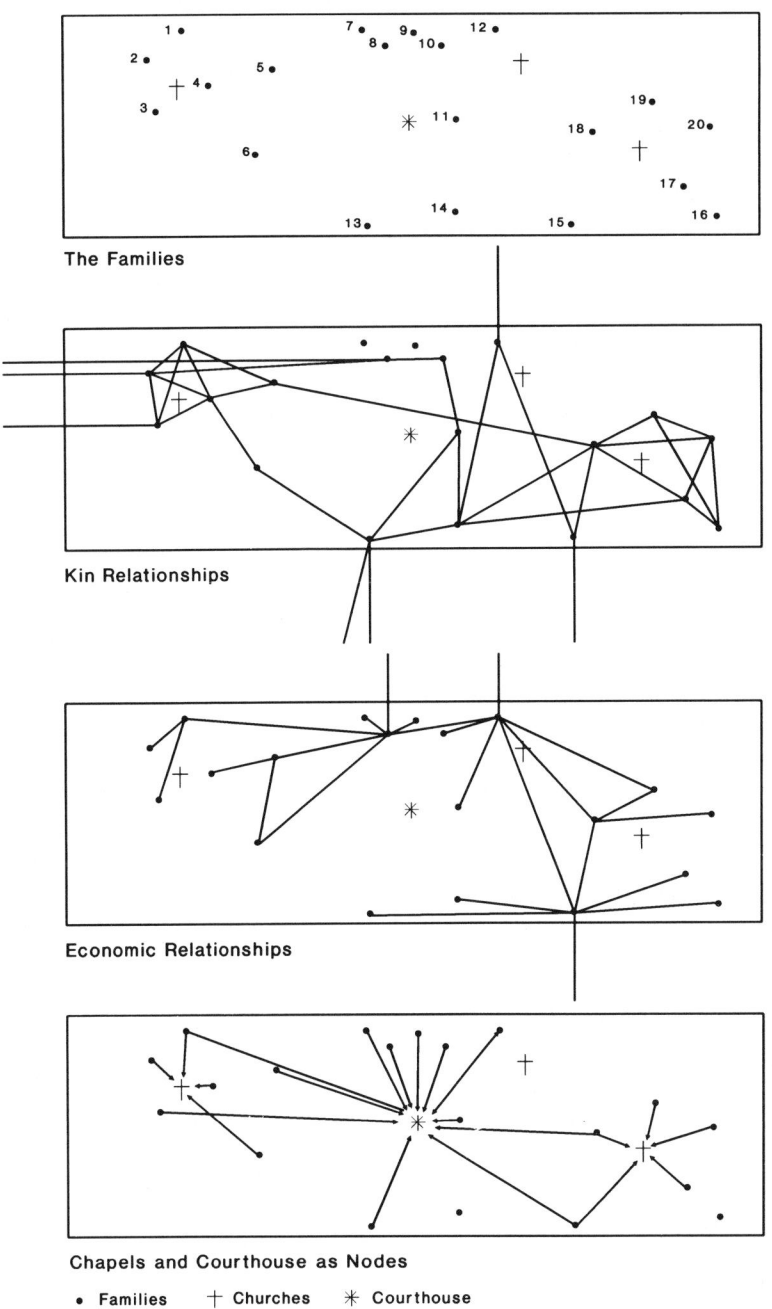

The Families

Kin Relationships

Economic Relationships

Chapels and Courthouse as Nodes

• Families + Churches ✳ Courthouse

Fig. 3.2. Hypothetical network analysis of a community

The four diagrams broadly depict fundamental aspects of the locale. The ratios of external to internal linkages in the second and third diagrams suggest that the political boundaries of the county do to an extent define a particular field of social activity. (A purely random aggregation surrounded by an imposed and meaningless boundary would have a random variant of 1 as a ratio of external to internal linkages.)[24] Yet the relative permeability of the boundaries of the field is equally clear. Those interpersonal relationships which underlie kinship linkages, for example, are more easily effected across the unobstructed western boundary and the narrow southern river than across the broad river to the north.

Within the county itself there are definite indications of clustering. Yet no physical barriers that might explain the phenomenon bisect the land. And there is a significant difference in the configuration of the kinship and economic clusters. In this situation we can contemplate the former as indicative of neighborhoods oriented inward on the churches (nodes) and constrained by spatial friction. The latter suggests that particular heads-of-family served as nodal points in the economic structure of the area.

Even to a casual glance, moreover, the diagram of kinship suggests that the eastern and western neighborhoods formed tighter clusters than did that in the center of the county; in the mathematics of network analysis, these outer clusters are characterized by a higher density. The last three diagrams together suggest one reason why this might be the case. The nodal points within the eastern and western neighborhoods (the chapels) had restricted ranges, while nodal points in the center (the county court and those heads-of-family centralizing the economic structure) served the entirety of the county, giving to the center a certain "cosmopolitan" cast denied the extremities.

The importance of this hypothetical reconstruction lies not in the particular conclusions, these and others, for even this overly simplified example can be pressed to yield more. We have focused on the overall pattern of associations within the locale. But it is equally valid to change the focus and concentrate on those vertical associations linking the locale to the broader society of which it was a part, tracking even into England, for example, the external lines emanating from the economic nodes that appear in the third diagram of figure 3.2. Similarly, it is valid to deal with the families by category. Is there a correlation between the socioeconomic

24. It is by no means axiomatic that political boundaries coincide with the boundaries of a meaningful social field; the local political structure will, however, involve to some degree a nodal point for those within the political boundaries. The latter statement rationalizes beginning a community study at the political level; the former constitutes a caution to those who too readily assume that their study of a political unit is prima facie a community study. See Rutman, "The Social Web," 66–68, 71.

position of families and the degree of embeddedness in the local network? Would we find a greater propensity for embeddedness in vertical networks at one socioeconomic level and relative confinement to horizontal networks at another? If so (and in the Chesapeake such is probably the case), where and how did the several levels link together?

The importance lies, rather, in the very fact that conclusions can be approached at all, that without concern for a sense of "community" (theorized in advance as a predominant or absent force), we can begin to delineate the local structure within which lives were lived in the particular time and place and the connecting points between that structure and the larger society. By comparison between times and places, moreover, we can begin to sense the variations of structure and the force of particular social variables. Presume for the moment that our western chapel was the mother church of a parish which crossed county lines (a situation not at all uncommon in early Virginia). Figure 3.3 depicts a completely hypothetical kinship network which might follow from this. Jump ahead one hundred years to a time when the churches represented not simply an Anglican mother church and two chapels but two distinct denominations. Figure 3.4, again hypothetical, depicts what might result. Contemplate the broad evolution of a local structure over time. The settlement process, we suggest, would be marked by the rapid appearance of a few nodal points and relatively dense networks. The modernization process of which so much is being made might well be measured by the proliferation of nodes and diffusion of networks.[25]

The relational variables we have used to exemplify a network approach are clearly not the only ones to be used. They are not even necessarily the best that ultimately will be used. For a major challenge to those who involve themselves in community studies in the immediate future will be the imaginative exploitation of difficult sources with the intent of delineating the most appropriate variables.

Neither is the approach we are outlining preclusive. On the one hand, a variety of methodological devices developed by those exploring life within communities can be applied to the study of the web of local associations. The application of formal demographic techniques in our particular case has underscored the fragility of life in the area and the social necessity for strong friendship and kinship ties.[26] The measurement of endogamous

25. Even in the absence of relevant historical work, it is already becoming common to associate particular network characteristics with Tönnies's gemeinschaft and gesellschaft. See, e.g., Kenneth N. Walker et al., "Social Support Networks and the Crisis of Bereavement," *Social Science and Medicine* 2 (1977): 35–41.

26. See Darrett B. and Anita H. Rutman, "Of Agues and Fevers: Malaria in the Early Chesapeake," *William and Mary Quarterly*, 3d ser., 33 (1976): 31–60; Rutman and Rutman,

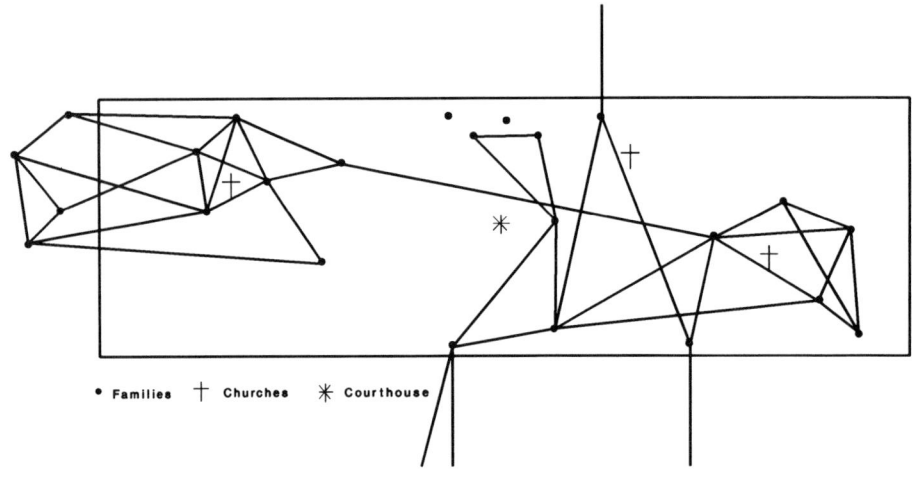

Fig. 3.3. Hypothetical kinship network assuming overlapping parish and county

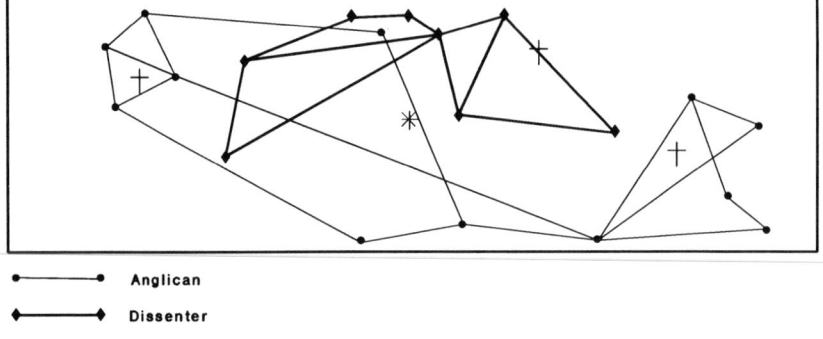

•——————• Anglican

◆——————◆ Dissenter

Fig. 3.4. Hypothetical kinship network assuming two denominations

and exogamous marriages — marriages between individuals from the single locale as against those between individuals from different locales — to some extent gives us a measure of the strength of the area under study as a bounded social field. The measurement of marriage "runs" (how far the parties in the marriage lived from each other) measures spatial friction. In the actual study upon which our hypothetical reconstruction is based, for example, 95 percent of all marriages over a five-year span were between persons living no more than five miles from each other; 36 percent were

"'Now-Wives and Sons-in-Law': Parental Death in a Seventeenth-Century Virginia County," in *The Chesapeake in the Seventeenth Century: Essays on Anglo-American Society*, ed. Thad W. Tate and David L. Ammerman (Chapel Hill, N.C., 1979), 153–75 [chaps. 9 and 10 below].

between persons living within half a mile, in effect virtual next-door neighbors.[27]

On the other hand, we must bring into the analysis what at first glance appears to be the very antithesis of the basic approach. The cold, sterile, mathematical analysis of networks is of necessity dependent in part upon the warm, human, ethnographic approach described so well by Rhys Isaac.[28] It is quite possible (although, as we shall see, it is hard work) to determine that this person was cousin to that person, or that a group of individuals was in regular face-to-face contact in church and court. Alan Macfarlane has made the point with regard to an English locale that "almost everyone who appears to have spent more than a few weeks . . . appears in the local records." Much the same could be said of our Virginia county. The records, however, speak only to behavior. Macfarlane: "We have a very large amount of information about how people interacted, but we know far too little about what they thought, felt, or even said they were doing."[29] To put the point bluntly: Behavior in bed might ultimately result in demonstrable cousinship, but did cousinship mean anything to the cousins? Before proceeding on the assumption that it did, we must demonstrate something more than the original bedroom behavior. A quantitative approach to such things as naming patterns and kinship marriages and the correlation of partial networks (Does, for example, kinship associate with membership in a friendship network? In an economic network?) will help. But in the end researchers will, in all likelihood, have at least some recourse to Isaac's controlled variant of the historian's traditional qualitative methodology. That is, they will have to search out those relatively few instances in the records which offer something more than the barebones of behavior, subject such incidents to the minutest of analyses to extract hints as to the attitudes underlying behavior, and generalize common attitudes from particular "social dramas."[30]

27. Rutman and Rutman, *A Place in Time: Middlesex*, 121.

28. Isaac, "Ethnographic Method in History: An Action Approach," *Historical Methods* 13 (1980): 43–61, repeated in the appendix to his *The Transformation of Virginia, 1740–1790* (Chapel Hill, N.C., 1982). But see also Macfarlane, "History, Anthropology, and the Study of Communities," 636–37, and Beeman, "New Social History and the Search for 'Community,'" 433–43. All seem to want the same thing, that is, to enlist an anthropological approach to field research to exercise control over the traditional historians' way of immersion in the materials to find a subjective truth through selective quotation. They draw primarily on Clifford Geertz, particularly his *The Interpretation of Cultures: Selected Essays* (New York, 1973), and Victor Turner's *Dramas, Fields, and Metaphors: Symbolic Action in Human Society* (Ithaca, N.Y., 1974) and his earlier work.

29. Macfarlane, "History, Anthropology, and the Study of Communities," 645–46.

30. Isaac's ethnographic approach is, however, a tool to be used for a particular purpose; the exclusive use of the single tool in historical reconstruction without regard for its limitations is, I believe, fraught with danger. I have elaborated on some of the dangers in "Encoun-

We do, however, stress that the work is neither quick nor easy. Consider the presumptions as to the utilization of sources that underlie the hypothetical reconstruction of figure 3.2. The first diagram presupposes that we can locate the families of the county spatially, the second and third that we can determine kinship and economic relationships between families. But how is this to be done? Sociologists and anthropologists, from whom we borrow so many concepts, have no data-gathering methods to offer us. Historians cannot undertake surveys or fieldwork among the dead. They must rely on remnants from the past, occasionally physical artifacts, more often than not documents. Implicit in the presumption that we can locate families spatially and track linkages, therefore, is the existence of an extensive documentary base and an extraordinarily deep and thorough exploitation of that base.

This sort of work cannot be done solely from censuses or occasional tax lists. One cannot "drop into" the population for a quick look via one or two such documents and make a ready return to the present to begin drafting. A single document such as the 1704 rent roll of Virginia might offer the historian the information that one George Goodloe of Middlesex County was obligated to pay quitrents on fifty acres, but only the methodical sifting and meshing of a dozen-odd scattered documents — patents, mortgages, conveyances, wills, and administrations — will locate Goodloe's seventy-three acres (not fifty; the rent roll is inaccurate) on the upper reaches of Middlesex's Briery Swamp, bounded on one side by the land of his son and on the other by that of his son-in-law. And only an even more extensive sifting through an even greater variety of sources will allow the location of a tenant, perhaps through a lease recorded among conveyances, or a suit for nonpayment of rent, or an isolated entry in the county's order book that the sheriff served a writ in a particular house occupied by the tenant.

A simple kinship problem exemplifies the meshing process and the necessity of casting the widest possible net. We are confronted by two individuals, Samuel Voll and Jonathan Roberts, and the question, Are these two related? The names themselves offer no hint of kinship. Given the nature of early American vital records, a direct search for evidence of birth and lineage might well unearth a series of scattered entries:

Sarah Brooks, married Andrew Voll, 1685
Samuel, son of Sarah and Andrew Voll, born 1686
Sarah, daughter of Samuel and Eleanor Drake, born 1663

---

ter with Ethnography: A Review of Isaac's *Transformation of Virginia*," *Historical Methods* 16 (1983): 82–86.

Mary, daughter of Samuel and Eleanor Drake, born 1664
Mary Drake, married Roger Roberts, 1681
Jonathan, son of Mary and Roger Roberts, born 1683

The entries suggest as genealogies:

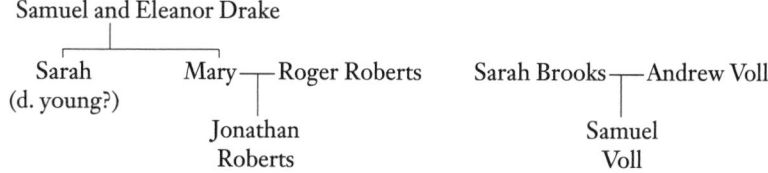

Still no kinship links can be established between subjects. If, however, we expand our exploitation of the materials beyond vital records, methodically break down all types of materials pertaining to the locale, and reassemble all on a name basis, two crucial entries from widely different sources surface:

> 1682: Eleanor Drake, about to marry Jonathan Spark, confirms to her daughters Sarah Brooks and Mary Roberts, two heifers marked with a notch on the right ear.

> 1684: Per petition, administration of the estate of William Brooks, deceased, is granted to Sarah, widow of the said William, and Andrew Voll her husband.

Obviously the genealogies must be redrawn to depict our subjects as cousins:

```
            Samuel Drake—(1)—Eleanor ?—(2)—Jonathan Spark
                                 |
                 _____|_____
                |                                 |
Andrew Voll—(2)—Sarah—(1)—William Brooks   Mary—Roger Roberts
        |                                        |
   Samuel Voll                            Jonathan Roberts
```


The ideal conclusion of this sifting and meshing of remnant materials — a technique with the awkward name "mass prosopography" — is the creation of a data base from which to accomplish an absolute mapping of whatever relational variables are being utilized. Tracking kinship or economic ties, the work ideally uncovers all linkages.[31] Even in the best of situations, however, we must acknowledge that we will fall short of the ideal. The historian's materials are simply not good enough. Statistical techniques offer some succor. The careful examination of what we have uncovered will suggest what still remains hidden, and if, as is likely, there is a pattern to what we have and have not discovered — if, for example, our material is full for the uppermost levels of the society and scattered for the lowest — we can either draw a stratified sample from our base or weight proportionately to reflect the reality.[32] But traditional historical methods offer succor, too. Even in the absence of any demonstrable linkages, we must presume that Matthew Kemp (number 15 on the first diagram of figure 3.2) is a nodal point of an economic cluster which extends beyond the county when we find that, by virtue of a particular Virginia statute, his tobacco notes were to pass current in both the area under study and the county to the south. A point already made bears repeating: The historian, even when unable to carry through the particular formal analysis because of the nature of the available materials, can still be guided by the logic underlying the analysis.

Nevertheless, the goal of completeness remains. The effort must be made. Community studies of any kind labor under a severe handicap: the suspicion that the locale under study is not representative and that conclu-

31. A distinction in degree (but not kind) is to be drawn between, on the one hand, "mass prosopography" as described here and, on the other, "reconstitution" and "record linkage." Record linkage to this point in time is limited to linkages within and between a few highly standardized record sets, e.g., vital records, censuses, tax lists, city directories. Reconstitution involves record linkage to reassemble family and sometimes household units. See E. A. Wrigley, ed., *An Introduction to English Historical Demography*, (New York, 1966), chap. 4, on reconstitution, and Wrigley, ed., *Identifying People in the Past* (London, 1973), on linkage. Periodic reports on various machine-linkage and reconstitution projects are to be found in such journals as *Historical Methods* and the *Journal of Family History*; Ian Winchester, "What Every Historian Needs to Know about Record Linkage for the Microcomputer Era," *Historical Methods* 25 (1992): 149–65, summarizes much of this literature. Mass prosopography attempts record linkage within the entirety of the record base associated with a locale and is not limited as to purpose, the broader approach following from the subject: the study of a total community. The Middlesex prosopography is described more fully, and tested, in Darrett B. and Anita H. Rutman, "'More True and Perfect Lists': The Reconstruction of Censuses for Middlesex County, Virginia, 1668–1704," *Virginia Magazine of History and Biography* 88 (1980): 37–74. See also Alan Macfarlane, *Reconstructing Historical Communities* (Cambridge, 1977). For a recent use of the method in European history, see David I. Kertzer and Dennis P. Hogan, *Family, Political Economy, and Demographic Change: The Transformation of Life in Casalecchio, Italy, 1861–1921* (Madison, Wis., 1989).

32. For an introduction to sampling, see R. S. Schofield, "Sampling in Historical Research," in *Nineteenth-Century Society: Essays in the Use of Quantitative Methods for the Study of Social Data*, ed. E. A. Wrigley (Cambridge, 1972), 146–90, and Melvyn A. Hammarberg, "Designing a Sample from Incomplete Historical Lists," *American Quarterly* 23 (1971): 542–61. On weighting, see Rutman and Rutman, "'More True and Perfect Lists,'" 50–54.

sions derived from the microcosm cannot be generalized to a macrocosm. The suspicion properly engenders caution, a call for ever more studies, and the hope that in the long run firm and broad generalizations as to social processes will emerge from the synthesis of many studies. But it should also engender a sense of obligation. The very raison d'être of local studies is the capability of dealing directly and in great depth with limited materials. Where other historians reap large fields and presumably miss much, we have chosen — hence are obliged — to glean and glean again our small fields.

Linkages and associations, clusters and nodes — the language of our approach seems to take us far from our early American past. A language of covenants and cavaliers, plantations and towns, Yankee merchants and tobacco factors, seems more evocative of the early American world. The method, too, takes us at times far from the ways of traditional historiography, a phenomenon deplored by some. "It takes months — even years — of laborious and painstaking work to assemble . . . even a few pieces" of data, James A. Henretta has complained. "The hours or days which might have been spent in reading diaries, newspapers, or letters — in discovering and then pondering the felt *meaning* of the lives and cultural values of the historical actors — are consumed instead by a quest for technical exactness and statistical finesse. . . . Consciousness and meaning have been usurped by data and diagrams."[33]

In a sense we sympathize with Henretta's complaint. Too often it seems a case of the historian choosing technical exactness or the traditional immersement in diaries, newspapers, and letters when it should be a matter of whatever exactness the materials allow and such immersement. Yet traditional methodology in the absence of the "laborious and painstaking work" Henretta seems to scorn is inherently subjective and noncumulative, nowhere more so than in community studies. One is never quite sure where the character of the ponderer gives way and the nature of that being pondered takes over. Moreover, the traditional language of "Puritans," "Yankees," and the like with which historians have been describing early America is one of assumed rather than derived contrasts. It delimits in advance of study the uniquenesses of specific times and places, and it

---

33. Henretta, "The Study of Social Mobility: Ideological Assumptions and Conceptual Bias," *Labor History* 18 (1977): 167. See also Myron P. Gutmann, "The Future of Record Linkage in History," *Journal of Family History* 2 (1977): 151–58, who argues that cost alone makes the labor Henretta deplores impossible. Gutmann's argument was perhaps pertinent to its time, but not to the 1990s. The personal computer "revolution" has intervened for those historians who take the time to learn that the PC is more than a mysterious "black box." At the moment each of the two machines I work on — neither particularly expensive — has more storage room and computing power than the main frame on which I began in the 1960s.

clouds commonalities. In community studies particularly the sole reliance on traditional language and traditional methodology will lead inevitably to that idiosyncracy so bedeviling to sociologists and anthropologists. Perhaps traditional language and method are serviceable by themselves if the historian's goal is simply poetic description. (Henretta quotes approvingly Theodore Roszak's quip "to map a forest means less than to write poems about it.")[34] But if the historians' purpose is to contribute to a body of knowledge within which comparisons can be made and social processes over time traced, they need the check of an objective method — that is to say, the requirements of a technical approach as a restriction upon their subjective immersion in the subject — and they need a language neutral as to time and place. Churches can serve as nodes whether they are covenanted congregations or Anglican chapels, while bars, racetracks, and factories can serve equally as nodes. And people individually live in a network of associations whether they live neatly around a village green, on scattered farms, or in a modern slum or suburb. The problem for community studies is indeed to draw maps, maps of the nodes and associations at particular times and places, and thereby identify the social parameters within which past lives were lived.

34. Henretta, "Social Mobility," 167n, quoting Roszak, *Where the Wasteland Ends: Politics and Transcendence in Postindustrial Society* (Garden City, N.Y., 1972), 410. Roszak (and Henretta) forget that value is essentially derived from need. I suspect that, lost at night in a snow-laden Vermont forest, they would rather have with them a map than Robert Frost's "Stopping by Woods on a Snowy Evening."

II

PRACTICE

4 The Mirror of Puritan Authority

What follows is one of the earliest direct challenges to the domination of intellectual history in the doing of American history in general and specifically of "Puritan" studies in the doing of New England history. Winthrop's Boston was in press at the time, and as a brash young scholar, I set out to slay dragons. In the way of polemics, the point is certainly overstated; the Puritan ideas dismissed so cavalierly here would have to be resuscitated in other works, for ideas do, indeed, play a role in human affairs. But to an extent the essay helped redirect attention — hitherto fixed on the minister's study — to the men and women in the village lane. And that was its purpose.

P uritanism" is a time-honored word in American history. On the highest level of scholarship it signifies a concept dear to historians who have made a life's work defining the American "mind." On the lowest level it is one of many catchwords and slogans that serve to half educate our youth, a capsule description to distinguish the New England colonies from those to the south and explain the course of New England's institutional and political development. On either level, the historians' "Puritanism" would seem to be their own creation, a stereotype which, as any intimate view of a "Puritan" community will show, has little to do with reality in New England.

The stereotype has arisen as the result of a tendency among historians of early New England, and particularly the intellectual historians who have dominated the field in the last generation, to limit themselves to the study of the writings of the articulate few on the assumption that the public professions of the ministers and magistrates constitute a true mir-

ror of the New England mind.¹ The historian seeking to understand a
New England concept of authority, for example, has familiarized himself
with the literature of England and Europe relative to the nature of man in
society. He has scanned the works of such lay leaders of early New England as John Winthrop, noting his "little speech" on liberty of July 1645
and his earlier "A Modell of Christian Charity": "God Almightie in his
most holy and wise providence hath soe disposed of the Condicion of
mankinde, as in all times some must be rich some poore, some highe and
eminent in power and dignitie; others meane and in subjeccion." He has
thumbed through the ministerial writings to find Thomas Hooker:
"However it is true, [that] the rule bindes such to the duties of their places
and relations, yet it is certain, it requires that they should *first freely ingage*
themselves in such covenants, and *then* be carefull to fullfill such duties."
Or perhaps he has dipped into the pages of John Cotton: "It is evident by
the light of nature, that all civill Relations are founded in Covenant. For,
to passe by naturall Relations between Parents and Children, and Violent
Relations, between Conquerors and Captives; there is no other way given
whereby a people . . . can be united or combined into one visible body, to
stand by mutuall Relations, fellow-members of the same body, but onely
by mutuall Covenant; as appeareth between husband and wife in the family, Magistrates and subjects in the Commonwealth, fellow Citizens in the
same Citie."²

On occasion, the historian has turned also to the law, noting that it is
replete with examples of the intrusion of authority into every aspect of
New England life: "Taking into consideration the great neglect of many
parents and masters in training up their children in learning, and labor,
and other implyments which may be proffitable to the common wealth,"
it is ordered that the selectmen of every town "shall henceforth stand
charged with the care of the redresse of this evill"; "forasmuch as in these
countryes, where the churches of Christ are seated, the prosperity of the
civil state is much advanced and blessed of God" and the ministers'
preaching of the word "is of generall and common behoofe to all sorts of

1. One takes judicial notice of the late Perry Miller's influence in molding our view of
New England. See his *The New England Mind: From Colony to Province* (Cambridge, Mass.,
1953), x: "As far as possible I have again employed the premise of my general title, that
'mind' means what was said and done publicly. Therefore I have made sparing use of diaries
or private papers."

2. James Kendall Hosmer, ed., *Winthrop's Journal "History of New England," 1630–1649*
(New York, 1908), 2:237–39; Winthrop, "A Modell of Christian Charity" (1630), in Massachusetts Historical Society, *Winthrop Papers* (Boston, 1929–47), 2:282; Hooker, *A Survey of
the Summe of Church Discipline* (London, 1648), pt. 1:69; Cotton, *The Way of the Churches of
Christ in New-England* (London, 1645), 4.

people, as being the ordinary meanes to subdue the harts of hearers not onely to the faith, and obedience to the Lord Jesus, but also to civill obedience and allegiance unto magistracy," it is ordered that "every person shall duely resort and attend" to church services; it is ordered that "hereafter, noe dwelling howse shalbe builte above halfe a myle from the meeteing howse."[3]

From such sources modern historians have drawn a picture of a highly cohesive and ordered social structure in which authority was omnipresent—the authority of the father in the family, of the minister in the church, of the magistrate in town and commonwealth. Both the cohesiveness of society and the authority were God-ordained, for man from the moment of Adam's fall was a degenerate being who required the oversight of his fellows in order to avoid the worst of sins. ("*In multitude of counsellers is safetie*," Cotton was fond of saying.)[4] Within the family, the father's authority was a natural concomitant to parenthood. But for the rest, man chose for himself. He submitted himself to the oversight of a congregation and through it a presbytery of ministers and elders and to the civil authority of a king or prince or magistrate. Having submitted, however, he was bound by a godly duty to "faithe patience, obedience." Thus the ministers wrote that the congregations were obliged to "yeeld obedience to their Overseers, in whatsoever they see and hear by them commanded to them from the Lord"; the magistrates that "we have our authority from God, in way of an ordinance, such as hath the image of God eminently stamped upon it, the contempt and violation whereof hath been vindicated with examples of divine vengeance."[5] To further the interests of the community as a whole, the individual's personal aspirations were to be sublimated. "Goe forth, everyman that goeth, with a publicke spirit, looking not on your owne things onely, but also on the things of others," Cotton commanded the settlers who sailed with Winthrop in 1630. And Winthrop echoed him: "Wee must be knitt together in this worke as one man." Magistrates and ministers, too, were committed to the welfare of the entire community. The ministry was to guide the community in the way of God's truth. The civil authorities were to preserve the community in its liberty to do "that only which is good, just, and honest." The "ultimate and supreme" goal of both was that "the common Good of the

3. Nathaniel B. Shurtleff, ed., *Records of the Governor and Company of the Massachusetts Bay in New England* (Boston, 1853–54), 2:6, 177–78, 1:157, 181.

4. Cotton, *Way of the Churches of Christ*, 45, and his *The Keyes of the Kingdom of Heaven* (London, 1644), 55.

5. Winthrop, "Modell of Christian Charity," 283; Cotton, *Keyes of the Kingdom*, 37; Hosmer, *Winthrop's Journal* 2:238.

Society, State or Kingdom" be preserved and *"God in all things . . . glorified."*[6]

The current view of New England Puritanism, of which this view of New England authority is but a part, rests upon two major implicit assumptions. The first is that there is such a thing as "Puritanism" — a term impossible perhaps to define, but capable nevertheless of being described — and that the acme of Puritan ideals is to be found in New England during the years 1630–50. After the latter date, it is asserted, degeneration set in and there was a gradual falling away from the Puritan ideal. George Lee Haskins, the outstanding writer on law and authority in early Massachusetts, reflects this assumption when he writes that "the initial decades of the Bay Colony's existence were the formative years" when, "under the pervasive influence of Puritan doctrine," government, law, ecclesiastical polity, and social structure were fully shaped; "the early social and political structure was to endure for several decades, but it gradually crumbled as primitive zeals began to wane and the religious aspects of life were subordinated to commercial interests."[7]

Haskins owes an unacknowledged debt to Cotton Mather and other New England Jeremiahs, for the notion of Puritan quintessence and decline goes back to Mather's day. Sitting down to pen his *Magnalia Christi Americana* at the end of the seventeenth century, Mather was convinced that the years in which he was living were degenerate ones, that the years preceding his — the founding years — had constituted a golden age of which he was one of the few pure survivors. By telling the story of the past and its leaders he hoped to call his own time to the dutiful obedience to God's will (in both religious and social matters) that had previously prevailed. Mather's motive was succinctly set forth in the introduction to his sketches of the lives of the early ministers: "Reader, behold these *examples*; admire and follow what thou dost behold *exemplary* in them. They are offered unto the publick, with the intention . . . that *patterns* may have upon us the force which *precepts* have not."[8]

This first assumption, though old, has proved of great pragmatic value to the modern historian. Having established that the first decades of New England were the acme of Puritanism, the historian can then turn around and describe Puritanism in terms of what he has found in New England

6. Cotton, *Gods Promise to His Plantation* (London, 1630), 20; Winthrop, "Modell of Christian Charity," 294; Hosmer, *Winthrop's Journal* 2:239; John Barnard, *The Throne Established by Righteousness* (Boston, 1734), quoted in Perry Miller and Thomas H. Johnson, eds., *The Puritans: A Sourcebook of Their Writings* (1938; reprint, New York, 1963), 1:275.

7. Haskins, *Law and Authority in Early Massachusetts: A Study in Tradition and Design* (New York, 1960), ix-x.

8. Mather, *Magnalia Christi Americana; or, The Ecclesiastical History of New-England* (1702; reprint, Hartford, 1852–53), 1:233.

during those early years. Hence, he can avoid the problem of defining Puritanism, a task which Samuel Eliot Morison once found distasteful but necessary.[9] The historian can also evade the issue of separating those facets of New England thought and character which were uniquely Puritan from those which merely reflected the way of life in England. Moreover, by accepting Mather's progression from golden age to degeneration, the historian can conceptualize Puritanism by drawing upon a vast quantity of material without worry whether he is using his sources out of context as regards time, place, or persons.[10] If Puritanism can "best be described as that point of view, that philosophy of life, that code of values, which was carried to New England by the first settlers in the early seventeenth century" and became "one of the continuous factors in Amerian life and thought," as a leading anthology by Perry Miller and Thomas H. Johnson asserts, then certainly (the historian reasons) one can postulate a unique and unchanging Puritan ideal of society in terms of the letters and tracts emanating from New England during the first two decades of settlement and, with increasing caution in view of the degeneration, from the whole of the seventeenth century.[11] The same anthology contains selections from Winthrop's 1630 "Modell of Christian Charity" through John Wise's 1717 *Vindication of the Government of New-England Churches* to exemplify a Puritan theory of state and society and concludes that:

> the most obvious lesson of the selections printed herein is that ... the theorists of New England thought of society as a unit, bound together by inviolable ties; they thought of it not as an aggregation of individuals but as an organism, functioning for a definite purpose, with all parts subordinate to the whole, all members contributing a definite share, every person occupying a particular status. . . . The society of early New England was decidedly "regimented." Puritans did not think the state was merely an umpire, standing on the side lines of a contest, limited to checking egregious fouls, but otherwise allowing men free play according to their abilities and the breaks of the game. . . . The state to them was an active instrument of leadership, discipline, and, wherever necessary, of coercion. . . . The commanders were not to trim their policies by the desires of the people, but to drive ahead upon the predetermined course. . . . There was no questioning that men who would not serve the purposes of the society

9. Morison, *Builders of the Bay Colony* (Boston, 1930), 54.

10. Miller, *From Colony to Province*, x: "I . . . have, on matters of larger concern, taken my illustrations indifferently from whichever writer seemed most to the point."

11. Miller and Johnson, *The Puritans* 1:1.

should be whipped into line. The objectives were clear and unmistakable; any one's disinclination to dedicate himself to them was obviously so much recalcitrancy and depravity.[12]

The second major assumption is that one is free to ignore the "if" in Winthrop's "little speech" on liberty: "If you stand for your natural corrupt liberties, and will do what is good in your own eyes, you will not endure the least weight of authority, but will murmur, and oppose, and be always striving to shake off that yoke."[13] Winthrop had, of course, no call to speak of those who "stand" for natural liberties unless there were individuals who did so. Similarly, one assumes oneself free to ignore the nature of the law; that law reflects not merely the assumptions of society but the antithesis of those assumptions. The law calling upon town selectmen to ensure the proper upbringing of children when their parents were neglecting to educate them to serve the community not only indicates that children were expected to receive such an education but implies strongly that some children were not being prepared in the prescribed manner.[14] The law requiring settlers to build their houses within a half mile of the agencies of social control — church and magistrates — echoes not only the ideal of a cohesive society but the fact that some persons were perfectly willing to break with the ideal and scatter across the New England countryside. One indication that the law (and the ideal it reflected) was being disregarded is a 1639 letter written by the Plymouth congregation to Boston's First Church "concerning the holding of Farmes of which there is noe lesse frequent use with your selves then with us . . . by means of [which] a mans famylie is Divided so in busie tymes they cannot (except upon the Lord's day) all of them joyne with him in famylie duties." The repeal of the Massachusetts law in 1640 on the grounds that it was unenforceable is still further substantiation.[15]

The assumption is not without its rationalization. If the historian accepts as a matter of faith that, as Richard Schlatter writes, "it was the Puritan leaders who shaped the culture of New England, whatever the rank and file may have wanted" — an extension of the notion of a Puritan oligarchy from the political to the social milieu — then it is easy to explain

12. Ibid., 183.

13. Hosmer, *Winthrop's Journal* 2:239.

14. A major point in Bernard Bailyn's *Education in the Forming of American Society: Needs and Opportunities for Study* (Chapel Hill, N.C., 1960).

15. John Reyner and William Brewster "in the name and with the consent of the rest" of the Plymouth Church to the "reverende brethren the church of Christ in Boston to the Elders there," 5 Aug. 1639, Cotton Papers, Prince Collection, Boston Public Library, Boston; Shurtleff, *Records of the Governor and Company* 1:291.

away those who disregarded the law or who stood for "natural corrupt liberties."[16] Once again, Mather has provided the modern historian with a ready-made answer. To him incidents of social and religious dissent were merely the "continual *temptation* of the devil," which was, at least in the early years, overcome by the pure in heart.[17]

That an ideal arrangement of society was visualized by some of the first comers to New England and that they contemplated realizing the ideal in the New World are patently obvious. One need only glance at Winthrop's "Modell of Christian Charity" to see it.[18] But was it uniquely Puritan? The thought that men, like the diverse parts of nature, ideally stood in ordered symmetry is to be found in Shakespeare's *Troilus and Cressida*:

> The heavens themselves, the planets and this centre,
> Observe degree, priority and place. . . .
> O, when degree is shaked,
> Which is the ladder of all high designs,
> The enterprise is sick! How could communities . . .
> Prerogative of age, crowns, sceptres, laurels,
> But by degree, stand in authentic place?[19]

The notion of men entering society by compact or covenant and thereby binding themselves to authority was a pervading theme in Western thought, although particularly relevant for the religious polemicists of the sixteenth and seventeenth centuries. One finds it, for example, in the *Vindiciae contra Tyrannos* of the French Protestants and in Anglican Richard Hooker's *Ecclesiastical Polity*. In Hooker's work, too, is found the idea of the divine nature of authority once established by man: "God creating mankind did endue it naturally with full power to guide itselv, in what kind of societies soever it should choose to live," yet those on whom power "is bestowed even at men's discretion, they likewise do hold it by divine right" for "albeit God do neither appoint the thing nor assign the person; nevertheless when men have established both, who doth doubt that sundry

16. Schlatter, "The Puritan Strain," in *The Reconstruction of American History*, ed. John Higham (New York, 1962), 26. The notion of a political oligarchy has been under sharp attack by, among others, B. Katherine Brown. See her "Puritan Democracy: A Case Study," *Mississippi Valley Historical Review* 50 (1963): 377–96.

17. Mather, *Magnalia Christi Americana* 2:490.

18. Darrett B. Rutman, *Winthrop's Boston: Portrait of a Puritan Town, 1630–1649* (Chapel Hill, N.C., 1965), chap. 1, analyzes the ideal in terms of Winthrop's "Modell"; Rutman, "God's Bridge Falling Down: 'Another Approach' to New England Puritanism Assayed," *William and Mary Quarterly*, 3d ser., 19 (1962): 408–21, briefly traces its fate.

19. Act 1, scene 3, lines 85–108.

duties and offices depending thereupon are prescribed in the word of God"; therefore, "we by the law of God stand bound meekly to acknowledge them for God's lieutenants."[20]

More importantly, was the ideal — so often expressed by the articulate few and commented upon by the intellectual historians — ever a reality in New England? Certainly conditions in America were not conducive to it. The very ideal contained a flaw, for while in England the social and religious covenant was an abstract principle to be toyed with by logicians, in New England it was, in town and church, transformed into practice. How does one convince the generality that the forms and personnel of authority are within its province, but that once established they are in God's domain and are to be honored as such? What spokesman for New England orthodoxy could surpass Ireland's Cuchulain in battling the waves of the sea? Moreover, the transition from old to New England constituted a break in the social fabric familiar to the individual. In an English borough or village the individual located himself according to well-established social and political relationships, but these were no more. Family ties in New England during the early years were relatively few. Ties to the traditional elements of authority — vestrymen, churchwardens, manor stewards, borough councillors, justices of the peace — had disappeared, to be created anew in the New England town, it is true, but such new relationships lacked the sanctity of long familiarity. And even when new ties existed, there was little stability in the New Englander's place in the social and political order. What mattered the regular assertion that God had ordained some to ride and some to walk when those who walked one day could, by virtue of the absence of traditional leaders, the presence of New World opportunities, and the application of their own diligence, ride another?

Such musings give a hint of the answer as to whether the ideal was ever a reality in New England. For more than a hint, however, one must turn to the New Englander's own habitat, his town. For many historians such research necessitates a shift to an entirely different set of sources. It means leaving behind published sermons, tracts, and laws and turning instead to town and church records. It calls for an end to the relatively comfortable perusal of the writings of a few and undertaking the drudgery of culling local records to identify the persons in a given town — their backgrounds, landholdings, economic activities, social and economic affiliations, and politics. Research of such nature is time-consuming, but the rewards are rich.

One such study is that of Sudbury, Massachusetts, undertaken by Sum-

20. Sir Ernest Barker, *Church, State, and Education* (Ann Arbor, Mich., 1957), 87–88; Hooker, *Of the Laws of Ecclesiastical Polity*, bk. 8 [London, 1648], chap. 2, pars. 5–6, 9.

ner Chilton Powell.[21] Sudbury was a small interior town devoted to the raising of cattle. It was not directly affected by the turn to trade and commerce in the 1640s, as were some other communities. Moreover, its population was relatively homogeneous during the period with which Powell dealt. One might expect, therefore, that all the generalizations respecting Puritan attitudes would be reflected in the activities of Sudbury's people. But Powell's story is far from that. The founders were acquisitive English yeomen, little touched by any formal Puritan movement in England. During the town's first years, its people were devoted to building and cultivating the land, using the "open-field" or common agricultural method that most of them had known in England. In the early 1650s, however, they felt the pinch of too little land and solicited the General Court for an additional tract. The subsequent enlargement opened a Pandora's box. One segment of the town demanded a shift to closed agriculture — large tracts individually operated — and a division by which "every man shall enjoy a like quantity of land"; another resisted. The issue became entangled with a second, the desire of some to build a new meetinghouse. Matters were complicated still further by a third issue, the desire of the older settlers to limit the number of cattle allowed on the town meadow. The heated debates that followed involved every person in the town, including minister Edmund Brown. Town meetings became "exciting and well-attended"; tempers flared. In the end the town split, one faction moving away to found Marlborough, Massachusetts.[22]

The debates divided the town into warring factions, Peter Noyes and Edmund Goodnow representing the first settlers and heads of families, John Ruddock and John How leading the younger men of the town, and minister Brown acting largely in his own interest. At one point Goodnow declared that "be it right or wrong, we will have [our way] . . . if we can have it no other way, we will have it by club law." At another point How threatened secession by the young men: "If you oppress the poore, they will cry out; and if you persecute us in one city, wee must fly to another." Pastor Brown called a meeting "to see to the constraining of youth from the profanation of the Lord's day in time of public service" and turned the session into a political harangue; subsequently the minister appeared at a town meeting to cry out he would "put it to a Vote, before I would be nosed by them." Townsmen refused to attend Sabbath lectures and services for fear of being "ensnared" by their political opponents. One party visited the minister "to desire him not to meddle," and Ruddock bluntly told his

21. Powell, *Puritan Village: The Formation of a New England Town* (Middletown, Conn., 1963). Powell is evidence of the hold that "Puritanism" as a historian's concept has, for his own evidence against the validity of the concept is forced into the conceptual framework.
22. Ibid., 119.

pastor that "setting aside your office, I regard you no more than another man." The Reverend Mr. Brown ultimately attempted to have the dispute submitted to a council of elders drawn from neighboring churches, but the various factions refused on the grounds that "it was a civil difference."[23] Where in this debate is there any indication that the New Englanders "thought of society as a unit, bound together by inviolable ties . . . all parts subordinate to the whole . . . every person occupying a particular status"?

In Boston, too, much the same story is to be found: actions quite contrary to attitudes so often generalized upon.[24] In 1634 the generality — again, a relatively homogeneous populace — challenged the town's leadership by demanding an immediate division of all available land on an equal basis. The response of the leadership was to some extent based on attitudes made classic by historians. Winthrop, thinking in terms of the community, argued against the allocation of more land than an individual could use, partly out of his desire "to prevent the neglect of trades, and other more necessary employments" and "partly that there might be place to receive such as should come after." To him, it would be "very prejudicial" if newcomers "should be forced to go far off for land, while others had much, and could make no use of it, more than to please their eye with it." But the townsmen would have none of it. Land was too much a way to personal gain.

The issue reached a climax in December when a committee of seven was elected to divide the town lands. Winthrop "and other of the chief men" failed of election. The townsmen feared "that the richer men would give the poorer sort no great proportions of land" and chose "one of the elders and a deacon, and the rest of the inferior sort." All the advocates of an ordered society were brought to bear to overturn the election. Winthrop spoke of his grief "that Boston should be the first who should shake off their magistrates," and the Reverend Mr. Cotton of "the Lord's order among the Israelites" by which "all such businesses" were "committed to the elders." "It had been nearer the rule," Cotton argued, "to have chosen some of each sort." The generality gave way for the moment and agreed to a new election. Subsequently a more proper committee was chosen "to devide and dispose" of the land, "leaving such portions in Common for the use of newe Commers, and the further benefitt of the towne, as in theire best discretions they shall thinke fitt."[25]

The battle, however, was by no means over. The pursuit of individual gain continued to prompt political activity. The prevailing economic view (and one not uniquely Puritan) was that all phases of the economy were

23. Ibid., 124ff.

24. The argument that follows is developed more fully in Rutman, *Winthrop's Boston.*

25. Hosmer, *Winthrop's Journal* 1:143–44; "Boston Town Records [1634–1660/61]," in *City of Boston, A Report of the Record Commissioners* 2 (Boston, 1877): 3.

subject to government regulation.[26] Town governments in Massachusetts had the authority to regulate land distribution, land usage, and the laying out of streets; in Boston the town government established embryonic building codes and licensed inns and wharves. Given this actual exercise of power over the various avenues of opportunity, it was to one's advantage to participate in public affairs.

Land, for a time, continued to be the principal issue. The town had a limited area into which it could expand. By the second decade it had become difficult to find plots for newcomers or additional acreage for older settlers. In 1641 popular pressure forced the selectmen to review the larger grants made in the 1630s, but this action served little purpose. Even where surveys indicated that a Winthrop, Oliver, or Cotton held more land than had been allocated, the selectmen took no remedial action.[27] During the following year the selectmen — in order to obtain more room on Boston's tiny peninsula for house lots — resurrected an earlier order denying the inhabitants permanent possession of their lots in the Boston fields. The result was an angry town meeting in which the order was repealed "for peace sake, and for avoyding of confusion in the Towne."[28]

Boston's turn to trade in the 1640s brought about a change. Opportunities for personal aggrandizement in land were gradually replaced by better chances for advancement in commerce and allied crafts such as coopering, leatherworking, and shipbuilding. For the artisan, participation in local government was equally as important as it had been for those persons interested in land. The leatherworker or butcher, subject to the selectmen under local regulations regarding the cleanliness of his establishment, or even his very right to carry on his trade within the town, of necessity participated in the town meetings to elect the men who could, in a moment, curtail or end his business activities. The retailer, subject to the inspection of clerks of the market operating under commonwealth law, was quick to make known his choice for such officials. Almost everyone engaged in any kind of economic activity — the laws limiting the electorate notwithstanding — sought to vote for the deputies to the General Court and the assistants inasmuch as these men wrote the commonwealth ordinances governing economic activity.[29]

26. E. A. J. Johnson, *American Economic Thought in the Seventeenth Century* (London, 1932), 17–18 et passim.

27. "Boston Town Records," 2:26, 59, 60, 61.

28. Ibid., 65.

29. E.g., in ca. 1655 a committee of the General Court protested that everyone, including "scotch servants, Irish negers and persons under one and twenty years," was voting for deputies to the General Court in contravention of the law (Dan[iel] Gookin and others to the General Court, Manuscript Photostats, box 7, Massachusetts Historical Society Library, Boston). The statement, although extreme, is by no means unique.

On the intertown level in Massachusetts, too, the desire for personal aggrandizement played havoc with the ideal of an orderly and cohesive society. Town rivalries arose; boundary disputes raged interminably between communities, the prize being a rich meadow or copse.[30] Craftsmen in one town were jealous of those in another. Shoemakers outside Boston, for example, objected to shoemakers within that town organizing a company and seeking exclusive privileges regarding shoes sold in the Boston market. Do not allow "our Brethren of Boston" to "have power put into their hands to hinder a free trade," they wrote to the General Court. "Keeping out Country shoomakers from Coming into the Market," they continued, "wil weaken the hands of the Country shoomakers from using their trade, or occasion them to Remove to boston which wilbe hurtful to Other townes."[31] Merchants and tradesmen in the northern towns — Ipswich, Salem, Newbury — bitterly resented the fact that "Boston, being the chiefest place of resort of Shipping, carries away all the Trade." They reacted in a series of political moves aimed at reducing Boston's central position in the commonwealth. An effort was made to move the seat of government from Boston; an attempt got under way to change the basis of representation in the House of Deputies to Boston's disadvantage; and an alliance was formed between northern towns and country towns to create a bloc within the house to oppose those towns immediately around Boston harbor.[32]

The political activity in and among the towns suggests that the people of Massachusetts Bay, and one can extrapolate to include the other New England colonies, were not acting within the concepts of authority and cohesive, ordered society that modern historians have so carefully delineated and pronounced to be characteristic of Puritanism and Puritan New England. Society was not something to which the people of the Bay commonwealth invariably subordinated their own interests. Indeed, the abstract concept of "society" seems to have held little meaning for a generality intent upon individual pursuits. Nor was authority a pervasive thing, obliging the individual through family, church, and state to sublimate personal aspirations to the interests of the community as a whole. The

30. Shurtleff, *Records of the Governor and Company*, and John Noble and John F. Cronin, eds., *Records of the Court of Assistants of the Colony of the Massachusetts Bay, 1630–1692* (Boston, 1901–28), vol. 2, are replete with such disputes.

31. Gowen Anderson and others to the General Court, 1648, Massachusetts Archives, State House, Boston.

32. J. Franklin Jameson, ed., *Johnson's Wonder-Working Providence, 1628–1651* (New York, 1910), 96. Lawrence Shaw Mayo, *John Endecott: A Biography* (Cambridge, Mass., 1936), 470ff., alludes to the existence of an "Essex Clique" in Massachusetts politics; the clique can be further identified by a close analysis of the officers and committeemen of the House of Deputies as found in vol. 3 of Shurtleff, *Records of the Governor and Company*.

"state" in Sudbury—in the form of either town or commonwealth government—could provide no other solution to the town's disputes than to permit the community to divide. The church—the Reverend Mr. Brown personally and the elders of the neighboring churches invited in by Brown—was unable to interpose its authority to settle matters. Family fidelity failed to check the personal aspirations of the "landless young sons" who followed Ruddock and How.[33]

The people of Massachusetts, it would appear, were coming to view the elements of authority as being divided rather than united. In particular, they viewed the church and state as distinct entities with well-defined (and to a large extent mutually exclusive) areas of operation. In Sudbury, for example, Pastor Brown's intervention in a civil affair led to his being asked not to "meddle." In Boston the calling of the Synod of 1646–48 by the commonwealth government roused strong opposition from those who lashed out against the interjection of "civil authority" in church business.[34] The conflict so begun would eventuate in a full-scale assault upon the imposition of ministerial authority within the church and of synodical authority among churches, further evidence that the historians' concept of authority and cohesiveness bears little resemblance to the New England reality. Historians might cite as evidence of the concept the Cambridge *Platform* which emanated from the Synod and pronounced ministerial and synodical authority to be part of the New England Way, but the deathbed utterances of the Reverend John Wilson are more to the point. Wilson cited as "those sins amongst us, which provoked the displeasure of God" the rising up of the people "*against their Ministers . . . when indeed they do but Rule for Christ*," and "*the making light of, and not subjecting to the Authority of* Synods, *without which the Churches cannot long subsist.*"[35]

The same dichotomy between church and state that one finds in the towns can be seen on the commonwealth level. Historians have noted all too often those laws passed by civil authorities to further the views of the church and those cases where the ministry advised the magistrates on civil matters. But they have paid far too little attention to the arduous efforts made to define the respective spheres of church and state. As John Cotton wrote in 1640, "The government of the Church is as the Kingdome of Christ is, not of this world, but spirituall and heavenly. . . . The power of the keyes is far distant from the power of the sword." To him, church and state in Massachusetts were involved in the same task, "the Establishment of pure Religion, in doctrine, worship, and [church] government, according to the word of God: As also the reformation of all corruptions in any of

---

33. Powell, *Puritan Village*, 137.
34. Hosmer, *Winthrop's Journal* 2:278ff.
35. Quoted in Rutman, "God's Bridge Falling Down," 416.

these." Hence the ministers, in whose care the word of God was placed, could logically press for "sweet and wholsom" laws and "civil punishments upon the willfull opposers and disturbers" of the church. But for the things of this world — "the disposing of mens goods or lands, lives or liberties, tributes, customes, worldly honors, and inheritances" — "in these the Church submitteth, and refereth it self to the civill state."[36]

For the most part, too, historians in the past few years have tended to overlook those cases where there was a clash between magistrates and ministers. In 1639 the General Court decided that too frequent and overly long church meetings were detrimental to the community and asked the elders "to consider about the length and frequency of church assemblies." The ministers promptly denounced the magistrates. The request "cast a blemish upon the elders," they said, one "which would remain to posterity, that they should need to be regulated by the civil magistrate."[37] The overanxious intervention of an elder in a matter before the Court of Assistants in 1643, on the other hand, drove one magistrate to exasperation. "Do you think to come with your eldership here to carry matters?" he shouted. On another occasion, when the elders of Essex County went beyond the bounds that Winthrop considered proper in espousing the cause of the northern towns against Boston — for when town argued with town the elders tended to identify with their communities — the governor lashed out. They "had done no good offices in this matter, through their misapprehensions both of the intentions of the magistrates, and also of the matters themselves, being affairs of state, which did not belong to their calling."[38]

In the division of authority that was taking place, it would seem that the church was freely conceded the power of opening and closing the doors of heaven. To whatever extent the individual sought heaven, he honored the authority of the church in moral and theological matters. But the keys to personal aggrandizement in this world were lodged with the state, and the generality was coming to look upon the state in a peculiarly modern way. In one sense the state was the servant of the individual, obligated to foster his welfare and prosperity. At the same time, it was to protect him from the aspirations of others, acting, so to speak, as an umpire for society, exercising authority in such a way as to avoid collisions between members of the community who were following their individual yet concentric

36. Cotton, *Way of the Churches of Christ*, 19, 50; Cotton, *Keyes of the Kingdom*, 50; Cotton, *A Briefe Exposition of the Whole Book of Canticles* (London, 1642), 251.

37. Hosmer, *Winthrop's Journal* 1:326. Note, too, Thomas Shepard's comment: "The Magistrate [must] kisse the Churches feet" and "meddle not beyond his bounds" ("The Autobiography of Thomas Shepard," Colonial Society of Massachusetts, *Publications* 27 [1932]: 397).

38. Hosmer, *Winthrop's Journal* 2:117, 190.

orbits. One can perceive such a view of society, however obliquely, in the political theory of the later New Englanders. For indeed, their writings on this matter are not all of a piece. There is a subtle difference between a Winthrop or Cotton for whom the goal of society was the pleasing of God; a Samuel Willard to whom a happy, contented people was most pleasing to God; and a John Wise to whom "the Happiness of the People, is the End of its [the state's] Being; or main Business to be attended and done."[39]

The view of society discernible in the New England community is quite different from that expounded by intellectual historians who have turned to the writings of the articulate few — and little else — as their mirror of New England's mind. Are we to discard their mirror and the "Puritan" concepts that they have seen in it? The purpose of intellectual history is to delineate the ideological framework within which a people acted. If the actions of the people under consideration do not fall within the framework created, it follows that the framework is invalid. It is not that simple, of course. In the case of New England, the intellectual framework erected over the past years has been firmly based upon the writings of the leading laymen and clergy in the society. We must accept such works as a valid expression of their ideals, even though their ideals might not apply to the people as a whole.

But what are we to describe as "Puritan," the ideals of the articulate few that, relative to society and authority, were neither unique nor pervasive or the actuality of the man in the street — more accurately, the man in the village lane — that does not fit the ideals? The very fact that such a question can be asked would seem to imply that the description of New England in terms of Puritanism, or of Puritanism in terms of New England, is erroneous. Certainly the concept of a Puritan golden age, followed by decline, disappears. Mather's degeneration is, in large part, nothing more than the insistence by the generality upon a relationship between the individual and society rather different from that held to by the leaders. And the golden age, as Mather himself admitted, was marked by continual controversies which "made neighbours that should have been like *sheep*, to 'bite and devour one another'" and inspired "unaccountable *party-making*," a symptom of that different relationship.[40]

The historian must, of course, address himself to the problem of New England's intellectuals. Isolated from reality as they were, they clung for almost half a century to ideals that grew more outdated with the passing of each day and then gradually and subtly accommodated their ideals to the

39. Willard, *The Character of a Good Ruler* (1694), in Miller and Johnson, *The Puritans* 1:254; Wise, *Vindication of the Government of New-England Churches* (Boston, 1717), 46.
40. Mather, *Magnalia Christi Americana* 2:490.

realities of the situation facing them. But their accommodation and the forces in society that caused them to make changes represent a much more important aspect of history than the mere description of "Puritanism." And the historian must dispense with the easy generalization that such leaders "shaped" New England's culture regardless of what "the rank and file may have wanted." He must seek instead to understand the rank and file, their motivations, aspirations, and achievements. For in the last analysis, which is more vital, an ideological "Puritanism" divorced from reality which has received so much attention over the years or the reality that has received so little attention but that was in essence laying down the basis for two-and-a-half centuries of American history ahead?

5 Children of the Fellowship

Rejecting a preoccupation with "Puritanism" as an intellectual system is by no means a rejection of Puritanism, for a history of New England without its ministers — and their influence — would be singularly incomplete. But how is "the man in the village lane" to be linked to the minister in his study? How is the very stuff of social history to be joined to the stuff of intellectual history to make one complete story? In a slim volume published in 1970 I attempted to sketch a way to approach the problem, envisioning Puritanism not as a concrete thing but as occupying an airy, transactional space lying between ministers of a particular persuasion and laymen and women who heard and in some degree and kind responded to them. The first of the four essays in the volume outlined the definitional problems (and errors) associated with the terms Puritan *and* Puritanism *and isolated as a beginning point a nexus of ardent preachers in old England; the second, included here, linked that nexus to New England and New Englanders.*

That Master John Cotton and Robert Keayne were on hand at the May meeting of the New England Company in 1628 — the one, a member of what has been described as a Puritan fellowship of ministers, to lecture; the other, a lay follower of the fellowship, to jot down the main points of the lecture — was not merely fortuitous. Nothing is clearer than the association of the fellowship with first the company and subsequently the great venture into Massachusetts Bay that proceeded from it.

The company had been founded as a result of the activities of Master John White of Dorchester and numbered among its earliest investors

Originally published as chapter 2 of Darrett B. Rutman, *American Puritanism: Faith and Practice* (Philadelphia: J. B. Lippincott Company, 1970). Copyright © by Darrett B. Rutman. Reprinted by permission of W. W. Norton & Company.

Master Hugh Peter, lecturer at St. Sepulchre's, London. Only a few days before Cotton addressed the assembled members of the company, Master Nathaniel Ward, curate of St. James, London, and soon to be rector of Stondon Massey, Essex, had spoken.[1] Masters White and John Davenport of London selected the ministers who would journey to New England in 1629 to serve the religious needs of the initial settlement at Salem: Samuel Skelton of Sempringham, Lincolnshire; Francis Higginson, a lecturing nonconformist from Leicestershire; Francis Bright, a young protégé of Davenport's. All of these were ministers of the fellowship. Indeed, in 1629 Master White would address "many reverend Divines" at the Cambridge commencement — a traditional annual gathering of the fellowship — issuing there "a call" for New England. And to read the roster of lay investors in the company is to read one after another the names of prominent lay followers of Puritan ministers.

Yet the initial motivation of the venture was basically profit, not religion. It had begun in the west country of England in the early 1620s. White and an association of Dorchester merchants had financed a fishing settlement on Cape Ann, a rocky peninsula jutting seaward to the north and east of Boston Bay. The settlement had brought no profit, and the merchants had abandoned the enterprise. But White, with a few others, persevered, sending supplies to the remaining settlers — who removed from Cape Ann to what would become Salem — and searching for new financing in England. By 1628 White had interested London merchant acquaintances in the venture, and a new association had been formed. Supplies and additional men were sent to the colony that year, and in the next the association obtained a royal charter as "The Governor and Company of the Massachusetts Bay in New England." Still the intention was profit.

In the course of his agitation, however, White had spread knowledge of New England among the lay followers of Puritan preachers in England's northeastern counties. And among them, sometime in early 1629, talk began of utilizing the company not for profit but as a vehicle by which to flee an England discerned as socially and religiously declining. With whom the idea originated we cannot say. Perhaps it arose first in the household of the earl of Lincoln at Tattershall, near Sempringham. Certainly that seems to have been an early center; among the leaders of the emigration were to be Isaac Johnson, the earl's son-in-law; Thomas Dudley, the earl's onetime steward; and Simon Bradstreet, Dudley's son-in-law and successor as steward. But it makes little difference. By mid-1629 John Winthrop of Groton, Suffolk County, had become the one whom the

---

1. A number of sermons to the company were recorded in Keayne's manuscript notebook of English sermons, 1620, Massachusetts Historical Society, Boston.

"chief undertakers" would not do without, for "the wellfare of the Plantation" depended upon his going.[2] By the end of March 1630, under Winthrop's leadership, the gentlemen had assumed control of the company, recruited settlers, gathered supplies, and set sail. What is important is that the gentlemen were children of the fellowship, sped on their way by Master Cotton himself, who delivered the farewell sermon, "God's Promise to His Plantation"; that the ministers who sailed with them were from the fellowship, as were those who would join them in New England in the years immediately after 1630; and that, given the fact that New England during its first twenty years was "an ecclesiastical country above any in this world" — Cotton Mather listing 77 practicing English ministers who arrived in New England in the years to roughly 1640; John Eliot in 1650 listing 37 practicing ministers in Massachusetts alone, one for every 415 people — New Englanders in general can be termed children of the fellowship.[3]

Children of the fellowship? What does that mean? It is an awkward way of saying that the New Englanders were Puritans, but the awkwardness is necessary if we are to keep in focus the descent of their Puritanism as we have conceived it — from the preachers to the laymen — and the nature of that Puritanism, that is, what they received from the ministers.

Here we are face to face with a crucial but extremely difficult problem. Our approach has been to delimit Puritanism in terms of the preachers. We have conceptualized Puritanism as a gift imparted to laymen who tucked it away in the storehouse of the mind, and we have described (or defined) it while still in the possession of the givers (the preachers) in order to avoid the confusion of trying to find the gift in the clutter of that storehouse. But when we shift from the preachers to the lay followers, from the giver of the gift to the recipient, we move headlong toward that clutter. We ought immediately to pause and reckon up our chances of finding anything at all there. For the mind does not neatly compartmentalize things. Puritanism as we have conceived it, once conveyed to laymen, does not sit solitary on a shelf apart from all the other bric-a-brac that the mind collects and stores away. Our metaphor of gift and storehouse is convenient from the standpoint of filtering out the component influences on men, but it is erroneous when trying to envision the actual working of any single idea or set of ideas upon them. A better metaphor with which to approach the latter is the mind as a melting pot in which all

2. Winthrop's gradual involvement in the Massachusetts venture is described in Darrett B. Rutman, *John Winthrop's Decision for America, 1629* (Philadelphia, 1975).

3. Mather, *Magnalia Christi Americana; or, The Ecclesiastical History of New-England* (1702; reprint, Hartford, 1852–53), 1:235–38; "John Eliot's Description of New England in 1650," Massachusetts Historical Society, *Proceedings*, 2d ser., 2 (1886): 46–50.

the impressions and ideas collected in life (plus a genetic heritage) flow together in a gooey mess — the source of that synaptic chain which leads from brain to muscle action. Psychologists, whose very subject matter is that goo, are divided over whether to plunge in or not. Insofar as they can, and admittedly they cannot for long, historians had best refrain.

If we ought to forbear entering the clutter of the mind or (mixing our two metaphors) swimming in its gooey mess to analyze, what should we do? Certainly we must do more than merely describe Puritanism in terms of the preachers, for this would be to do very little. Certainly, too, we cannot simply assert that the ministers' ideas were Puritan ideas equally ascribable to ministers and laymen. This would be (and is, for historians have frequently proceeded this way) an act of faith in the efficient transmission of ideas which defies all reason — a point requiring elaboration.

It is a truism to say that what one who speaks (or writes) intends to convey is not necessarily what the hearer (or reader) understands. Words filter through the preconceptions, values, and concerns for the particular condition of both speaker and listener. To use a simple example, a preacher might offer the phrase "saving faith" in the context of a broad theological system, using the word *saving* as a qualification: that faith which proceeds from justification and is consequently efficacious. But a listener might accept "saving" as a consequence of faith rather than a qualification: To have faith is to be saved. Or the preacher might urge godliness in the sense of an elaborate morphology of conversion, but the hearer might understand only the necessity for leading an outwardly moral life. The minister might condemn as sinners those who are not embarked on what he defines as the necessary Christian quest; the hearer might understand as sinners only those who frequent the public houses or the Southwark theaters and make of a negative attitude toward public houses and theaters the essence of whatever he or she is receiving from the preachers.[4] The idea that filters past the preconceptions, values, and particular concerns of the imparter, travels the sound waves or light rays to the recipient, filters past the recipient's preconceptions, values, and concerns, mixes in the melting pot that constitutes the recipient's mind with all the other notions and impressions stored there, and finally moves out again to be conveyed to a third party or transformed into action — such an idea (and all ideas follow this track) cannot retain its purity. Hence, from the layman's standpoint, the gift of Puritanism from preacher to layman can never be conceived of as

4. William Prynne, for example. Note his early activity in William M. Lamont, *Marginal Prynne, 1600–1669* (London, 1963). Thomas Lechford, a devotee of Prynne's, was moved enough by this sort of interpretation of the preachers' gift to come to New England; but when, in New England, he received a deeper impression of what the preachers were saying, he turned back to English orthodoxy. See my introduction to Lechford's *Plain Dealing; or, News from New England* (1642; reprint, New York, 1969).

anything more than an influence. We cannot, therefore, ascribe the ministers' Puritanism to the laymen and let it go at that.

And, finally, we cannot simply accept as an act of faith the assumption that the ministers' gift of Puritanism changed the lives of lay recipients so completely that what they did after receiving the gift was entirely the result of it. With regard to American Puritanism, this would lead us to the logical series:

$$
\begin{array}{c}
\text{Preachers'} \\
\text{gift} \\
\text{(Puritanism)}
\end{array}
\rightarrow
\begin{array}{c}
\text{New} \\
\text{Englanders}
\end{array}
\rightarrow
\begin{array}{c}
\text{New England} \\
\text{action}
\end{array}
=
\begin{array}{c}
\text{Preachers'} \\
\text{gift} \\
\text{(Puritanism)}
\end{array}
$$

The solution to our predicament might lie in detouring around the layman's mind completely—neither enter it to attempt to analyze nor depend upon it to generalize—and concentrating on behavior. If we can establish normal patterns of life and behavior in England without Puritanism, deviation from the norm on the part of those with Puritanism might be construed as the result of that Puritan element in the lay mind which otherwise defies the historian.[5] If, for example, the normal pattern in England is to attend church four times a year while individuals whom we can associate with Puritan preachers (hence by assumption receiving the gift of Puritanism) go four times a week, we might conceivably say that one element of the layman's Puritanism was an increased attention to churchgoing. The problems are manifold, however, and we must beware of them. How are we to discriminate between the effect of that with which we are concerned (Puritanism) and the effect of other but irrelevant variables? Are we to say that an effect of Puritanism is longevity if we find that the normal life expectancy of an infant born in England of, say, 1620 is 32 years, while in a community served by a Puritan preacher men are living to an average of 71.8 years?[6] Perhaps it is true, but probably not. Common

5. This is, of course, an expression in pure form of a statistical measurement of variance, and it is improbable that we could ever use it in such a pristine fashion. One question pinpoints the major problem: Where could we possibly find a viable control group completely devoid of any possibility of Puritan influence? There is, consequently, the problem of a lack of statistical precision inherent in the nature of the materials upon which we must depend. We have to content ourselves with using as a control rough norms based upon England as a totality—actually, rough norms drawn from particular communities and extrapolated into English norms—counting on the size of the base to overcome the error of incorporating into the control group the very deviation we want to measure. The inability to use a pristine methodology should not stop us, for one can suggest that the results will be more exact than results gained by extrapolating from a few items of literary evidence. It should, however, warn us against pretending that history is an exact science.

6. Thirty-two is the actual life expectancy at birth for England in the 1690s as given by Gregory King and used in Peter Laslett, *The World We Have Lost* (New York, 1965), 93; 71.8

sense will be an invaluable tool. How are we to accommodate the effect of time? Puritanism, in terms of the preachers, was not a static corpus of ideas but an evolving thing from the 1570s into the 1630s; lay behavior emanating from Puritanism, consequently, cannot be construed as static but changing. And how are we to take into account the fact that behavior resulting from the infusion of Puritanism in the mind will vary both in degree and kind?

Let us develop this last. True, we have considered the ministerial fellowship as a rough entity, accenting common elements among the preachers as a necessary step in reducing the complexity of the past generally and our concept of Puritanism specifically to manageable proportions. But here, as always, we must be aware of the intrinsic artificiality of conceptualization — the historian's ordering of the past to make it comprehensible. When we shift our attention from the common elements to the individual ministers of the fellowship, we find that each put a peculiar stress on one or ignored another of the common elements. Thus, for one preacher a national regeneration might be paramount, and he will accent the jeremiad, threatening and cajoling a wayward England with little reference to the dialectic of salvation. To another the dialectic is all-important, and he will urge personal preparation and the inner search for assurance. Still a third might be more concerned with the mixture of the godly and ungodly in his parish and will have traveled far along that line which led through the gathering of the godly into informal associations to the claim that such gatherings constituted the essentials of a visible church. Here a minister of the fellowship will accept the covenant that bound a gathering together and the standards that it imposed upon its members; there a minister will be more concerned with the individual faith that lay behind the gatherings. Among the ministers themselves, while in England, these differences could be balanced by the very raison d'être of the fellowship, the necessity for those at variance with society and dissenting from the episcopacy to cling together, giving a bit more substance to the fellowship than merely a historian's artificial categorization. A man might differ but still be a friend, an ardent preacher, and a fellow worker in the Lord's vineyard, hence a companion in this ambiguous fellowship. As one minister would write of the doctrine and preaching of another, his reasons "do not satisfy me, though the man I reverence as godly and learned."[7] Among laymen associated with a Puritan preacher, however, it was the preaching not of the

---

is the life span of thirty male settlers of Massachusetts as reported by Philip J. Greven, Jr., "Family Structure in Seventeenth-Century Andover, Massachusetts," *William and Mary Quarterly*, 3d ser., 23 (1966): 239.

7. John Cotton to Samuel Skelton, 2 Oct. 1630, in Thaddeus M. Harris, *Memorials of the First Church in Dorchester* (Boston, 1830), 55.

fellowship as a whole but of the specific preacher that had its effect, and the effect we measure by measuring the deviation of the individual or community from the norm will not be the effect of the common elements of Puritanism but of the peculiar elements stressed by that preacher. Between "Puritan" and "Puritan," consequently, we ought to expect — and be prepared to cope with — wide differences.

Moreover, we have used the phrase "associated with the preachers" perhaps too easily. Certainly it is necessary to have some clearly stipulated criteria governing who among the laymen is to be considered Puritan and to keep them ever in mind, if for no other reason than to avoid the tendency to make of empirical findings based on the criteria the criteria themselves. To repeat a hypothetical example already used: Laymen associated with Puritan preachers attended church four times a week as against the normal four times a year; increased attention to churchgoing is, therefore, an element of Puritanism. So far we are on relatively firm ground (if, of course, our empirical evidence supports us, and we rule out factors other than association with Puritan preachers as the cause of action). But to go on and say such-and-such a person (or group of persons) displays an increased attendance to churchgoing and is therefore Puritan is to convert the finding into a criterion and will hazard error after error as we read additional deviation on the basis of the conversion — that is to say, from the individual or group newly defined as Puritan by the substitute criterion.[8]

But how are we to understand "associated"? Robert Keayne, to judge from his notebook, listened to Puritan preachers regularly for some seven years before leaving for New England in the early 1630s. Peter Noyes, a yeoman of the parish of Weyhill, Hampshire, who would eventually go to Sudbury in New England, was a distant cousin of the Reverend Thomas Parker of the fellowship. Is the association of both of them with the fellowship such as to label them equally as Puritan laymen, and will their deviation from an English norm, when subjected to measurement, tell us something about Puritanism?

One caveat here is obviously to beware of a too facile association of laymen and preachers, hence too facile a choice of the individuals whose behavior and life structure are to be measured for the extent of the deviation. A less obvious caveat is that degree will undoubtedly be a factor. The effect of the preachers will not be an absolute. Keayne might be deeply affected, and this be indicated in his behavior, as a result of strong associa-

---

8. Some might smile at the patent ridiculousness of the error and say it cannot have occurred. But framed differently it should be familiar: Puritans were such-and-such people; such-and-such people came to New England; therefore we can read the meaning of Puritanism in what we find in New England. In the last statement we have converted the finding into the criterion.

tion; Noyes might be affected so slightly as to deviate from the normal behavior almost infinitesimally as a result of peripheral association. Moreover, degree will enter into consideration as a result of susceptibility. Any single Englishman might cross paths with the fellowship once, twice, a hundred times or more; one contact might be enough to change his behavior or a hundred-plus insufficient to affect him in the slightest way. And susceptibility might depend on elements otherwise irrelevant to our subject. Of three men equally associated with the fellowship, one might be so involved in satiating his desire for material wealth that he is completely unaffected; a second might be simply breaking even in this world and so look forward with a modicum of interest to the next and be affected somewhat; the third might be the proverbial loser and, giving up in this world, pin all his hopes on the next and on the good preacher who shows him the way into it.

Despite the methodological difficulties, however, we must — if we are to get anywhere at all — proceed by categorization and measurement. The caveats are simply to put us on guard, not forestall us. We can categorize New England as Puritan if such categorization implies no more than that in New England we find preachers of the fellowship and laymen in clear association with the preachers, thus maintaining the preachers and association with the preachers as our criteria of Puritanism and refraining from converting to other criteria. And we can proceed to measure the effect of Puritanism in New England if we accept the possibility that measurable deviation from the English norm might be accountable to irrelevant variables rather than Puritanism (geography, for example, or the exigencies of the transit of culture from old England, or simply the passage of time), and if we accept the further possibility of variation within New England resulting from the fact that individual ministers of the fellowship varied and that men reacted to the fellowship in different ways and to different degrees. In reading the deviation from the norm and accounting it to Puritanism, it will be far safer to err by being too conservative rather than too liberal, that is, to account less to Puritanism than more.

Let us attempt a cursory first measurement.

Prima facie, we can say that some degree and kind of quickened religiosity is part of the gift passed from preacher to laymen. One asserts this prima facie, for to do otherwise would be to argue that the preachers were singularly unsuccessful in what they considered they were about: bringing men and women to the realization of the necessity of the Christian quest as the preachers tended to define that quest. But beyond this, the data tend to conform. When we find laymen in close association with the preachers, we almost invariably find them to be more clearly religious than the average Englishman in terms of the preachers' peculiar morphology of conversion—more knowledgeable of that morphology; more diligent in pursuing religion via the preachers' principal device, the sermon; and more religiously introspective in that they were inclined to examine themselves for signs of the workings of God's will upon them.[9]

We will return to religiosity.[10] For the moment we need only mention it, noting further that measurement in terms of religiosity is relatively easy, particularly when religiosity is defined in terms of the specific points of polity and doctrine attributable to the fellowship. To go beyond religiosity, however, and call for measurement of a deviation in terms of economics, or politics, or social structure is to court difficulties. The calling is easy; the accomplishment is not. In devastating fashion historian J. H. Hexter has assaulted the "tunneling" phenomenon among historians, writing that they have "split the past into a series of tunnels, each continuous from the remote past to the present, but practically self-contained at every point and sealed off from contact with or contamination by anything that was going on in any other tunnel."[11] His particular bête noire was thematic tunneling—the artificial division into themes such as political history, intellectual history, economic history, social history, ad infinitum. Let us add geographic tunneling, particularly that which has divided the history of the seventeenth century as it was played out on the western shore of the Atlantic from that as played out on the eastern shore. In truth, the historian of early America too often has been either ignorant of all but the most general features of the work of English historians of the Tudor-Stuart-Georgian years or deluded by his search for a unique American past into believing that the crossing of the ocean or the influence of the frontier wrought such a traumatic change that one can stop at the landing beach in the quest for American beginnings. The measurement in question, however, calls for the early American historian to become as familiar with the other side of the Atlantic as he or she is with this side.

But this necessity for the early Americanist to learn something new is only part of the difficulty. The simple fact is that until very recently historians—even English historians—have paid little attention to the fundamentals of sixteenth- and seventeenth-century societies. Quite rightly did Carl Bridenbaugh open his 1968 social history of the English people for the years 1590–1642 with the line: "The ordinary men and women of any epoch of English history have seldom attracted the atten-

9. See, for example, Edmund S. Morgan's delineation of John Winthrop's religiosity in *The Puritan Dilemma: The Story of John Winthrop* (Boston, 1958), chap. 1.

10. In a subsequent chapter of *American Puritanism*.

11. Hexter, *Reappraisals in History: New Views on History and Society in Early Modern Europe* (Evanston, Ill., 1961), 194.

tion of historians."[12] Rightly, too, has Peter Laslett, an English historian of the Tudor-Stuart years, asked:

> Why is it that we know so much about the building of the British Empire, the growth of Parliament and its practices, the public and private lives of English kings, statesmen, generals, writers, thinkers and yet do not know whether all our ancestors had enough to eat? Our genealogical knowledge of how Englishmen and their distant kinsmen overseas are related to the English-men of the pre-industrial world is truly enormous and is grow-ing all the time. Why has almost nothing been done to discover how long those earlier Englishmen lived and how confident most of them could be of having any posterity at all? Not only do we not know the answers to these questions, until now we never seem to have bothered to ask.[13]

We can add to Laslett's questions a whole series of queries about the society from which the New Englanders came: What sort of lives did most Englishmen of that day lead? How did society operate on a day-to-day basis? What were the assumptions of the men in England's village lanes and town streets? Without the answers we have no English norm from which to measure, and we are only now beginning to find the answers.

We do, however, have data for the New England side of the Atlantic, although not nearly enough along certain lines. Lengthy tomes have elab-orately dissected the "mind" of New England, and if the dissection has been based only on the writings of a few leading laymen and clerics, it nevertheless clearly delineates the publicly pronounced values and as-sumptions of those few. We have, too, voluminous works elaborately por-traying various aspects of New England's society—the family; the work-ings of towns, villages, and churches; the law; manners and morals; servants and town officers; crime and punishment. Yet the one blind gen-eralization that New England was Puritan and that therefore all that we find in New England is Puritan clouds the view. If we glimpse a criminal being turned off the ladder in Boston in the 1630s or 1640s, we do not put it down as simply English justice being done but as Puritan justice; if a law is discerned which limits wages or prices, it is immediately labeled a Pu-ritan law; and if we discern a strong family orientation with domination by

---

12. Bridenbaugh, *Vexed and Troubled Englishmen, 1590–1642* (New York, 1968), vii.

13. Laslett, *The World We Have Lost*, 127. Such quotations from the mid- and late 1960s should remind us of how very young social history is even in Great Britain. We now (1993) know considerably more.

the father, we refer to familialism and the patriarch as elements of Puritanism.

With the basic facts of English life only now being studied in depth and of New England life too rashly generalized as Puritan, any attempt at measurement is begun unpropitiously. But we can begin, using what we are slowly understanding about the former (English life) and what we think we know about the latter (New England). And to proceed is to be immediately struck by a curious impression: With the exception of religious attitudes and institutions, the measurable difference between New and old England that need be accounted for by the influence of the preaching fellowship — our criterion for Puritanism — is minimal.[14] Simply put, little to nothing in the way of social polity discernible in New England is not to be found in old England. It cannot be stressed in strong enough language that this conclusion is tentative and that it is based upon only the beginning of sophisticated research into the ordinary lives on both sides of the ocean. But with one after another of the "Puritan" traits turning out to be nothing more than English traits, one can hardly avoid suggesting that further work will merely add to the impression.

Let us exemplify the case in the simplest way possible. What follows is a sampling of statements from historians of New England society;[15] ap-

---

14. Perry Miller was undoubtedly aware of this. See the "Introduction" to Miller and Thomas H. Johnson, eds., *The Puritans: A Sourcebook of Their Writings* (1938; reprint, New York, 1963), 1:7: "Most accounts of Puritanism . . . attribute everything that Puritans said or did to the fact that they were Puritans; their attitudes toward all sorts of things are pounced upon and exhibited as peculiarities of their sect, when as a matter of fact they were normal attitudes for the time. . . . About ninety per cent of the intellectual life, scientific knowledge, morality, manners and customs, notions and prejudices, was that of all Englishmen," leaving only 10 percent uniquely Puritan. "When we come to trace developments and influences on subsequent American history and thought, we shall find that the starting point of many ideas and practices is as apt to be found among the ninety per cent as among the ten." The problem is that Miller neither elaborated nor stipulated a definition by which the unique could be extracted from the general.

15. Edmund S. Morgan, ed., *Puritan Political Ideas, 1558–1794* (Indianapolis, 1965), xvii; Richard L. Bushman, *From Puritan to Yankee: Character and the Social Order in Connecticut, 1690–1765* (Cambridge, Mass., 1967), 14; Edmund S. Morgan, *The Puritan Family: Religion and Domestic Relations in Seventeenth-Century New England* (1944; reprint, New York, 1966), 76–77; Thomas Jefferson Wertenbaker, *The Puritan Oligarchy: The Founding of American Civilization* (New York, 1947), 42–44; Ola Elizabeth Winslow, *Meetinghouse Hill, 1630–1783* (New York, 1952), 50–51; Stuart Bruchey, ed., *The Colonial Merchant: Sources and Readings* (New York, 1966), 91–92; Joseph Gaer and Ben Siegel, *The Puritan Heritage: America's Roots in the Bible* (New York, 1964), 87; Edmund S. Morgan, "The Puritans and Sex" (1942), as reprinted in *Pivotal Interpretations of American History*, ed. Carl N. Degler (New York, 1966), 1:6. In all fairness it must be added that in some cases the authors of these passages go on to note the English custom, Morgan writing for example that "the custom of placing children in other families already existed in England in the sixteenth century" (*Pu-*

pended at the right are statements about Tudor-Stuart English society in general, all drawn from a single work by social historian Peter Laslett:[16]

New England	England
[Note] the often repeated Puritan warning that every man, for the good of society, must remain in the place to which God had called him. [Governor] Winthrop could remind the emigrants of Massachusetts that God had so ordered the condition of mankind that "in all times some must be rich some poore, some highe and eminent in power and dignitie; others means and in subjection," and he was properly shocked when a servant suggested to a master who was unable to pay him that they change places.	In this society, subordination and politics were founded on tradition. . . . This submissive cast of mind is almost universal in the statements made by the men about themselves. "There is degree above degree, As reason is. . . . " "Take but degree away, Untune that string, And hark what discord follows." It would seem that once a man in the traditional world got himself into a position where he could catch a glimpse of his society as a whole, he immediately felt that degree, order, was its essential feature. Without degree, unquestioning subordination, and some men being privileged while all the others obeyed, anarchy and destruction were inevitable. Any threat to the established order was a danger to everyone's personality.
Weakness in the family endangered the entire social order, for the Puritans knew that the pattern of submission set in the home fixed the attitude toward authority throughout life and that strong family government prevented disorder in the state. The father was the model for all authority — magistrates were called the fa-	The duty of Christian obedience rested on the commandment *Honour thy Father and thy Mother*. . . . What more familiar sentiment for the beneficed rector or the itinerant preacher to appeal to when the children of the village community were being instructed in their Christian duties? Submission to the powers that be went

---

ritan Family, 77). But the context of the discussions, the constant reiteration of the adjective *Puritan*, and the casualness of the admission of the English custom (when acknowledged), all tend to sublimate the parallel custom to the notion of a peculiar Puritan attribute.

16. Laslett, *The World We Have Lost*, 173–74, 177–78, 19–20, 12, 60, 74, 118, 35, 130.

thers of their people — and the biblical commandment to honor parents was expanded to include all rulers.

To strengthen control at the primary level, the General Assembly ordered that every young person submit himself to family government.

Puritan children were frequently brought up in other families than their own even when there was no apparent educational [or economic] advantage involved. . . . In explanation I suggest that Puritan parents did not trust themselves with their own children, that they were afraid of spoiling them by too great affection.

It could not have been by chance that each group of settlers turned to the English manor as the model for their town, not in political or religious matters, but in its agricultural, industrial and, to some

very well with the habit of obedience to the head of the patriarchal family, and it had the extremely effective sanction of the universal fear of damnation to the defiant. "Short life," so the doctrine went, "was the punishment of disobedient children."

Only the recognition that people came not as individuals, but as families, makes it possible to begin to come closer to the facts. . . . It goes without saying, of course, that no one in a position of "service" was an independent member of society, national or local. . . . Such men and women, boys and girls, were caught up, so to speak, "subsumed" is the ugly word we shall use, into the personalities of their fathers and masters.

Sometimes, we have found, [the ordinary Englishman] would prefer to send out his own children as servants and bring in other children and young men to do the work. This is one of the few glimpses we can get into the quality of the emotional life of the family at this time, for it shows that parents may have been unwilling to submit children of their own to the discipline of work at home.

Though the detailed arrangements for the working of the land were no longer undertaken at the manor court, and though that court might be dying as an institution, nevertheless, the community

extent, social features. The manor was a dying institution in England.... Their natural impulse would have been to ignore this relic of medieval times, and divide their land into farms. But against this, it seems certain, their advisors warned them in most emphatic terms, pointing out that to scatter themselves throughout their town would not only militate against the unity so essential to a new community, but might so discourage the advancement of religion as to defeat the chief purpose of their migration.... The creation of the agricultural village is a tribute to the foresight of Winthrop, or Dudley, or Endicott, or whoever it was that thought this matter through, for it became the corner stone of Puritan New England.

still had its affairs to run co-operatively. The church had to be administered.... The poor law had to be carried out; the roads had to be kept up; the constable appointed to maintain the peace. The more important the common responsibilities of any community, presumably, the stronger the association between its members, because each one's interest is engaged. But living together in one township, isolated, spatially, from others of comparable size, of very much the same structure, inevitably means a communal sense and communal activity.... The strength of this sense of community in the English villager can be seen when he removed himself beyond the ocean, and settled again, surrounded by the alien, virgin land, which required new household groupings. In the final years of the traditional order in England, when the English were establishing their townships on the eastern seaboard of the North American continent, the village community at home was of course the model.

On Sunday it was always "going to meeting" or "going to preaching"; never going to church. In the town mind, as well as on the Town Book, this was not God's holy temple; it was an all-purpose place of assembly. In a typical phrase which expressed the current view for more than a century it was "our meetinghouse, built by our own vote, framed by our own

Every meeting of the village community took place in the Church.... This function of the church building as a meeting place for all purposes of the community, must be stressed. Here they were, these farming householders, not all of whom could read, sitting in the building put up by their fore-runners many centuries before, and which they, in

hammers and saws, and by our own hands set in the convenientest place for us all." Accordingly, no particular sacredness attached to the building itself. On Sunday the town assembled here for preaching; on town meeting Monday essentially the same group met in the same place to vote "fence repairs," convenient "Horse Bridges," rings for swine.

their turn, annually repaired and even beautified. In the place where they came so often to Christian service they chose their neighbors for the traditional offices, secular and spiritual. When English villagers found themselves in America, one of the first buildings which they put up for the new village was the *Meeting House*, for the town meeting had a great deal to decide in starting all anew. The *Meeting House* was also, of course, the Christian church of the village being born.

Agrarian in outlook and deeply religious, they strongly supported the emphasis of the church on the restrictive elements within the Puritan heritage [with regard to economics]. . . . Note particularly the provision for selectmen "to set reasonable rates upon all commodities and proportionately to limit the wages of workemen and labourers."

Once we are alive to the real possibility of famine the perpetual preoccupation of the authorities of that era, governmental and municipal, with the supply of food for the poor takes on a new significance. The insistence on fair prices for all victuals and especially of bread is a reminder that people might starve even where supplies were available. . . . Hence the strict control of all dealings in breadstuffs and all handlers of them.

Even the well-covered woman was not beyond censure or punishment if her attire was considered too expensive, affected, or simply beyond her social station. Such indulgence was a clear indication of overweening pride. This applied also to men.

Private correspondence is full of resentment at common people wearing the clothes reserved to the socially superior.

Toward sexual intercourse outside marriage the Puritans were as frankly hostile as they were favor-

The code of moral behavior in the traditional world can be looked upon . . . as an essential part of the

able to it in marriage. They passed laws to punish adultery with death, and fornication with whippings. Yet they had no misconceptions as to the capacity of human beings to obey such laws. Although the laws were commands of God, it was only natural — since the fall of Adam — for human beings to break them. Breaches must be punished lest the community suffer the wrath of God.

workings of the general social scheme. Here was a nation-wide community of persons . . . living under agrarian conditions and not far above subsistence level. It was a community which made of the nuclear family the unit for nearly all activity, only adding other persons to it as servants, when that was necessary. If the shape of the society was to be maintained, Pauline morality had to be enforced. . . . Ordinary people can rarely be heard on this subject. But when they spoke their minds as witnesses in ecclesiastical courts they left no doubt that sexual intercourse outside marriage was universally condemned.

Enough of juxtaposing quotations. To continue would undoubtedly bore the reader without materially adding to the clear impression that New England, considered apart from religion, far from being a distinct culture, its deviation from the English norm subject to ready measurement, was really — to use Laslett's word — traditional within that English norm.

Let us see the situation clearly and, for a moment, widen our sights to include areas other than New England to which Englishmen went in the seventeenth century. Englishmen settling in New England seem to have tended to reestablish as closely as possible the traditional culture that, through the works of such as Laslett, we are now beginning to understand. Did all Englishmen do this? Apparently not. The Virginians do not seem to have. They did not settle in tight-knit communities, did not — and I paraphrase Laslett here only to indicate that the restrictions of tunnel history work both ways, that he seems to know as little about the western shore of the Atlantic as early American historians know of the eastern — did not establish townships using the village community of England as their model, did not construct as one of their first buildings a meetinghouse and troop in periodically to deal with the multifarious business incumbent in starting anew. Indeed, we can interpret various actions (all abortive) of the Virginia Company of London and later of the crown as attempts to induce artificially the traditional culture — the imposition, for example, of semimartial (can we call it patriarchal?) law in the early years of the colony, the periodic attempts to have Virginians abandon their dispersed population pattern and congregate in towns. Of course, this is only a surface glance. Historians have not yet penetrated very far into any seventeenth-century Anglo-American society except that of New England. There might well be — to use but one example — traditional family attitudes and patterns hidden in the extant records. But this surface glance would seem to indicate that the Virginians were atraditional, that their culture was something new in the English-speaking world and in sharp contrast to the traditional New England culture — this despite the more general view that considers the Virginians the transplanters par excellence.[17] One can, in effect, suggest a reversal of the normal way of dealing with New England and Virginia. New England differed from Virginia not because the Virginians were typically English and the New Englanders were trying to make a new (and to their lights a better society), but because the New Englanders were attempting to transplant the image of a traditional society and the Virginians were straying from that image.

If one accepts this reversal, one immediately comes to the question of causation. Why did Virginians stray from traditional? Why did the New Englanders attempt to remain within the tradition? The answer is certainly not simplistic. It involves, of course, the concept of cultural baggage: Men brought their social and cultural experiences with them to the New World and, in building anew, built with what they knew; they deviated from the known only under pressure; cultural inertia, consequently, was a force for the traditional.[18] But the answer might also involve the cultural area of old England from which the settlers of one part of Anglo-

17. For Virginians as "transplanters," see Daniel Boorstin, *The Americans: The Colonial Experience* (New York, 1958), 97ff. The view expressed here is not at variance with that of Jack P. Greene, *Pursuits of Happiness: The Social Development of Early Modern British Colonies and the Formation of American Culture* (Chapel Hill, N.C., 1988), that Chesapeake society reflected to a far greater extent than did that of New England the English society of the moment. My argument in *American Puritanism* was — and remains — that New England reflected an English conceptualization of society that we can call "traditional," that this traditional conceptualization was more and more at odds with evolving English society, and that it was seized upon by the Puritan ministers and their lay followers who made it central to a social (as against strictly religious) jeremiad against the course of events in old England and carried it to New England. Subsequent scholarship does, however, amend the argument of *American Puritanism*. We have today a far better view of the complexity of Chesapeake society than we had in 1970 — it was, in effect, more communally organized than we thought — while studies such as Joseph Sutherland Wood, "The Origin of the New England Village" (Ph.D. diss., Pennsylvania State University, 1978), and Stephen Innes, *Labor in a New Land: Economy and Society in Seventeenth-Century Springfield* (Princeton, N.J., 1983), have depicted a reality in New England more reflective of English society than of the traditional conceptualization of society.

18. Robert F. Berkhofer, Jr., "Space, Time, Culture, and the New Frontier," *Agricultural History* 38 (1964): 24–25.

America came as against the area from which came the settlers of another part.[19] It might involve the very nature of initial settlement — by individuals in Virginia (recall that the very first settlers were all male, and males predominated among newcomers throughout the seventeenth century), by families (in terms certainly of influence if not numbers) in New England.[20] And the answer might well involve geography and the evolving agricultural systems. New England's agriculture, as it developed, was little different from old England's agriculture; indeed, what drove New England into commercial endeavors seems to have been the fact that the section produced exactly the same commodities that old England produced, and that as a consequence the section had to take to the sea to find non-English markets for its produce.[21] Virginia's agriculture came to center on a system of tobacco cultivation alien to England. A traditional society could fit New England's traditional agriculture; a new society had to evolve to encompass the new agriculture of Virginia. We cannot, however, discount the possibility that the answer might involve Puritanism as well: the influence of the ministerial fellowship.

Earlier we noted that the gentlemen who led the Winthrop migration were children of the fellowship, that the ministers who sailed with them and in the years immediately following were from the fellowship, and that by 1650 the number of practicing ministers in Massachusetts alone was 37, one for every 415 people. What of Virginia? True, the fellowship touched that colony in its earliest years. Ships arriving in England in November 1609 reported that "unhappy dissension" had fallen out among the settlers "by reason of their Minister, who being, as they say, somewhat a Puritan, the most part refused to go to his services and hear his sermons, though by the other part he was supported and favored."[22] Master Alexander Whitaker arrived on the James River in 1611 and died in 1617. Family and education link Whitaker to the fellowship. (Among his uncles was the Reverend Laurence Chaderton.) And from Virginia, Whitaker wrote to others of the fellowship, his letters marked by the very

19. The argument of David Hackett Fischer's *Albion's Seed: Four British Folkways in America* (New York, 1989). For variation within New England itself, see David Grayson Allen, *In English Ways: The Movement of Societies and the Transferal of English Local Law and Custom to Massachusetts Bay in the Seventeenth Century* (Chapel Hill, N.C., 1981).

20. An argument vigorously restated by Virginia DeJohn Anderson, *New England's Generation: The Great Migration and the Formation of Society and Culture in the Seventeenth Century* (Cambridge, 1991).

21. Darrett B. Rutman, "Governor Winthrop's Garden Crop: The Significance of Agriculture in the Early Commerce of Massachusetts Bay," *William and Mary Quarterly*, 3d ser., 20 (1963): 396–415 [chap. 6 below].

22. J. Beaulieu to William Trumbull, 30 Nov. 1609, Trumbull MSS, Berkshire Record Office, utilizing microfilm in the Virginia Colonial Records Project, Virginia State Library and Archives, Richmond.

spirit of the group. There were, too, other ministers in early Virginia who can be linked, although only tentatively in some cases, to the fellowship.[23] Yet this entry into the South never developed. In the face of Virginia's succession of disasters, none of the earliest ministers was blessed with longevity. There were always too few ministers for the size and dispersal of the colony's population. And, as in England, as Anglicanism rose vis-à-vis dissent, the government in Virginia tended to brand the few ministers of the fellowship who arrived as dissenters and exercise the law against them. One effect of this was to leave even fewer ministers in Virginia than there might otherwise have been. In 1649 a group of newcomers, arriving after a particularly hazardous journey from England at the home of a settler in Northampton County on Virginia's Eastern Shore, thought to give thanks in a church for a safe arrival. It was Sunday, and "we would have been glad to have found a church for the performance of our duty to God," one wrote, "to have rendered our hearty thanks to him in the public assembly . . . but we were not yet arrived to the heart of the country where there were churches, and ministry perform'd."[24] The writer erred only in thinking that things would be better "in the heart of the country." For in all Virginia at the moment there were only 6 ministers, one for every 3,239 persons.[25]

Clearly, the presence of ministers in large numbers relative to the population in New England and the absence of ministers in any significant numbers in Virginia is a measurable distinction between the two areas. If we assume that ministers generally are a force for traditional social organization and behavior, for traditional culture, the distinction can be worked into the explanation for the overt traditionalism of New England and Virginia's deviation. The ministers' voice was, in New England,

23. Harry Culverwell Porter, "Alexander Whitaker: Cambridge Apostle to Virginia," *William and Mary Quarterly*, 3d ser., 14 (1957): 317–43; Alexander Brown, ed., *The Genesis of the United States* (London, 1890), 1:497ff.; George M. Brydon, *Virginia's Mother Church and the Political Conditions under Which It Grew*, (Richmond and Philadelphia, 1947–52), 1:20–30; Perry Miller, "Religion and Society in the Early Literature of Virginia," in Miller, *Errand into the Wilderness* (Cambridge, Mass., 1956), 99–140, originally published in two installments in *William and Mary Quarterly*, 3d ser., 5 (1948) and 6 (1949).

24. Colonel Norwood, *A Voyage to Virginia*, in Peter Force, comp., *Tracts and Other Papers, Relating Principally to the . . . Colonies in North America* (Washington, D.C., 1836–47), vol. 3, tract 10:48.

25. Based upon a survey of known ministers in the colony, the principal sources for which were Edmond Neill, *Notes on the Virginia Clergy* (Philadelphia, 1877); Edward L. Goodwin, *The Colonial Church in Virginia* (Milwaukee, 1927); George M. Brydon, "Addendum to Goodwin's List of Colonial Clergy," typescript, Virginia State Library and Archives; Frederick L. Weis, *The Colonial Clergy of Virginia, North Carolina, and South Carolina* (Boston, 1955); and my own research. Population figures for both Virginia and New England are, of course, best estimates and subject to the many reservations stipulated in Darrett B. Rutman, *Winthrop's Boston: Portrait of a Puritan Town, 1630–1649* (Chapel Hill, N.C., 1965), 293–94.

added to whatever force there was in cultural inertia, initial settlement by families, and the agricultural potential; the lack of a ministerial voice in Virgina in effect removed an impediment to straying from the traditional when other factors (the predominance of single males among the settlers and a tobacco-based agriculture) encouraged that straying. But we can go one step further. Perhaps the voice of the fellowship — as the laymen heard it — was more loudly a voice for tradition than that of the ordinary English minister.[26] If this was the case, we should expect that New England would be more intensely traditional than even England, our norm. And perhaps the intensity of adherence to tradition is a deviation from that norm which we ought to seize upon as a primary effect of the preachers' gift upon the laity of New England.

26. The subsequent chapter of Rutman, *American Puritanism*, argues just this point.

6 Governor Winthrop's Garden Crop

"The first premise of all human existence, and, therefore, of all history," Marx wrote, is that men and women "must be in a position to live in order to 'make history.'" And living implies involvement in an economy of some sort. It follows, therefore, that in order for New England to offer us a "Puritanism" to study, New Englanders had first to survive economically in a land in which there was no guarantee of survival. What follows speaks narrowly to the issue of New England's early economy. But it also has application to what has become a central question in American history: the "transition" from a culturally determined marketplace to a homeostatic "free" market, from a premodern economy to "capitalism." In the early 1640s New Englanders — from the governor of Massachusetts in Boston to the villagers in Dedham and Springfield and Hartford — all came to realize that in order to buy what they needed, they had to sell what they had in a market which they might be able to open but could not control.

There is a paradox in the history of early Massachusetts — indeed, one applicable to all of New England in the first decades. It is that of an agricultural land in which the trades of the sea were dominant; a land largely devoted to crops where — if the tenor of historical writing is to be accepted — profits were made in other endeavors.

On the one hand, there is the frequent description of New England's "cold climate and rocky soil," and the conclusion that agriculture was "not an encouraging business." The New Englanders simply made a good

Presented originally at a session of the American Historical Association's annual meeting, Washington, D.C., December 1961 and subsequently published as "Governor Winthrop's Garden Crop: The Significance of Agriculture in the Early Commerce of Massachusetts Bay," in the *William and Mary Quarterly*, 3d ser., 20 (1963): 396–415. Copyright 1963 by the Institute of Early American History and Culture. Reprinted with the permission of the editor.

thing of a bad bargain during the first years of settlement, building a short-term prosperity by selling their agricultural surplus to new arrivals. But when the tide of newcomers ebbed and depression broke upon them in 1640, they turned to trade, shipbuilding, fish. In the words of a recent writer, they abandoned the plow "for the rising star of ocean commerce."[1]

On the other hand, there is the unavoidable fact that the land dominates town and commonwealth records both before and after 1640. The General Court of Massachusetts Bay regularly designated land for new towns in the interior — away from the sea and ships. The towns themselves were always in the throes of a new distribution of land. Court records indicate farm after farm being leased, with the owner receiving agricultural products as rent; probate records show land passing from father to sons, while estate inventories list page on page of farm equipment.[2] Contemporary descriptions of the commonwealth reiterate the impression given by the records. Edward Johnson, writing in 1651, described the Bay settlement as a chain of agricultural communities. Dorchester, he wrote, boasted "Orchards and Gardens full of Fruit-trees, plenty of Corne-Lande"; Roxbury was "this fertill Towne" of "very goodly Fruit-trees, fruitfull Fields and Gardens, their Heard of Cowes, Oxen and other young Cattell of that kind about 350"; Ipswich was a "very good Land for Husbandry, where Rocks hinder not the course of the Plow." Even Boston, though its center on Shawmut Peninsula was by this time devoted exclusively to commercial pursuits, included purely agricultural areas at Muddy River, Winnisimmet, Rumney Marsh, and Pullen Point.[3]

Only occasionally have writers hinted at the resolution to this paradox. Charles M. Andrews, in surveying the extant cargo manifests of the period, concluded that ships from New England carried away cargoes consisting of one-third fish, one-third wood products, and one-third wheat and other grains. Bernard Bailyn, in examining the seventeenth-century New England merchant, noted the existence of a trade in provisions to the wine-producing islands of the eastern Atlantic (the Cape Verde Islands, Madeira, the Azores) and to the sugar-producing islands of the Carib-

1. Max Savelle, *The Foundations of American Civilization* (New York, 1942), 145; George Lee Haskins, *Law and Authority in Early Massachusetts: A Study in Tradition and Design* (New York, 1960), 109.

2. The conclusions presented here were drawn in large part from research that ultimately emerged in Rutman, *Winthrop's Boston: Portrait of a Puritan Town, 1630–1649* (Chapel Hill, N.C., 1965), and Rutman, *Husbandmen of Plymouth: Farms and Villages in the Old Colony, 1620–1692* (Boston, 1967).

3. J. Franklin Jameson, ed., *Johnson's Wonder-Working Providence, 1628–1651* (New York, 1910), 69–70, 72, 96. For Boston, see the various town divisions, grants, and property transfers in "Boston Town Records [1634–1660/61]," and "The Book of Possessions," both in City of Boston, *A Report of the Record Commissioners* 2 (Boston, 1877).

bean.[4] Yet the extent of these agricultural exports and the interaction of commerce and agriculture — the fact that neither could have existed without the other, that New England itself could probably not have persisted without both — has been left unexplored.[5]

Such an exploration must begin with the peculiar and highly inflationary economy that had evolved in the 1630s: that economy based upon the production of an agricultural surplus and the consumption of the surplus by new arrivals.[6] Each year, before 1640, five, ten, twenty ships dropped anchor in Boston harbor. Every arrival was a signal: Out from the town hurried the lighters carrying merchants and shopkeepers eager to take from the ships' inventories those English goods for which their customers on shore waited; back in the same lighters came the passengers from the ships. The newcomers brought little in the way of material goods, having transformed their possessions into cash in England. They were now eager to transform that cash into new possessions in Massachusetts. From the already established settlers they bought the Indian corn and wheat, the timber, and, particularly, the cattle needed to start life anew. For their part, the established settlers hastened to their local merchants to transform the newcomers' cash into English pots and pans, plows and cloth, even lace and frills. From the towns and villages to the Boston merchants who served to supply the local communities, the coin made its way, and from the merchants to the ships that came in steady procession. Where cash was not sufficient, credit was obtained; the colony was prosperous and expanding; bills would eventually be paid.

In 1640, however, with surprising suddenness, the cycle collapsed. The three preceding years had been tremendously prosperous. In 1637 and 1638 the tide of immigrants had run strong. But in 1639 there had been a

---

4. Andrews, *The Colonial Period of American History* (New Haven, 1934–38), 1:516; Bailyn, *The New England Merchants in the Seventeenth Century* (Cambridge, Mass., 1955), 83ff.

5. The best general work on agriculture in this period is still Percy W. Bidwell and John I. Falconer, *History of Agriculture in the Northern United States, 1620–1860* (Washington, D.C., 1925), 5–66, though it fails to recognize any large export of agricultural products from New England and notes (p. 42) a regular import of wheat, rye, barley, and the like into the section "not entirely due to inability to raise a sufficient supply of these grains at home, but in part at least to the realization of the advantages of specialization in fishing, trading, and shipbuilding."

6. For descriptions of the economy as it developed in the 1630s and of the depression of the early 1640s see John Winthrop to Sir Nathaniel Rich, 22 May 1634, Massachusetts Historical Society, *Winthrop Papers* (Boston, 1929–47), 3:166–68; James Kendall Hosmer, ed., *Winthrop's Journal "History of New England," 1630–1649* (New York, 1908), 1:112, 2:6, et passim; Jameson, *Johnson's Wonder-Working Providence*, 209; Marion H. Gottfried, "The First Depression in Massachusetts," *New England Quarterly* 9 (1936): 655–59; Bailyn, *New England Merchants*, 32ff., 45–49; Rutman, *Winthrop's Boston*, 178–94.

slackening.[7] For a time the momentum of the earlier years kept the economy operating, though fatal cracks had opened. The settlers found their surplus harder to dispose of as the market created by the flood of newcomers contracted; the store of cash in the coffers of the Boston merchants diminished as the specie contributions of the newcomers failed to keep pace with the outgoing payments for imports.[8] In 1640 the ships entering the harbor from England, encouraged by "the store of money and quick markets" of prior years, carried enlarged inventories.[9] But the diminished supply of specie would not even cover old bills, let alone permit the contracting of new ones. Shippers found the market steadily worsening through the summer and fall and grumbled over poor profits. More important was the position of the settler. The market for his surplus, contracting since the previous year, all but disappeared. He offered his produce in payment of goods and debts, but the merchants "would sell no wares but for ready money."[10] In consequence, commodity prices plummeted, wheat from seven shillings a bushel in May to four shillings in October; Indian corn from five shillings to three, then, by June 1641, to nothing.[11] Cattle prices fell from £20 and £30 a head to £4 and £5. But even at this price there was no market. The very land lost value.[12] In the

7. Charles E. Banks, *The Planters of the Commonwealth* (Boston, 1930), 190, 201–2. The peak year was 1638, with 3,000 arrivals, but for 1639 Banks cites only three ship arrivals. In 1640 there was a recovery in the number of immigrants, 1,575 passengers aboard ten ships. See William B. Weeden, *Economic and Social History of New England* (Boston and New York, 1890), 1:165. But this was too late to contribute to a recovery from the recession that had already set in. And probably the arrivals of 1640 carried less specie than they had previously. See Thomas Gostlin to John Winthrop, 2 Mar. 1640, *Winthrop Papers* 4:212; *New Englands First Fruits* (1643), in Samuel Eliot Morison, *The Founding of Harvard College* (Cambridge, Mass., 1935), 444. The almost complete stoppage of immigrants came in 1641.

8. Repeated warnings of the shaky condition of the economy mark the correspondence of 1639–40. See, e.g., Hugh Peter to John Winthrop, ca. 10 Apr. 1639, John Tinker to Winthrop, 28 May 1640, *Winthrop Papers* 4:112–13, 249–52; "Report of Edmund Browne" to Sir Simonds D'Ewes, Sept. 1639, in Colonial Society of Massachusetts, *Publications* 7 (1905): 78.

9. Hosmer, *Winthrop's Journal* 2:6.

10. Ibid., 17. That at least some cash transactions took place this year is illustrated by the presence of £300 aboard the *Mary Rose* of Bristol when she exploded and sank in the harbor, 27 July 1640 (ibid., 10).

11. Nathaniel B. Shurtleff, ed., *Records of the Governor and Company of the Massachusetts Bay in New England* (Boston, 1853–54), 1:214, 304; Hosmer, *Winthrop's Journal* 2:31, 92; William Coddington to John Winthrop, 25 Aug. 1640, Henry Smith to Winthrop, 2 Nov. 1640, *Winthrop Papers* 4:279–80, 296.

12. The highest cattle price noted during the inflation of the late 1630s was the sale of six cows for £301 payable over seven years (Thomas Mayhew's mortgage to Simon Bradstreet, 29 Sept. 1638, Chamberlain Manuscripts, Boston Public Library, Boston, A.1, 1–63). The decline can be traced in Edward E. Hale et al., eds., *Note-book Kept by Thomas Lechford, Esq., Lawyer in Boston, from June 27, 1638, to July 29, 1641* (Cambridge, Mass., 1885); *Winthrop*

disaster the possiblity arose of a wholesale desertion from the Puritan commonwealth of people who could not conceive of a way to live there. "The times of Unsettled Humyrs of many mens spirits to Returne for England," John Cotton called the early 1640s. "Why should a man stay untill the house fall on his head and why continue his being ther, where in reason he shall destroy his subsistence?" wrote Thomas Hooker; and John Winthrop declared, "They concluded there would be no subsisting here, and accordingly they began to hasten away."[13]

The crux of the economic problem facing the settlers was the existence of an unsalable agricultural surplus. The newcomers had constituted one market for that surplus. Now that market had been lost. The solution in this situation — when, as a Puritan rhymester put it, "men no more the Sea passe o're, and Customers are wanting"[14] — was nothing other than finding new customers at home or abroad. The leaders of the commonwealth did not realize this. Their response to the plight was dictated by prevalent economic theory, which accented the position of the merchant.[15] Reduce imports — hence the encouragement given to domestic cloth manufacturing, the ironworks, the passage of a series of sumptuary laws — and increase exports — thus the renewed attempts to spur a domestic fish industry, the support given to various trading ventures — and the net result would be (in their minds) a favorable flow of trade, a consequent increase in the merchants' specie and credit, a quickening of imports from England, and prosperity.[16] That the merchants could not import unless the

---

Papers, vol. 4; Shurtleff, *Records of the Governor and Company*, vol. 1; Hosmer, *Winthrop's Journal*, vol. 2. On land values, see ibid., 2:17, 19.

13. [Cotton] to Richard Saltonstall, ca. 1649, Cotton Papers, Prince Collection, Boston Public Library, Boston; Hooker to Thomas Shepard, 2 Nov., 1640, Hutchinson Papers, Massachusetts Archives, State House, Boston; Hosmer, *Winthrop's Journal* 2:82. Note, too, the specific incidents of ships carrying passengers out of New England, e.g. ibid., 1:333–35, 2:11, 33–34, 207; Thomas Lechford, *Plain Dealing; or, News from New England*, ed. J. Hammond Trumbull (Boston, 1867), 113–14; Edward Winslow, *New-Englands Salamander* (1647), in Massachusetts Historical Society, *Collections*, 3d ser., 2 (1830): 120. Note also Winslow's comment (p. 141) on "the many thousands . . . that came from New England" and were in old England at the time of his writing.

14. *Good News from New-England* (1648), in Massachusetts Historical Society, *Collections*, 4th ser., 1 (1852): 204.

15. Joseph Dorfman, *The Economic Mind in American Civilization, 1606–1685* (New York, 1946), 1:6; E. A. J. Johnson, *American Economic Thought in the Seventeenth Century* (London, 1932), 150–53.

16. On cloth, see Gottfried, "The First Depression in Massachusetts," 664–66; on the ironworks, E. N. Hartley, *Ironworks on the Saugus* (Norman, Okla., 1957), 47ff.; on the fisheries, Harold A. Innis, *The Cod Fisheries* (Toronto, 1954), 75ff., and Raymond McFarland, *A History of the New England Fisheries* (New York, 1911), 53–69; on fur trade, Arthur H. Buffinton, "New England and the Western Fur Trade, 1629–1675," Colonial Society of

general populace bought and that the general populace could not buy unless it could sell the products of the countryside did not occur to them.

The finding of new customers for excess agricultural products was, therefore, accidental. In 1640 and 1641, probably through their connections with English merchants, a few men in the Bay colony became cognizant of the existence of a market for wood products in Spain and the Atlantic islands — merchant George Story arranging for the shipment of 8,500 clapboards in 1640, presumably to the islands; Samuel Maverick in 1641 dealing with William Lewis of Malaga, Spain, for the sale of clapboard.[17] Undoubtedly it was through such contacts that clever traders among the men of Massachusetts learned of a market across the Atlantic for the cheap wheat and other grains glutting the Bay area. Edward Gibbons, a leading Bay merchant, was early in seeing the possibility. In October 1641, at his urging, the General Court gave official encouragement to the preparation of a grain ship. It commanded the colonists to forgo bread and cakes made of wheat flour inasmuch "as it appeareth to this Court that wheate is like to bee a staple commodity, and that a ship is withall convenient speede to bee set fourth, and fraited with wheate, for the fetching in of such forraine commodities as wee stand in need of." Little is known of the actual shipment. Presumably the various towns of the colony "adventured" their local surplus under Gibbons's direction. Presumably, too, it sailed for Spain or the islands before May 1642.[18] Certainly, however, the commonwealth had struck at the heart of its problem, though its approach in limiting consumption to create an exportable surplus when a surplus already existed displays the economic ignorance of the time. Grain values, minimal in 1641, steadied in 1642, the General Court in September reflecting the market price in ordering that wheat and barley be received for taxes at four shillings a bushel, rye and pease at three shillings four pence, and Indian corn at two shillings six.[19]

In the years immediately following, the trade in agricultural products grew quickly to major proportions: wood products, which had first found an overseas market and were in these years a product of the agricultural

Massachusetts, *Publications* 18 (1917): 160–92, and Francis X. Moloney, *The Fur Trade in New England, 1620–1676* (Cambridge, Mass., 1931).

17. Hale et al., *Note-book Kept by Thomas Lechford*, 327; *A Volume Relating to the Early History of Boston Containing the Aspinwall Notarial Records from 1644 to 1651*, in Registry Department of the City of Boston, *Records Relating to the Early History of Boston* 32 (Boston, 1903): 71–72, hereafter cited as *Aspinwall Notarial Records*.

18. Shurtleff, *Records of the Governor and Company* 1:337; William H. Whitmore, *A Bibliographical Sketch of the Laws of the Massachusetts Colony from 1630 to 1686* (Boston, 1890), xxiii. At the same time, the making of malt out of wheat was prohibited. The order was repealed 20 May 1642.

19. Shurtleff, *Records of the Governor and Company* 2:27; *New Englands First Fruits*, 444.

community as farmers cut timber in their off-season and sold it to the coopers of Boston and elsewhere to be cut and shaped into pipe staves, treenails, clapboard, and the like; grains, principally wheat but including also quantities of rye, barley, dried pease, and Indian corn; and packed and salted beef.[20] The extent of the trade can be followed in the ship arrivals and departures from the Bay.[21] In the fall following the sailing of Gibbons's grain ship, John Winthrop recorded the departure of six ships "laden with pipe staves and other commodities of this country"; four others had sailed "a little before." At least one of these vessels had initiated its voyage in the new market itself, coming from Madeira with wine specifically to pick up and return with New England produce. During the winter following, as the governor reported, the "much corn spent in setting out the ships, ketches, etc.," in addition to a bad crop in 1642, caused a reversal of the earlier market glut and created a temporary scarcity of grain.[22]

Indications of voyages in 1643 are confused, but it is evident that the trade continued and grew: at least five vessels returned to Boston harbor with wine and sugar, and two ships sailed. Early in 1644 the sixty-ton *Hopewell* of Boston sailed for the Canaries with a cargo of wheat-in-bulk; six other identifiable vessels sailed in the trade that year. The year following, the *Edmund and John* of London carrying at least 3,000 bushels of pease, wheat, and Indian corn, the *Dolphin* of London with 7,000 bushels or more, and five other identifiable vessels made the journey.[23] During this one year, 1645, a total of some 20,000 bushels of grain valued at approximately £4,000 in Boston prices were exported from the commonwealth; so much indeed that the provisions market in the Canary Islands was temporarily surfeited.[24] In terms of bulk this grain equaled the exports of fish and wood products; hence the average cargo would conform to

20. On wood products, see N. Sylvester to John Winthrop, Jr., 7 Apr. 1655, in Massachusetts Historical Society, *Proceedings*, 2d ser., 4 (1889): 274; William B. Trask et al., eds., *Suffolk Deeds* (Boston, 1880–1906), 1:122–23; Hugh Peter and Emmanuel Downing to John Winthrop, 13 Jan. 1641, John Endecott to Winthrop, 28 Jan. 1641, *Winthrop Papers* 4:304–5, 311–12. For the various efforts to regulate local timber cutting, see "Boston Town Records."

21. Figures reflecting ship arrivals and departures in Boston harbor are drawn from a shipping list for the years 1640–50 compiled from ship mentions in a variety of sources, most notably *Aspinwall Notarial Records*; *Winthrop Papers*, vols. 4, 5; Hosmer, *Winthrop's Journal*, vol. 2; Hale et al., *Note-book Kept by Thomas Lechford*; Trask et al., *Suffolk Deeds*, vols. 1, 2; and Massachusetts Archives, State House, Boston.

22. Hosmer, *Winthrop's Journal* 2:85, 89, 92.

23. For the *Hopewell*, see ibid., 154; for the *Edmund and John* and *Dolphin*, *Aspinwall Notarial Records*, 395, 397.

24. Hosmer, *Winthrop's Journal* 2:245; Stephen Winthrop to John Winthrop, ca. Mar. 1646, *Winthrop Papers*, 5:62.

Andrews's formula of equal thirds. But fish, while more substantial in terms of value — between £4,000 and £10,000 worth being exported this year — was far less to the benefit of the area as a whole.[25] Grains profited the farmers who produced them, the local merchants who sent them on to Boston, and the Boston merchants who sold them for shipment abroad; fish, on the other hand, profited a scattering of fishermen located primarily along the northern coast, the English houses that, as Bailyn and others have pointed out, controlled the trade in this early period, and those Boston merchants acting as agents for English firms.[26] Wood products were to the general profit of the Bay; but, subjected to heavy freight charges and bringing low prices in comparison to bulk, they were a poor third in terms of value. In one case, for example, pipe staves brought but £18 per 1,000 delivered at Madeira. At this price (which was probably high) it would have required roughly 225,000 pipe staves to equal the value of grain exports in 1645 and as much as one-half million to equal the value of the fish exports. Yet the average shipment seldom exceeded 10,000.[27]

Thus far and through 1646, when six identifiable vessels made the journey to the Atlantic islands and the Iberian Peninsula (including the locally built *Malaga Merchant*, a 250–300-ton ship whose name proclaimed her intended trade), agricultural exports flowed principally eastward across the ocean.[28] But a second outlet, in the Caribbean, was opening up.[29] From the early 1640s Massachusetts men had been sporadically

25. Robert Child to Samuel Hartlib, 24 Dec. 1645, in Colonial Society of Massachusetts, *Publications* 38 (1959): 52, estimates a catch valued at £10,000. But see Hosmer, *Winthrop's Journal* 2:42, 321: 300,000 fish sent to market in 1642 (approximately 7,500 quintals worth about £6,750) and £4,000 worth taken in local fisheries during the winter season of 1646–47.

26. Despite the occasional claims of writers on the subject — e.g., Innis's quoting with approval (in *Cod Fisheries*, 76) C. L. Woodbury's 1880 statement that "it was the winter fishery that placed on our coasts a class of permanent consumers, and gave to agriculture the possibility of flourishing. . . . It . . . gave to the industrious the great boon of independence, the foundation of character in the individual, and in the State. Agriculture followed with halting steps where it led the way" — the factual evidence presented by Innis, McFarland, Bailyn, and others fails to show the existence of any large fishing operations in southern New England or extensive profit to the settlers of the Bay during the first two decades. On the contrary, there is a great deal of evidence indicating that the fisheries brought very little profit to the colony.

27. *Aspinwall Notarial Records*, 244–45. This was in 1649. In 1646 a shipment brought £14 per 1,000 delivered to the ship at Boston; in 1648 pipe staves were used to satisfy a debt on the basis of £3 per 1,000 (ibid., 47, 125). With regard to freight charges, note the shipment of £270 worth of pipe staves in 1646 at a charge of £91 16s.(ibid, 47). The same was true of other wood products — bolts, shaken casks, treenails.

28. Ibid., 46, 47, 180–81, 403–4.

29. Contacts southward had existed during the 1630s but were not of great importance. Hosmer, *Winthrop's Journal* 1:126, 222, 260, et passim; Thomas Mayhew to John Winthrop,

exchanging provisions for raw cotton, tobacco, indigo, and sugar, John Winthrop reporting to his son that "Our Pinnaces had very good receitts" during the 1646 trading season. Large-scale trading began in 1647, however. That year West Indian ships, particularly from Barbados, appeared in Boston harbor "to trade for provisions for the belly," a plague of six months' duration having struck the islands and the settlers there having become "so intent upon planting sugar [introduced in 1641] that they had rather buy foode at very deare rates than produce it by labour."[30] Boston merchants immediately responded, shipping out grain, beef, bread, fish, and eventually live cattle and horses.[31] The following year, for the second time in the decade, grain exports from the Bay, southward and across the Atlantic, were so great as to cause a local scarcity in the commonwealth. A temporary order of the General Court prohibited the export of Massachusetts-grown grain. Prices, which had been steadily rising — wheat from four shillings a bushel to four shillings six pence in 1647 — turned sharply upward during the scarcity, then fell to five shillings as the 1649 crop relieved the situation, remaining at that level into the 1650s.[32]

The trade in agricultural produce inaugurated by Massachusetts men was very quickly incorporated into that evolving trade network emanating from the merchant houses of England. New Englanders moving out to barter for a profitable return in the peninsula and the island markets during the early 1640s found established English merchants already there. At times they were driven to make connections with these merchants by the reluctance of foreign traders and officials to deal with them as independents. The *Hopewell* of Boston, for example, on coming to Tenerife in the Canaries in 1643 found resident English agents there and an of-

---

Jr., 22 Apr. 1636, Hugh Peter to John Winthrop, 15 July 1637, *Winthrop Papers* 3:253, 450; Hale et al., *Note-book Kept by Thomas Lechford*, 46–47.

30. John Winthrop to John Winthrop, Jr., 14 May 1647, Richard Vines to John Winthrop, 19 July 1647, *Winthrop Papers* 5:161, 172.

31. See, e.g., *Aspinwall Notarial Records*, 80, 83–84, 140–41, 177–78; Trask et al., *Suffolk Deeds* 1:106; Hosmer, *Winthrop's Journal*, 2:346. Similarly, a Virginia trade was developing through the 1630s and 1640s, though it too became a major factor only ca. 1647. See ibid., 1:64 et passim; John Noble and John F. Cronin, eds., *Records of the Court of Assistants of the Massachusetts Bay, 1630–1692* (Boston, 1901–28), 2:25; correspondence in *Winthrop Papers* 2:337–38, 3:31, 156, 255, 276, 345; Virginia Colonial Records Survey Project, *Report No. 707*, 1; *Aspinwall Notarial Records*, 115–16, 236–38. By 1647, of thiry-one ships in Virginia at one time, seven were New England vessels. *A Perfect Description of Virginia* (London, 1649), in Peter Force, comp., *Tracts and Other Papers, Relating Principally to the . . . Colonies in North America* (Washington, D.C., 1836–47), vol. 2, tract 8:14.

32. Hosmer, *Winthrop's Journal* 2:341; Shurtleff, *Records of the Governor and Company* 2:215, 286, 3:212, 245, 359; Edward Hopkins to John Winthrop, Jr., 19 May 1649, *Winthrop Papers* 5:346.

ficialdom which refused to deal unless the ship gave bond through these agents that it would not trade on to Portuguese Madeira.[33]

More frequently, however, the Massachusetts merchants sought relations with English houses and their agents, selling their produce through them in order to build up credits in England against the purchase of goods for importation into the commonwealth. Samuel Maverick's first efforts in sending clapboard to William Lewis in Spain had been to build credits through Lewis with his London supplier. Subsequently, Massachusetts men were themselves sought out by English merchants to supply New England products to the Atlantic community in return for imports.[34] By the mid-1640s the local merchants were shipping abroad in their own and English ships in payment of goods advanced to them from England. Stephen Winthrop, for example, is found in partnership with Edward Gibbons and Thomas Fowle exporting 7,000 bushels of grain, 12,000 pipe staves, 40 hogsheads of packed beef and pork, and 1,000 quintals of fish to the Canary Islands for the account of a London firm, presumably in payment of earlier shipments of cotton goods, silk, window glass, iron, pewter, brass, shoes, and nails. In 1646 three Bostonians — Barnabas Fower, James Mattock, and John Spoore — agreed to deliver 60,000 pipe staves to the waterside at Boston as payment for linen and woolen cloth dispatched to them by Bristol merchants. The following year Nicholas Davison of Charlestown shipped pipe staves and rye to Madeira to satisfy in part his account with the estate of a London merchant. Richard Ludlow in 1648 received goods from an English merchant at Boston on condition that he load wheat and pease aboard a vessel to be dispatched to Boston by the merchant the following year. At about the same time, merchant Thomas Breedon entered the New England scene — where eventually he would rise to great heights — with a cargo loaded by an English house at Malaga on his promise to return "wheate fish or Tobacco" in payment.[35] The West Indian trade also became involved in this Atlantic complex, though it always remained more open to enterprising persons venturing small cargoes on their own than did the Atlantic trade. In 1649, for example, Ralph Woory of Charlestown, probably acting as agent for William Peakes of London, bought 5,000 quarter-pound loaves of bread from Bostonian James Oliver, paying with bills of exchange drawn on Peakes in London; the bread was to be carried on the ship *Planter* to Barbados and sold, presumably for sugar delivered to Peakes in England.[36]

33. Hosmer, *Winthrop's Journal*, 2:154.

34. The nature of the developing relationships between New England and English merchants is amply explored in the early chapters of Bailyn's *New England Merchants*.

35. *Aspinwall Notarial Records*, 75, 137, 202, 379–80, 394, 397.

36. Ibid., 225.

All the while, too, as the trade developed, English ships were moving into Boston harbor to seek grain on an open market, paying in English goods or bills of exchange. This was apparently the case in 1645 when a "store of linen, woollen, shoes, stockings, and other useful commodities" was brought from England and "the ships took pay in wheat, rye, peas, etc." In 1651 Hezekiah Usher, the Boston bookseller who was to establish one of the leading merchant families in the Bay, was building credits with Londoner Thomas Bell by selling wheat to Bell's agent aboard the ship *Sarah*.[37]

Direct exports to the Caribbean or across the Atlantic constituted but one outlet for agricultural produce. Another outlet was the outfitting and provisioning of ships attracted to the Bay by the facilities and cheap food-stuffs there. Begun in 1641 and 1642 when privateers began outfitting in the port before operating in the Caribbean and when storms and accidents at sea forced more legitimate vessels to make port in a depressed Boston, outfitting and provisioning had become a major industry by the end of the decade.[38] Then, Edward Johnson could write of the "store of Victuall both for their owne and Forreiners-ships, who resort hither for that end."[39]

The activities of John Parris, the merchant-uncle of the future mint-master John Hull, exemplify the extent of this branch of the agricultural trade of the commonwealth. Parris, having first visited the Bay in 1642 from Madeira, eventually based his operations in Barbados and in the late 1640s sent ship after ship to Boston to fit and provision for slave voyages to the African coast. On one occasion 3,698 pounds of cured beef, 4,200 quarter-pound loaves of bread, 100 bushels of pease, and a variety of other commodities were loaded aboard a Parris vessel. Again, English ships voyaging to the fishing areas of the northern coast and Newfoundland, the Atlantic islands and the Caribbean time after time are found making Boston a port of call, in part to load New England produce but in part to outfit and provision. In 1649, for example, the owners of the ship *Mary* of London lodged a protest against Boston workmen "for delay of time (these eight dayes) to fitt and furnish her out uppon her voyage to fyall Maderas or else where and so to Virginia." Merchants such as bookseller Usher profited greatly in the trade; Usher and a partner on one occasion provided £850 in "wheate pease fish and other provissions" for the crew of

37. Ibid., 381; Hosmer, *Winthrop's Journal* 2:245.

38. Hosmer, *Winthrop's Journal* 2:55–56, 57, 153. Note, too, that in restricting the use of grain in 1642 before the stocking of Gibbons's grain ship, the General Court exempted the making and selling of "bisket of wheate meale for the use of ships" (Shurtleff, *Records of the Governor and Company* 1:337).

39. Jameson, *Johnson's Wonder-Working Providence*, 71.

the ship *Castle Frigate*.[40] But the whole port community of Boston and Charlestown profited: the shipwrights, cordwinders, smiths and carpenters, and wharfers who fitted and loaded the ships; the butchers who transformed cattle into packed and salted beef; the coopers who built the casks to hold it; the millers and bakers who transformed wheat into bread and biscuits; even the doctor who on one occasion treated an injured sailor.

This thriving commercial community was intimately connected to the surrounding countryside. For the trade in grain and provisions necessarily stretched not only outward from the harborside but inland into the very heart of the commonwealth and even beyond to the towns of Connecticut, Rhode Island, and New Haven. The records of the internal trade between port and country are scant but clear: Settlers in the outlying towns bought goods and paid their debts and taxes in grain and other produce; local merchants were supplied with their stock from Boston and forwarded as payment the agricultural goods they had received from their own customers. Prices at various places in Massachusetts reflect the flow, increasing as commodities passed from hand to hand. In 1647 wheat brought four shillings six pence at Boston, but far in the interior at Springfield it was three shillings ten, with prices for pease and Indian corn proportionately lower; in late 1648 wheat was five shillings in the port, but in the outlying areas around Boston it could be bought directly from the farmers for four shillings eight pence.[41] The monetary expressions were only a convenience, of course, for even in Boston, as Robert Keayne commented, "the way of trade" was "not so much for ready money as for exchange," cloth, tools, pewterware, and such items from England "for Corne, Cattle and other Comodities."[42]

In this constant exchange of goods transportation was a vital consideration, and the records show an intense interest on the part of the authorities to keep open vital lines of traffic. Roads were difficult to build and maintain, but the commonwealth, even in this early period, tried to insist on a minimum upkeep "so as a loaden horse carrying a sack of Corne may passe," with a lessening effect as distance from the port increased. Produce moved easily into Boston from towns just back from the coast. Dedham's inhabitants, according to one commentator, found that the capital's

40. *Aspinwall Notarial Records*, 210, 285–87; Trask et al., *Suffolk Deeds* 1:45. Usher seems to have supplied the payroll for the ship's crew, receiving payment in bills of exchange drawn on London.

41. Mason A. Green, *Springfield, 1636–1886* (Springfield, Mass., 1888), 95; Shurtleff, *Records of the Governor and Company* 2:215; *Aspinwall Notarial Records*, 188–89. The cost of transportation accounts for part, but not all, of the differential.

42. "The last will and testament of me, Robert Keayne," in City of Boston, *A Report of the Record Commissioners* 10 (Boston, 1886): 12.

"coyne and commodities" lured them into making "many a long walk" to supply "the Markets of the most populous Towne"; another described Dedham as a town of "many Bisquette makers and Butchers" who had "Vent enought for their Commodities in Boston." Ipswich at the end of the 1640s was sending "many hundred quarters" of beef to the Boston market yearly, as was Weymouth, whose constable in 1655 decided that wood products and grains were too difficult to transport. Collecting local taxes in cattle, he drove the herd to Boston to sell. (So great, indeed, was the influx of cattle that by 1648 Boston petitioned the General Court for two fairs a year, the second exclusively "for Cattle to make provision both for or selves and shipping.") On the other hand, Sudbury, nineteen miles west of Boston, was considered too far from the "Mart Towns" by Edward Johnson in 1651, though it made possible its continued existence by taking "in Cattell of other Townes to winter." Andover, twenty miles from Boston and fifteen from Salem, suffered from the same isolation.[43] The area of adequate land transportation steadily expanded, however, and in 1660 Samuel Maverick wrote of Rehoboth that "it is not above 40 Miles from Boston, betweene which there is a Comone trade, carrying and recarrying goods by land in Cart and on Horseback." But Andover seems to have been isolated through most of the century, its inhabitants complaining to the General Court of Massachusetts in the 1680s that they were "burthened" with "such rocky impassable ways as indanger the lives and limbs of ourselves and beasts" and asking for the opening of "the nearest and best way to . . . Salem which is the nearest Market Towne."[44]

Far easier were connections by water, and in this respect Long Island Sound was the great artery of the Bay's internal trade, imported goods moving along the sound as far westward as Fairfield on the border of New Netherland and New England's agricultural produce moving eastward to the Bay for transshipment into the Atlantic community. In the late 1640s the artery branched to the north at several points: at Narragansett Bay at the eastern entrance to the sound, at Thames River to John Winthrop, Jr.'s New London in Pequot country, at the Connecticut to the river towns and William Pynchon's Springfield in the far backcountry of Massachu-

43. Noble and Cronin, *Records of the Court of Assistants* 2:84 et passim. The subject of roads and bridges is continually stressed here and in Shurtleff, *Records of the Governor and Company*, vols. 1, 2, 3. The descriptions are from Jameson, *Johnson's Wonder-Working Providence*, 96, 179, 196, 249; Samuel Maverick, "A Briefe Discription of New England and the Severall Townes Therein," ca. 1660, Massachusetts Historical Society, *Proceedings*, 2d ser., 1 (1885): 238; Petition of Nicholas Morton, late constable of Weymouth, 2 Nov. 1655, Photostats, box 7, Massachusetts Historical Society Library, Boston; Petition of the town of Boston to the General Court, ca. Oct. 1648, vol. 119, Massachusetts Archives, State House, Boston.

44. Maverick, "Briefe Discription," 243–44; Sarah Loring Bailey, *Historical Sketches of Andover, Massachusetts* (Boston, 1880), 57.

setts, and at New Haven. It also branched to the south to Long Island; in 1649 wheat was moving along the artery from as far west on the island as Hempstead in Dutch territory.[45] The Connecticut River towns were the most productive points along this route. Robert Child referred to them as "exceedingly abounding in corne . . . the fruitfullest places in all new England," and as early as 1644 and 1645 the area was dispatching many thousands of bushels of grain to Boston.[46] Farther upriver, William Pynchon of Springfield recorded in his account books shipments of 1,500 bushels of grain in the single year 1652.[47]

Along the coast itself were located small merchants who bought in bulk from Boston, retailed among the coves and islands of the sound, and collected produce to be returned to Boston: men like Richard Smith of Wickford, Rhode Island, who in April 1649 is glimpsed leaving Providence "to Newport, bound for Block Iland and Long Iland and Nayantaquit for Corne," or the Quaker merchant Nathaniel Sylvester, busy several years later retailing English goods for grain, pipe staves, and cattle at Shelter Island, Rhode Island, and New London.[48] Not all such shippers bringing grain into Boston were honest. In 1655 the Massachusetts General Court, "taking into . . . consideration the complaynts of severall in reference to the abuses committed by divers seamen, who, bringinge corne from Conectecott and other places, so measure the same as by experience is found will not yeeld so much, altho presently measured agayne, by fowre or five percent," empowered the selectmen to appoint official measurers of grain.[49] That same year, too, imports of wheat into the Bay were of such magnitude as to break the five shilling per bushel price that had been maintained since 1649.[50]

45. Roger Williams to John Winthrop, Jr., 13 June 1649, *Winthrop Papers* 5:353; *Aspinwall Notarial Records*, 170, 202, 240, 386–88. See also Sidney H. Miner and George D. Stanton, Jr., eds., *The Diary of Thomas Minor, Stonington, Connecticut, 1653 to 1684* (New London, Conn., 1899); virtually every year either Minor or one of his sons drove horses and cattle overland to sell in Massachusetts Bay, a journey difficult enough to cause him on one occasion to write his will in case "I never returne from Bostowne" (p. 203).

46. Child to Samuel Hartlib, 24 Dec. 1645, in Colonial Society of Massachusetts, *Publications* 38 (Boston, 1959): 51. The river towns "the last yeare . . . spared 20000 bushell [of corn], and have already this yeare sent to the bay 4000 bushell at least."

47. Bidwell and Falconer, *Agriculture* 1:12; Sylvester Judd, *History of Hadley* (Springfield, Mass., 1905), 368. See, in general, Stephen Innes, *Labor in a New Land: Economy and Society in Seventeenth-Century Springfield* (Princeton, N.J., 1983). It is hard not to ascribe the commercial activity that Innes found on the basis of the fortuitous survival of the Pynchon Records to other locations along the Connecticut River and Long Island Sound.

48. Roger Williams to John Winthrop, Jr., ca. April 1649, *Winthrop Papers* 5:326; letters of Sylvester to John Winthrop, Jr., 1654–55, in Massachusetts Historical Society, *Proceedings*, 2d ser., 4 (1889): 271–74.

49. Shurtleff, *Records of the Governor and Company* 3:375.

50. Ibid., 394. At the time the General Court temporarily barred imports of malt, meal,

Typical of the operations of small resident merchants on the great artery were those of John Winthrop, Jr., at New London, a settlement intended from the beginning for agriculture and laid down "on fruit-bearing land without rocks, arable with a goodly number of planting fields."[51] In 1649 Robert Scott, a onetime servant, a member of the First Church of Boston, and, in partnership with Robert Harding, a large-scale exporter of grain, forwarded a bark laden with cloth and other imports to Winthrop for resale to the New London settlers; "if you send corne" in payment, Scott's agent wrote, "mr. scott will exspeckt wheate and Rye or pease as well as Indian an equall proportion of each." The relationship between Winthrop as the local merchant and Scott as his supplier was already an established one, for Winthrop is reminded that £2 17*s.* was "Resting upon the Booke of old." The year prior, Winthrop sent "soe many fatt Cattle" to Charlestown as to satisfy a debt there. The cattle were to be dispatched on the hoof to be butchered, salted, packed, and shipped in the Bay area. In 1649 Winthrop inquired about the price of beef in Boston and was advised by his father "not to sende any for it will not yeild above 3*d.* the li. at most." At the same time the younger Winthrop was making arrangements for the pickup of cattle at the mouth of Thames River. Some months later he was meeting debts by selling beef packed and salted at New London.[52]

The internal trade of New England — the products of the land flowing one way to the harbor at the head of Massachusetts Bay, English imports the other way to the towns and villages of the hinterland — tied New England's agricultural and commercial communities together. The outward flow of grain, cattle, and other products provided a market for the agricultural community. In the Bay commonwealth alone there were by 1650 some 15,000 people, perhaps 3,000 families.[53] If averages hold good,

---

flour, wheat, barley, biscuit, beer, and salted beef to protect local farmers from the competition of other areas of southern New England.

51. William R. Carlton, "Overland to Connecticut in 1645: A Travel Diary of John Winthrop, Jr.," *New England Quarterly* 13 (1940): 505.

52. Benjamin Negus to Winthrop, Jr., 12 April 1649, Nicholas Davison to Winthrop, Jr., 29 July 1648, Winthrop to Winthrop, Jr., Mar. 1649, Thomas Olcott to Winthrop, Jr., 2 Mar. 1649, John Clark to Winthrop, Jr., 8 Oct. 1649, *Winthrop Papers* 5:330–31, 240, 311, 314, 373. On Scott, see MS Records of the First Church of Boston, copy in Massachusetts Historical Society Library, under date of 15 Dec. 1633; *Aspinwall Notarial Records*, 145–46, 188–89, 405.

53. Population figures for the colony vary, that in the text being calculated on the basis of ship arrivals to 1643: approximately 200; the average number of passengers carried computed from the passenger lists in Banks, *Planters of the Commonwealth*: 84; less estimated numbers of those returning to England or moving on to the settlements in Connecticut and Rhode Island: approximately 3,000 by 1638, according to a "Petition of Planters in Conecticut," Bancroft Transcripts, New England, 1:337-[42], New York Public Library, New

each family held between twenty and thirty acres, of which between ten and twenty were in cultivation, probably three or four planted in grain earmarked to be sold and ultimately exported.[54] These three or four acres would yield 60 to 100 bushels of wheat, or £12 to £20 in English goods per year when exchanged with the local merchant. This constituted probably the greater part of the annual income (discounting the home consumption of farm products) of the Bay family during these years, with additional income from the sale of stock, garden produce, and the like.[55] Yet this agricultural community was absolutely dependent on the merchants of the ports who sent its products away and returned to it the necessary imports from England and elsewhere, a dependence recognized by Captain Edward Johnson when he attributed the farmers' resistance to the sporadic attempts of the authorities to promote the home manufacture of cloth to a fear that "if the Merchants trade be not kept on foot . . . their corne and cattel will lye in their hands." The magistrates of the commonwealth, too, recognized the dependence. In 1650 they drafted a letter to their agent in England: "Wee . . . have a Competencie of Cattle of all Sorts and allso of Corne for Subsistence and Some to spare, whereby with the help of some fish here taken wee formerly have procured Clothing and other necessaries for our families by means of some Traffique in bothe

York; plus a calculated natural increase to 1650. See Evarts B. Greene and Virginia D. Harrington, *American Population before the Federal Census of 1790* (1932; reprint, Gloucester, Mass., 1966), 12–13.

54. For average landholdings and land utilization see Bidwell and Falconer, *Agriculture*, 38; Jameson, *Johnson's Wonder-Working Providence*, 154. These averages agree with actual property descriptions available in various town and probate records, though some extremely large holdings and extremely small holdings are in evidence, e.g. Thomas Dexter of Lynn with 600 acres, 80 of which were "plowed up," and "Bostian Ken Commonly called Bus Bus Negro of Dorchester" who in 1656 was raising 4½ acres of wheat (Trask et al., *Suffolk Deeds* 1:69, 2:297). Kenneth A. Lockridge, "Land, Population, and the Evolution of New England Society, 1630–1730," *Past and Present* 39 (1968): 62–80, revises the average holding upward but not the average acres in cultivation.

55. For agricultural yield, see Thomas Jefferson Wertenbaker, *The Puritan Oligarchy: The Founding of American Civilization* (New York, 1947), 4, which gives the English yield at 10 bushels of wheat per acre; John Winthrop's exaggerated estimate to the earl of Warwick, ca. Sept. 1644, *Winthrop Papers* 4:492, of 30 to 40 bushels per acre; the General Court's underestimate of 6 to 8 bushels per acre in its draft letter to Edward Winslow, ca. 1650, vol. 106, Massachusetts Archives; and the eighteenth-century figure of 20 bushels in Lyman Carrier, *The Beginnings of Agriculture in America* (New York, 1923), 150. Reversing the figures in the text and multiplying the average yield by the number of families gives 18,000 to 30,000 bushels of wheat exported per year at the end of the decade, not an overly high estimate in view of the 20,000 bushels exported in 1645. That the great bulk of wheat grown was exported is indicated by Martha Johanna Lyon's comment to John Winthrop, Jr., 23 Mar. 1649 (*Winthrop Papers* 5:323), that the use of wheat flour was above ordinary people. On New England farm practices in general, see Robert R. Walcott, "Husbandry in Colonial New England," *New England Quarterly* 9 (1936): 218–52; Rutman, *Husbandmen of Plymouth*.

Barbadoes and some other places." But if this should fail — possibly by the Dutch underpricing New England commodities — they were undone, for then "the generallitie of people are exceedingly [distressed] and in small Capacitie to Carrie through their ocasions."[56]

This dependence of the agricultural community upon the commercial community centered in Boston and Charlestown extended beyond the Bay colony, however. For the fact that through the 1640s the Bay merchants, by virtue of their exports, constituted the largest market for the agricultural products of the settlements of Narragansett Bay, Long Island Sound, and Connecticut River gave to those merchants an economic domination over southern New England which would remain unbroken, a domination recognized in the common appellation of the time, "Boston in New England."[57] Only the Massachusetts men managed to develop the broad connections in the Atlantic trading complex necessary to expedite imports and exports; hence the other settlements had always to buy from the Bay and sell to it. Only the Bay was able to establish the complex internal trade necessary to the distribution of imported goods to the hinterland. John Eliot, for example, in 1650 advised those "who ever would send any thing to any Towne in New England" to send it to Boston or Charlestown "for they are haven Townes for all New England and speedy meanes of conveyance to all places is there to be had."[58] Ultimately a small direct trade from the southern settlements to the West Indies would develop, but largely as a branch of the Massachusetts commercial system.[59]

The commercial community was, conversely, just as dependent upon the countryside. A prosperous population in the hinterland constituted an indispensable market for the goods imported by the merchants from England. But more: The agricultural products of the hinterland afforded the merchants entrée into the greater world of Atlantic commerce. Agricultural products largely filled the holds of the first Massachusetts-built ships; their export introduced the merchants to the profitable commerce of the Iberian Peninsula, the Atlantic islands, the Caribbean; the avail-

56. Jameson, *Johnson's Wonder-Working Providence*, 211; Draft of a letter from the General Court to Edward Winslow in England, ca. 1650, vol. 106, Massachusetts Archives.

57. John Clark, *Ill Newes from New-England* (1652), in Massachusetts Historical Society, *Collections*, 4th ser., 2 (1854): 23; Albert Matthews, "The Name 'New England' as Applied to Massachusetts," Colonial Society of Massachusetts, *Publications* 25 (1924): 382–90.

58. "John Eliot's Description of New England in 1650," Massachusetts Historical Society, *Proceedings*, 2d ser., 2 (1886): 50. See also "Answers of the General Court of Connecticut to Certain Queries of the Lords of the Committee of Colonies," 15 July 1680, Massachusetts Historical Society, *Collections*, 1st ser., 4 (1795): 220–23. The smaller towns attempted to effect direct connections with the Atlantic community during the 1640s but failed.

59. For example, the position of Peleg Sanford in Rhode Island in the Hutchinson family complex, sketched by Bailyn, *New England Merchants*, 88–90.

ability of cheap provisions attracted Atlantic shippers to Boston for outfitting, contributing immeasurably to the port's development. In the Atlantic complex where the Bay merchants were establishing themselves, their greatest asset in these years was their control of the cattle and grains and wood products of New England's farms and villages: their staple products.[60] Without the produce that flowed into them from the countryside and out through them to the Atlantic, they would have been as unable to purchase the all-important English imports as they had been during the depression of 1640 and 1641.[61]

Already the merchants were expanding their activities beyond the trade in agricultural produce. They were developing and controlling a domestic fishing industry and tapping the timber and fish resources of the northern coast. But in expanding their operations they were proceeding generally from the strength of the agriculturally based economy and specifically from the strength of their own trade in agricultural goods. Merchants who first entered the fish trade as agents for English houses during the 1640s — men like Valentine Hill — were equally at home in the provisions trade and — like Thomas Fowle — they regularly resorted to grain to meet their obligations when fish failed them.[62] Again, as Massachusetts men began going abroad as resident agents for New England, they went first as agents of the provisions trade. Robert Harding, for example, a onetime resident of the Bay, operated from London after 1646 but retained his connections with Bay merchants and in 1648, in partnership with Boston and Ipswich men, was collecting wheat for export. Stephen and Samuel Winthrop traveled to Tenerife early in 1646 with a cargo of wheat and fish. Stephen traded along the Spanish coast (at least in part on behalf of those at home), then went on to London. Samuel remained at Tenerife briefly, then moved on to the Caribbean on the advice of his father, setting up shop for a time at Barbados, fully expecting "imployment [from] my Freinds . . . especially our New england Marchants" in receiving their produce shipments. So many New Englanders were attracted south by the provisions trade that within a few years a Barbadian street would be referred to as "the New-England street."[63]

60. Jameson, *Johnson's Wonder-Working Providence*, 246–47; Samuel Danforth, *Almanac for 1648* (Cambridge, Mass., 1648), under November.

61. At which time the General Court had spurred on shipbuilding out of fear that the lack of returns would dissuade English shippers from making the colony a port of call.

62. *Aspinwall Notarial Records*, 8, 9.

63. William L. R. Marvin, "Robert Harding," Bostonian Society, *Publications* 6 (1910): 127–28; *Aspinwall Notarial Records*, 188–89; Stephen Winthrop to John Winthrop, Jr., ca. Mar. 1646, 23 Aug. 1646, 16 Mar. 1649, Samuel Winthrop to Winthrop, Jr., 16 May 1647, *Winthrop Papers* 5:62–64, 97–98, 320–21, 163; "The Diaries of John Hull," American Antiquarian Society, *Archaelogia Americana* 3 (1857): 235.

The expanding interests of the merchants should not cloud either the agricultural basis from which their expansion developed or the continued interaction between the world of commerce and the acres of corn and meadow. For though agriculture undoubtedly declined in the villages and towns along the immediate coast as the inhabitants turned to winter fisheries after 1650, the growing population of the inland areas had no other source of income but agriculture.[64] The internal commerce in farm produce and the export of that produce continued. Even the appearance of the wheat blight that destroyed the primary agricultural export — first along the Massachusetts coast in the summer of 1663, then gradually farther west until it struck the wheat of the river towns and New Haven in 1665 — did not halt the process.[65] In that very year "pork, beef, horses, and corn" were indicated among the leading exports of New England by commissioners dispatched by the crown; in 1675 a similar report cited "horses, beef, pork, butter, cheese, flour, peas, biscuit" as major exports of the section; in 1689 an anonymous writer commented that "the other *American plantations* cannot well subsist without *New England*" inasmuch as the section was supplying them "with provisions, beef, pork, meal, fish, etc."[66]

Commerce and agriculture — interacting, interdependent — it was on this basis that the economy recovered from the depression of the early 1640s. And it was from this basis that the economy proceeded. In the countryside prices for grains, cattle, and wood products rose steadily through the second decade, though never to the inflated levels of 1639. In contrast to the dark days of ten years before, the General Court could comment in 1652 on "mens outward estates . . . increasing in their hands," and one New Englander could write of his land "being grown more worth; to such value as we thought it was at the hiest."[67] In the port towns the foundations of widespread operations and family fortunes were being laid down by busy merchants and artisans.

"Let me tell thee who are like to reap benefite by transporting themselves to those colonies," a pamphleteer for New England wrote in 1648:

64. Note the petition to the General Court of the inhabitants of the town of Lynn, ca. 27 Oct. 1648: "Wee wold not envy our neighbour townes which are of the risinge hand by tradinge or other wayes[.] we rather wishe theyr prosperity[.] but for our selves we are neither fitted for or inured to any such course of trade but must awayt Gods blessing alone upon our Lands and Cattell" (Massachusetts Archives, vol. 100).

65. "The Diaries of John Hull," 208, 210, 213, 218.

66. Noel Sainsbury, ed., *Calendar of State Papers, Colonial Series, America and West Indies, 1661–1668* (London, 1880), 346; ibid., *1675–1767* (London, 1893), 221; "A brief Relation of the Plantation of New England . . . 1689," in "Hutchinson Papers," Massachusetts Historical Society, *Collections*, 3d ser., 1 (1825): 98.

67. Draft "Declaration concerning the advancement of learning in New Engl: By the genrall Court," Oct. 1652, and "A Replye to the resenes of Mr. Philop Nelson" by Richard Dommer, May 1656, vols. 58 and 15(B), Massachusetts Archives.

merchants "skild in commerce with forraigne nations lying near the Indies," seamen "skild in Navigation," and "Husband-men" who "are like to
benefit themselves much, all sorts of cattell increasing exceedingly, and
tillage prospering, that thousands of Acres are broken up yearly."[68] Here
was a new formula for prosperity to replace that which had failed in 1640:
farmers to produce, merchants to deal in their products, and ships to carry
the products to faraway markets. In this formula the paradox of an agricultural land where the pursuits of the sea predominated — a paradox posed
by historians looking at commerce and agriculture separately — disappears.

68. *Good News from New-England*, 218.

People in Process:
The New Hampshire Towns of the Eighteenth Century

7

What follows displays some of the new demographic and modeling techniques — not always applied well or wisely — that were coming into use in the early days of the "new social history." Equally important, however, it displays the challenge and counterchallenge that were in the air. Historical positions were hypotheses to be tested and refined, not certainties to be espoused. Kenneth Lockridge's overpopulation thesis was (and remains) one of the most important products of the moment, while James Henretta's morphology of town development was a daring attempt to order the disparate results of the various town studies that were appearing. Yet neither moved unthinkingly into the literature.

The study of early New England society, from the beginning of settlement to the beginning of the mills, has in the last decade altered dramatically. From the vantage point largely of the study of specific locales, young scholars have been chorusing a suggestive if not always harmonious medley. The starring soloists are familiar: John Demos, Philip J. Greven, Jr., Kenneth A. Lockridge. But the chorus is larger than its soloists, and significant parts are being sung by others. The major motif is familiar, too. Lockridge expressed it in 1968: "Clearly there were evolutionary patterns present within the society of early New England, patterns which reflect most significantly on the direction in which that society was heading. . . . A finite supply of land and a growing population, a population notably reluctant to emigrate, were combining to fragment and reduce landholdings, bringing marginal lands increasingly into cultivation, and raising land prices. Ultimately, the collision of land and population may

Presented originally at a conference on "The Family, Social Change, and Social Structure" held at Clark University, Worcester, Mass., in April 1972 and subsequently published in the *Journal of Urban History* 1 (1975): 268–92. Copyright © 1975 by Sage Publications, Inc.

have been polarizing the structure of society." More recently James A. Henretta has written of "a morphology of societal evolution" being played out in the New England towns, an "intricate interaction between land, population, technology, and culture"; "three distinct phases, corresponding roughly to the passage of generations, appear to characterize the social life of the towns." "The 'traditional' community of the first generations, with its emphasis on patriarchy, hierarchy, and stability," was "inexorably superseded by an 'expanding' society with very different social characteristics. And this, in turn, gave way to the 'static' town of the late eighteenth century."[1]

Compelling as this motif may sound, however, its weaknesses must be noted. First, it is unclear whether this evolutionary pattern, in whole or in part, was being played out only in towns laid down in the early and mid-seventeenth century and extending into the eighteenth — Lockridge's Dedham, Greven's Andover — or whether it was discernible in all New England towns, perhaps all Anglo-American communities, as a pattern initiated by the founding of a community, whenever that took place, and extending three or four generations into the community's future. Certainly Henretta implies the former, although he works the eighteenth-century town of Kent, Connecticut, into his analysis. Second — and more important a weakness — is the limited evidence on which the motif is constructed. In all of New England by the late eighteenth century there were some thousand-odd towns; a dozen-odd have been or are being subjected to the type of analysis that initially suggested the morphology.

Commendably, all scholars involved have been quick to admit the inadequacy of building generalizations on too thin a base, their papers and prefaces abounding with calls for further town studies. But while it is true that each new study in which the course of events of a particular town is discerned as conforming to the morphology will add further credence to it, one can easily calculate the time and effort required to build a sample adequate to the generalizations offered. What follows is an attempt to test and refine the morphology, at least in part, in a less arduous and time-consuming way by using as a sample the towns, for the most part established in the eighteenth century, of the single province of New Hampshire.

One hundred and ninety-eight inhabited towns spanned New Hampshire in 1790, extending from its narrow seaboard north and west into and beyond the White Mountains.[2] For each a variety of data have been gath-

---

1. Lockridge, "Land, Population, and the Evolution of New England Society, 1630–1730," *Past and Present* 39 (1968): 74; Henretta, "The Morphology of New England Society in the Colonial Period," *Journal of Interdisciplinary History* 2 (1971): 380, 388, 391.

2. The word *town* is not used in a legal sense but is to be construed as an inhabited location generally identified as a particular place at the time; legally, it might be a town, parish,

ered. The age of each has been established, defining age as the number of
years elapsed since the first permanent settlement in the area that would
become the town.[3] Early nineteenth-century gazetteers and maps have
provided a starting point for estimating time-specific areas for each town,
a laborious process of addition and subtraction as boundaries were adjusted and readjusted, and as one town spawned another.[4] Modern soil and
topographical materials have been used to establish a true profile of the
agricultural potential of each, while petitions from the towns, travelers'
accounts, and gazetteers have been drawn on to estimate that potential as
the eighteenth-century inhabitants might have envisioned it.[5] Key demographic indices have been compiled from occasional town inventories and
from five successive censuses — the first in 1767, the last in 1790 — and
rates of change between censuses have been established.[6] And, finally,

---

precinct, or unincorporated but inhabited grant. This is the unit definition of the 1790
census. U.S., Bureau of the Census, *Heads of Families at the First Census of the United States
Taken in the Year 1790: New Hampshire* (Washington, D.C., 1907), lists 205 localities in the
state. Adjusting for double counting, unsettled places, and the like reduces the number to
198. Note that not all localities have values for all dates; hence the size of the groups dealt
with here will vary. Gosport — on an island seven miles off the coast and marked by extreme
values in 1767 because of the peculiarities of its situation — has been generally omitted from
consideration.

    3. Settlement dates have been established through particular town histories and from the
documents and headnotes of Nathaniel Bouton et al., eds., *Documents and Records Relating to
the Province [Towns and State] of New Hampshire (1623–1800)* (Concord, N.H., 1867–1941),
hereinafter cited as *Provincial and State Papers*, particularly vols. 9, 11–13 *(Town Papers)*, 24–
26 *(Town Charters)*, and 27–29 *(Masonian Papers)*.

    4. The process has been to establish a base area from Eliphalet and Phinehas Merrill,
comps., *Gazetteer of the State of New Hampshire* (Exeter, N.H., 1817); John Farmer and Jacob
B. Moore, comps., *A Gazetteer of the State of New Hampshire* (Concord, N.H., 1823); and the
Philip Carrigain map of New Hampshire of 1816 and MS Town Plans, 1803–8, in the Office
of the Secretary of State of New Hampshire, Concord; supplementing these with Alonzo J.
Fogg, comp., *The Statistics and Gazetteer of New Hampshire* (Concord, N.H., 1874); *Town and
City Atlas of the State of New Hampshire* (Boston, 1892); then working backward to establish
age-specific areas on the basis of adjustments indicated in *Provincial and State Papers* and a
variety of early maps.

    5. Categorization of modern soil data was done by John T. Engle of the University of
New Hampshire, largely on the basis of U.S. Department of Agriculture county surveys
(both published and unpublished) and U.S.D.A. reports. The best and most extensive of the
travel accounts surveyed was Timothy Dwight, *Travels in New England and New York*, ed.
Barbara Miller Solomon and Patricia M. King (Cambridge, Mass., 1969). Petitions were
surveyed in *Provincial and State Papers*. Key phrases describing the agricultural potential were
extracted from the Merrills' and Farmer and Moore's gazetteers cited in note 4.

    6. The most valuable of the colonial censuses — for their completeness and because they
can be combined with figures for rateable estates and polls — are those of 1767 and 1773. See
"[Rateable Estates and Polls (1767), Census (1767)]," *Provincial and State Papers* 8:166–170;
"Census of 1773" and "[List of the Rateable Estates of the Several Towns]," ibid., 10:625–
36, 7:326–29. For the "Census of New Hampshire, 1775," see ibid., 7:724–81; for the

town histories and the papers of the province and state government have been searched for indications of economic opportunities other than agricultural and of the cohesiveness of each town, or lack of cohesiveness.

At first glance this mass of data seems but a confused mélange. In 1790 the towns varied in age from 4 to 167 years old; in area from less than a quarter square mile — the island town of Gosport — to slightly over 127 square miles; in population from 6 to Portsmouth's 4,700-odd. Soils ranged from sand to rich alluvium to exposed bedrock; topographies ranged from plains and valley floors to rolling uplands and mountains; expressed potential from a disgusted "very poor Baron Brooken and uneaven" to a delighted "beautiful interchange of small hills and valleys. . . . The scenery pleasant, and the soil rich." Densities ranged from less than 1 person per square mile to 372; sex ratios from 79 to 200 males per 100 females; widows, from none to over 16 percent of the female population; annual rates of population change over the years 1767 to 1790 from a population loss of almost 5 percent per year to a gain of just over 17 percent. Some towns seem shattered by confused associations and were towns in legal form only; indeed, one even disappeared as a town, its land and people divided almost as spoils of war by contiguous but contentious neighbors.[7] But other towns seem somnolent and undisturbed, the quintessence of Michael Zuckerman's "peaceable kingdoms."[8]

Can the mélange be made to give way to order? The morphology hypothesized — if it is to be applied to all towns regardless of founding date — depicts the towns as progressing through age-related stages, much as schoolchildren progress through age-related grades; hence, just as the confusion of the playground, where all ages play together, gives way to the ordered ages of the classroom, the confusion of unordered data on the towns can be expected to give way when the towns are separated by age into what are already being conventionally referred to as "generations."[9]

"Census of 1786," ibid., 10:637–89. All of these are aggregations by towns and counties; only the 1790 census (see note 2) contains an enumeration by name. Occasional town inventories are to be found in *Provincial and State Papers*, particularly in those volumes specifically cited in note 3, and in a manuscript volume of "Town Inventories" in the New Hampshire State Archives, Concord.

7. Monson was divided between Amherst and Hollis in 1770.

8. Zuckerman, *Peaceable Kingdoms: New England Towns in the Eighteenth Century* (New York, 1970).

9. The basic generational scheme of Philip J. Greven, Jr., *Four Generations: Population, Land, and Family in Colonial Andover, Massachusetts* (Ithaca, N.Y., 1970), appropriately resulted in "generational" conclusions. Others have adopted the generational terminology with only vague justification and at times even vaguer definition. See, e.g., Henretta, "Morphology of New England Society," 38off., and Kenneth A. Lockridge in an "Afterthought" included in *Colonial America: Essays in Politics and Social Development*, ed. Stanley N. Katz (Boston, 1971), 485–91. In order to conform to the hypothesized morphology here and in

Such, indeed, seems to be the case with regard to certain key demographic indices. Table 7.1 summarizes the data for density, white sex ratio, and population change as grouped in a generational schema. Generation by generation density — the number of people per square mile — rises until, in the oldest towns in 1790, there are on average but 37-odd acres of a town's land (good, bad, and indifferent) available for each household.[10] Generation by generation the sex ratio — the number of males per 100 females in the population — declines. And generation by generation the average annual rate of population change declines until, among the oldest towns, a percentage increase per year shifts to a percentage decrease and almost half the towns are in the losing column, steady exporters of people.[11] Specifically, the relationship between the rate of population change and age is curvilinear; at the earliest ages towns gain population at an extraordinary rate, but that feverish increase quickly subsides into a long, shallow, downward curve until it shifts imperceptibly from an annual gain to an annual loss. And approximately 55 percent of the variation among the towns in terms of their population change is accounted for by their differing ages.[12] Density and age are related in a more linear than curvilinear fashion, with approximately 50 percent of the variation in density accounted for by age. But correlating sex ratios and age reveals a break in the pattern of strong associations. The ratios plunge abruptly from extremes of several hundred males per 100 females in towns of one and two years old into what seems a near-random sprinkling around the 100 mark (100 males per 100 females), with here and there an aberrant community. At most, 14 percent of the variation in the sex ratio is accounted for by the age of the town.

What can be demonstrated with three demographic variables can be demonstrated with others. Some show a fairly strong association with age — the percentage of males over sixty, for example, and the percentage

---

table 7.1, I have adopted a generational grouping, defining a generation as thirty-three years, the sum of three such generations being the conventional three-life lease in England. To obtain a better fit of data to the groupings, however, I have had to separate from the first generation the first three years of settlement.

10. In contrast, towns aged 3 through 33 years offer a figure of just over 240 acres available per household. One stresses the crudeness of these figures, arrived at by dividing the average number of persons per household in 1790 in the towns as grouped (5.78 in the older towns, 5.62 in towns aged 3–33) into the average density of the group in 1790, and the results into 640, the number of acres per square mile.

11. The annual rate of population change has been computed as $LOG(P/100 + 1)/N$ where P equals the percentage change of population between two censuses and N equals the number of elapsed years.

12. Using eta as the most appropriate measure of a curvilinear relationship and eta squared to approximate the proportion of variance in the dependent variable "accounted for" by the independent variable.

Table 7.1. Density, white sex ratio, and population change of New Hampshire towns by age, 1767 and 1790

Age of towns	Number		Mean density		Mean sex ratio		Population change, 1767–90			
	1767	1790	1767	1790	1767	1790	N	N losing	% losing	Mean annual % change
3 & under	12	0	2.7	—	180.0	—	12	0	0.0	9.56
4–33	37	103	11.8	14.8	113.9	106.8	36	3	8.3	5.29
34–66	25	48	30.4	33.8	103.5	100.7	25	5	20.0	1.63
67–99	1	11	—	37.1	—	96.8	1	0	—	—
100 & above	17	20	84.2	98.3	96.6	94.9	17	8	47.1	−0.14
All towns	92	182	29.3	30.3	116.7	103.3	91	16	17.6	3.78

Sources and note: See notes 2–6 for sources. Gosport (age 100+) is excluded from 1767 data and from the computation of the rate of population change.

of females widowed, indicative of the interrelationship between the age of the population and the age of the town. Others show surprisingly weak associations: the age of the town and the percentage of children in the population.[13]

But is age the most appropriate basis on which to organize the demographic data of the towns? Demographic historians have suggested, in the context of European peasant societies, a cyclic, homeostatic adjustment of birth, death, and marriage rates as populations "sought" — and one realizes the anthropomorphism of the word — a rough equilibrium between the shifting levels of the economy and the size of the population to be supported. More to the point with regard to Anglo-American society, where economic conditions never brought on the crisis situation needed to trigger such adjustments, is the demographers' suggestion of a systematic link between the level of economic opportunity and migration.[14] The barebones of that linkage in an Anglo-American context are charted in figure 7.1.

Obviously there can be no system in the absence of people; hence we must initiate one by introducing a population through migration into the area of what will become a town. A simple identity basic to demography gives us a next step: that a population at a subsequent point in time is the product of the population at a previous point plus births, minus deaths (the net natural increase); plus in-migration, minus out-migration (the net migration figure). Much effort has already been expended on the phenomenon of natural increase, and all that has been said elsewhere by a variety of authors writing on birth and death rates can be construed as implicit in the model. But what of in- and out-migration? What are the conditions governing these? The word *governing* is used with calculation, for it immediately suggests the analogy of a governor — a servomechanism, if you will — with the task of controlling or governing the system.[15]

Two have been introduced into the model. The second — "Optimal

13. The censuses do not give a figure for children per se; they do, however, give a figure for "boys" — ambiguously defined as males "under 16 years of age" and "16 years and under." The number of children has been arbitrarily constructed by doubling the number of boys; it is, consequently, a gross estimate and, when converted to a percentage of total population, can be quite erroneous in the youngest towns where (as noted below) adult men and boys tended to open the area in the absence of females.

14. See E. A. Wrigley, *Population and History* (New York, 1969), 112–13; George W. Barclay, *Techniques of Population Analysis* (New York, 1958), 204–6. Daniel Scott Smith has more recently summarized the position in "A Malthusian-Frontier Interpretation of United States Demographic History before circa 1815," in *Urbanization in the Americas: The Background in Historical Perspective*, ed. Woodrow W. Borah et al. (Ottawa, 1980), 15–24.

15. See Walter Buckley, *Sociology and Modern Systems Theory* (Englewood Cliffs, N.J., 1967), particularly 36ff., 52ff.

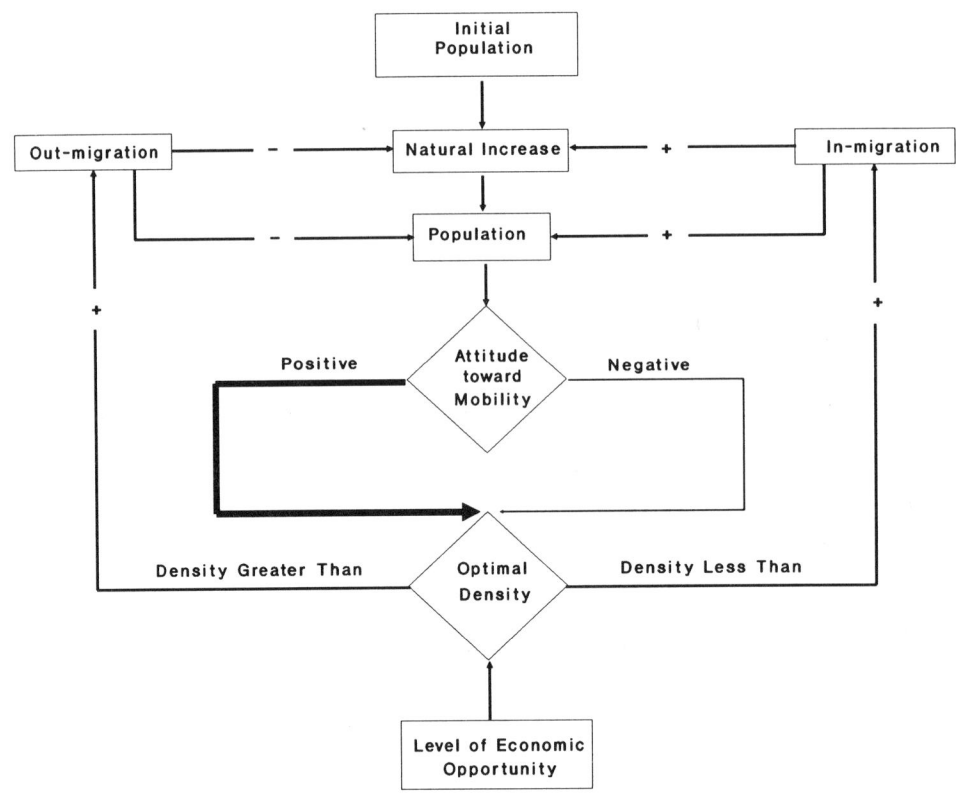

Fig. 7.1. A Malthusian model of population behavior

Density" — is the operative device, continually reading the atmosphere of the system, specifically the population density, and testing density against an optimum established by the level of economic opportunity. When the governor senses that density is below optimum, it triggers in-migration much as a thermostat sensing a temperature below its setting triggers a heating device; when the governor senses density above the optimum, it calls for out-migration. Information is fed into our demographic thermostat through a prior governor, however, one set by communal and personal attitudes toward the very concept of in- and out-migration. Given a low level of acceptance of the notion of mobility (in or out), either because of outright hostility to, or simple ignorance of, the possibility or the benefits of movement, the operation of the primary governor is curtailed, while the higher the level of acceptance, the more freely the primary can operate. But like all cultural switches, this screening switch seems faulty. No matter how low the level of acceptance of mobility may be, there is leakage through the switch and the primary governor operates to some extent.[16]

Neither governor is introduced here as a startling discovery. The stress of Lockridge, Greven, and others, for example, on the reluctance of the seventeenth-century son to leave the town of his birth and family even when economic conditions would seem to dictate a departure is a recognition of the dampening effect of the cultural switch. The model, with its governors, is introduced only to shift attention from age — a measure of elapsed time from the initiation of the system and certainly important in that context — to the system itself.

In the New Hampshire materials the initiative phase of the system is clear. Extreme sex ratios in the least dense and newest towns — towns of the "eastern frontier" — suggest the pattern by which town populations were first established in the mid- and late eighteenth century: men journeying, frequently without women, to the site of the new town to begin the process of clearing and building. Yet new populations did not long exist in an imbalanced condition. One index after another suggests that these were largely young and middle-aged married men (possibly with a hired hand to help temporarily) and that their wives and children, if not present from the beginning, would follow within a year or so.[17]

Table 7.2 aggregates the towns of 1767 by density and displays group means for comparative purposes. The extreme sex ratio of the lowest-density group drops radically toward the range of well-settled towns as density rises. The percentage of single males in the male population, which in the towns of least density is twice that of settled communities, halves as density rises to between 2 and 5 per square mile. The preponderance among females of those married over those single in low-density towns is reversed (and normalized) as density rises; towns with densities of 5 to 8 in this respect differ little from towns with densities of 60 and above. That a large proportion of the married couples in the low-density towns were young and either at or just beyond the beginning of their child-rearing activities is indicated by the near absence of elderly males and widows and by the percentage of children in the total population — low as

16. For example, even while arguing for Dedham as a closed system in the mid-seventeenth century, Lockridge must acknowledge a trickle of movement in and out. See his "The Population of Dedham, Massachusetts, 1636–1736," *Economic History Review*, 2d ser., 19 (1966): 322.

17. The same conclusion, on the basis of literary evidence, is offered by Charles E. Clark, *The Eastern Frontier: The Settlement of Northern New England, 1610–1763* (New York, 1970), 221. The "eastern frontier" is, in this regard, similar to the later frontier investigated by (among others) Jack E. Eblen, "An Analysis of Nineteenth-Century Frontier Populations," *Demography* 2 (1965): 399–413.

Table 7.2. Key demographic indices of New Hampshire towns, 1767, grouped by density

Density of towns	N	Mean age	Mean density	Mean % of males				Mean % of females			Mean sex ratio	Mean % of children in population
				16 & under	17–60 single	17–60 married	Over 60	Single	Married	Widowed		
2.0 & under	7	3.0	1.3	35.5	36.2	28.0	0.3	40.0	59.8	0.1	246.5	46.3
2.01–5.0	14	8.2	3.6	48.4	17.5	33.1	1.0	58.6	40.5	0.8	121.7	52.9
5.01–8.0	13	19.7	6.8	52.6	14.5	30.3	2.6	61.8	36.3	1.9	114.6	56.0
8.01–11.0	10	24.6	9.4	50.9	15.5	30.4	3.2	62.7	34.3	3.0	104.9	51.8
11.01–15.0	10	32.4	12.7	50.6	15.2	30.1	3.7	61.9	34.7	3.4	108.5	52.3
15.01–35.0	12	54.5	26.8	52.4	15.5	26.8	5.3	61.8	33.3	4.8	106.7	53.6
35.01–60.0	11	77.8	47.3	47.5	16.4	30.6	5.4	61.9	32.9	5.3	94.4	45.8
60.1 & above	17	102.5	91.7	48.0	18.4	27.9	5.7	61.8	31.0	7.1	97.3	46.4

Sources and notes: See notes 2–6. Gosport (density = 1,136) is excluded from the computation of the mean density of the last category. Mean age has been computed using only the 93 towns of 1767 for which age is established; hence the sample size for the second category is 13.

some men arrived in the town without their families, rising above the level of the more densely settled towns as the preponderantly young married couples brought children into the world, then dipping back into the range of the settled towns as the population aged, couples left the child-rearing years, and their children, spread in age, gradually entered married life and begat children of their own. Older couples were never entirely missing from the population, however, and density does not rise very high before one sees a significant percentage of the male population over sixty and of widows among women. In sum, halfway through the first "generation" and with density still well below 10 per square mile, the mean town among New Hampshire's eighteenth-century frontier towns had achieved a balanced population only slightly different from that of the more settled towns, largely because of the relatively young age of its married couples. The population, in effect, had been initiated.

A surviving census, complete with enumeration, taken in the town of Orford in 1772 catches one town in the course of its rapid journey toward settled "normalcy."[18] Seven years after the first entrance of a population, the town contained 149 people (density equaling 3.4 per square mile). Fourteen of its people were indicated in the census as unattached single men, 6 of them as servants or transient laborers; 10 were characterized as married men making improvements on their land in the absence of families; the remaining 125 persons were subsumed in twenty-six family units, one of them extended in the sense that a nineteen-year-old son and his bride still resided in the father's household. Of the twenty-seven couples, eleven were childless, four had one or two children living in the household; the remaining twelve had between three and nine children, an average of just over five. In all, children sixteen years and under amounted to approximately 43 percent of the town's population.

From the standpoint of the model, the most interesting demographic index is the annual percentage change in the size of the population. Table 7.3 summarizes the growth rates of the towns grouped by density for the period 1767–73.[19] As is to be expected, extraordinarily high growth rates mark the initiation of populations, ranging in the lowest three density groups from means of 10 percent to 17 percent per year. (The percentage

18. In *Provincial and State Papers* 9:645ff. there are three lists. The first and third are censuses, the second is a memorandum of improvements. The second and third are dated 1772. The first is undated. Comparison of the two censuses suggests that the undated first is some six to eight months earlier than the dated second. See also Alice Doan Hodgson, *Thanks to the Past: The Story of Orford, New Hampshire* (Orford, N.H., 1965).

19. The annual percentage changes of population in 1767–90 are included in the table for the purpose of comparison. Note, however, that the figures for the longer period will axiomatically show less increase inasmuch as the years of lowest density (and in the main highest annual rates of growth) for any given group are subsumed in the longer span of years.

Table 7.3. Population change, 1767–73, 1767–90, among New Hampshire towns of 1767, grouped by density

| | Mean annual population change | | | |
| | 1767–73 | | 1767–90 | |
Density of towns	N	%	N	%
2.0 & under	7	17.1	7	11.3
2.01–5.0	13	11.2	13	7.5
5.01–8.0	11	9.7	13	5.8
8.01–11.0	9	7.5	9	4.6
11.01–15.0	10	6.1	10	3.9
15.01–35.0	11	2.7	12	1.4
35.01–60.0	11	0.8	11	−0.1
60.01 & above	16	−0.2	16	−0.5

Sources and note: See notes 2–6. Gosport excluded.

figure can be translated into people in Orford: With 75 persons and a density of less than 1 per square mile in 1767, Orford more than tripled in population over the succeeding six years, averaging an annual growth rate of just over 18 percent; at least 122 of the increase were newcomers to the town, and the remainder a high estimate of the net natural increase.)[20] The population initiated, the feverish growth rates slackened. But these were still high-opportunity towns in terms of low densities and available agricultural land. The system's governors called for continuing growth through in-migration but at steadily decreasing rates as in-migration combined with natural increase to raise densities and consequently limit opportunity.

The group means reflect the process as growth rates drop from 7.5 percent per year (for towns of densities of 8 and 10 per square mile) to 6, 3, and 1 percent. And the figures gain significance when we realize that rates of 1 and 2 percent per year actually indicate that net in-migration has become a negligible factor in increasing the population, that what growth there is, is being maintained by natural increase, and that, indeed, out-

20. The natural increase has been separated from the migration-related increase by a simulation operating on the basis of a transposition of the basic demographic identity $P_2 = P_1 + B - D + M$ (where P_2 equals the population in the year or period in question, P_1 the population in the preceding year or period, and B, D, and M are the number of births and deaths and net migration figure, respectively), i.e., $M = P_2 - (P_1 + B - D)$, with values for succeeding populations, births, and deaths estimated by the use of given birth and death rates and the rate of population change. Birth and death rates have been adopted from Robert Higgs and H. Louis Stettler, "Colonial New England Demography: A Sampling Approach," *William and Mary Quarterly*, 3d ser., 27 (1970): 282–94, and Lockridge, "Population of Dedham," 318–44. The procedure is crude and unrealistic, but the intent is to produce a minimal figure as an estimate of net migration.

migration quite possibly has begun. A specific town makes the point: Wilton, in the south central highlands, was a town of just over 1,000 in 1786 and growing at a rate of 2.1 percent per year in the period 1786–90, but it gained approximately 89 persons by natural increase, leaving only 7 to be accounted for as the difference between in- and out-migration.[21]

One might anticipate that our mean population change should, in terms of the model, ultimately decline to zero and remain there, indicative of an optimum relationship between density and opportunity being maintained by a steady overflow of the excess population, departures from zero being indicative of a change in the level of economic opportunity either downward (forcing a greater part of the population out) or upward (drawing in population). But such anticipation assumes a precision perhaps uncharacteristic of social mechanisms in general and certainly uncharacteristic of our ability to perceive them. And it ignores a fundamental characteristic of both the mobile population and of the model, one which seems to make overcorrection — a population loss in excess of that demanded by the system — inevitable.

We have seen who, in the main, is attracted into a high-opportunity agricultural town: preponderantly the young man with wife and children. Such is consequently the type attracted from an existent agricultural town. The economy being male- and adult-dominated, the system being governed by the relationship of density and economic opportunity, only the adult male was truly excess, and yet when he left, he took more than himself away. Indeed, the outflow of a relatively few young, adult males could remove a significant proportion of a town's youth, leaving what remained relatively older and, as a group, incapable of sustaining the prevailing level of natural increase.

New Hampshire's Epping, a prosperous southeastern agricultural town, exemplifies the point. In 1767 the town contained just over 1,440 people in 20.5 square miles, density equaling roughly 69 per square mile. By 1773 density had risen to over 80, but in the succeeding years the population steadily declined, dipping to 1,255 by 1790 (density equaling 61). Between 1773 and 1790 an estimated 600 persons must have left in order to account for the net loss and the continuing natural increase of those left behind. In terms of the system, the balance of density and opportunity seems to have been restored by the departure of roughly 100 adult males; the relationship of adult males to land in 1767 (40.4 acres per male) had deteriorated by 1773 (34.8) and nearly recovered by 1790 (38.3).[22] But a good portion of the young families of the town had gone,

21. Birth and death rates for Wilton were computed from Jeremy Belknap, *The History of New Hampshire* (1812; reprint, New York, 1970), 2:187.

22. Computed by dividing males 16 years of age and older (325 in 1767, 377 in 1773, 338

and where in 1767 over 53 percent of the population had been children, in 1790 the children amounted to just under 41 percent. By the early nineteenth century, possibly reflecting a continuing outflow, certainly reflecting the fact of fewer children maturing and having children of their own, the population had dipped still further, to 1,100-odd.[23]

Mean rates of change in the 1767–73 period — 0.8 and a minus 0.2 in our highest density groups in table 7.3 — seemingly reflect both attributes of the model: its tendency toward overcorrection and its imprecision. We can suggest that these towns are, as a group, roughly balanced at the crucial junction of density and economic opportunity. But the latter attribute — imprecision — makes negligible our chance of spotting minor yet meaningful changes in the rates, that is to say, those changes resulting from minor changes in the level of economic activity. We cannot make, for example, any comment on the advent of occupational specialization in essentially agricultural towns. That process by which additional opportunities were incorporated into agricultural economies, thereby increasing the number of people capable of being supported and decreasing the pressure for out-migration, was far too gradual to be silhouetted by the crude instrument we are using.[24]

Raw density figures, however, do reflect major differentiations in the level of economic activity. Very broadly, sixty acres of land can be considered the optimum farm for a single-family household in eighteenth-century New Hampshire. Below that figure the householder approaches and ultimately falls below subsistence; above, the land, if it is to be worked, requires more than the single family.[25] The optimum density in a purely

---

in 1790) into the area of the town. In terms of acres per household: 52.3 in 1767, 44.8 in 1773, 58.8 in 1790.

23. By 1820 the population had fallen to 1,158, or 58 per square mile (Farmer and Moore, *Gazetteer*, 120). No mills came to Epping to provide economic opportunities that might have reversed the trend.

24. Such a process was argued as an alternative to Lockridge's overcrowding thesis (and rejected by Lockridge) from the very beginning. See his "Afterthought," 485–91. But Lockridge's plea for an end to arguing generalities and for historians to "go back to the evidence and build a structure of hard data and rigorous analysis" (p. 491) has been largely ignored. Bonnie Barton's exploration of population growth and economic opportunities ca. 1650–1800 in "The Creation of Centrality," *Annals of the Association of American Geographers* 68 (1978): 34–44, is a refreshing exception.

25. There are many estimates of the optimal size of the eighteenth-century "family farm." See Charles S. Grant, *Democracy in the Connecticut Frontier Town of Kent* (New York, 1961), 36–38, where he arrives at between 40 and 89 acres. The figure offered in the text is a best, but still crude, estimate based on such factors as the agricultural techniques of the time (I suspect they had not changed radically from those described in Darrett B. Rutman, *Husbandmen of Plymouth: Farms and Villages in the Old Colony, 1620–1692* [Boston, 1967]) and the requisite size of the woodlot (itself an estimate, combining the needs of the household and

agricultural town, consequently, lies around 60 per square mile.[26] Given the broadness of this estimate, however, a 20 percent margin seems in order; hence the parameter falls between 48 and 72 persons per square mile. Among the New Hampshire towns of 1767, nine had densities above this range; the census of 1773 adds three additional towns to the list. But four of the twelve dropped back below the limit of a density of 72 by 1790. Like Epping, they seem to have pressed beyond a limit, triggered out-migration as a corrective, and reflected the corrective by dipping below the critical value. Of the rest: one (Portsmouth) was the leading entrepôt of the province, and another (Newcastle) its ancillary; two (Exeter and Dover) were long-established secondary centers with substantial mercantile and artisan activities; two (Gosport and Rye) were fishing towns; one (Seabrook) combined fishing and the construction of small boats purchased and used by seamen all along the coast from mid-Maine to Boston. Only one, Kensington, seems devoid of economic activity other than agriculture. The consistently high mean density of this subgroup (140 in 1767, 148 in 1790) reflects the high level of economic activity in these towns and their consequent ability to maintain relatively large populations, while their removal from the group of highest-density towns in table 7.3 reduces the mean of the group to 69.6, a value better reflective of the essentially agricultural economies of the towns.

Categorizing the towns by density rather than age is clearly in order, age being simply a measure of elapsed time in a process governed in the main by density.[27] Indeed, categorization by age hazards confusion. Henretta's use of Kent, Connecticut, in a generational morphology is a case in point. Kent, below the midpoint of its second generation (forty-odd years), is at a stage which Henretta associates with the third and fourth generations. Among the New Hampshire towns, a geographic cluster in the southeastern hinterland is placed, in a categorization by age, with a cluster along the middle Merrimack, but the towns of the former were obviously at and beyond optimum densities and displayed rates of population change between 1767 and 1790 indicative of significant out-migration, while those of the latter seem well under optimum densities and were

---

the regrowth rate of woodlands: on the first, see the high estimate in Ralph H. Brown, *Historical Geography of the United States* [New York, 1948], 108; on the second, Dwight, *Travels* 1:75). Given the uncertainty of the numbers, however, the wide error margins in the text are an absolute necessity.

26. Using 5.7 persons per household. The figure for optimum density obviously would not apply to towns with extensive waste areas. But in the period in question all of the towns of high density were located in the southeastern part of New Hampshire where wastage was minimal.

27. Lockridge himself shifted to a density model in his "Social Change and the Meaning of the American Revolution," *Journal of Social History* 7 (1973): 406–7.

receiving newcomers at a substantial rate.[28] One can speculate on the reasons for towns to pass through the demographic process at different speeds. The southeastern towns were easily, hence more quickly, settled from old, contiguous towns, while the middle Merrimack was more isolated and necessitated a longer trek for would-be settlers; the southeast was relatively protected during the Indian wars, which did not end until the late 1750s, while the middle Merrimack was an exposed salient; the southeastern towns were outside of a proprietary system which, it has been argued, tended to slow settlement elsewhere. One can also contemplate the possibility that speed through the process varied distinctively between the seventeenth and eighteenth centuries, with the earliest agricultural towns (Andover, for example) consistently requiring a full three generations to move from the initiation of a population to excessive density and out-migration.

But the question here is which variable gives the soundest basis for generalizing on a broad process applicable to all the towns all the time? The extent to which anomalies disturb the generalizations in terms of age is indicated by the strength of the explanatory power of age cited earlier. Consideration of the towns in terms of density is not without anomalies, certainly, but in the main density explains more of the demographic variation among the towns. With regard, for example, to settled agricultural towns — that is, removing from the sample towns in the process of initiating populations and towns known to have economic opportunities other than agricultural ones — density in 1767 can be said to explain 73 percent of the variation among the 1767–90 rates of population change.[29]

The strong relationship between density and population change, as well as the clear contrast between what we can term towns of low and high economic opportunity, is strong support for our bare-bones model. And yet it cannot be stressed too much that it is bare-bones, that there are secondary processes within it, and that these need and deserve extensive investigation. Density, for example, was not significantly related to the sex ratio, and yet the sex ratio appears to some extent a governor affecting the flow of single males and, surprisingly, females among the settled towns.[30]

28. In the southeastern cluster (Brentwood, Kingston, East Kingston, South Hampton, Newton, Plaistow) a mean age in 1767 of 45 was matched with a mean annual population change in 1767–90 of minus 0.4 percent and a density in 1767 of 58; the middle Merrimack cluster (Bow, Concord, Canterbury, Pembroke) had a mean age of 39, mean annual population change of 3.5 percent, and a mean density of 13.3.

29. Reporting r^2 as a percentage. For the same subset, age and rates of population change computed an r^2 of .43. Within this particular subset the relationships proved linear rather than curvilinear.

30. A simulation using a regression model and varying the values of the percentage of single males among total males and the sex ratio to establish the direction of the single

Marriage potential, as well as economic opportunity, seems to have been an important determinant in directing the flow of population.

What the model does explain, however, it explains despite variations in soil (both real, in terms of modern soil data, and in the minds of eighteenth-century men) and in topography. No categorization of the towns according to these variables produced significant and distinctive groupings of the demographic data. The demographic process men and women were caught up in seems more determinative than the soil on which they lived.

What of other aspects of the morphology postulated? Lockridge has suggested overpopulation and the appearance of a rural proletariat. There is no support for this thesis in the New Hampshire materials. The cultural governor seems wide open (a radical change from the seventeenth century, perhaps even the early eighteenth century), allowing the economic opportunity governor to operate freely. Towns surpassing an allowable density, moving toward the red zone that Lockridge described so well, readily exported their young and fell again into the safe green. With one exception (Kensington), New Hampshire towns remaining above the critical point are demonstrably towns with economic opportunities other than agricultural. One underscores that this is an expected result in the Lockridgean scheme. In his initial essay, while contemplating the interrelationship of overpopulation and the Revolution, he nevertheless resuscitated Frederick Jackson Turner's "safety valve," albeit in a purely agricultural setting, suggesting its operation after 1790.[31] It was, however, operative in New Hampshire well before that date, indeed, through the last half of the century at least. At the same time, however, the New Hampshire materials underscore the most severe criticism of Lockridge: that he tended to ignore economic opportunities other than agricultural. When observed density in what is presumed to be a totally agricultural area rises and remains above a safety line determined by the type and structure of agriculture employed, it is absolutely obligatory to look for a shift upward in the level of economic opportunity, that is to say, a shift of some degree away from agriculture. Only where density exceeds the safety line and there is no shift can we speak of overpopulation.[32]

---

female population (increasing or decreasing) in particular towns gave correct prediction in 75 percent of the cases. The errors, moreover, were almost entirely in towns with opportunities additional to agriculture; hence they indicated that the simulation did not take into account a relevant factor and that with that factor entered success of prediction would be in the 90 percent range.

31. Lockridge, "Land, Population, and the Evolution of New England Society," 77–78.

32. Lockridge's Dedham, for example, from which he drew so much of his thesis, is ranked in the highest "commercial-cosmopolitan" group in the most sophisticated classification of eighteenth-century towns to date, that of Van Beck Hall in *Politics without Parties: Massachusetts, 1780–1791* (Pittsburgh, 1972), chap. 1. Hall's classification, constructed for a

What of the changing social climate that, proceeding from Lockridge and Zuckerman, Henretta built into the morphology and linked to a demographic process? The two can be conjoined only in a limited sense. We can conceive of the demographic process in the earliest seventeenth-century towns, when the cultural governor was set low and mobility restrained, ultimately contributing pressure that tended to change attitudes and open the cultural switch to allow density to affect migration. We can conceive of mobility, once a significant reality, affecting attitudes and opening the switch still further. And we can conceive of changing attitudes toward community and an enlarged role for the family — both phenomena imbedded in Henretta's morphology — as concomitant with changing attitudes toward mobility. The linkage of the demographic process and changing attitudes can be phrased generationally in the sense that the early seventeenth-century towns lived two or three generations with one set of attitudes which subsequently (in the third or fourth generation) shifted. But this is not a course to be rerun in each town — a point on which there must be no confusion. First-generation towns of the eighteenth century did not revert to the attitudes of the first-generation towns of the seventeenth and did not reexperience an attitudinal change in response to an inexorable demographic process. The new towns were founded in the milieu of the new attitudes; "the history of . . . [eighteenth-century] settlements" — Henretta's words stressed here — "would not be completely congruent with that of . . . [seventeenth-century settlements] despite the existence of certain demographic similarities."[33] Orford exemplifies the new attitude toward mobility, for the town is not marked by a population gathering in the first years and settling in as a unit for a multigenerational stay. On the contrary, 63 percent of Orford's families as listed in 1772 would be gone from the town by 1790.[34] Mobility was a continuing factor, as it was not in the settlement of the seventeenth-century towns. Orford suggests, too, the enlarged role of the family, for these were in many cases entire families disappearing from the early town and moving on — Ebenezer Baldwin, his wife, and four children, Noah Dewey and wife, Shubel Cross, his wife, and two children — and in the absence of strong community ties, as Henretta wrote, the family might well be taking on "more of the tasks of socialization and acculturalization

---

period later than Lockridge's, cannot be applied to the earlier period, of course, but it is suggestive, particularly in the light of Barton, "Creation of Centrality," 42, a graphic depiction of Dedham's nonfarm economic activity, 1650–1800.

33. Henretta, "Morphology of New England Society," 393. This is a reservation on Henretta's part that serves to blunt completely the central thrust of his "morphology."

34. Figures generated by a name analysis of the Orford census cited in note 19 and the entry for Orford in U.S., Bureau of the Census, *Heads of Families at the First Census.*

... smoothing the passage from one generation and one community to the next."[35]

Clearly the attitudinal shift, however firmly linked to the demographic process, was time specific; only the demographic process itself was timeless. What of a shift in political attitudes, the "direct causal link between the growth of population and certain types of political change" that Henretta asserts?[36] Again, the linkage can be conceived of as time specific. The inexorable demographic process through which the earliest seventeenth-century towns passed might have something to do with the breakdown of a pattern of "patriarchy, hierarchy, and stability" in those towns. But it does not follow that there was a constant linkage. If shifting social attitudes were not timelessly linked to the demographic process — if first-generation towns of the eighteenth century did not revert to the social attitudes of the seventeenth century's first-generation towns and reexperience a demographically inspired attitudinal shift — is it logical to assume a timeless link between shifting political attitudes and the demographic process? But beyond logic, if the various "types of political change" are construed as reflected in (or reflective of) political disputes within the New Hampshire towns, there is little demonstrable relationship in the eighteenth century between the demographic process and the political climate. Disputes were related to topography as sections of towns separated by mountains, rivers, marsh, or simple distance argued and more often than not divided; to religion as churches of different persuasions sought support from limited resources; to the proprietary system as all parts of a town fought the tax-free status of unimproved proprietary lands. And disputes broke out as freely at any one age, and at any one stage of the demographic process, as at any other.[37]

Succinctly put, what does this excursion into the granite hills of New Hampshire suggest?

Contextually, it would seem to demonstrate that there was indeed a demographic process at work in the towns of early New England, but one best generalized about in terms of population density and level of economic opportunity rather than age qua "generations." Overpopulation and the appearance of an agricultural proletariat as general phenomena, however, are suspect, for the Turnerian safety valve opened soon enough

35. Henretta, "Morphology of New England Society," 397.

36. Ibid., 391.

37. While there is a slight indication of a link between the rate of population change and disputes (defined as intratown disputes, 1765–78, reaching the New Hampshire province or state government via petitions from one or more parties to the dispute), the analysis is not significant enough to support a hypothesized relationship between disputes and a particular position in the developmental model.

in eighteenth-century New Hampshire to avoid that Lockridgean culmi-nation of the process and to substitute another: mobility.[38]

Methodologically, it underscores a cardinal distinction for those histo-rians with a bent toward a social science approach between a timeless hypothesis of social behavior and a time-specific hypothesis. In the highly generalized "morphology of societal evolution" with which we opened, the two seem confused, while in the eighteenth-century excursion they have stood forth as separate. The process keyed to density and oppor-tunity seems timeless in that there seems little difference, except in terms of time in process, between the demographic course run in these towns and that described as running in seventeenth-century Massachusetts towns. The particular impact of that demographic process on social and political attitudes, however, was time-specific in that attitudinal changes were cumulative and the demographic process impacted on successive rather than repetitive sets of attitudes.

Finally, in terms of potential, the excursion seems to offer fruitful ave-nues for reflection. Our culmination — mobility — links to a broad spec-trum of current scholarship. A relatively easy accommodation to sustained population growth, for example, links far easier than does Lockridge's portentous overcrowding and rural proletariat to James H. Hutson's re-cent suggestion of an interrelationship between a consciousness of demo-graphic growth and Revolutionary optimism.[39] The link to studies of the family is clear in the proposition that changed attitudes toward mobility (hence the acceptance both in new towns and in the older towns that spawned them of at least a partial disruption of family ties) were prerequi-sites to actual mobility, while a changed role for the family was a conse-quence. And the mobility of the villagers links to the extensive work under way on American cities and on urban mobility. Two questions asked re-cently by Stephan Thernstrom and Peter Knights seem as applicable to the New Hampshire towns of the latter half of the eighteenth century as they are to the nineteenth-century city: "If American city-dwellers were as restless and footloose as our evidence suggests, how was any cultural continuity — or even the appearance of it — maintained? . . . American society in the period considered here was more like a procession than a stable social order. How did this social order cohere at all?"[40] Perhaps the

38. The demographic process seems general along the Anglo-American coast. See, e.g., Darrett B. and Anita H. Rutman, *A Place in Time: Middlesex County, Virginia, 1650–1750* (New York, 1984), 236–39.

39. Hutson in rebuttal to Jesse Lemisch and John K. Alexander, "The White Oaks, Jack Tar, and the Concept of the 'Inarticulate,'" *William and Mary Quarterly*, 3d ser., 29 (1972): 141–42.

40. Thernstrom and Knights, "Men in Motion: Some Data and Speculations about

changing role of the family suggested by the morphology for mobile villagers is a part of the answer with regard to both mobile villagers and mobile urbanites.

Urban Population Mobility in Nineteenth-Century America," in *Anonymous Americans: Explorations in Nineteenth-Century Social History*, ed. Tamara K. Hareven (Englewood Cliffs, N.J., 1971), 40.

8 Magic, Christianity, and Church in Early Virginia

The subtle social analysis of the American past that is so often termed the "new social history" began in the 1960s with early New England as its subject. But studies of New England were studies in isolation. Comparisons and generalizations were impossible in the absence of similar studies of other areas of Anglo-America. Indeed, the problem of identifying the unique consequences of Puritanism was unresolvable, for how could any particular phenomenon observed in New England be called a consequence of Puritanism when we had only vague notions of phenomena elsewhere. It was with this thought in mind that in the early 1970s I turned my attention to Virginia, exploring first the religious life of the "Cavaliers." An invitation to lecture at the fourth annual Lawrence Henry Gipson Symposium at Lehigh University in 1976 gave me an opportunity to order my thoughts on the subject. The theme of the symposium was "Religion, Philosophy, and a Revolutionary World."

Religion in the era of the Revolution. The phrase immediately conjures up the enlightened rationalism of a Franklin, Jefferson, or Paine: "I believe in one God, and no more; and I hope for happiness beyond this life. I believe in the equality of man; and I believe that religious duties consist in doing justice, loving mercy, and endeavoring to make our fellow-creatures happy." But it should also evoke an image of the evangelicals, of Virginia Baptists gathering in June 1771: "The multitude stood round weeping, but when we sang *Come we that love the lord . . .*

Originally delivered in September 1976 and subsequently published as "The Evolution of Religious Life in Early Virginia," in *Lex et Scientia: The International Journal of Law and Science* 14 (1978): 190–214. Copyright © 1978 by Westminster Publications, Inc. Reprinted with permission of the editor.

they were so affected that they lifted up their hands and faces toward heaven and discovered such chearful countenances in the midst of flowing tears as I had never seen before." It should provoke, too, a picture of the formally religious, the good parson "preaching wholly by a written copy" and seemingly addressing himself more "to the cushion, than to the congregation." And it should provoke a picture of the barely religious, of those who invited Virginia's Devereux Jarratt to "frolic and dance"; Jarratt declined and told them his reason, that his mind was "turned to religion." "This put some damp on their spirits," he wrote, "though they allowed that all people ought to be better than they were — but they thought I had overshot the mark. . . . 'We all ought to be good, say they, but sure there can be no harm in *innocent mirth.*' "[1]

Rationalism, evangelicalism, formalism, and what, for want of a better word, we can call indifference are the main strands that scholars have isolated in the religious life of the Revolutionary era. Over the past years some few have pushed forward from that watershed, excitedly sketching the conquest of America by "republican millennialism" on the one hand and "civil religion" on the other.[2] I should like to push backward, into the seventeen decades of change and change again that preceded (and formed) the period of the Revolution, specifically addressing myself to Virginia. The subject is obviously not virgin ground; indeed, that is its challenge. It is a subject heavy with conventional (but incomplete) wisdom.

Throughout the literature on religion in the Old Dominion, the planting of the Anglican church and a Virginia colony are held to constitute a single event. True enough, there was a desultory Puritanism in the very earliest years, perhaps even, as Perry Miller described it, a brief cycle of "religious dedication, disillusionment, and then reconciliation to a world

1. Thomas Paine, *The Age of Reason* (1794), in *The Complete Writings of Thomas Paine*, ed. Philip S. Foner (New York, 1945), 1:464; "Journal of Daniel Fristoe," in *Imprisoned Preachers and Religious Liberty in Virginia*, ed. Lewis Peyton Little (Lynchburg, Va., 1938), 243; Jarratt, *The Life of the Reverend Devereux Jarratt Written by Himself* (1806; reprint, New York, 1969), 22, 42–43.

2. E.g., Perry Miller, *The Life of the Mind in America: From the Revolution to the Civil War* (New York, 1965), 49–72; Sidney Mead, "The 'Nation with the Soul of a Church,' " *Church History* 36 (1967): 262–83, and in his other works; Robert N. Bellah, "Civil Religion in America," *Daedalus: Journal of the American Academy of Arts and Sciences* 96 (1967): 1–21; the essays in *The Religion of the Republic*, ed. Elwyn A. Smith (Philadelphia, 1971), notably J. F. MacLear, "The Republic and the Millennium," 183–216; Nathan O. Hatch, "The Origins of Civil Millennialism in America: New England Clergymen, War with France, and the Revolution," *William and Mary Quarterly*, 3d ser., 31 (1974): 407–30, the last starting from the post-Revolutionary culmination and tracing back through New England's ministerial literature. Hatch went on to develop the theme in *The Sacred Cause of Liberty: Republican Thought and the Millennium in Revolutionary New England* (New Haven, 1977).

in which making a living was the ultimate reality" to mirror the longer and stronger cycle he envisioned for New England.[3] But thereafter it was a question of the central government asserting an Anglican orthodoxy in legal statutes and of the Virginia gentlemen, in their vestries, molding the establishment to their peculiar American condition. Daniel Boorstin, for example, was echoing traditional scholarship when he wrote of the church of "The Transplanters": "The Church of England, in becoming the Church of Virginia, had not altered its theology one iota, [but] it had undergone a sea-change in institutions."[4] A bishop's church without bishops led inevitably through fights over induction and presentment, glebe rights and salaries, to the gentlemanly parish of the eighteenth century. One shifts without change from scholar to scholar—from Boorstin to Alhstrom, from Alhstrom back to Bruce, from Bruce to Goodwin to Brydon, from Brydon to Seiler: "The harsh conditions imposed by a foreign and hostile environment, geographical separation from the mother country, and the absence of a competent episcopal form of organization led the colonists to apply their own distinctive modifications to the structure and operation of the church in Virignia. In the absence of direct English control a colonial control was substituted. The Assembly, the governor, and, most important in the development of local self-government, the parish vestry, assumed essential roles in the emergence of the Anglican Church in Virginia."[5]

Serviceable enough in many ways, this conventional knowledge nevertheless has an essential flaw. It deals with religion largely as a matter of law and institutional arrangements, barely touching upon religiosity as an internal state or quality of mind. That the Virginians were religious is simply a given, proceeding from the fact that they went to the bother of having an established church at all. Beyond that, the kinds and degrees of their religious feelings have been approached independently by citing in potpourri fashion the books of practical piety resting upon the shelves of various Virginia gentlemen, the godly expressions of their last wills (Rob-

3. Miller, "Religion and Society in the Early Literature of Virginia," in his *Errand into the Wilderness* (Cambridge, Mass., 1956), 139, originally published in two installments in *William and Mary Quarterly*, 3d ser., 5 (1948) and 6 (1949).

4. Boorstin, *The Americans: The Colonial Experience* (New York, 1958), 125.

5. Sydney E. Ahlstrom, *A Religious History of the American People* (New Haven, 1972), 184–93; Philip Alexander Bruce, *Institutional History of Virginia in the Seventeenth Century* (New York, 1910); Edward Lewis Goodwin, *The Colonial Church in Virginia* (Milwaukee, 1927); George M. Brydon, *Virginia's Mother Church and the Political Conditions under Which It Grew* (Richmond, 1947–52); William H. Seiler, "The Church of England as the Established Church in Seventeenth-Century Virginia" and "The Anglican Parish Vestry in Colonial Virginia," *Journal of Southern History* 15 (1949): 478–508; 22 (1956): 310–37. The quotation is from Seiler's "The Anglican Parish in Virginia," in *Seventeenth-Century America: Essays in Colonial History*, ed. James Morton Smith (Chapel Hill, N.C., 1959), 122.

ert Dunster bequeathing "his soul to God and his sin to the Devil"), the legal enforcement of the Sabbath, and the punishment of moral offenders.[6] And always, religious feelings have been approached cautiously. The Christian nation to come required a Christian past, but Cavalier joie de vivre had always to be set up in contrast to the crabbed, introspective Puritan to the north. Miller, of course, was not bothered by this last consideration, but even he seems to suggest that religiosity, as he conceived it, came to an end in Virginia in 1624 with the completion of his cycle of dedication, disillusionment, and worldly reconciliation.

It is, however, precisely at the point of the state or quality of the mind that a study of religion ought to begin. There is no intention here of branching off into a long philosophic and semantic discussion of the nature of the religious phenomenon. Anthropologists, sociologists, psychologists, and historians and philosophers of religion have all grappled eloquently with the problem. Suffice it to say that at the nub of the human mind there seems to lie an aching awareness of the unknown and uncontrollable. Consciously and unconsciously the mind questions nature. Why does the rain come to nurture the seed one spring and not another? Why does the lightning strike my house and not my neighbor's? Why was I born poor and another rich? Why does success reward another's efforts and not my own? Why does this child die and not that? Why death itself? Why life? Where nature offers no answers, a transcending, or super, nature is conceived — or revealed. In effect, the unknown is systematized that it might become known, perhaps even controlled.[7] Protestantism, the

6. Quoted in Bruce, *Institutional History of Virginia* 1:18.

7. See J. Milton Yinger, *The Scientific Study of Religion* (New York and London, 1970), 7–8: "The quality of being religious, seen from the individual point of view, implies two things: first, a belief that evil, pain, bewilderment, and injustice are fundamental facts of existence; and, second, a set of practices and related sanctified beliefs that express a conviction that man can ultimately be saved from those facts.... In this sense, religion can be thought of as a kind of residual means of response and adjustment. It is an attempt to explain what cannot otherwise be explained; to achieve power, all other powers having failed us; to establish poise and serenity in the face of evil and suffering that other efforts have failed to eliminate." Such a broad — in this case functional — conceptualization of religion, although common in other disciplines, has not fared well among historians. Thus John F. Wilson's "The Status of 'Civil Religion' in America," in *Religion of the Republic*, ed. Smith, 1–21, is a complete rejection of sociologist Robert Bellah's "Civil Religion in America" on the grounds that the phenomena Bellah cites as religious do not match those "conventionally or historically designated" as such. More recently Robert W. Doherty's use of sociologist Thomas Luckmann's conceptualization of "a universal human trait which changes its forms under differing conditions," in his "Sociology, Religion, and Historians," *Historical Methods Newsletter* 6 (1973): 161–69, has been rejected by Harry S. Stout and Robert Taylor, "Sociology, Religion, and Historians Revisited: Towards an Historical Sociology of Religion," ibid., 8 (1974): 29–38. Doherty's application might well be flawed, but Stout and Taylor's insistence (p. 35) that "a more effective approach . . . would be one that proceeds from basic intellectual distinctions

articles of England's faith promulgated in 1558, and Virginia's Anglican-ism are all subsets of a systematization which we call Christian. But the world of magic, witchcraft, sorcery, and conjuring, of cunning men and astrologers, involves such a systematization as well. And Keith Thomas's remarkable study of magic in premodern England is a convincing demon-stration of the coexistence of both as resolutions of what Max Weber called the "metaphysical needs of the human spirit" in the England from which the first Americans came.[8] True, one can postulate differences (al-though possibly no more than heuristic) between the religious and the magical. Religion, for one thing, can be discerned as tending more toward explanation of the unknown—God's in his heaven, all's right with the world even given its perplexities; the devices of magic as tending more toward control of it. But a response on one modern sociologist's question-naire is enough to suggest at least a consanguinity between the two, the respondent believing "in astrology because he doesn't believe in God."[9]

What we can call a thirst to systematize the unknown—to explain or control the natural world by bridging to a transcendent world—is a nec-essary first dimension of the study of religion in early Virginia. The Vir-ginians must be conceived as having to some degree such a thirst. The concept of cultural baggage—a far more persuasive way of looking at the early American scene than its opposite, "sea-change"—together with the findings of Thomas about the prevalence of witchcraft in England, sug-gest the very wide parameters within which the early Virginians might have attempted to quench this thirst.

The thesis is quickly stated. Culture is well defined as "a normative system," "the blueprint or design for behavior" that "prescribes what ought to be done, delimits what may be done, and defines what exists"; as the "values, norms, and beliefs" that shape "the nature of the institutions in a society and the roles a person plays in them." Culture as such is carried by people as they move from an old to a new environment, and it is

whereby belief systems emanating from institutions are considered as indispensable struc-tural elements in social organization" seems to consign religious history to the study of creeds and practices—hardly an advance!

8. Thomas, *Religion and the Decline of Magic* (New York, 1971). I stress my debt to Jon Butler who first pointed out to me the importance of Thomas's work. My reliance in large measure on the model of early American religious development that Butler presented in his short essay *Religion and Witchcraft in Early American Society* (St. Charles, Mo., 1974) will be obvious to all who read it. Butler subsequently developed his ideas in "Magic, Astrology, and the Early American Religious Heritage," *American Historical Review* 69 (1979): 317–46, and *Awash in a Sea of Faith: Christianizing the American People* (Cambridge, Mass., 1990).

9. T. W. Adorno et al., *The Authoritarian Personality* (New York, 1950), 738. From Max Weber through Bronislaw Malinowski to the present, enormous effort has been expended in the attempt to distinguish magic and religion, but empirically all distinctions tend to fail. Yinger, *Scientific Study of Religion*, 69–79, is a good summary.

not difficult to accept the fact that it plays a significant part in determining their behavior in the new surroundings.[10] Thomas suggests that the cultural milieu from which the Virginians emerged was not monolithically Christian in regard to this thirst for systematization of the unknown, and that Christianity, which relates the natural and transcendent through an epic of creation, reprobation, and the redemptive nature of Christ, was in the process of diffusion through the culture rather than a pervasive feature of it. The suggestion is startling, but it follows from his evidence.

What else is one to make of the deathbed examination of an elderly man who had all his life sat patiently through Sunday and weekday sermons, two or three thousand in all? "Being demanded what he thought of God, he answers that he was a good old man; and what of Christ, that he was a towardly young youth; and of his soul, that it was a great bone in his body; and what should become of his soul after he was dead, that if he had done well he should be put into a pleasant green meadow." What are we to make of the conversation (in 1681) between Oliver Heywood and a country boy on Hardger Moor? "I begun to ask him some questions about the principles of religion," Heywood recorded in his diary. "He could not tell me how many gods there be, nor persons in the godhead, nor who made the world nor anything about Jesus Christ, nor heaven or hell, or eternity after this life, nor for what end he came into the world."[11] One suspects, however, that the boy well understood the magical purposes of the straw men or "corn dollies" put outside the farmhouse door on Allhallows Eve, a surviving custom, incidentally, still seen in northern New England.

Startling as it is, however, the suggestion explains—and at the same time tends to be substantiated by—the constant complaint of the evangelical Puritan minister that too many of his hearers were dead to religion, and his proclivity for categorizing Englishmen as Christian, superstitious (i.e., Catholic), or "dumb."[12] The last, perhaps, were not simply deaf to a Puritan message but, like the boy on Hardger Moor, essentially ignorant of Christianity itself. More to the point here, the conjunction of cultural baggage theory and Thomas's suggestion associates with the story of religion in early Virginia phenomena that have been tucked off to the side as quaint curiosities. The most obvious, of course, are the telltale signs of a magical bridge to the transcendent.

Witchcraft certainly was transplanted to Virginia.[13] At least three in-

10. Robert F. Berkhofer, Jr., "Space, Time, Culture, and the New Frontier," *Agricultural History* 38 (1964): 24, 25, 30.

11. Minister William Pemble, quoted in Thomas, *Religion and the Decline of Magic*, 163; Heywood quoted in ibid., 151.

12. Darrett B. Rutman, *American Puritanism: Faith and Practice* (Philadelphia, 1970), 21.

13. Conjoining witchcraft and magic subsumes a great deal of subtle difference. But essentially they perform the same function. One can seek relief from the anxiety of the

stances of the hanging of witches aboard the ships coming to the Chesapeake are on record. The first is a curt notation in the Virginia General
Court records of 1654 that one Captain Bennett "had to appear at the
admiralty court to answer the putting to death of Kath. Grady as a witch at
sea." The third involved shipowner Edward Prescott, accused in 1659 in a
Maryland court of the hanging of Elizabeth Richardson. That the witch
was hanged was not denied, but Prescott was relieved of responsibility on
a technicality. The second, again on record in Maryland, affords a full
description of the hanging of the witch Mary Lee by the aroused crewmen
of the ship *Charity* in 1654. With their ship leaking and buffeted by contrary winds, the crew seized upon Mistress Lee as the cause of their plight.
The captain, pressed by his men, "thought fitt, Considering our . . .
Condition to Satisfie the Seamen in a way of trying her according to the
Usuall Custome in that kind whether She were a witch or Not." But
before the trial could begin, two crewmen seized and stripped the woman,
found what they took to be the witch's "teat," then called the captain to
have a look. Captain and crew apparently argued the evidence overnight,
leaving Mistress Lee tied to the capstan, but in the morning, when she
confessed that she was indeed a witch, the captain conveniently took
himself to his cabin and left the crew to rid the ship of the maleficent
presence.[14]

In addition to these shipboard cases, Virginia's county and colony records indicate that nineteen Virginians were either formally charged with
witchcraft or referred to as witches by their neighbors between 1626 (the
case of Joane Wright) and 1705 (the case of Grace Sherwood).[15] That so

---

unknown by appealing to the magician (or witch) to wield his or her powers or by verbalizing
the anxiety "in a framework that is understandable and which implies the possibility of doing
something," i.e., accusing the witch who is "potentially controllable by the society." See
Clyde Kluckhohn, *Navaho Witchcraft* (Cambridge, Mass., 1944), 60–61. The latter conceptualization underlies the exciting work on early American witchcraft being done by John
Demos, e.g., "Underlying Themes in the Witchcraft of Seventeenth-Century New England," *American Historical Review* 75 (1970): 1311–26, work culminating in his *Entertaining
Satan: Witchcraft and the Culture of Early New England* (Oxford, 1982).

14. Conway Robinson, "Notes from the Council and General Court Records, 1641–
1664," *Virginia Magazine of History and Biography* 8 (1900–1901): 162 (also to be found in H.
R. McIlwaine, ed., *Minutes of the Council and General Court of Colonial Virginia, 1622–1632,
1670–1676, with [Robinson's] Notes* [Richmond, 1924], 504); William Hand Browne et al.,
Archives of Maryland, vol. 41, *Proceedings of the Provincial Court of Maryland, 1658–1662*, ed.
Bernard Christian Steiner (Baltimore, 1922), 327–29; ibid., vol. 3, *Proceedings of the Council of
Maryland, 1636–1667*, ed. William Hand Browne (Baltimore, 1885), 306–8.

15. For the Wright case, see McIlwaine, *Minutes of the Council and General Court*, 111–12,
114; the Sherwood documents are gathered together in Edward W. Jones, "Grace Sherwood, the Virginia Witch," *William and Mary Quarterly*, 1st ser., 3 (1894–95): 96–101, 190–
92, 242–44, 4 (1895–96): 18–22. My own survey of the records was consciously independent
of that of Richard Beale Davis. See his "The Devil in Virginia in the Seventeenth Century,"

many of these recorded instances (ten) were actions for slanderous defamation brought by those called witches against reviling neighbors, that the plaintiffs in these actions in some instances received negligible damages or none or even saw their cases dismissed, that of those apparently charged (eight), three were exonerated while only one seems to have been found guilty and punished (William Harding was whipped and banished in Northumberland in 1655 after conviction "of Witchcraft Sorcery &c" by a jury of twenty-four men) — all this indicated to Richard Beale Davis that the Virginians were incredulous and skeptical in such matters. "The Devil in Virginia," to use Davis's title, was conspicuous for his near absence, and in classic anti-Puritan fashion Davis notes that "there are here none of the melodramatic events testified to by children and adults in Salem Village."[16] Perhaps. But for the moment the point is that the evidence of witchcraft — a major stone in the magical bridge between the natural and the transcendent — is well documented in Virginia. In sound mind and with a clear conscience a Virginian could ascribe his poor hunting to the spell of another (1626), hold that only the horseshoe over his door protected his sick wife from the evil intentions of a neighbor woman

---

originally published in *Virginia Magazine of History and Biography* 65 (1957): 131–49, but most conveniently consulted in his *Literature and Society in Early Virginia, 1608–1840* (Baton Rouge, La., 1973). That our surveys produced essentially the same list would seem to bear out his note (p. 25) that while "there may be a few other cases entered" in the manuscript county records, "this seems unlikely." I have included (where Davis has not) two particular references: the first, the deposition of Mary Samborne of 13 Oct. 1659 as evidence of a probable charge of witchcraft against the wife of one Thomas Stevenson, this on the basis of the tone of the deposition, specifically the deponent's paraphrasing of Goodwife Stevenson's words to the wife of Richard Carter: "And at their parting she told her she would be revenged of her and would do her a mischiefe by day or night" (Beverley Fleet, ed., *Virginia Colonial Abstracts*, vol. 11, *Charles City County Court Orders, 1658–1661* [Baltimore, 1961], 53); the second, the deposition of Thomas Hickman, recorded in Northumberland County in Jan. 1667, referring to Thomas Barrett as having performed "jugling tricks that people said could not be done without aid of the Devil" (ibid., vol. 19, *Northumbria Collectanea, 1645–1720* [Baltimore, 1961], 75).

16. Fleet, *Virginia Colonial Abstracts*, vol. 2, *Northumberland County Records, 1652–1655* (Baltimore, 1961), 69; *William and Mary Quarterly*, 1st ser., 1 (1892–93): 127. The outcome of four cases in which there seems to have been a formal charge is unknown, as is the outcome of the second trial of Barbara Winbrough in 1658 (she had been acquitted in 1657). The ultimate exoneration of Grace Sherwood is assumed (Davis, *Literature and Society*, 29). See also ibid., p. 41: "Satan seemed to at least a few to continue to honor Virginia with his presence. But the average Virginian of 1700 was apparently not at all convinced that Evil was incarnate, that it employed supernatural means through chosen human beings to tempt mankind. A few individuals, usually simple and superstitious country folk resentful of personal loss in family or property, looked around for a cause or outlet for their emotions. A busybody neighbor who might seriously or playfully pretend to occult powers was a natural candidate for suspicion. But for decades the Virginia justices and juries had critically weighed the charges of intercourse with Satan."

who perforce passed under it on her way to saying black prayers at his wife's bedside (1671), could attribute to a witch the death of his pigs and withering of his cotton (1698), and, in court, faced with a suit for slander, insist that "to his thoughts, apprehension or best knowledge" two witches "had rid him along the Seaside & home to his own house" (again 1698).[17] Magic was commemorated among Virginia's toponyms. In Charles City County a marsh was known locally as "Conjurer's Field"; in Princess Anne the inlet where Mistress Sherwood was tried by water is even now known as "Witchduck."[18] And the law took cognizance of the magical. As late as 1691 and 1692 commissions of the peace issued for Northampton and Essex counties by Governor Francis Nicholson strictly enjoined the justices to inquire not only into cases of felony, trespass, and forestalling but ones of witchery as well, while in 1736 a handbook for the justices published in Williamsburg outlined the dimensions of such inquiry, just as had the classic English handbook of 1618, Michael Dalton's *Countrey Justice*, which the Lower Norfolk justices cited as their guide when, in 1675, they examined Joan Jenkins "concerning her beeing familier with evell spiritts and useing witchcraft &c."[19]

At least one instance of countermagic (of a sort) is to be found in early Virginia materials as well. When, on the eve of Bacon's Rebellion, the son of the king of the Doeg Indians was captured, the boy was in a trance state, "eyes and mouth shutt, no breath discern'd." Captain George Brent diagnosed bewitchment — presumably by an Indian witch — and noted "that he had heard baptism was an effectuall remedy against witchcraft." Baptism followed "by the church of England liturgy" with Brent and Captain George Mason as godfathers and Mrs. Mason as godmother. Shortly after, the source narrates, the child's eyes fluttered, and with the further assistance of brandy, he recovered.[20] And white magic — resort to the supernatural to help rather than to hurt — is also to be found. The presence of

17. Cases of Wright and Sherwood cited in note 15; case of the wife of Capt. Christopher Neal in Northumberland County, Order Book, 1666–72, 179–81, 186–87, Virginia State Library and Archives, Richmond, and "The Good Luck Horseshoe," *William and Mary Quarterly*, 1st ser., 17 (1909): 247–48; case of John and Anne Byrd, "Witchcraft in Virginia," ibid., 2 (1893–94): 59–60.

18. Nell Marion Nugent, *Cavaliers and Pioneers: Abstracts of Virginia Land Patents and Grants, 1623–1666* (Richmond, 1934), 32, 87, 137; Davis, *Literature and Society*, 39.

19. Bruce, *Institutional History of Virginia* 1:283; George Webb, *The Office and Authority of a Justice of the Peace* (Williamsburg, Va., 1736), 361–62; case of Joan Jenkins, *William and Mary Quarterly*, 1st ser., 3 (1894–95): 163–65.

20. [Thomas Mathews], "The Beginning, Progress, and Conclusion of Bacons Rebellion in Virginia," in Peter Force, comp., *Tracts and Other Papers, Relating Principally to the . . . Colonies in North America* (Washington, D.C., 1836–47), vol. 1, tract 8:9. Wilcomb E. Washburn, *The Governor and the Rebel: A History of Bacon's Rebellion in Virginia* (Chapel Hill, N.C., 1957), 21, identifies Brent and Mason.

white magic, by virtue of the nature of our available sources, is harder to detect than black or maleficent magic; we must for the most part rely on court records, and these are invariably weighted toward the black, for few would accuse the magical Samaritan, nor would the magical Samaritan tend to take umbrage at a bit of advertising and bring suit against those who called him or her "witch." In the only systematic analysis of English witchcraft, for example, Alan Macfarlane established for one county 503 indictments for witchcraft, of which 492 involved black magic and only 11 white.[21] The nineteen Virginia cases offer no opportunity for a definitive classification, but one suspects that in at least some cases the offense was white, not black. William Harding, for example, might well have been more a cunning man than a maleficent witch, both the fact that he was presented by a minister (in England the ecclesiastical jurisdiction tended more to encompass white magic than black) and the lightness of his punishment hinting as much.[22] Certainly, however, George Webb's *The Office and Authority of a Justice of the Peace* of 1736 refers to the practice of white magic when it defines petit witchcraft — the use, for example, of charms "to provoke Love" — to be punished by a yearlong imprisonment and quarterly pillorying.[23] And in 1735 William Byrd of Westover makes matter-of-fact reference to white magic in a letter to Londoner John Hanbury: "I am glad to hear your ship the Williamsburgh got home well, and that Crane agreed with a witch at Hampton for a fair wind all the way."[24]

The point of citing the presence of magic in early Virginia is that magic and Christianity were, in a very real sense, competitive systems. Both Thomas and Macfarlane make this clear in the English context. And no one stated it more directly than an Essex minister, whose remarks on white magic are quoted by Macfarlane: "As the Ministers of God doe give resolution to the conscience, in matters doubtfull and difficult; soe the Ministers of Satan, under the name of Wise-men and Wise-women, are at hand by his appointment, to resolve, direct and helpe ignorant and unsetled persons, in cases of distraction, losse, or other outward calamities."[25] True, both are related to that fundamental thirst to systematize the unknown. True, too, magic can merge with Christianity — ride piggyback, so to speak. The medieval propensity toward a magical interpretation of

21. Macfarlane, *Witchcraft in Tudor and Stuart England: A Regional and Comparative Study* (New York, 1970), 25.

22. Ibid., 69–72, 115.

23. Webb, *Office and Authority of a Justice*, 361–62. Compare this with the relevant English statute in Macfarlane, *Witchcraft*, 14–15.

24. Letter of 22 Oct. 1735, *The Correspondence of the Three William Byrds of Westover, Virginia, 1684–1776*, ed. Marion Tinling (Charlottesville, Va., 1977), 2:463.

25. William Perkins quoted in Macfarlane, *Witchcraft*, 121.

Catholic rites is an example, as is Captain Brent's resort to baptism to counteract witchcraft. But as historians we can move a step ahead in our effort to understand by envisioning them as competing systems, and their practitioners as purveying to the societies of premodern England and Virginia two distinct products.

We are a step ahead, too, when we envision the Christian side of the magic/Christianity dichotomy in similar terms. To put the point bluntly, men thirsted for a systematization of the unknown; both magical and Christian systematizations were available to them; and within the Christian category there was offered a variety of subsets to essentially uncommitted men and women.

We need not pause long to document the familiar facts of Virginia's religious history. Virginia's laws clearly and constantly stipulated that the colony was to be Anglican, that there was to be "an uniformitie" in the churches "as neere as may bee" to the "the cannons and constitutions of the church of England," that for the preservation of the purity of doctrine and the unity of the church all ministers were to conform to the orders and constitutions of the church in England, that nothing be taught except that by the canons appointed and inserted into the Book of Common Prayer. Yet the Virginians clearly and constantly demonstrated that they were far less particular than their laws would suggest, for when any ostensible man of God presented himself, they seem to have been quick to put him in a pulpit.[26]

At mid-seventeenth century Nansemond County Virginians, despairing of attracting ministers, sent away to New England—a veritable nursery of men of God—and while those who responded to the call were soon sent packing by the government at Jamestown, there were others in the colony of roughly Puritan persuasion: masters Thomas Harrison and William Durand of Lower Norfolk County, certainly; Charles Grymes of York County in all probability; Daniel Richardson of Hungars Parish, Northampton, and later Settingbourne Parish, Rappahannock; Francis Doughty of Hungars. In 1677 the bishop of London knew of the state of affairs and complained to the Committee for Trade and Plantations that the laws of the colony were not being duly executed and that "persons" were being allowed "to exercise the Ministry without proofe that they are in [Anglican] orders." In the 1680s Presbyterian-types James Porter, Josias Makie, and Andrew Jackson were all incumbent ministers of osten-

---

26. The examples are from William W. Hening, ed., *The Statutes at Large: Being a Collection of All the Laws of Virginia . . . [through 1792]* (Richmond and Philadelphia, 1809–23), 1:153, 277, 2:47. There is a convenient list of such statutes in the appendixes of Brydon, *Virginia's Mother Church*, vol. 1, and a more extensive typescript extract of "Legislation in Colonial Virginia concerning Religion" prepared by Brydon in the Virginia State Library and Archives.

sibly Anglican parishes.[27] Traveling Quakers were received — the "public," proselytizing Friends — and where they passed, Quaker meetings sprang up.[28] Historians working in the context of the orderly, denominational Christianity that was to develop have tended to read back into this farrago to accent the particular persuasions, talking of an Anglican Virginia and of dissenting Puritans, Presbyterians, Quakers. We are, however, closer to understanding the early Virginians when we envision them as being of no particular persuasion at all but instead as merely responding to any man who offered a systematic bridge to the transcendental. At least on the lower socioeconomic levels they were like Thomas's elderly Londoner who conceived of his soul as a great bone or the ignorant lad on the moor. In some measure, at least, this was their cultural heritage. The ordered niceties of particular Christian subsets were largely irrelevant to them, and like thirsty men and women anywhere, they drank regardless of the size or shape of the container bearing the water. Certainly one Virginian, the perspicacious William Byrd, was aware of this phenomenon. On his way to survey the dividing line between Virginia and North Carolina, he passed two Quaker meetinghouses, and the sight led him to observe that the Quakers flourished only where there was no competing Anglican ministry. This thought drew him on to wonder why no popish Marylanders or New England precisionists had appeared "to labor in this neglected vineyard." For "people uninstructed in any religion are ready to embrace the first that offers. 'Tis natural for helpless man to adore his Maker in some form or other."[29]

A generalized thirst for an ordering of the unknown is one dimension of the story of religion in early Virginia. It explains the presence of magic (and witchcraft) as simply one of two systems competing for the minds of

27. William L. Saunders, ed., *The Colonial Records of North Carolina* (Raleigh, N.C., 1886), 1:234. A survey of the Virginia ministry based upon Edmond Neill, *Notes on the Virginia Clergy* (Philadelphia, 1877); Goodwin, *Colonial Church in Virginia*; Brydon, "Addendum to Goodwin's List of Colonial Clergy," typescript, Virginia State Library and Archives; Frederick L. Weis, *The Colonial Clergy of Virginia, North Carolina, and South Carolina* (Boston, 1955); and my own research in county materials indicates for the period to 1690 at least thirty ministers whose doctrines or practices would have dissatisfied the bishop of London. Babette M. Levy, "Early Puritanism in the Southern and Island Colonies," American Antiquarian Society, *Proceedings* 70 (1960): 69–348, would add more names, but the method utilized is suspect; she insists that a Puritan populace can be identified as such by virtue of its acceptance of a Puritan minister, and that a minister can be identified as Puritan by virtue of his serving in one of her Puritan areas.

28. William W. Hinshaw et al., *Encyclopedia of Quaker Genealogy* 6 (Ann Arbor, Mich., 1950): 5–13, 21–25, 39–43, 145–50.

29. Byrd, "History of the Dividing Line betwixt Virginia and North Carolina Run in the Year of Our Lord 1728," in Louis B. Wright, ed., *The Prose Works of William Byrd of Westover* (Cambridge, Mass., 1966), 193. See also Stanley Pargellis, ed., "An Account of the Indians in Virginia," *William and Mary Quarterly*, 3d ser., 16 (1959): 242.

men, the other being Christianity; similarly, it accounts for the diversity within the proferred Christian system and the propensity of the Virginians to slake their thirst in any vessel offered. It is not, however, the only dimension.

The enormous social function that the Christian institution was expected to perform is an obvious second dimension. For Christianity has historically involved more than a "transcendental reference" for the individual; the phrase is that of sociologist Talcott Parsons, but the concept suggests our thirst for the ordering of the unknown. Christianity has also been, to borrow from Emile Durkheim, a "social thing," a "means by which the social group [defines and] reaffirms itself periodically."[30]

In one sense this affirmation involves simply the use of the religious institution to serve particular social purposes, the purpose, in the process, being both accomplished and "sacralized" or hallowed. Most obvious, of course, is the hallowing of family formation via marriage; less obvious is a whole array of social responsibilities devolving upon the church. In law and practice in Virginia, for example, we note society utilizing the parish to care for its orphaned and bastard children and for its poor: Mary Clay, "a poore Indigent woman" and widow, was maintained by Christ Church Parish, Middlesex County, for twenty-three years, and the same parish regularly expended between a fifth and a quarter of its income on such "welfare" tasks. We note, too, the parish being used to identify property boundaries in the "rite" of perambulation, even to identify the persons of the community by virtue of the charge given it to keep the records of births and deaths. The church was also used as a physical nexus for the local community: its door was plastered with notices of lost boats and animals; its incumbent minister or lay reader was legally enjoined to inform the community of proclamations and new laws; its services were as much occasions for social interchange as for spiritual reflection.[31]

The church was expected, too, to affirm the moral boundaries of the society by serving as the focal point of enunciation and example. Thus laws required Sunday sermons on morality and, at the same time, called upon the ministers to shun excess in drinking, idleness, and gambling and instead to occupy themselves with honest study, "haveinge always in mynd that they ought to excell all others in puritie of life, and should be

---

30. Quoted in Thomas F. O'Dea, *The Sociology of Religion* (Englewood Cliffs, N.J., 1966), 4, 12. Peter Berger, *The Sacred Canopy* (New York, 1967), is a major statement of this idea.

31. Based upon a survey of parish expenditures by Christ Church, Middlesex, to 1726. The parish accounts are to be found in C. G. Chamberlayne, ed., *The Vestry Book of Christ Church Parish, Middlesex County, Virginia, 1663–1767* (Richmond, 1927). See also Darrett B. and Anita H. Rutman, *A Place in Time: Middlesex County, Virginia, 1650–1750* (New York, 1984), 122–25, 195–200.

examples to the people, to live well and christianlie."[32] In 1701 a leading Virginian wrote that while "it may not be convenient to force all People to be of one Religion, yet it may be requisite to oblige every one to profess and practise some sort of Religion or other" for "it is to be wish'd, that some Care were taken to instruct the people well in Morality, that is, what all Perswasions either do, or pretend to desire." A few years later another Virginian left his parish church 100 pounds sterling to underwrite preaching four quarterly sermons against the four reigning vices of atheism and irreligion, swearing and cursing, fornication and adultery, and drunkenness. And in 1723 the vestrymen of Christ Church, Middlesex, commended their minister, who was said to be "without any Blemish in his life and conversation but has always like a good Minister Set us Pious Examples by Living a righteous, Sober, and Godly life."[33] When the moral boundaries were broken, the religious institution was used (again in Durkheim's words) to "heal the wounds" inflicted by offenses against the "collective sentiments" of the society, both by fulfilling its charge to present moral offenses to the county courts and by providing a place of ceremonial degradation: "Whereas Joane the wife of William Thomas was arested to this [County] Court by Mr. Thomas Griffen on an action of slander for throwinge severall Aspersions & scandalls on the said Griffen & Sarah the wife of John Philips, which haveinge been sufficiently proved against her, the said Joan, the Court hath therefore ordered that shee shall at the next time that the Minister officiates in the uper parts of the river make publique acknowledgement of her said offence & her sorrow for the same."[34]

In still another sense the Christian institution affirmed the society by adjusting its internal hierarchy to that of the society at large. For example, not just anybody took a seat on the governing board of a Virginia parish;

32. Hening, *Statutes at Large* 1:158. The law cited is that of 1632, but its thrust was common through the period.

33. Louis B. Wright, ed., *An Essay upon the Government of the English Plantations on the Continent of America (1701)* (San Marino, Calif., 1945), 22–23, 39; Will of William Churchill, 18 Nov. 1710, *William and Mary Quarterly*, 1st ser., 7 (1898–99): 187; Chamberlayne, *Vestry Book of Christ Church, Middlesex*, 188; William Stevens Perry, comp., *Historical Collections Relating to the American Colonial Church* (Hartford, 1870–78), 1:348–50. The first has been attributed to Ralph Wormeley of Middlesex by Virginia White Fitz, "Ralph Wormeley: Anonymous Essayist," *William and Mary Quarterly*, 3d ser., 26 (1969): 586–95; support for the attribution can be found in Robert Carter to Francis Lee, 15 July 1702, Wormeley Estate Papers, 1701–16, with Christ Church, Lancaster Processioners' Returns, 1711–83, Virginia State Library and Archives.

34. Emile Durkheim, *The Division of Labor in Society*, trans. George Simpson (Glencoe, Ill., 1960), 108; Lancaster County, Deeds, etc., no. 1, 1652–57, 99, Virginia State Library and Archives.

on the contrary, as an intensive study of one well-functioning parish clearly shows, an invitation to join the vestry followed as night the day the achievement of high economic status within the community. Thus the religious institution, in effect, was used to signify the "arrival" of a new community leader. Neither did one sit just anywhere within a Virginia church or chapel, as Mistress Jones of Christ Church Parish, Middlesex, quickly learned. As the housekeeper and perhaps mistress of Colonel Christopher Wormeley, a position which in her eyes raised her status, she attempted to sit "above her Degree," only to be bodily "displaced" by the churchwarden, a displacement which was fully approved by the vestry. Richard Price of St. Mary White Chapel in nearby Lancaster learned a similar lesson. For his "rude irreligous & uncivill" intrusion "into the seate purposely designed & made use off by his Majesties Justices of the peace," in the course of which he "did rudely force backwards upon his seate" the high sheriff of the county, Price was dispatched by Lancaster's gentlemen justices to Jamestown and the governor for judgment and punishment. To the justices the whole affair tended "to the dishonor of God Almighty, the contempt of his Majesty and Ministers, offence of the congregation, scandall to religion & evill example of others."[35]

In none of this, of course, were the Virginians unique. Any consideration of the English church, and of the English parish in particular, makes obvious the large and multifaceted social role it played. Moreover, and a more important point, it played this role regardless of the particulars of doctrine and ceremony preached and exercised under its cover. Whether a Catholic populace crowded the church to impart a magical significance to the miracle of transubstantiation, or solemn Puritans gathered around a kitchen table to commemorate the Last Supper — to cite two extremes — the Christian institution functioned socially in much the same way.[36] That it should do so was an element of the cultural baggage carried to Virginia, and it is for this reason that I have referred to the people's "expectation" that religion would play an enormous social role. The social functioning

35. Chamberlayne, *Vestry Book of Christ Church, Middlesex*, 63; Lancaster County, Orders, etc., no. 1, 1666–80, 206, Virginia State Library and Archives. See also Rutman and Rutman, *A Place in Time: Middlesex*, 143–52, 161–62, and *A Place in Time: Explicatus* (New York, 1984), chap. 10.

36. See, e.g., Toulmin Smith, *The Parish* (London, 1854); Edward L. Cutts, *Parish Priests and Their People in the Middle Ages in England* (London, 1898); Sidney and Beatrice Webb, *English Local Government from the Revolution to the Municipal Corporations Act: The Parish and the County* (London, 1906); Sedley L. Ware, *The Elizabethan Parish in Its Ecclesiastical and Financial Aspects* (Baltimore, 1908); pertinent sections of A. Abram, *English Life and Manners in the Later Middle Ages* (New York, 1913); Eleanor Trotter, *Seventeenth Century Life in the Country Parish, with Special Reference to Local Government* (Cambridge, 1919); A. R. Powys, *The English Parish Church* (London, 1930); William E. Tate, *The Parish Chest: A Study of the Records of Parochial Administration in England* (Cambridge, 1946).

of the Virginia church was not, as it developed, exactly the same as that of its English parent, certainly; neither was it the only implement for fulfilling such social tasks, for church and Sabbath day on the one hand, and county court and court day on the other, shared much the same set of social functions. But that is another story. The point here is that, again, we are faced with an imperative in the evolution of early Virginia's religion: The church was expected to perform a social function, and, as in England, the social function expected of the religious institution was not related to the particular Christian subset preached from the pulpit. In brief, it did not matter in Virginia whether the incumbent conformed to the canons and constitutions of the Church of England or deviated from those canons, provided that the church, as it in large measure inevitably did, performed its social role. Even the Quaker "churches" did so, as is evidenced by the records of the Chuckatuck Monthly Meeting, established in Nansemond in 1672 and flourishing at century's end. Its record book is little different from, say, the parish book of Middlesex's Christ Church or Gloucester's Petsworth: a record of care for the poor, for widows, for children; of moral and marketplace discipline; of the community's births, marriages, and deaths; of recognition of social status by the admission into the offices of the meeting of the community's preeminent men.[37]

The two dimensions outlined—the thirst for an ordering of the unknown on the one hand and the expectation that the Christian institution play a particular social role—offer us a setting for the evolution of religion in Virginia, one far more complex than the simple citation of the law—"Ordered, That there be a uniformitie throughout this colony . . . to the canons and constitutions of the church of England"—would imply and the assertion of an Anglican transplantation and sea change can explain. Seventeenth-century Virginia was a colony where magic rubbed shoulders with Christianity; where "honest, able, sober, pious and orthodox ministers" were solicited from London, and "Anythingarians" were accepted into parish pulpits; where men and women, in the absence of ministers of any sort, gravitated toward Quakerism with its rationalization of a ministerless structure and, in at least one case, attached to their meetinghouse a steeple more appropriate to an Anglican church, this last, wrote William Byrd, a "piece of foppery" unexpected "from a sect of so much outside simplicity." Why? Because the Virginians were acting more in response to basic psychological and social needs than to the tenets of any particular creed.[38]

37. Typescript copy of "The Chuckatuck Record" labeled "Lower Virginia Monthly Minutes and Register of Births, Deaths, Marriages, 1647–1756," Virginia State Library and Archives.

38. Quoted in Brydon, *Virginia's Mother Church* 1:426; Byrd, "History of the Dividing Line," 193. The term "Anythingarians" was actually applied by John Urmstone to North

Magic, of course, as it did in England, receded. It did not disappear completely, however; we must keep in mind Byrd's Hampton witch of 1735. The nineteen identifiable cases involving witches suggest the pace of this recession: of the nine cases between 1626 and 1665, five seem to have involved actual charges brought against witches, while three were suits brought by persons called witches against their defamers; of the ten cases between 1668 and 1705, only three involved actual charges, while the remaining seven were suits for defamation. Many reasons have been offered for the decline of magic. One can suggest that three, very much entangled with each other, are to the point here. The first is the competitive press of Christianity itself, in effect slowly conquering the minds of men and women. The second is the very nature of magic. Magic is extemporaneous in the sense that it is resorted to in response to particular situations.[39] It does not, therefore, tend to maintain a "standing order" — an institutional form — and without institutionalization it cannot perform a broad social role. Rich and poor can resort to magic in response to specific events, but magic (in contrast to the Christian institution) does not assume the general care of the poor or affirm the general social pre-eminence of the rich. Christianity, simply because its institutional form assumed so many social tasks, had a "leg up," so to speak, on its rival.[40] The third is the classical formulation of anthropologist Bronislaw Malinowski: Magic thrives when man's knowledge and his ability to control his environment and destiny are weak and tends to wither when such knowledge and control grow stronger.[41] For the Virginians this third reason would seem particularly applicable. The whole process of settlement — the act of removing from England to America and of bringing even a small part of the wilderness into cultivation, the promise (and to some extent the reality) of material self-improvement — was an assertion of an ability to control one's destiny, and even nature itself.[42]

Carolina in 1711 (Saunders, *Records of North Carolina* 1:769), but it seems equally applicable in this sense to an earlier Virginia.

39. In either sense described in note 13: appealing to the magician or accusing the witch.

40. A theme developed at length in Butler's *Awash in a Sea of Faith*.

41. Malinowski, "Magic, Science, and Religion," in *Science, Religion, and Reality*, ed. Joseph Needham (New York, 1925), 19–84. Thomas, *Religion and the Decline of Magic*, 647–56, summarizes and applies the thesis to England. One need not espouse all of Malinowski in accepting this broad generalization.

42. Still a fourth argument is that the rise and fall of witchcraft per se in sixteenth- and seventeenth-century England are associated with a shift from a traditional communitarianism to a new individualism. The essence of this argument is that the accusation of witchcraft is a transfer of guilt from the egocentric individualist to the object of his or her discomfort, i.e., the old man or woman who has solicited help on the basis of communitarian values and been refused in the context of individualistic values. Macfarlane, *Witchcraft*, chap. 16, develops the argument. The application to Virginia is confused. Some, but not all, of the

One can suggest, moreover, that Malinowski's formulation offers insight into the nature of the Virginians' evolving religiosity as well. To the extent that religion and magic have a common root in the psychological need to order and control the unknown, whatever reduces the necessity for a magical resolution equally reduces the need for a religious resolution. Concomitantly, those areas of religion which tend most readily to assume magical attributes — the exercise of particular rites, for example, which gain their efficacy by the form of their doing — grow less important.[43] The argument conceivably explains the increasing appeal of latitudinarianism in the Virginia situation. Anglican dogma and liturgical ritual would become relatively unimportant; Christianity would become important more for its broad placement of man in a cosmic scheme and less for its immanent God, ready at hand to act on the human situation; and the Christian institution itself would come to be valued largely for the social rather than the spiritual role it played. An important reservation must be entered, however; the trend toward latitudinarianism and secularization would not be equal across all social categories within the society. It would instead occur most prominently among those who believed themselves to be capable of controlling their own destinies and less commonly among those who felt themselves to be less capable of exerting such control. Latitudinarianism, a distant God, and a socially oriented church would be most comforting to the gentry, less and less comfortable as one descended through the ranks of the commonality — a point to which we will return.

Latitudinarianism in its practical rather than ideological aspect was a lay phenomenon. And thus far we have been concerned with the lay dimensions of religion in early Virginia. But there is still a third dimension to be considered: the character of the purveyor of the Christian system — the Anglican priest, the "dissenting" minister, the Quaker "Minister of Truth." For convenience call the type, regardless of persuasion, simply "minister." Much ink has been used to point up the theological distinctions among the ministers of the seventeenth century, all to very good purpose. But here let me make the point of their essential similarity.

Heuristically we can distinguish in religion both a function — the psychological and social needs that the religion serves — and the form in which that function is performed. Certainly in the seventeenth century the burdens of fulfilling forms were largely borne by the minister. He was,

---

witchcraft accusations fit easily. But one would expect many more cases, given what is generally assumed to be the Virginians' individualistic behavior. The argument, moreover, applies only to the accusation of magic, not to the application to magic.

43. "The most essential point about magic and religious ritual is that it steps in only where knowledge fails." Conversely, magic and religious ritual "step out" where knowledge succeeds. Malinowski, *The Foundation of Faith and Morals* (London, 1936), 34.

by commitment and training, the professional, the expert in the things pertaining to form: polity, creed, and practice. Moreover, he was, to use the terms of modern sociology, a "problem-area specialist." As such, to paraphrase Roland L. Warren, we can envision the ideal type as "task oriented and highly specialized; his expertise less situational and more abstract; likely to have many of his answers before confronting his problems; a purveyor of a particular program and axiomatically inimical to a consideration of alternatives; paternalistic and tending to lean toward the side which knows what is right and insists that right prevail."[44] The paraphrase, of course, describes the dogmatic specialist in general; the ministerial specialist of the seventeenth century was even more dogmatic, for he had the deity on his side. He was the expert on the Godhead from which flowed what he conceived as a single truth relative to religious form. On the question of the nature of this truth, the ministers might divide; on the question of its existence and the necessity of its implementation among men, they agreed. Indeed, in implementing forms derived from the Godhead, the seventeenth-century ministers tended, in our terms, to elevate the particulars of form above the very function of religion (although such terms would be inconceivable to them, for the function of religion was, to them, indistinguishable from its form). Their very profession, moreover, they derived from the Godhead, and they had a clear and rigid concept of their role within society and the respect toward their persons that the role demanded. They were, in their own eyes, the shepherds of God's flock, the academicians of the Lord, and, in the separate but coordinate divisions of society into church and state, the proper administrators of the former.

Prima facie the ministerial type and an implicit latitudinarianism would be antithetical. And the extant records of seventeenth-century Virginia offer evidence of sharp confrontations between the two, with laymen soliciting the function of religion and ignoring the form, and ministers purveying form and aghast at the formal laxity of the laity. On the Carolina border, for example, the Quaker "Minister of Truth" William Edmundson discerned the irreligion of those who flocked to hear him in the fact that "they came and sat down . . . smoking their pipes." In York County, Master Charles Grymes "would admitt of none to receive the sacrament but such as came to be examined and instructed in his Chamber." His standards were high, for some individuals who came to him for instruction were refused it, he "biding them learne better." But one Daniel Holland would have none of this and stayed away entirely, pleading the

44. Quoted in Darrett B. Rutman, "The Social Web: A Prospectus for the Study of the Early American Community," in *Insights and Parallels: Problems and Issues of American Social History*, ed. William L. O'Neill (Minneapolis, 1973), 93. See also Max Weber, *The Sociology of Religion*, trans. Ephraim Fischoff (Boston, 1964), 30.

minister's scrupulosity when presented to the county court for his absten-
tion.[45] The records offer abundant evidence, too, of the sharp conflict
between the clerical view of the ministerial position (God's shepherd) and
a lay view (the minister as functionary). To the laity of Petsworth Parish,
Gloucester, for example, their assessment of Master Thomas Vicaris's
performance of "his Ministerial Function" was properly affected by their
approval of his "life & conversacon"; to Master Morgan Goodwyn, however, such ministers as Vicaris were "most miserably handled by their
Plebian Junto's, the *Vestries*; To whom the *Hiring* (that is the usual word
there) and Admission of *Ministers* is solely left."[46]

Anglican form could only be purveyed by ministerial minds of an Anglican persuasion. And through much of the seventeenth century the Anglican ministry in Virginia suffered from both the paucity of its ministers and
their isolation — an isolation in part physical and induced by the scattered
nature of Virginia's population but in part institutional in the sense that
the very form they espoused denied the ministers a corporate identity
apart from an episcopal structure they did not have.[47] As a consequence
there was little to be done in defense of form except complain against its
absence, as Goodwyn did, and Roger Green, or to work quietly on behalf
of form within particular parishes.[48]

In the 1670s and 1680s, however, the number of ministers in Virginia
tripled, the new arrivals coming directly from England and reflecting the

45. Saunders, *Records of North Carolina* 1:216; Fleet, *Virginia Colonial Abstracts*, vol. 26,
York County, 1648–1657 (Baltimore, 1961), 8. The reports home of American missionaries
dispatched by the Society for the Propagation of the Gospel in Foreign Parts (on microfilm
at the Library of Congress, Washington, D.C.) are replete with such examples; there were no
missionaries to Virginia, but some of the North Carolina reports are readily available in
Saunders.

46. C. G. Chamberlayne, ed., *The Vestry Book of Petsworth Parish, Gloucester County, Virginia, 1677–1793* (Richmond, 1933), 14, 17; Goodwyn, *The Negro's and Indians Advocate
Suing for Their Admission unto the Church* (London, 1680), 168.

47. The ministers themselves recognized this duality, the Anglicans calling for both a
bishopric and a concentration of the Virginians into towns — e.g. R[oger] G[reen], *Virginia's
Cure: or, An Advisive Narrative concerning Virginia* (1662), in Force, *Tracts*, vol. 3, tract 15:5 —
and the dissenters for simply towns — e.g., Francis Makemie, *A Plain and Friendly Perswasive
to the Inhabitants of Virginia and Maryland for Promoting Towns and Cohabitation* (1705), in
Virginia Magazine of History and Biography 4 (1896–97): 255–71. Compare the ready recourse to corporate effort by ministers unshackled by a commitment to episcopacy in New
England and the Delaware River Valley as described by Robert F. Scholz, "Clerical Con-
sociation in Massachusetts Bay: Reassessing the New England Way and Its Origins,"
William and Mary Quarterly, 3d ser., 39 (1972): 391–414; Scholz, "'The Reverend Elders':
Faith, Fellowship, and Politics in the Ministerial Community of Massachusetts Bay" (Ph.D.
diss., University of Minnesota, 1966); Jon Butler, *Power, Authority, and the Origins of American
Denominational Order: The English Churches in the Delaware Valley, 1680–1730* (Philadelphia,
1978), which includes the corporate efforts of Quaker "Ministers of Truth."

48. In their works cited in notes 46 and 47.

strong church position of the English Anglican revival.[49] And in 1689 episcopal authority of a sort arrived in the person of Master James Blair, newly appointed commissary of the bishop of London. Under his aegis the orthodox Anglican clergy met at Jamestown and considered at length the dearth of qualified candidates for Virginia's pulpits, the number of unorthodox ministers occupying many of those pulpits, and the dependence of the ministry on the lay vestries. The first problem, they agreed, was to be solved by the erection of a college "to the end that the Church of *Virginia* may be furnish'd with a Seminary of Ministers of the Gospel"; the second by soliciting an order requiring the ouster of all ministers not properly in episcopal orders; the third by the payment of the ministry out of quitrents rather than by parish levies. Memorials to the crown and civil authorities of the colony were prepared to effect these reforms. But the most important work was the organization of an "Ecclesiastical Jurisdiction" in Virginia which would effect "a speedy Reformation of the lives of both Clergy and Laity." "The Ecclesiastical laws against all cursers Swearers & blasphemers, all whoremongers fornicators and Adulterers, all drunkards ranters and profaners of the Lords day and Contemners of the Sacraments" were to be revived "and put in execution," and, with the consent of the meeting, Blair appointed four "Substituts and Surrogats" to "exercise the Ecclesiastical jurisdiction" within the various "precincts" of Virginia. Twice a year the surrogates, with the whole clergy of their precincts, were to hold court, while an annual "General meeting" at Jamestown was to act as a superior court for "difficult and intricat" cases. Blair's own periodic visitations of the parishes would complete the system. Quite clearly the ministers intended to establish a structure which could define and enforce an Anglican orthodoxy.[50]

The Anglican effort of 1690 failed of its immediate purpose. Blair subsequently sped for England to solicit quitrent money for both college and clergy, and while he was successful in obtaining royal funds for the college and his own salary, his attempts to collect monies in Virginia ran afoul of the necessity to spend monies for defense.[51] The ecclesiastical court structure was no sooner set up in 1691 than it was struck down, Blair's surro-

49. Largely as a result of the activities of Henry Compton, bishop of London from 1675 to 1713. See Edward Carpenter, *The Protestant Bishop* (London, 1956), chaps. 14, 15; J. H. Bennett, "English Bishops and Imperial Jurisdiction, 1660–1725," *Historical Magazine of the Protestant Episcopal Church* 32 (1963): 175–88; William Wilson Manross, comp., *The Fulham Papers in the Lambeth Palace Library: American Colonial Section, Calendar and Indexes* (Oxford, 1965), sec. 14–16.

50. Brydon, *Virginia's Mother Church* 1:279–83; Henry Hartwell, James Blair, and Edward Chilton, *The Present State of Virginia and the College* (1699), ed. Hunter Dickinson Farish (Williamsburg, Va., 1940), 65–68, 72.

51. Virginia Colonial Records Survey Project, *Report No. 401*, 10.

gate, Master Samuel Eburne, being summoned before the governor and council to acknowledge the error of such ways.[52] And while the governor and council, in response to the ministers, once more ordered that no parish "entertain any minister . . . who doth not in all things comply with the Canons of the Church of England," the vestry of Christchurch Parish, Lancaster, as late as 1704 would report that it was well satisfied with Master Andrew Jackson, "although not Quallified with Episcopall Orders."[53] For our purposes, however, the fact of immediate failure is less important than the fact of the attempt itself, exemplifying as it does the ministerial dimension of Virginia's religious course.

In the last analysis religion in early Virginia seems fragmented by the three dimensions suggested. An innate drive to order the unknown came to be satisfied by a basic Christian outlook, one discernible certainly among the gentlemen of Virginia. Life, wrote William Fitzhugh in 1698, is "but going to an Inn, no permanent being. By God's [will] I continue the same, good thoughts & notions." "I believe," wrote William Byrd, "that man must have continu'd under [God's] curse to all eternity had not Jesus Christ[,] the first born of the creation, by whose ministry God made the World, been pleas'd to offer himself to be a propitiatory Sacrifice. . . . I believe that Jesus Christ while he livd in the World was [the] most perfect Teacher and most perfect Pattern of virtue and holiness."[54] That the social expectations were met is exemplified by the pervasiveness from an early date of the functional parish and by what Philip Fithian would describe in 1774 as "the three grand divisions of time at the Church": "Before Service giving & receiving letters of business, reading Advertisements, consulting about the price of Tobacco, Grain, &c. & settling either the lineage, Age, or qualities of favourite Horses. . . . In the Church at Service, prayrs read over in haste, a Sermon seldom under & never over twenty minutes, but always made up of sound morality, or deep studied Metaphysicks. . . . After Service is over three quarters of an hour spent in strolling round the Church among the Crowd, in which time you will be

52. John P. Kennedy and H. R. McIlwaine, eds., *Journals of the House of Burgesses of Virginia, 1619–1776* (Richmond, 1905–15), 2:366–67. In part the quick collapse of the ecclesiastical courts seems to have resulted from the bishop of London's own limited view of the proper role of his commissary. See Manross, *Fulham Papers*, 165; Bennett, "English Bishops and Imperial Jurisdiction," 182–83.

53. H. R. McIlwaine and Wilmer L. Hall, eds., *Executive Journals of the Council of Colonial Virginia, 1680–1754* (Richmond, 1925–45), 1:176; "Replies of the Vestries in Virginia in 1704 to Governor Nicholson upon the Subject of Induction of Ministers," Brydon, *Virginia's Mother Church* 1:531.

54. Richard Beale Davis, ed., *William Fitzhugh and His Chesapeake World, 1676–1701: The Fitzhugh Letters and Other Documents* (Chapel Hill, N.C., 1963), 358; Louis B. Wright and Marion Tinling, eds., *The Secret Diary of William Byrd of Westover, 1709–1712* (Richmond, 1941), xxviii.

invited by several different Gentlemen home with them to dinner."[55] And the ministerial mind (of the Anglican persuasion), over time and by the weight of numbers and perseverance, did indeed impose the appearance of Anglican form upon the churches. Christchurch, Lancaster, although loyally supporting Master Jackson in 1704, was clearly apologetic about his deviation from an emerging norm. They would, the vestrymen wrote, "upon removall of our present Minister . . . embrace it as a Singuler blessing of heaven both upon our Selves and posterity to be Supplied with another good one in his room whose Conversation as well as Doctrine may becom his Character." The same year Gloucester's Petsworth vestry made a point of hearing their minister, Emanuel Jones, "read Common Prayer . . . both in the forenoon & afternoon . . . according to the form and order prescribed & Directed by the book entituled the book of Comon prayer & administration of the Sacraments," noting that "immediately after reading the Same [he] made a declaration of his unfeigned Assent & Consent to all the matters & things therein Contained."[56]

But the ministerial mind imposed itself at a cost paid in the eighteenth century. In part, the coin paid was the encouragement of nascent denominationalism and pluralism, for as the century progressed, enough of a recognizable Anglican orthodoxy appeared to deter Presbyterian- and Baptist-types from adhering (as they had through the seventeenth century). And barred from this emerging orthodoxy, men and women of such persuasions necessarily sought identification with other emerging orthodoxies; a small group from Hanover County, for example, determining "that Luther was a noted Reformer, and that his book had been of special use to us," declared themselves Lutherans, then discovered a copy of the *Confessions of Faith of the Presbyterian Church of Scotland* and accepted the designation Presbyterian.[57] In part, too, however, the coin was the surrender to lay latitudinarianism and the acceptance of the church as primarily a social institution. The laymen wanted no "scholars and stoicks, or zealots too rigid in outward appearance," no "quarrelsom and litigious ministers, who would differ with their parishioners about insignificant trifles." And they got none. The best of Virginia's parsons came to accept "the Practical Part of Religion" as "the Chief part of our Pastoral Care;" the worst mumbled a quick, formal sermon to the cushion, then went off

55. Hunter Dickinson Farish, ed., *Journal and Letters of Philip Vickers Fithian, 1773–1774: A Plantation Tutor of the Old Dominion* (Williamsburg, Va., 1957), 167.

56. "Replies of Vestries . . . in 1704," Brydon, *Virginia's Mother Church* 1:532; Chamberlayne, *Vestry Book of Petsworth Parish*, 82.

57. William Henry Foote, *Sketches of Virginia: Historical and Biographical* (Philadelphia, 1850), 124.

to dine with the local squire.[58] Yet the lay latitudinarianism to which the ministers surrendered was not, recall, spread equally through the society. Under the aegis of a distant God and social church, a gentry-oriented society could and did flourish, largely indifferent to the deeper aspects of its own creation, nurturing here and there a Jeffersonian rationalism. But for those less comfortable in society, more anxiety prone — perhaps a growing number, if we accept the thrust of recent social historians — the social church offered little.[59] Eighteenth-century evangelicalism, speaking more to psychological needs than did Virginia's polite Anglicanism, would find its converts largely among these.[60] With that, it seems, we come full circle. For having started with religion in the era of the Revolution — with rationalism, evangelicalism, formalism, and indifference — our exploration of the antecedent evolution in the religious life of Virginia returns us to the same place.

58. Hugh Jones, *The Present State of Virginia*, ed. Richard L. Morton (Chapel Hill, N.C., 1956), 117–18; Commissary Blair in 1722, quoted in Davis, *Literature and Society*, 157.

59. Kenneth A. Lockridge's "Land, Population, and the Evolution of New England Society, 1630–1730," *Past and Present* 39 (1968): 62–80, and "Social Change and the Meaning of the American Revolution," *Journal of Social History* 7 (1973): 403–39, are the seminal pieces, but recent work on Chesapeake society is tending to conform, e.g., Russell R. Menard, "From Servant to Freeholder: Status, Mobility, and Property Accumulation in Seventeenth-Century Maryland," *William and Mary Quarterly*, 3d ser., 30 (1973): 37–64; Carville V. Earle, *The Evolution of a Tidewater Settlement System: All Hallow's Parish, Maryland, 1650–1783*, University of Chicago, Department of Geography, Research Paper no. 170 (Chicago, 1975), 217; Rutman and Rutman, *A Place in Time: Middlesex*, 236–40.

60. It is at this point that the present work links to that of Rhys Isaac, specifically "Religion and Authority: Problems of the Anglican Establishment in Virginia in the Era of the Great Awakening and the Parsons' Cause" and "Evangelical Revolt: The Nature of the Baptists' Challenge to the Traditional Order in Virginia, 1765 to 1775," *William and Mary Quarterly*, 3d ser., 30 (1973): 3–36 and 31 (1974): 345–68; "Preachers and Patriots: Popular Culture and the Revolution in Virginia," in *The American Revolution: Explorations in the History of American Radicalism*, ed. Alfred E. Young (DeKalb, Ill., 1976), 125–56.

9 Of Agues and Fevers: *Malaria in the Early Chesapeake*

With Anita H. Rutman

Religion was the bridge that carried me into the Chesapeake world. But the material rather than mental conditions of life rapidly became the dominant concern. A small band of Chesapeake scholars centered on the Maryland Hall of Records in Annapolis was already at work, and one of their earliest findings was the extraordinary mortality among the men of seventeenth-century Maryland. The Rutman and Rutman collaboration, concentrating on Middlesex County, Virginia, was able to confirm this conclusion and extend it into the eighteenth century and to women; indeed, to demonstrate that women in the main had an even shorter life span than men, a demographic anomaly. The anomaly required explanation, a requirement which led us far beyond the traditional literature of the historian, into Index Medicus, *and eventually to malaria. But a malarious Chesapeake, in turn, raised questions about the ways a society copes, and how to disentangle our vantage point in the twentieth century from judgments about the past, in this case about what so many came to regard as simply a demographic and consequently social disaster. For the most part the questions — raised in the form of suggestions in "Of Agues and Fevers" — still await answers.*

On Tuesday, April 25, 1758, Landon Carter of Sabine Hall, Virginia, recorded in his diary the imminent death of his daughter Sukey. "Her face, feet and hands are all cold and her pulse quite gone and reduced to the bones and skin that cover them and dying very hard. . . .

Presented originally at a conference on early American social history at the State University of New York, Stony Brook, N.Y., June 1975 and subsequently published in the *William and Mary Quarterly*, 3d ser., 33 (1976): 31–60. Copyright 1976 by the Institute of Early American History and Culture.

Severe stroke indeed to A Man bereft of a Wife and in the decline of life."
Sukey was probably about seven; Carter was forty-seven but thought of
himself as old, and he had lost three wives in all.[1]

Carter's diary entry records as personal tragedy what historical demography is presenting more formally: the fragility of life in the early Chesapeake. Life spans were in the main far shorter than today, shorter even
than in seventeenth- and eighteenth-century New England; childhood
deaths were commonplace; and women in their childbearing years ran a
greater risk of death than did their husbands, the latter often being left
widowers.[2] What were the roots of that fragility? How may it have affected the mind and form of Chesapeake society? Answers to these questions may emerge from an understanding of the endemic nature of malaria in the region.

A caveat is immediately in order. Any entry into the medical life of the
past must be undertaken cautiously. On the one hand, Carter and his
contemporaries referred to disease in archaic terms and in the context of
an archaic medical paradigm. On the other, the nature of modern symptomatology can delude the historian, for while the clinical and laboratory
manifestations of disease are carefully delineated in modern textbooks,
the past had neither the conceptions nor the means to discern the latter,
and the former seldom appeared in pristine form. "Typicality" is vitiated
by the unique circumstances of the particular patient, by the fact that
discrete diseases can combine in unfamiliar manifestations, and by the fact
of treatment itself: In the seventeenth century what effect might phlebo-
tomy (bleeding) have had on the course of a malarial attack? And in the
twentieth century how many physicians have seen an absolutely untreated
case of malaria through its full course?[3] In brief, the past with respect to
discrete diseases is indistinct. Literary references to the maladies and

---

1. Jack P. Greene, ed., *The Diary of Colonel Landon Carter of Sabine Hall, 1752–1778*
(Charlottesville, Va., 1965), 1:221.

2. Lorena S. Walsh and Russell R. Menard, "Death in the Chesapeake: Two Life Tables
for Men in Early Colonial Maryland," *Maryland Historical Magazine* 69 (1974): 211–27.
Subsequent scholarship has confirmed time and again the appalling mortality in the region
that Walsh and Menard first suggested. See, for example, Daniel Blake Smith, "Mortality
and Family in the Colonial Chesapeake," *Journal of Interdisciplinary History* 7 (1978): 408–15;
appendix 2 of Darrett B. and Anita H. Rutman, "'Now-Wives and Sons-in-Law': Parental
Death in a Seventeenth-Century Virginia County," in *The Chesapeake in the Seventeenth
Century: Essays on Anglo-American Society*, ed. Thad W. Tate and David L. Ammerman
(Chapel Hill, N.C., 1979), 177–82; Rutman and Rutman, *A Place in Time: Explicatus* (New
York, 1984), 37–59; Allan Kulikoff, *Tobacco and Slaves: The Development of Southern Cultures
in the Chesapeake, 1680–1800* (Chapel Hill, N.C., 1986), 62–63.

3. The classic caution was entered by Charles Creighton, *A History of Epidemics in Britain*
2 (Cambridge, 1894): 1–2. Donald G. Bates, "Thomas Willis and the Epidemic Fever of
1661: A Commentary," *Bulletin of the History of Medicine* 39 (1965): 393–412, is a brilliant
modern restatement and elaboration.

ailments of seventeenth- and eighteenth-century Chesapeake colonists abound in surviving letters, diaries, travelers' accounts, scientific works, and the like, but no single reference points unerringly to malaria as it is described today. Hence historians can only build an inferential case for its prevalence, combining the available literary evidence with a contemporary understanding of the disease so that the two are consonant with each other, then test their case against the known attributes of the society — in the present instance, its demographic attributes.

These cautions lead to a first question: Malaria — what is it? Put succinctly, malaria is a febrile disease arising as a reaction of the body to invasion by parasites of the genus *Plasmodium*.[4] The life cycle of the *Plasmodium* forms a complex system involving as hosts a female anopheline mosquito and a vertebrate. In anthropomorphic terms the human host serves as the nursery within which the parasite spends its asexual "childhood"; its sexual "adulthood" is spent in the mosquito. Figure 9.1 illustrates this complex system in a more "*Plasmodia*-centric," but still simple, form. A highly idealized clinical reaction in the human host is illustrated in figure 9.2. From infection by the bite of the female *Anopheles* mosquito through a tissue stage in the liver, the reaction is nil. Only as the parasites enter the blood to attack the red cells do the body's defenses rise to do battle and clinical reactions begin. Headache and general malaise are occasional premonitory symptoms, but the internal battle is most marked by fever paroxysms, with the parasite's cycle setting the tempo. Relatively slight paroxysms follow the first entry into the blood; as the cycle proceeds, wave after wave of parasites are rhythmically released, and the host's fever rises and falls in response. Fever "spikes" climb progressively higher, frequently accompanied by antecedent chills and postcedent sweatings. Associated with the paroxysms are secondary symptoms. The host may experience headache (sometimes with an accompanying eye pain), loss of appetite, nausea, generalized aches and pains and specific abdominal pain, and occasional respiratory difficulties, weakness, and vertigo. An observer might discern vomiting, skin eruptions, palpable enlargement of the spleen and liver and a generalized swelling of the limbs,

---

4. The cumulative nature of scientific writing, with its periodic "position papers," has been our key to an understanding of malaria. As basic references and guides to the pre-1972 literature we have used *A Symposium on Human Malaria with Special Reference to North America and the Caribbean Region*, ed. Forest Ray Moulton (Washington, D.C., 1941); *Malariology: A Comprehensive Survey of All Aspects of This Group of Diseases from a Global Standpoint*, ed. Mark F. Boyd (Philadelphia, 1949); G. Robert Coatney et al., *The Primate Malarias* (Bethesda, Md., 1971); and *Proceedings of the Inter-American Malaria Research Symposium*, ed. Robert G. Scholtens and José A. Nájera, printed as a supplement to the *American Journal of Tropical Medicine and Hygiene* 21 (1972): 604–851. *Cumulated Index Medicus* (Chicago, 1960–) provided entry to the most recent studies.

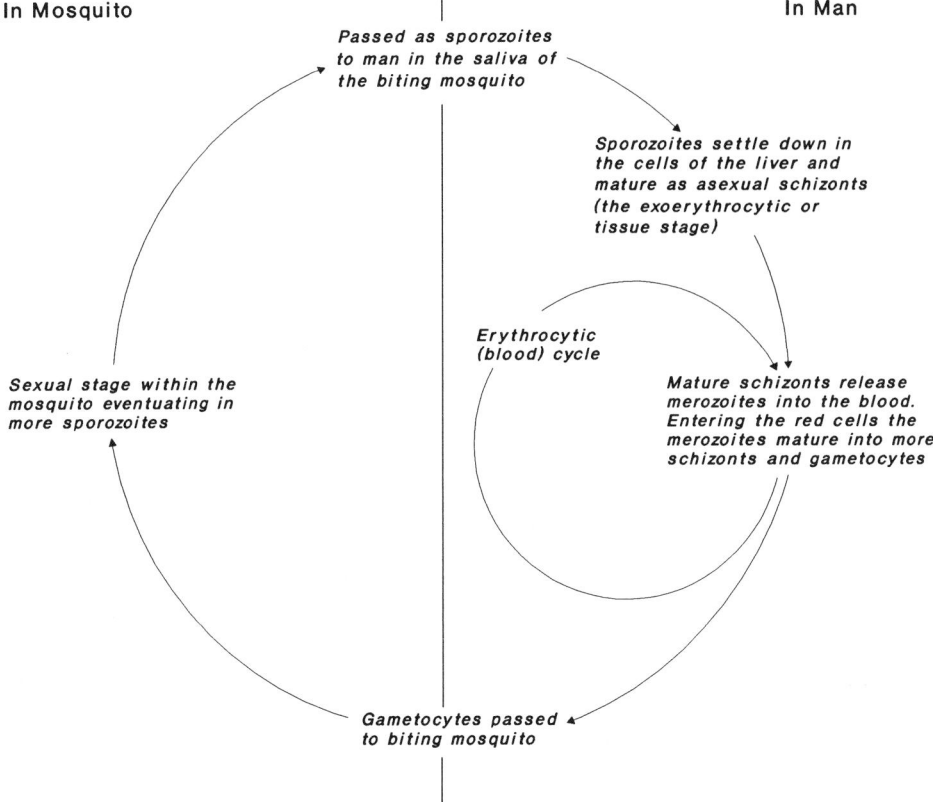

In Mosquito | In Man

Passed as sporozoites to man in the saliva of the biting mosquito

Sporozoites settle down in the cells of the liver and mature as asexual schizonts (the exoerythrocytic or tissue stage)

Erythrocytic (blood) cycle

Sexual stage within the mosquito eventuating in more sporozoites

Mature schizonts release merozoites into the blood. Entering the red cells the merozoites mature into more schizonts and gametocytes

Gametocytes passed to biting mosquito

Fig. 9.1. The life cycle of the malaria parasite. Adapted from G. Robert Coatney et al., *The Primate Malarias* (Bethesda, Md., 1971), 30.

nosebleed, diarrhea, jaundice, and pallor, the last indicative of severe anemia. If the body's defenses ultimately prevail, the cycle is broken and at least the parasites in the blood are destroyed. Remission and recovery follow.

From long association with humans, however, *Plasmodium* has evolved its own defenses against theirs. Defeated in the blood, the parasites can remain ensconced in some manner in the liver.[5] Within eight to ten months after the primary attack, they will again enter the blood. The cycle begins anew, and the fever returns, calling forth counterdefenses on the part of the host. The initial attack starts a process by which an immunity is acquired, and each successive relapse strengthens the immunity until all outward symptoms disappear. The immunity does not last long—only a few years. But the reintroduction of *Plasmodia* by the bite of a female

5. The relapse mechanism of the parasite is not clearly understood. Coatney et al., *Primate Malarias*, 31–37, succinctly reviews the state of knowledge as of 1971.

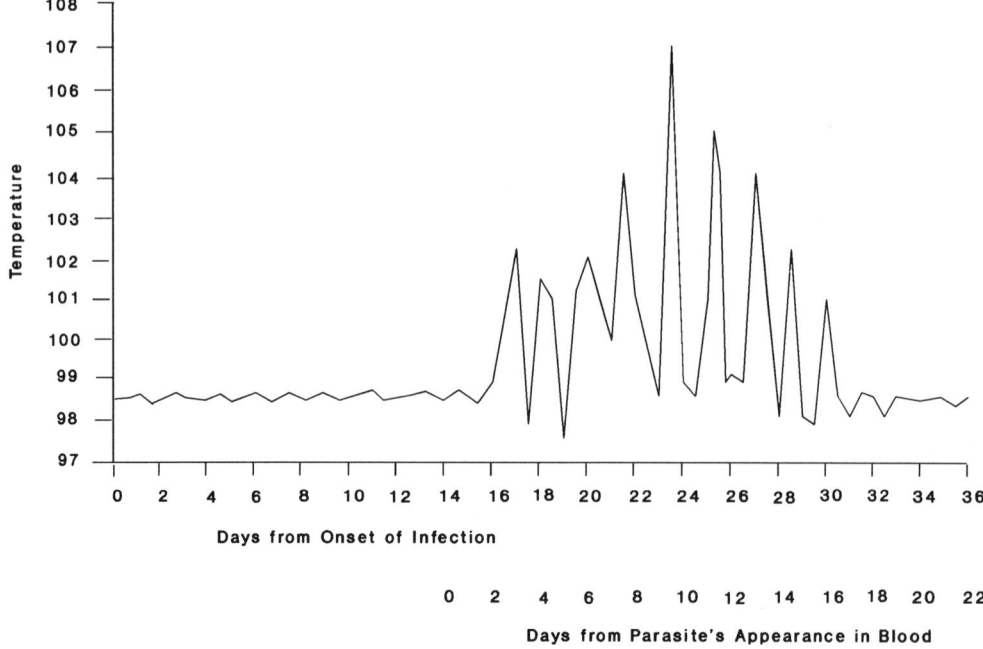

Fig. 9.2. Hypothetical clinical reaction to invasion by malaria *Plasmodium vivax* (a primary attack). Adapted from C. Merrill Whorton et al., "The Chesson Strain of *Plasmodium vivax* Malaria," pt. 3, "Clinical Aspects," *Journal of Infectious Diseases* 80 (1947): 237–49.

Anopheles brings on enough of an internal reaction to reinvigorate the immunity, even though it may not result in an observable reaction in the host.

Thus far our intent has been to sketch quickly and in idealized terms the principal features of malaria, in order to lay the ground for a more complicated discussion. First, our reference has been to genus *Plasmodium*, but genus implies species, and indeed there is a multiplicity of species. Four of these infect humans, two of them commonly: *Plasmodium vivax* and *Plasmodium falciparum*.[6] Between these two species there are clear differences in the reaction of the human host. The patterns of fever spikes vary, reflecting different patterns of parasitic development within the body. The intensity of the disease also varies, *vivax* being the more benign, *falciparum* the more virulent; mortality directly associated with untreated *vivax* is estimated at under 5 percent, while mortality associated with untreated *falciparum* can rise as high as 25 percent.[7] The classic relapse

6. *P. malariae* and *P. ovale* have been rarities in North America and hence are omitted here.
7. Emilio Pampana, *A Textbook of Malaria Eradication*, 2d ed., (London, 1969), 19.

pattern is that of *Plasmodium vivax*, there being little or no relapse associated with *falciparum*.

Acquired immunity likewise varies between species. Immunity to *vivax* is rapidly acquired and relatively long-lived (approximately three to five years); that to *falciparum* is more solid but shorter-lived and more dependent on regular reinfection for prolongation. And while there is a pronounced innate immunity to *vivax* among blacks, there seems to be no race-specific immunity to *falciparum*. Whites and blacks are clearly susceptible to infection — indeed, a significant portion of modern research on *falciparum* malaria takes place in black Africa — but blacks seem to tolerate an attack somewhat better than whites. Among both whites and blacks can be found what is termed the "sickle-cell trait," which seems to confer a resistance to infection, although the interdependence of this genetic trait and malaria on the one hand and the long association of blacks with a malarious Africa on the other have made the trait generally more common among blacks than among Caucasians.[8]

Within species, moreover, there are strains — an unknown number, of which only a few have been isolated in the laboratory — and there are clear differences in the reaction of the host to particular strains of the same species. Again, the pattern of fever spikes will vary slightly, but more important with reference to both species and strains is the fact that acquired immunities tend to be species- and strain-specific. A person who is infected by *Plasmodium vivax*, St. Elizabeth strain, for example, tends to develop resistance only to that strain.

Second, we have referred to the mosquito vector as simply the female anopheline, but this masks a complex reality involving a genus *Anopheles* (within the family Culicidae and tribe Anophelini), six subgenera, and a variety of species and subspecies that vary in range, breeding habitat, and biting characteristics, and also as carriers of the parasite. *Anopheles atropos* and *Anopheles bradleyi*, for example, breed in the saltwater pools and marshes of the coast from Texas to Maryland, but *atropos* prefers water with a high salt content, *bradleyi* a low; and while *bradleyi*, in common with most *Anopheles*, tends to confine its biting to dusk, *atropos* will swarm and bite in bright sunlight. *Anopheles crucians* is a species of the southeastern coastal plain, frequenting fresh to slightly brackish swamps and pools and the margins of ponds and lakes. In the early twentieth century it was

---

8. Coatney et al., *Primate Malarias*, 283: "There appears to be no racial or innate immunity among Negroes against falciparum malaria as has been observed for vivax malaria. . . . However, the Negro does have a tendency to be able to clinically tolerate falciparum malaria infections better than the Caucasians. The presence of genetic traits which inhibit parasite multiplication or survival, such as sickle cell hemoglobin and enzyme deficiencies, have been reported but are not universally accepted." Cf. Peter H. Wood, *Black Majority: Negroes in Colonial South Carolina from 1670 through the Stono Rebellion* (New York, 1974), 88–89.

suspected as the primary vector in tidewater Virginia, because of its high density in the area and its propensity to enter houses to bite.[9] *Anopheles punctipennis* has the greatest range of any North American species, breeding in shaded springs and pools or along the margins of streams from southern Canada to New Mexico and along the Pacific coast. It bites only outdoors, entering houses in late fall only to hibernate. *Anopheles quadrimaculatus* prefers open sunlit waters for breeding, and although it is one of the *anopheles* most susceptible to *Plasmodium* (hence most likely to carry the parasite back to human beings), it seems to have a decided preference for the blood of cows and horses. All of the anopheline mosquitoes share certain characteristics. They are creatures of short flight, normally ranging no more than one to two miles from their breeding places. They are highly affected by the weather. Optimal conditions for biting include a bright moonlit night, humidity about 85 percent, and a temperature in the low to mid-eighties. In a temperate climate the onset of cold weather brings on a suspension of all anopheline activity.

Species and strains of *Plasmodium* on the one hand; variety of *Anopheles* on the other — yet we have only touched on some of the many variables involved in what malariologist Mark F. Boyd has described as the most complex and contradictory of disease systems.[10] A third set of complications relates to the behavior of malaria in communities.

In the malarial system the disease manifestation in humans is only one part. *Anopheles* must be infected by a human host, who, in turn, must be infected by *Anopheles*, with the circular transmission dependent on both. An anopheline mosquito must have access to, and must bite, a person (and not a nearby horse or cow) when the blood of that person is carrying the single form of the parasite that will infect the mosquito — in general, during or shortly after a malarial attack. After enough time has elapsed to allow the completion of the parasitic cycle within the mosquito, the mosquito must bite again, passing on the single form of the parasite that will bring about reinfection. To use technical terms, an *Anopheles* with a sporozite-clear saliva biting a person free of gametocytes will have no more effect than to provoke a swat and a scratch! Within any given malarial community the degree to which the system is established is clearly dependent on the rate of transmission of the parasite from *Anopheles* to human being and back to mosquito through properly timed bites. At the lowest levels of endemicity, few infected mosquitos are abroad, few in the human population play host to the parasite, and transmission is only occa-

9. James Stevens Simmons, "The Transmission of Malaria by the *Anopheles* Mosquitoes of North America," in *Symposium on Human Malaria*, ed. Moulton, 114; Stanley B. Freeborn, "Anophelines of the Nearctic Region," in *Malariology*, ed. Boyd, 1:388.

10. Boyd, "Epidemiology of Malaria: Factors Related to the Intermediate Host," in *Malariology*, ed. Boyd, 1:552.

sional. At the very highest levels of endemicity — hyperendemicity — virtually all anopheline mosquitoes are infected, and they are so numerous that no member of the human population can avoid being bitten every night. Human infection is then virtually 100 percent, and transmission is virtually constant. Between these extremes lie an indefinite number of levels of endemicity.

To speak of levels of endemicity is not to speak directly of levels of clinical morbidity, that is, the number of persons in the population displaying observable symptoms. Recall that malarial infection results in the human host in a species- and strain-specific immunity but one of limited duration that is dependent for prolongation on reinfection (although not necessarily morbidity). In a malarial community the development of individual immunities tends to create a degree of group immunity. How effective that group immunity will be depends on the transmission level, or the level of endemicity. In communities of low endemicity individuals will be infected less often and group immunity will be lower than in areas of high endemicity. Clinical morbidity, group immunity, and endemicity levels interact to force a curvilinear relationship between the first and last, as sketched in figure 9.3. If we were to measure the endemic and clinical morbidity levels of a number of communities, we would find that morbidity climbs as endemicity rises, since a greater percentage of infectious bites by *Anopheles* leads to symptomatic malarial attacks. Yet the rate of morbidity will be balanced at some point by the rate of immunities in the population and then will begin to decline until, in a hyperendemic situation, morbidity is largely limited to children, nonimmune newcomers to the community, and pregnant women. Moreover, within any given community the level of endemicity (and consequently clinical morbidity) will tend to stabilize at a fixed figure. The figure may rise or fall as the number of anopheline mosquitoes in the area rises or falls, or as the number of nonimmune people changes, or when the onset of a new strain or species makes prior immunities irrelevant, or even as the spatial organization of the society shifts: a trend toward urban clustering, for example, will tend to decrease the proportionate access of mosquitoes to the population and bring a decline in the endemic level. But although the level of endemicity may change, there will invariably be a tendency toward stasis.[11]

Two other aspects of the malarial system in communities must be sketched before we turn to the subject at hand — malaria in the early Chesapeake region. First, whatever the endemic or morbidity level of a population, there is an areal definition to that population. The point is

11. A few malariologists, notably Ronald Ross, and statistician Alfred J. Lotka have attempted to reduce the malarial system to a mathematical model. See Mark F. Boyd, "Epidemiology: Factors Related to the Definitive Host," ibid., 683–87.

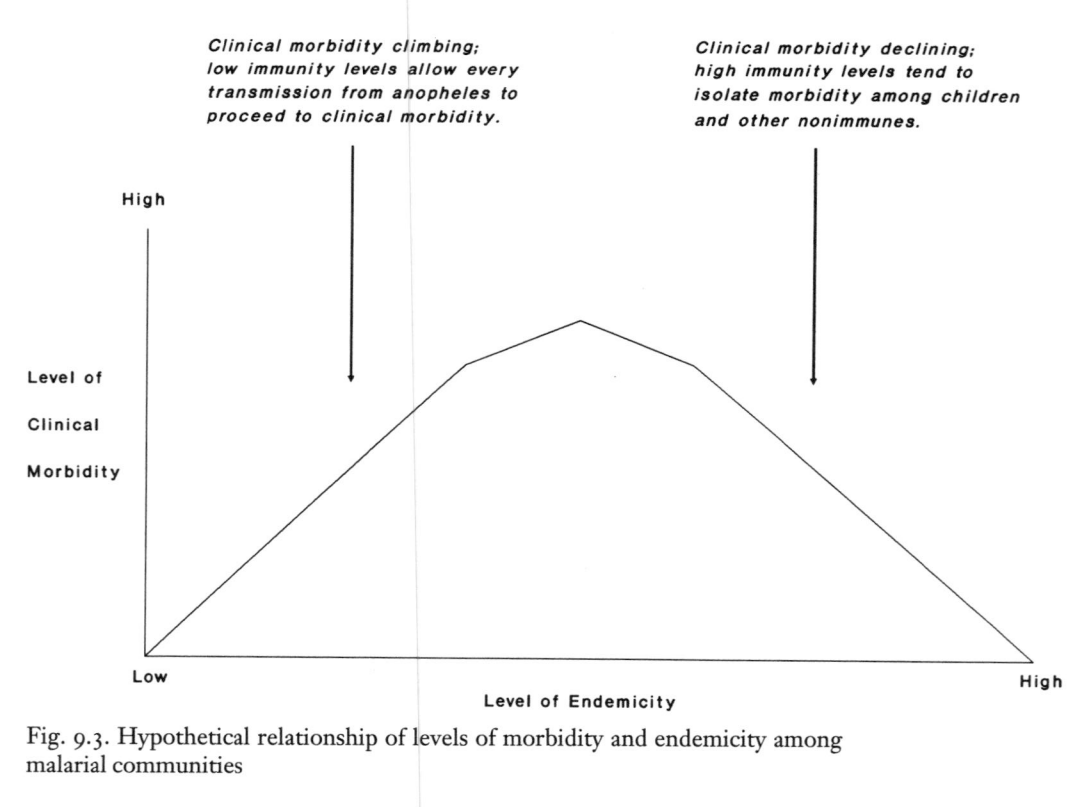

Fig. 9.3. Hypothetical relationship of levels of morbidity and endemicity among malarial communities

best made by an example. Consider a village located beside a saltwater swamp in which *Anopheles bradleyi* breed. Given the flight and breeding limitations of *bradleyi*, it is clear that even if our exemplifying village is highly endemic, another one, four miles away beside a freshwater pond need not be. The areal boundaries of the malarious population are thus defined by the mosquito. Presume that the pond by our second village is a breeding area for *Anopheles quadrimaculatus*. What then? It will remain malaria free only if no one laden with gametocytes travels to it from the first village. In this case the areal boundaries are set by levels of population mobility as well as by the mosquito. The example may seem exaggerated, but the abruptness of areal boundaries was clear even in the 1890s when Walter Reed noted that while malaria was endemic among the soldiers of Washington Barracks, on the low flats bordering the Anacostia and Potomac rivers in the District of Columbia, it was significantly less prevalent "among those who live in the more elevated section of the city" away from the flats.[12]

Second, in a temperate climate such as that of the Chesapeake malaria cannot achieve the hyperendemic level that follows from near-constant transmission. As we have noted, the onset of cold weather inhibits anopheline activity and thus regularly interrupts transmission. In the absence of transmission, morbidity declines, individual immunities diminish, and the nonimmune increase; group immunity thus deteriorates, leaving the population vulnerable to what is to come. Latent infections will persist over the winter; and as these bring on a few malarial attacks in the spring, as cases of *vivax* contracted during the previous fall reappear as relapses, and as mosquitoes start biting again, transmission restarts and the malarial system is reinvigorated. The endemic level, having declined during the winter, rises again. Symptomatic morbidity steadily increases through the spring and summer to a peak in the autumn, then abruptly declines with the coming of another winter. Figure 9.4, a seasonal plot of 614 malaria cases treated at the Johns Hopkins University Hospital in the early 1890s, displays the seasonality of the two major species of malaria then current in the Chesapeake area.

Was there malaria in the early Chesapeake? Historiographically, the question has been asked mainly with reference to Virginia, and the answer has been mixed. Thomas Jefferson Wertenbaker, reflecting a traditional view, wrote in 1914 of the "great swarms of mosquitoes" that rose from "the stagnant pools" around Jamestown and attacked the settlers of 1607 "with a sting more deadly than that of the Indian arrow or the Spanish musket ball." In 1930 the tradition was challenged by Wyndham B. Blan-

---

12. Hugh R. Gilmore, Jr., "Malaria at Washington Barracks and Fort Myer: A Survey of Walter Reed," *Bulletin of the History of Medicine* 29 (1955): 348.

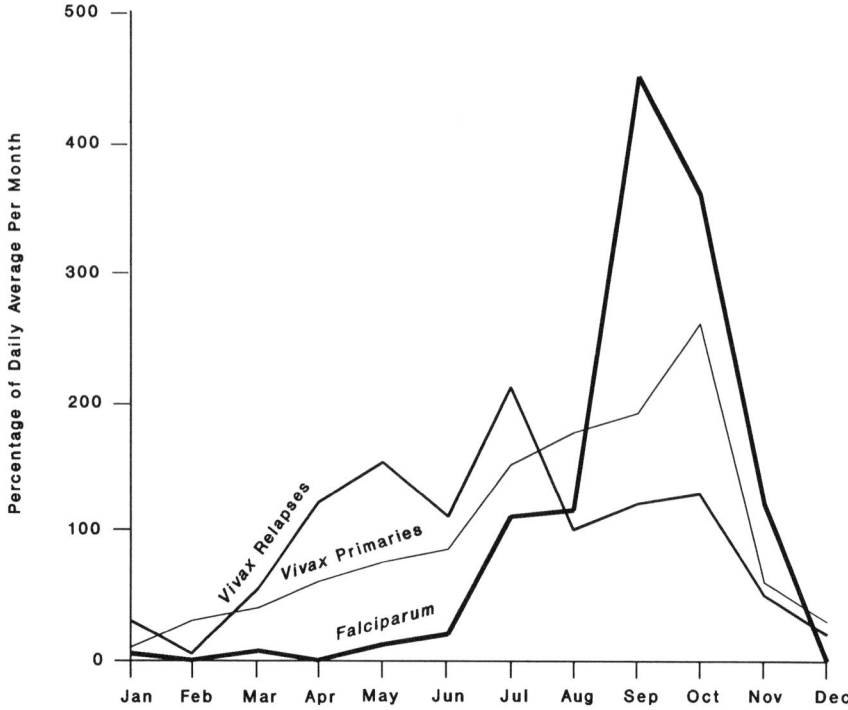

Fig. 9.4. Seasonal distribution of malaria cases treated at Johns Hopkins Hospital, Baltimore, 1889–94. Adapted from *Malariology: A Comprehensive Survey of All Aspects of This Group of Diseases from a Global Standpoint*, ed. Mark F. Boyd (Philadelphia, 1949), 1:557. The distribution is expressed as the percentage of daily average per month to allow comparison of different sample sizes and to minimize the effect of months of different lengths. The percentage is arrived at by a series of divisions: $[(Em/Dm) / (Ey/365.25)] \times 100$ where Em = the number of events in a month, Dm = the number of days in a month, Ey = the total number of events in the sample. February is assigned 28.25 days.

ton. "No one doubts that there were marshes, mosquitoes and sickness along the James River," but "there is no evidence . . . that malaria was responsible for a preponderating part of the great mortalities." Blanton was rebutted by John Duffy in 1953: with malaria in the Carolina lowcountry to the south and among the French and English to the north, "it is highly improbable that the early settlers in Virginia were exempt." In 1957 Blanton replied that there was no natural habitat around Jamestown for *Anopheles quadrimaculatus* (even if this was true, Blanton ignored the fact that *quadrimaculatus* is but one of many species). He also contended that malaria was not introduced until late in the century — by which time the colonists, by clearing the forests, had created a habitat for mosquitoes — and that it was brought by slaves from the malaria-infested areas of the west African coast.[13] This mini-debate was in reality a nondebate, for the participants had different frames of reference. Blanton's gaze was fixed on the great mortalities of the years to the mid-1620s, from which he extrapolated forward; Duffy, with a broader view of the whole colonial period, inferred from the whole to the part.[14]

All indications are that malaria was imported into the Americas by Europeans. The disease in its milder form (*vivax*) is thought to have been general in Europe in the sixteenth and seventeenth centuries; Oliver Cromwell seems to have been only one of the more prominent sufferers. The more virulent *falciparum* is thought to have been prevalent in large parts of Africa. But the Americas appear to have been free of the disease until the arrival of Europeans.[15] G. Robert Coatney and his colleagues find the evidence of pre-Columbian malaria too scant to be convincing, while to Saul Jarcho the existence of the mosquito in precontact America is certain, of *Anopheles* probable, and of malaria improbable although not impossible.[16]

If malaria was not indigenous to the Americas, it could only have been introduced by the entry of infected individuals into areas where *Anopheles* breed. When or from where such persons arrived in Virginia — directly from England or by way of the Caribbean — is irrelevant and certainly indeterminable. Although a variety of strains and perhaps even both major species may have been introduced by diverse carriers at a fairly early date, a more probable model, given the flow of immigration and the prevalence of *vivax* in Europe and *falciparum* in Africa, would have strains of the former entering during the first half of the century, followed by the grad-

13. Wertenbaker, *Virginia under the Stuarts, 1607–1688* (Princeton, N.J., 1914), 11; Blanton, *Medicine in Virginia in the Seventeenth Century* (Richmond, 1930), 54; Duffy, *Epidemics in Colonial America* (Baton Rouge, La., 1953), 207n. Duffy made good use of St. Julien Ravenel Childs, *Malaria and Colonization in the Carolina Low Country, 1526–1696* (Baltimore, 1940), but to that study must be added Wood, *Black Majority*, chap. 3, and Blanton, "Epidemics, Real and Imaginary, and Other Factors Influencing Seventeenth Century Virginia's Population," *Bulletin of the History of Medicine* 31 (1957): 454–62. For a malariologist's answer to the general question of the historical development of malaria in North America, see Mark F. Boyd, "An Historical Sketch of the Prevalence of Malaria in North America," *American Journal of Tropical Medicine* 21 (1941): 223–44.

14. Hence Blanton could make a part of his chain of evidence for the whole seventeenth century the "happy, intelligent, and vigorous" nature of the Powhatan Indians of 1607, arguing that they would have been otherwise if malaria had been prevalent, for "malaria notoriously destroys happiness, intelligence and vigor" ("Epidemics, Real and Imaginary," 457).

15. Frederick F. Cartwright and Michael D. Biddiss, *Disease and History* (New York, 1972), 138–44.

16. Coatney et al., *Primate Malarias*, 7; Saul Jarcho, "Some Observations on Disease in Prehistoric North America," *Bulletin of the History of Medicine* 38 (1964): 6–9.

ual establishment (perhaps spotty) of areas of stable, low-level endemicity. The shattering of this picture would occur as blacks in numbers began arriving from a variety of African areas, bringing with them *falciparum*, as well as new strains of *vivax*.[17] In this model, symptomatic morbidity — the number of clinical cases — would rise gradually to about 1650, by which time the occasional, seemingly random cases of the early decades would be giving way to seasonal outbreaks. Through the remainder of the century epidemiclike incidents would mark the entry of each new strain or species, the general level of malaria morbidity rising a bit higher in the aftermath of each such outbreak.[18] The model also suggests that a qualitative change occurred sometime in the second half of the century as *falciparum* entered the colony, precipitating more virulent and wracking attacks, a phenomenon also noted by Peter Wood in his study of South Carolina slavery. The evidence from Carolina suggests to Wood that the benign *vivax* was prevalent in the 1670s but was supplanted by the more virulent *falciparum* in the 1680s.[19]

The literary evidence for Virginia supports this model, although in relating the archaic and imprecise terminology of the sources to the modern symptomatology of the disease, we enter on the most treacherous ground of medical history. Blanton, for example, keyed his search for malaria on the uses of the word "ague" as referring to the combination of chills and fevers so generally associated in the popular mind with the disease. But chills may accompany fevers other than malarial, and malarial fevers are not always accompanied by chills. In a modern study of 201 paroxysms, 137 were found to be unaccompanied by chills, leading the investigators to conclude that "the term 'chills and fevers' inadequately describes" a malarial attack.[20] Similarly, the words "intermittent" and

17. White susceptibility to diseases prevalent among blacks would be the other side of the coin with regard to Philip D. Curtin's thesis of black susceptibility to diseases prevalent among whites. See Curtin, "Epidemiology and the Slave Trade," *Political Science Quarterly* 83 (1968): 190–216.

18. This is the picture drawn by a 100-year simulation based on the mathematics in Boyd, "Epidemiology: Factors Related to the Definitive Host." It has been extended to incorporate elementary shifts in the human population and changes in the immunity level to reflect assumptions as to the sequential introduction of species (*vivax* followed by *falciparum*) and the periodic introduction of new strains. Jon Kukla subsequently elaborated upon this model, accentuating to a greater degree the English origins of the disease, in "Kentish Agues and American Distempers: The Transmission of Malaria from England to Virginia in the Seventeenth Century," *Southern Studies* 25 (1986): 135–47.

19. Wood, *Black Majority*, 87.

20. G. Robert Coatney and Martin D. Young, "A Study of the Paroxysms Resulting from Induced Infections of *Plasmodium vivax*." *American Journal of Hygiene* 35 (1942): 141. C. Merrill Whorton et al., "The Chesson Strain of *Plasmodium vivax* Malaria," pt. 3, "Clinical

"remittent," used in the sources as adjectives for "fever," may or may not refer to the characteristic fever spikes of malaria, as may "quotidian," "tertian," and "quartan" used to describe the timing of the spikes. References to chinchona or its synonyms — Peruvian bark, Jesuit bark, or simply "the bark" — may also be indicative of malaria, for chinchona was introduced into Europe as a specific remedy for what is generally considered to have been malaria. But such references are not infallible, for the bark was sometimes utilized for fevers other than malarial, and its efficacy was widely questioned; hence it was not invariably given.[21] Nevertheless, we must have a measure of confidence: even if many of the references to ague, the varieties of fever, and "the bark" are misapplied, the remainder correctly point to malaria. From the sources it seems clear that the "agues and fevers" that were only occasional in the first fifty years in Virginia became more general and more severe (reflecting the entry of *falciparum?*) in the second fifty and on into the eighteenth century.

There is no need here to review the occasional evidence for seventeenth-century malaria cited by Blanton.[22] Clearly, by the 1680s the "seasoning" — that period of illness which almost inevitably befell a newcomer to the Chesapeake — was associated with what we can take for malaria. Newcomers might assume any sickness that struck them to be a "seasoning," as Robert Beverley noted in his *History of Virginia* and as George Hume did in 1723. To Hume a whole succession of illnesses — from "a severe flux" to a "now and then" bout with "the fever and ague" — added up to "a most severe" seasoning.[23] But the longtime resident of Virginia was more precise. William Fitzhugh noted in 1687 that his newly arrived sister had had "two or three small fits of a feaver and ague, which now has left her, and so consequently her seasoning [is] over." And again, in another letter: "My Sister has had her seasoning . . . two or three fits of a feaver and ague." John Clayton, Virginia's scientific parson, wrote of

Aspects," *Journal of Infectious Diseases* 80 (1947): 241, reported chills in only 46 percent of 158 primary attacks.

21. A. W. Haggis, "Fundamental Errors in the Early History of Chinchona," *Bulletin of the History of Medicine* 10 (1941): 417–59, 568–92.

22. Blanton found six references up to 1700. See his *Medicine in the Seventeenth Century*, 52–53, and "Epidemics, Real and Imaginary," 458. A few escaped him, notably John Clayton's cited below in note 24. To some extent the number of references is a function of the quantity and types of materials extant from the period rather than of the prevalence of the disease.

23. Beverley, *The History and Present State of Virginia*, ed. Louis B. Wright (Chapel Hill, N.C., 1947), 306: "The first sickness that any New-Comer happens to have there, he unfairly calls a Seasoning, be it Fever, Ague, or any thing else, that his own folly, or excesses bring upon him"; George Hume to Ninian Hume, 20 June 1723, *Virginia Magazine of History and Biography* 20 (1912): 397–400.

"Seasonings, which are an intermiting feaver, or rather a continued feaver with quotidian paroxisms," in describing that same year the "distempers" among the English.[24]

By the 1680s sharp geographical differences in levels of health were being noted in the colony. To a French traveler of 1686–87 the inhabitants of tidewater Gloucester County "looked so sickly that I judged the country to be unhealthy"; those of Stafford and old Rappahannock were obviously healthier, "their complexions clear and lively." The Virginians gave him a reason he considered "quite plausible": "Along the seashore, and also along the rivers which contain salt, because of the tide, the inhabitants in these places are rarely free from fever during the hot weather; they call this a local sickness; but the salt in the rivers disappears about twenty leagues from the seas, just as one enters the county of Rappahannock, and those who live beyond that point do not suffer from it." Clayton, too, noted the geographic difference, adding a hint of autumnal seasonality: "So far as the Salt Waters reach the Country is deemed less healthy. In the Freshes they more rarely are troubled with the Seasonings, and those Endemical Distempers about *September* and *October*."[25] All three phenomena are commensurate with a hypothesis of widespread malaria. As we have seen, autumnal seasonality is inherent in temperate-zone malaria; so too are the susceptibility of newcomers — they must develop immunities to the specific species and strains of *Plasmodia* present in an area — and the sharp boundaries between infected and uninfected populations, although in this case the boundaries would seem to have been only temporary. Time would be required to create in newly settled areas the conditions necessary to maintain the endemic levels that existed in older areas.[26]

24. William Fitzhugh to Henry Fitzhugh, 18 July 1687, Fitzhugh to Dr. Ralph Smith, 1 July 1687, in Richard Beale Davis, ed., *William Fitzhugh and His Chesapeake World, 1676–1701: The Fitzhugh Letters and Other Documents* (Chapel Hill, N.C., 1963), 229, 230; Clayton to Dr. Nehemiah Grew, 1687, in Edmund and Dorothy Smith Berkeley, eds., *The Reverend John Clayton, a Parson with a Scientific Mind: His Scientific Writings and Other Related Papers* (Charlottesville, Va., 1965), 26. Richard H. Shryock, *Medicine and Society in America, 1660–1860* (New York, 1960), 87, generally associated malaria with the colonial "seasoning"; so did travelers describing the entry of newcomers into the malarious Mississippi Valley of the nineteenth century. See Michael Owen Jones, "Climate and Disease: The Traveler Describes America," *Bulletin of the History of Medicine* 41 (1967): 256.

25. Gilbert Chinard, ed., *A Huguenot Exile in Virginia: or Voyages of a Frenchman Exiled for His Religion with a Description of Virginia and Maryland* (New York, 1934), 130, 174; Clayton to the Royal Society, 1688, in Berkeley and Berkeley, *John Clayton*, 54. Clayton went on to suggest that an investigation of the phenomena might result in "several beneficial Discoveries, not only in relation to those Distempers in *America*, but perhaps take in your *Kentish Agues*." The latter phrase has generally been understood to refer to malaria.

26. In contrast to descriptions of other parts of Virginia, John Banister's description of the falls area of the James makes no mention of illness and disease, implying a relatively disease-

For the eighteenth century the literary evidence is clearer, and there is no question among historians as to the prevalence of malaria. John Oldmixon, who presumably drew some of his information from William Byrd II, wrote at the turn of the century that "the *Seasoning* here, as in other parts of *America*, is a Fever or Ague, which the Change of Climate and Diet generally throws new Comers into; the Bark is in *Virginia* a Sovereign Remedy to this Disease." Beverley wrote of the Virginians' "Intermitting Fevers, as well as their Agues," as "very troublesome" and cited "*Cortex Peruviana*" as a remedy that "seldom or never fails to remove the Fits." Byrd dosed with the bark his family, himself, and his fellow commissioners of the North Carolina boundary survey. In 1735 he referred to the shipment of "infused" bark to Virginia by England's "Drugsters and Apothecarys" — that is, bark which had been steeped in water, the water being used in England and the residual bark shipped to the colonies — as "almost as bad as Murder." Hugh Jones wrote of a people "subject to feavers and agues, which is the country distemper, a severe fit of which (called a seasoning) most expect, some time after their arrival." Chinchona was "a perfect catholicon for that sickness . . . which being taken and repeated in a right manner, seldom fails of a cure."[27]

Sources from the latter half of the century contain abundant references to what can be construed as malaria, leading Blanton to conclude that "hardly any section . . . escaped the inevitable 'Ague and Fever.' "[28] Indeed, here and there in the literature are such detailed accounts that one is tempted to diagnose individual cases — Landon Carter's Sukey, for example. Autumnal fevers were pronounced in both 1756 and 1757, Carter

---

free area during the late seventeenth century (Joseph and Nesta Ewan, *John Banister and His Natural History of Virginia, 1678–1692* [Urbana, Ill., 1970]). At the end of the eighteenth century, Thomas Jefferson wrote that "Richmond was not well chosen as the place to shake off a fever and ague in the months of Aug. Sep. and Oct. till frost. All it's inhabitants who can afford it leave it for the upper country during that season" (Wyndham B. Blanton, *Medicine in Virginia in the Eighteenth Century* [Richmond, 1931], 67). In the nineteenth and twentieth centuries no malarial "fall line" existed as was suggested by the earlier distinction between "the salts" and "the freshes." See the county morbidity and mortality statistics for 1927–32 in Frederick L. Hoffman, *Malaria in Virginia, North Carolina, and South Carolina* (Newark, N.J., 1933).

27. Oldmixon, *The British Empire in America*, 1 (London, 1708): 294; Beverley, *History of Virginia*, 306; Louis B. Wright and Marion Tinling, eds., *The Secret Diary of William Byrd of Westover, 1709–1712* (Richmond, 1941), 232, 372–73, 386–89, 538, 589; Louis B. Wright, ed., *The Prose Works of William Byrd of Westover: Narratives of a Colonial Virginian* (Cambridge, Mass., 1966), 102, 130, 189, 340–42, 348; William Byrd to Mrs. Otway, 2 Oct. 1735, *Virginia Magazine of History and Biography* 36 (1928): 121, in which Byrd, as Clayton had earlier (see note 25 above), associated the Virginia "distemper" with "your Kentish Distemper"; Jones, *The Present State of Virginia*, ed. Richard L. Morton (Chapel Hill, N.C., 1956), 85.

28. Blanton, *Medicine in Virginia in the Eighteenth Century*, 67.

writing of the fall of the latter year that it was a "very Aguish Season" when nothing "but the barke" would do and noting that "it has been more usefull this year than common." During the autumn of 1756 Sukey was among the sixty-odd in his family and labor force to take sick. A year later, in the midst of a still worse fever season, Sukey came down again, falling into a monthly pattern of attacks that extended through the autumn and early winter, subsided during the coldest weather, then reappeared in March 1758. In describing his daughter's illnesses, Carter noted time and again the secondary symptoms associated with malaria, from nausea and vomiting to pains and pallor. But most telling is his running account of the course of Sukey's fever. In figure 9.5 the description of five days of Sukey's first 1757 fever in August is superimposed on a modern fever chart of a quotidian (intermittent-remittent type) clinical attack of *Plasmodium falciparum*. Was Sukey's a case of malaria? Diagnosis from such evidence is impossible; all the historian can hope for is consonance between historical evidence and medical understanding. The literary description of Sukey's illness seems entirely consonant with malaria.[29]

Presuming that, from the literary evidence, a circumstantial case can be made for the presence of malaria in the Chesapeake region, or at least in Virginia, in the seventeenth and eighteenth centuries, what demographic effects might follow? Can we discern these effects and substantiate to an extent the literary case already made? In other words, does the hypothesis of malaria fit, perhaps even explain, the empirical evidence? The question requires consideration of as much as possible of the demographic analysis of early America done to date. It requires, too, the drawing of analogies between early America, for which no direct measurement of malaria or its effects is available, and malarious areas of the world where measurements have been made during the twentieth century.

Since 1967, when Philip J. Greven, Jr., formally introduced early Americanists to the startling possibilities for research opened by French demographic historians, a great deal of sophisticated demographic work has been done on New England and, recently, on the early Chesapeake region.[30] This work has varied in quality and to some extent in methodology. It has been confined for the most part to explorations of particular

29. Sukey's illness can be followed to her death in Greene, *Diary of Carter*, 1:127–222. In the case of prominent men, even more positive "diagnosis" is common, for example, the diagnosis of Washington as suffering from "chronic malaria" in Blanton, *Medicine in Virginia in the Eighteenth Century*, 309.

30. Greven, "Historical Demography and Colonial America: A Review Article," *William and Mary Quarterly*, 3d ser., 24 (1967): 438–54. Maris A. Vinovskis, "Mortality Rates and Trends in Massachusetts before 1860," *Journal of Economic History* 32 (1972): 184–213, is a good introduction to, and critique of, the New England work, particularly that of Greven, Kenneth A. Lockridge, Susan L. Norton, and Vinovskis's own. The Chesapeake work is cited in note 2 above.

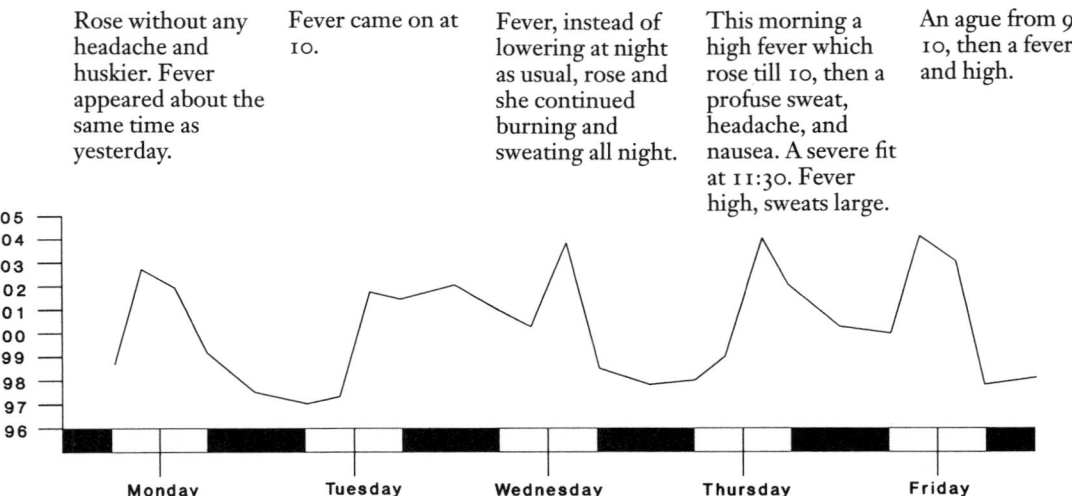

Fig. 9.5. Eighteenth-century fever description arising from an infection of *Plasmodium falciparum* super-scribed on a twentieth-century fever chart. Fever description paraphrased from Jack P. Greene, ed., *The Diary of Colonel Landon Carter of Sabine Hall, 1752–1778* (Charlottesville, Va., 1965), 1:165–67; fever chart adapted from S. F. Kitchen, "The Infection in the Intermediate Host: Symptomatology, *Falciparum* Malaria," in *A Symposium on Human Malaria with Special Reference to North America and the Caribbean Region*, ed. Forest Ray Moulton (Washington, D.C., 1941), 198, case no. 1164. Monday was the second day of fever.

locales, and for both regions such local studies are few. Investigation has nonetheless advanced to the point where a few basic phenomena seem to be coming into focus — four in particular with regard to mortality. First, radically different mortality schedules seem to have obtained in New England and the Chesapeake region. Men and women in the northern colonies tended to live considerably longer lives than did their contemporaries to the south. Second, in the Chesapeake and in seventeenth-century Salem, Massachusetts (but not apparently in other New England areas studied so far), women fifteen to forty-five years, the childbearing years, seem to have run a substantially greater risk of death than did males of the same age. The third finding emerges from the second: even within a particular region and time period mortality rates in general, and sex-specific mortality rates in particular, seem to have varied by locality. Finally, in New England at least, mortality rates shifted over time. In the eighteenth century life expectancies rose from seventeenth-century levels in some areas and for some segments of the population and fell in others, the net effect being a tendency toward convergence — the "washing out" of differences. All four of these phenomena can be seen in table 9.1, drawn from studies of Andover and Salem, Massachusetts, and Middlesex County, Virginia. But the table also suggests, in its confusion of sample definitions and age groupings, that such cross-study comparisons furnish grounds for only very broad general statements.

Still, the broad statements are enough to prompt questions. Why a difference in mortality between New England and the Chesapeake? Why a shift in mortality over time within New England? Why, in the seventeenth century, a sex-related difference in mortality during the years between fifteen and forty-five? Piecemeal explanations have been offered with respect to the New England data. Rising mortality rates and falling life expectancies between the seventeenth and eighteenth centuries have been attributed to the rise of population density to the point where infectious diseases could be supported. Although this plausible supposition accounts for some of the data, it does not explain those from Salem where mortality rates tended to fall slightly. Maris Vinovskis has related high death rates among Salem's females in the seventeenth century to maternal mortality; but were the conditions of childbirth so very different between Salem and nearby Ipswich where Susan Norton has found "no significant attrition of the female population during the years when . . . married women would be bearing children"?[31] Did the care of women in childbirth improve so greatly in the eighteenth century as to account for the

---

31. Vinovskis, "Mortality Rates," 201; Susan L. Norton, "Population Growth in Colonial America: A Study of Ipswich, Massachusetts," *Population Studies* 25 (1971): 442.

Table 9.1. Comparative adult life expectancies: the Chesapeake region and New England (expressed as expected years yet to live)

Achieved age	Andover, Mass. b. 1670–99		Salem, Mass. d. 17th century		Middlesex Co., Va. b. 1650–1710		Salem, Mass. d. 18th century		Andover, Mass. b. 1730–59	
	Male	Female	Male	Female	Male	Female	Male	Female	Male	Female
15	—	—	—	—	—	24.9	—	—	—	—
20	44.8	42.1	36.1	21.4	28.8	19.8	35.5	37.0	41.6	43.1
25	—	—	—	—	23.7	16.3	—	—	—	—
30	38.7	35.9	29.2	20.0	19.4	13.6	30.3	32.6	36.3	36.5
35	—	—	—	—	15.8	10.7	—	—	—	—
40	31.4	29.0	24.1	20.9	13.0	8.6	25.3	26.3	28.4	30.9
45	—	—	—	—	10.0	9.2	—	—	—	—
50	23.5	22.4	19.1	14.4	7.7	9.3	19.6	21.1	24.5	25.0
55	—	—	—	—	7.7	7.7	—	—	—	—
60	15.2	15.9	14.5	16.2	5.8	7.9	14.5	16.4	17.2	18.8
65	—	—	—	—	5.0	5.0	—	—	—	—
70	10.2	11.9	10.0	10.0	3.6	3.7	10.0	10.0	10.9	12.0
75	—	—	—	—	2.9	5.2	—	—	—	—
80	6.7	9.5	—	—	—	—	—	—	7.1	8.3
85	—	—	—	—	—	—	—	—	—	—
90+	5.0	6.2	—	—	—	—	—	—	5.0	5.0

Sources and notes: Achieved age represents the lower inclusive boundary of a group. In the case of Middlesex: 15–19, 20–24, 25–29, etc.; Andover: 20–29, 30–39; 40–49, etc.; but N.B. Salem: 21–30, 31–40, 41–50, etc., with an estimate of 10 inserted for 71-plus. For Andover and Salem, see Maris A. Vinovskis, "Mortality Rates and Trends in Massachusetts before 1860," *Journal of Economic History* 32 (1972): 198–99 (drawing upon the work of Philip J. Greven, Jr., and James K. Somerville, respectively). For Middlesex, see appendixes 1 and 2 of Darrett B. and Anita H. Rutman, " 'Now-Wives and Sons-in-Law': Parental Death in a Seventeenth-Century Virginia County," in *The Chesapeake in the Seventeenth Century: Essays on Anglo-American Society*, ed. Thad W. Tate and David L. Ammerman (Chapel Hill, N.C., 1979), 175–82. The Middlesex table, both here and there, is based upon data for subjects known to have achieved marriageable age and to have chosen to marry. Both sources discuss at length the population and procedures underlying the tables.

congruence of male and female life expectancies found by Vinovskis in Salem and reflected in table 9.1? Most importantly, none of the piecemeal answers applies to the sharp contrast between New England and Chesapeake mortality.

Does a consideration of malaria suggest a more general answer? The most obvious impact of malaria is on the general level of public health. Malaria is not notorious as a "killer" disease: the 5 and 25 percent mortality rates cited earlier are extremes. It is rather "the great debilitator"; it lowers the level of general health and the ability to resist other diseases. One modern study estimates that for every death ascribed to malaria in an infected population, five additional deaths are actually due to malaria acting in concert with other diseases.[32] Carter's Sukey is a case in point. Weakened by her bouts with a malarial fever, and undoubtedly anemic, she died in the spring of 1758 from what appears to have been a respiratory infection.

That an inverse relationship exists between the degree of malaria morbidity and the death rate is indicated in modern Guatemala. A malaria eradication program was initiated there in 1957, and the death rate declined 20 percent between 1958 and 1963. In Ceylon, where both eradication and a concerted attempt to expand medical facilities began immediately after World War II, the death rate declined by two-thirds between 1946 and 1953, with roughly 23 percent of the decline attributable to the malaria eradication program.[33] Thus a hypothesis of a malarious Chesapeake and a relatively nonmalarious New England might well explain a considerable part of the disparity between New England and Chesapeake mortality rates.

Note, however, that we refer to New England as "relatively" free of malaria. We mean to imply a difference of degree rather than an absolute difference, for there is evidence of malaria in seventeenth-century New England. Duffy describes "attacks of pernicious malaria" in Boston in 1658, western Connecticut in 1668, Salem in 1683, and Boston again in 1690. For some reason, however, the northern boundary of malaria shifted in the eighteenth century, leaving New England entirely free of the disease after roughly the mid-century mark.[34]

32. Peter Newman, *Malaria Eradication and Population Growth, with Special Reference to Ceylon and British Guiana* (Ann Arbor, Mich., 1965), 77.

33. S. A. Meegama, "Malaria Eradication and Its Effect on Mortality Levels," *Population Studies* 21 (1967): 207–8, 232. The effect of eradication on mortality rates is the subject of an intense debate, one largely fought out in the pages of *Population Studies*. We have adjusted Meegama's figures to reflect R. H. Gray, "The Decline of Mortality in Ceylon and the Demographic Effects of Malaria Control," ibid., 28 (1974): 226–27.

34. Duffy, *Epidemics*, 206–7, 213. Oliver Wendell Holmes's "Dissertation of Intermittent Fever in New England," *Boylston Prize Dissertations* (Boston, 1838), is, from start to finish, a compendium of quotations indicative of malaria in New England.

The whole question of endemic (as distinct from epidemic) disease is undeveloped in early American historiography in general, and for New England specifically, but one can make a calculated guess that malaria had only a marginal foothold in New England even in the seventeenth century and that levels of endemicity varied among the closed populations of the area.[35] Among some, the disease was virtually nonexistent (but the population, lacking immunity, would be susceptible to sudden, short-lived periods of morbidity); among others, malaria was relatively well established.

This view would be consonant with the findings of modern malariologists who break down national malariometric and morbidity rates into regional and even village rates and find enormous variety. It would also be consonant with the diversity of mortality rates being found by historians of New England and—if we assume that Salem was an area of relatively well-ensconced malaria—with the two peculiarities of Salem's mortality schedule presented by Vinovskis. The first is the suggestion that while in other New England towns that have been studied mortality rose in the eighteenth century, Salem's mortality declined, that there was, in effect, a tendency among the towns for mortality to converge. Such a tendency would be very familiar to students of eradication programs; and what was the disappearance of malaria from eighteenth-century New England but a form of natural eradication?[36] The second is the high death rate for women in their childbearing years, which, although unique to Salem among the seventeenth-century New England towns studied, was shared with Middlesex in tidewater Virginia.

Exaggerated maternal mortality can be directly associated with endemic malaria, a relationship intuitively perceived in the malarious South of a half century ago by country doctors who routinely dosed their pregnant patients with quinine and more recently demonstrated in a controlled study of 250 pregnant women in urban Nigeria.[37] The nature of

---

35. Richard H. Shryock's complaint in his "Medical Sources and the Social Historian," originally published in the *American Historical Review* 41 (1935–36): 458–73, and reprinted in Richard H. Shryock, *Medicine in America: Historical Essays* (Baltimore, 1966), is that historians in general, and medical historians specifically, have emphasized the story of medical disasters (epidemics). "It is easier to find records of a sudden 'visitation' than it is to trace obscure, endemic conditions; and once written, the former makes more spectacular reading. Hence the universal attention accorded 'the Black Death.' Hence also the neglect of contemporary endemic diseases, which in the long run were more fatal and perhaps equally significant in their social consequences" (p. 278).

36. For example, Gray, "Decline of Mortality," 226–27.

37. Warren K. Stratman-Thomas, "The Infection in the Intermediate Host: Symptomatology, *vivax* Malaria," and S. F. Kitchen, "The Infection in the Intermediate Host: Symptomatology, *falciparum* Malaria," in *Symposium on Human Malaria*, ed. Moulton, 187–88, 203–4; H. M. Gilles et al., "Malaria, Anaemia, and Pregnancy," *Annals of Tropical Medicine and Parasitology* 63 (1969): 245–63. See also P. Tilly, "Anaemia in Parturient Women, with Special Reference to Malaria Infection of the Placenta," ibid., 109–15; C. A. Gill, "The

the linkage is still undetermined, but the indirect evidence indicates that pregnancy tends to nullify immunities, paving the way for a buildup of parasites, morbidity, and pronounced anemia, with a consequent hazard of abortion, premature labor, and the childbirth death of both mother and infant. Modern medical researchers cannot, of course, measure mortality directly, for of necessity they intervene to stop the course of the disease. Neither can modern medical research duplicate the conditions that exaggerated the hazards in the seventeenth and eighteenth centuries: large households crowded into small houses, exposing anemic, periodically feverish mothers-to-be to contagious ailments; living conditions that can only be described as dirty, with a consequent exposure of the mother to septicemia; and above all, a counterproductive medical practice: the bleeding and stringent dieting that William Byrd imposed on his pregnant and presumably malarious and anemic wife could hardly have been efficacious.[38]

Analogy can, to an extent, supply what the medical research leaves out. Puttalam district, Ceylon, in the late 1930s was an area roughly comparable to Middlesex County, Virginia, in the late seventeenth and early eighteenth centuries. Both were rural; both were devoid of modern medicine; in both, childbirth was managed by traditionally rather than medically oriented midwives; and both (Puttalam district for a certainty and Middlesex for the sake of argument) were malarious. Figure 9.6 graphs age- and sex-specific death rates for each area. The values are obviously different — for one reason because the figures are based on different statistical populations — but the similarity of the general configuration of the curves is significant.[39] In both areas females in their fertile years ran an exaggerated risk of death in comparison to males. The link between the two areas might well have been malaria, and for the historian who must work from

---

Influence of Malaria on Natality with Special Reference to Ceylon," *Journal of the Malaria Institute of India* 3 (1940): 201–52; and R. Menon, "Pregnancy and Malaria," *Medical Journal of Malaya* 27 (1972): 115–19.

38. For example, Wright and Tinling, *Secret Diary*, 141–42, 344, 364.

39. Only a very general comparison can be made because of the different age groups used (Puttalam has been graphed on the basis of the midyears of the age groups 5–14, 15–24, 25–34, 35–44, 45–54, 55–64, and age 70 for the cohort 65-plus; Middlesex on the basis of smoothed data for the midyears of 5-year groups), the different species and strains of *plasmodium* prevalent in the two areas, and, above all, the differences in the populations at risk. In Puttalam the entire population of the district, 1937–38, was at risk; for Middlesex the population at risk is married and widowed adults, the figures being based on the experience of subjects born over the span of years 1650–1710 who both survived to a marriageable age and chose at some time to marry. If the Puttalam population at risk had been so restricted, the resulting "bulge" of female deaths during the fertile years would undoubtedly have been somewhat greater. More complete, but comparable, Middlesex data are reported in Rutman and Rutman, *A Place in Time: Explicatus*, 52.

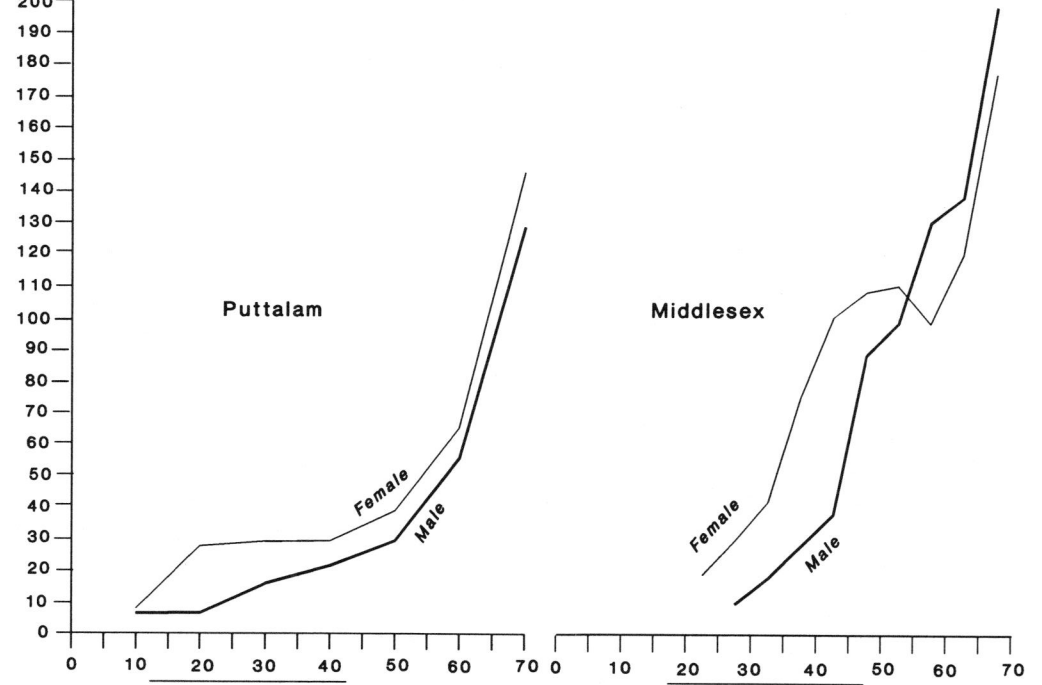

Fig. 9.6. Age-specific death rates, Puttalam District, Ceylon, 1937–38, and seventeenth- and early eighteenth-century Middlesex County, Virginia. See S. A. Meegama, "Malaria Eradication and Its Effects on Mortality Levels," *Population Studies* 21 (1967): 225; Darrett B. and Anita H. Rutman, "'Now-Wives and Sons-in-Law': Parental Death in a Seventeenth-Century Virginia County," in *The Chesapeake in the Seventeenth Century: Essays on Anglo-American Society*, ed. Thad W. Tate and David L. Ammerman (Chapel Hill, N.C., 1979), 177–82. High maternity cohorts are underlined. N.B.: The populations at risk varied. See note 39.

highly tangential evidence, the extent to which female deaths exceed male deaths in a given area may well be a rough measure of the hold of malaria on that area. If the suggestion is sound, Middlesex and whatever part of the Chesapeake region it accurately reflects were highly malarious.

What of the social ramifications of malaria? Although disease is biologically defined, it is also to an extent culturally defined. The sickly appearance of Gloucester County men and women in 1687 and the ghostly pallor of those who lived about the Great Dismal Swamp in 1728 invited comment by Durand de Dauphiné and William Byrd, respectively; but did the inhabitants look upon themselves as diseased and sick?[40] Probably not. Even the periodic "agues and fevers" of malaria could be culturally normative rather than culturally exceptional. This is the implication of the almost casual language with which Fitzhugh reported the end of his sister's illness: "and so consequently her seasoning [is] over." Even in Carter's diary most of the seizures are noted in a commonplace way: "Judy's fever left her this day. Lucy her ague and fever at 5 this eve."[41] Only in extreme situations did illness become something more than commonplace, as it did for Carter in the terrible year 1757. "It is necessary that man should be acquainted with affliction," Carter wrote in exasperation toward its end; "and 'tis certainly nothing short of it to be confined a whole year in tending one's sick Children. Mine are now never well."[42] It is, perhaps, this cultural definition of illness that underlies the diverse reactions to endemic and epidemic diseases commented on by Richard Shryock; the former are "taken for granted," the latter provoke hysteria.[43]

That said, however, we propose three ways in which endemic malaria, even if matter-of-factly accepted by its victims, conceivably affected their society. What follows can only be quick, tentative, and suggestive. The subject of the interrelationship of disease and society is only now coming into prominence under such rubrics as "medical anthropology," and potentially useful models from contemporary studies are still few and rudimentary.[44] In addition, we have been able to associate the disease only generally with Virginia through literary evidence, and only with regard to one small tidewater area — Middlesex — can we make even a rough statement as to degree. Still, a beginning seems in order.

40. Chinard, *Huguenot Exile*, 130; Wright, *Prose Works of William Byrd*, 202.

41. Davis, *Fitzhugh and His Chesapeake World*, 229; Greene, *Diary of Carter* 1:203.

42. Greene, *Diary of Carter* 1:194.

43. Shryock, *Medicine and Society*, 93–95.

44. For example, V. F. P. M. Van Amelsvoort, *Culture, Stone Age, and Modern Medicine* (Assen, The Netherlands, 1964). Burton A. Weisbrod et al., *Disease and Economic Development: The Impact of Parasitic Diseases in St. Lucia* (Madison, Wis., 1973), chap. 2, is a good overview of this literature, but see also Gerald Gordon et al., *Disease, the Individual, and Society* (New Haven, 1968), pt. 1.

The most obvious interrelationship between disease and society is that defined by economics. What is the cost to the society of an endemic disease such as malaria? In modern economic scholarship the question has been posed in terms of the economic gain to a society of an eradication program, and the answer seems to be coming back as a negative. Robin Barlow has summarized the findings: eradication of malaria brings about a population rise by reducing the death rate and, more important, by raising both the birthrate, as more children are successfully delivered, and the rate of survival through childhood. Moreover, the reduction of mortality, morbidity, and debility increases the quantity and quality of labor output. An immediate economic gain follows, but the society loses in the long run as the added population makes increasing demands on the public sector for services, reduces per capita income, and curtails capital formulation.[45] This econometric approach is cold and impersonal, and it runs counter to the historian's normal prejudice by requiring an "if" proposition: What if there had been no malaria in the Chesapeake? But there is some profit in applying it, if only to discount any quick generalization as to malaria and economic backwardness. Without malaria the rate of natural increase in the Chesapeake and the number of people living there would have been greater. This probably would not have resulted in an increased demand for public services, for the concept of public service was weakly defined; yet an increase in a population, dependent on a single cash crop and a finite market, would have resulted in greater production and lower prices, and consequently lower per capita income. Only if receiving lower prices for tobacco had led Virginians to an earlier and more energetic acceptance of economic diversification would the overall economy have improved.[46]

Another approach is perhaps more revealing. The agricultural economy of the Chesapeake region was labor-intensive; in the main a person's economic position depended on the application of labor to land. But disease in general and malaria in particular strike directly at labor.[47]

45. Barlow, "The Economic Effects of Malaria Eradication," *Papers and Proceedings of the Seventy-Ninth Annual Meeting*, in *American Economic Review* 57 (1967): 130–48. See also Barlow, *The Economic Effects of Malaria Eradication* (Ann Arbor, Mich., 1968); Newman, *Malaria Eradication*; and Gladys N. Conly, "The Impact of Malaria on Economic Development: A Case Study," in *Proceedings of the Inter-American Malaria Research Symposium*, ed. Scholtens and Nájera, 668–74, a preliminary report on an attempt to measure microeffects using 300 farm families in eastern Paraguay before and after an eradication program.

46. John C. Rainbolt, *From Prescription to Persuasion: Manipulation of [Seventeenth] Century Virginia Economy* (Port Washington, N.Y., 1974), discusses the early and unsuccessful diversification attempts. Avery Odelle Craven, *Soil Exhaustion as a Factor in the Agricultural History of Virginia and Maryland, 1606–1860* (Urbana, Ill., 1926), 69, dates tidewater diversification at about the mid-eighteenth century.

47. Wood, *Black Majority*, 91, argues that in South Carolina the combination of malaria (together with yellow fever), black resistance to both diseases, and the labor-intensive econ-

Hence in the Chesapeake one's economic position was constantly jeopardized by disease, as the marquis de Chastellux observed when, with reference to "epidemical disorders" common among the slaves of the Virginians, he reported that "both their property and their revenue" were "extremely precarious."[48] The risk, however, was unevenly spread. The planter who relied on his own labor, with that of his wife and perhaps a single servant or slave, chanced disaster more than did the planter who had built up a labor force of ten or twenty persons. Imagine the small planter struck down by a malaria attack at the moment most appropriate for the transplantation of tobacco seedlings from seedbeds to fields, or when the ripe tobacco leaves had to be cut and housed. A good percentage, perhaps even all, of his year's income might be lost. The intensity of the dependence on labor is illustrated by Peter Mountague of Middlesex County whose one male servant ran away at harvest time in 1701, causing Mountague to complain to the county court in 1702 that he had sustained as a consequence "the whole loss of the last crop."[49] It is true that larger planters could be hard hit. Armistead Churchill of Middlesex lost thirty slaves in one six-month period in 1737.[50] But a large labor force ensured against catastrophe. Even at the height of his troubles in 1757 Carter still had laborers in his fields. Moreover, in a society in which working lives were short, the amassment of capital provided defense against the economic effects of death. The short-lived planter, large or small, frequently left orphaned children.[51] But the chances that the orphans of the large planter would start their working years with enough capital in the form of labor to protect them from disaster were far greater than those of orphans of the small planter. Generation after generation, the latter had to begin their working lives with no more, and sometimes less, than their fathers had begun with. These inequalities may well have contributed to economic polarization over time.[52] For the planter who, by virtue of ability,

---

omy "must have done a great deal to reinforce the expanding rationale behind the enslavement of Africans." Wood attempts to demonstrate that South Carolina's whites, from an early date, thought of the blacks as more resistant to disease, in sharp contrast to Winthrop D. Jordan, *White over Black: American Attitudes toward the Negro, 1550–1812* (Chapel Hill, N.C., 1968), 259–65. We have found no evidence in Virginia to substantiate Wood's thesis.

48. Marquis de Chastellux, *Travels in North America, in the Years 1780, 1781, and 1782*, 2d ed. (London, 1787), 2:297.

49. Middlesex County, Order Book No. 3, 1694–1705, 483, Virginia State Library and Archives, Richmond.

50. *The Parish Register of Christ Church, Middlesex County, Va., from 1653 to 1812* (Richmond, 1897), 275–76. In this case the loss might well have been to yellow fever, a disease then entering the colony.

51. See chap. 10 below.

52. Darrett B. Rutman, "The Social Web: A Prospectus for the Study of the Early American Community," in *Insights and Parallels: Problems and Issues of American Social History*,

energy, or luck, lived insulated from the economic consequences of disease had a far better chance to improve his economic position and, consequently, still greater insulation.

A consideration of disease and economics has led to one aspect of the structure of Chesapeake society: exaggerated economic polarization. But disease interacts with social structure in other ways as well. Provision must be made for illness. This was in part an individual matter, as it was for Dennis Conyers when he sold one hundred acres on the Piankatank River in Middlesex to Peter Godson on the condition that "the said Peter . . . administer Physick or Physical means to the said Dennis for his own person for the space of one year."[53] For the whole society the provisions for illness take on a more general form. The phenomenon of every planter his own practitioner has long been noted. Equally to the point are the phenomena of every claimant to the title "doctor" being engaged as one and, notwithstanding the aspersions of a Byrd, the high esteem accorded physicians in the Chesapeake area.[54] On a still higher level of generalization one can suggest that illness and early death were related to the basic social organization of the Chesapeake. In the continuing study of Middlesex County of which this chapter is a part, the region is emerging not as an area of isolated plantations and individuals but as a mosaic of close-knit neighborhoods and kinship groups. Few aspects of life reflect this mosaic more clearly than do illness and death. Illness brought visitation, and kin and neighbors clustered about the sickbeds of the county.[55] Death, particularly the death of parents with the consequent orphaning of children, evoked kinship obligations, and relations (including such relations as godparents) moved to care for the parentless. The effect was a society of open

---

ed. William L. O'Neill (Minneapolis, 1973), 85, 85n, 112–13, briefly compares polarization in New England and Middlesex.

53. Lancaster County, Deeds, etc. [Wills and Settlements of Estates], no. 2, 1654–1702, 116–17, Virginia State Library and Archives.

54. Philip Alexander Bruce, *Economic History of Virginia in the Seventeenth Century* (New York, 1896), 2:231ff. See Byrd to Dr. Hans Sloane, 20 Apr. 1706, *William and Mary Quarterly*, 2d ser., 1 (1921): 186: "Here be some men indeed that are call'd Doctors: but they are generally discarded Surgeons of Ships, that know nothing above very common Remedys." Oldmixon, *British Empire* 1:294, presumably reflecting Byrd, wrote that the Virginians "reckon it among Blessings" that they had few doctors, "fancying the Number of their Diseases would encrease with that of their Physicians." These attitudes are in sharp contrast to the social position accorded physicians in Middlesex society.

55. The phenomenon can be glimpsed in depositions submitted to the county court in cases involving disputed wills, for example, the probate proceedings surrounding the will of John Burnham in Middlesex County, Deeds, etc., no. 2[1a], 1679–94, 22, Virginia State Library and Archives. Here and there, too, it can be seen in literary sources, William Byrd, for example, hovering about the sickbed of John Bowman of Henrico County (Wright and Tinling, *Secret Diary*, 89–94).

and mixed households. The home was not an isolated castle but a neighborhood focal point. The typical family was not the neat nuclear one of mother-father-children but a mixed affair of parents, stepparents, guardians, natural children, stepchildren, and wards.[56] It could hardly have been otherwise, given the prevalence of illness, the frequency of early death, and the necessity of caring for the sick and orphaned; and it can be argued that in the Chesapeake region the form and strength of the social bonds were direct corollaries of the fragility of life.

Finally, one can suggest an impact of disease on the culture of the Chesapeake, for while culture to an extent defines disease, the relationship is reciprocal. The associations are so tenuously perceived that questions seem more in order than statements. If there is validity in the ideal *mens sana in corpore sano*, then, conversely, the ill do not think clearly. Might this have been related to the low level of intellectual activity in the early Chesapeake, a level frequently contrasted to that of New England? Dr. John Mitchell's biographers, writing of his years in Urbanna, Middlesex, imply as much. "Continuous bouts of malaria . . . left him with little energy and even less *joie de vivre*," and most of Mitchell's significant work was done after he removed to England.[57] What would be the attitudes of a population which had a relatively high rate of illness and short life expectancy? Richard S. Dunn's comparison of New England and the English Caribbean is provocative, assuming that the Caribbean and Chesapeake were both areas of high malarial morbidity. "The Caribbean and New England planters were polar opposites in social expression. . . . The contrast in life style went far beyond the obvious differences in religion, slavery and climate. The sugar planters 'lived fast, spent recklessly, played desperately, and died young.' . . . Their family life was broken, and since the colonists were predominantly young people without effective guidance, they behaved in a freewheeling, devil-may-care fashion."[58]

Applied to Virginia, Dunn's description probably would be an exaggeration, but Virginia can certainly be described, in comparison with New England, as a present-minded society which was more involved, in Wordsworth's phrase, with "getting and spending" than with abstractions or ideals. Do the Virginians' attitudes toward death reflect the fact of frequent illness and early death? Robinson Jeffers's "patient daemon" was much on the minds of colonials north and south, but while the New

56. A point elaborated upon in the following chapter and in Darrett B. and Anita H. Rutman, *A Place in Time: Middlesex County, Virginia, 1650–1750* (New York, 1984), 94–127.

57. Edmund and Dorothy Smith Berkeley, *Dr. John Mitchell: The Man Who Made the Map of North America* (Chapel Hill, N.C., 1974), 59.

58. Dunn, "The Social History of Early New England," *American Quarterly* 24 (1972): 675, quoting his *Sugar and Slaves: The Rise of the Planter Class in the English West Indies, 1624–1713* (Chapel Hill, N.C., 1972). See the latter, pp. 302–3, regarding malaria in the English Caribbean.

Englanders seem to have been both enamored of and terrified by death, the Virginians apparently discerned death more as a matter of fact, of "Dissolution"—William Fitzhugh's word—and of business, the willing and disposing of property.[59] The comparison can only be highly tentative, for little work has been done on the subject, but two vignettes are suggestive. In September 1658 William Price of Lancaster County told of his last conversation with Roger Radford: "I came into the room where Mr. Radford was sitting upon his bed sick. I asked him how he did. 'Pretty well,' he said. 'You are not, I think, a man for this world. Therefore you had best to make your peace with God and set everything to rights with Mr. Cocke.' He answered: 'No, for he is more engaged to me than I to him.' 'What do you give Polly Cole?' [I asked.] 'I give Polly Cole my land.' "[60] The second vignette was recorded by Philip Fithian toward the end of the eighteenth century. The sudden death of a black child "with the Ague and Fever" was "the Subject of Conversation in the House." "Mr. *Carter* observed, that he thought it the most desirable to die of a Short Illness. If he could have his Wish he would not lie longer than two days; be taken with a Fever, which should . . . gradually increase till it affected a Dissolution—He told us that his affairs are in Such a state that he should be able to dictate a Will which might be written in five Minutes, and contain the disposal of his estate agreeable to his mind—He mentioned to us the Substance."[61]

Economy, social structure, culture—all conceivably bore the imprint of malaria in the early Chesapeake. We do not mean to assert a direct causal association, for the question of the relation of disease to society is far too complex, the variables far too many, and the evidence far too slim. We do mean to suggest that malaria was endemic in the early Chesapeake (and relatively absent in New England), and that it is in the nature of societies to adjust to the disease environment in which they exist. These, we argue, should be informing assumptions in early American history, and the processes and consequences of such adjustments, varying by time and place, require the attention of historians.

59. Jeffers, "The Bed by the Window" (1931), in *The Selected Poetry of Robinson Jeffers* (New York, n.d.), 162; David E. Stannard, "Death and Dying in Puritan New England," *American Historical Review* 78 (1973): 1305–30; William Fitzhugh to Mrs. Mary Fitzhugh, 30 June 1698, in Davis, *Fitzhugh and His Chesapeake World*, 358.

60. Lancaster County, Deeds, Etc. [Wills and Settlements of Estates], no. 2, 1654–1702, 56–57, Virginia State Library and Archives. The quotation has been modernized.

61. Hunter Dickinson Farish, ed., *Journal and Letters of Philip Vickers Fithian, 1773–1774: A Plantation Tutor of the Old Dominion* (Williamsburg, Va., 1957), 182. The deeply religious Fithian noted that "our School make it [the death] a Subject for continual Speculation; They seem all to be free of any terror at the Prescence of Death; *Harry* in special signified a Wish that his turn may be next." Cf. David E. Stannard, "Death and the Puritan Child," *American Quarterly* 26 (1974): 456–76.

10 "Now-Wives and Sons-in-Law": *Parental Death in a Seventeenth-Century Virginia County* With Anita H. Rutman

At a working conference of early American historians in the early 1980s, a very good friend (and a very good historian of New England) mentioned in passing that "of course, there were no communities in the Chesapeake." A few years later at another such conference, still another historian, in commenting upon the high mortality rates found in the Chesapeake, went on to say that they "augured poorly for any sort of well-ordered, cohesive family." "There was simply too much death . . . and too few watchful elders for the forces of authority and tradition to prevail as they so clearly did in New England." Remarks of that sort betray a continuing tendency among American historians generally to measure such things as "community" and "family" against a New England standard. Comparison is important, of course. But when we set aside arbitrary standards and simply draw conclusions from the materials we have — as in the case of what follows, delivered in 1974 and first published in 1979 — we find that it is not a matter of the Chesapeake being devoid of families and communities but, by virtue of different conditions, of its forming families and communities of a different kind.

In the name of God Amen. . . ." With the customary words Maximilian Petty, "planter" and undersheriff of Middlesex County, Virginia, "sick and weake in Body," began his last will and testament in the closing days of

Presented originally at a conference on the seventeenth-century Chesapeake held in November 1974 at the University of Maryland, College Park, and St. Mary's, Maryland; published subsequently (with appendixes) in *The Chesapeake in the Seventeenth Century: Essays on Anglo-American Society*, ed. Thad W. Tate and David L. Ammerman (Chapel Hill: University of North Carolina Press for the Institute of Early American History and Culture, Williamsburg, Va., 1979), 153–75. Copyright © 1979 by the University of North Carolina Press. Reprinted with the permission of the publisher.

1687. To his God he bequeathed his soul, to the grave his body, and to his wife and children "those Worldly Goods the Lord hath lent me." Within a matter of weeks after writing his will Petty was dead; his wife, Christian, was a young widow; and his two children, Maximilian and Ann, were fatherless. Young Max was just ten, Ann seven and a half.[1]

To us in the twentieth century there is a sadness to such a death. The plight of young widowhood and of fatherless children is enough of an anomaly in our society to give us pause. But there was no such anomaly in late seventeenth-century Virginia. Indeed, few of the children of this time and place reached their majority without losing at least one parent, while over a third lost both. Parental death was a part of the fabric of life.

The extensiveness of parental death in early Virginia shows itself in the course of an in-depth study of community organization and lifestyle in one county — Petty's own Middlesex.[2] A long splinter of land bounded by the Rappahannock River and Chesapeake Bay on the north and east, the Piankatank River and Dragon Swamp on the south and west, Middlesex was first settled about mid-century. From York River and the Eastern Shore, from Northumberland on the Potomac, and from England, men and women had entered the land, some simply to take up acreage, resell, then move on, but most to settle permanently, raising corn and tobacco, cattle and children. (Richard Perrott, Jr., born in February 1651, was, as the parish register carefully noted, "the first Man Child that was gott and borne In Rappahannock River of English parents.")[3] Servants and free laborers arrived, worked for a time, then moved on or found land in the county to patent, buy, or rent. Very quickly a permanent, stable population appeared. By the late 1660s, when both the county and the coterminous parish of Christ Church had been organized, the area was home to some 90 families. In 1687 a militia report on the households of the county capable of supplying horses and arms for defensive purposes gives indication of 142 families, while a best estimate places the total population at 1,225.[4] Just over a generation later (1724) the minister of Christ Church

1. Middlesex County, Wills, etc., 1675–1798, pt. 1, 54; *The Parish Register of Christ Church, Middlesex County, Va., from 1653 to 1812* (Richmond, 1897), 36. All manuscript county records cited in this chapter are to be found in the Virginia State Library and Archives, Richmond.

2. Published as Darrett B. and Anita H. Rutman, *A Place in Time: Middlesex County, Virginia, 1650–1750* (New York, 1984) and *A Place in Time: Explicatus* (New York, 1984). The principal source for the specific examples and conclusions offered in this and the following chapter is the prosopography described in chap. 3 above and in *A Place in Time: Middlesex*, 30–33, 296. Full citation of the specific sources of that prosopography would be overly extensive and redundant; hence the footnotes in both chapters are confined to direct quotations and a few salient points.

3. *Parish Register of Christ Church*, 41.

4. Tithable List, Nov. 1668, Lancaster County, Orders, etc., no. 1, 1666–80, 86–87,

reported to the bishop of London that there were some 260 white families in his parish, while the total population can be estimated at 1,560 white men, women, and children and 820-odd blacks.[5] Names from the earliest days of the county—Perrott, Wormeley, Kemp, Minor, Tuggle—were still there one, two, three generations later (some are even still there today). Some names disappeared as surnames but cropped up subseqently as first names, indicative of family memories of family ties. There are no Eltonhead surnames in the parish register, for example, but the 1678 entry of the birth of Eltonhead Stanard is in a real sense a memorial to four Eltonhead sisters who underlie so many Middlesex families—Agatha, who married first Ralph Wormeley, then Sir Henry Chicheley; Alice, who married, in order, Rowland Burnham, Henry Corbin, and Henry Creek; Eleanor, wife of Middlesex's William Brocas, then Lancaster's John Carter (living just across the Rappahannock on Corotoman Creek); and Martha, who married Edwin Conaway and was the grandmother of the Eltonhead Stanard of 1678. Marriage and remarriage was a way of life, and in its complexities one first senses the magnitude of parental loss.[6]

Mary, the wife of George Keeble, for example: Her parentage is unknown, but from her gravestone we know that she was born about 1637

---

extracting those residing in what would become Middlesex; Militia List, 1687, Middlesex County, Order Book no. 2, 1680–94, 317–19; for tithable counts for 1686, 1687, and 1688, see ibid., 274, and C. G. Chamberlayne, ed., *The Vestry Book of Christ Church Parish, Middlesex County, Virginia, 1663–1767* (Richmond, 1927), 51, 57, 60. A crude multiplier to convert from tithables to population—1.9—can be constructed from the count of tithables and untithables forwarded by the county court in 1701 (C.O. 5/1312, 19, 10, Public Record Office, London). Every test indicates it is a sounder multiplier for this specific place and time than the general multiplier offered by Evarts B. Greene and Virginia D. Harrington, *American Population before the Federal Census of 1790* (1932; reprint, Gloucester, Mass., 1966), xxiii. For an extended discussion of such multipliers, see Darrett B. and Anita H. Rutman, "'More True and Perfect Lists': The Reconstruction of Censuses for Middlesex County, Virginia, 1668–1704," *Virginia Magazine of History and Biography* 88 (1980): 42–48. The militia list is very inaccurately transcribed in William Armstrong Crozier, ed., *Virginia Colonial Militia, 1651–1776* (New York, 1905), 98–99.

5. William Wilson Manross, comp., *The Fulham Papers in the Lambeth Palace Library: American Colonial Section, Calendar and Indexes* (Oxford, 1965), 177.

6. Here and there in the literature of Anglo-America one finds allusions to parental loss. Peter Laslett, *The World We Have Lost* (New York, 1965), 95–96, refers to the evil stepmother of fairy tales and to his Clayworth study (in May 1688, 35.5 percent of all the children alive in Clayworth were orphans) in commenting upon "the society of the pre-industrial world" being "inured to bereavement and the shortness of life." Joseph E. Illick, in a parenthetical expression in his "Child-Rearing in Seventeenth-Century England and America," in *The History of Childhood*, ed. Lloyd deMause (New York, 1974), 321, notes that "the likelihood of both natural parents surviving until a child reached his majority was not high" and cites five autobiographies and "the popularity of such tales as *Cinderella*" (p. 344). But we have found no systematic study of the extent of such loss or any suggestions as to its ramifications.

and had seven children presumably by Keeble before finding herself widowed at about twenty-nine years of age. At least four of these children (Walter, Mary, George, and Margaret) were alive when she married Robert Beverley in 1666, shortly after Keeble's death. By Beverley she had five more children (Peter, Robert, Harry, John, and Mary). She died in 1678 at the age of forty-one, and Robert Beverley almost immediately remarried. His new wife, Katherine, was herself recently widowed by the death of Major Theophilus Hone. So quick was the remarriage that Major Hone's personal property was already in the Beverley house by the time the inventory of it was taken.[7] Dropping into the Beverley household in 1680, just after this most recent marriage, we conceivably would have found Keeble children (those of Mary and George), at least one Hone child (Theophilus, Jr.), Beverley children by Robert and Mary, and the first of four Beverley children by Robert and Katherine — William Beverley, born in 1680. Thomas, Katherine, and Christopher Beverley would follow before Robert Beverley's death in 1687. His widow, Katherine, immediately married Christopher Robinson; in the vernacular of genealogists she was now Katherine (Armistead) Hone-Beverley-Robinson.[8] Robinson himself was a widower, having lost his wife Agatha Hobert in 1686 (four of their children survived: Anne, Christopher, Agatha, John); Katherine would bear four more children before her death in 1692 (Elizabeth, Clara, another Theophilus — her earlier son by Major Hone having died[9] — and Benjamin). The chain of marriages and remarriages finally broke the next year with the death of Christopher Robinson. In sum, the progeny of six marriages among seven people amounted to twenty-five known children. Not one of these children could have grown to maturity without losing at least one parent and passing through a period under a stepparent.

Such examples could be multiplied. Another Armistead — Elizabeth — married Ralph Wormeley in 1688. Wormeley was at the time a widower with two known children by his first wife, née Katherine Lunsford, who herself had been a widow when she married Ralph. Three children are known to have been born to Ralph and Elizabeth. Widowed in 1701, Elizabeth married the widower William Churchill, whose wife Susanna

7. Middlesex County, Order Book no. 1, 1673–80, 208.

8. The assumption that Katherine was an Armistead rests on "Will of Christopher Robinson, 1693," *Virginia Magazine of History and Biography* 7 (1899–1900): 17–23. See also the note pertaining to Maj. Theophilus Hone, ibid., 4 (1896–97): 4. Recent evidence adds even more to the family complications; see Brent Tarter, "Major Robert Beverley (1635–1687) and His Immediate Family," *Magazine of Virgina Genealogy* 31 (1993): 166–67.

9. The frequent practice of giving subsequent children the same names as earlier children who had died explains other name duplication in this section, but not all. Note Christopher, son of Katherine and Robert Beverley, and Christopher, son of Agatha and Christopher Robinson.

had been a widow with two known children. Churchill and Elizabeth themselves had three known children. In all, five marriages among seven people are known to have produced ten children. Only two of these ten — Susanna Churchill's two children by her first husband — could possibly have grown to maturity without knowing the loss of a parent, and that possibility exists solely because we cannot determine with certainty the children's birth dates. Even when the complex skein of marriage and remarriage is not in evidence, reconstituted families exemplify parental loss. Richard Perrott, Jr., Rappahannock River's first English "Man Child," married only once. His fifteen-year-old bride, Sarah Curtis Half-hide, was already a widow, but presumably her marriage to William Half-hide had been brief and childless. In 1693 both Richard and Sarah died; of the eight known children of their twenty-one-year marriage, the eldest was nineteen at the time of his parents' death, the youngest four, and six in all were under fifteen.

For all the examples of children losing parents, however, there are examples to the contrary. Four of the five known children of Ezekias and Elizabeth Rhodes who survived to maturity were married by the time Ezekias died in January 1717. (His widow lived on until 1727.) The fifth child, William, was eighteen at the time his father died. Peter and Eleanor Brummell's four known children were married before their parents' death. So, too, were the four surviving children of John and Mary Brim. With examples on both sides, the question becomes one of representativeness: Which set of examples best states the main trend?

The answer in part lies in vital statistics for Middlesex's men and women. At what age did they marry? At what age die? How many of the children of their marriages could they possibly see to maturity? Seventeenth-century observers have left suggestive hints about the demographic situation. A traveler to Virginia in the late 1680s noted that he had "met few old people"; in the same decade John Clayton, Virginia's scientific parson, wrote that "if the English live past 33, they generally live to a good age," but "many die between 30 and 33"; and William Fitzhugh, writing in 1687, when he was thirty-six, looked upon himself as in his "declining age."[10] But this sort of fragmented and subjective information does not give us the precision and the neutral vantage point that are required to answer the questions we have set.

10. Gilbert Chinard, ed., *A Huguenot Exile in Virginia: or Voyages of a Frenchman Exiled for His Religion with a Description of Virginia and Maryland* (New York, 1934), 173; Clayton to Dr. Nehemiah Grew, 1687, in Edmund and Dorothy Smith Berkeley, eds., *The Reverend John Clayton, a Parson with a Scientific Mind: His Scientific Writings and Other Related Papers* (Charlottesville, Va., 1965), 39; Fitzhugh to Nicholas Hayward, 30 Jan. 1687, in Richard Beale Davis, ed., *William Fitzhugh and His Chesapeake World, 1676–1701: The Fitzhugh Letters and Other Documents* (Chapel Hill, N.C., 1963), 203.

No seventeenth-century source offers us the vital statistics we need, nor does any single source offer data on all the vital events necessary to construct such statistics. Middlesex's first generation was an immigrant generation; hence evidence of birth dates is scattered through the records of older counties and in England. Marriages and deaths within the county were recorded in the parish register, but how complete is the register? Marriages and deaths occurring outside the county are obviously not recorded in it; beyond that, we must always assume that some proportion of the vital events within the county were missed. Despite such difficulties, however, enough data on the first and second generations (those born through 1710) can be gathered to allow the construction of a tentative table of life expectancies (see table 10.2) while an availability sample allows a tentative estimate of the median age of first marriage.[11] On the basis of these figures we can hypothesize Middlesex's median couple, a highly idealized concept, we stress, a couple which does the most improbable of all things: live strictly according to statistical expectations. Presuming that, for both husband and wife, the marriage was a first marriage, he would be just turned 24, she just 20. In the course of their marriage they would have between four and six children, perhaps one of which would die in infancy, in some instances leaving no record but a gap in the progression of recorded births or baptismal dates of children born to the mother. Four or five would survive, however. In the normal course of events, and leaving room for the probability of a fetal death or a child who did not survive, these children would be born when the wife was 21, 24, 30, 34, and 37. The wife of this median marriage could be expected to die at 39, leaving in her husband's care children who were 18, 15, 9, 5, and 1. The husband, 43 at the death of his first wife, would probably remarry almost immediately and have still other children. But he could be expected to die in turn at 48. The children of his first marriage, now orphaned, would be 23, 20, 14, 10, and 6, respectively; any children of his second marriage, also losing their father, would be even younger.

The marriage sketched above (and in fig. 10.1) is hypothetical and based on tentative statistics. Yet that it reflects, very roughly, a reality is suggested by a sample of 239 children for whom the requisite data as to dates of their birth and death dates of their parents exist.[12] The sample

11. The procedures by which such data were gathered and tested for biases are described in Rutman and Rutman, "'More True and Perfect Lists,'" 37–74, and in appendix 1 — "A Note on the Sources and Method" — of the original publication of this essay in *The Chesapeake in the Seventeenth Century*, ed. Tate and Ammerman, 175–77.

12. The subject children were those born to the wives of men listed in the 1687 militia list for whom firm information as to date of birth and parental death dates was available. Given the nature of the list — ranging from older men with many years of marriage behind them to young men newly married, but more of the latter than the former — the distribution of birth

Husband's Achieved Age	Wife's Achieved Age	Children's Achieved Ages				
		First	Second	Third	Fourth	Fifth
24 Married	20					
25	21	Born				
26	22	1				
27	23	2				
28	24	3	Born			
29	25	4	1			
30	26	5	2			
31	27	6	3			
32	28	7	4			
33	29	8	5			
34	30	9	6	Born		
35	31	10	7	1		
36	32	11	8	2		
37	33	12	9	3		
38	34	13	10	4	Born	
39	35	14	11	5	1	
40	36	15	12	6	2	
41	37	16	13	7	3	
42	38	17	14	8	4	Born
43	39	18	15	9	5	1
44	Dead	19	16	10	6	2
45		20	17	11	7	3
46		21	18	12	8	4
47		22	19	13	9	5
48		23	20	14	10	6
Dead						

Fig. 10.1. Age profile of an idealized early Middlesex County, Virginia, marriage

indicates that almost a quarter of Middlesex's children suffered the loss of one or both parents by the time of their fifth birthday, and over half by the time of their thirteenth birthday. And 73.2 percent had lost one or both parents by the time they reached twenty-one or married, whichever came first (table 10.1).[13] To put the results another way: The 239 children of the sample were the products of sixty-eight marriages; at the end of sixty-two (91 percent) of these marriages, minor children were left in the care of the surviving spouse; the subsequent death of the survivor left orphaned minors in forty-one (60 percent) of the cases.[14]

dates of the subject children, as expected, concentrated in the period immediately surrounding the date of the list yet spanned a range of years with large enough subsets to allow testing for a trend over time. Of the subject children, 15.2 percent were born in the years 1655–79, 49.6 percent in the years 1680–94, and 35.2 percent in 1695–1724.

13. The awkwardness of this last category follows from the ambiguity of the concept of "majority." In law, Virginia girls were of age at eighteen, boys at twenty-one; but in point of fact marriage endowed maturity regardless of age.

14. The sample computes to 3.5 children per marriage, roughly half the rate found in early New England. But this Middlesex figure cannot be used as a fertility index, for only marriages productive of children for whom specific data were known were entered into the sample. Moreover, a figure for births per marriage is extremely crude as a comparative index for it does not take into account potential variation in years per marriage. Stronger, more formal, indices of fertility are offered in Rutman and Rutman, *A Place in Time: Explicatus*, chap. 5. The same work offers more refined data on mortality (chap. 4) and parental loss

Table 10.1. Parental loss in early Middlesex County, Virginia

Achieved age	Children known to survive to age	Children with both parents at age	Children with but one parent at age	Children orphaned at age
1	239 (100%)	222 (92.9%)	17 (7.1%)	0 (0.0%)
5	227 (100%)	174 (76.7%)	47 (20.7%)	6 (2.6%)
9	211 (100%)	124 (58.8%)	67 (31.8%)	20 (9.5%)
13	194 (100%)	90 (46.4%)	66 (34.0%)	38 (19.6%)
18	173 (100%)	57 (32.9%)	62 (35.8%)	54 (31.2%)
*	164 (100%)	44 (26.8%)	61 (37.2%)	59 (36.0%)

Source and note: See note 12. * indicates age 21 or age at marriage, whichever came first.

Obviously the society had to accommodate the many children losing parents. Apprenticeship absorbed some of the children of the poor, the one fact about orphanhood generally commented upon.[15] Indigent orphans were bound out by the parish vestry and churchwardens or, more often, by the county court. Thus James Merritt, whose father's estate was administered by Cuthbert Potter as chief creditor, was bound by the court in 1679 "till he comes of Age" to Christopher Robinson.[16] But an indigent widow who by virtue of age, incapacity, or the paucity of her estate was not a candidate for remarriage might well apprentice one or more children as well. Mary Gibbs, for example, left a widow with three sons by the death of her husband Gregory in 1683 (and pregnant with a fourth son), that same year bound her ten-year-old eldest to Richard Willis, who contracted "to teach him the art and trade of a shooemaker and to finde him sufficient Diet and Cloathing"; another son was put to apprenticeship four years later. Mary lived on in widowhood until 1726, her third son, John, presumably staying with her. The fourth son, Charles, baptized in September 1684, apparently died young.[17]

Yet apprenticeship absorbed only a few of the children. The children of the affluent, of the "middling sort," even of most of the poor, were expected to stay with the surviving parent, who more often than not remar-

---

(chap. 6), but those data do not change any of the conclusions offered here; indeed, they strengthen the conclusions.

15. See, for example, Philip Alexander Bruce, *Institutional History of Virginia in the Seventeenth Century* (New York, 1910), 1:85, 545–46; Arthur W. Calhoun, *A Social History of the American Family* 1 (1917; reprint, New York, 1960): 307–8. Other works — such as Mary Newton Stanard, *Colonial Virginia: Its People and Customs* (Philadelphia, 1917), and Edmund S. Morgan, *Virginians at Home: Family Life in the Eighteenth Century* (Williamsburg, Va., 1952) — do not consider orphans or parental loss at all.

16. Middlesex County, Order Book no. 1, 1673–80, 177.

17. Middlesex County, Order Book no. 2, 1680–94, 135, 308.

ried, endowing the child with a stepparent. In the case of the remarriage of
the surviving wife, the stepfather normally became the guardian of the
child. But for good and sufficient reasons — the failure of the guardian to
educate the child as befitting its parentage and estate, for example, or, as in
the case of the son of Elizabeth Maguire, abuse by the guardian — the
county court could intervene and place the child in the custody of someone else. And the child itself, at the age of fourteen, had the right to go
before the court and request a new guardian, as did Henry, Edwin, and
Martha Thacker in 1681, following the remarriage of their mother,
Eltonhead, to William Stanard.[18]

Orphanhood, an event for almost 20 percent of the children before
their thirteenth birthday and for over 30 percent before their eighteenth,
required still other arrangements. The county court had general oversight
of the children. On its own, or at the request of a child of fourteen or
older, it could specify custody and guardianship. But the wishes of parents
expressed in their wills were, by law, paramount. Tobias Mickleburrough
provided that his minor son by a first marriage "remain and abide" with
his second wife (the child's stepmother) "provided shee deals well and
kindly by him"; otherwise the designated overseers of the will were to
"remove and place him where in their discression they shall See most
Convenient." Due care was to be taken for the child's education "that he
may be Instructed and taught to read write and Cipher so far that he may
be well capable of doing any ordinary Business."[19] Frequently wills designated that orphaned children be put into the charge of an elder brother or
stepbrother, sometimes even an elder sister or stepsister. (In half the cases
of our sample of marriages where the orphanhood of minors resulted,
elder brothers or sisters had already reached majority.) James Dudley, for
example, survived three wives and was survived by five children; in writing
his will he charged his eldest son (born to Dudley's second wife) with the
care of his two youngest children (born of the third marriage), requiring
him "to bring them up in the fear of God and to put the[m] to Schoole in
Moderation, the girle for to read and the boy for to Read and Rite and
Siffer if it be possible he can." Thomas Stiff, leaving two grown children
and two minor children (ages nine and seven), named his eldest son executor "and required him to take care" of the two minors. William Daniell

18. For the laws, see, e.g., William W. Hening, ed., *The Statutes at Large: Being a Collection
of All the Laws of Virginia . . . [through 1792]* (Richmond and Philadelphia, 1809–23), 2:92–
94, 3:371–76. The Maguire case is to be found in Middlesex County, Order Book no. 2,
1680–94, 503; that of the Thacker children, ibid., 47. The abuse of the Maguire child lay in
his not being raised in a Christian manner. Middlesex displays no such abuse as the rape of a
minor girl by her stepfather and subsequent infanticide that occurred on the Eastern Shore
(*Virgina Magazine of History and Biography* 4 [1896–97]: 185–97).

19. Middlesex County, Will Book A, 1698–1713, 139–41.

survived two wives and was survived by children ranging in age from thirty-four to four; in his will he stipulated that his three youngest daughters remain on the plantation bequeathed to his eldest son, William, "till they are marryed." Thomas Kidd provided that his four "smallest" (ranging in age from eight to eleven) remain upon the plantation left to them and be brought up by his daughters, Frances, twenty-two, and Mary, eighteen. Thomas Toseley, in writing his will, assumed that his two minor children would remain with their mother, his second wife, but provided that, should she die, the two sons of his wife's first marriage (in other words, not Toseley's sons at all) "manage and looke after My Children and their Estates." Thomas Tuggle left his children (ranging from Mary, nineteen, to Henry, ten) in the care of their elder half brother by his wife's first marriage but seems to have anticipated problems: They were all to live together on the plantation left to Tuggle's eldest son, if they could do so "contentedly"; if not, the half brother was to build a fifteen-foot-square house on the property and live by himself, leaving the children in the main house.[20]

Children were left in the care of uncles as well. When, for example, James Blaze died in February 1701, two young nieces were living with him: Agatha Vause, who had lost her father at age two and remained with her mother through two remarriages before being orphaned, and Mary Osborne, age two when her mother died, twelve at the death of her father. In his will Blaze provided inheritances to maintain the girls and expressed his desire that they "have two yeares Sculeing a pees and then to Returne Home and Learne Houseold work of my wife" Elizabeth.[21] On occasion, godparents took their godchildren into their homes or, as in the case of the widow of minister John Sheppard, the godchild of the deceased spouse; Richard Robinson, minister Sheppard's godson, was thirteen when his mother died, eighteen when his father died, and was living with Mistress Sheppard at age nineteen (1694) when he testified in her behalf in a suit against Francis Dodson.[22] Even simple friends had to be relied upon to care for one's orphans. Anne Chowning, widow of Robert Chowning and mother of seven children ages fifteen through four, made no other arrangement than to ask friends Richard Allen and Richard Shurley "to Act and doe" for the children "for their best advantage."[23] Such designated overseers seem to have been expected to take the children in and act as guardians in the absence of kin. And in a society in which orphans were so

20. Ibid., 245–46, 231, 236–37; Will Book B, 1713–34, 267–68, 311, and Wills, etc., 1675–1798, pt. 1, 27–28.

21. Middlesex County, Wills, etc., 1675–1798, pt. 1, 136–38.

22. Middlesex County, Order Book no. 2, 1680–94, 679. Mrs. Sheppard was also Robinson's distant cousin.

23. Middlesex County, Will Book B, 1713–34, 132.

common and where wives and husbands could reasonably expect that their own children might require accommodation, the widow Chowning's trust in her friends seems not undue. Edwin Conaway anticipated no problems when he interceded in behalf of the orphans of Elias Edmonds. Their estate was being rapidly dissipated by bad management (or so he thought); hence he suggested to one of the justices of the court new managerial arrangements. In anticipation of objection he added that "you will say who will keep the Children upon those terms. I answer I will find those that shall keep them and give them better Education than those in whose Custody they are."[24]

Conaway's letter points up a very real problem associated with the death of parents in this society, although not one to be overstated. The children were heirs and heiresses of property and personalty large and small. Partible inheritance was the rule, sons generally sharing realty equally (after deduction of the dower rights of the widow), although the eldest son was frequently favored, sometimes with an augmented share, more often by the bequest to him of the improved home property, while unimproved realty went to younger sons. (Daughters generally inherited realty only in the absence of sons.) Sons and daughters shared personal property (again after the deduction of the widow's share), the most frequent bequest by a father to a daughter being specific cattle and the increase thereof. The expense of rearing minor children was an appropriate deduction from the income, even at times the capital, of the inheritance. Hence those to whose charge the minors fell — widows and guardians — had the control of inheritances until children came of age or, in the case of a girl, married.[25] To both the father of the children and the society at large, the central concern was to effect the transfer of the property from the testator, through the minority of the child (when the inheritance was under the control of others), to the mature adult in as nearly intact a condition as possible. A multitiered system by which estates were handled — in some cases fathers named executors and overseers as well as guardians to watch after their children's estates — was a defense mechanism. But beyond that, fathers sought to protect their children's inheritances by prescribing and proscribing, in their wills, the actions of guardians. Thomas Tuggle, for example, charged the potentially troublesome half brother to preserve the property of the children, taking care to remove "no fences . . . nor to sell any timber from the land but to Make use of no more then will serve the

24. Conaway to Toby Smith, 27 Mar. 1654, Lancaster County, Deeds, etc. [Wills and Settlements of Estates], no. 2, 1654–1702, 1–2.

25. One result was that the law was extremely restrictive regarding the marriage (even the solicitation to marriage) of minor girls. See, e.g., Hening, *Statutes at Large* 2:281, 3:149–51, 441–46.

plantation." James Blaze stipulated that his wife Elizabeth was to have the use of his plantation during her lifetime, but she was "neither to sell nor Give Aney of the timber," cutting only "for hur owne ocashon to build with." "If she Cannot Keep Hands upon the plantation In the Ingan necke and Keepe the Houseing in Repare Shee may Lease it and Like wise to Keepe the plantation In Repare wheare on I nowe Live." James Dudley required his designated overseers, in the event his wife remarried, to "take good and Sufficient Security for the Money left to my Dear Children and also to see that none of my Lands be cleared which I have given to my Son James nor no timber cut off of it further than what is Necessary for repaireing the houses and for tobo: Caske for the said Plantacon."[26] The gentlemen justices of the county court, for their part, required performance bonds of most guardians and administrators, set aside special court days for "Orphans' Court," when the guardians were to bring in accounts for auditing, and acted promptly to protect the estates of orphans when malfeasance was called to their attention. And in the colony's assembly the same sorts of men — fathers and gentlemen justices — passed one after the other general laws to protect and preserve the estates of orphans.

All of this is testimony to the realization that great opportunity existed to despoil the parentless. And, indeed, examples of spoliation or attempted spoliation can be found. In 1664 the children of Oliver Seagar and Humphrey Owens sought the assistance of the court against Humphrey Jones, who had assumed their guardianship by marrying their common mother, Eleanor. In response to their assertion that Jones was claiming (as part of Eleanor's dower) a goodly portion of their estates, the court empaneled "a Jury of the ablest and neerest inhabitants" to make a just division. When, in 1681, Henry, Edwin, and Martha Thacker went to court to obtain a guardian other than their mother's new husband (William Stanard), it was obviously because the children — or at least Henry, the eldest at eighteen — suspected that their new stepfather would act against their interest. In 1686 Henry, on behalf of himself and the other children, brought suit against Stanard for mishandling of their estates, and Stanard fled the county. In 1685 the county court acted quickly to preserve the estates of John Gore and George Ransom from the spoliation of John Ascough, who had married the mother of the children and was "about Selling all his [and their] estate" before sailing for England. The court ordered that all of Ascough's property and that of the children, be forestopped "from any Sale or Alienacon untill the Said Orphts. estates be well Secured." And in 1706 the court moved to protect the children of the deceased Richard Stevens. His "considerable personall estate" was "likely

26. The Dudley, Blaze, and Tuggle wills are cited above, notes 20, 21.

to be Imbezelled away" by the "ill Management and Riotous Liveing" of his widow Sarah "and the orphans of the sd. decd. thereby ruined"; hence the court placed the estate in the hands of the county sheriff.[27]

But given the extensiveness of parental loss and the number of children whose estates were vulnerable, the number of assaults upon the estates of orphans seems relatively few. Most men involved with the estates were like Edwin Conaway, scrupulously attentive to the welfare of the Edmonds children when in 1654 he questioned the management of their estate, or like Robert Carter, one of the five overseers of the estate of Ralph Wormeley a half century later. Every page of the extant Wormeley estate record testifies to Carter's concern for the young heirs to the largest fortune in Middlesex, in this case particularly vulnerable heirs inasmuch as young Ralph and John were completing their education in England and the main Wormeley property, called Rosegill, was in the hands of their mother and her new husband, William Churchill. When in 1706, after five years' oversight of the estate, Carter heard that the boys were to return, he wrote that it was "high time"; "Col. Churchills living upon the place together with his relations have given him the Opportunity to fix himself absolutely in the Government of the Estate, the management whereof is become very much a trouble to all concerned, I believe, to me I am sure it is."[28] One suspects that care and scrupulosity in such matters were in effect products of the situation: What men such as Conaway and Carter did for the children of others, they could hope other men would do for theirs.

Parental loss and orphanhood were pervasive in this early Virginia society. So much is clear. Children from every socioeconomic level and from every birth cohort from the earliest period to well into the eighteenth century were involved. No breakdown of our sample of children has produced significant deviation from the percentages cited. Parental loss was a constant over time, as witness the Chowning family: Robert Chowning, Jr., lost his father at the age of fifteen; when Robert, Jr., died in 1698, he left seven children ranging in age from fourteen to two; his eldest son died in 1721, leaving six children ages fourteen to one. This prevalence of loss, and its pervasiveness, had great implication in the society and for our study of it.

Households tended to be mixed and complex affairs. We have noted the

27. Lancaster County, Deeds, etc. [Wills and Settlements of Estates], no. 2, 1654–1702, 307; Middlesex County, Order Book no. 2, 1680–94, 100, 240, and Will Book A, 1698–1713, 179.

28. Wormeley Estate Papers, 1701–16, with Christ Church, Lancaster Processioners' Returns, 1711–83, Virginia State Library and Archives. Extensive extracts are printed with the Wormeley Genealogy in *Virginia Magazine of History and Biography* 36 (1928): 287–91. The quotation is from the printed version, p. 290.

phenomenon in passing. In the Beverley household in 1680, just after the marriage of the widow Hone and Robert Beverley, we found Keeble, Hone, and two sorts of Beverley children, conceivably ranging in age from unmarried children in their early twenties to the just born. Had we dropped into just about any other household in Middlesex, we would have found much the same thing: orphans, half brothers, stepbrothers and stepsisters, and wards running a gamut of ages.[29] The father figure in the house might well be an uncle or a brother, the mother figure an aunt, elder sister, or simply the father's "now-wife" — to use the wording frequently found in conveyances and wills. Neither the romantic depictions of Alice Morse Earle or Mary Newton Stanard nor the connotations of social science terminology — the image of the nuclear family with its slowly graying parents and maturing children — applies. Historians more prone than we to use psychoanalysis can (and perhaps will) make great use of the mass trauma and the disruption of childhood implied.[30] They need only cite the case of Agatha Vause: By the time she was ten she had lost a father, two stepfathers, a mother, and her guardian uncle. But we must accept that what we take for traumatic loss was the norm for these children. To use the symbolism of Johann Sebastian Bach, death was a singing watchman in their world, teaching them from an early age that life was transitory. A planter of nearby Stafford County, referring back to his childhood, put the matter succinctly in a letter to his mother: "Before I was ten years old as I am sure you very well remember, I look'd upon this life here as but going to an Inn, no permanent being."[31] And what we might take for the disruption of childhood involved, conversely, a system for rooting the parentless child within the society.

Kinship and quasi-kinship were the essentials of the system. One can

29. Given the current emphasis on the makeup of the household, it is surprising that this phenomenon has not been more widely noticed. Michael Anderson, however, has found it extensively in mid-nineteenth-century Britain. See the revised version of his "Family, Household, and the Industrial Revolution," in Michael Gordon, ed., *The American Family in Social-Historical Perspective* (New York, 1973), 59–75. Elizabeth Wirth Maverick in "Nature versus Nurture: Patterns and Trends in Seventeenth-Century French Child-Rearing," in *History of Childhood*, ed. deMause, 288–89, suggests much the same thing, writing that "a high mortality and remarriage rate introduced a complex kinship relationship into the households." But she inexplicably links her statement to that of Marc Bloch on the decisive influence of the French grandparent. As is pointed out below, high mortality vitiates the influence of grandparents.

30. That they are turning in this direction is indicated by William Saffady, "The Effects of Childhood Bereavement and Parental Remarriage in Sixteenth-Century England: The Case of Thomas Moore," *History of Childhood Quarterly* 1 (1973): 310–36. See also Daniel Blake Smith, "In Search of the Family in the Colonial South," in *Race and Family in the Colonial South*, ed. Winthrop D. Jordan and Sheila L. Skemp (Jackson, Miss., 1987), 21–36.

31. William to Mrs. Mary Fitzhugh, 30 June 1698, in Davis, *Fitzhugh and His Chesapeake World*, 358.

even argue that they were accentuated in the society in large measure in response to the expectation of parental death and parentless children. Even in the earliest days in the area of what would become Middlesex, the county's people linked themselves together. It does not seem simply fortuitous that two separate branches of Robinson family men should settle in the county, or that a third, covert line should be represented by Frances Robinson and her children. Neither does it seem fortuitous that four husbands of Eltonhead sisters should seat themselves within a few miles of each other, or that Henry Corbin, busily establishing himself financially in Northumberland, should move to Middlesex immediately following his marriage to an Eltonhead widow. Brothers-in-law (and their children and stepchildren) would be kin to one's own children, ready at hand to step in when death left children parentless.[32]

In the years to and after 1700 the cementing and recementing of kinship by cousin marriages, the marriages of stepbrothers and stepsisters, of wards and natural children, the extension of kinship through godparentage and by virtue of sequential marriages that made quasi-kin of unrelated children proceeded at such a pace as to leave the best of genealogists far behind. That such relationships were meaningful is attested to by the regularity of bequests to godchildren, to sons- and daughters-in-law (the seventeenth century's dual expression for stepsons and stepdaughters as well as for children's spouses), to nephews, nieces, and cousins. And such relationships were called upon when death made children parentless. The Edmonds guardian whom Edwin Conaway challenged in 1654 was the children's mother's first husband's son by a prior marriage. When young Humphrey Jones was orphaned, there was on hand to look after him Randolph Seager: Young Humphrey was his father's son by a third marriage; Seager was the son of Humphrey's father's second wife by a prior marriage; and Seager's wife was Humphrey's half sister. Garrett Minor designated two Vivion brothers-in-law and a Montague cousin to serve as trustees for his children. And that Edwin Thacker was the grandson of the sister of Ralph Wormeley's children's grandmother (their first cousin twice removed) was enough to allow Wormeley in 1701 to consider Thacker a "relative" and call upon him to serve as co-overseer of the children's inheritances. For children, stability lay not so much in transitory parents but in the permanent network of relatives and quasi-relatives in which they were embedded. Instability, for children and for parents contemplating their children's parentless future, lay in being outside the system. James Jordan, new to the county when he wrote his will in 1710, had not even friends to rely upon: "If it Should please God to take my wife whilst my Children [are] younge and Uncapeable of Governing themselves," he

---

32. A point elaborated upon in Rutman and Rutman, *A Place in Time: Middlesex*, 47–52.

wrote, please God "the Worshipfull" county court would "take them under theire tuition and Care and then what Small Estate there may be to be Equally devided Amongst them."[33]

One suspects that in their situation the children of Middlesex matured early. There seems little enough of that emotional content of family life which gives meaning to childhood as we know it, little time for it given the fact of many children and the shortness of life itself. Only in one of the many wills surviving from Middlesex in this period does one catch a hint of that whimsy which proceeds from the love of a parent toward a child, when George Ransom leaves to his daughter Elizabeth a "Jack in the box."[34] The strictures as to education that have been quoted here and there as we proceeded reflect a pragmatic outlook toward a life of work and property: Let the boy learn "to reade, write, and Cast Accots"; let the girl learn the rudiments of "housewifery."[35] And the very fact that children were heirs and heiresses matured them. We catch sight of children in their early teens acting to preserve inheritances — the Thacker children moving against their stepfather Stanard — and of fathers, in their efforts to protect their orphaned children's estates, attempting to push sons into an early legal maturity. As early as 1656 the law allowed orphans at seventeen to control the produce of their own labor, while increasingly in the eighteenth century men attempted to lower the age of majority by testamentary declarations. John Summer, for example, in 1703 specified that his son of sixteen was of age to dispose of his estate with the advice of designated executors, while Thomas Norman in 1727 declared it to be his will that his seventeen-year-old son Robert "Act and do for himself."[36]

Even when fathers lived to see their sons into maturity — when death did not take the parent and leave the boy fatherless but propertied — fathers seem impelled to set up sons independently, as Richard Perrott, Sr., did when he turned property over to his son, Richard, Jr., when the latter was twenty-two.[37] (The norm being early parental death and youthful inheritance, it almost seems as if the long-lived father felt obliged to keep his son equal to his peer group.) Authority within the community, too, was shared with the young. Matthew Kemp was sitting on the parish

33. Middlesex County, Will Book B, 1713–34, 42.

34. Middlesex County, Wills, etc., 1675–1798, pt. 1, 1.

35. Will of Jane Cocke, ibid., 92.

36. Hening, *Statutes at Large* 1:416–17; Middlesex County, Will Book A, 1698–1713, 146–47 and Will Book B, 1713–34, 306.

37. Middlesex County, Deeds, etc., no. 2[1a], 1679–94, 15. The many conveyances of this sort have the advantage of providing a date at which a son was established independently; the same phenomenon, but without the date, can be observed in wills where a son is left "the plantation whereon he now lives" (will of Marvell Moseley, Middlesex County, Will Book B, 1713–34, 238).

vestry and county court by age twenty-one; young Perrott was named to the vestry and court at twenty-six; so, too, was Robert Dudley. Indeed, the "fathers" of the community — meaning the vestrymen and justices — ranged in age in 1687 from young Kemp to Abraham Weekes and John Mann, the two senior members at fifty-six years of age; over half were under forty. Fifteen years later the same situation prevailed. Half were under forty, with the members ranging in age from William Wormeley at twenty-four to John Wortham at fifty-seven. In this context George Washington's eighteenth-century career does not seem particularly unusual. Born in 1732, losing his father at eleven, raised by various relatives (including his half brother Lawrence), inheriting Mount Vernon at age twenty, Washington was a militia lieutenant colonel commanding at Fort Necessity at age twenty-two and a burgess at twenty-six; at twenty-seven he married a widow with two small children, and at forty-three he commanded the Revolutionary army.

We cannot help but contrast what we have found in this early Virginia community with what current scholarship is depicting for New England. No direct comparison can be made; New England's scholars have been relatively mute on the subject of parental death and orphanhood. Philip J. Greven, Jr., for example, does not even index "orphans" in his study of Andover, Massachusetts. John Demos has much to say in his study of Plymouth, but while his picture of the testamentary provisions regarding the parentless is very much like that found in Middlesex, his picture is based on limited sources.[38] Moreover, Demos's discussion of orphans, his mortality figures (together with Greven's seventeenth-century figures), and his and Greven's figures for mean age at first marriage offer a conundrum. Demos does not write as if orphanhood was an exceptional circumstance in Plymouth society; yet the mortality figures, arranged to form a table of life expectancies (as in table 10.2), suggest that the potential for orphanhood was all but nonexistent.[39] In Middlesex, where first-married men and women could expect to die in their late forties and late thirties, respectively, parental death and orphanhood were (as we have seen) inherent in the highly idealized median marriage. The mean child could not escape the loss of parents.[40] But in New England, if the figures offered by

38. Greven, *Four Generations: Population, Land, and Family in Colonial Andover, Massachusetts* (Ithaca, N.Y., 1970); Demos, *A Little Commonwealth: Family Life in Plymouth Colony* (New York, 1970). Demos relies very heavily on the 1631 will of Mary Ring. He also seems to construe the accommodation of parentless children as servitude (p. 115).

39. The same type of conundrum is offered by the matter-of-fact approach to remarriage by Demos (but not by Greven). If the mortality figures are correct, the potential for remarriage would be minimal, and remarriage exceptional. Greven notes the exceptional nature of remarriage (using it to substantiate his mortality figures); Demos does not.

40. The same is suggested by life tables constructed on the basis of data from other areas

Table 10.2. Comparative life expectancies: the seventeenth-century Chesapeake and New England

| | One can expect to live until age | | | | | | |
| | Middlesex Co., Va. | | Maryland | Andover, Mass. | | Plymouth Colony | |
Having achieved age	Married males $N = 259$	Married females $N = 258$	Males $N = 153$	Males $N = 192$	Females $N = 108$	Males	Females $N = 645$
20	48.8	39.8	46.0	64.6	62.1	69.2	62.4
25	48.7	41.3	47.7	—	—	—	—
30	49.4	43.6	50.4	69.3	65.3	70.0	64.7
35	50.8	45.7	53.0	—	—	—	—
40	53.0	48.6	55.6	71.8	68.7	71.2	69.7
45	55.0	54.2	59.5	—	—	—	—
50	57.7	59.3	62.0	73.5	72.1	73.7	73.4
55	62.7	62.7	65.6	—	—	—	—
60	65.8	67.9	69.3	75.6	76.4	76.3	76.8
65	70.0	70.0	74.4	—	—	—	—
70	73.6	73.7	77.0	80.3	81.9	79.9	80.7
75	77.9	80.2	78.5	—	—	—	—
80	—	—	—	86.6	89.6	85.1	86.7
85	—	—	—	—	—	—	—
90	—	—	—	95.0	95.8	—	—
95	—	—	—	—	—	—	—
100	—	—	—	—	105.0	—	—

Sources and notes: Middlesex: Appendixes 1 and 2 of Darrett B. and Anita H. Rutman, "'Now-Wives and Sons-in-Law': Parental Death in a Seventeenth-Century Virginia County," in *The Chesapeake in the Seventeenth Century: Essays on Anglo-American Society*, ed. Thad W. Tate and David L. Ammerman (Chapel Hill, N.C., 1979), 175–82; Maryland: Russell R. Menard and Lorena Walsh, "Death in the Chesapeake: Two Life Tables for Men in Early Colonial Maryland," *Maryland Historical Magazine* 69 (1974): 211–27; Andover: computed from data in Philip J. Greven, Jr., *Four Generations: Population, Land, and Family in Colonial Andover, Massachusetts* (Ithaca, N.Y., 1970), 27, 108; Plymouth: John Demos, *A Little Commonwealth: Family Life in Plymouth Colony* (New York, 1970), 192. N.B.: Demos's first achieved age is 21 rather than 20. The computation technique has been adopted from George W. Barclay, *Techniques of Population Analysis* (New York, 1958), chap. 4.

Demos and Greven are to be accepted, the mean marriage ended with the death of the wife at around sixty-three, the widower dying at around seventy; the eldest child of the marriage would be approximately forty at the time of the mother's death and forty-four when the father died, while the youngest child would be twenty-three and twenty-seven. Either orphanhood was an exceptional circumstance in New England — and the contrast with Virginia startling, to say the least — or the mortality figures offered are incorrect.[41]

If New England's mortality figures stand, however, together with the startling contrast, where does that leave us? Certainly it suggests that we are dealing with two entirely different types of childhood along the seventeenth-century Anglo-American coast: In New England one lived

---

of the Chesapeake region, one of which is included in table 10.2 for comparative purposes. See Lorena S. Walsh and Russell R. Menard, "Death in the Chesapeake: Two Life Tables for Men in Early Colonial Maryland," *Maryland Historical Magazine* 69 (1974): 211–27; Daniel Blake Smith, "Mortality and Family in the Colonial Chesapeake," *Journal of Interdisciplinary History* 8 (1978): 403–27. That four samples drawn independently are so alike (and so variant from the New England samples) tends to substantiate all four.

41. Terry L. Anderson and Robert Paul Thomas, "White Population, Labor Force, and Extensive Growth of the New England Economy in the Seventeenth Century," *Journal of Economic History* 33 (1973): 634–67, developed their argument in large part by equating a stable population model to Greven's data, specifically the United Nations model life table Level 45, Female, and Level 65, Male, as presented in United Nations, Department of Economic and Social Affairs, *Population Studies*, no. 22, *Age and Sex Patterns of Mortality: Model Life-Tables for Under-Developed Countries* (New York, 1955); no. 25, *Methods for Population Projections by Sex and Age* (New York, 1956); and no. 39, *The Concept of a Stable Population: Application to the Study of Populations of Countries with Incomplete Demographic Statistics* (New York, 1968). As early as 1931, Alfred J. Lotka, the "father" of stable population theory, sketched a method for assessing the extent of parental loss from life-table data in "Orphanhood in Relation to Demographic Factors: A Study in Population Analysis," *Metron: Rivista Internazionale di Statistica* 9 (1931): 37–109. Applying Lotka's shorter method (unadjusted for posthumous and puerperal orphans) to the tables suggested as pertinent by Anderson and Thomas leads to a crude estimate of 10 percent of New England's children losing their fathers by age 15, 14 percent losing their mothers, and 1.5 percent losing both. But is the designated model life table (and the data from which it is extrapolated) appropriate? Linda Auwers Bissell in a study of "From One Generation to Another: Mobility in Seventeenth-Century Windsor, Connecticut," *William and Mary Quarterly*, 3d ser., 31 (1974): 79–110, notes in passing (p. 93n) that of a sample of 99 sons born between 1650 and 1669, 31 received land before their sixteenth birthday but after the death of their fathers — 31.9 percent of the sample, a figure more to be expected in Middlesex than in New England. If the phenomenon of fatherless sons proves so alike, it will be hard to understand divergent mortality schedules and life expectancies. The potential for error (particularly errors resulting from name confusion) is enormous. Greven and Demos were working in the "pioneer days" of such research, before that potential was fully understood; Greven, for example, assumed that "adult deaths were almost always recorded" (*Four Generations*, 109). Mortality is so crucial both for understanding New England society and for comparative purposes, and the works of Demos and Greven are proving to be such influential studies, that perhaps a retest of the Andover and Plymouth data is in order.

more in a parental situation; in the Chesapeake area one lived more in a kinship situation. It suggests, too, an ancillary but equally startling contrast between the societies: that in Virginia we ought not to expect the generational tension of which the New England scholars have been making so much.[42] When, as in Middlesex, half of the sons (50.6 percent of our sample) lost their fathers before reaching legal maturity or marriage — and the tendency with respect to the other half was for fathers to set mature sons up independently in their early twenties — the potential for tension hardly existed.[43] And it means that we ought not to expect much of tradition in this Virginia society, again in contrast to New England, whose scholars are suggesting the great strength of tradition.[44] For tradition on a folk level tends to pass from a society's elderly to its youth, from grandparents to grandchildren. Few of Middlesex's children ever knew their grandparents.[45]

"In the name of God Amen," Maximilian Petty wrote, to return to the scene with which we began. A year after Petty's death his widow, Christian, married again, giving young Maximilian and Ann (now eleven and eight and a half, respectively) a stepfather. The marriage, to William Briscoe, a former servant of Petty's and his successor as undersheriff of the county, was hardly successful; there were no children, and in 1692 Briscoe was jailed for sexually assaulting Mrs. Margaret Whitaker. In mid-1700 he died, and Christian was free to marry again; her new husband, John Viv-

42. See, for example, Sumner Chilton Powell, *Puritan Village: The Formation of a New England Town* (Middletown, Conn., 1963), chap. 8; Kenneth A. Lockridge and Alan Kreider, "The Evolution of Massachusetts Town Government, 1640 to 1740," *William and Mary Quarterly*, 3d ser., 23 (1966): 567; Greven, *Four Generations*, 279–82; James A. Henretta, "The Morphology of New England Society in the Colonial Period," *Journal of Interdisciplinary History* 2 (1971): 388–91, and his *The Evolution of American Society, 1700–1815: An Interdisciplinary Analysis* (Lexington, Mass., 1973), 36–37.

43. One can argue that relatively early male mortality and the early independence of sons had an effect upon the Chesapeake labor system as well. The New England scene of a man and one or more sons at work on the family fields — or, given the nature of agricultural labor, lolling in the barn in off-seasons and during inclement weather, a phenomenon that Edmund S. Morgan has rightly observed but perhaps overburdened in "The Labor Problem at Jamestown, 1607–1618," *American Historical Review* 76 (1971): 595–611 — simply could not apply in Virginia. How, then, was labor supplied to the "family farm"? In the context of this question, servants and ultimately slaves — at least on the smaller holdings — might well be construed as substitutes for sons. See also Morgan, "Slavery and Freedom: The American Paradox," *Journal of American History* 59 (1972): 5–29.

44. Philip J. Greven, Jr., "Historical Demography and Colonial America: A Review Article," *William and Mary Quarterly*, 3d ser., 24 (1967): 453; Kenneth A. Lockridge, *A New England Town, the First Hundred Years: Dedham, Massachusetts, 1636–1736* (New York, 1970); Darrett B. Rutman, *American Puritanism: Faith and Practice* (Philadelphia, 1970), 47–51.

45. In contrast, note John M. Murrin's aside in an extensive "Review Essay" on New England social history in *History and Theory* 11 (1972): 238, that it may well be that grandparents were a New England invention.

ion, was a widower twice over with five children. Christian was the "now-wife" to whom Vivion left the use of his land and the care of two of his own minor children when he died in 1705. Of Maximilian, Jr., we know little; presumably he died soon after his mother's remarriage. Ann, however, grew to propertied womanhood. By the time she married Thomas Smith in 1698 (at age eighteen) she was twice an heiress, once by the will of her father and again by the will of her godfather, Augustine Cant. In 1700 her stepfather Briscoe would, in a way, make her an heiress again, leaving his estate to her husband and children (although giving his widow, Christian, its use through her life). Ann's marriage to Smith lasted until her death in 1704. Two children are known to have been born to the marriage, both of them minors when left motherless, the younger but a few months old. The next year Smith died, and they were orphaned children.

11 The Genesis of a Chesapeake Town

With Anita H. Rutman

The infrequency, even absence, of towns and villages has long been held to be characteristic of the early Chesapeake. Somehow we imagine that the economy of the region was integrated by shipboard merchant-captains roaming its broad rivers, and Thomas Jefferson's remark is quoted time and again: "Our country being much intersected with navigable waters, and trade brought generally to our doors, instead of our being obliged to go in quest of it, has probably been one of the causes why we have no towns of any consequence." One wonders, however, what river capable of carrying the traffic of the Atlantic into and out of the interior serviced Monticello on its mountaintop. And one wonders about the twenty-five towns that Jefferson actually listed. How did they come into being? Rural sociologists of the 1930s described the American countryside, North and South, in terms of "open-country neighborhoods" surrounding small retail centers. Has this geography no history?

Today, where a small creek joins the Rappahannock River on the north shore of Middlesex County, Virginia, lies the town of Urbanna. Except in terms of the county itself, it has never had much importance. True, it was the earliest town on the Rappahannock, but it was quickly surpassed by upriver towns — Tappahannock, Falmouth, Fredericksburg. How it came to exist at all, however, in an otherwise unremarkable tidewater county of Chesapeake tobacco growers, tells us something about the way counties like Middlesex were linked to a larger world of trade and commerce, a merchant community which sprinkled the Atlantic with myriad sailing ships and imparted value to the tobacco crop the county's planters tended. It tells us, too, something about the making of our contemporary rural landscape: small towns, sometimes little more than crossroad hamlets, set here and there amidst tilled fields and wood-lands.

We can begin some thirty years after the area was first opened to settle-ment (1650), at a time when there was no town in Middlesex, and specifi-cally with Tobias Mickleburrough.[1] From the early 1680s on, Micklebur-rough kept a store on the south branch of Sunderland Creek. His was by no means a store in the modern sense. His business was conducted any-where and everywhere: in the hall of his house, while standing in the entry, at church during the time before and after service devoted to "strolling round" and "consulting," and at court day. It was an almost casual matter of a neighbor mentioning needs, Mickleburrough answering in terms of items on hand or to be had through his "connections," a bargain struck — so much in goods in return for so much tobacco when the crop was made — and its careful recording in "a book of Sales."[2] Most of the goods he had on hand Mickleburrough kept in a storeroom, probably a separate building, but others were tucked here and there about his house. In all, his "store goods" amounted to roughly £20 current money, or 5 percent of Mickleburrough's personal belongings as inventoried after his death.[3] For, notably, he was a planter as well as storekeeper, owning twenty blacks in 1703, a home plantation of just over two hundred acres, another, largely undeveloped, of six hundred acres some two miles away, and he was oper-ating still a third as guardian for a minor in his care.

It is the store goods that interest us, however, for they allow a glimpse of what he and his neighbors needed in the way of imports: nails in a variety of sizes from threepenny to twenty, cloth and thread, buttons, bone combs, mirrors, pewter, gunpowder, a variety of locks and hinges, window glass, linseed oil, and the white and red lead that, when mixed, made colored paint. But the last was probably not for sale; in all likelihood it was the "oyle and Colours" that Mickleburrough had laid aside for his own new house. The inventory of another storekeeper with a somewhat larger stock adds to the list: again nails and cloth, but also "5 women's Gownes" and "a Girls petticoate," "a parcell shoe buckles," hatbands, pots and pans, hoes and axes, two hammers, a saw, and "3 horne books."[4]

1. All manuscript county records cited in this chapter in the Virginia State Library and Archives, Richmond. See note 2 in the preceding chapter on the sources of the prosopogra-phy.

2. The phrase is from a 1692 case at law involving the estate of Oswald Cary, another merchant (Middlesex County, Order Book no. 2, 1680–94, 541).

3. Middlesex County, Will Book A, 1698–1713, 141–45.

4. Ibid., 104–6.

A list of thirty debtors compiled by the executors of Mickleburrough's estate, moreover, allows us a glimpse of his customers. When plotted on a map, they form a tight circle extending three miles in every direction about his house. Twelve were renters; seventeen were small planters with holdings ranging from 50 to 272 acres and averaging 124; only one was another major holder, Mickleburrough's brother-in-law Henry Thacker with 1,375 acres. Their debts to Mickleburrough, too, were small, ranging from 16 pounds of tobacco to 850 and averaging just over 300. Were all the tobacco owed him in February 1703 collected and packed in hogsheads for shipment, it would amount to roughly seventeen hogsheads, by no means the equivalent of the fifty-three hogsheads shipped by Middlesex's major planter, Ralph Wormeley, in 1701. It was, nevertheless, a significant quantity, particularly when we add the hogsheads from Mickleburrough's own land; if Wormeley's tobacco made up roughly a quarter of a ship's cargo, Mickleburrough's would have made up a tenth.[5]

In our mind's eye we must envision small retail operations such as Mickleburrough's spread all across Middlesex at the end of the seventeenth century, the "merchants . . . seated with their Stores in their Country Plantations, and having their Customers all round about them," as commented on in a contemporary pamphlet, the "Men in Number from ten to thirty" on every Chesapeake river who "take care to supply the poorer sort with Goods and Necessaries."[6] Seldom do we see such operations in any detail. Most often our information comes in the form of sparse hints entered in the records for one purpose or another: a judgment against Edward Spark "to be paid in a Store" (1691), another judgment using the same language (1693), the trial of two slaves (1696) accused of theft "out of the Stoore" of a planter whose court actions and inventory imply retail trading.[7] They were, however, the top opening of a funnel through which the produce of the small and middling planters of Middlesex flowed out to the Atlantic. Still, storekeeping planters like Mickleburrough were only part of a larger structure.

Mickleburrough himself was but one of several customers of another

---

5. Wormeley Estate Papers, 1701–16, with Christ Church, Lancaster Processioners' Returns, 1711–83, 148, Virginia State Library and Archives. A Middlesex hogshead (of sweet-scented tobacco) held roughly 500 to 600 pounds at this time. On a ship's cargo, see William Fitzhugh's proposal to load a ship for Thomas Clayton, 1686, in Richard Beale Davis, ed., *William Fitzhugh and His Chesapeake World, 1676–1701: The Fitzhugh Letters and Other Documents* (Chapel Hill, N.C., 1963), 180–83.

6. Henry Hartwell, James Blair, and Edward Chilton, *The Present State of Virginia and the College* (1699), ed. Hunter Dickinson Farish (Williamsburg, Va., 1940), 12–13; John Oldmixon, *The British Empire in America* (1708), quoted in Lewis Cecil Gray, *History of Agriculture in the Southern United States to 1860* (Washington, D.C., 1933) 1:410.

7. Middlesex County, Order Book no. 2, 1680–94, 521, 634 and no. 3, 1694–1705, 132.

Middlesex man, William Churchill, who had what Mickleburrough did not, that is, those close relationships with merchants in England that, by virtue of mutual trust, allowed the conduct of business across three thousand miles of water. A Virginian of a later date put the matter neatly. Asked by a friend to send tobacco to a particular merchant in England (who in turn would sell it, deduct costs, and use the proceeds to establish an account against which the Virginian could draw to pay debts or buy goods for import into Virginia), John Custis at first refused on the grounds that "Mr Hanberry" — the merchant in question — "is an utter stranger to me." Subsequently Custis agreed, but cautiously, giving to "Mr Hanberry . . . (who I understand is your particular friend) the trouble of a small consignmnt." "The gentleman is an utter stranger to me," he repeated, "but I depend he is a man of honor and probity otherwise you that understand mankind so well would never have listed him in your friendship. . . . If Mr. Handberrys uses me well [and] if I live we may have greater dealings."[8]

Churchill, entering Middlesex from England in 1675 as a young man of twenty-five and buying land along the lower Rappahannock, had such relationships from the start, specifically with his "kinsmen," merchants Nicholas and John Goodwin of London. To these he added others over time, and, importantly, he acquired Middlesex connections — Christopher Robinson, for one, who also had extensive English ties. In partnership or alone, Churchill bought, sold, rented, mortgaged, and foreclosed land throughout the county. He traded with a variety of English mariner-merchants — men whose ships plied the rivers on an itinerant basis, putting off English goods and taking on tobacco. He entered into a variety of engagements with his English connections, acting for them as agent or factor, gathering cargoes for them, and selling their goods. But he also traded on his own account, sending tobacco on consignment to one or another English merchant to create a balance upon which he could draw. Like Mickleburrough, he operated a store; in 1688 he had a servant working there exclusively. But he also wholesaled goods to others, including Mickleburrough, advancing them English goods on the promise of a return in tobacco. In 1703 Mickleburrough owed Churchill just under £400. So extensive were Churchill's operations in the county that at one time he engaged William Kilbee, who lived in its lower reaches, to serve as his factor and to collect debts owed him. By 1698 Churchill was styling himself "William Churchill and Co."[9]

Mickleburrough served the small and middling planters in effecting the

8. E. G. Swem, ed., "Brothers of the Spade: Correspondence of Peter Collinson of London, and of John Custis, of Williamsburg, Virginia, 1734–1746," American Antiquarian Society, *Proceedings* 58 (1948): 68, 79–80.

9. Middlesex County, Order Book no. 3, 1694–1705, 276.

vital exchange of tobacco for English goods; so, too, did Churchill to an extent. But Churchill also served Mickleburrough, giving a structured appearance to trade within the county. In sum, Churchill was Mickleburrough's "connection," while Churchill's own connections led outward to the mariner-merchants and London houses. The arrangement was by no means unique. Indeed, when we track the various credit arrangements in the county through lawsuits and the like, territorial hegemonies begin to suggest themselves.

In his early years Churchill's network of debtors within the county was confined to its lower reaches. Matthew Kemp held sway in the south-central area, operating in both Middlesex and Gloucester counties from holdings on the lower Piankatank River, with Richard Stevens and Robert Dudley having to him the same relationship as Mickleburrough had to Churchill. Robert Beverley, Christopher Robinson, and Richard Willis divided the rest of the county. (The Wormeleys, Middlesex's great planter family at Rosegill plantation, had little part in these intracounty credit relationships; with their own connections in England, they exported and imported largely for themselves.) Notably, the connections abroad and within the county that allowed these hegemonies did not automatically pass from father to son as land and personal property did but shifted from one planter-merchant to another. Beverley had fallen heir to the connections of John Burnham, a major planter-merchant of the 1670s who died in 1681. When Beverley died in 1687, Robinson's area of influence grew. When Robinson died in 1693, Churchill's influence spread from the lower part of the county into the center, while Gawin Corbin — scion of a major family with extensive relations both in Middlesex and England — entered the scene to take Robinson's place in the county's upper reaches on the Rappahannock. And when Willis died in 1701, Corbin's and Churchill's influence swelled to fill the vacuum. Willis was much married but child-less; his lands went to a nephew, John Alden, but Alden never assumed the merchant role of his uncle.

If credit relationships suggest an element of rationality in the economic structure of the county, we must nevertheless confess that the point escaped observers at the time. Each year toward the end of the seventeenth century, some 150 ships arrived in the Chesapeake in the late fall carrying goods consigned to planter-merchants at their various locations or sent on speculation to be bartered for tobacco on the spot. For three to four months the ships sailed the waters of the bay and its rivers, each taking its own course until, their English goods gone and their holds filled with tobacco, they set canvas for England.[10]

10. In war the ships arrived and departed in convoy. See Arthur Pierce Middleton, *Tobacco Coast: A Maritime History of Chesapeake Bay in the Colonial Era* (Newport News, Va., 1953), chap. 10.

Viewing the comings and goings from his vantage point in Gloucester County, just south of Middlesex, the Reverend John Clayton was led to comment that "the great number of Rivers and the thinness of the Inhabitants distract and disperse a trade. So that all Ships in general gather each their Loading up and down an hundred Miles distant; and the best of Trade that can be driven is only a sort of *Scotch* Pedling." To others, merchants such as Churchill and Mickleburrough lived "the best of any" but still were "subject to great Inconveniencies in the way of their Trade." "They are obliged to sell upon Trust all the Year long, except just a little while when Tobacco is ready," "drive a pityful retail Trade to serve every Man's little Occasions, being . . . in Effect but Country Chapmen," and all the while pay damaged tobacco and high freight rates for the "scrambling Manner" in which the ships offloaded and loaded their cargoes.[11] The apparent disorder suggested towns as a cure, for with towns business could be centralized and the crop assembled in but a few spots, allowing the ships a quick and orderly unloading and loading. The thought linked to a concern (at least among some) for the scattering of the population across the landscape — "our wild and Rambling way," one Virginian called it — and the lack of "cohabitation," and hence a lack of the "Christian Neighbourhood" and "brotherly admonition" that the English mind associated with towns. And both thoughts linked to a more general concern over Virginia's single-minded attachment to tobacco and the failure of every attempt to encourage diversification: Towns, some felt, would attract craftsmen and artisans, even manufacturers, and these in turn would lessen the dependence on English imports and the tobacco that paid for them.[12]

Over the years such concerns had provoked occasional action from Virginia's government. In the 1650s the legislature of the colony ordered that in every county there be established "one or two places and no more" where "the marketts and trade of the county shall be and not else where," and the county court designated two places in Middlesex "for Stoars and Markets." But "markets" on paper were not markets in fact. The ineffective act was soon replaced by another that simply provided that if any

11. Edmund and Dorothy Smith Berkeley, ed., *The Reverend John Clayton, a Parson with a Scientific Mind: His Scientific Writings and Other Related Papers* (Charlottesville, Va., 1965), 53; Hartwell, Blair, and Chilton, *Present State of Virginia*, 10–11.

12. Nicholas Spencer to Mr. Secretary Coventry, 9 July 1680, quoted in John W. Reps, *Tidewater Towns: City Planning in Colonial Virginia and Maryland* (Williamsburg, Va., 1972), 67; R[oger] G[reen], *Virginia's Cure: or, An Advisive Narrative concerning Virginia* (1662), in Peter Force, comp., *Tracts and Other Papers, Relating Principally to the . . . Colonies in North America* (Washington, D.C., 1836–47), vol. 3, tract 15:5; John C. Rainbolt, *From Prescription to Persuasion: Manipulation of [Seventeenth] Century Virginia Economy* (Port Washington, N.Y., 1974), 49–50, 149–50.

county or particular person set up a place "whether the merchants shall willingly come for the sale or bringing of goods such men shall bee lookt uppon as benefactors to the publique." Governor William Berkeley attempted to force the development of Jamestown and, by ordering the tobacco ships to anchor only where they could be protected by forts, other towns as well. "If the shipps had soe ridd," wrote a commentator later, "and the tobacco of every County had beene brought to p'ticular places," it would be very advantageous in "causeing Warehouses to be built, and soe in p'cess of times Townes."[13]

In 1680, under the leadership of Middlesex's own Robert Beverley, acting as clerk of the House of Burgesses, the Virginia legislature passed a comprehensive bill "for Cohabitation and encouragement of Trade and Manufacture" under which the colony's trade would be funneled through twenty towns to be established in the various counties, including one in Middlesex. The authorities in England suspended the bill late in 1682, objecting largely to provisions that might have encouraged diversification and taken Virginians away from tobacco. Beverley tried again in 1685, only to have the effort swamped in the wake of, first, an Anglo-American constitutional squabble, and then England's Glorious Revolution, which saw the replacement of James II by William of Orange and Mary, his Stuart wife. Finally, in 1691 another port bill, only slightly different from that of 1680, was passed. This, too, was rejected by English authorities, as was another drafted by Beverley's son, also Robert, and passed in 1705.[14] But the whole sequence of acts created enough of a legal framework to

13. William W. Hening, ed., *The Statutes at Large: Being a Collection of All the Laws of Virginia . . . [through 1792]* (Richmond and Philadelphia, 1809–23), 1:412–14, 476; Lancaster County, Deeds, etc., no. 1, 1652–57, 201; [William Sherwood], "Virginias Deploured Condition: Or an Impartiall Narrative of the Murders Comitted by the Indians there, and of the Sufferings of his Majesties Loyall Subjects under the Rebellious Outrages of Mr. Nathaniell Bacon Junior," Massachusetts Historical Society, *Collections*, 4th ser., 9 (1871): 164.

14. For the acts in general, see Edward M. Riley, "The Town Acts of Colonial Virginia," *Journal of Southern History* 16 (1950): 306–23; Rainbolt, *Prescription to Persuasion*, 113–17, 132–35, 157–68. For the growth of towns in Virginia and the South in general — a matter unfortunately confused by the use of the words "urban" and "urbanization" — see Joseph A. Ernst and H. Roy Merrens, "'Camden's turrets pierce the skies!': The Urban Process in the Southern Colonies during the Eighteenth Century," *William and Mary Quarterly*, 3d ser., 30 (1973): 549–74; Hermann Wellenreuther, "Urbanization in the Colonial South: A Critique," *William and Mary Quarterly*, 3d ser., 31 (1974): 653–71; Jacob M. Price, "Economic Function and the Growth of American Port Towns in the Eighteenth Century," *Perspectives in American History* 8 (1974): 123–86; Carville Earle and Ronald Hoffman, "Staple Crops and Urban Development in the Eighteenth Century South," ibid., 10 (1976): 7–78; Earle and Hoffman, "The Urban South: The First Two Centuries," in *The City in Southern History: The Growth of Urban Civilization in the South*, ed. Blaine A. Brownell and David R. Goldfield (Port Washington, N.Y., 1977), 23–51.

allow prominent Virginians here and there to proceed with the business of erecting towns. In Middlesex the effort first pitted the county's cosmopolitan merchants against Ralph Wormeley of Rosegill, and then a group of young men aspiring to be cosmopolitan merchants against those whose aspirations had already been fulfilled.

Scion of important families on both sides and heir to both a substantial fortune and the most significant landholdings in Middlesex County, Ralph Wormeley was the embodiment of that baronial elite or "aristocracy" so often commented on by historians as characteristic of Virginia's past. His home plantation, Rosegill, fronting on the Rappahannock in mid-county, contained 10 percent of the labor force of the county in 1668, and a traveler in the 1680s described it as "a rather large village" of "at least twenty houses."[15] By both ruthless legal maneuvers and using his crown offices to force lands to escheat, then taking title to them, Wormeley sought constantly to enlarge the estate. His additions seem clearly designed to extend his property holdings across the county from the Rappahannock on the north to the Piankatank on the south, dividing the county in half. The mother church of the county was located in the middle of Rosegill and, embellished with Wormeley silver and linens, was, in his mind, his manor church. If a town was to be built in Middlesex, it seems, he would have it his manor town.

The act of 1680 first specified where any town in Middlesex would be located: on a fifty-acre tract on the upriver side of Rosegill Creek—Wormeley land. It was to Wormeley, therefore, that the leading planter-merchants of Middlesex applied when, each presumably acting because he saw his own profit in the venture, they sought through the county court to make the town a reality. A bare six weeks after the passage of the act, the Middlesex court designated Robert Beverley and John Burnham its agents or "feoffees" to arrange the purchase of the land for ten thousand pounds of tobacco and receive it on behalf of the public. The same order charged the feoffees with laying out streets and half-acre town lots—Beverley to do the actual surveying—and empowered them to "make Sale and [pass] good and Sufficient Deeds and Conveyances to all [and] every Person . . . that shall Desire [to] Purchase." Beverley's survey seems to have been completed in October 1681. In November the court anticipated moving itself to the town, ordering Beverley and Christopher Robinson to contract with "workmen" for a courthouse to be built there "of Such Dimentions and with Such Conveniency as in their discretions they Shall thinke Convenient." For all the activity, however, nothing happened. Certainly nobody moved into the town. More importantly, later events indicate that

15. Gilbert Chinard, ed., *A Huguenot Exile in Virginia: or Voyages of a Frenchman Exiled for His Religion with a Description of Virginia and Maryland* (New York, 1934), 142.

while Wormeley accepted the ten thousand pounds of tobacco for the town site, he withheld passing formal title.[16]

Still, the matter of a town of their own remained in the minds of the gentlemen. In late 1684 — before the abortive town act of 1685, hence not an action taken in response to that act — the justices of the county court approached Wormeley about the possibility of building a courthouse on the town land. Wormeley seemed amenable, promising at the January 1685 court to give answer in Febuary. At that court he and Beverley undertook to build the courthouse. But before the actual work was to begin, three of the court's members were to negotiate with Wormeley and sign on behalf of "this Court and all the Inhabitants of this county" what were referred to as simply "Articles of Agreement or other Wrightings." There is no hint at this time of what Wormeley was requiring. But in the end nothing happened. Except for a Wormeley warehouse, the town land remained vacant.[17]

In June 1690 — well before the passage of the 1691 port bill, hence, again, not specifically a response to it — the matter rose anew in the Middlesex court. Matthew Kemp, William Churchill, and Robert Dudley were delegated "to Waite upon" Wormeley at Rosegill and "discourse his honor about the Land . . . for to build a Town upon" and particularly about building a courthouse there. The records are mute as to the outcome, but a year later, with a new town act on the statute books (at least temporarily), the court bestirred itself again. In an unusual step the justices first announced where and when they would meet to consider the matter of "the Towne Land," then charged the sheriff to "give Notice to the Severall Gentlemen." On the appointed day they designated new feoffees — Matthew Kemp, Christopher Robinson, and William Churchill — but also charged their clerk with drawing up a deed of sale. Their language was unequivocal: The deed so drawn was to "be presented to the said Ralph Wormeley Esqr." by the whole court meeting on the town land at seven o'clock on the morning of July 27. And inasmuch as Wormeley had "allready received the Consideracion of the aforesaid fifty Acres of Land," they would require him to sign.[18] Clearly a dispute was in progress and a denouement imminent.

Wormeley did not appear at the town land to meet the justices on the appointed morning. Perhaps he let them know in advance that he would ignore their summons, saving them the trip. There is, however, a hint in the sterile language of subsequent court depositions that he simply ig-

16. Middlesex County, Order Book no. 1, 1673–80, 41a, 42, 50, 509–10; Hening, *Statutes at Large* 3:59; John P. Kennedy and H. R. McIlwaine, eds., *Journals of the House of Burgesses of Virginia, 1619–1776* (Richmond, 1905–15), 2:181.

17. Middlesex County, Order Book no. 2, 1680–94, 193, 200–201.

18. Ibid., 474, 508–10.

nored the matter, in which case the justices waited for him in vain, shuffling about in the damp grass. In any event, the feoffees and some others did go to Rosegill's great house later in the day. Admitted, they demanded of Wormeley "an Assurance and Conveyance of a good and absolute" title to the land. The deed prepared by the clerk was laid before him. Wormeley curtly refused to sign. The document, he said, did not contain certain reservations that "hee had agreed formerly."

What reservations?

"One Eare of Indian Corne or a pepper Corne yearly" as an "acknowledgement" or quitrent for the land, "with other limitattions that None liveing in the Towne should keepe a Dove Howse nor keepe any hoggs but in a Sty nor any horse but in the howse."

The feoffees refused reservations that to all intents and purposes summed up to lordship. The law was on their side, they said, citing the provisions of the 1691 statute to the effect that if the owner of lands designated for a town refused to pass title, "such denial shall ipso facto be taken for a forfeiture to the feoffees." By simply noting his refusal, the feoffees told Wormeley, they would have the land for the town.

"Soe doe if you will," the master of Rosegill is recorded as replying.[19]

With that the deputation left. Later they recorded their account of the visit in the county's order book, together with those of the clerk and two witnesses — "ipso facto" evidence of Wormeley's intransigence, hence of his forfeiture. It did them no good. The town land was laid out in streets once again, and particular locations were designated for "Church-yard markitt place and fortification"; fourteen lots were actually sold.[20] But when the court contracted with James Curtis and John Hipkins for "a good Strong, Substantiall . . . Built house, for a Court House" in the town in April 1692 and the builders started work, Wormeley sent his servants across the creek to stop them. The court could only dispatch another deputation "to Know his Reasons for hindering" Curtis and Hipkins. The answer is unrecorded, but in early 1693 the court relieved the builders of their obligation to continue and took possession of what materials remained. Subsequently they sent another deputation to Wormeley, not to protest — that apparently was futile — but to attempt to "agree" with him "for the Building and Erecting of a Court house" on the land. No agreement was possible, and the court proceeded to make other arrangements for quarters. In October 1693 Christopher Robinson had a "house frame" on the town land, the only private construction recorded. Presumably

19. Ibid., 512, 515–18.

20. Ibid., 572–73. See also Wesley Newton Laing, "Urbanna's Tobacco Warehouse," Association for the Preservation of Virginia Antiquities, *Report on a Building at Urbanna, Virginia* [Richmond, 1961].

Wormeley had stopped Robinson's builders as he had stopped the county's.[21]

In the early years of the new century, the town again became a matter of contention. The situation, however, was altogether different. Old economic networks once paramount in the county — what we have referred to as hegemonies — had waned while new ones waxed. Robert Beverley's death in the mid-1680s saw the rise of Christopher Robinson, who married his widow, assumed the administration of the estate, and added Beverley's English connections to his own. Beverley's eldest sons left Middlesex to take up lands and careers elsewhere; a younger son, Harry, remained in Middlesex on land he controlled by virtue of marriage to Elizabeth Smith, Wormeley's ward. Then Christopher Robinson died. His 1693 will left his "true Friend Mr. William Churchhill" principal executor of the estate and, for a brief time, of the Beverley estate as well.[22] Robinson's death also left Churchill heir to Robinson's English connections, most notably the Jeffreys of London, for whom Robinson had served as principal factor and who now looked to Churchill. Churchill seems also to have taken charge of Robinson's two minor sons, Christopher and John, and until they came of age in 1701 and 1703 respectively, of the lands devised to them by their father. Ralph Wormeley died in 1701, and two years later Churchill married his widow. Wormeley's sons, like the Robinson brothers, were minors, and they were in England at the time; hence Churchill moved onto Rosegill, adding its resources to his own.

Churchill's rise to preeminence on the one hand and, on the other, the presence in the county of three young sons of once preeminent fathers — Christopher and John Robinson and Harry Beverley — set the stage for what followed. Churchill, together with Gawin Corbin from his plantation on the Rappahannock at the upper end of the county and Matthew Kemp on the Piankatank, dominated the trade of the county by virtue of their near monopoly of vital connections with English merchants. The young men seem to have seized upon the notion of a town as a vehicle by which to make such vital connections for themselves.

The issue was joined in June 1704 when Beverley and the Robinson brothers presented a petition to the county court asking that feoffees for the town be revived and themselves appointed.[23] Corbin, as one of the executors of Wormeley's will, and Churchill, "as marrying the Widdow,"

---

21. Middlesex County, Deeds, etc., no. 1, 1687–1750, 10–11, and Order Book no. 2, 1680–94, 559, 610–11, 627, 654.

22. "Will of Christopher Robinson, 1693," *Virginia Magazine of History and Biography* 7 (1899–1900): 21; Middlesex County, Order Book no. 2, 1680–94, 718–19.

23. Kemp and Churchill, among the old feoffees, were still alive and active.

both members of the court, left the bench — an act carefully noted later as testimony to their "impartiallity" in a matter involving their own interest — and from the bar "offered such reasons against [the petition] as then occurred to them." Beverley and John Robinson, also justices, apparently kept their places, voted for their own petition, and saw it carry.[24] Exactly what Churchill and Corbin offered by way of argument is not stated. It is possible, but unlikely, that they propounded old Ralph's lordly "reservations," although certainly they cited those reservations and the forfeiture proceedings as putting at least a question mark on the county's title to the land. And we can only guess at what lay behind their opposition. Churchill's change of mind seems the key. He had been an advocate of the town and a feoffee himself in the 1690s when he was building his English connections. Now he, with Corbin and Kemp, had those connections secure and conceivably saw no need for a town.[25] Still, at this point, the difference that had surfaced seems relatively minor.

Within two months, however, the affair became a major contretemps. The nagging question of a courthouse for the county had arisen again the year before when the justices realized that their lease on the current building would soon expire and began considering "the best ways and meanes for the Speedy building and Erecting" of a new courthouse, referring the matter from one court to another. Finally, at an evening meeting on March 15, 1704, after earlier ordering the sheriff to "make Proclamacion" of their intent "to the end all workmen may have notice," they read aloud the specifications of the building they had in mind, the century's way of inviting bids on public works. They also designated justices John Smith, Harry Beverley, and John Robinson to survey a two-acre site for a courthouse in Smith's old field, a location on the county's main road a mile or so below the then location. Presumably, too, the three were to accept

24. Middlesex County, Deeds, 1703–20, 70–72.

25. When at a later date the same sort of movement arose on the upper James, William Byrd II expressed what undoubtedly were Churchill's sentiments as the fight over Urbanna developed, and perhaps Wormeley's before him: "I erected a very covenient [ware]house . . . over against the falls, which is so well customed that it brings me in at least £50 per annum. But a powerful family in those parts finding the storage of their goods . . . to be very chargeable, intend to push hard . . . to have a town laid out there, that they may build warehouses of their own, and perhaps if an act should pass in their favour, the publick may give me twenty shillings an acre for 50 acres. Now behold the great injustice of this proceeding. In the first place I would not sell 50 acres, in this place for £5 an acre, if I were not compelld to it. . . . In the next place what compensation shall I have for £50 a year I make by the warehouses, when others will have such warehouses as well as I" (Byrd to Micajah Perry, 27 May 17[29], *The Correspondence of the Three William Byrds of Westover, Virginia, 1684–1776*, ed. Marion Tinling [Charlottesville, Va., 1977], 1:398). Byrd would lay out Richmond at the site a few years later. It seems that the same sort of processes were at work at different locations in the Chesapeake but proceeding within different time frames.

securities from whichever workmen took up the contract and oversee the work.[26]

But Beverley and the Robinson brothers had a different idea—the town. Winning the feoffeeship in June and outweighing John Smith on the committee, they ignored a July order of the court to get on with the business of the courthouse as planned, suggested informally that a Robinson building near or on the town land could be fitted out for the court at a lower cost than building anew, and then in August petitioned "for the Courthouse to be built upon the Town land." At the same time they asked that a public landing be established on the opposite side of Rosegill Creek from the town and for "maine roads" to be built "up and down the County," connecting the town to the network of existing roads. The landing entirely and the roads for the most part would perforce be built on Rosegill. In a heated session the court rejected their petitions, agreed summarily with John Hipkins to build the courthouse for twenty-five thousand pounds of tobacco, and named Churchill, Smith, and John Grymes to lay out a site on land that had been donated near the present courthouse.[27]

In the aftermath of the court's action, something new in the ever-changing situation in the county shows itself. All of the principals in these affairs were among the cosmopolitan few, marked by status and wealth, of course, but also by outlook—a comprehension, if you will, of a society and economy larger than the single county as a stage for their actions. But where earlier there had been among such great men no disjunction between economic and political influence, one now appeared. Churchill, Corbin, and Kemp controlled the economic ties that led outward from the county; the young men were virtually without such ties. Yet strands of kinship led outward from Robinsons and Beverleys to prominent families elsewhere in Virginia—to Peter Beverley, for example, clerk of Gloucester County and at the time speaker of the House of Burgesses in Williamsburg; to William Byrd of Charles City County, whose sister Ursula had been wife to Robert Beverley the younger. Time and an inexorable demographic dynamic were weaving an elaborate spiderweb of relationships at the highest level of Virginia's society. One consequence was that the young men had a political awareness and influence quite apart from the economic networks that tied Virginia to the commerce of the Atlantic. They lost no time utilizing their influence.

By September 1704 the young men had a petition before the governor and council in Williamsburg "complaining of diverse irregular Proceedings of the Court" in Middlesex. By October there was another, "praying

26. Middlesex County, Order Book no. 3, 1694–1705, 525, 528, 536, 544, 546.
27. Ibid., 570, 578; Middlesex County, Deeds, 1703–20, 70–72.

the building of the courthouse may be stopped until the petitioners be heard." To the second was attached "a Paper signed by the Major part of the Freeholders" of the county, complaining that "the building of the . . . Court house in the Place appointed by the Court is a Grievance." The governor and council concurred with the second petition to the extent of ordering construction stopped until the whole matter could be disposed of by the General Assembly of the colony. In February 1705 there was still a third petition from the three before the council, "praying" for authority to take "Depositions of witnesses for proving their Complaint against the Court." Either the council had had enough, or, more likely, the counterinfluence of Churchill, Kemp, and Corbin finally proved effective. The council determined not "to meddle further" in the business and refused the last petition.[28]

We need not follow the tortuous path of this long and complicated dispute. At one juncture four of the justices formally complained to the governor about a fifth as "a person most notorious by abusive, prophane, and Imoral Qualities, so misbecoming the seat of Justice, that we humbly desire to be excused Sitting with him." At another, Harry Beverley approached justice John Grymes as the latter sat under the mulberrry trees outside the courthouse; an argument ensued and Beverley raised his cane and struck. Grymes rose, his own cane in the air.

"Strike," shouted Beverley.

"No, I will not!"

"Hypocrite!" And Beverley struck again.[29]

Passions, however, should not detour us from the essential elements of the matter. It was, as we have said, a quarrel among the cosmopolitan few, those who occupied the very highest niche in Virginia (not just Middlesex) society. But the county was inevitably drawn into the battle and changed by its outcome.

The county court was one arena of battle. William Churchill and Christopher Robinson, each for his own reasons, had formally withdrawn from the court. Each returned, however, Churchill to attend regularly during the period of dispute until appointed to the colony's council in 1705, Robinson to attend only twice at crucial sessions, although he could always rely on the attendance of Beverley and his brother.[30] Less well

28. H. R. McIlwaine and Wilmer L. Hall, eds., *Executive Journals of the Council of Colonial Virginia, 1680–1754* (Richmond, 1925–45), 2:391, 403, 433.

29. Middlesex County, Order Book no. 3, 1694–1705, 602–3; Middlesex County, Deeds, 1703–20, 85–86; William P. Palmer et al., eds., *Calendar of Virginia State Papers and Other Manuscripts [1652–1869]* 1 (Richmond, 1875): 88.

30. Robinson had refused to join the court when first appointed in 1701; Churchill formally withdrew in 1702 after fairly regular attendance from 1687 on (Middlesex County, Order Book no. 3, 1694–1705, 394, 401). It is quite likely that Robinson had a long-standing

connected justices perforce took sides according to the ties that linked them to one side or the other. Thus John Hay stood with his brothers-in-law, the Robinsons; Roger Jones and George Wortham with Churchill who was godfather to and namesake of the Jones children and Wortham's major creditor.

County men of lesser status — the plain freeholders and inhabitants — were caught up in the fray as well. The feoffees sent their friends "about the County to all meetings, horseraces and feasts and to Peoples houses" to solicit signatures to the "paper" they dispatched to the council in Williamsburg. The response of Churchill's faction was couched in terms of condemnation against the "depth of the Selfe Interest Intrigues" of Beverley and the Robinsons.[31] And in still another way the county as a whole seems to have been drawn into the dispute. When the affair began in 1704, Churchill and Corbin represented the county in Virginia's House of Burgesses. As chance would have it, new general elections were called for the fall of 1705 when the dispute was at its height. We have no knowledge of the candidates or electioneering (except that Churchill, named to the governor's council that year, could not have stood for reelection); only the indirect evidence of the results indicates that the feoffees carried their case to the hustings. When the balloting was over, Christopher Robinson and Harry Beverley were the county's new burgesses, and Gawin Corbin and Matthew Kemp, "in Behalf of Themselves and others the Freeholders," were unsuccessfully protesting the outcome.[32]

In the end the larger community of cosmopolitan gentlemen resolved the affair, not the county. In May 1705 the feoffees' petitions had been considered in the House of Burgesses, and the house attempted a compromise by ordering that the courthouse be built where it had been begun but that a road be laid out from the lower end of the county, across Rosegill, to a "Convenient Landing upon The Creek Side" opposite the site of the town.[33] The compromise was not initially successful. While the courthouse was completed by early 1706, Churchill fought the road and landing. Partisans of one side or the other refused to sit on the court with their opponents, forcing adjournments for lack of a quorum. The governor attempted amelioration but eventually was forced to name a new court; still the quarreling continued. The road and landing were built, but the former was "stopt," presumably by Churchill. Petitions and cross peti-

---

and deep grievance against Churchill, perhaps reciprocated, possibly dating from Churchill's activities with regard to the estate of the elder Robinson. The formality of their refusals in 1701 and 1702 might be a result. In any event the two were together in attendance at a court or vestry meeting only three times from 1701 to 1710, years when both were active.

31. Middlesex County, Deeds, 1703–20, 70–72.

32. Kennedy and McIlwaine, *Journals of the House of Burgesses* 4:134, 139.

33. Ibid., 4:94, 100, 102.

tions clogged the court; at one session in 1707 partisans of one side or the other challenged so many justices as parties interested in the outcome that a quorum was lost. Ultimately the whole matter was again referred to Williamsburg by way of a judicial appeal from a decision of the court, in this instance one adverse to Churchill, Corbin, and young Ralph Wormeley, who had come of age and was assuming control of his patrimony. The appeal was summarily denied. In 1708 young Ralph carried another appeal to Williamsburg, but without success.[34] The long affair was at an end, perhaps in part because by then Urbanna was a fact.

Through all the long controversy, the young men — Beverley and the Robinson brothers — never seem to have lost sight of what they were about. Between June 1704, when they were designated feoffees, and March 1708, twenty-three lots in the town were sold.[35] The long-empty town site throbbed with the sounds of hammers and saws as houses and outbuildings were erected. Indeed, with building going on so generally in the county, Middlesex's own force of carpenters and craftsmen seems to have been inadequate. Between 1706 and 1710 the number of laboring adults in the county surged upward as a result of the temporary sojourn of itinerant laborers drawn or brought into the county to serve the building boom.[36]

As the feoffees had hoped, merchants were attracted to the town, minor merchants at the moment, but some would build rapidly from an Urbanna base. (The town finally received its name in 1706.) Among them were the Walker brothers, James and Richard. James had been involved in minor trading along the Rappahannock in Middlesex and Essex counties since 1698. In 1704 he was one of those circulating the feoffees' popular petition, and in November of that year he and his brother each bought lots in the town. Edmund Hamerton was another circulating the petition who bought a lot. A minor trader along the coast, he was a friend of the Walkers and at the same time something of an antagonist of Churchill, Kemp, and Corbin, against whom he had suits pending. Samuel Brown and his cousin William Gordon were attracted in from Maryland. Gordon, to judge from the inventory of his books following his death, might well have been a Catholic. Perhaps it was his presence that prompted the opponents of the town in the heat of 1704 to write of Urbanna's being intended as a "harbour for disaffected people."[37] Men from the county moved into the town as well. Christopher Robinson built a house there. So, too, did James Curtis, his cousin, whose farm abutted the town land on

34. Middlesex County, Order Book no. 4, 1705–10, 112, 122, 124, 154, 179, 202.

35. Laing, "Urbanna's Tobacco Warehouse," 8.

36. Darrett B. and Anita H. Rutman, *A Place in Time: Explicatus* (New York, 1984), chap. 3.

37. Middlesex County, Deeds, 1703–20, 72.

the south. In February 1707 Curtis was licensed "to keep an Ordinary at his dwelling house in the Burgh of Urbanna," giving bond to provide "good wholesome and Cleanly lodging and dyet for travelers and Stableage . . . for their Horses" and promising that he "Shall not Suffer or permitt any unlawful gameing in his house Nor on the Sabboth day to Suffer any person to Tipple or drink more than is Necessary." By August of that year, there was a second ordinary licensed, and Curtis was appointed "Constable for the City of Urbanna."[38]

"City," of course, was simply a grandiloquent embellishment. At the time Urbanna straggled along the creekside, not half its lots built upon; at its zenith later in the century, it would be no more than what a traveler called Yorktown, "a delicat Village" encompassing at the most no more than thirty houses, a hundred-odd buildings if all its kitchens, warehouses, stores, and sundry outbuildings were counted. But even then it would appear to a visitor as simply an extension of the countryside. Chickens scratched in its dusty streets, scurrying away from the hooves of passing horses. Cows grazed its backyards. Thomas Tuke's home and tailor shop were in the town in the 1720s, as were his cow, calf, and heifer. In the 1730s the physician John Mitchell's two-acre lot would boast a barn for his horse, vegetable and herb gardens, fruit trees, and a "physic garden" where he grew the medicinal plants that he processed into the emetics, purges, lenitives and alexipharmics he prescribed to his patients and sold in his apothecary shop.[39]

To some extent, the growth of Urbanna — and of the other small trading towns appearing in Virginia at about the same time — is associated with the colonywide efforts to improve the quality of Virginia's export. In 1713 and again in 1730, these efforts took the form of warehouse acts. The first, pried from Virginia's legislature by the then governor, Alexander Spotswood, required that public warehouses be constructed throughout Virginia and that all tobacco used in payment of taxes or debts be delivered to a warehouse for inspection by tobacco agents who, if they found it acceptable, would hold the tobacco, issuing receipts or notes that could pass as money until ultimately used to redeem the tobacco for export.[40] Virginians of all sorts objected to the act, lesser planters com-

38. Ibid., 122; Middlesex County, Order Book no. 4, 1705–10, 80, 131.

39. Gregory A. Stiverson and Patrick H. Butler III, eds., "Virginia in 1732: The Travel Journal of William Hugh Grove," *Virginia Magazine of History and Biography* 85 (1977): 21; Middlesex County, Will Book B, 13–1734, 364–65; Edmund and Dorothy Smith Berkeley, *Dr. John Mitchell: The Man Who Made the Map of North America* (Chapel Hill, N.C., 1974), 17–20. The description can be applied to the vast majority of America's towns and villages until well into the twentieth century. See, e.g., Leslie C. Stewart-Abernathy, "Urban Farmsteads: Household Responsibilities in the City," *Historical Archaeology* 20 (1986): 5–15.

40. Waverly Winifree, ed., *The Laws of Virginia, Being a Supplement to Hening's The*

plaining of the fees that the agents were to collect, major planters of both the fees and the fact that tobacco — even theirs — would pass through public facilities on its way to market rather than through their own warehouses and docks. The major planters appealed to the populace, and in assembly elections in 1715, most of those who had supported the act in the legislature were ousted. The appeal fired the populace, inspiring agitated meetings that here and there gave over to riot. The sheriff of Essex County, Middlesex's sister county to the west, wrote that "the peoples' inclinations" were "so great against The Tobacco law that they have not meet me to pay their Dues [levies]" and had signified "Their Dissatisfaction" further "by burning one of Mr. Buckners' Storehouses, with some Tobacco and his Scales in it." Not popular clamor but complaints from major planters to their English merchant friends resulted in pressure leading the government overseas to disallow the act in 1717.[41] Within thirteen years, however, the major planters of the colony and the English tobacco merchants had undergone a change of mind. With their support a second warehouse act was passed (in 1730), a near duplicate of the first but with even stronger provisions for inspection, including the burning of inferior tobacco by the agents.[42] The act survived English scrutiny and became a permanent part of the Virginia scene.

All of this history was echoed in Middlesex. The Robinson brothers represented the county in the legislature that passed the 1713 act, Christopher having served from 1705 and John from 1710. The brothers supported the governor and were rewarded for it, Christopher contracting to build Middlesex's warehouse and a dock in Urbanna for an annual rental of three thousand pounds of tobacco or £15 current money and John moving into Urbanna in 1713 and assuming the position and fees of agent when the act went into force in November 1714.[43] Cleavages among the gentlemen show themselves in petitions submitted from Middlesex to the legislature. In 1714 some of the county's gentlemen asked that tobacco agents be prohibited from trading on their own account or serving as a factor for others, a provision which would have reduced John's agency to little more than a clerk's role. The next year the gentlemen asked that a second warehouse be designated for Middlesex, to be erected outside

Statutes at Large, 1700–1750 (Richmond, 1971), 75–90; D. Alan Williams, "Political Alignments in Colonial Virginia Politics, 1698–1750" (Ph.D. diss., Northwestern University, 1959), 142–44.

41. Palmer et al., *Calendar of Virginia State Papers* 1:181; Winfree, *Supplement to Hening*, 119–24; Middleton, *Tobacco Coast*, 120–22.

42. Hening, *Statutes at Large* 4:247–71.

43. Middlesex County, Order Book no. 5, 1710–21, 155, 167; Middlesex County, Deeds, 1703–20, 361; "The Present State of Virginia . . . 1714," *Virginia Magazine of History and Biography* 2 (1894–95):8.

Urbanna, presumably in the lower end of the county where so many of the major holdings were located.[44] There is no evidence of rioting in the county, but in the elections of 1715 the brothers Robinson were both ousted from the legislature. Edmund Hamerton, who had failed in Urbanna and had settled for marriage to a widow near the Essex line, and William Blackburn, a middling planter from the lower reaches of the county, were returned to a short session of the legislature in 1715, while major planters Gawin Corbin and John Grymes replaced them for the next session in 1718. The 1730 act, establishing public warehouses in Middlesex at both Urbanna and on Kemp property in the lower end, provoked no ripple of controversy in the county.

The benefits accruing to Urbanna by virtue of the warehouse acts were conceivably many. From late 1714 through 1717 and again after 1730, tobacco flowed into the town as a matter of law, its presence there in quantity, together with facilities for ready loading and unloading, attracting ships to the town. The boon to any stores that might be established in the town was twofold. The ships attracted to the town carried in English goods, while the county men carrying their tobacco to the warehouses were ready customers for them. The tobacco notes, moreover, constituted a handy medium of exchange; the county man had only to pass over notes in payment for goods or old store debts, while storekeepers need only keep the notes, leaving the tobacco in the warehouse until the ships arrived, then redeeming inspected and approved hogsheads to make an outward-bound cargo.

Nevertheless, we ought not overestimate the effect of the acts in forwarding the town. Urbanna was devoted to stores and storekeepers from the very beginning, before the act of 1713, and was already dominant in the trade of the county by 1730 and the second warehouse act. Indeed, the ready acceptance of the second act can be accounted for in part by the fact that, in effect, it was legislation attuned to an existing situation.

The earliest merchants attracted to the town — the Walkers, Hamerton, Brown, Gordon — used it initially as a base from which to conduct the itinerant trading to which they were accustomed, all running sloops along the Rappahannock and across the bay to Virginia's Eastern Shore. Brown died soon after arriving. Hamerton, as we have noted, failed; undercapitalized and overindebted, he seems to have stopped trading by 1710. But Gordon and the Walker brothers succeeded. And more and more they came to rely less on itinerant trading than on the settled trade of the county, sinking their capital into goods and maintaining stocks of tools and cloth and luxuries the like of which had not been matched in the county before. Gordon's — "William Gordon and Company" as early as

44. Kennedy and McIlwaine, *Journals of the House of Burgesses* 5:83, 133.

1707 — had not only the usual assortment of nails and such in stock when Gordon died in 1720 but pewter plates and spoons, shoemakers' tools in abundance, earthenware, eyeglasses, forty-four dozen coat buttons, calico curtains and valances, "one pound and a gram of Indigo," Madeira wine and French brandy, "eighteen paper pictures," and even six "flower potts" — an inventory of almost five hundred separate items "in the store" alone.[45] The Walkers' store inventory was too diverse even to be listed in detail by the appraisers following James's death in 1721; they simply entered the stock in trade as a single item of £406 value. Richard Walker's inventory (1727) and the careful instructions that he inserted in his will to guide his executors in finishing the year's business afford a glimpse of the operations of a store. On the one hand, Richard bought goods in England, added a 25 percent markup, and put them on sale in Urbanna; on the other, he bought tobacco for shipment on account to a number of separate English merchants, paying 12s. 6d. per hundred pounds tobacco if cash was what the seller wanted but preferring to pay in store goods or credit, for which he offered a premium 16s. 6d. The latter allowed him a double profit, first on the tobacco and second on the marked-up goods.[46]

Energetic and astute men, Gordon and the Walker brothers were committed to trade, specialists if you will, devoting their lives to their craft. With their profits they obtained land and laborers, Gordon purchasing 400 acres in the county in 1710 and adding an adjoining 350 acres two years later. When he died he had thirty-one black slaves and seven white servants. James Walker, at his death, had land and blacks in Middlesex and Essex counties; Richard, 1,400 acres in Spotsylvania. The merchants linked themselves to the county by marriage. James Walker, for example, married Clara Robinson, sister of Christopher and John, in 1707. Ultimately the merchants took seats on the county court and vestry (Gordon excepted, another hint of his Catholicism). But they lived in Urbanna; trade and the operation of their stores were always their paramount concerns. In this they differed from, and gained an immediate advantage over, planter-merchants like Churchill who had dominated the county's trade earlier but for whom merchandising had been simply one of many ways to profit. It was not, however, their only advantage.

Their stores offered variety to the men and women of Middlesex and a more stable source of goods than had the planter-merchants. A Middlesex man (or his wife) in need of a particular item could count more readily on

45. Middlesex County, Order Book no. 4, 1705–10, 117, and Will Book B, 1713–34, 347–50.

46. Ibid., Will Book B, 252–56, 303–5, 335–42. Patrick Cheap's markup was higher, on some goods 35 percent, on others 55 percent (ibid., Will Book C, 1740–48, 214–32). See also Jacob M. Price, *Capital and Credit in British Overseas Trade: The View from the Chesapeake, 1700–1776* (Cambridge, Mass., 1980), 149–50.

its immediate availability and judge its quality on the spot. Indeed, Say's Law seems applicable in the sense that the rich supply of goods offered in Urbanna's stores provoked demands that planter-merchants, operating their own stores more casually, could not meet. The stores offered ready credit as well, actually pursuing store accounts; recall that by virtue of Walker's pricing policy, our Middlesex man and his wife could buy a third more goods by promising tobacco in payment than they could paying cash. Six volumes of Gordon's store accounts dating from 1708 to 1720 testify to the extent of the network of credit emanating so quickly from Urbanna.[47] The very size of the operations of the stores, moreover, and the limited number of middlemen involved tended to free their debtors from harassment. Accepting credit from a Mickleburrough in the 1690s, for example, tied one to a complex network of transactions inasmuch as Mickleburrough was simply one of many indebted to Churchill, who in turn was a creditor to many and himself indebted to English merchants; should Churchill fall behind for some reason — perhaps because the death of a major debtor, by throwing the estate into probate, delayed payment to him — he would be pressed by his English connections and would in turn press Mickleburrough, who would press his debtors. Notably the Urbanna merchants were involved in few suits for debt before the county court, while Churchill and Mickleburrough had been regularly before the court as both defendants and plaintiffs. And the Urbanna merchants acted in concert in their own interest. In 1727, for example, they petitioned the governor to remove the customshouse from the home of a major planter and place it in the town as "the most proper and Convenient place" inasmuch as "the far greater part of the Tobacco Exported from this River, is purchased in the Country for merchants at home" by the men of Urbanna. Not a single countryman (as distinct from townsman) was among the signers.[48]

Given such advantages, Urbanna and its stores brought about a reorientation of the internal trade of the county, one strengthened, not inspired, by the Warehouse Act of 1730. Major planters retained their own connections to English merchants, sending tobacco on consignment and buying English goods for themselves directly. But as Urbanna rose, the evidence of their retailing to their Middlesex neighbors declined. Small stores still sprinkled the countryside, although even they changed character, being more reflections of Urbanna's establishments in the variety of their stock and the single-minded attachment to trade of their owners than continuations of Mickleburrough's casual trading. Even peddlers made their ap-

47. Referred to in the inventory of his estate in Middlesex County, Will Book B, 1713–34, 347, but not located.
48. Palmer et al., *Calendar of Virginia State Papers* 1:212–13.

pearance, stocking pack animals in Urbanna, then crying up a trade in small goods along the more remote roads and paths of the county and beyond.[49] But a new sequence of hegemonies appeared to serve the small and middle planters, successors to but different from the hegemonies of Burnham, the first Robinson, and Churchill in being town-based rather than plantation-based: Gordon and the Walker brothers until 1720, Christopher Robinson II as Gordon's principal executor and Richard Walker until both died in 1727, James Reid and Patrick Cheap thereafter. The last — Reid and Cheap — were even more single-minded in their devotion to trade than their immediate predecessors. Entering the county from Scotland in the mid-1720s and remaining unmarried until their deaths (Cheap in the 1740s, Reid in the 1760s), they never owned more in the way of land than their Urbanna lots. In this sense they lived apart from the countryside that surrounded Urbanna, as their predecessors had not. But a scene enacted countless times on any given day not only in their store but in countless stores in the Chesapeake and elsewhere — a rangy tobacco farmer talking price and credit with the storekeeper or his clerk, the farmer's wife picking through the bolts of buckram and dimity, children eyeing a bin or jug of sugar lumps — links town and farm firmly together in the American past.

49. For evidence of a country store (Price's in the upper part of the county), see Middlesex County, Will Book B, 1713–34, 298–300, Will Book C, 1740–48, 429, and Deeds, etc., no. 1, 1687–1750, 133. For peddlers see ibid., Will Book A, 1698–1713, 153–54, Wills, etc., 1675–1798, pt. 1, 212, and Will Book C, 1740–48, 423–24; Hening, *Statutes at Large* 5:54–57. The second Middlesex warehouse established under the 1730 act (at Kemp's on the Piankatank) seems to have served the major planters in the lower part of the county and across the river in northern Gloucester (Kennedy and McIlwaine, *Journals of the House of Burgesses* 6:202–3, 207, 424; Hening, *Statutes at Large* 4:380–93).

12 The Village South
With Anita H. Rutman

In the mid-1980s I thought to draw together the various strands I had been following so long into a single synthetic volume on the American community. As I read, I noted that everywhere in the literature small towns and villages bulked large — except in descriptions of the antebellum South, where they appeared hardly at all. But what of Urbanna, I asked myself? Established in the first decade of the eighteenth century, it still existed. I had walked its streets! Was Urbanna simply an anachronism? Curious, I glanced at the itineraries of the great tours of the early South: George Washington's in 1791, the marquis de Lafayette's in 1825. These grand gentlemen did not proceed from great plantation to great plantation but from town to town. I surveyed the accounts of travelers in the Southeast from Virginia through Georgia during the years from the late eighteenth century to the Civil War and saw the southern town regularly depicted. Gradually the impression grew that, somehow, something vital was being overlooked.

To Harper Lee the depression South in twentieth-century America could be epitomized by a town, and through her ingenue, Scout, she described it: "Maycomb was an old town, but it was a tired old town when I first knew it. In rainy weather the streets turned to red slop; grass grew on the sidewalks; the courthouse sagged in the square." It was in a town, too, that William Faulkner's Emily died, while Faulkner's Flem Snopes began his Yaknapatawpha County career in Frenchmen's Bend, a "hamlet" containing store, cotton gin, a combined gristmill and blacksmith's shop, livery stable, boardinghouse, and a schoolhouse and church with

An initial version of this essay — drawn from ongoing research on "The Village South" — was presented to the faculty and graduate students of the University of Florida in January 1990 as part of the Department of History's Colloquium Series.

"perhaps three dozen dwellings within sound of both bells." And Carson McCullers found Miss Amelia Evans's sad café in a town, dreary perhaps — "Not much is there except the cotton mill, the two-room houses where the workers live, a few peach trees, a church with two colored windows, and a miserable main street only a hundred yards long" — but a town nevertheless.[1] Yet the town as a significant element in southern culture has a truncated history. In our conventional wisdom we label the antebellum South rural, apply exquisite analysis to its most blatant characteristics, the plantation, slavery, a nonslaveholding "yeomanry," and, following the litany of the late nineteenth-century "New South" movement, assign the town-based South to the years following the Civil War.[2]

What follows is not intended to overturn this conventional wisdom altogether; the fact of the essentially agricultural nature of the whole of

1. Lee, *To Kill a Mockingbird* (1960; reprint; New York, 1962), 9; Faulkner, "A Rose for Emily," in *Collected Stories of William Faulkner* (New York, 1950), 119; Faulkner, *The Hamlet* (1940; reprint; New York, 1956), 28; McCullers, "The Ballad of the Sad Café," in *The Ballad of the Sad Café: The Novels and Stories of Carson McCullers* (Boston, 1951), 3. Faulkner's "hamlet" is, in terms of the definitions used here, more appropriately a "village."

2. For example, Ralph V. Anderson and Robert E. Gallman, "Slaves as Fixed Capital: Slave Labor and Southern Economic Development," *Journal of American History* 64 (1977): 42 — Towns "were few, small, and widely separated. There was no rich history of farm and village or town interaction"; David L. Carlton, *Mill and Town in South Carolina, 1880–1920* (Baton Rouge, La., 1982), 9 — "The rise of the town [after the Civil War] . . . provided an opening wedge with which modern forms of social organization . . . could penetrate a south whose economic and social life had long revolved around autonomous white planters and small farmers"; Gavin Wright, *Old South, New South: Revolutions in the Southern Economy since the Civil War* (New York, 1986), 24 — "The antebellum South had few large cities, but the sparsity of *small towns* was an even more striking feature"; Don H. Doyle, *New Men, New Cities, New South: Atlanta, Nashville, Charleston, Mobile, 1860–1910* (Chapel Hill, N.C., 1990), 1 — "The South claimed only fifty-one of the nation's nearly four hundred urban places. . . . Critics of the South saw the absence of towns as one of the most striking distinctions of the region" and "blamed slavery and the plantation system." See also Frederick F. Siegel, *The Roots of Southern Distinctiveness: Tobacco and Society in Danville, Virginia, 1780–1865* (Chapel Hill, N.C., 1987), 63; in the course of making an otherwise startling case for the small town in southwestern Virginia, Siegel listed among "the distinctive elements of . . . Southern backwardness. . . the absence of towns and cities." The relationship of the Old and New South is a matter of hot dispute at the moment. Dan T. Carter, "From the Old South to the New: Another Look at the Theme of Change and Continuity," in *From the Old South to the New: Essays on the Transitional South*, ed. Walter J. Fraser, Jr., and Winfred B. More, Jr. (Westport, Conn., 1981), 23–32, succinctly summarizes positions to ca. 1980, while the lead paragraphs of successive books and articles bring them up to date. See, for example, Lacy K. Ford, Jr., "Rednecks and Merchants: Economic Development and Social Tensions in the South Carolina Upcountry, 1865–1900," *Journal of American History* 71 (1984): 294–98; James Michael Russell, *Atlanta, 1847–1890: City Building in the Old South and the New* (Baton Rouge, La., 1988), 2–5. The extent and nature of the antebellum southern town system would seem crucial to this debate.

colonial and antebellum America would bar such.[3] It is meant simply to put the town and village and hamlet back into our understanding of the early South. Neither is what follows a perverse or isolated argument. Indeed, a regular, albeit minor, theme of the social history of the past few decades has sought — to use David Goldfield's imagery — to plant magnolias on America's Main Street. Unfortunately, however, the theme has been obfuscated by its surroundings, for the effort has, for the most part, been undertaken in the guise of "urban history." Thus Goldfield's imagery leads ultimately to a call "to develop an urban view of southern history."[4] If by "urban view" we are to understand something of the aura of Louis Wirth's classic definition of "urbanism as a way of life" distinct from the rural or as the crèche in which modern entrepreneurialism and anomie were swaddled, then the effort properly invites criticism, even rejection.[5] To restate the obvious: The early and antebellum South was essentially agricultural. The problem is not an urban South apart from the countryside but rather the town, village, and hamlet as integral to the structure of this (or any) agriculturally based society.[6]

3. It is almost trite to cite the numbers: In 1800 well over 90 percent of the population lived in the countryside, five out of six did so in 1860, two out of three in 1900. See, for example, Steven Hahn and Jonathan Prude, "Introduction," in *The Countryside in the Age of Capitalist Transformation: Essays in the Social History of Rural America*, ed. Hahn and Prude (Chapel Hill, N.C., 1985), 3.

4. Goldfield, *Urban Growth in the Age of Sectionalism: Virginia, 1847–1861* (Baton Rouge, La., 1977), 283. See also his "Pursuing the American Dream: Urban Growth in the Old South," in *The City in Southern History: The Growth of Urban Civilization in the South*, ed. Blaine A. Brownell and Goldfield (Port Washington, N.Y., 1977), 52–91; David F. Weiman, "Urban Growth on the Periphery of the Antebellum Cotton Belt: Atlanta, 1847–1860," *Journal of Economic History* 48 (1988): 259–72; Frank J. Huffman, Jr., "Town and Country in the South, 1850–1880: A Comparison of Urban and Rural Social Structures," *South Atlantic Quarterly* 76 (1977): 366–81; Leonard P. Curry, "Urbanization and Urbanism in the Old South: A Comparative View," *Journal of Southern History* 40 (1974): 43–60; Lyle W. Dorsett and Arthur H. Shaffer, "Was the Antebellum South Antiurban? A Suggestion," ibid., 38 (1972): 93–100.

5. Wirth, "Urbanism as a Way of Life," *American Journal of Sociology* 44 (1938): 1–24.

6. Only a few historians have noticed the towns apart from urbanization, the most notable among them being Orville Vernon Burton, *In My Father's House Are Many Mansions: Family and Community in Edgefield, South Carolina* (Chapel Hill, N.C., 1985), 28–33, and James Oakes, *The Ruling Race: A History of American Slaveholders* (New York, 1983), 91–94. The latter, relying heavily on Joseph H. Ingraham's *The South-West, by a Yankee* (1835; reprint, New York, 1969), makes the towns central to his thesis of slaveholders "adrift" in an unstable world. See also such state studies as John Hebron Moore, *The Emergence of the Cotton Kingdom in the Old Southwest: Mississippi, 1770–1860* (Baton Rouge, La., 1988), 177–203; Weymouth T. Jordan, *Ante-Bellum Alabama: Town and Country* (1957; reprint, University, Ala., 1987), 22–40; and Clement Eaton's more general *The Growth of Southern Civilization, 1790–1860* (New York, 1961), 247–70. There are only a handful of studies of specific towns and villages (as distinct from cities). Some Georgia examples: James C. Bonner's *Milledge-*

A map of any antebellum southern state highlights the problem: The state appears dotted with names. Isolate a single county in a state — Houston County, Georgia, on William G. Bonner's 1847 map, for example (map 12.1). A spiderweb of roads radiates from a place called Perry, one road heading northwest to Fort Valley, another north to Busbayville, another northeast to Wilna and Wellborn's Mills, still another southeast to Hayneville, another directly south to Henderson, and finally a road winding south-southwest to Minerva.[7] Faced with this plethora of names, one might simply smile (with Frederick Law Olmsted) at the obvious conceit and pass on to the more important subject of the planter and his slaves: "I found that many a high sounding name," Olmsted wrote, "indicated the locality of merely a grocery or two, a blacksmith shop, and two or three log cabins. I passed through two of these map towns without knowing that I had reached them."[8] Or one might do as a contemporary historian has done, acknowledge that "villages and small towns abounded" but consider them as simply extensions of the slave and plantation South, hence adequately covered by the study of slaves and plantations. "Southern towns primarily reflected the countryside," Elizabeth Fox-Genovese asserts on her way to ignoring them. "Most, especially the politically and culturally influential towns, were centers and extensions of the plantation region."[9] Even historians more inclined to see an antebellum urban South — Goldfield himself, for example — tend to denigrate what they find: Southern cities "were what sociologist Edgar Thompson termed 'plantation cities,' entertainment and marketing adjuncts to those self-sufficient agricultural units that were the mainsprings of the antebellum southern economy. 'Mere trading posts,' W. J. Cash called the best of them, and that is precisely and only what they were. . . . White painted towns dozing in the summer sun, strewn about with hogs, dogs, and a few people; a river lazily

ville: Georgia's Antebellum Capital (Athens, Ga., 1978); E. Merton Coulter, Auraria: The Story of a Georgia Gold-Mining Town (Athens, Ga., 1956) and his Old Petersburg and the Broad River Valley of Georgia: Their Rise and Decline (Athens, Ga., 1965); Bird and Paul Yarbrough, eds., Taylors Creek: A Story of the Community and Her People, 1760–1986, 2d ed. (Greenville, S.C., 1986); Huffman, "Town and Country" (on Athens); Anne S. Larcom, "East Point, Georgia: Overview of a Century," Atlanta History 32 (1988–89): 39–59.

7. Map of the State of Georgia Compiled under the Direction of His Excellency George W. Crawford by William G. Bonner, Civil Engineer, Milledgeville, Entered . . . 1847 by William G. Bonner in the Clerk's Office of the District Court of Georgia, no scale but ca. 1:360,160, 58½ by 51¼ inches, engraved and printed by Sherman and Smith, New York, published by Wm. G. Bonner, 1847, Georgia Department of Archives and History, Atlanta.

8. Olmsted, A Journey in the Back Country (1860; reprint, New York, 1970), 159–60.

9. Fox-Genovese, Within the Plantation Household: Black and White Women of the Old South (Chapel Hill, N.C., 1988), 74, 78. It is difficult to understand her insistence on applying a census definition (population greater than 2,500) to locate an urban South while opening the door to smaller places in the North that simply met "urban standards" (pp. 75–76).

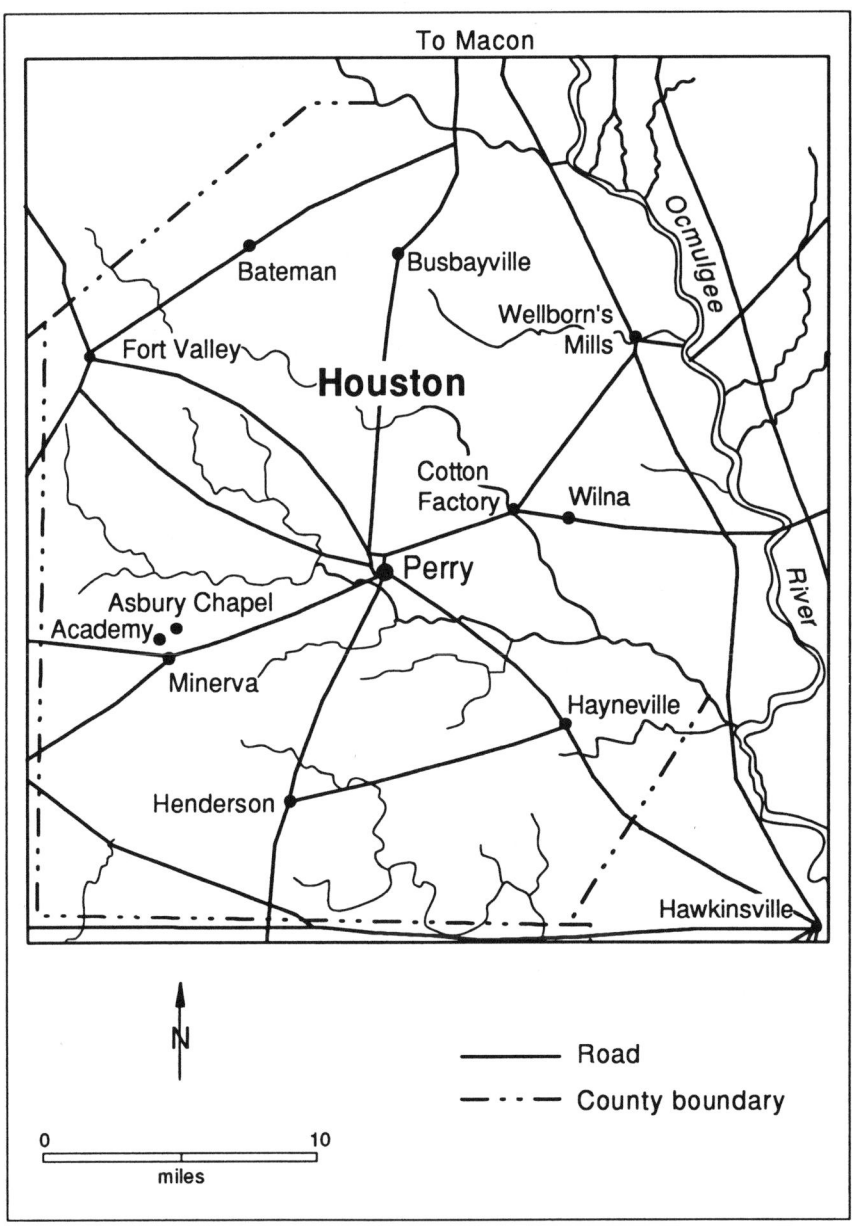

Map 12.1. Houston County, Georgia, in the late 1840s. Redrawn from the Bonner Map of 1847 cited in note 7.

lapping against rotted wood pilings; a languid populace briefly awakening with the arrival of a steamboat . . . and then quickly resuming its 'at ease' posture waiting for nothing more than supper."[10]

All this is to beg the obvious questions, however. Who lived in the Perrys, Wilnas, and Haynevilles of Georgia's Houston County, however mean and straggling? Indeed, what proportion of the southern population lived in such places? And why? Why were they not out on their "self-sufficient" plantations and farms, on the former playing the patriarch (and plantation lady) and overseeing the growing of cotton, on the latter playing the role of staunch, independent yeoman? What did the denizens of such places do for a living? Above all, what role (if any) did they and their villages and towns play in southern society as a whole, and what role (if any) did town and village play in the making of a southern *mentalité*? Such questions cannot be approached with the historian's customary distinction in mind between urban and rural, dichotomous states inappropriate as analytical tools when applied to an agricultural society. Southern cities do not fit neatly into a category devised in the twentieth century for the Chicagos, New Yorks, Birminghams, and Londons of the world — Goldfield's resorting to Thompson's "plantation cities" is testimony to this — while the small settlements of the region have no place at all until *urban* and *urbanization* are redefined to allow "the study of urbanization" in the absence of "urban communities."[11] But more generally, if rural and urban

---

10. Goldfield, *Cotton Fields and Skyscrapers: Southern City and Region, 1607–1980* (Baton Rouge, La., 1982), 32. Lacy K. Ford, Jr., *Origins of Southern Radicalism: The South Carolina Upcountry, 1800–1860* (New York, 1988), 89, echoes Goldfield with regard to "upcountry towns": They were "somnolent courthouse villages which came to life once or twice a month on sales day or during court week." Note, also, the ambiguity expressed by Joan N. Sears, "Town Planning in White and Habersham Counties, Georgia," *Georgia Historical Quarterly* 54 (1970): 23–25: Courthouse towns "were the center of transportation, commerce, schools, the professions, and government. . . . Travellers headed for these centers. . . . Here came the judges when the court was in session. . . . Here the newspaper was printed and here our battles and heroes were commemorated, and here that climax of all festivities, the fourth of July, was traditionally celebrated." Yet, "it is important to realize that the people who settled in Habersham County were not town builders. They had been and intended to remain rural folks. To put the town in its correct perspective, we must recognize it as an equal but not overly important part of the tidy jigsaw pattern of the county civil and social life."

11. Carville Earle and Ronald Hoffman, "The Urban South: The First Two Centuries," in *The City in Southern History*, ed. Brownell and Goldfield, 23. The argument for functional urbanization in the absence of urban areas (cities) — ridiculed by Erik H. Monkkonen, *America Becomes Urban: The Development of U.S. Cities and Towns, 1780–1980* (Berkeley, Calif., 1988), 256 — is associated largely with historical geographers studying the eighteenth century. See, for example, Joseph A. Ernst and H. Roy Merrens, "'Camden's turrets pierce the skies!': The Urban Process in the Southern Colonies during the Eighteenth Century," *William and Mary Quarterly*, 3d ser., 30 (1973): 549–74; Merrens, *Colonial North Carolina in the Eighteenth Century: A Study in Historical Geography* (Chapel Hill, N.C., 1964), 142–72;

history are two sides of the same scholarly coin — as Robert P. Swierenga
has asserted — our conceptualization must connect the two, not separate
them.[12] It would seem more appropriate to envision rural and urban as
simply two extremes on a continuum, with the Chicagos, New Yorks,
Birminghams, and Londons at one end, farm life at the other, and a range
of places in between. That, in any event, is the conceptualization applied
here.

Consider first the extensiveness of town and village life in the antebellum South. For purposes of illustration our case in point is Georgia, a
state chosen because within its boundaries was reflected something of
both the temporal and geographic variety to be found in the larger South.
Here, for example, were eighteenth-century settlements maturing in the
nineteenth, and a nineteenth-century frontier ballooning westward from
the middle Savannah toward the Chattahoochee River and Alabama, then
southward toward Florida and northward into the mountains. Here, too,
were coastal rice-growing counties, pine and limesink barrens behind, and
behind the barrens a rich cotton land cutting across the state from east to
southwest, fading into the piedmont to the north, and beyond the piedmont, the mountains (map 12.2).

The decennial censuses are of little help in finding Georgia's towns and
villages. Census marshals north and south were eclectic in their labeling of
the aggregations they reported, and historians who accept their labels at
face value do so at their own peril. For the North, "townships" are too
often mistaken for towns in our sense, while for the South towns are for

---

Earle, *The Evolution of a Tidewater Settlement System: All Hallow's Parish, Maryland, 1650–
1783,* University of Chicago, Department of Geography, Research Paper no. 170 (Chicago,
1975), 62–100; Earle and Hoffman, "Staple Crops and Urban Development in the Eighteenth-Century South," *Perspectives in American History* 10 (1976): 7–78. Goldfield, *Cotton
Fields and Skyscrapers,* 28, uses the phrase "urbanization without cities" in a different way,
viz., urbanization without familiar-looking cities.

12. Originally in Swierenga, "Toward the 'New Rural History': A Review Essay," *Historical Methods Newsletter* 6 (1973): 111–22, and reiterated subsequently in his "The New Rural
History: Defining the Parameters," *Great Plains Quarterly* 1 (1981): 211–23; "Theoretical
Perspectives on the New Rural History: From Environmentalism to Modernism," *Agricultural History* 56 (1982): 495–502; "Agriculture and Rural Life: The New Rural History," in
Ordinary People and Everyday Life: Perspectives on the New Social History, ed. James B. Gardner
and George Rollie Adams (Nashville, 1983), 91–113. Despite the avowal of a relationship,
few of the "new rural historians" do more than juxtapose town and countryside. Hahn and
Prude, in *Countryside in the Age of Capitalist Transformation,* 9–10, for example, argue for
"seeing rural and urban history as distinct but linked aspects" so that "the special rhythms
and textures of rural history" can be better studied, while Hal S. Barron, "Rediscovering the
Majority: The New Rural History of the Nineteenth-Century North," *Historical Methods* 19
(1986): 141–52, after summarizing the literature, concludes (p. 150) that rural "patterns . . .
differed in significant ways from urban and industrial society" although city and countryside
"became increasingly interdependent and intertwined."

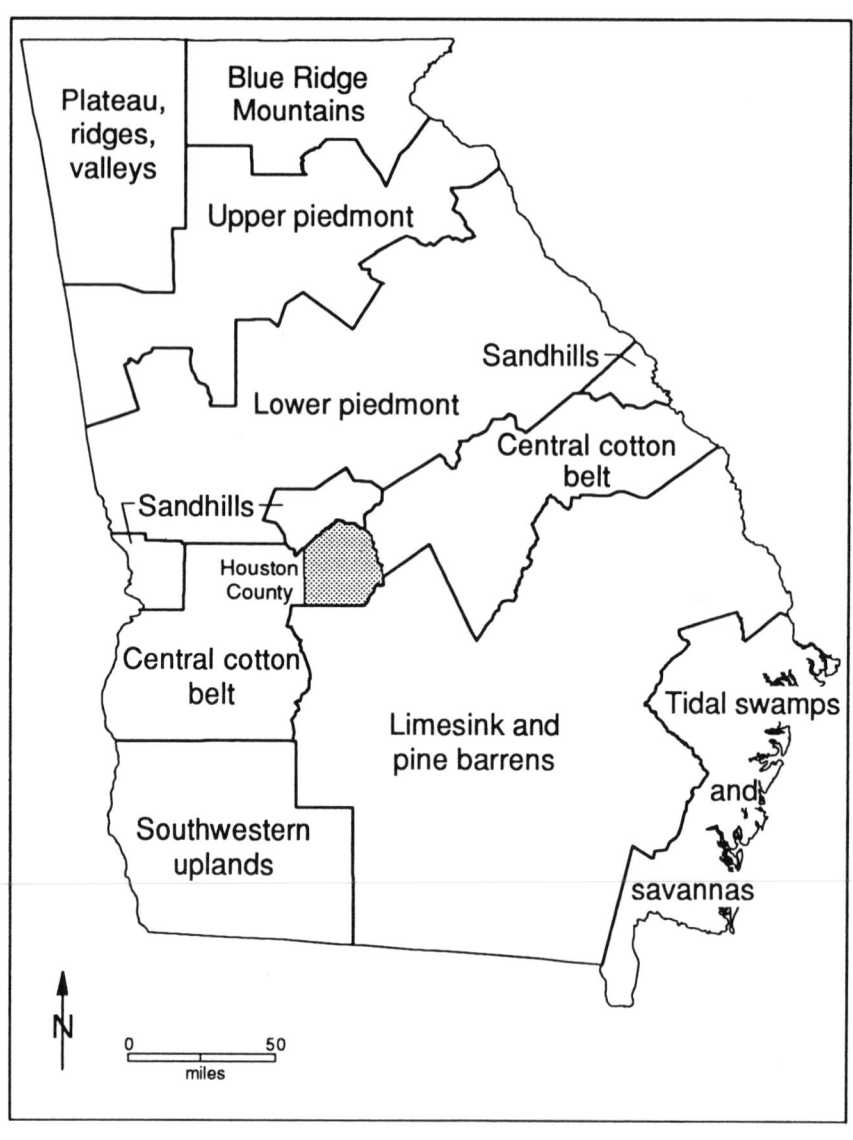

Map 12.2. The regions of mid-century Georgia. Adapted from Frederick A. Bode and Donald E. Ginter, *Farm Tenancy and the Census in Antebellum Georgia* (Athens, Ga., 1986), 76, as described in note 37.

the most part subsumed in counties.[13] Only two of the five censuses through mid-century isolated for Georgia more than a handful of towns, that of 1810 which reported the populations of twenty-eight towns — in all encompassing 5.4 percent of the free population of the state — and that of 1850 which isolated nineteen, "all the towns that can be ascertained from the schedules."[14] The disarray of the census in this regard was not unnoticed, the superintendent of the 1850 census, J. D. B. De Bow, commenting that "in New England and the Northern States, what are returned as cities, and towns, often include whole rural districts" while "especially" in the South and West "hundreds of important towns and cities . . . are not even distinguished on the returns from the body of the counties in which they are situated."[15] In an attempt to rectify the situation, De Bow's office went to the effort of compiling a list of some 4,800 discrete places and their populations, including thirty-one Georgia towns additional to the nineteen previously reported, which was published in the 1854 *Statistical View of the United States*.[16] The two lists combined — that contained in the original census report and De Bow's additions — constitute the most inclusive single listing of Georgia's antebellum towns.

13. Note, for example, Timothy R. Mahoney, *River Towns in the Great West: The Structure of Provincial Urbanization in the American Midwest, 1820–1870* (New York, 1990), appendix A. When the "number of towns" he reports for the counties of Illinois and Iowa in 1850–52 is multiplied by what he reports as the "population per town," the result in thirty-seven of thirty-eight instances approximates the total population of the county; i.e., he has confused "town" and "township." Stanley Elkins and Eric McKitrick, in "A Meaning for Turner's Frontier," *Political Science Quarterly* 69 (1954): 321–53, 565–602 — often cited to support the argument that the South boasted few towns (e.g., by Wright, *Old South, New South*, 24, 277) — clearly understood the problem with regard to northern towns and supplemented the census data with those from state gazetteers, but they accepted the census count of southern towns without question, hence in effect offered a fallacious "apples and oranges" comparison. See particularly 341–42n.

14. U.S., Bureau of the Census, *Return of the Whole Number of Persons within the Several Districts of the United States* . . . ([Washington, D.C.], 1801); *Amount of Each Description of Persons Within the United States of America* . . . (Washington, D.C., 1811); *Census for 1820* (Washington, D.C., 1821); *Fifth Census; or, Enumeration of the Inhabitants of the United States, 1830* . . . (Washington, D.C., 1832); *Compendium of the Enumeration of the Inhabitants and Statistics of the United States* . . . (Washington, D.C., 1841); *The Seventh Census of the United States, 1850* . . . (Washington, D.C., 1853) — the quotation is from p. 366. *The Seventh Census* took note of an 1852 local census of Augusta but did not include Augusta in its list of "Cities and Towns"; we have used an 1850 count cited below at note 19.

15. De Bow, *Statistical View of the United States* . . . *Being a Compendium of the Seventh Census* (Washington, D.C., 1854), 192.

16. The Georgia additions are subsumed in the national listing in ibid., 338–93. All are indicated as total populations — that is, combining free and slave — and as drawn from sources other than the census. That the figures are largely estimates rather than the products of local censuses is indicated by the fact that sixteen of the thirty-one end with a zero, an unlikely occurrence if they were real counts.

There are, however, problems in merging the two lists to establish the total population of the towns. The original broke down the population of its various places by sex within the categories "Whites," "Free Colored," and "Slaves" but noted that in three instances slaves were not "defined" in the schedules; hence no total population was offered. But even where slaves were "defined" it is unclear whether they were actually town-dwelling slaves or simply the property of town-dwelling whites who held agricultural lands and slaves apart from the towns. For its part, the *Statistical View* of 1854 offered only total populations with no indications of the number free and slave. Given such problems, our solution has been to concentrate on the free population, extracting it directly from the original list and estimating it in the case of the thirty-one towns added in 1854.[17] On this basis the fifty towns and villages of the two lists combined were home to 40,942 of the state's half million free population, almost 8 percent of the total.[18]

Despite the additions of 1854, the work of the Census Office is far from adequate. To gain even an approximation of the extent of town and village life at mid-century, we must push further. When we do, we find that census manuscripts themselves offer population figures for four places not included on either of the Census Office's published lists.[19] George P. White's *Statistics of . . . Georgia* of 1849 included population estimates for sixty-eight additional places, plus a count of houses or families or male inhabitants for still another eleven.[20] An 1849 newspaper account of the Etowah Iron Works offers evidence of over 200 workers and their families at that Cass County site, a figure translated into "a village of 800 people"

---

17. The estimates were obtained by the computation $P - (P(R + D))$ where P is the total population of a place, R the proportion of the population that was slaves for the county in which the place lay, and D the average difference between the proportion of the county population that was slaves in 1850 and (where known) the proportion of the town population that was slaves. The computation $R + D$ has been capped at 0.5 to reflect the assumption that no population aggregation was greater than 50 percent slave. The procedure was tested using those cases in which both a free and a slave population were unequivocally given, the total being subjected to the procedure to obtain an estimated free population which was subsequently compared to the known figure. The estimating procedure returned 91.4 percent of the known. When the same test was made of the estimating procedure as applied to the southeastern states of Maryland, Virginia, and North and South Carolina, the results varied by state from 85.5 percent in South Carolina to 98.9 percent in Maryland. In other words, the estimates invariably erred on the conservative side, being understatements of the known town-dwelling free population of the five states.

18. Georgia's total free population (whites and free blacks) in 1850 was 524,503.

19. Carnesville (Franklin County), Covington and Oxford (Newton), Augusta (Richmond). See MS Census Returns, Georgia, Seventh Census, 1850, Social Statistics, 225, 600, 738, Baker-Wilkinson Collection, Duke University Library, Durham, N.C..

20. White, *Statistics of the State of Georgia . . . Together with a Particular Description of Each County* (Savannah, 1849), 204–617.

in the memoirs of Mark A. Cooper, Etowah's owner.[21] In another newspaper account Bibb County's census marshal reported to the public what he did not report to the Census Office, the population of Macon's suburbs of Vineville (850 people) and East Macon (315).[22] John P. Campbell's *Southern Business Directory* of 1854 adds Paulding County's Dallas, population 130, while the stock book of the Cedar Shoals Water Power Company offers a description of a Newton County factory village of "two fine large dwelling houses and eighteen smaller ones," a store, church, school, and "four negro houses."[23] When we incorporate all such isolated numbers from a variety of sources, we have an additional 28,862 people living in ninety-four places ranging in size from Meriwether County's tiny Sandtown (free population 55) to Cobb County's Marietta (1,500) and Augusta, Richmond County (5,329). The roughly 8 percent of the free population in towns has been increased to over 13 percent.[24]

And still more: A systematic search through the various editions of

21. *Georgia Journal and Messenger* (Macon), 29 Aug. 1849; MS Memoirs of Major Mark A. Cooper, P. K. Yonge Library of Florida History, University of Florida, Gainesville, 9.

22. *Georgia Journal and Messenger* (Macon), 11 Sept. 1850.

23. Campbell, ed., *The Southern Business Directory and General Commercial Advertiser* (Charleston, S.C., 1854), 280–81; Newton Historical Society, *History of Newton County, Georgia* (Covington, Ga., 1988), 191. For other examples, see E. Merton Coulter, "Scull Shoals: An Extinct Georgia Manufacturing and Farming Community," *Georgia Historical Quarterly* 48 (1964): 43–44; Thaddeus Brockett Rice, *History of Greene County, Georgia, 1786–1886*, ed. Carolyn White Williams (Macon, Ga., 1961), 63–64, 66, 71; Susie Blaylock McDaniel, *Official History of Catoosa County, Georgia, 1853–1953* (Dalton, Ga., 1953), 24–25; William H. Davidson, *Brooks of Honey and Butter: Plantations and People of Meriwether County, Georgia* (Alexander City, Ala., 1971), 2:320–22.

24. White, *Statistics of Georgia*, does not indicate whether his population estimates were of total population or free population, but we have assumed them to be the latter on the basis of a number of tests. In thirty-nine instances we have both White's figures and a total population (free and slave) from the 1850 census; in twenty-nine cases White is under the census figure, an abnormally high incidence if both were reporting on the same basis. Campbell, *Southern Business Directory*, 261, 268, offers a breakdown into whites, free blacks, and slaves for two places drawn from a lost state census; in both instances White's figures conform to the free population. Other sources offer twelve additional population figures with no indication whether or not slaves are included. In the absence of any ability to test the figures offered — and in the interest of arriving at a conservative estimate — we have assumed the figures to be total population and adjusted downward to an estimate of the free population using the procedure described in note 17. Ten family counts and two house counts have been converted to an estimate of the free population by multiplying them by the number of free persons per family or house as computed from the 1850 census for the county in which the place was located. The free white populations at Troup Factory, Troup County — for which we have only a count of males — has been estimated by multiplying by half the county rate of free whites per family. Converting house counts in the fashion we do ignores the potential impact of multiple-family dwellings, hotels, boardinghouses, factory dormitories, and the like. But the error is again on the conservative side, leading to an underestimate of the town-dwelling population.

Adiel Sherwood's gazetteers of the state (1827, 1829, 1837) offers a further forty-eight towns with some indication of their size, either Sherwood's own population estimate or his count of houses or families, all of which towns are known to have continued in existence after 1854 but none of which have been included to this point. Estimating their free population in 1850, we have located another 9,192 town and village inhabitants, giving us a grand total of 78,996, or 15 percent of the free population of the state.[25] But still we are not done.

Every gazetteer cited to this point — White in two editions (the second in 1854), Sherwood in four (the fourth appearing in 1860), Campbell combining the information of a gazetteer with commercial advertisements in his *Business Directory* — together with their counterparts from earlier in the century, took note of what Sherwood, after completing his description of a county and its towns, would list simply as "other post villages and public places." Heard County's Houston, for example: In January 1847 the federal Post Office advertised for mail carriers to ride the route from LaGrange to Houston to Stroud's Creek and Fredonia, Alabama; White in his 1849 edition referred to Houston as a "thriving" village; John T. Smith in his *Commercial Tax Digest and Directory* of 1851 listed it among the 201 "principal towns and villages" of the state; Campbell in 1854 located a post office, four dry goods merchants, and a coeducational academy there; but Sherwood in 1860 simply listed it, without comment, as a post village in the southwestern part of the county.[26] Glen-

---

25. Sherwood, *Gazetteer of the State of Georgia* (Charleston, S.C., 1827), 21–115; Sherwood, *A Gazetteer of the State of Georgia*, 2d ed. (Philadelphia, 1829), 51–177; Sherwood, *A Gazetteer of the State of Georgia: Embracing a Particular Description of the Counties, Towns, Villages, Rivers, etc.*, 3d ed. (Washington, D.C., 1837), 110–252. One population figure has been converted to an estimate of the free population by the procedure described in note 17 above, forty-four house counts and three family counts by the procedures described in note 24. Estimates through 99 and between 100 and 249 inclusive were adjusted upwards from the date of the original observation to accommodate a demonstrable average annual increase in populations of this size of 5.12 and 2.08 percent per year, respectively. These percentages were established using 148 cases for which two population figures or estimates at least four years apart were available. The computations used both to establish growth rates and extrapolate from an earlier estimate to one applicable to 1850 were drawn from George W. Barclay, *Techniques of Population Analysis* (New York, 1958), 28–33. For a theoretical validation of declining growth rates in a newly settled area, see Darrett B. Rutman, "People in Process: The New Hampshire Towns of the Eighteenth Century," *Journal of Urban History* 1 (1975): 268–92 [chap. 7 above].

26. *Milledgeville Federal Union*, 5 Jan. 1847; White, *Statistics of Georgia*, 321; Smith, *Georgia Commercial Tax Digest, and Directory: Containing a Complete List of the Names of Merchants and Copartnerships . . . Amount of Stock in Trade . . . as Returned to the Office of the Comptroller General by the Receivers of Tax Returns for 1850, with an Appendix Containing a List of the Principal Towns and Villages* (Milledgeville, Ga., 1851), 90; Campbell, *Southern Business Directory*, 260; Sherwood, *Gazetteer of Georgia: Containing a Particular Description of the State; Its Resources, Counties, Towns, Villages*, 4th ed. (Macon, Ga., 1860), 80. Of Smith's 201 "princi-

alta, Marion County, is another example: to Sherwood (1860) it was simply a post office ten miles west of the county courthouse, but White in 1849 wrote of its post office, store, "doctor's shop, etc."[27] Alapaha in Lowndes County is mentioned by White but not by Sherwood, yet there was a post office there in 1846, and Campbell in 1854 listed three dry goods merchants and a grocer doing business in the village.[28] In all, 612 such examples could be piled up, "post villages and public places," all of which can be located on contemporary maps of the state in 1850 but all of unknown size.[29]

Thus far, by moving beyond the published federal census and De Bow's addition to it, by scouring census manuscripts, gazetteers, newspapers, and the like, we have found references to a total of 804 places — potentially the towns, villages and hamlets in the state in 1850. Yet we still do not know the full proportion of the state's free population living in such places.

In this regard another element of the 1850 census is suggestive. De Bow, by way of annotating the *Statistical View of the United States* of 1854, wrote that "the rural population" — by which he obviously meant the actual farm-dwelling population of a state — "might be ascertained by multiplying the number of farms into the average of persons existing upon

pal" places, 58 (28.9%) are identified in other sources as simply "post villages and public places."

27. Sherwood, *Gazetteer* (1860), 95; White, *Statistics of Georgia*, 411.

28. *Milledgeville Federal Union*, 5 Jan. 1847; Campbell, *Southern Business Directory*, 262.

29. All places included to this point have been located on maps of Georgia from the period. The most useful for this purpose have been: Geographical, Statistical, and Historical Map of Georgia Drawn by F[ielding] Lucas, Jr., J. Yeager, Sculp., no scale but ca. 1:2,217,600, 11½ by 8½ inches, printed in H[enry] C. Carey and I. Lea, *A Complete Historical, Chronological, and Geographical American Atlas* (Philadelphia, 1822), no. 24; Georgia, Entered According to Act of Congress in the Year 1842 by Sidney E. Morse and Samuel Breese, no scale but ca. 1:1,564,000, 14 by 11 inches; A New Map of Georgia with its Roads & Distances, Entered ... 1846 by H. N. Burroughs in the Clerk's Office of the Eastern District of Pennsylvania, no scale but ca. 1:1,267,200, 14 by 11 inches, printed by S. Augustus Mitchell, Philadelphia, [1846]; the 1847 Bonner map cited in note 7 above; Bonner's Map of the State of Georgia with the Addition of Its Geological Features, the Geological Representations Entered ... 1849 by W. Thorne Williams in the Clerk's Office of the District Court of Georgia, no scale but ca. 1:1,140,480, 19¾ by 17½ inches, printed at Ackerman's, New York, published by W. T. Williams, Savannah, 1849; Lloyd's Topographical Map of Georgia from State Surveys before the War Showing Railways, Stations, Villages, Mills, no scale but ca. 1:633,600, 35½ by 33¼ inches, printed by J. T. Lloyd, New York, 1864, and reprinted at ca. 1:887,040, 25 by 21 inches, no additional publication data but ca. 1980. All of these maps are on file in the Georgia Department of Archives and History, and some in the P. K. Yonge Library, University of Florida, Gainesville. Also useful: George B. Davis et al., *Atlas to Accompany the Official Records of the Union and Confederate Armies* (Washington, D.C., 1891–95), reprinted as *The Official Military Atlas of the Civil War* (New York, 1978), particularly plates 142–48; James C. Bonner, *Atlas for Georgia History* (Milledgeville, Ga., 1969); Thomas W. Hodler, *The Atlas of Georgia* (Athens, Ga., 1986).

each."[30] Assuming that on each Georgia farm there was at least one dwelling and using the census count of dwellings to establish the average number of free persons per dwelling (5.74 for the state), we readily compute a farm-dwelling free population of 298,999, or 57 percent of the state's free population. Yet in our own search for towns and villages we have managed to estimate a nonfarm-dwelling free population of only 78,996. More than 147,000 people are missing, lost to errors and undercounts on both sides of an equation (farm plus nonfarm dwellers) which must add up to the free population of the state. If we assign a quarter of these to cover both our underestimates of the free population of the towns and villages to this point and the known but as yet unpopulated villages and hamlets in question, the hamlet-, village-, and town-dwelling free population of Georgia rises to at the very least 115,000, almost 22 percent — roughly one in five — of the free population of the state.

Postal records suggest that this crude calculation is not at all out of line. Among the various series produced by the nineteenth-century Post Office Department were biennial reports of the net revenues of the nation's post offices by name, county, and state and of the annual compensation of their postmasters. Both compensation and revenues reflect the volume of mail passing through each office. And there is a clear theoretical link between the volume of mail handled by a post office and the size of the place immediately surrounding the office, one demonstrated empirically by Allan R. Pred with regard to early nineteenth-century cities and by Richard W. Helbock with regard to small towns.[31] The applicability of theory to antebellum Georgia is easily demonstrated.

Postal records for the year July 1, 1850, to June 30, 1851, indicate that there were 656 post offices spread across the ninety-five counties of Georgia.[32] The records, aggregated by county, can be linked to county-based data drawn from the federal census of 1850 and state tax registers.[33] Once

30. De Bow, *Statistical View of the United States*, 193.

31. Pred, *Urban Growth and the Circulation of Information: The United States System of Cities, 1790–1840* (Cambridge, Mass., 1973), 78–103; Helbock, "Postal Records as an Aid to Urbanization Studies," *Historical Methods Newsletter* 3 (1970): 9–14.

32. "Auditor's Report, Showing the Compensation of Postmasters [of Georgia], and Nett Proceeds at Each Office, from July 1, 1850 to June 30, 1851," in U.S., Department of State, *Register of All Officers and Agents, Civil, Military, and Naval, in the Service of the United States* (Washington, D.C., 1851), 289–309. In the listing, the periods covered by the reports from the various post offices are sometimes given with specific dates, e.g., "to May 30." These have been rounded to the nearest number of quarters and extrapolated to a yearly figure by dividing the revenue or compensation by the number of quarters reported and multiplying by four. Atlanta made no return in 1850–51; in the analysis that follows we have made use of the city's 1849–50 report.

33. Specifically with the data in De Bow, *Statistical View of the United States*, 206–17, and Smith, *Georgia Commercial Tax Digest*, the latter an extraction of data on individuals and firms recorded as paying a merchant tax on the 1850 county tax registers returned to the comptroller general of the state.

Table 12.1. Georgia postal revenues, 1850–51, correlated with selected county variables

Variable	Product-moment correlation (r) with postal revenue	
	All counties	Excluding counties with major cities
Value of stock in trade	.922**	.847**
Amount of taxes paid by merchants	.899**	.874**
Number of merchants and tradesmen	.833**	.737**
Hands employed in manufacturing	.646**	.703**
Capital invested in manufacturing	.590**	.637**
Free population	.348**	.454**
Density of free population	.473**	.449**
Density of slave population	.622**	.487**
Number of farms	−.118	.305*
Number farms per square mile	−.006	.313*
Average value of farms	.714**	.319*
Total number of families	.413**	.464**
Total number of dwellings	.400**	.462**
Dwellings in excess of farms	.682**	.513**
Excess dwellings per square mile	.773**	.527**
Value of staple production per farm	.639**	.227

Sources and notes: See notes 32 and 33 for sources. $N = 95$, the number of counties in the state in 1850, for the first column; 91 for the second, where the counties containing Savannah, Augusta, Columbus, and Macon are excluded. The asterisks indicate the significance level: * significant at the .01 level; ** the .001 level.

linked, the relationship between postal revenues and other measurable phenomena — the free and slave populations of the county, for example, the number of farms and the value of their staple crops, the value of stock-in-trade in the hands of the county's merchants and tradesmen and the amount of taxes they paid — can be assessed, as in table 12.1. The formal correlation statistics suggest a strong relationship between postal revenues and both the number of merchants and tradesmen in a county and the extent of their activities (indicated by the value of their stock-in-trade and the amount of capital invested in manufactories). The strong relationships hold even when we exclude from the analysis those counties containing the four known "cities" of the state — Savannah, Augusta, Macon, and Columbus. Conceivably the post offices, merchants, storekeepers, and manufactories could have been scattered across the open countryside of the counties, tucked singly among the plantations and farms rather than gathered in towns and villages; indeed, that is the implicit assumption of those noted earlier who argue for an essentially townless South. Such might be the case in some instances — we cannot ignore the probability of the isolated country store and post office — but not generally. Table 12.2

Table 12.2. Georgia post office revenues, 1850–51, correlated with selected town and village variables

Variable	Product-moment correlation (r) with postal revenue	
	All towns and villages	Excluding major cities
Estimated free population	.959	.797
Number of merchants and tradesmen	.867	.727
Amount of taxes paid by merchants	.966	.823
Value of stock in trade	.961	.782
Value of real property of merchants	.976	.719
Number of members of Masonic lodge	.526	.461

Sources and notes: See notes 32 and 34 for sources. $N = 160$ for the first column, 156 for the second. All correlations are significant at the .001 level.

takes the analysis below the county level, linking 160 Georgia post offices to places for which we already have estimates of the free population, and these in turn with data on the economic and Masonic activity in these places.[34] Post office revenues are clearly and strongly related to the extent of such activities within the particular places of the counties.

The strong statistical relationships reported in table 12.2 suggest a final opportunity for estimating the free populations of at least some of those villages and towns of 1850 which have thus far eluded us. For if, in effect, we can use such variables as post office revenues, merchant activity, and the number of Masons in a place to duplicate with a fair degree of accuracy the free populations we already know, it is a reasonable step to use the same variables to estimate the free populations we do not know.[35] In table

34. Smith, *Georgia Commercial Tax Digest* lists 3,309 merchants and firms, their stock in trade, number of slaves, amount of real property, and tax paid, but only by county. Other sources — notably Campbell, *Southern Business Directory*, and the R. G. Dun & Co. Collection, Baker Library, Harvard University Graduate School of Business Administration, Boston — allow individual merchants listed in Smith to be placed in particular towns and villages. Freemasonry in Georgia's towns and villages is briefly discussed in chapter 13; the lodges and membership of 1850 utilized here are listed in *Proceedings of the . . . Grand Lodge of Georgia at Its Annual Communication . . . 1850* (Macon, Ga., 1851), 41–125.

35. Our procedure has been to construct a regression equation using a data base of 116 places for which we have both postal revenues and a firm estimate of the free population, the latter serving as the dependent variable with a series of independent variables chosen for their logical relationship to population, viz.: the postal revenue attributed to the place and the percentage of the postal revenue of the surrounding county represented by that figure; the number of merchants and members of the Masonic order located in the place; the number of hands employed in manufacturing in the place; the total number of dwellings in the county minus the number of farms. We also introduced a series of dummy variables representing the geographic location of the place within the state according to the regional scheme described in note 37. The mean of the free population "predicted" by the regression was 315, of the original values (i.e., known populations) 362, with 70 percent of the latter

Table 12.3. Estimated free population of Georgia places, 1850, by source of estimate

Source of estimate	Number of places	Mean estimate	Sum of estimates
Published census	19	1,395	26,505
De Bow's additions	31	466	14,437
Census MS additions	4	1,536	6,145
White	79	247	19,518
Sherwood	48	191	9,192
Other literary sources	11	291	3,199
Regression analysis	405	78	31,395
Total	597	185	110,390

Source and notes: See text for the derivation of the various estimates. Twenty additional locations satisfied the criteria for the regression analysis, but the resulting population estimates failed the minimum test for "hamlet" developed in table 12.5 and they were dropped. Evidence suggests the existence of still another 207 places, but in the absence of any way to estimate their populations they, too, were dropped.

12.3 we append the estimates derived in this fashion to those established in other ways and already discussed. It is obvious that the procedure is catching some of the smallest villages and hamlets of the state: Note the mean estimated size of seventy-eight. But in sum we have added over 31,000 free persons to the number of town, village, and hamlet dwellers, bringing the total to just over 110,000 or 21 percent of Georgia's free population, again, roughly one in five of the state's free men and women. We are not, it seems, dealing with an insignificant phenomenon.[36]

The 597 places that we have been able to locate and (at least by way of estimation) to populate — not in all likelihood the totality of Georgia's towns and villages in 1850 but certainly an adequate sample — were located in every part of the state. Their distribution, however, varied among the state's geographic regions. Map 12.3 visually depicts this variation, locating our places with reference to a regional breakdown of the state (see map 12.2 for the regions).[37] Table 12.4 restates the distribution in

---

subsumed in the model (reporting r^2 as a percentage). The regression equation, derived from known populations, was subsequently used as a predictive equation to estimate unknown populations. A full description of the procedure, together with a demonstration that hands employed in manufacturing in Georgia in 1850 were overwhelmingly white, will appear in Darrett B. and Anita H. Rutman, *The Village South: Antebellum Georgia, a Case Study* (forthcoming).

36. It is important to note that while estimates on the basis of the regression are used in the aggregations here, the populations of individual towns offered as examples are always values obtained in other ways.

37. No regional categorization of Georgia's antebellum counties is fully satisfactory. The most sophisticated is that of Frederick A. Bode and Donald E. Ginter, *Farm Tenancy and the*

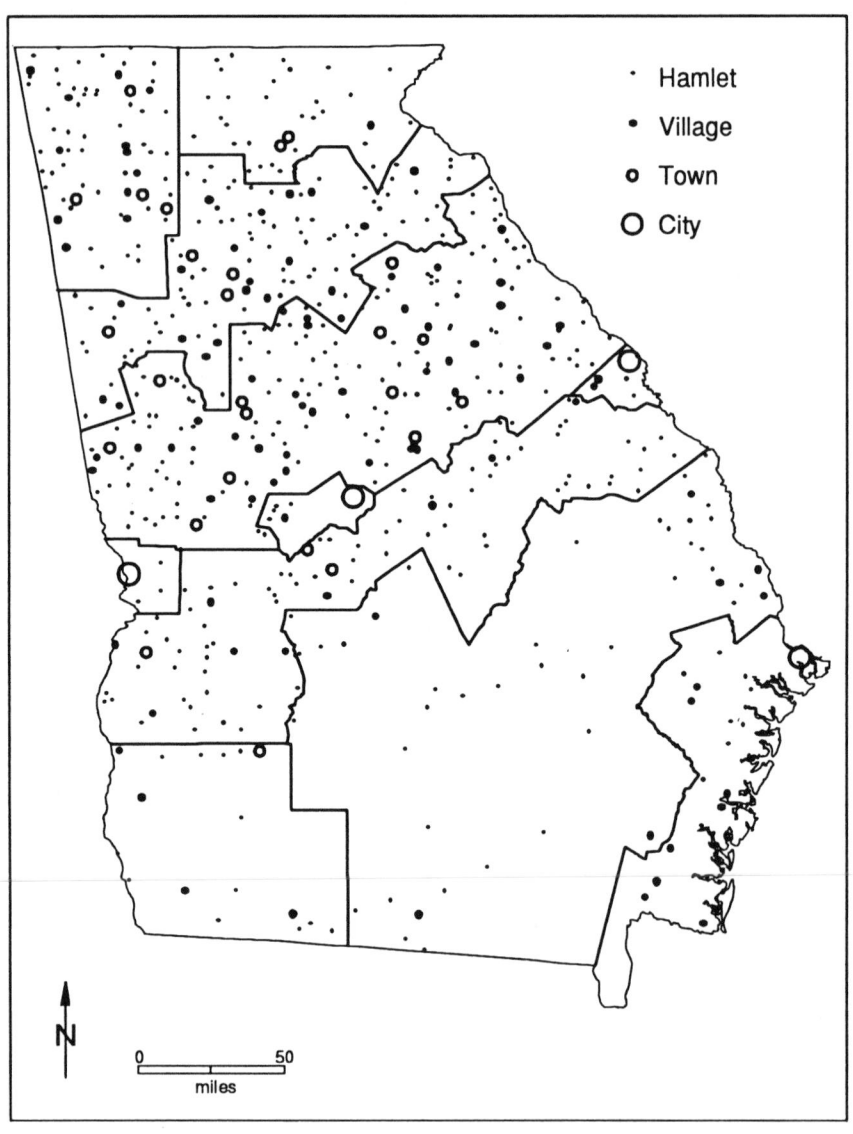

Map 12.3. Georgia's mid-century hamlets, villages, towns, and cities. The interior lines delineate the regions of the state labeled in map 12.2. See table 12.5 for the definitions of hamlet, village, town, and city.

Table 12.4. Population aggregations of Georgia, 1850, by geographic region

Region	Number of places	Places per 100 square miles	Mean population	% of free population in all places	Farms per 100 square miles	Staple production per farm ($)	% of slaves in population
Plateau, ridges, valleys	70	2.0	185	22.4	119.2	68.08	19.2
Blue Ridge Mountains	33	1.0	110	10.9	90.4	0.79	7.6
Upper piedmont	105	1.7	141	13.4	188.2	96.31	20.9
Lower piedmont	199	1.9	175	24.2	146.8	562.20	54.2
Sandhills	22	1.7	718	52.2	126.0	422.27	46.4
Central cotton belt	87	1.0	120	14.7	91.6	574.43	49.2
Limesink & pine barrens	43	0.3	73	7.4	34.6	143.51	31.8
Tidal swamps & savannas	21	0.6	583	70.9	27.6	1,453.37	67.2
Southwestern uplands	17	0.4	157	15.2	40.8	505.97	47.7

Sources: See text for the identification of places and population estimates, note 37 for the regional breakdown. Regional areas used in computing densities have been established using county areas as given in George White, *Statistics of the State of Georgia . . . Together with a Particular Description of Each County* (Savannah, 1849), corrected by reference to the 1847 Bonner map of the state cited in note 7. The free population, number of farms, and number of slaves used in the various computations have been drawn from J. D. B. De Bow, *Statistical View of the United States . . . Being a Compendium of the Seventh Census* (Washington, D.C., 1854), 206–17. Staple production per farm in dollars has been computed using the census report of rice and cotton production per county converted to dollar values using (in the case of the coastal counties) rice and cotton prices compiled by Alfred Glaze Smith, *Economic Readjustment of an Old Cotton State: South Carolina, 1820–1860* (Columbia, S.C., 1958), 220–26, adjusted to accommodate the sea island/short staple differential as reported in the Charleston *Courier*, 25 Oct. 1849, and (in the case of interior Georgia) using the average prices current for cotton, 1849–51, as reported in the Athens *Southern Banner*, the Macon *Georgia Journal and Messenger*, and the Columbus *Enquirer*.

numeric terms, offering the number of places per 100 square miles and the mean size of places by region but adding information necessary to an understanding of the role of our places in the structure of an agricultural society, not simply the slave and staple society of the South: the number of farms per 100 square miles and an indication of the commitment of each of Georgia's regions to slavery and staple agriculture. The distribution of towns and villages and hamlets had more to do with the first (the density of farms in the surrounding countryside) and less to do with the last two (slaves and staples).[38]

Small places, it seems, were necessary social and economic rendezvous for the farmers of any country neighborhood; hence where there were farmers, there were small places. We glimpse this in James Silk Buckingham's 1842 account of his travels in Georgia. Crossing by road from Macon to Columbus in the lower piedmont, he noted post offices every ten or twelve miles along the way, "very humble buildings, and often mere sheds" but, "like the old barbers' shops in English villages a century ago — places for the idle and gossiping to assemble and discuss the news." Usually the post office was itself a "confectionery" dispensing "liquors of all kinds" or a general store proffering "dry-goods, hardware, earthenware, medicines." If not, "confectionery" and store stood nearby, together with a blacksmith shop, perhaps a tannery, a mill, a church. On leaving a slightly larger place — one more recognizable as a village — Buckingham passed thirty saddled horses "fastened to the branches of trees by their

Census in Antebellum Georgia (Athens, Ga., 1986), 76, who adapted to the 1860 county boundaries the 1880 regionalization developed in Richard C. Sutch and Roger L. Ransom, *Economic Regions of the South in 1880*, Southern Economic History Project, Working Paper Series no. 3 (Berkeley, Calif., 1971). We have adapted Bode and Ginter to the 1850 counties but subsumed their "Cumberland Plateau" region (one county in 1850) into their "Ridge and Valley" region, joined their "Limestone Barrens" and "Pine Barrens" into one region, and divided their "Piedmont" region into an "Upper piedmont" and "Lower piedmont" following Steven Hahn, *The Roots of Southern Populism: Yeoman Farmers and the Transformation of the Georgia Upcountry, 1850–1890* (New York, 1983), 7, 9n; i.e., our "Upper piedmont" is comparable to Hahn's "Upcountry," although, unlike Hahn, we did not drop DeKalb County (containing Atlanta) as an up-country anomaly.

38. In formal terms, among the counties statewide there was a strong linear correlation between the number of population aggregations (cities, towns, villages, and hamlets) per 100 square miles and the number of farms per 100 square miles ($r = .792$, significant at the .001 level) and a slight negative correlation with the value of staples produced per farm ($-.116$) and the percentage of the total population that was slave ($-.014$), the last two coefficients suggesting the dampening effect of the plantation economy. When the analysis is confined to the fifty-three counties of the upper and lower piedmont and the cotton belt, the correlation coefficients are, respectively, .703, $-.166$, $-.131$. The coefficients indicate that 50 to 65 percent of the variation in the density of population aggregations in the various counties is to be "explained" by the variation in the density of farms. An analysis of variance of town densities across the various regions of the state with farm density entered as a covariant subsumes 87 percent of the variance (reporting r^2 as a percentage); with the value of staples per farm and the percentage of the population that was slave added as covariants, 88 percent.

bridles"; inquiring of his guide, he learned "that the farmers who come in from the country to effect sales of stock, or make purchases of supplies in the village" habitually tethered their horses outside "to save the expense of stabling."[39] We glimpse the linkage of town and farm again in newspaper advertisements in which the proximity of the former was put forward as an advantage to the latter; this from *The Soil of the South* of October 1853, for example: "Fowle Town Plantation for Sale. . . . in the county of Lee, adjoining the village of Palmyra, and five miles from the city of Albany. . . . Here is a market for everything; good society, church, school, daily mail."[40]

Yet if farmers needed hamlets and villages, even more determinative was the fact that hamlets and villages needed a minimal number of nearby farmers in order to exist; hence in such diverse regions as the Blue Ridge in the far northeast and the coastal savannas and swamps of the southeast, villages were relatively few. The latter area boasted the highest concentration of slaves in the state and the greatest commitment to commercial agriculture. Here were located Savannah, Georgia's major city, truck farmers growing garden produce for its supply in the immediate environs, and a sprinkling of minor ports.[41] But the rest of the region was a countryside of broad, flat, open plains, tidal swamps, and sea islands. Along the rivers and on the islands of the coast were the holdings of the wealthiest planters in the state, their fortunes tied to rice, sea island cotton, and blacks; inland were stock farmers. But among both groups holdings were large (Liberty County's averaging over 1,400 acres) and relatively few (244 spread across the county's 800 square miles). Few, too, were the region's hamlets and villages. For its part, the mountainous northeast was an almost direct contrast. While coastal region elevations seldom rose higher than 15 or 20 feet above mean sea level, the valleys of the Blue Ridge — let alone the peaks — were 1,600 to 1,800 feet high, too high (and cold) for all but the hardiest crops. Yet here in a land of few slaves and little commitment to the great staples of the South, villages and hamlets were almost as

39. Buckingham, *The Slave States of America* (1842; reprint, New York, 1968), 1:233–34, 2:145; John Melish, *Travels through the United States of America* (1812), in *The Rambler in Georgia*, ed. Mills Lane (Savannah, 1973), 27–28.

40. *Soil of the South* (Columbus), Oct. 1853, 703.

41. When data on agricultural production of such items as potatoes, butter and cheese, slaughtered animals, and garden and orchard products from De Bow, *Statistical View of the United States*, 210–17, are mapped by county, there is a clear hint of von Thünen rings about Savannah and Macon (implying commercial agriculture serving an urban aggregation) but not Augusta and Columbus. On von Thünen rings, see the editor's introduction to Johann Heinrich von Thünen, *Von Thünen's Isolated State: An English Edition of "Der Isolierte Staat,"* ed. Peter Hall, trans. Carla M. Wartenberg (Oxford, 1966); Richard J. Peet, "The Spatial Expansion of Commercial Agriculture in the Nineteenth Century: A von Thünen Interpretation," *Economic Geography* 45 (1969): 283–301; Howard F. Gregor, *Geography of Agriculture: Themes in Research* (Englewood Cliffs, N.J., 1970), 57–58.

sparse as along the coast, and for the same reason: Few valleys in these mountains — even with farms a third the size of those on the coast — could support enough farm customers to support in turn the "confectioneries," stores, and blacksmiths, even churches, of a village.

All across the state the same relationship prevailed. Farms were few on the acidic soils of the barrens and, for the most part, were concentrated on the alluvial bottomlands of the rivers; there, too, were to be found the region's few hamlets and occasional villages. North and west of the barrens lay Georgia's central cotton belt with far better soil, a greater number of farms, and a higher village density. Yet here subregional variation showed itself, the uniformly strong soils of the eastern cotton belt giving way increasingly to a mixture of good and bad as one progressed toward the oak and hickory lands of the southwestern uplands, the change reflected in farm density and in the number of villages. The sandhills constituted the border country between cotton belt and piedmont. Here was the fall line where the narrow, relatively fast moving rivers of the north dropped abruptly and widened to become the slow, meandering rivers of the south. Acidic soils, quickly leeched, and a lack of bottomland made this a poor region for agriculture. But the sandhills marked a transit point for river traffic, giving rise to a belt of large towns (or small cities) — Augusta on the Savannah, Macon on the Ocmulgee, Columbus on the Chattahoochee — each with a circlet of satellite villages, some commercial (East Macon, for example, with four or five stores), some residential (Vineville, "a delightful retreat from the noise and heat" of Macon), some industrial (Griswoldville to the northeast of Macon, "a pretty village, occupied chiefly by Mr. Griswold and his workmen, in the gin-making business").[42] For its part the piedmont was a varied land, higher and increasingly hilly as one progressed northward and crossed the invisible line between its lower and upper parts, its soils discontinuously strong and weak. Cotton dominated the lower piedmont but gradually gave way with elevation to corn, grain, and cattle until the piedmont proper gave way to the ridges, valleys, and plateau of the northwest and mountains of the northeast, where cotton all but disappeared. Yet throughout the piedmont and on into the valleys of the northwest, farm density, and with it the occurrence of villages and hamlets, tended to be well above that of the rest of the state.

Our 597 places were distributed by size as well as geographically, and with size by function within a structure of places well defined where farm density was high (the upper piedmont, for example), atrophied where it was low (the barrens). Table 12.5 summarizes.

The post office hamlets that Buckingham noted echoed the definition

42. Campbell, *Southern Business Directory*, 217–18; White, *Statistics of Georgia*, 112; Sherwood, *Gazetteer* (1837), 90; ibid. (1860), 87.

Table 12.5. Georgia's hamlets, villages, towns, and cities of 1850 by region

Region	Number and, in parentheses, mean population of			
	Hamlets	Villages	Towns	Cities
Plateau, ridges, valleys	54 (77)	11 (242)	5 (1,232)	—
Blue Ridge Mountains	30 (53)	1 (298)	2 (872)	—
Upper piedmont	82 (56)	19 (272)	4 (1,230)	—
Lower piedmont	147 (84)	41 (269)	11 (1,035)	—
Sandhills	12 (87)	7 (339)	—	3 (4,127)
Central cotton belt	74 (72)	10 (301)	3 (687)	—
Limesink & pine barrens	37 (48)	6 (227)	—	—
Tidal swamps & savannas	12 (79)	8 (276)	—	1 (9,081)
Southwestern uplands	12 (60)	4 (346)	1 (564)	—

Sources and notes: See text for the identification of places and population estimates. On the definition of a hamlet, see Glenn T. Trewartha, "The Unincorporated Hamlet: One Element of the American Settlement Fabric," *Annals of the Association of American Geographers* 33 (1943): 37. We have accepted his upper boundary (free population 150) and operationalized his lower boundary, viz., at least 4 residences (therefore a minimum of 4 times the average number of free persons per dwelling computed for the county in which the place lies) and evidence of activity apart from farming. With the exception of hamlets (which they define as 50–200 people), we follow the implicit categorization of Stanley Elkins and Eric McKitrick, "A Meaning for Turner's Frontier," *Political Science Quarterly* 69 (1954): 341–42n, in defining a village as 151–500 people and a town as over 500, arbitrarily isolating Savannah, Augusta, Macon, and Columbus as cities.

of what De Bow in 1854 contemplated as the minimal subcounty unit for the nation as a whole, "places having an aggregation of over fifty or a hundred persons, with a store, tavern, blacksmith shop or school house and post office, or some or all of these."[43] But Buckingham also described a step up on a continuum of places, writing of Franklin County's Carnesville as "a very perfect specimen of a gradually forming American village, rising into the dignity of a county-town."[44] Carnesville represented a type of place that served an administrative function additional to the social and economic functions of even the smallest hamlet, for it was the county seat and, by definition, a focal point for the farmers of the county who perforce had recourse to its clerks and courts. Where farmers congregated, of course, one found the inevitable store and confectionery and blacksmith. But Carnesville had, to an extent, a life of its own. Clerks and courts meant people, some permanent residents, others transients — the justices and lawyers who followed the circuit, for example — who, in turn, made necessary hotels and inns and boardinghouses, hence more permanent resi-

43. De Bow, *Statistical View of the United States*, 192.
44. Buckingham, *Slave States of America* 2:144.

dents in the form of hotel and inn keepers and their families. And the aggregation fed upon itself to add still others — a doctor, perhaps a dentist and a printer, churches with their ministers, a school and its teachers, specialized shops with their shopkeepers. Buckingham caught some of this in describing Carnesville. "In its centre," he wrote, "was the Court House of the district, and within a few yards of this were the sign-posts of three hotels. Not far off was seen the symbol of a doctor of medicine, with his name and title at full length, under a rudely delineated pestle-and-mortar, as the emblem of his profession. Right opposite to him, in a small wooden cabin of a single room, was the office of another professional man, the attorney-at-law; and within a few doors of these were the shops of a blacksmith, a carpenter, and a saddler, with one large grocery store, at which everything sold by grocers, ironmongers, drapers, stationers, and haberdashers, in larger places, were to be found."[45] In offering this snapshot of Carnesville, however, Buckingham missed what might well be the town's most significant feature. He saw it as "a gradually forming" village in the process of "rising." In point of fact, it was already an old town and had long before become what it would be in the foreseeable future. Settled shortly after the Revolution, it had boasted a courthouse and some twenty houses in the 1790s. Thirty years later it was still the same size: courthouse, clerk's office, school, five stores, fourteen dwellings. And in 1850 — ten years after Buckingham's visit — it was no larger; by White's count there were but seventeen houses, while the census marshal of 1850 counted a population free and slave of 250.[46] Serving as the administrative and economic center of a limited district, Carnesville was inherently limited in size and social complexity, as were all such towns.[47]

45. Ibid., 144–45. William Lamar Cawthon, Jr., "Clinton: County Seat on the Georgia Frontier, 1808–1821" (M.A. thesis, University of Georgia, 1984), is indicative of the rich materials available for the study of such towns.

46. Jedidiah Morse, *The American Gazetteer* (Boston, 1797), under Carnesville; Sherwood, *Gazetteer* (1829), 88; White, *Statistics of Georgia*, 258; MS Census Returns, Georgia, Seventh Census, 1850, Social Statistics, 225, Baker-Wilkinson Collection, Duke University Library, Durham, N.C.

47. There is a tendency to attach the adjectives "stagnant" or "stunted" to such towns — Ford uses both in *Origins of Southern Radicalism*, 63, 89 — as though growth were implicit in place. It is a curious modern attitude which defies past realities. Most villages did not rise to become towns or cities, a point made indirectly by Stuart M. Blumin, "When Villages Become Towns: The Historical Contexts of Town Formation," in *The Pursuit of Urban History*, ed. Derek Fraser and Anthony Sutcliffe (London, 1983), 54: Relative to the number of towns with a population of over 5,000 at the beginning and end of the nineteenth century (18 versus 745), "the sheer number of rural villages that grew into towns was certainly very great"; relative to the number of villages, however, it was not very great at all. In 1909 the U.S. Bureau of the Census estimated 2,027 "minor civil divisions" in the eighteen states enumerated in the 1790 census and 11,667 in those same states in 1900 (*A Century of Population Growth From the First Census of the United States to the Twelfth, 1790–1900* [Washington, D.C., 1909], 77). Still, Blumin points to the appropriate question: Why do some

Still, there were larger and more complex places. Albany, on the Flint River in the southwest with a free population of around 550, five stores, a drugstore, ten lawyers, eight doctors, and "a number of mechanics"; Marietta, free population around 1,200, "one of the most pleasant towns in north Georgia," with six dry goods merchants, seven grocers, two druggists, two clothing stores, shoestore, crockery store, bookstore; Griffin, 1,500 free persons, three churches, three or four hotels, five warehouses, forty to fifty stores, "besides a large number of mechanics' shops"; Athens, with a free population of some 1,650, site of Franklin College (now the University of Georgia) and, "consequently," home to "more persons of education, taste, and good manner, than is generally found in so small a community" but boasting, too, sixteen general merchants, six grocers, four clothiers, and a variety of stores and shops purveying hats, caps, boots, shoes, carriages and wagons, watches and books; Macon on the dividing line between cotton belt and piedmont, with a free population of 3,367 and solidly devoted "to business"; Columbus, stretching a mile and a quarter along the Chattahoochee, 3,684 whites and free blacks.[48] Such towns served the farmers of their immediate neighborhoods in much the same fashion as did the country villages, Buckingham writing of "many of the country people coming" into Macon, "some on horseback, some in waggons, and some on foot."[49] And their dynamics were much the same, their very size promoting an enlargement and sophistication of goods and services offered, which, in turn, increased their size.

In the structure of our places, however, what set such towns apart was the fact that their merchants served as the linchpins connecting the countryside with the larger national and international economy, trading country produce for goods in Augusta, Savannah, and even beyond, in New York, then wholesaling the goods for country produce to the stores of the surrounding villages and hamlets. One hint of this is to be found in table 12.6, a breakdown by region of the merchants of Georgia and the value of their stock in trade as identified in the state's tax digests for 1850.

The penetration of merchants into every part of the state is clear, albeit the degree of penetration varied; in this respect—and logically so, for merchants were based in towns and villages—the distribution of merchants across the state closely resembled that of towns and villages. But the variation in the stock in trade per family in the region is to the point here. If we assume that, collectively, the merchants of a region held stock

---

villages grow and others not? So, too, does geographer Edward K. Muller in "Regional Urbanization and the Selective Growth of Towns in North American Regions," *Journal of Historical Geography* 3 (1977): 21–39.

48. White, *Statistics of Georgia*, 112, 120, 443–45; Campbell, *Southern Business Directory*, 231, 236–37; Buckingham, *Slave States of America* 2:70–71.

49. Buckingham, *Slave States of America* 1:210.

Table 12.6. Georgia's merchants and their stock by region, 1850

Region	Number of merchants	Stock in trade in dollars	
		Total	Per family
Richmond (Augusta)	345	1,023,004	657.46
Chatham (Savannah)	347	775,150	391.69
Sandhills	359	1,038,450	258.64
Tidal swamps & savannas	79	95,700	68.26
Southwestern uplands	92	176,500	56.09
Lower piedmont	843	1,199,251	47.33
Central cotton belt	295	331,400	26.30
Plateau, ridges, valleys	292	216,050	22.17
Upper piedmont	453	383,450	20.16
Limesink & pine barrens	115	99,400	13.91
Blue Ridge Mountains	89	69,600	12.34

Sources and notes: John T. Smith, *Georgia Commercial Tax Digest and Directory: Containing a Complete List of the Names of Merchants and Copartnerships . . . [and] Amount in Stock in Trade . . . as Returned to the Office of the Comptroller General by the Receivers of Tax Returns for 1850* (Augusta, Ga., 1851); J. D. B. De Bow, *Statistical View of the United States . . . Being a Compendium of the Seventh Census* (Washington, D.C., 1854), 206–17. The "Number of merchants" counts each partnership or firm as one; the "Regions" are exclusive, i.e., Richmond (Augusta) is not included among the counties of the sandhills, nor is Chatham (Savannah) included among the counties of the tidal swamps and savannas.

in trade for retail purpose in the amount of no more than $30 per free family of the region, then any amount in excess of this figure can serve as a rough index of wholesale activity.[50] In the table Chatham and Richmond counties (Savannah and Augusta) have been isolated at the top; as might be expected, the two stand out in this regard, the merchants of the two counties combined holding almost $1.8 million in stock in trade, $657 and $392 per free family respectively, twenty-two and thirteen times the $30 figure. But so, too, do the counties of the sandhills containing Macon and Columbus, with stock in trade exceeding $30 by a factor of almost nine. When we isolate a further group of counties known to contain significant town populations — Baker (Albany), Baldwin (Milledgeville), Clarke (Athens), Cobb (Marietta), DeKalb (Atlanta), Floyd (Rome), Pike (Griffin), and Troup (LaGrange) — wholesale trading is again indicated, the merchants in these counties holding stock in trade in the amount of $74 for every free family in the counties as grouped.

Other hints are to be found in newspaper notices and advertisements.

50. The $30 figure approximates the statewide average computed using Smith, *Georgia Commercial Tax Digest* and the number of families given in De Bow, *Statistical View of the United States*, when Chatham, Richmond, Bibb, and Muscogee (i.e., Savannah, Augusta, Macon, and Columbus) are excluded from the computation, viz., $30.47.

Sims and Cheever, Apalachicola, Florida, commission merchants, operated shallow barges up and down the Flint River; in January 1851 the *Albany Patriot* announced the arrival of two of their barges loaded with "groceries" for their outlet in the town and the subsequent departure of the barges loaded with cotton. Savannah's H. A. Crane, "Wholesale Grocer and Commission Merchant," invited "Planters and Country Merchants . . . to call and examine" his advertised goods "for themselves." Macon's *Georgia Journal and Messenger* periodically published lists of its advertisers broken down by the goods they offered — "Groceries and Staple Goods," "Carriages, Harnesses," "Hardware, Tin-Ware" — urging "our country friends . . . to preserve the list, and to be sure to give the parties a call before buying elsewhere." Ross & Brothers maintained a retail establishment on Macon's Cotton Avenue, advertising "a fine stock of Staple and Fancy Goods" for "the city and country trade." But they referred to themselves as "Wholesale Grocery and Dry Goods Merchants" and in a separate establishment across the avenue kept "constantly on hand large and splendid stocks of everything in the Grocery, Produce, and Dry Goods line; which they sell very low for Cash or Barter, for any kind of marketable trade, or on reasonable credit to punctual Dealers," respectfully soliciting "all country and retail merchants to call and examine their style of goods and prices."[51]

Commentators extolled the successes of such places. Albany, White noted, did "a thriving trade," shipping out 10,000 to 12,000 bales of cotton a year — by the late 1850s the figure would increase to 30,000 — and serving as the marketplace not only for its own Baker County but for Irwin and Sumter counties as well. Marietta "does considerable business," serving as the market for Cobb, Cherokee, and parts of Lumpkin, Forsyth, Gilmer, Paulding, and Carroll counties. Griffin's merchants did "a large amount of business. . . . Probably over $400,000 worth of goods are annually sold" throughout Meriwether, Henry, Pike, and portions of Troup, Fayette, Upson, Monroe, and Butts counties. Athens "commands a heavy trade with the surrounding country." Macon, with its "heavy grocery, produce and cotton trade," sold annually some $2 million worth of goods, sending merchandise to, and collecting the produce of, thirteen surrounding counties. Columbus's trade topped Macon's by $200,000.[52]

51. *Albany Patriot*, 11 Jan. 1850; Joseph Bancroft, *Census of the City of Savannah, Together with Statistics Relating to the Trade, Commerce, Mechanical Arts, and Health of the Same* (Savannah, 1848), 67; *Georgia Journal and Messenger* (Macon), 26 Dec. 1849; Campbell, *Southern Business Directory*, 219. See also Richard Keily, *A Brief Descriptive and Statistical Sketch of Georgia . . . with a Map and Description of Lands for Sale in Irwin County* (London, 1849), 14–15, on Columbus and Macon; Robert S. Davis, Jr., ed., "Georgia on the Eve of the Civil War: The Insurance Reports of C. C. Hine," *Atlanta History* 31 (1987): 48–56, on Atlanta, Rome, Griffin, Macon, and Columbus.

52. George P. White, *Historical Collections of Georgia* (New York, 1855), 260; White,

To this point the focus has been on mid-nineteenth-century Georgia and on imparting a rough order to its various places. Yet time is the historian's milieu, and we must recognize that the mid-century scene was the product of a long history within which towns, villages, and hamlets were as integral as plantations and slaves.

James Oglethorpe's founding of Savannah in 1733, of Frederica on St. Simon's Island in 1735, and of Augusta as an upriver trading post in 1736 is familiar. Savannah persisted to become Georgia's major city, its role in passing the colony's (and subsequently the state's) produce into the Atlantic commercial world and receiving in return a variety of finished goods recognized by commentators from almost the very beginning. Augusta was virtually destroyed during the Revolution but revived in its aftermath. Frederica faded into a hamlet of ten houses and a post office by 1827.[53] Oglethorpe's establishment of German and Scottish enclaves at Ebenezer and Darien, respectively, is also familiar. Darien was abandoned, resettled, and ultimately persisted as a minor port. Ebenezer, upriver from Savannah, prospered until the Revolution and declined thereafter. In the early 1770s John Bartram described it as "a delightful village incompassed with gardens, orchids, cornfields and pasture grounds . . . good mills both for grist and sawing lumber"; to Buckingham in 1839 it was only "a small cluster of humble dwellings."[54]

Less familiar are towns such as Wrightsborough and Sunbury. The former was settled by North Carolina Quakers in the late 1760s in what would become Columbia County, northwest of Augusta. Bartram found it a town of twenty houses and "several traders" selling "Sugar, Rum, Salt, and dry Goods"; on the eve of the Revolution it boasted 60 families in the village itself and 200 farm families in the surrounding area.[55] Sunbury was

---

Statistics of Georgia, 111, 188, 471; Sherwood, *Gazetteer* (1860), 60; Campbell, *Southern Business Directory*, 213, 230.

53. While the original fort and town of Frederica fell to ruins, the nearby hamlet of St. Simon's (some 20 families in 1800; 10 houses in 1827) replaced it. See Charles C. Jones, Jr., *The Dead Towns of Georgia* (1878; reprint, Atlanta, 1974), 45–136; Lucian Lamar Knight, *Georgia's Landmarks, Memorials, and Legends* (Atlanta, 1913–14) 1:59–65; Andrew Ellicott, *The Journal of Andrew Ellicott* (1803; reprint, Chicago, 1962), 268; J. B. Dunlop, "A Scotsman Visits Georgia in 1811," ed. Raymond A. Mohl, *Georgia Historical Quarterly* 55 (1971): 268; Sherwood, *Gazetteer* (1827), 27–29, 57, 121.

54. William Bartram, *Travels in Georgia and Florida, 1773–74: A Report to Dr. John Fothergill*, American Philosophical Society, Transactions, new ser., 33, pt. 2 (Philadelphia, 1942), 136; Buckingham, *Slave States of America* 1:154. George Fenwick Jones, *The Salzburger Saga: Religious Exiles and Other Germans along the Savannah* (Athens, Ga., 1984), is the best study of Ebenezer and the other German villages mentioned here.

55. Bartram, *Travels . . . 1773–74*, 137, 139; John Gerhard William De Brahm, *History of the Province of Georgia . . . Now First Printed* (Wormsloe, Ga., 1849), 25. See also Ralph C. Scott, Jr., "The Quaker Settlement of Wrightsborough, Georgia," *Georgia Historical Quarterly* 56 (1972): 210–23.

established in 1758 by Liberty County planters who felt a need for a port more convenient than Savannah. Bartram visited here, too, describing it as a "pretty town" of "about one hundred houses . . . neatly built of wood framed, having pleasant Piasas around them."[56] All but unknown are a sprinkling of lesser places: Abercorn, a short-lived village between Savannah and Ebenezer, its inhabitants bought out in the 1770s and their lands incorporated into a rice plantation; Goshen, an outlying settlement of Germans from Ebenezer; Hampstead, Highgate, and Vernonsburg near Savannah, the last persisting into the nineteenth century when Sherwood described it as "a small cluster of houses . . . now nearly gone to decay." Hardwick was laid out in 1755 and contemplated as a new capital for Georgia by the then royal governor; twenty-seven of its lots were sold within the year, but not becoming the capital, it "became scarcely more than a village."[57] Chance alone gives us a glimpse of another persisting colonial hamlet, Thunderbolt, a river settlement five miles southeast of Savannah. In 1735 the earl of Egmont noted its twenty-eight "souls"; a century later Emily Burke, a New Hampshire schoolteacher engaged in the city, discovered it while riding in the countryside. It was "a little settlement of fishermen upon the bank of the river, where boats of all sizes might be seen upon the water or drawn upon the shore. . . . Fishing nets and lines were spread all around to be dried, and many an old fisherman might be seen here, taking his noon-day nap beneath the shade of a weeping willow."[58]

There is an ephemeral quality to many of these earliest towns and villages. They appear now and again in the historical record, then all too frequently disappear. But the important point is that they appeared at all, and largely in a region (the coastal savannas and swamps) which, by virtue of geography and settlement pattern, was not particularly conducive to their formation. When the Bureau of the Census attempted in the early part of this century "to ascertain from outside sources the names of . . . villages and other settlements which existed in 1790 but were not reported at the First Census," its labors produced a list of thirty-nine Georgia localities. Our own systematic review of travelers' accounts and gazetteers — the basic sources — excised "ghosts" from the list, dropped villages abandoned by 1790 and those not yet founded, and added some not identified by the bureau to arrive at much the same total — thirty-seven —

---

56. Bartram, *Travels . . . 1773–74*, 135.

57. Sherwood, *Gazetteer* (1827), 110; Knight, *Georgia's Landmarks* 2:605–7; Jones, *Dead Towns of Georgia*, 140, 224–32, 245–55.

58. Diary of the earl of Egmont, 19 June 1734, cited in Evarts B. Greene and Virginia D. Harrington, *American Population before the Federal Census of 1790* (1932; reprint, Gloucester, Mass., 1966), 180; Burke, *Pleasures and Pain: Reminiscences of Georgia in the 1840s* (1850; reprint, Savannah, 1978), 22.

containing, by a very rough estimate, some 15 percent of the state's free population.[59] Equally important, however, the very appearances and disappearances of these towns and villages illustrates a truism: They survived or failed not by virtue of human intent but to the degree they fit an ecological niche framed by nature — in this case the broken coast with its tidal swamps, broad savannas, pine barrens behind — and by men and women applying their efforts to the environment in the interest of survival and prosperity.

Sunbury and Darien are perfect examples. The first was a planned enterprise, its design — reminiscent of Savannah's — reflecting in its 496 rectangular lots and three public squares what the mind of the moment thought a town ought to be.[60] But rivaling Savannah was merely a wish, never a reality. Sunbury was built where Midway River entered St. Catherine's Sound, the river itself little more than a broad creek running inland a bare twenty miles; even if a contemplated canal had been completed to join the Midway and Newport rivers, the waterway created would hardly

59. U.S., Bureau of the Census, *Century of Population Growth*, 73. The survey of travelers was based upon (but not limited by) Thomas D. Clark, *Travels in the Old South: A Bibliography* (Norman, Okla., 1956–59), and Garold Cole, *Travels in America: From the Voyages of Discovery to the Present. An Annotated Bibliography of Travel Articles in Periodicals, 1955–1980* (Norman, Okla., 1984). Among gazetteers surveyed were (in addition to those cited elsewhere): Jedidiah and Richard C. Morse, *A New Universal Gazetteer, or, Geographical Dictionary, Containing a Description of . . . the Known World* (New Haven, 1821); William Winterbotham, *An Historical, Geographical, Commercial, and Philosophical View of the American United States and of the European Settlements in America and the West Indies*, 2d ed., (London, 1799); R. Brookes, *Brookes' General Gazetteer Improved, or, A New and Compendious Geographical Dictionary Containing a Description of the . . . Known World* (Philadelphia, 1806); Mathew Carey, *American Pocket Atlas . . . with a Brief Description of Each State and Territory*, 4th ed. (Philadelphia, 1814); David Baille Warden, *A Statistical, Political, and Historical Account of the United States* (Edinburgh, 1819); William Darby, *Darby's Universal Gazetteer, or, New Geographical Dictionary* (Philadelphia, 1827). John Melish's *Travels in the United States in the Years 1806 & 1807, and 1809, 1810, & 1811* (Philadelphia, 1815) is more gazetteer than travel description. Travelers and gazetteers were supplemented by local histories. For guides to these, see William P. Filby, *A Bibliography of American County Histories* (Baltimore, 1985); Marion J. Kaminkow, *United States Local History in the Library of Congress: A Bibliography* (Baltimore, 1975); and Clarence S. Peterson, *Consolidated Bibliography of County Histories in Fifty States in 1961, Consolidated 1835–1961* (Baltimore, 1963). The survey resulted in seven locations with no indication of size, seventeen with house counts for the period 1757–1826, four with family counts 1734–86, nine with population counts 1734–1810, and two with counts of the free population in 1790 and 1820. The rough estimate of the percentage of the free population dwelling in villages and towns was obtained by extrapolating to 1790 and applying the ratios of free persons per dwelling, free persons per family, and percentage of free population as given in *Century of Population Growth*, 86, 96, 102.

60. See Sylvia Doughty Fries, *The Urban Idea in Colonial America* (Philadelphia, 1977), particularly chap. 5 on Savannah; James L. Machor, *Pastoral Cities: Urban Ideals and the Symbolic Landscape of America* (Madison, Wis., 1987), chap. 3. Jones, *Dead Towns of Georgia*, 140, reprints a contemporary plat of Sunbury.

have matched that which Savannah could tap. The town's trade, consequently, was inevitably local and its mercantile infrastructure oriented more to transshipment through the larger port than toward building overseas trading contacts. And even then its trade was limited, for Sunbury was located in the midst of rice plantations; rice was a wealthy man's crop; and wealthy men were far more likely to do their business in Savannah than locally.[61] At the same time the town, by virtue of its peninsular location on a much broken coast, was too inconveniently located to play the part of country village. It was, in a very real sense, at the end of a road rather than in the center of a road network. Locally oriented stores, even the Liberty County courthouse in 1797, shifted to Riceborough, a cluster of houses emerging in the 1790s around a bridge crossing Newport River eight miles inland and commanding both river and road traffic. Sunbury lingered on, but only as a resort — wealthy planters bought lots, built houses, and moved "to town" in the summer, exchanging the sultry heat of their rice plantations for the town's ocean breezes — and as an educational center. Its greatest asset was clearly William McWhir, an Irish cleric and schoolteacher who took over Sunbury Academy in 1793 and for a quarter century held forth to some seventy students a year. Planters' tastes changed, however; Georgia's hill country was ultimately discerned as a more healthy resort than its coast. And after McWhir's retirement the academy declined, its very buildings torn down in 1842. By then Sunbury was all but abandoned.[62]

Darien, by way of contrast, was an unplanned town. Oglethorpe placed his Scots near the mouth of the Altamaha only as a buffer against Spanish St. Augustine, and when the immediate danger had passed, the surviving settlers abandoned the town to spread out on farms along the river and northward on the path to Savannah. With farms and plantations in the immediate vicinity, a network of paths and roads to link it to the countryside, the broad stream at its door, and ready access to the sea (and by sea to Savannah), the site could serve a function which Sunbury could not, and the town was soon resettled. In 1839 Fanny Kemble would write of its "houses scattered about here and there, apparently without any design," looking "for the most part either unfinished or ruinous." But to George Sibbald in 1801 it was already "a thriving town." In 1811 a traveler wrote of its thirty houses, an inn "crowded with People waiting to hear the News" brought in by stagecoach, and a trade consisting of "exporting the produce" of "the banks of the river." Joshua Shaw's 1822 *United States*

61. Lewis E. Atherton, *The Southern Country Store, 1800–1860* (Baton Rouge, La., 1949), 20–21. Based largely on materials from Louisiana and Mississippi, Atherton's remains the only extensive study of the retail trade of the South.

62. Jones, *Dead Towns of Georgia*, 141–223. See also Paul McIlvaine, *The Dead Towns of Sunbury, Ga., and Dorchester, S.C.*, 3d ed. (Hendersonville, N.C., 1976).

Directory described it as "a place of some importance" with a bank, newspaper, two dry goods stores, a hotel, two boardinghouses, four commission merchants, a tailor, watchmaker, two lawyers, and two physicians. Even Kemble perforce took note of its merchants, "thoroughbred Yankees [although not necessarily Yankee-born], with the true Yankee propensity to trade, no matter on how dirty a counter, or in what manner of wares."[63]

What was true early in coastal Georgia was true later and inland. Towns and villages and hamlets came into being in a variety of ways and either fit an ecological niche or disappeared. Georgia's post-Revolutionary population growth centered on the middle Savannah, up- and downstream from Augusta, with settlers arriving from the Carolinas and Virginia and moving westward into the central cotton belt and lower piedmont, then north and south, their pace measured by successive acquisitions of Indian lands. In the early years, before the cotton gin made short staple cotton a viable crop, men thought in terms of an extension of tobacco culture, of towns as riverside collection and inspection points, and a score or more such towns were established, each touted as "the grand Warehouse, for the riches of the Western frontier."[64] One such was Petersburg, founded by Dyonysius Oliver on the point of land where the Broad River meets the Savannah fifty miles above Augusta and named for Oliver's hometown of Petersburg, Virginia. By 1799 there were twenty-one "Stores for Dry Goods and Groceries" in the town; over 3,000 hogsheads of tobacco worth a quarter-million dollars passed through its two warehouses that year. Two years later it boasted a hundred houses and was referred to as "a Town which has risen out of the woods in a few years, as if by enchantment," second only to Augusta in the up-country by virtue of its "situation and commercial consequence." But Petersburg was already at its peak. Tobacco was replaced by cotton, which could be carted or floated uninspected to the most convenient store or merchant's warehouse. The tobacco towns lost their raison d'être and, in the case of Petersburg, had

63. G. Arthur Gordon, "The Arrival of the Scotch Highlanders at Darien," and Alexander R. MacDonnell, "The Settlement of the Scotch Highlanders at Darien," both in *Georgia Historical Quarterly* 20 (1936): 199–209, 250–62; Frances Anne Kemble, *Journal of a Residence on a Georgian Plantation in 1838–1839*, ed. John A. Scott (New York, 1961), 115–18; Sibbald, *Notes and Observations on the Pine Lands of Georgia. . . . To Which Is Added a Geographical Sketch of the State* (Augusta, Ga., 1801), 65; Shaw, *United States Directory for the Use of Travellers and Merchants, Giving an Account of the Principal Establishments of Business and Pleasure throughout the Union* (Philadelphia, 1822), 121–22. See also J[ohn] C. Kayser Company, *Commercial Directory of the United States: Containing Topographical Descriptions, Extent, and Productions of Different Sections of the Union, Statistical Information Relative to Manufactures* (Philadelphia, 1823), 47–48.

64. Sibbald, *Pine Lands of Georgia*, 61, writing of Federaltown on the east bank of the Oconee.

nothing with which to replace it. Like Sunbury, its peninsular position between two broad rivers placed it on the periphery of its county; Elberton, in the center, became the county seat, and Petersburg faded into a hamlet, then disappeared altogether.[65]

Cotton and the very process of settlement had their own dynamic, however. Settlement was not simply a matter of farmers, planters, and slaves but of storekeepers, taverners, millers, tanners, and smiths, of lawyers, doctors, clerics, and schoolteachers who gathered in towns and villages and hamlets to serve the settling farmers. And moving cotton from farm to market (and market goods back to the farm) required the rough structure of places described earlier. Most places were hamlets, emerging as if from thin air, Greene County's Cove Shoals, for example, appearing in the 1820s around a combined grist and lumber mill whose owners began selling liquor and general merchandise on the side.[66] Others grew up around rural academies: Oglethorpe County's Hermon, a "village, like many others in the state . . . built for the purpose of supporting the academy" and declining when the academy failed and Hermon had no other reason for being; Hancock's Powelton, whose two academies "were the attractives which drew the people around them that their children might enjoy the advantages of education"; Clarke County's Salem, the schools of which "may be said to have *created* the village" of twenty-one houses, two stores, three offices, seven shops, and a tannery supplying "a large section of country with leather"; Athens, emerging around Franklin College.[67] In mid-1803 a young man from Petersburg visited the last and described its two stores, post office, mill, toll bridge over the Oconee, and five or six houses. "The place may, perhaps, rise into considerable importance, but is not at present very attractive or worthy of admiration." Fifteen years later there were thirty-two houses; Sherwood counted seventy-two in 1826; Buckingham a hundred in 1839, by which time Athens was the major market town of northeastern Georgia.[68] The presence of the courthouse axiomatically attracted a population but guaranteed neither prosperity nor persistence. Clarke's county seat was Watkinsville — 240 people,

65. Virginia Steel Wood, ed., "A Connecticut Yankee's Field Reports: Shaler Hillyer's Impressions of Petersburg and Elbert County, Georgia, in 1800," *Georgia Historical Quarterly* 70 (1986): 280–87; Knight, *Georgia's Landmarks* 2:721–23; Elmer T. Clark, J. Manning Potts, and Jacob S. Payton, eds., *The Journal and Letters of Francis Asbury* (London, 1958) 2:312; Sherwood, *Gazetteer* (1827), 86–87.

66. Cove Shoals Mill, Greene County, MS Account Book, 1819–21, 1825–27, Georgia Department of Archives and History.

67. Sherwood, *Gazetteer* (1827), 62, 88, 94; ibid. (1837), 177; Buckingham, *Slave States of America* 2:73–75.

68. Hugh C. Bailey, "The Petersburg Youth of John Williams Walker," *Georgia Historical Quarterly* 43 (1959): 131; Sherwood, *Gazetteer* (1827), 24–27; Buckingham, *Slave States of America* 2:73.

free and slave, in 1849 — rather than bustling, advantageously located Athens seven miles to the north on the Oconee.[69] For its part, the court-house could be usurped altogether, as was the case in Coweta County. Already a village with two churches, a store, and doctor, Bullsboro was originally named the county seat in 1827 but lost first its churches when the nearby town of Newnan offered them free building lots, then its store and courthouse, and finally its entire population. In 1837 Newnan had forty-five dwellings, nine stores, three confectioneries, three churches, two doc-tors, four lawyers, three blacksmiths, two carriage makers, two shoe shops, a saddler, and three taverns. The site of Bullsboro had been incorporated into a farm.[70]

Georgians and travelers alike sensed the concurrent appearance of both towns and farms. Sherwood waxed eloquent: "Almost all the towns on the west side of the Ocmulgee seem to have sprung into existence as if by the plastic hand of magic. Four or five years ago, the whole territory was a solitary wilderness . . . but now industry has converted it into beautiful plantations and ornamented it with many lovely villages." So, too, did the Swedish traveler C. D. Arfwedson, who, on viewing Columbus rising along the Chattahoochee, was prompted to recollect "how often" he had "heard of towns sprung up in the midst of wilderness, with . . . commerce and trades of various kinds, courthouses, stages and steamers, schools, churches and prisons; all as if created by magic! Other towns disappear with the same rapidity: what in Europe is formed or undone in the lapse of ages is here effected in as many months."[71] Others applied a more jaun-diced eye to the evolving scene. Buckingham, traveling from Knoxville to Talbotton in the western part of the state, wrote of "log huts and rising settlements, hardly yet amounting to villages . . . the edge of the road being favourable for sending produce to market and receiving supplies." Charles Joseph LaTrobe in 1835 noted the "frequent towns springing up . . . which will doubtless become more frequented. But the names! What do you say to Suspendersville? So euphonious." Still, "it was one of the prettiest places on our road." Basil Hall visited Macon in 1828, five years after it was laid out along the Ocmulgee. It was "exactly such a town as Utica or Syracuse in the North, or any other of those recently erected towns in the western parts of the State of New York." Trees were "still growing in some of the streets, and the stumps were not yet grubbed up in

69. White, *Statistics of Georgia*, 179–80; E. Merton Coulter, "The Politics of Dividing a Georgia County: Oconee from Clarke," *Georgia Historical Quarterly* 57 (1973): 475–92.

70. Knight, *Georgia's Landmarks* 1:484–86; Sherwood, *Gazetteer* (1829), 140; ibid. (1837), 207; Mary G. Jones and Lily Reynolds, eds., *Coweta County Chronicles for One Hundred Years* (Atlanta, 1928), 57–58.

71. Sherwood, *Gazetteer* (1827), 55; ibid. (1829), 108–9; Arfwedson, *The United States and Canada* (1834), in *Rambler in Georgia*, ed. Lane, 104.

others. The houses looked as if they had been put up the day before, so that you smellt the saw-mill everywhere. The signs and sign-posts were newly painted; the goods exposed before the doors were piled up, as if just lifted out of the wagons; the bars at the numberless grocery stores, alias grog-shops, were glittering with new bottles and glasses." Hall sensed the uncertainties of the scene, "the mushroom growth of rapid and unthinking speculation" and, too frequently, the subsequent "withering." Even Macon was, he thought, in jeopardy. It was founded in the hope of using the Ocmulgee as a route to the sea, but from Macon southward for some forty miles the river was shoal-ridden and subject to long periods of low water. "Expectation not being realized, the rage for settling there had given place to newer fashions; other situations had been preferred, and this city, which, in the opinion of its founders, was to have been one of the greatest in all the South, it was feared would soon vanish altogether."[72]

Macon did not wither and die, of course. Changes in transportation, communication, manufacturing, and in the practice of doing business in general were as rapid in the first half of the nineteenth century as at any other time before the mid-twentieth century; Georgia's townsmen — oriented toward the movement and exchange of goods, toward business — were struggling with equations for matching aspirations to possibilities that they barely understood. There were difficulties, some national (a volatile economy with periodic crashes and depressions), others particular to slavery and cotton (among them a chronic shortage of capital for non-agricultural ventures and a world market periodically surfeited with cotton). And false solutions to difficult equations abounded. Coastal townsmen contemplated (and began) canals, unmindful of a geography which placed a hundred miles of pine and limesink barrens between themselves and the cotton-producing hinterland. Those advocating internal improvements — largely townsmen — could not decide which way the future, "whether *railroads, turnpikes or canals*"; in 1831 a general convention at Putnam County's Eatonton (free population under 400) urged a survey of the state to determine its "fitness" for any or all of these.[73] Even Maconites, whose future ultimately would be made by railroads, vacillated. They struggled with their uncooperative river, contemplating a variety of projects to improve it. In the early 1830s "a few of the wealthier and more enterprising citizens determined to make a trial with steamboats," building one "by way of an experiment" with shallow draft and flat bottom; in

72. Buckingham, *Slave States of America* 1:231; LaTrobe, *The Rambler in North America* (London, 1835), 2:64–5; Hall, *Travels in North America* (1828), in *Rambler in Georgia*, ed. Lane, 79–80. LaTrobe's "Suspendersville" remains unidentified.

73. John C. Butler, *Historical Record of Macon and Central Georgia* (1879; reprint, Macon, Ga., 1958), 101–2.

1834 four steamboats were on the river; by 1837 there were seven. When railroad fever, arising first in Eatonton and Athens, swept the towns of the cotton belt and lower piedmont, Maconites quickly espoused a proposal emanating from the town of Forsyth to build a railroad northward which would carry cotton into the town but were initially reluctant to support a railroad to Augusta or Savannah which, they thought, would vitiate their efforts to make use of the Ocmulgee. Columbians, too, because it would compete with their Chattahoochee River traffic, resisted a railroad east-ward toward Macon until the 1850s.[74]

But Maconites and Columbians — and Georgians in general — in time embraced the railroads. And railroads engendered their own false starts and expectations. When Maconites pushed a railroad into the southwest, a speculator bought land along the route, platted the town of Oglethorpe, and began selling lots. Financial difficulties halted the railroad just there for a few years, and Oglethorpe boomed, its population swelling to 2,500 by 1852. "Speculation in lots and dwellings was a profession, and every-body desired to be in Oglethorpe, as if *bewitched* by some unaccountable hallucination." By 1854 the town boasted the county courthouse (moved from nearby and nearly eclipsed Lanier), a newspaper, eighty "business houses," and eight hotels; cotton-laden wagons crowded its street and country folk its stores. "Wealth flitted before the people of the city." Then the railhead was pushed on to Americus and "magnificence faded." Houses were "sold to planters and removed." By 1860 Oglethorpe was reduced to simply another country town of 268 whites, 2 free blacks, and 184 slaves.[75] For their part the directors of the Central of Georgia Rail-road linking Savannah and Macon thought that the line alone would engender towns and, consequently, rail traffic, ignorant or forgetful of the fact that the barrens tended to preclude farmers who were necessary to towns.[76]

Farms and towns: This was the vital linkage in Georgia and in the South in general. Townsmen and villagers were not out to change the slave and

74. Arfwedson, *United States and Canada*, 101; James H. Stone, "Economic Conditions in Macon, Georgia, in the 1830s," *Georgia Historical Quarterly* 54 (1970): 209–225; Butler, *Macon and Central Georgia*, 101, 121, 142; Ulrich Bonnell Phillips, *A History of Transportation in the Eastern Cotton Belt to 1860* (New York, 1908), 221, 225, 226, 257, 265.

75. Knight, *Georgia's Landmarks* 2:854; Sherwood, *Gazetteer* (1860), 93, 151–52n. Notices and advertisements for Oglethorpe appeared throughout the state. See, for example, *Georgia Journal and Messenger* (Macon), 28 Nov. 1849 (an advertisement) and *Albany Patriot*, 4 Jan. 1850 (a notice to the effect that the depot for the Southwestern Railroad was "perma-nently fixed" at Oglethorpe). White's *Statistics of Georgia* of 1849 did not list Oglethorpe. In his *Historical Collections of Georgia* of 1855 he commented on its rapid growth and noted that it was "so situated as to command the trade of a large portion of southwestern Georgia" (p. 543). By then, however, the bubble was on the verge of bursting.

76. Phillips, *Transportation in the Eastern Cotton Belt*, 293.

staple nature of their society, hence should not be charged by historians with their failure to do so. Their intent was simply to serve their own aspirations within the society as they found it, a point made clear when Macon's Mechanics Society was accused of being antislavery because the mechanics objected to the competition of slave labor. To the contrary, the society responded; it was the "owners and masters" of slaves who, by allowing "negroes to make contracts and dispose of their own time," were "virtually emancipating and placing negroes upon an equality with white labor." Indeed, the mechanics declared, "we repudiate and disavow, as abusive calumny, all intention to interfere with the just and lawful rights of slaveholders, some of us being of that class."[77] The same was true with the turn to manufacturing, particularly in the 1840s. The mills — thirty-six of them by mid-1849 — introduced new elements into the scene.[78] There were factory villages like Rosewell in Cobb County, whose owner — anticipating the better-known Graniteville, South Carolina, by a half-dozen years — provided stores, church, and school but no tavern (temperance was "strictly enforced") for a thousand inhabitants.[79] And there were factory girls — "brunettes of the piney woods," William Cullen Bryant's guide called them as Bryant toured a factory near Augusta — who arrived at the factory gates from family farms in the barrens "barefooted, dirty, and in rags" and were "scoured, put into shoes and stockings, set to work and sent regularly to the Sunday-schools where they are taught what none of them have been taught before — to read and write." To some extent the mills exacerbated racial issues. Bryant's millworkers, for example, would not work "side by side" with blacks, and the millowners "decided at length upon banishing" blacks altogether.[80] And, given the increasing siege mentality of the South, the mills, to some, appeared a defense against a rapicious North "bloated by the profits wrung from the labors of our planters." "The true and wise policy of the South, *is to manufacture all we can our-*

77. *Georgia Journal and Messenger* (Macon), 7 Nov. 1849.

78. According to a list in the *Georgia Journal and Messenger* (Macon), 27 June 1849. At that time stock had been subscribed for an additional six mills. The 1850 census counted only thirty-five mills (De Bow, *Statistical View of the United States*, 180). See also *The Autobiography of Henry Merrell: Industrial Missionary to the South*, ed. James L. Skinner III (Athens, Ga., 1991), 128; Randall Martin Miller, *The Cotton Mill Movement in Antebellum Alabama* (New York, 1978), 171; Richard W. Griffin, "Textile Industry," in *Encyclopedia of Southern History*, ed. David C. Roller and Robert W. Twyman (Baton Rouge, La., 1979), 1226–29; Robert S. Davis, Jr., "The First Golden Age of Georgia Industry, 1828–1860," *Georgia Historical Quarterly* 72 (1988): 699–711; Griffin, "The Origins of the Industrial Revolution in Georgia: Cotton Textiles, 1810–1865," ibid., 42 (1958): 355–73; Richard. H. Shryock, "The Early Industrial Revolution in the Empire State," ibid., 11 (1927): 110–28.

79. White, *Statistics of Georgia*, 189; White, *Historical Collections of Georgia*, 402; Campbell, *Southern Business Directory*, 236; Sherwood, *Gazetteer* (1860), 52.

80. Bryant, *Letters of a Traveller; or, Notes of Things Seen in Europe and America* (New York, 1850), 345–48.

selves, to render her as independent as possible of the North."[81] But the important point is that in the same way Georgia's towns and villages were devoted to moving products to and from its farms, the state's developing factories and foundries were devoted largely to processing the products of farms into goods for farms. Of some eleven million dollars invested in Georgia's manufactories in 1860, over two million were in cotton mills producing the coarse cloth worn by slaves growing cotton and the twine and bagging used in its shipment, another million in woolen mills, a million and a quarter in ironworks and foundries producing the gears and engines that processed and transported cotton, a million and a half in flour mills, and almost two million in lumber mills and turpentine distilleries.[82] Capital unbundled from agriculture per se (land and slaves) was put to use in support of agriculture.

The description of Georgia's Houston County presented earlier falls into place now. Houston was a cotton-belt county some twenty miles south of Macon, 750 farms in 1850, 1,138 white families, almost 10,000 slaves. From the land came corn (over a half-million bushels a year), wheat, rye, oats, and potatoes to feed its stock and people and about eight million pounds of cotton. So much the census tells us. But the names sprinkled about the map represent towns and villages and hamlets in which were concentrated the amenities and service elements of this country district. Perry—founded with the county in the early 1820s, twenty houses in 1826, twice that a decade later, population between three and five hundred in 1850—was the county seat and the administrative center of the county; here, too, were three churches, two schools, a debating society, a physician doubling as druggist, four taverns, a racecourse, "mechanics" of various sorts, and the general stores: Bateman and Talton's, Felder's, Mann's, Thompson and Son. Henderson and Hayneville to the south of Perry were as old; Solomon Henderson had opened his store at what would become the former even before the county was established. White wrote of them as "small but pleasant villages," population 150 and 140 respectively. Each serviced its neighborhood with one or more churches, stores, and schools. Minerva, to the west, was even smaller: a half-dozen houses, a church, a school. In the eastern part of the county, grist and saw mills had appeared early along the small streams feeding the Ocmulgee, giving rise to the creekside hamlets of Wellborn's Mills, presumably named for Carlton Wellborn who entered the county in 1828, and Wilna. Near the latter, Daniel Parr built first a gristmill, then a flour mill, and in 1843 a water-powered cotton mill. When the last burned

81. *Georgia Journal and Messenger* (Macon), 11 July 1849.
82. U.S., Bureau of the Census, *Manufactures of the United States in 1860 Compiled from the Original Returns of the Eighth Census* (Washington, D.C., 1865), 61–82.

down, Joseph Tooke, the county's largest planter with over 5,000 acres and 600 slaves, bought the property, rebuilt the mill, and hired Parr to operate it. Tooke was no stranger to such investments; at one time or another he owned a distillery, a furniture factory, and a steamer plying between Hawkinsville (downriver on the Ocmulgee) and Savannah. To the north of Perry, Busbayville and Bateman were small hamlets clustered around their general stores; Fort Valley was a twin in size and services to Hayneville and Henderson. But Fort Valley vied briefly with Perry as the route of the Southwestern Railroad was being laid out, won handily when its citizens subscribed $700 as against Perry's nothing, and by the mid-1850s was outpacing the county seat with a population approaching 1,000, a half-dozen stores, and two railroad hotels.[83]

Contemplating this map we can envision a single highway leading from the farms and plantations of the state — and the South in general — through hamlets (Wilna, Busbayville), villages (Henderson and Hayneville), towns (Perry and Fort Valley), to market centers such as Macon. There is constant movement in both directions along this highway. On the one hand we glimpse the Reverend B. F. Tharpe "almost daily passing" between his house in Perry and his farm in the countryside, "high silk hat" shining in the sun, the wheels of his sulky squeaking to the tune of "Preach-er! Preach-er!" On the other, there is the weekly wagon carrying cloth from the cotton mill to sell in Macon, a sign on its side boasting the cartage of "the Pride of Perry." "This sho wuz a busy place," an ex-slave said of Greene County; "six mule wagon trains going to Greensboro every day, carrying cloth [from countryside mills] an bringin' back cotton goods, and mail for all dis country."[84]

All our places were connected in fact. And, indeed, there was easy passage for people as well as goods between town and farm. George W. Paschal's father was a failed storekeeper who removed his family from Lexington, Oglethorpe County, to a nearby farm; young George studied the law and ultimately resettled himself as an attorney and his mother as a hotelkeeper in Lumpkin County's Auraria. Buckingham, that indomitable

83. All of the sources cited earlier have been drawn upon for this sketch of Houston, but see also Bobbe Smith Hickson, *A Land So Dedicated: Houston County, Georgia* ([Perry, Ga.], 1976), 48–105; Warren Grice, ed., *First Hundred and Ten Years of Houston County, Georgia, 1822–1932* (Chelsea, Mich., 1983), 1–178; Ralph B. Flanders, "Two Plantations and a County of Antebellum Georgia," *Georgia Historical Quarterly* 12 (1928): 1–37; "Statement of the Number of Polls, Slaves, Quantity of Land, &c in Houston County," *Georgia Journal and Messenger* (Macon), 19 Nov. 1848, 26 Sept. 1849; "Statistics of Houston," *Southern Cultivator* (Augusta), 11 Jan. 1849; MS Houston County Tax Digest, 1849, Georgia Department of Archives and History.

84. Grice, *First Hundred and Ten Years of Houston*, 24, 26; "Grandma" Lawrence, quoted in Edward L. Ayers, *Vengeance and Justice: Crime and Punishment in the 19th-Century American South* (New York, 1984), 107.

traveler, having crossed the line from Georgia to Alabama, ran into a young inn-keeping couple who, "having been brought up without having been taught the proper value of money," were no sooner married than bankrupt. "In this extremity," they had only two choices, go to Texas or "purchase a small piece of land in some rising village near home, and by a little harder labour and more rigid economy, get on quite as well, though not quite so fast, as in Texas." An advertisement in the *Albany Patriot* informs us of another kind of easy passage between town and country, announcing the establishment of "R. S. Hardwick and Cooke, Factors and Commission Merchants": "Mr. Hardwick is a Planter of Hancock County, and, of course, identified in feeling and interests with his brother Planters. Mr. Cooke is a citizen of Savannah, and thoroughly acquainted with all branches of the Commission Business."[85] Yet somewhere along the continuum of places extending outward from the farm an invisible line was crossed, and men and women began thinking of themselves as "of the country" or "of the town."

"Lexington formed a society of its own, and gave tone to the surrounding country," Paschal reminisced. The Lexington he was recalling had barely two hundred people, white and black. And from James Lamar's recollections of farm life eight miles from Columbus: "Sometimes grandfather, who lived a mile further on, would come by on his way to town, and . . . I would 'get to go.' The ride was long and slow and hot, but no matter. It was going to town with all its strange sights and sounds."[86] Townsmen laughed at their country neighbors. In Macon, Buckingham was regaled with anecdotes of "the country people," one of which recounted the story of Macon's first church bell. "When it rang for the hour of worship . . . crowds of persons from the country would assemble in groups to see it, and watch its upward and downward motions with all the eagerness of children witnessing for the first time the movements of a new toy."[87] Or they took umbrage, Mary Bryan, a young girl of Thomasville (population around 500) writing a correspondent huffily of her plans for the day being ruined by the untimely and uninvited visit of one of her

85. George W. Paschal, *Ninety-Four Years: Agnes Paschal* (Washington, D.C., 1871), 34–35, 44–137, 233–34; Buckingham, *Slave States of America* 1:252; *Albany Patriot*, 4 Jan. 1850. This is not to argue that planter participation in mercantile firms was common. Only 34 of 899 partners in all Georgia firms in 1850 as identified in Smith, *Georgia Commercial Tax Digest* (3.7 percent) were "planters" by the classic definition of ownership of land and 20 or more slaves; only 82 of all 2,822 merchants listed—partners and independents—were planters (2.9 percent); only 811 owned land and any number of slaves at all (28.7 percent). Cf. Ford, *Origins of Southern Radicalism*, 90: "The overwhelming majority of the most successful mercantile firms in Upcountry towns [in South Carolina] were either owned or backed by planters."

86. Paschal, *Ninety-Four Years*, 31; James S. Lamar, *Recollections of Pioneer Days in Georgia* (Washington, D.C., 1916), 8–9.

87. Buckingham, *Slave States of America* 1:224.

mother's "country friends."[88] Country folk responded in kind. Buckingham, again: "Planters and farmers" think that "as they are the only people who rise early and work hard, they ought to be exempt from taxation, while the townspeople, whom they consider as a class of mere idlers, ought to pay the public burthens, however heavy they may be."[89] The attitudes emerged in formal debate, the Reverend George F. Pierce, in an 1853 address to the Southern Central Agricultural Society, complaining of "the increasing disposition in the best of our Country population to congregate in towns and villages of the land." "Oh, these towns, with their dram-shops, their evil agents, and their thousand snares, they ruin our sons despite our piety and prayers." An agricultural monthly published in Columbus printed Pierce's address but also answered it, quoting from the *Prairie Farmer* — "If the town grows, the country grows" — and adding: " 'Town *vs*. country,' 'country *vs*. city!' Did you ever see the two blades of a pair of scissors worrying and bullying and fighting each other. . . . They are not head and tail, nor lord nor peasant; they are rather the two arms and levers by which the world moves."[90]

All that has been said sums to one salient fact: Georgia — and by extrapolation the South as a whole — was as much a land of villages and towns as of planters, slaves, and yeoman farmers. These pages are too few to do justice to the full fabric of village and town life and the elaborate rabbeting that united town and country into a single (albeit variegated) society. That exposition is still to come. It is enough for the moment to make the point of the towns themselves, one the Georgians (and southerners) would themselves have readily understood.[91] Which brings us full circle.

Having begun with Harper Lee, William Faulkner, and Carson McCullers in the twentieth century, we end with Joseph Baldwin, Augustus B. Longstreet, William Tappan Thompson, and Joseph B. Cobb in the mid-nineteenth century. For indeed, just as there was an antebellum village South preceding the town-based New South, there was an antebellum town-based literature anticipating in setting (but not, admittedly,

88. James S. Patty, ed., "A Georgia Authoress Writes Her Editor: Mrs. Mary E. Bryan to W. W. Mann," *Georgia Historical Quarterly* 41 (1957): 424.

89. Buckingham, *Slave States of America* 2:115–16.

90. *Soil of the South* (Columbus), June 1854, 170–71; July 1854, 209.

91. The awareness, even centrality, of towns among Georgians themselves is evident in the very fact that it is by virtue of their gazetteers that we identify so many of their towns. But there are all sorts of other indications. Two very different examples: In 1846 the state administration contemplated a revision of the tax system and estimated revenues from city and town lots and improvements ($30,000) at one-half the estimated revenues from landed estates and improvements ($60,000) (Georgia Treasury Department, *Annual Report of the Treasurer . . . Made to the Legislature in November, 1846* [Milledgeville, Ga., 1846], 14). And in 1849 a correspondent reporting on a "Fancy Dress Ball" at the McIntosh House, Indian Springs, identified twenty of the Georgians present by town, only five by county (*Georgia Journal and Messenger* [Macon], 19 Sept. 1849).

in literary quality) the Lees and Faulkners and McCullers of our century. Lawyer Baldwin wrote lawyer stories inevitably set in courthouse towns. Longstreet was another lawyer, but his *Georgia Scenes* were more broadly social. They were, however, equally oriented to the town: "The Horse Swap," opening with the scene of a young man galloping up and down a village street; "The 'Charming Creature' as a Wife," recounting the courtship and unfortunate marriage of a farmer's son turned town lawyer and Evelina, "the only child of a wealthy, unlettered merchant, who, rather by good luck than good management, had amassed a fortune"; "The Fox Hunt" sallying from a country village. Thompson's "Pineville" springs to life in quick vignettes: A circus — "the great attraction" — comes to town; the widow Stullings's amiable daughters are pursued by "the village beaux"; "Josiah Perkins, of Ticklegizzard settlement" visits town in company with two or three neighbors "on a trafficking expedition," disposing of "their stock in trade . . . of a few dozen eggs, as many pounds of butter, and a few quarters of whortleberries . . . and their proceeds expended in the purchase of sundry articles of prime necessity, such as homespun, rum and tobacco." Georgia-born (Lexington) Cobb wrote of Mississippi's Columbus, but his town — which is virtually a character in his stories — could have been anywhere in the South: Church Street on a Sunday morning with its "numerous throng of shining carriages. . . . Flashy-looking negroes, in linen and broadcloth . . . mounted on their lofty boxes"; Main and Market with their stores, for, "small as Columbus is, we have yet here a sufficiency of all necessary materials to paint a miniature of the world"; again, as in Pineville, the country folk in for a day, this time beguiled into buying what they did not need by canny clerks; the panoramic view from the Tuscaloosa Road of "a Mahometan city, rising suddenly to the vision in the interior of a country not famed for its improvements." "Surely," Cobb wrote, and historians ought to listen, "our dull, dry, stale Columbus (as it is often called) is not wholly without its claims to interest."[92]

92. Baldwin, *The Flush Times of Alabama and Mississippi: A Series of Sketches* (1853; reprint, Baton Rouge, La., 1987); Longstreet, *Georgia Scenes: Characters, Incidents, &c. in the First Half Century of the Republic* (1835; reprint, Savannah, 1975), 20, 91, 94, 197; Thompson, *The Chronicles of Pineville; or, Sketches of Georgia Scenes, Incidents, and Characters* (Philadelphia, 1845), 11, 15, 106; Cobb, *Mississippi Scenes; or, Sketches of Southern and Western Life and Adventures* (Philadelphia, 1851), 17, 27, 32, 41–53.

III

EXTENSIONS

13 Myths, Moralities, and Megatheories: *The Case of the Antebellum American South*

> *The literature on the antebellum South is truly voluminous. But as I pushed my exploration of America's towns and villages forward — following a strand which began in* Winthrop's Boston *and ran through Middlesex's Urbanna and the streets of antebellum Georgia — I sensed more and more that the literature on the South stood in splendid isolation. Planters, slaves, and an upland yeomanry staunchly resisting modernity dominated, and all the pressing questions asked of other areas of the United States seemed, at least by virtue of their not being asked, irrelevant. But were they? Perhaps another blinding paradigm was at work. A return visit in 1991 to Moscow — where a Marxist-Leninist paradigm was being unceremoniously abandoned, and scholars were searching almost feverishly for a replacement — gave me the opportunity to consider the question, however briefly. The subject of the conference was historical synthesis, and I opened with a text, a line from Werner Karl Heisenberg: "What we observe is not nature itself, but nature exposed to our method of questioning."*

That a historian should open with a maxim drawn from quantum mechanics, with an aspect of Heisenberg's uncertainty principle itself, one of the fundamentals of that field, might at first blush seem surprising.[1] Yet when the point at issue is historical synthesis and its problems, uncertainty is the appropriate starting point. Synthesis is, ideally, a matter of meshing speculation and discrete observations to form ever broader and ever more uncertain hypotheses about whatever reality is

Presented to an international conference on "Social History and Problems of Synthesis" sponsored by the Russian Academy of Science and Institute of General History, Moscow, October 1991.

1. Werner Karl Heisenberg, *Physics and Philosophy: The Revolution in Modern Science* (New York, 1958), 58.

under study, a difficult task. Historical synthesis, however, has more often than not been a matter of building upon myths, moralities, and megatheories assumed to be certain and therefore certainly encompassing the discrete observations we marshal for our readers' contemplation. The larger lessons of history, in other words — our generalizations — tend less to conjoin speculation and historical observation and more to organize observations according to the historian's judgment as to what is right and what is wrong and where the world is (or ought to be) heading. In this sense our problem is not so much the creation of synthesis — in history that is too readily and too facilely done — but the introduction of uncertainties into the syntheses we create.

Consider the case of nineteenth-century America and in particular the pre-Civil War American South. In the United States two related megatheories today dominate consideration of the topic.

First: In the early nineteenth century the United States was in the throes of a "great transition." In its past lay a precapitalist world of prideful craftsmen and independent yeoman farmers, of small, organic communities marked by a wide distribution of land and wealth, by social and economic cooperation, and by a subsistence rather than market economy. In its future lay capitalism, the dominance of a national, even international, marketplace, the separation of labor from the tools of production, the onset of bourgeois values, inequities of wealth, and (for some) the anomie of urban and factory life.

But the second megatheory: This transition was confined to the northern states of the American Union. The South, shaped by its peculiar institution, by slavery, evolved as an anachronism, beyond feudalism, certainly, integrated into a world market by virtue of its dedication to staple crops but barred from the consequences of that integration by its pseudo-feudal labor system, "a brave, if deeply flawed, new world," one scholar has called it, not merely "a copy or recreation of the precapitalist European society out of which it, like the North, had grown."[2] The South was divided, true. There were the fiercely independent yeomen of its up-country and the great planters of its cotton belt and coastal plains. Yet the

---

2. Elizabeth Fox-Genovese, *Within the Plantation Household: Black and White Women of the Old South* (Chapel Hill, N.C., 1988), 55. The historical debate as to how to classify the slaveholder — as a "profit-maximizing" and "bourgeoisified" capitalist or "seigneurial" pseudocapitalist — is irrelevant; in context, the slaveholding planter is inevitably painted as a tertium quid, i.e., neither one nor the other. Fred Bateman and Thomas Weiss, *A Deplorable Scarcity: The Failure of Industrialization in the Slave Economy* (Chapel Hill, N.C., 1981), for example, frame their analysis of the planter in terms of rational economic behavior, clearly indicate that "large-scale slave farms . . . earned a considerably higher return" than did manufacturing (p. 138), then manipulate their definitions to conclude that planter failure to invest in manufacturing supports "the traditional notion of 'planter irrationality' " (p. 140).

region was one, and unique, by virtue of slavery and the hegemonic politics and *mentalité* of its planters.[3]

Two megatheories, then. The debt of the first to Karl Marx and an even larger megatheory is obvious. So, too, is its mythic quality, for in this American version of Marx the precapitalist world of the yeomanry appears more often than not Edenesque, a landscape of contented, cooperative, sharing men and women, devoid of the sins of avarice and greed. Indeed, applied to the narrative of American evolution, it offers an attractive morality play to critics of contemporary American society. Capitalism, like Eve's snake, is an invidious force in Eden. One need only note the language used. Capitalism has "tentacles." It "probes" and "penetrates." "Sturdy yeomen" flee before it but are ultimately "absorbed," "conquered."[4]

The second megatheory, too, has mythic and moral qualities. It is, for one thing, predicated too much — albeit silently — on Margaret Mitchell's Scarlett O'Hara and baronial Tara and too little on the hardscrabble life of most southern farmers. Consider, for example, the implications of a passing, almost banal line in a recent *Interpretation of the Old South*: "On most plantations slaves worked in gangs under the direct supervision of the owner or his representative." "Gangs" were working groups of ten to twelve slaves; to have even one gang implies a holding of at least twenty slaves in all. But in one of the five richest cotton counties of central Georgia in 1850 (Houston) three-quarters of the farmers had fewer than twenty slaves. The author's *Interpretation of the Old South* is reduced to an

---

3. Lengthy citations regarding the two would be gratuitous, but see for representative presentations the essays in Steven Hahn and Jonathan Prude, eds., *The Countryside in the Age of Capitalist Transformation* (Chapel Hill, N.C., 1985); Prude's own *The Coming of Industrial Order: Town and Factory Life in Rural Massachusetts, 1810–1860* (Cambridge, 1983); Hahn's *The Roots of Southern Populism: Yeoman Farmers and the Transformation of the Georgia Upcountry, 1850–1890* (New York, 1983); Allan Kulikoff, "The Transition to Capitalism in Rural America," *William and Mary Quarterly*, 3d ser., 46 (1989): 120–44 and his *The Agrarian Origins of American Capitalism* (Charlottesville, Va., 1992); Rachel N. Klein, *Unification of a Slave State: The Rise of the Planter Class in the South Carolina Backcountry, 1760–1808* (Chapel Hill, N.C., 1990); Christopher Clark, *The Roots of Rural Capitalism: Western Massachusetts, 1780–1860* (Ithaca, N.Y., 1990); Charles Sellers, *The Market Revolution: Jacksonian America, 1815–1846* (New York, 1991). It is difficult to square the social historians' insistence on an anachronistic South standing apart from the "great transition" with political historians such as J. Mills Thornton III, *Politics and Power in a Slave Society: Alabama, 1800–1860* (Baton Rouge, La., 1978), and Marc W. Kruman, *Parties and Politics in North Carolina, 1836–1865* (Baton Rouge, La., 1983), who make varied responses to the evolving market (i.e., the "great transition") central to their depiction of the development of political parties in the antebellum South.

4. Fox-Genovese, *Within the Plantation Household*, 54, 55; Hahn, *Roots of Southern Populism*, 4; Prude, *Coming of Industrial Order*, 261; Kulikoff, "Transition to Capitalism," 124, 142.

interpretation of a part.[5] Moreover, the very insistence on a unique South flows at least in part from a moral question. In American scholarship slavery is the great, and peculiarly American, wrong; hence it—and the South that hosted it—must be set apart from the nation as a whole. Only in this context does the reception of Fogel and Engerman's *Time on the Cross* make sense. It was not simply the narrowness or even the quantitative methods of the work that provoked the outcry against it, but the work's essential amorality. It attempted to measure the profitability of slavery without condemning it.[6]

For all of that, however, our two megatheories are not to be dismissed out of hand. They are loosely rooted in the empirical, for there was, indeed, a transformation of some sort taking place in nineteenth-century America, and North and South did differ. The essential problem lies not in the megatheories themselves but in their effect.

Taken together, the two have truncated the social history of the antebellum nation. For the North we have countless studies of the great transition, of the onset of manufacturing and the development of the marketplace, of revolutions in transportation and finance and law, of mill towns and the appearance of urban conglomerations, of the coming of class and the appurtenances of class as new determinatives of social relations. For the South we have a steady stream of studies informing us of slaves and planters and yeomen and the unique world they made for themselves. But the two literatures never mingle. Our megatheories, in effect, have posited two distinct and separate lines of scholarly inquiry that—except in terms of contrasting cultures which must ultimately clash in Civil War—are all but oblivious to each other.[7]

5. James Oakes, *Slavery and Freedom: An Interpretation of the Old South* (New York, 1990), 11. The banality is surprising in the light of Oakes's earlier work, notably *The Ruling Race: A History of American Slaveholders* (New York, 1982).

6. Robert W. Fogel and Stanley L. Engerman, *Time on the Cross* (Boston, 1974). Note Fogel's rejoinder to this attack—by redefining the immorality of slavery and discarding what he terms "the assumption that productivity is necessarily virtuous"—in his *Without Consent or Contract: The Rise and Fall of American Slavery* (New York, 1989), 388–411.

7. There are, of course, exceptions: Oakes, *Slavery and Freedom*, for example. Edward Pessen's "How Different from Each Other Were the Antebellum North and South?" *American Historical Review* 85 (1980): 1119–49, summarizes the literature to 1980, while the response of critics to his modest plea for considering similarities is revealing of the general thrust of scholarship. Accepting the fact of similarities, Stanley L. Engerman immediately turned back to differences "possibly crucial in the antebellum period, possibly of potential subsequent importance. . . . However similar the motivations of planter capitalists and industrial capitalists, however efficiently each section followed its comparative advantage, and however rapidly both sections were growing economically, one section included a slave-based agriculture and the other had, in addition to a commercial agriculture based on family farms, a developing industrial sector based upon wage labor. One section was more influ-

Urbanization, for example, is an element of the great transition in the North. Yet because the South was a priori unique, because it was proceeding in its own fashion and not in conformity with that great transition, the section cannot be conceived of as having had towns and cities such as were appearing in the North. What towns and cities there were must be uniquely southern. And so they appear in the work of the foremost scholar of southern urbanization. "There were, of course, towns and cities in the Old South," David R. Goldfield has written, "but none that . . . [a] New Yorker was likely to find familiar. Even the largest cities — New Orleans, Charleston, Memphis, Mobile — were what sociologist Edgar Thompson termed 'plantation cities,' entertainment and marketing adjuncts to those self-sufficient agricultural units that were the mainsprings of the antebellum southern economy. 'Mere trading posts,' W. J. Cash called the best of them, and that is precisely and only what they were."[8] In such curt terms the scholar dismisses the setting within which at least 20 percent of the inhabitants of the state of Georgia lived in 1850.[9] There is no effort to disentangle the subtle role that cities, towns, and villages undoubtedly played in southern life. That role flows axiomatically from megatheory; a planter's world obviously needed only "plantation" cities. (Did not the farmer's world of the North need farm cities?) Neither is there concern for southern manufactories, the role of southern merchants, rather than farmers, in their establishment, and the lives of the factory laborers (largely white) who operated them — the factories of Georgia's sandhill cities, for example, arising in the 1840s and giving to the state the sobriquet "Empire State of the South."[10] Nor is there curiosity about commonalities that northern and southern cities, railroads, mercantile networks, and factories might have shared. Megatheory establishes in advance that there were none.

---

enced by planter-slaveowners, the other more by merchant and industrial capitalists. . . . These differences, even with some basic similarities in belief and behavior, in conjunction with the importance of attitudes toward race and slavery, had obvious implications for national political and social life" (ibid., 1159).

8. Goldfield, *Cotton Fields and Skyscrapers: Southern City and Region, 1607–1980* (Baton Rouge, La., 1982), 32.

9. See chap. 12 above.

10. Studies of antebellum southern manufacturing tend to be tucked away and forgotten in state historical journals, but see John R. deTreville, "The Little New South: Origins of Industry in Georgia's Fall-Line Cities, 1840–1865" (Ph.D. diss., University of North Carolina, 1986), especially p. 232; Mary A. DeCredico, *Patriotism for Profit: Georgia's Urban Entrepreneurs and the Confederate War Effort* (Chapel Hill, N.C., 1990), chap. 1; *The Autobiography of Henry Merrell: Industrial Missionary to the South*, ed. James L. Skinner III (Athens, Ga., 1991) — the last an appropriate companion volume to Theodore Rosengarten's *Tombee: Portrait of a Cotton Planter* (New York, 1986).

There is no intention here of subjecting Goldfield — or any author — to singular criticism. I am quick to admit that we are vastly richer for his work in a variety of ways.[11] My point is simply that in accepting mega-theories as certainties he — indeed, all of us — are made slaves to mega-theory. In his research Goldfield pounced upon one quotation from a northern traveler in the South who exclaimed in exasperation, "Where's your towns?" But he did not notice another visitor writing of Macon, Georgia, in 1829, "Macon appeared to be in the South, exactly such a town as Utica or Syracuse in the North, or any other of those recently erected towns in the western parts of the State of New York."[12] Mega-theory imparts importance to the first — the quotation fits — while at the same time blinding Goldfield to the second. Goldfield asks rhetorically why "southern cities retain[ed] a rural aspect long after their northern counterparts had forgotten the value of trees . . . and the use of space to liberate rather than to crowd" and answers in terms of southern unique-ness: "The agrarian city existed because staple-crop agriculture not only dominated the fields but came to hold the hearts and minds of the region as well." But in so doing he passes by the ruralization of northern cities, the parks and cemeteries that David Schuyler has called "the first physical expression of the evolving definition of urban form and culture," and he misses the implicit unity of North and South.[13] Southerners — if not Goldfield — knew that to some extent at least the ruralization of their

11. Goldfield's generalizations in *Cotton Fields and Skyscrapers* are very much at variance with his earlier call for an "urban view of southern history" in his *Urban Growth in the Age of Sectionalism: Virginia, 1847–1861* (Baton Rouge, La., 1977), 283. The former, however, reflects the common view of southern towns and town life described in chap. 12. The most significant exception is Oakes, *The Ruling Race*; relying largely on the account of a single traveler, Oakes makes towns central to his thesis of slaveholders "adrift" in an unstable world. The blindness of American historians with regard to antebellum southern towns is most noticeable in synthetic works such as David Hamer's *New Towns in the New World: Images and Perceptions of the Nineteenth-Century Urban Frontier* (New York, 1990), a study of the role of towns in the opening up "new societies" in nineteenth-century Australia, New Zealand, Canada, and the United States in which there is virtually no mention of an ante-bellum southern town.

12. Goldfield, *Cotton Fields and Skyscrapers*, 32, quoting Daniel R. Hundley, *Social Relations in Our Southern States* (New York, 1860), 26; Basil Hall, *Travels in North America* (1829), in *The Rambler in Georgia*, ed. Mills Lane (Savannah, 1973), 79. The Hundley quote is fre-quently used — see, e.g., Don H. Doyle, *New Men, New Cities, New South: Atlanta, Nashville, Charleston, Mobile, 1860–1910* (Chapel Hill, N.C., 1990), 1; I have never seen the Hall quotation used!

13. Goldfield, *Cotton Fields and Skyscrapers*, 29, 33; Schuyler, *The New Urban Landscape: The Redefinition of City Form in Nineteenth-Century America* (Baltimore, 1986), 37. See also Thomas Bender, *Toward an Urban Vision: Ideas and Institutions in Nineteenth Century America* (Lexington, Ky., 1975), 80–93; Sylvia Doughty Fries, *The Urban Idea in Colonial America* (Philadelphia, 1977), chaps. 3 and 5; James L. Machor, *Pastoral Cities: Urban Ideals and the Symbolic Landscape of America* (Madison, Wis., 1987).

cities was part of a national, not simply regional, phenomenon. George White of Georgia, for example, offered a description of Macon's Rose Hill Cemetery in 1849 in terms that Schuyler could easily have used to generalize about the nation as a whole. And the link between Rose Hill and northern developments was explicit: "Another spot could scarcely be found in any section of our country so much diversified, and comprising so many distinct objects and combinations going to form a perfect picture of rural beauty. Many who have visited the Cemeteries of the North, and even the far famed Mount Auburn [in Massachusetts], think it far inferior in natural beauty and location to Rose Hill."[14]

Megatheories as certainties not only lead and blind us but confuse us as well. Masonry and Antimasonry are cases in point. The Ancient and Honorable Fraternity of Free and Accepted Masons was, of course, an eighteenth-century import into what would become the United States. Americanized during the Revolution and Republicanized in its aftermath, this secret society — despite sporadic attacks upon it — had grown to spectacular proportions by the mid-1820s when perhaps one in every twenty to twenty-five adult white males was a member. Then disaster. In September 1826 one William Morgan, a stonemason and former Mason who had threatened to divulge the secret rites and mysteries of the order, disappeared while under arrest in Canandaigua, New York, probably murdered by Masons. The incident precipitated a paroxysm of rage that culminated in the formation of an Antimasonic party, the presidential candidacy of William Wirt in 1832, and the near destruction of the society during that decade.[15]

Masonry and Antimasonry have been recurrent problems in American historiography. What lay behind the rise of the order and its near destruction? What does the incident tell us about American society in general? The current consensus lodges the whole furor in the context of the great transition to capitalism. In the most recent major study, Paul Goodman has insisted that Masonry and Antimasonry must be viewed against the backdrop of a painful and traumatic adjustment to a "new world built on a mobility ethic, conspicuous consumption, a volatile market economy, and

14. George P. White, *Statistics of the State of Georgia . . . Together with a Particular Description of Each County* (Savannah, 1849), 109.

15. Dorothy Ann Lipson, *Freemasonry in Federalist Connecticut* (Princeton, N.J., 1977), 13–79; Steven C. Bullock, "A Pure and Sublime System: The Appeal of Post-Revolutionary Freemasonry," *Journal of the Early Republic* 9 (1989): 359–73; Bullock, "The Revolutionary Transformation of American Freemasonry, 1752–1792," *William and Mary Quarterly*, 3d ser., 47 (1990): 347–69; Ronald P. Formisano and Kathleen Smith Kutolowski, "Antimasonry and Masonry: The Genesis of Protest," *American Quarterly* 29 (1977): 139–65. On the growth of the order, see Henry Leonard Stillson, ed., *History of the Ancient and Honorable Fraternity of Free and Accepted Masons, and Concordant Orders* (Boston, 1906), 877–92.

modern class structure." In this context Masonry "proffered a universal therapeutic to an emerging bourgeoisie." "Made up mostly of business and professional men, Masonic Lodges reflected the emerging system of social relations based upon a modern class system." For their part Antimasons "sensed that the [precapitalist] idea of an organic community was in jeopardy, . . . that a new class system which located people on an impersonal spectrum according to wealth, occupation, education, and appearance fractured communities in ways that social differences had not in Early America." Uncomfortable in the great transition to modernity, Antimasons made Masonry the "master symbol" of their disgruntlement.[16] Goodman even goes so far as to correlate the extent of Masonry (and, consequently, the strength of its antithesis) with the degree of involvement in the marketplace. Thus, while "Masonry grew all over the country as a modern middle-class emerged along with the spread of the market economy," it grew more slowly in the state of New Hampshire where "the business and professional elements . . . were less numerous."[17]

All well and good. But what of the South? Here the acceptance of megatheories as certainties weaves confusion and illogic. Neither Goodman nor the foremost scholar of the politics of Antimasonry could find a trace of Masonry's great enemy in the South. Why was it absent from the section? Because, Goodman argued, the South stood apart from the great transition. "The failure of Antimasonry to penetrate significantly into the southern states . . . highlights different ways Northerners and Southerners experienced change. In the South the market system failed to penetrate

16. Goodman, *Towards a Christian Republic: Antimasonry and the Great Transition in New England, 1826–1836* (New York, 1988), 41–42, 52–53. Others place both Masons and Antimasons on the side of the bourgeoisie. See, e.g., Ronald P. Formisano, *The Transformation of Political Culture: Massachusetts Parties, 1790s-1840s* (New York, 1983), 197, 217, 199: "Antimasonic voters were . . . not very different from Masons or from other voters"; "the state's Antimasonic leaders were in fact usually upwardly mobile, aspiring individualists, fully attuned to the spirit of 'improvement,' and, compared with Masons, more involved in nontraditional enterprises. Most had experienced improvement in their own condition and eagerly sought it for their fellow men as well." "The quarrel" between the two was, consequently, not between those on contrary sides of a premodern/modern or precapitalist/capitalist divide but "was essentially cultural and religious, between descendants of the Puritans who were very similar in socioeconomic status . . . but whose values clashed in fundamental ways." A spate of recent studies accents Masonic maleness and places the growth of the order and other such fraternities in the context of gender relations but without denying the relationship to the great transition. Note Joan Jacobs Brumberg and Faye E. Dudden, "Masculinity and Mumbo Jumbo: Nineteenth-Century Fraternalism Revisited," *Reviews in American History* 18 (1990): 370, in which a study of this kind is applauded for making the point "that the rise of industrial capitalism in nineteenth-century America problematized manhood as well as womanhood."

17. Goodman, *Christian Republic*, 110.

extensive areas.... This left the South less vulnerable to social tensions that elsewhere encouraged" the tumult. Perhaps. But William Gregg's words to the legislature of South Carolina in 1857 could just as easily have been addressed by a Lowell or Cabot to the legislature of Massachusetts, Gregg reminding the legislature that in the prosperous period of 1833–37 "every man expected to be a *millionaire*, and there was scarcely a successful merchant in the country that was not preparing to branch his concern, and spread his business to the winds. Soap and candle-men had become *wholesale* merchants, and looked forward to the day when they would be ranked among the Rothschilds." Pertinent quotes can be missed, of course, particularly those that do not fit preconceptions. But, good scholar that he is, Goodman could not ignore the empirically obvious, that Masonry existed in the South from the beginning, and that by the eve of the Civil War, for example, there were more Masons per 1,000 whites in the southern state of Georgia than in any other state of the Union. The fact led him not to question his correlation of Masonry and great transition but to conclude that southern Masonry "flourished" because there was no "powerful Antimasonic movement" to check it.[18] Yet how can this be? How can the Antimasonic advocacy of a precapitalist social order fail because the South was immune from the great transition while Masonry — the product and symbol of that transition — flourished?

Again, I do not call up Goodman for singular criticism. My intent is to illustrate the power of megatheories to blind and confuse us all. I could, quite literally, call up virtually any subject to make the same point. In his 1978 study of northern evangelicalism, for example, Paul E. Johnson argued that "evangelicalism was a middle-class solution to problems of class, legitimacy, and order generated in the early stages of manufacturing."[19] Applied to southern evangelicalism — of which we have abundant evidence — Johnson's correlation destroys either southern uniqueness or itself! The appearance of voluntary associations has in the main been associated with the rise of an American "middle class" ethos; without studies of southern voluntary associations, we presume their absence and the absence of a southern middle class. But is the assumption valid? In one of the few studies of voluntarism to extend south of the Mason-Dixon Line, Anne Firor Scott found abundant evidence of women's organizations and concluded that "there is no case to be made for southern ex-

<hr />

18. Ibid., 235; William Preston Vaughn, *The Antimasonic Party in the United States, 1826–1843* (Lexington, Ky., 1983), 170; Broadus Mitchell, *William Gregg: Factory Master of the Old South* (Chapel Hill, N.C., 1928), 189.

19. Johnson, *A Shopkeeper's Millennium: Society and Revivals in Rochester, New York, 1815–1837* (New York, 1978), 138.

ceptionalism from the voluntary association evidence." "Evidently these groups were a response to something more than simply industrialization or 'modernization.' "[20]

To return to Goodman: In actuality, his comment on the South was simply an aside in a study of Masonry and Antimasonry properly sited (according to the dictates of megatheory) in the North. He did not really bother to look at the subject in a southern context. Why should he when he axiomatically associated the phenomena with the great transition and held to the view of a unique South immune to that transition? Had he bothered to look, however — had he stepped aside from the prevailing megatheories — anomalies might well have forced a healthy uncertainty.

So it was in my case. Quite recently, and quite by chance, I came across a series of Masonic minute books detailing the membership and activities of a number of Georgia lodges in the 1830s, 1840s, and 1850s. Curious, I began tracking down the membership and comparing the results with northern studies that undergird the interpretation of the order as a repository of middle-class values. The similarities were immediately apparent. Sixty-five percent of the members of one particular Georgia lodge — located in an upper piedmont county ostensibly dominated by precapitalist yeomen — in 1829 were storekeepers, tradesmen, merchants, lawyers, doctors, and the like; in two other lodges in up-country counties the percentages in 1850 were 67.4 and 60.9; in a comparable area of the North, 59 percent of the Masons fell into the same category.[21] My interest

20. Richard D. Brown, "The Emergence of Voluntary Associations in Massachusetts, 1760–1830," *Journal of Voluntary Action Research* 2 (1973): 64–73; Mary P. Ryan, *Cradle of the Middle Class: The Family in Oneida County, New York, 1790–1865* (Cambridge, 1981), 142; Stuart M. Blumin, *The Emergence of the Middle Class: Social Experience in the American City, 1760–1900* (Cambridge, 1989), 302; Scott, *Natural Allies: Women's Associations in American History* (Urbana, Ill., 1991), 195.

21. Mary G. Jones and Lily Reynolds, eds., *Coweta County Chronicles for One Hundred Years* (Atlanta, 1928), 61–64, gives the 1829 membership of Burns Lodge, Newnan from its Secretary's Book and allows the compilation of occupations. The 1850 membership of Golden Fleece Lodge, Covington, Newton County, and the 1849 roll of Lafayette Lodge, Cumming, Forsyth County, have been drawn from Grand Lodge of the Most Honourable Fraternity of Free and Accepted Masons of the State of Georgia, *Proceedings [for 1849]* (Macon, Ga., 1849), 90–91, and *Proceedings [for 1850]* (Macon, 1851), 45–46, and linked to the 1850 MS Census Schedules and the MS state tax digests for 1851 (Newton) and 1853 (Forsyth), Georgia Department of Archives and History, Atlanta; John T. Smith, *Georgia Commercial Tax Digest, and Directory: Containing a Complete List of the Names of Merchants and Copartnerships . . . Amount of Stock in Trade . . . as Returned to the Office of the Comptroller General by the Receivers of Tax Returns for 1850, with an Appendix Containing a List of the Principal Towns and Villages* (Milledgeville, Ga., 1851); John P. Campbell, ed., *The Southern Business Directory and General Commercial Advertiser* (Charleston, S.C., 1854); the R. G. Dun & Co. Collection, Baker Library, Harvard University Graduate School of Business Administration, Boston; and appropriate county histories. The comparison is to data drawn from Genesee County, New York, by Kathleen Smith Kutolowski, "Freemasonry and Commu-

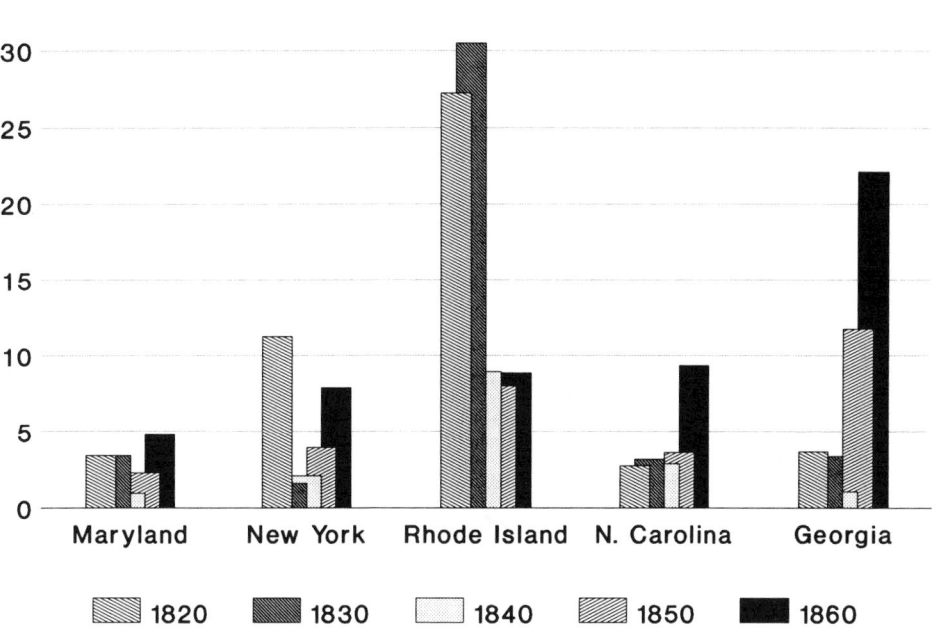

Fig. 13.1. Masonry in five states, 1820–60 (Masons per 1,000 free white population). From Henry Leonard Stillson, ed., *History of the Ancient and Honorable Fraternity of Free and Accepted Masons, and Concordant Orders* (Boston, 1906), 877–92, corrected in the case of Georgia with reference to William Henry Rosier and Fred Lamar Pearson, Jr., *The Grand Lodge of Georgia Free and Accepted Masons, 1786–1980* (Macon, Ga., 1983); U.S., Bureau of the Census, *The Statistical History of the United States from Colonial Times to the Present* (New York, 1976), 24–37.

piqued, I looked about for signs of Antimasonry, and it was not long forthcoming: an abrupt decline in membership and a dissolution of lodges concomitant with the period of northern Antimasonic fervor (see fig. 13.1); defensive speeches in the general meeting of the statewide organization; calls in the Georgia press for the order to dissolve itself in the interest of "peace and harmony"; an up-country Baptist church querying its conference as to what action the church should take with regard to church members who were also members of the Masonic fraternity. (Answer: Such members should be given the choice of leaving the Masons or leaving the church.)[22] Stunned by so much evidence of a middle-class

nity in the Early Republic: The Case for Antimasonic Anxieties," *American Quarterly* 34 (1982): 543–61. Kutolowski's is the most thorough research to date. A similar exercise using lodges in two cotton-belt counties (Houston Lodge, Perry, Houston County, and Cross Lodge, Lumpkin, Stewart County) produced percentages of 41.1 and 47.2, respectively.

22. See William Henry Rosier and Fred Lamar Pearson, Jr., *The Grand Lodge of Georgia*

Masonry and its precapitalist antithesis where megatheory establishes they should not be, I could only conjecture that we misunderstood the nature of Masonry and its relationship to the great transition, the great transition itself, the uniqueness of a South standing apart from that transition, or all three.

Which returns me to Heisenberg's uncertainty principle, my starting point. Its application in particle physics is simplicity itself: Given our limitations, we can establish either the location of a particle at a given moment or its movement, but not both; it is ours to choose which we do, and not the choice of the particle that we study. The more general epistemological implication is equally simple: "To 'understand' something is to give up some other way of conceiving it."[23] It is a truism that historians should take to heart. As we struggle with syntheses — old or new — we must keep in mind their artificiality. We make them, and in the doing we gain particular understanding, but at the cost of other understandings. If we can but keep this in mind, we will be ever ready to stand aside from the syntheses we create, consider our historical observations — our data — anew, and speculate as to what other understandings there might be.[24]

Free and Accepted Masons, 1786–1980 (Macon, Ga., 1983), 43–71, for the decline of membership and dissolution of lodges, p. 62 for the address of Samuel Rockwell, Deputy Grand Master, to the Grand Lodge, 1831; Milledgeville *Southern Recorder*, 16 June 1831; Don. L. Shadburn, ed., *Pioneer History of Forsyth County, Georgia* (Roswell, Ga., 1981), 1:138, quoting the records of the Baptist Union meeting of 10 May 1844. Lipson, *Freemasonry*, 313, aptly distinguishes between "political" and "social" Antimasonry, the one epitomized by the formal party, the other by the sorts of Antimasonic sentiment evidenced in Georgia. Goldman and Vaughn are quite right; there is no sign of formal, political Antimasonic activity in the state.

23. Gary Zukav, *The Dancing Wu Li Masters: An Overview of the New Physics* (New York, 1979), 310.

24. The alternative is simply to wait until the mass of ill-fitting empirical evidence grows to such an extent that it overcomes in a rush the ruling paradigm — what I here call megatheory. See Thomas S. Kuhn, *The Structure of Scientific Revolutions* (Chicago, 1962). Building uncertainty into the paradigms themselves would result in a better-paced expansion of understanding.

14 Community: *A Sunny Little Dream*

Somehow in the nineteenth century, in literature and in works of scholarship by such giants as Ferdinand Tönnies and Emile Durkheim, the Western world seems to have accomplished a mental shift. Sir Thomas More's Utopia *of 1516 was centered on the city; William Dean Howells's* Altruria *of 1894 exalted the countryside and its villages. In that reversal the small, personal community was endowed with all the good things of life. Kurt Vonnegut expressed it well in a* Playboy *interview in 1973: "This is a lonesome society that's been fragmented by the factory system. . . . People don't live in communities permanently anymore. But they should: Communities are very comforting to human beings." It is a theme expressed regularly by scholars, would-be reformers on both left and right, politicians, and just plain people. But in the same interview Vonnegut expressed doubt as to whether the community of popular sentiment ever really existed. "Have you done any research on this?" the interviewer asked. "No. I'm afraid to. I might find out it wasn't true. It's a sunny little dream I have of a happier mankind." Having spent a very long time trying to understand the "small worlds" of the past that are used to legitimatize such sunny little dreams, I have come to realize that Vonnegut's fear was well founded. And invited to deliver a talk as part of a dialogue between scholars and the general public, I said as much.*

On a narrow plain toward the bottom of Olduvai Gorge in east central Africa, close to what some one or two million years ago was the beach of a lake, there sits a circle of stones roughly three meters in diameter. It is, we are assured by archaeologists, not a natural grouping but manmade, or, rather, protohuman-made, the foundations of some sort of

An initial version of this essay was delivered as the second annual Humanities Lecture, the University of Florida, December 1985. Portions subsequently appeared in Darrett B. Rutman, "Assessing the Little Communities of Early America," *William and Mary Quarterly*, 3d ser., 43 (1986): 163–78. Copyright 1986 by the Institute of Early American History and Culture. They are included here with the permission of the editor.

crude windbreak. It has given rise to a fantasy common to archaeologists the world over, one involving a band of these prehuman creatures camping by the lakeside, gathering roots and berries, killing, when they can, some of the animals drawn to the water, scavenging the kills of other predators. In and around the camp they make their stone tools, butcher the animals they have killed, eat, and then disperse to sleep. "Suddenly a nearby volcano becomes active" — the words are those of a paleoanthropologist retelling the fantasy. It spews out "clouds of poison gas, dust, ash, and red-hot particles, killing all the animals" and the sleeping near humans in their shelters. "The hominids and their tools and prey would thus be perfectly preserved under a thick blanket of protective ash" for some scholar a million-plus years later to find, excavate, and analyze.[1] What is most vivid in this fantasy (to me) is that the paleoanthropologist — the most skilled and knowing of scholars in terms of the murky time when humankind emerged — envisioned the hominids living in a social group, or, to use another word, in a "community."

Another scene: It is the late 1940s, and we are with a cultural, rather than paleo-, anthropologist. This particular scholar follows in the tradition of Ferdinand Tönnies, the German sociologist who first dichotomized *Gemeinschaft* (community) and *Gesellschaft* (society), associating the first with an old, warm, personal, and friendly way of village life which he viewed with sadness as disappearing from his late nineteenth-century Germany and the second with what he considered the cold, impersonal, fragmented, urban life emerging. Our particular anthropologist is exploring the nooks and crannies of the British Isles, looking for a small and isolated and forgotten place where, he is convinced, he will "find something of the old [gemeinschaft] tradition still alive." Eventually he comes to a village in the islands off Scotland's northern coast, virtually as far from the great conurbation of London as he can get and still remain in Great Britain. He stays his appointed time, nagging the natives with questions and assiduously jotting their answers in his notebooks. Ultimately the notes become a sprightly volume in which our anthropologist reflects upon "the significance of Island life — not so much for the past, which cannot be changed," he writes, "as for the future, which can." The significance lies, he concludes, "in the intensity" of his villagers' "communal traditions, extinguished elsewhere. . . . Comprehension of this break-up of community brings out the value of the enduring elements of communal life still recorded, remembered, and surviving in the 'Outermost' Hebrides."[2]

1. Robert J. Wenke, *Patterns in Prehistory: Mankind's First Three Million Years* (Oxford, 1980), 128.

2. The text silently conjoins the words of two anthropologists, Conrad M. Arensberg, *The Irish Countryman: An Anthropological Study* (1937; reprint, Garden City, N.Y., 1968), 37, and

And one final scene: We are peering over the shoulder of an unrepentant rebel of the New Left of the 1960s, a little older now, a little more pragmatic, but no less intense. He (or she, for it could well be either) no longer attempts to block public buildings while insisting on a "dialogue" over some list of "nonnegotiable" demands; our rebel is now with an institute devoted to encouraging and organizing "citizen advocacy" and "neighborhood power." He is writing a book as well. What is our goal, he asks rhetorically? "Community. Dancing, singing, fighting, taking care of each other, helping each other out," a "return to the roots of being human."[3]

These three brief scenes lay out the ground I have chosen for myself. The first suggests that the human is, indeed, one of many social species, and for most of its existence its basic social groupings have been small. The second reflects the fact that sometime in the nineteenth and early twentieth centuries, at least in the Western world, the idea emerged that the small, intimate, face-to-face society somehow embodied all that was good in humankind, that it was a natural state in sharp contrast to the unnatural world of city, contract, bureaucracy, and technology that was rapidly developing. The third underscores a tendency, certainly in Britain and America, to embrace the image of the small community as an antidote for all that is felt to be wrong in modern society: size, and with it complexity and impersonality; the rule of contract rather than trust, of law rather than culture; above all, the pursuit of individual comfort rather than taking comfort in the comfort of the group. "Small is beautiful," wrote British economist E. F. Schumacher. "What is so wonderful about being big?" B. F. Skinner echoed in *Walden Two.* "The world is suffering from the ills of bigness."[4] And from the fringes of the American political spectrum, Sheldon Wolin writes: "A political being is not to be defined as the citizen

---

Arthur Geddes, *The Isle of Lewis and Harris: A Study in British Community* (Edinburgh, 1955), 14, 22.

3. Again, I have conjoined authors: Harry C. Boyte, *The Backyard Revolution: Understanding the New Citizen Movement* (Philadelphia, 1980), 198; David Clark, *Basic Communities: Towards an Alternative Society* (London, 1977), 17.

4. Schumacher, *Small Is Beautiful: Economics As If People Mattered* (1973; reprint, New York, 1975); Skinner, "Walden Two Revisited," in his *Walden Two* (1948; reprint, New York, 1976), ix. The tradition of lodging reform in the small community is as old as modern industrialization and urbanization. See, e.g., Mark Holloway, *Heavens on Earth: Utopian Communities in America, 1680–1880* (London, 1951); Paul K. Conkin, *Tomorrow a New World: The New Deal Community Program* (Ithaca, N.Y., 1959). The latter (p. 52) quotes Franklin K. Lane, secretary of the interior in 1919, to the effect that the only solution to the social problems of the early twentieth century was "to develop a new rural life with all the urban advantages. . . . The United States should turn to the farm village . . . or to settlement around a community center which could contain the advantages of city life. Co-operation could banish isolation; there could be motion pictures and baseball teams, and 'there'll be a dance every week in the community house.'"

has been, as an abstract, disconnected bearer of rights, privileges, and immunities, but as a person whose existence is located in a particular place and draws its sustenance from circumscribed relationships: family, friends, church, neighborhood, workplace, community." Parker J. Palmer elaborates: "We live in a culture of brokenness and fragmentation. Images of individualism and autonomy are far more compelling to us than visions of unity, and the fabric of relatedness seems dangerously threadbare and frayed. . . . We have all but lost the vision of the public [understood as] our oneness, our unity, our interdependence upon one another," our sense of community. Karl Hess: "There is not a single large institution or organization in the world today that is satisfactorily performing all of the functions people have assigned to it. They are creaking, cracking, and even crashing under their own weight. Everywhere people sense that things are going to hell." His solution: community, "a *place* in which and a *way* in which people can live peacefully, socially, cooperatively."[5] Philosophizing academics put the point more politely, arguing for a retraining of the *Habits of the Heart* and a consequent renewal of "community and democracy in America," for a renewal of the "civil society," an eighteenth-century notion translated by Daniel Bell for twentieth-century America as "a return to a manageable scale of social life," to "voluntary associations, churches, and communities," to locally made decisions rather than decisions emanating from "the state and its bureaucracies."[6] Reforming politicians echo the theme: America is suffering from a "sleeping sickness of the soul," Hillary Rodham Clinton has said; Americans lack a "sense that our lives are part of some greater effort, that we are connected to one another, that community means that we have a place where we belong no matter who we are." But even those who see little wrong in American life tend, from their different perspectives, to lodge what is right in the community: Ronald Reagan in 1984 celebrating as America's "bedrock" the little community "where neighbors help one another, where families bring up kids together, where American values are born," New York's Mario M. Cuomo

5. Wolin (1982) as quoted in Harry C. Boyte, *Community Is Possible: Repairing America's Roots* (New York, 1984), 212; Palmer, *The Company of Strangers: Christians and the Renewal of America's Public Life* (New York, 1982), 19–20; Hess, *Community Technology* (New York, 1980), 1, 5.

6. Robert N. Bellah et al., *Habits of the Heart: Individualism and Commitment in American Life* (Berkeley, Calif., 1985); Charles H. Reynolds and Ralph V. Norman, "The Longing for Community: Civic Ecology, Narrative, and Practices," in *Community in America: The Challenge of Habits of the Heart*, ed. Reynolds and Norman (Berkeley, Calif., 1988), 1; Bell, "American Exceptionalism Revisited: The Role of Civil Society," *Public Interest* 95 (1989): 56. For a careful exposition (and rejection) of "civil society" as expounded in both Europe and the United States, see Adam B. Seligman, *The Idea of Civil Society* (New York, 1992).

in 1987 referring to community as "the reality on which our national life has been founded."[7]

My argument here is simplicity itself: The idea of the small community and its indiscriminate use as both the bedrock of our good society and as a panacea for our social ills is an idea whose time is long past. It neither adequately describes the historical reality from which we have proceeded nor maps a social reality to which we can logically aspire.

Let us first establish exactly what it is that we are talking about when we use this word *community*. In common parlance it is, of course, simply a synonym for the people of any particular place or kind; it is in this sense that newscasters report that "the community was outraged," that politicians take their cases "to the community," and that faculty wonder about their reputation in "the community of scholars." But *community* also expresses an idealization or sentiment, referring in the words of a modern glossary to a "mythical state of social wholeness in which each member has his place and in which life is regulated by cooperation rather than competition." And *community* is a contemporary scholars' term, referring specifically to that network of human relationships "observable and analysable with reference to location as a focus of attention."[8] In this last sense the word implies a research strategy and a series of questions. Any place is a potential social field occupied by points, but are the points of a particular place individuals, or are they families, or groups? In what ways, to what degree, and through what nodal points do they connect to each other? What constraints operate to enforce these relationships and to preclude others?[9] Obviously, community as a research strategy is in sharp contrast to community as an idealization or sentiment. The former probes the nature of relationships in a place. The latter declares an answer: The relationships within a community make for an ordered, cooperative whole. Obviously, too, scholarship is not immune to sentiment, as witness the anthropologist of our second scene who, having the sentiment in mind as he looked, readily found and reported on a sentimental community. And still again obviously: Such scholarship as that of our anthropologist's — and there has been a great deal of it over the years since Tönnies, emanating not merely from anthropologists but from sociologists, psy-

7. Clinton quoted in Michael Kelley, "Hillary Rodham Clinton and the Politics of Virtue," *New York Times Magazine*, 23 May 1993, 25; Reagan and Cuomo in Robert B. Reich, "Secession of the Successful," ibid., 20 Jan. 1991, 16.

8. Charles Abrams, *The Language of Cities: A Glossary of Terms* (New York, 1971), 59–60; Talcott Parsons, "The Principal Structures of Community," in *Community*, ed. Carl J. Friedrich (New York, 1959), 250.

9. For elaboration, see Darrett B. Rutman, "Community Study," *Historical Methods* 13 (1980): 29–41 [chap. 3 above].

chologists, political scientists, historians — has given validity to the sentiment, assuring the sentimental that there once was, in reality, such a
village Camelot.[10]

It is, however, the last sense of the word that guides me: community as a
research strategy. And over the past few years I have been engaged in a
systematic digesting of the works of historians, anthropologists, sociologists, and the like who have scrutinized particular places. The reading has
taken the form of concentric circles centered on my basic field of early
American history (which offers well over a hundred such studies) and
extending across space to early modern England and the Continent, and
across time from Sir Thomas More in the early sixteenth century to the
present — in all perhaps half-a-thousand volumes with a thousand and a
half still to go before I can sit down to draft the book I have in mind: a
study of the idea and reality of community in the West as these things have
changed over the past four hundred years. What follows is, therefore,
tentative, an early pressing of the grapes with all the grapes not yet in the
vat. And for the moment it is purposefully limited inasmuch as it deals
only with places generally considered unaffected by those complex mac-
roevents which we sum up as "industrialization," "urbanization," "the
transit to capitalism" and to which we more often than not attribute the
decline of community. The limitation is directly pertinent. I am, in fact,
using community as a research strategy in an attempt to find and assess the
sentimental community in the "premodern" West.

Recollecting the premodern places that I have scrutinized — largely vi-
cariously, of course, that is, through the eyes of other scholars — I am
struck first by their diversity. Each place is unique, the product of its own
history, while between and within the various regions of the West particular places display enormous variation in such things as the pattern, size,
and tenure of landholdings, rules of inheritance, the crops planted and the
crafts followed, marketing arrangements, labor systems, status hier-
archies. Place itself is identified according to different terminologies —
village, town, county, society, parish, canton, commune — and these in
turn reflect different ecclesiastical and civil polities. Individual scholars,
moreover, perpetually muddy the mélange by bringing to their work subjective understandings of the sentimental community and, more often
than not, attempting to establish its presence or absence in their particular
place. Yet the diversity gives way and one begins to sense the fundamental
social arrangements that encompassed the vast majority of the inhabitants

10. Kurt Vonnegut, Jr., quoted in the headnote from his *Wampeters, Foma, and Gran-
falloons (Opinions)* (New York, 1976), 241, 243, was a student of anthropologist Robert
Redfield at the University of Chicago and writes (ibid., 177) of taking his own "sunny little
dream" from Redfield's "lovely dream which he called 'The Folk Society,'" published in
American Journal of Sociology 52 (1947): 293–308.

of this premodern Western world when the findings of the various scholars are restated in the common language of community as research strategy. Everywhere the points in the social fields delimited by the scholars' places tend to be nuclear families. Virtually everywhere, too, they tend to be agricultural families faced with the same essential problem: how to extract from what land and skills they have the wherewithal to meet the family's needs and wants. And everywhere the relationships between families tend to form neighborhood networks, sometimes coterminous with the ecclesiastical or governmental unit that gives the place its name, sometimes forming clusters encompassed by the larger unit. For most of the families the distances spanned by the network of relationships in which they were enmeshed were relatively short, and the relationships themselves were multistranded in the sense that one dealt with the same group of "others" over and over again in a variety of ways.

Life, in brief, was lived "face to face" in these small societies and on a scale easily described — relative to that in which we live today — as small, intimate, and essentially cooperative. Life was, moreover, lived slowly and in tune to its own cycles and the seasons of the year. There was none of our contemporary hustle and bustle as people rush about doing this or that in the firm belief that they are in control of their own destinies (all the while relying on public- and private-sector "safety nets" to catch them when it turns out that they are wrong and fate, chance, or impersonal economic forces put them in jeopardy). Neither was there instant response to great events such as those discerned in three-minute television spots in our electronic world. Indeed, studies of the premodern West are consistently suggesting that what we, from a vantage point in their future, deem the great events of the time actually crept upon the populace all unawares and effected minimal immediate change in the lifestyle: the English Revolution of the 1640s passing through W. G. Hoskins's Midland village of Wigston Magna, for example, or the American Revolution passing through Robert A. Gross's Concord, Massachusetts, the world of the minutemen, or Napoleon's armies passing through Mack Walker's Weissenburg.[11] The events important to the men and women of these small places were themselves small and, for the scholar who reads more than a dozen-odd such studies, dull in their predictability: in terms of the individual, the events of the life cycle — birth, dependent childhood, marriage and (for males) a consequent independence, the appearance of one's own children, old age, death; in terms of the group, the monotonous season-

11. Hoskins, *The Midland Peasant: The Economic and Social History of a Leicestershire Village* (London, 1957); Gross, *The Minutemen and Their World* (New York, 1976), and "Culture and Cultivation: Agriculture and Society in Thoreau's Concord," *Journal of American History* 69 (1982): 42–55; Walker, *German Home Towns: Community, State, and General Estate, 1648–1871* (Ithaca, N.Y., 1971), 217–47.

ality of an agricultural world, with spring work giving way to that of summer, summer's to that of autumn, autumn's to winter's, and winter's to spring work again, the rhythm broken now and again by crop or market failures, by epidemics, and (in early America particularly) by squabbles over where to locate a church or courthouse and how much to expend on it, where to build a road or bridge, how much to pay the minister, with squabbles frequently giving way to secession as one neighborhood or the other came to feel itself ill-served by the whole and set itself up as a whole unto itself.

Equally to the point, life in the small places of the premodern West was lived within a web of reciprocal obligations and responsibilities. In villages and open-country neighborhoods alike, we seem always to be in a world of good neighbors, of borrowing and lending, sharing and caring, of "harmonious and co-operative relationships among . . . householders" that overcame personal, even familial, isolation. One scholar, looking at seventeenth-century England, has written of an internalized "moral community," a set of "minimum standards below which a neighbour fell only at risk of losing the benefits of local goodwill" (peaceableness, a recognition of customary obligations, the avoidance of placing unreasonable burdens upon the neighborhood) and of prescriptive standards (a recognition of the obligation to render aid and support, "a willingness to accept the neighbours as a reference group in matters of behaviour"). Such neighborliness, he suggests, was even the essence of folk religion, much to the consternation of clergymen who pressed elaborate creeds and beliefs. "Godly living," he quotes one villager as telling a minister, is to "say no body no harme, nor doe noe body noe harme and do as he would be done to." When the minister convinced him that more was required for salvation and the villager bemoaned his own damnation, a friend came to the rescue: "Damned Man, what speak you of damning. I am ashamed to heare you say so. For it is well knowne that you are an honest man, a quiet liver, a good neighbour."[12] Carlo Ginzburg's Menocchio pushes such "good neighbor" thinking back to the Continent of the mid-sixteenth century, the heretical miller of the Friuli explaining that he "would want us to believe in the majesty of God, to be good, and to do as Jesus Christ commanded: . . . 'Love God and your neighbor.' "[13] The seventeenth-century diary of Thomas Minor of Stonington, Connecticut, brings it across the ocean to early America.

12. Keith Wrightson, *English Society, 1580–1680* (New Brunswick, N.J., 1982), 53–54, 205. Heléna M. Wall, *Fierce Communion: Family and Community in Early America* (Cambridge, Mass., 1990) offers a compelling picture of the proscriptive and prescriptive aspects of "village" life in an early American setting.

13. Ginzburg, *The Cheese and the Worms: The Cosmos of a Sixteenth-Century Miller*, trans. John and Ann Tedeschi (Baltimore, 1980), 9.

Little emotion shows in the terse, unembellished sentences of this diary. It is largely the recording of a farmer's plowings and reapings, what he planted and built, borrowed and lent, bought and sold, of his meetings with neighbors and of the comings and goings of his family. The emotion that does show, however, inevitably suggests the value that the diarist placed on his position in the neighborhood and on friendship. There is apparent pride when in 1669 he self-consciously listed the offices he was holding for the year: "Select man[,] the Townes Tresurer[,] The Townes Recorder[,] The brander of horses . . . the head officer of the Traine band. . . . one of the Fouer that have the Charge of the milisheia of the whole Countie . . . sworne Commissinor and one to assisst in keeping the Countie Courte." There is defensiveness. For a brief period in the late 1660s, the diarist and his wife withdrew from Sabbath meetings; no reason is given. On returning, he carefully noted that at his own "desier" the minister formally queried "an assembly of the Inhabitants . . . whether they as neighbours had ought against Thomas minor or his wife" and that "none objected against them." There is chagrin when he wrote of a failed friendship: "I went To speake with a frend: but found I none: this is the second time I tried a man: but I wile for beare the third if that I can." And there is anger, secretly, not publicly, expressed: "I went astray in Companie of Two: that professed they loved me well: . . . my Children when I am dead: let none els but your selves This reade: but do take heed of being with your professed frends misled: the two Il nam to you: remember well the time and you will finde it true: Thomas Stanton and William Cheesbrough wer the men."[14]

Small, face-to-face, cooperative in fact even when in mind (as when Minor regarded his false friends) bitterness was hidden — thus far we seem to have found at least a semblance of the community of sentiment in our past. But we must press on.

These small places were not isolates, not little chunks of humanity contentedly sitting apart from all other chunks. They were complex entities in and of themselves, and at the same time parts of still larger social entities. John Donne's line can be rewritten to make the point — no place "is an *Iland*, intire of it selfe" — while Donne's seventeenth-century English world and two specific places within it can illustrate the point, the parishes of Terling, as reconstructed by historians Keith Wrightson and David Levine, and Myddle, as seen through the scholarship of David Hey.[15]

14. Sidney H. Miner and George D. Stanton, Jr., eds., *The Diary of Thomas Minor, Stonington, Connecticut, 1653 to 1684* (New London, Conn., 1899), 189–90, 207–8.

15. Donne, *Devotions upon Emergent Ocasions* (1624), ed. John Sparrow (Cambridge, 1923), 98; Wrightson and Levine, *Poverty and Piety in an English Village: Terling, 1525–1700*

Families were the basic building blocks of these English places. "The family was the basic unit of residence"—Wrightson's words—"of the pooling and distribution of resources for consumption" and for the most part of production as well. "Within the family, individuals found security and identity and the satisfaction of both physical and emotional needs." "Through the family, society reproduced itself; children were born and reared and property was transmitted from generation to generation," each father by the adroit distribution of what he had to give by way of gifts, bequests, and other "supports" attempting to maximize "the opportunities of as many children as possible." One father's plaint to an overly demanding son is evocative in this context: "I can supplye you no further," he wrote; "I have many other children that are unprovided, and I see my life is uncertain. I mervaile at your great undertakinges, havinge no means, and knowinge how much I am in debt allreadye."[16]

Families formed collectivities centered upon the parish church. That at Myddle, Hey writes, united the families of the parish "into a community, a unit to which people were conscious of belonging, and which distinguished them from their neighbors in adjacent parishes." Yet into the church on a Sunday trooped families not only from Myddle village but from a half-dozen satellite hamlets. The parish collectivity, the "community," obviously had parts. And when the young men and women of the families came of appropriate age, they found the pool of eligible mates within the narrow confines of the parish too small. Between a half and two-thirds found brides and grooms in surrounding parishes (most within a ten-mile circuit), leading Hey in the end to resort to the notion of a "neighborhood of north Shropshire" of which Myddle itself was only a part.[17]

Terling, too, we are told, constituted a collectivity with "its own integrity as a social unit." "The villagers lived and worked in close proximity to one another. . . . The parish had a distinct identity of which its inhabitants were demonstrably aware."[18] Yet Terling also had its parts and was itself a part of a cluster of parishes, again roughly ten miles in circuit, delimited by marriage runs, debt and credit relationships, and a degree of local migration which shocked historians when first discerned as a general phenomenon in the English scene.[19] No single parish, it seems, was complete

---

(New York, 1979); Hey, *An English Rural Community: Myddle under the Tudors and Stuarts* (Leicester, Eng., 1974).

16. Wrightson, *English Society*, 66; Wrightson and Levine, *Poverty and Piety*, 99; John to Henry Winthrop, 30 Jan. 1629, Massachusetts Historical Society, *Winthrop Papers* (Boston, 1929–47), 2:67.

17. Hey, *An English Rural Community*, 201, 208, 218.

18. Wrightson and Levine, *Poverty and Piety*, 74–75.

19. One of the earliest announcements of this finding was Peter Laslett and John Har-

enough to offer a livelihood to all, hence the regular exchange of population (largely young) between parishes and a steady stream of emigration from country parishes into England's towns and cities, particularly London, which, given prevailing notions of hygiene, proved a great sink for excess population. A majority of the emigrants to London died without issue.[20]

No single parish, moreover, could stand as a total economy; Donne's world, it seems, incorporated a complex and relatively efficient economic system of fairs, open markets, and private trading which ignored parish boundaries and from which no parish was isolated. We glimpse the fact in Myddle, far in the west of England, in the Welsh Marches. Richard Gough, Myddle's seventeenth-century chronicler whose work forms the basis of Hey's reconstruction, wrote of drovers and traders frequenting the village inn and under the heading of "conveniences that beelong to the parish . . . which are noe small advantages to it" noted that "the greatest . . . is the benefit of good marketts." In all there were at least eight in the immediate neighborhood of North Shropshire. But even London — some 150-odd miles away — drew from Myddle, Gough writing of the parish's John Foden who had "a good teame of horses with which hee carryed goods" to the city.[21] Indeed, in the early eighteenth century Daniel Defoe would write of "the general dependence of the whole country upon the city . . . for the consumption of its produce."[22] But if London bulked large, every town with inhabitants spending more time and effort in making things or rendering services than in gardening, tillage, or grazing was itself the center of an economic vortex, drawing nearby villagers to its market cross.

If these small places were not isolated, neither were they static, timeless, unchanging. We are not looking at a motionless past eventually set in motion (toward destruction according to the critics of modernity) by rising capitalism, industrialism, and urbanization. The timeless village structure of the Continent can itself be dated, while the very stones and

---

rison, "Clayworth and Cogenhoe," in *Historical Essays, 1600–1750, Presented to David Ogg,* ed. H. E. Bell and R. L. Ollard (London, 1963), 157–84. Note p. 174: "The startling fact is that a settled, rural, perfectly ordinary Stuart community could change its composition by well over half, getting on in fact for two-thirds, in a dozen years. So surprising is it that we do not yet know quite what to make of it."

20. E. A. Wrigley, *Population and History* (New York, 1969), 95–98.

21. Gough, *The History of Myddle,* ed. David Hey (Harmondsworth, Eng., 1981), 265–66; Hey, *An English Rural Community,* 194. See the map of market towns in western England and Wales ca. 1500–1640 in Alan Everitt, "The Marketing of Agricultural Produce," in *The Agrarian History of England and Wales,* vol. 4, *1500–1640,* ed. Joan Thirsk (Cambridge, 1967), 470.

22. Defoe, *A Tour through England and Wales* (1724–26; reprint, London, 1927), 1:3.

timbers of England's villages and neighborhoods speak of change. Villages disappeared — the familiar deserted village — while new villages were spawned from old. Persisting villages literally shifted their position on the ground. Within villages the houses themselves were built, rebuilt, and rebuilt again, changing their shapes, sizes, alignments, even positions.[23] The church of St. Peter in Hey's Myddle had indeed a Saxon foundation, but "nothing of the ancient fabric survives." Its steeple dates from 1634, the interior plan was in flux in the sixteenth and seventeenth centuries, and the whole was rebuilt in 1744. The Lordship of Myddle predates the Norman Conquest, but the process of clearing the woods of the parish, draining ponds, and hiving off "colony" hamlets from the original settlement went on "in fits and starts" from the beginning and would continue after 1813. In the 150 years of the late fifteenth through early seventeenth centuries some 1,000 new acres, roughly a quarter of the total acreage of the parish, were transformed from "waste" to cultivation.[24] Village economies changed, too, as witness five antique parishes in the Forest of Arden studied by Victor Skipp; over the years between 1570 and 1674 the parishes shifted from beef-centered agriculture to dairying as their farmers took advantage of an upsurge of population, with a consequent enlargement of the labor pool and the opening of new markets.[25] And populations changed. Limited resources on the one hand and the inexorable press of demography on the other — what anthropologist Marvin Harris has generalized as the perpetual encounter between belly and womb — underlay the high level of migration already mentioned.[26] Fathers begetting too many sons to share too little land, or too many daughters for too few suitors, perforce sent children into the world beyond the village to reencapsulate themselves (if they could) in places where the luck of the demographic draw had produced an opposite situation. One result was that within a generation no more than half a village's population could trace its neighborhood ancestry back beyond itself to an earlier generation. An-

23. Fredric Cheyette, "The Origins of European Villages and the First European Expansion," *Journal of Economic History* 37 (1977): 182–206; J. G. Hurst, "The Changing Medieval Village in England," in *Man, Settlement and Urbanism*, ed. Peter J. Ucko, Ruth Tringham, G. W. Dimbleby (London, 1972), 531–41; R. A. Dodgshon, "The Early Middle Ages, 1066–1350," and R. A. Butlin, "The Late Middle Ages, c. 1350–1500," both in *An Historical Geography of England and Wales*, ed. Dodgshon and Butlin (London, 1978), 95, 140; J. T. Smith, "The Evolution of the English Peasant Houses to the Late Seventeenth Century," *Journal of the British Archaeological Association*, 3d ser., 33 (1970): 122–47; W. G. Hoskins, "The Rebuilding of Rural England, 1570–1640," *Past and Present* 4 (1953): 44–59; R. Machin, "The Great Rebuilding: A Reassessment," ibid., 77 (1977): 33–56.

24. Hey, *An English Rural Community*, 18, 32, 39.

25. Skipp, *Crises and Development: An Ecological Case Study of the Forest of Arden, 1570–1674* (Cambridge, 1978), 52.

26. Harris, *Cultural Materialism: The Struggle for a Science of Culture* (New York, 1979), ix.

other result, of course, was the peopling of English America, a process to be understood — in Bernard Bailyn's words — as "an extension outward and an expansion in scale of domestic mobility in the lands of the immigrants' origins."[27]

Above all, individuality was not subsumed to the communality of these premodern places. We sense this when we encounter change in the village. The farmers of Arden did not shift from one form of agriculture to another as a way to perpetuate their community but seized the main chance to perpetuate and prosper individually. We sense it more generally when we shift our attention from the village or neighborhood as a whole — the social field, the community if you will — to the neighbors themselves, the points within the field. Looking at the whole, of course, we see the whole and marvel at its compactness. The close-knit web of relationships impresses itself upon our mind. But when we shift to a single point within the field — in effect gaze out into the network of relationships from the dooryard of one of its members — the nature of the whole is quite different. It is a machine of sorts which serves the purpose of the individual. A line from an ancient Greek comes to mind, Hesiod in his *Works and Days*. (He, too, was describing village life.) "Take fair measure from your neighbor and pay him back fairly with the same measure, or better, if thou can; so that if you are in need afterwards you may find him sure."[28] That this pertains to our small places comes clear on those rare occasions when we can probe the everyday affairs of one of our neighbors. Diaries such as those of Thomas Minor of Connecticut and Ralph Josselin, farmer and curate of Earls Colne, Essex, from 1641 into 1683, clearly display the calculation involved in the reciprocity of the village: Josselin, for example, cultivating a relationship one day and converting it into a loan on another; Minor jotting down that one John Morgan trimmed his cider barrels on an August day and a month later was "made even with" when Minor "payd" him four and a half bushels of corn. On another occasion Minor noted that he had to come out ahead from such exchanges by £101 a year if he was to keep the family venture that he headed afloat and prospering.[29]

But enough of particulars. Allow me to return to the general. My thesis involves "community," an idea which for some both describes an ideal past and maps an ideal future, an idea, too, which is clothed in the guise of a natural attribute of mankind. Recall the unrepentant rebel of the third of my opening scenes: He would have us "dancing, singing, fighting, taking

27. Bailyn, *The Peopling of British North America: An Introduction* (New York, 1986), 20.

28. Quoted in Karl Polanyi, *The Livelihood of Man*, ed. Harry W. Pearson (New York, 1977), 153.

29. Alan Macfarlane, *The Family Life of Ralph Josselin: A Seventeenth-Century Clergyman* (Cambridge, 1970), 55–56, 154–55; Miner and Stanton, *The Diary of Thomas Minor*, 50, 104–6.

care of each other, helping each other out," in a phrase, returning "to the roots of being human." Poor soul! As nothing else, he reminds me of John Winthrop, a visionary of the seventeenth century who led the English migration into New England in the 1630s. Winthrop, too, thought of his world — the premodern village world, mind you — as sick, diseased, collapsing.[30] His words are somewhat archaic, but the meaning is familiar.

"We are growne to that height of Intemperance in all excesse of Riott, as noe mans estate allmost will suffice to keepe saile with his aequalls: and he, whoe failes herein, must live in scorne and contempt."[31] Translation: Rampant individualism, consumerism!

"This Land growes weary of her Inhabitantes, soe as man whoe is the most praetious of all creatures, is here more vile and base then the earth we treade upon . . . masters are forced by authority to entertaine servants, parents to mainetaine there owne children, all townes complaine of the burthen of theire poore . . . and we use the authoritie of the Law . . . urginge [the execution of] the Statute against Cottages, and inmates."[32] Translation: The family is declining; bureaucratic control is being substituted for social cooperation!

"The Fountaines of Learning and Religion are soe corrupted as (besides the unsupportable charge of there education) most children (even the best witts and of faierest hopes) are perverted, corrupted, and utterlie overthrowne by the multitude of evill examples and the licentious government of those Seminaries, where men straine at knatts, and swallowe camells . . . but suffer all ruffianlike fashions, and disorder in manners to passe uncontrolled."[33] Translation: Schools are not teaching values, faculty would rather do research than teach, and the kids are going to pot!

Winthrop's solution, too, is familiar. He would encapsulate his New Englanders in what we easily recognize as the idealized or sentimental community, telling those sailing with him aboard the *Arbella* to be "knitt together in this worke as one man." "Wee must," he went on, "entertaine each other in brotherly Affeccion, wee must be willing to abridge our selves of our superfluities, for the supply of others necessities, wee must uphold a familiar Commerce together in all meekenes, gentlenes, patience and liberallity, wee must delight in eache other, make others Condicions our owne[,] rejoyce together, mourne together, labour, and suffer

30. Writes Barry Wellman, "The Community Question Re-Evaluated," in *Power, Community, and the City: Comparative Urban and Community Research*, ed. Michael Peter Smith (New Brunswick, N.J., 1988), 82: "It is likely that pundits have worried about the impact of social change on communities ever since human beings ventured beyond their caves."

31. Winthrop, "Reasons to be considered for justifieinge the undertakeres of the intended Plantation in New England" (1629), *Winthrop Papers* 2:139.

32. Ibid.

33. Ibid.

together . . . as members of the same body."[34] (His religious scruples, of course, prevented him from urging dancing, singing, or fighting together.)

And finally, Winthrop (just as our remnant rebel) thought of his solution in terms of a natural condition for humankind, although emerging from a religious tradition, the nature he had in mind was that prevailing in the biblical Eden: "Adam in his first estate was a perfect modell of mankinde in all theire generacions, and in him [a] love [for fellow man] was perfected. . . . But Adam[,] Rent in himselfe from his Creator, rent all posterity allsoe one from another, whence it comes that every man is borne with this principle in him, to loue and seeke himselfe onely." We regain our natural state only through grace, for then "the Spirit . . . gathers together the scattered bones of perfect old man Adam . . . knitts them into one body againe," and fashions the resurrected Adams (and their Eves) into one Edenic community.[35]

Social forms, however, do not emerge from wishful thinking. Winthrop's words, as it turned out, were but whispers in the wind; in the end, his New England — indeed, early America in general — owed far less to him and far more to the old England from which it sprang. And England (and the premodern West as a whole) was a world of relatively tight-knit — but by no means isolated, unchanging, impervious — neighborhoods, not because of some kind of ruling altruism but simply because it had to be that way.

The production of goods — primarily agricultural — dominated that world. Why? The answer lies in a calculus of energy inputs and caloric outputs. After all, that was a world in which fields were laid out with reference to how far an ox could pull a plow before the ox tired, while the yield of land once plowed and planted was but ten or twelve to one: only ten or twelve kernels of wheat gained from each kernel planted as seed. The very necessity of feeding itself required that 80 to 90 percent of the population be involved in agricultural production.

It was a world of small places, where relationships were direct, personal, and multiplex. Why? Again, a calculus, this time of energy inputs and communication outputs. To most individuals, the world was effectively limited to the distance to be walked or ridden in a day, communication to the distance a voice could travel. Given these constraints, how else was the world to be organized but on the basis of the small, direct, personal?

And this world was one of cooperation. But again, it was such by virtue of necessity. In cooperation lay the means for the subsistence of the individual, and the individual — not the group — was the core of the society.

34. Winthrop, "A Modell of Christian Charity" (1630), ibid., 294.
35. Ibid., 290.

Rodney C. Loehr demonstrated some years ago the inappropriateness of the notion of self-sufficiency when applied to a single farm, and Bettye Hobbs Pruitt has demonstrated that a substantial part of the population of rural Massachusets of 1774 could not even garner its daily bread except through reciprocal exchanges with neighbors.[36] Robert McC. Netting has demonstrated the specific relationship of cooperation to material necessity in his study of the Swiss village of Törbel, marvelously entitled *Balancing on an Alp*: Cooperation ruled those aspects of village life involving the ecologically fragile Alpine fields; without it, the fields would have been destroyed by undercare and overtillage. But individual effort prevailed in all other aspects of village life.[37] Even the *mentalité* of the villages—the "moral community" with its emphasis on good neighborliness that Wrightson describes—is to be associated with individual necessity. Consciousness flows from condition, it can be argued, from which it follows that to the degree the necessity of being a good neighbor was required by the material and social world within which one lived, good neighborliness was internalized.

This above all is what the sentimental notion of community misses: the centrality of the individual within any social form. Winthrop and our remnant rebel alike would sublimate the individual to the group, and both in their own way call this arrangement "natural." I hope I will be pardoned for my bluntness, but this is unadulterated nonsense. If we are to speak of "natural," let us truly do so. Samuel Butler once quipped that a chicken is but an egg's way of making more eggs. We can rephrase the quip: The human is a gene's way of making more genes.[38] Peter A. Corning put the thought more generally: "At heart, a human society is a collective survival enterprise."[39] Any way it is expressed, however, it is this line of reasoning—from gene to individual to group—which offers us the sociological truism *"Man is a social being obliged by nature to live with others as a member of society,"* legitimizes a paleoanthropologist's fantasy of digging up the totality of a protohuman society—we have always lived in groups—yet at the same time undermines the sentimentalization of one social form (the village community) over all other forms.[40] In this reasoning there is no

36. Loehr, "Self-Sufficiency on the Farm," *Agricultural History* 26 (1952), 37–41; Pruitt, "Self-Sufficiency and the Agricultural Economy of Eighteenth-Century Massachusetts," *William and Mary Quarterly*, 3d ser., 41 (1984): 333–64.

37. Netting, *Balancing on an Alp: Ecological Change and Continuity in a Swiss Mountain Community* (Cambridge, 1981), 64.

38. David Barash, *The Whisperings Within* (New York, 1979), 21.

39. Corning, *The Synergism Hypothesis: A Theory of Progressive Evolution* (New York, 1983), 27.

40. Gerhard E. Lenski, *Power and Privilege: A Theory of Social Stratification* (New York, 1966), 25.

natural social form, no ideal. All forms are equal which serve equally well as a "survival enterprise"; particular forms are the product of the environment (both material and social) in which the constituent individuals must exist. With reference to other species we would be talking about fitting into an ecological niche. Why not with reference to the human species? Hunter-gatherer bands fit a hunting and gathering world. Village communities fit a world of agricultural production and limited energy. And our contemporary "communities of limited liability" — sociological jargon that boils down to the neighbors among whom we reside and with whom we voluntarily involve ourselves in the interest of particular and well-identified purposes of our own — seem to fit the calculus of our high-energy Western world, one in which few are engaged in agricultural production and only a few more in production of any kind, while the great majority are involved in distribution, the administration of distribution, and the provision of services to one another.[41] From this perspective the modern form is as "natural" as the premodern. So, too, is our natural history, our "progress," if you will, as premodern forms evolved in an American landscape into our complex, bureaucratic, technological, individualistic present.[42]

I began with a fantasy; let me end with one — a fantasy prompted by the whole issue of our "natural" state but inspired by a few sentences from a contemporary novelist, Robert A. Heinlein. "There are," he wrote, "hidden contradictions in the minds of people who 'love nature' while deploring the 'artificialities' with which Man has spoiled 'Nature.' The obvious contradiction lies in their choice of words, which imply that Man and his artifacts are *not* part of 'Nature' — but beavers and their dams *are*."[43]

Join me, if you will, in contemplating a beaver colony; I leave to you the task of extracting the moral.

Our particular colony is small, composed of but two young beavers who came together just as the ice was breaking in the spring, when they moved onto the stream on which we find them. The time is late fall. Obviously the intervening months have been busy ones in beaver terms. Their dam has been built, backing up the water of the stream to form a large pond several acres in extent. Their lodge, too, has been built, a heap of intertwined branches and saplings in the middle of the pond. Scattered about

41. Gerald D. Suttles, *The Social Construction of Communities* (Chicago, 1972), 47–48, drawing from Morris Janowitz, *The Community Press in an Urban Setting: The Social Elements of Urbanism*, 2d ed. (Chicago, 1952).

42. An evolution sketched in broad strokes in Darrett B. Rutman, "Assessing the Little Communities of Early America," *William and Mary Quarterly*, 3d ser., 43 (1986): 163–78, and Robert F. Berkhofer, Jr., "The Organizational Interpretation of American History: A New Synthesis," *Prospects* 4 (1979): 611–29.

43. Heinlein, *Time Enough for Love: The Lives of Lazarus Long* (New York, 1974), 245.

the pond are the bare trunks of once-great oaks jutting up from water-logged roots, in effect killed by the beavers. Where lesser trees once stood, there are only stumps, their ends knawed to sharpened points, each surrounded by a litter of twigs and small branches. Here and there virtually intact trees, brought down by the beavers but abandoned, lie half in and half out of the water. We spot the beavers themselves at twilight, sitting atop the newly constructed lodge, resting from their day's work, gazing about at a world of their own creation.

"Henry," says one, "this is disgusting!"

The other — obviously Henry — stirs and, in rodent fashion, perches on his hind feet to get a better view.

"What do you mean? It looks grand to me. Real homelike. Comfortable."

"But we've killed the trees! We've driven out the birds that nested in them. We've filled up this beautiful valley with stagnant water. Henry, it's wrong! It's *unnatural!*"

The diatribe initiates a long conversation extending through the night and a week of nights thereafter, the course of which we need not follow. The upshot, however, is of interest. Henry, being a compliant creature and easily swayed, finally agrees with his companion that they ought to seek out an "alternative lifestyle," one which would not require them to build dams and ponds and lodges and the like, one which, in brief, would allow them to "return to the roots of being beaver." (I should add that in coming to this decision, our beavers consulted several tomes emanating from faculty at nearby Beaverbrook College, one of which convincingly demonstrated that dam building was a modern imposition on beaver culture sustained by current modes of socialization.)

As a consequence of their decision, our beaver couple move from the pond to the woods, nibbling bark only from those branches which storms blew down and restraining any impulse to use their foreteeth to bring down branches of their own. They were, as they construed it, living "naturally." One soon died of starvation; the other froze to death in the first snow of winter.

Index

Index